THE LONG WAY HOME

Book Two of the Celestial Wars Saga

Karen Buckeridge

Karen Buckeridge

Title: The Long Way Home: Book Two of the Celestial Wars Saga
Author: Buckeridge, Karen (1971–)

This story is entirely a work of fiction. No character in this story is taken from
real life. Any resemblance to any person or persons living or dead is accidental
and unintentional. The author, their agents and publishers cannot be held
responsible for any claim otherwise and take no responsibility for any such
coincidence.

Cover design and creation by: Nevena Jevtić
Images from: commissioned original.

PROLOGUE

Nights in Yaru were short in comparison to other realms, and as such, Clarise lifted herself up onto one elbow to observe her sleeping husband and smiled at the peaceful expression on his face. In all her long eons of education, not once had her personal governesses mentioned the Mystallian culture, which should have been her first clue to their apparent incompatibility.

But love rarely listened to anyone else, and Clarise's heart had been won the moment she and her sisters caught sight of the visiting Mystallians.

Avis in particular.

Over the next few days she had followed him discreetly, using her ranged senses to observe his likes and dislikes from a distance. She'd heard him mention in passing how his youngest brother Chance had the "pretty boy eyes of the family" which told her Avis liked liquid gold eyes. She'd also overheard him say to his sister Armina that he'd slit her throat in her sleep if she ever cut off her long hair.

At the time, she hadn't realised what an incursion into Armina's personal space that statement had been, and she'd been horrified by the subsequent brawl that ensued. Neither was trying to permanently harm the other, but the two had rolled across the ground until Griffith and Tal pulled them apart. All parties were laughing by this point, but Avis had also muttered under his breath that women built like men were the bane of his existence. To Clarise, that meant he liked long hair (the colour of which she based on the fact that all of the Mystallian siblings had jet black hair) and he liked his women petite. With each new piece of information, she'd crafted what she'd thought would be Avis' ideal Mystallian female.

And that night, on the floor of her father's conservatorium, all her work came to fruition when they came together and created Cora.

The time that followed were difficult to put it mildly, but that was the past. They were truly together now and had all eternity to make up for a few rough years. Her only current regret was her parting treatment of her bastard son, Charon.

Charon was the son she'd given birth to, to prove to herself that not all men were as cruel as her husband had been. When Avis came back into her life, she'd been forced to leave Charon with his father in Hell. Avis still had no idea she'd been unfaithful to him, and that deception weighed heavily on her mind. A Highborn Hellion's loyalty to family was absolute.

That thought brought her attention to Columbine. She really was such a darling child. Clarise loved all of her children, but of the three, Columbine best suited the Highborn Hellion way of life. Cora, by contrast, was Mystallian through and through. If ever that fact had been in doubt, it was gone now that her father had re-entered their lives. Cora had blossomed under his native guidance until very little remained of the Highborn Hellion she had once been.

As she settled down alongside her husband and drifted back to sleep, she knew one thing for certain.

They were never going to be separated again.

CHAPTER ONE

"Avis."

Avis stood at the bow of an elaborate Yarusian ship with his arms folded and his feet braced for the rocking impacts of the waves. The wind jerked at his cloak, whipping it around his sides and knees like a flag. Beating down on him from overhead, the rich orange sun seemed determined to bake him alive so long as he continued to wear the black leathers and fabric of his Mystallian uniform that covered him from neck to toe.

Stupid sun. Whether Ra was behind its searing brutality or not, Avis had been incarcerated in the deepest pits of Hell for over two years. If the realm most famous for its fire couldn't make him shed the uniform, the heat of a single sun wasn't likely to achieve it either. Two months into Yaru, he was still proudly wearing the Mystallian Uniform.

He cast his eyes over the dark, churning waters of the Nun Sea before them and breathed out slowly. Nothing but water in all directions. Despite the two Highborn Hellion Guards perched on either end of the guardrail behind him and a third atop the mast, Avis didn't like the growing sense of exposure. He had to assume he had no friends in this realm. It was safer that way. The three years he'd been on the run from the forces of Hell had left wide-spread carnage in his wake. He'd made a lot of enemies. Enemies that would do anything to hurt him, and the easiest way to hurt him these days was to come after those he cared about more than his powerbase of Life itself.

His eyes skimmed the waves again, searching for any hint of something other than blue between their ship and the distant horizon. Anything at all. Yaru's seventeen-hour days and seven-hour nights were playing havoc on his young family. Only eleven of those daylight hours were spent riding through the sky as fast as the demon steeds could go in the hopes of being gone before the Yarusians knew they were there. The rest of the time was spent on this very vessel ... waiting.

Clarise, his beautiful and clever shape shifting wife, had created a Yarusian style ship that blended in with the realm around them in the hopes that they would avoid discovery. So far, it had worked, but the lingering threat of discovery ate at his last nerve. He dared a quick glance at the sun overhead and added it to the list of things he cursed about this realm. If the Yarusians had a night and day balance like Mystal, their party would be under the cover of darkness by now instead of waiting another five hours for nightfall, and the risk of detection would be greatly reduced.

This—this floating on the Nun Sea like a cork with the sun high overhead highlighting their exact location—was like waiting for a boot to drop. They were too vulnerable, exposed like this ...

The scent of lavender filled his senses moments before a smaller pair of arms (bearing the same black leather gloves and doublet sleeves as him) slid around his waist from behind. He felt her face press into his back between his shoulder blades. "Avis," Clarise repeated, though her reprimand was muffled by his cloak. He was confident he knew what this was about, which was why he'd ignored her in the first place. They had opposing views on the matter, and since neither was prepared to concede to the other, he'd bought himself short reprieves by pretending he hadn't heard her. That was until she realised he was doing it deliberately. Cue the light huff at his back right now.

His lips pinched as he fought to swallow back the smirk, even as he turned inside her arms to face the small woman at the centre of his existence. "Yes, my love?" he asked, widening his eyes to feign innocence as he draped his arms over her shoulders and interlocked his fingers behind her neck.

Clarise stared up at him frostily; the gold in her irises hardening into sharp peaks. For a woman who didn't make it to his shoulder, she was one of the few people who had the power to call him on his bullshit and survive. "As I have said numerous times before, beloved. It defeats the purpose of blending in with the realm if you insist on standing on the open bow of our vessel with your Mystallian uniform on full display."

Just as he'd thought. The argument had been ongoing ever since they first crossed the Chaotic-Yarusian border a month ago and Avis still hadn't thought of a conclusive way to win it once and for all. It wasn't that she was wrong. He just … he couldn't leave it alone. With his enemies everywhere, sitting here in the middle of the Nun Sea under the bright Yarusian sun and waiting for something to find them while he remained tucked away out of sight …

… it gave him hives just thinking about it.

"We have four Highborn Hellion Guards, Avis. Each capable of doing their job without your input."

Avis knew that too.

By dint of sheer savagery, the Highborn Hellion Guard had earned the moniker of 'brute squad' throughout the Known Realms. Each had three solid legs that could change length at will to stabilise their large forms on any given terrain and four arms that were each capable of a different, independent attack from the rest. Their short head plates spun atop their shoulders taking in everything around them at once and huge, armoured wings with a tell-tale demonic claw at the tip made them just as aerially combative. But their most effective weapon by far was their speed. It was staggering. Avis had never seen anything move that fast before, and the key inference was 'never saw it'. Once something was identified as an enemy, these things became a blur of violence that couldn't be tracked by the naked eye, and that was terrifying.

No pantheon in existence could stand up to them for long, but that didn't pacify the trepidation that swamped him every time he went to look away from the water. As the Mystallian God of Life, his immortality was guaranteed. This wasn't about him. This was about his unestablished wife and their two unestablished children who could be taken from him and killed at any time if he didn't stay on top of things.

The mere thought of it had his eyes once again sliding to the water on either side of their ship. He was the eldest son of Order itself. He would stay in control, regardless of the realm he was in …

The impact of Clarise's flattened palm against his chest snapped his focus back to her. "You need to tone it down, beloved." She spoke the words slowly, enunciating every syllable to make sure he heard her. It was the same patronising tone she used with their children, and he had little care for being the target of it. She might have *wanted* him to tone it down, but that didn't mean he *had to* ... "Your heightened expectation of an ambush at any moment is affecting Columbine."

Oh.

Well, that changed everything.

Avis lifted his eyes to the small, gilded boxroom where he assumed both girls were waiting for their evening meal. He couldn't physically see either one of them, which meant he couldn't crawl inside their heads and poke around either, but as they shared the same blood as him, he could sense two of his own in there.

Columbine, their younger daughter, wasn't like any other child who'd come before her. Many celests liked to make that boastful claim about their children, but unfortunately for him and his wife, this was absolutely true of Columbine. Technically, both of their daughters fitted into the category of 'unique', though Columbine was by far the more different of the two. All other celestials naturally fell into two categories: mind bending and shape shifting. That power gave them the ability to be the absolute masters in their field.

As a child, the dominant power would reveal itself and remain in effect until the child reached puberty, where aspects of the other will come into their own, depending on the strength of that other side's bloodline. In the case of Columbine's older sister Cora, the two powers were equally matched because he was the son of Order, and her mother, the daughter of Chaos. Neither power would yield to the other. As such, the girl had both as a foetus and developed the mental capability of an adult as soon as a male Mystallian made physical contact with her after her birth. That male hadn't been him; something he now regretted every second of the day. He hadn't so much as laid eyes on her for over five years, save for a brief glance as a newborn, until they were reunited six months ago. Over the last few months, the two had more or less made their peace with what happened back then, though the Mystallian in his older daughter let him know on occasion that she wasn't as over it as he was.

He sucked in a tiny breath and huffed it out over Clarise's head. All he had to do was keep Cora alive, and he'd have the rest of eternity to rectify that. Ironically, being able to go verbally toe to toe with another Mystallian was like a breath of fresh air for him. Conversations with Clarise were subdued in comparison, and those he had with Columbine made him think the smallest raised voice would crush her. Cora was more like him, and both believed the shouting matches they shared were ... palate cleansing, since neither of them had to watch their Ps and Qs. The two were given the room, and after the walls were soundproofed to ensure the other half of their family couldn't hear them, all the vile language he missed so much came to the fore. Cora gave as good as she got. It really was like facing off with an adult from home ... if he ignored the fact that she only came up to the bottom of his ribs. They'd argued about everything from his unwillingness to try new things to the way she'd slip up and call him 'sir' (that was cathartic, as he really wanted to shout that one more so at Columbine but didn't dare).

They argued about colours. They argued about the use of contractions in a sentence. They argued about pretty much anything that came to mind, and then they stopped for drinks. The first time Cora had demanded access to the same ambrosia he had when she'd only been given fruit juice, brought a smile to his lips. His answer had been simple. Not until she could hold the form of an adult for the length of time it took for alcohol to burn its way through her system. While she was still stuck in the body of a child, she was still stuck with the drinks of one. Her snarkish "Fuck you!" had started another round of ranting, though that may have been because he grinned and deliberately took another deep swig of his ambrosia right in front of her.

Probably not the best parental approach, and certainly not one he shared with his wife, but it worked for him and Cora. Any tension they'd felt as a result of their circumstances was cleared up after they'd verbally vented at each other. Lines were drawn early on as to what would and wouldn't be acceptable subjects of conversation, but on the whole, they were getting there.

Back when he'd first learned of her adult intellect and dual power, he'd thought that was the most mind-blowing thing he had to learn about his children.

Then he met Columbine.

Columbine was born a celestial empath. A naturally occurring celestial empath. Where celestial power flowed from most powerful to least like water flowing downhill, Columbine genuinely felt all the emotions of everyone around her, regardless of their station. If they were feeling them strongly enough, she'd react to them as if they were her own. And she didn't even need line of sight to do it (unlike every other bender or shifter in existence). Celestials despised aberrations, and if anyone discovered what she could do, she'd either be killed on sight or enslaved for celestial gain.

Avis ground his teeth as his lips curled into an aggressive snarl. Neither would happen, so long as he breathed.

"Avis," Clarise warned again, and the Mystallian had to close his eyes for a moment to clear the anger from his thoughts. That was the hardest part of all. As a ruling god in his own right, Avis had billions of eons under his belt and never before had he had to keep his emotions in check. Ranting and raving were two of his oldest friends, and they didn't take kindly to being curtailed like this.

Not wanting to cause Columbine any undue stress, Avis took a very deep breath and released it, using the motion to empty his lungs and all the pent-up rage he felt with it. *Sorry, princess.* The silent apology was lame, but he was determined to get his emotions under control. Not the easiest thing for a hothead like him, but once he set his mind to something, he stuck at it.

Clarise hooked her hand around the back of his neck and pulled his head down for a quick, distracting kiss. In that moment, Avis forgot all about why he was so angry and pulled her in for a more passionate one.

Eventually, Clarise pressed her hands against his chest and pushed until their lips parted in a lusty sigh. "I actually came to tell you the evening meal will be ready shortly," she said, wrapping both her arms around his right elbow as if he might try to escape. "If you would care to join us."

Avis looked down at her and pursed his lips in annoyance. This wasn't the first time she'd used the evening meal as a means of drawing him away from his silent vigil and he really didn't like it. "Did I ever tell you how much I hate being played?"

Whether totally oblivious to his surliness, or knowing she was in no real danger, Clarise's expression softened and she smiled up at him until the gold in her eyes turned molten. "You may have mentioned the importance of your family eating together whenever possible, once or twice. If I choose to use that knowledge to my advantage, does that not merely prove me to be an avid listener?"

As much as Avis hated being played, he hated losing an argument even more. But it seemed whenever he found himself locking horns with his petite wife, the latter was happening with ever-increasing frequency. Which (not so coincidentally) led back to his earlier defence of ignoring her. "Fine," he conceded, answering all of her questions and demands in that single word even as he rolled his eyes to the cloudless sky overhead. "Lead the way, sweetheart."

To give him most of his arm back, Clarise slid her hands down to his wrist and held it tightly against her chest as she stepped around the throne, forcing him to come with her. It seemed she knew better than to assume he would follow of his own accord. Probably because in the last week or so … he hadn't.

He chuckled quietly to himself, ducking under the fabric canopy which shaded the golden throne facing the middle of the ship. Clarise's shorter height allowed her to walk beneath it unhindered.

Despite the heavy winds that pushed them through the water, a row of eight well-built Yarusian oarsmen lined either side of the ship. They stood with their bare backs to him, each densely packed with muscles that rippled every time they stepped forward as one and dragged the ship at an even keel through the water. Over and over. Perfect repetition despite not having a coxswain at the helm to keep them on course or belt out a rhythm to keep them in time.

Because they didn't need one.

On that first evening of arriving in Yaru, Clarise had created this ship with globs of body-sized formless mass at each rowing station. Avis had been about to ask what they were for when Frash, (a trusted hellion servant of Clarise's whom Avis despised with a passion) extended a thick tendril from herself and punched it into the nearest mass. That mass swelled up like an inflating balloon until a fully capable rower gripped the oar. Another tendril then shot out into the next one. And so on and so on. Avis watched as two full octads of oarsmen were in place in a matter of minutes. "What's stopping Hell from having an army of demons on any given battlefield, instead of an army of individuals?" Avis knew they fought as individuals. He knew it firsthand.

"Two things," Clarise had admitted, after taking a moment to consider her words carefully. "Both relate to the dangers that make it non-conducive to warfare. The first and most obvious reason is that all those forms still only possess one mind." She had looked up at him and smiled mischievously. "And why in the realms would we ever give one of your kind a veritable army to control with a single thought, beloved?"

Avis had to give her that. It'd be stupid to have all that muscle with only one mind, begging for a touch or ranged bender like him to assume control of it. "There are no touch benders outside the Nexus, sweetheart, and only a few ranged benders. So, what's the other reason?"

Clarise immediately sobered, and Avis hated himself for ending her playfulness. "They are all interconnected, beloved. Harm one, and they are all weakened. Kill one, and they all die. The more bodies you are in control of, the more risk you run."

"Because they can't all be looking everywhere at once?"

"No, each extension works independently of the whole. Like the cells of a non-shifter's body. The risk is that they are all one. If one gets hurt or sick, they all get hurt or sick in rapid succession."

"And I'm assuming you can't just expel the sick or hurt ones from the collective?"

"Imagine how difficult it would be to sever a portion of string from a roll without losing contact with either side of the problem area. We would lose everything beyond that point if all contact were severed, and then each being would need to be reintegrated, one being at a time. By the time we shifted matter around the problem area without losing contact with the other side, that problem would have spread its circumstance to more of the whole."

Avis could appreciate that analogy where regular Highborn Hellions, hellions and demons were concerned. Most shifters had the changing rate of chilled molasses. At four and a half years old, Columbine once again proved her uniqueness because she could shapeshift instantaneously, provided she didn't need to add or remove any extra mass. An added layer of protection should things become problematic for her, so to speak.

CHAPTER TWO

A forward movement drew Avis from his daydream, and he quickly realised Clarise was about to step off the dais and onto the main deck of the vessel two steps below. He reached past her and placed a stabilising hand on the second canopy post ahead of her while the other went under her palms for added support. He'd never seen Clarise stumble, but he wasn't willing to risk a first time either. Not if it could be avoided.

Avis helped her down to the deck, then moved onto the first step as she led him towards the gilded cabin in the middle of the ship. Jewel encrusted gold veneering was the dominant form of decoration to the Yarusians. The entire vessel was covered in both from bow to stern, making Avis feel as if he was standing on an elaborate jewellery box rather than a working ship. Even the rigging had threads of the yellow metal woven into the ropes, allowing them to glint in the bright sunlight. It was gaudy in Avis' opinion, to have so much gold on display. While it was true that his own palace had a gold-tiled roof and plenty of gold within, but the walls and floors were white marble, and the splash of polished timber and metal accents along with tasteful artworks scattered throughout the palace made all the difference between gaudy and exquisite.

The second step of the dais had been hollowed out, allowing the two octads to be connected without having an obvious umbilical cord running between them. (Yes, the demons called the fleshy vine that joined all the different bodies together an umbilical cord.) Technically, he couldn't argue the definition, but comparing it to what a mother and child shared before childbirth didn't sit well with him. It just wasn't right.

The only reason Clarise modified the step to hide the umbilical cord was because of Avis. When he'd found out how vulnerable it made Frash, he'd 'accidentally' smashed his booted heel into it, crushing it as hard as he could into the deck. The chorus of yelps, grunts, snarls and howls to be shouted from every oarsman on the ship simultaneously was music to his ears. It hadn't been a malicious act at all. The fact he hated that particular servant and was going to end her once she'd outgrown her usefulness was purely coincidental. Honestly—*ish*.

He followed Clarise down the deck, not missing the way the oarsmen's eyes followed him with wary caution. Good. It was about time that servant figured out he was never going to forgive her for the 'this is for your own good' bullshit she'd laid on him while he was still recovering in Hell. She'd treated him like a mindless invalid, and the first opportunity he got, he was going to get even with her for every realm-damned thing she forced him through during that convalescence. Some people thought the Devil had a good memory when it came to holding a grudge, but the Mystallians all knew Belial didn't hold a candle to Avis. If Clarise didn't rely on the bitch so heavily, he'd have killed her months ago. Just because he could.

Avis ducked his head under the transom and stepped through the open doorway into the only shaded space on the ship, except for the canopy-covered thrones on either end of the vessel. The outside measurements of this central room were barely four metres by three; not even the size of an ensuite in their former accommodations. Avis hated the cramped space, and looking around the tiny room once more, he remembered why. The area was divided into a further two sections. A small room at the back permanently housed a bathroom. The rest of the space filled every other role they required. Meals at mealtime. Beds at bedtime.

Above the bathroom door was a small shelf the length of Avis' forearm that housed four tiny, golden horse figurines with bright red diamond eyes, not unlike a set of children's toys. Avis often caught himself staring hard at those figurines, especially at their spindly legs. Clarise had said that the demon steeds could maintain that lifeless pose indefinitely, but Avis was convinced he could catch them moving if he just watched them long enough. So far, except for the way their red diamond eyes sparkled in the light, they'd never given away the hellion beast that lurked within.

Which was just as well, because, if there wasn't enough room for the family, there certainly wasn't enough room to adequately stable four demon steeds born of hellfire. Luckily, everything from Chaos was shifter by nature, and size, as well as shape, meant nothing at all to them. The same would never be said of his own precious mystallions back home. The mystallions were a species of proud, winged equines from which his pantheon took its name, and none of the herd would forgive him if he authorised such a vile and humiliating respite for them. He remembered one time when his sister of War had been needed to defend the Mystallian borders on short notice, and she didn't have time to saddle Gladiator properly. The pair had fulfilled their thrall, and the battle was won easily once they arrived at the border, but it didn't stop Gladiator from mule kicking Armina straight through the stable wall as soon as they were back in Pandess. That had been his way of expressing displeasure over being ridden bareback like a feral animal. To avoid further difficulties, Armina now kept Gladiator fully saddled at all times and aligned their powerbase to make the change permanent, and peace between Mystallian and mystallion was restored.

Turning them into a shelf full of children's trinkets would have had the whole herd ready to shed blood.

The first night Avis had laid eyes on the ridiculously tiny room, he'd told Clarise to take the hull down another level or ten to make things more comfortable for everyone. It seemed the obvious solution to the cramped space. But Clarise pointed out that not all the gods of Yaru were land-based (even though most of them were), and any who were swimming below them would see the ridiculously overextended hull of the ship if she did. Discretion demanded they stay within the conforms of the realm. And that was the end of that.

In the farthest corner from him stood the fourth member of the hellion brute squad. Two sets of upper arms were folded across its chest, and its head spun endlessly. It was explicitly tasked with the safety of Columbine, the younger of their two children. In Avis' mind, Cora was a five-year-old adult who was more than capable of handling herself.

Avis eyed the cramped space from wall to wall one last time before following Clarise towards the table. This was no way for a god and his family to travel, though he seemed to be the only one with a problem with it. The girls were already seated with their plates piled high. Clarise released his hand and moved to her side of the table facing him. While the second of Clarise's gangly servants stepped forward to help her into her seat, Clarise smiled at him, encouraging him to take his seat at the head of the table with a slight movement of her eyes in that direction. The stench of heavily cooked spices wafted up from the table, filling his nose with the burnt flavours of Yaru. It was as intense as it was overpowering, and he needed to take a moment to get his gag reflex under control. He managed to by reminding himself of what he'd been forced to eat at the beginning of their journey.

But there was a very big difference between the two. Untainted food was a scarce commodity back then, and his young family had been in an 'Eat-Or-Die' situation. That wasn't the same now. Clarise and her servants had access to all the mass they could use to create any meal his wife wanted, and these disgusting meal choices were one hundred percent her fault. In her infinite wisdom, she'd decided to make their journey a learning experience for herself and the girls, and whether he liked it or not, he was being dragged along for the ride. Whichever realm they happened to be in, Clarise wanted their family to sample the local cuisine. "To give them all an appreciation for the variety," she'd said at the time.

Well, Avis appreciated Mystallian food just fine. He didn't need or want to try anything else. Especially nothing that smelt that nauseatingly spicy. *Bleh.*

"What exactly do we have here, Tilu?" he asked, after taking his seat and running his eye over the meal suspiciously. There were a lot of browns and oranges on the table and little else. Everything seemed to be cooked within an inch of its corporeal existence.

The sister to the hellion controlling the oarsmen outside glanced up at him from her place behind Clarise, then dipped her head at him reverently before opening her mouth to speak. That right there was why Avis preferred this one. She knew her place. "*Ta'amia, ma'moul, baba ganoush, dulcis coccora …*"

"Mystallian!" Avis snapped, caring as little for the native names of the dishes that were as stupid as the food choices themselves.

"Chickpea balls with parsley, egg white and flour, deep-fried on a bed of garlic sauce. Crumbed fishcakes and spiced roast beef and vegetables done in a honey glaze …" Without moving from her place behind Clarise, Tilu extended her arm two full body lengths and moved her elbow to roughly where her fingertips had been. A second elbow allowed her to bend the limb unnaturally from above and she gestured to each plate as she spoke.

Avis followed her explanations with his eyes, the muscle under his right eye spasming as he found each description more asinine than the one before. Chicken peas? Cakes made of fish? But the one that had him snapping his attention to her in a combination of shock and horror was that third one. "You put honey on roast meat?" he barked, appalled by the very thought. There couldn't possibly be a worse way to spoil a deliciously savoury meat than to douse it in honey … or any other sweetener for that matter. Gravy was what you put on roast meat. Sweets were supposed to come *after* the meal, hence the name *dessert*. You didn't mix savoury with sweet at the same time. Everyone knew that. Who in their right mind put fish into cakes, and honey on roast? "Are you mad, woman?"

Clarise reached forward and encased his hand top and bottom with hers. She rubbed her thumbs across his knuckles in delicate circles, attempting to soothe his temper. "Try it, before you decide, beloved," she suggested. "It may surprise you."

Avis dropped his eyes to Clarise and frowned. "I really don't enjoy these culinary experiments of yours, sweetheart," he complained, shaking his head. "If we were meant to enjoy these Yarusian foods, we'd be Yarusian."

"Appreciation for another realm's food does not automatically grant you citizenship, beloved."

Avis mashed his lips together and slid his hand from hers. Just as Clarise knew when he'd been ignoring her, so too, he'd learned that when Clarise appeared to misunderstand his intent, it was rarely due to ignorance. More often than not, she knew exactly what he meant and was pretending otherwise to distract him. He'd fallen for it in the past, going off on a tangent that explained what he really meant instead of dealing with the matter at hand, but no more. His comment had nothing to do with citizenship – a fact she knew too damn well. But if he said anything else right now, it would end in an argument between them in front of their children; something they both agreed would never happen.

"It is good, Father," Cora agreed, utterly oblivious to the tension between her parents. She held up a thick slab of meat that she'd cut into three smaller pieces to pacify her mother, then stuffed all three into her mouth at once—completely defeating the purpose.

Even Columbine seemed to be enjoying the strange style of food, though she did eye him from time to time from the corner of her peripheral vision.

Fucking hell. Controlling his temper around her was going to be the death of him. With nothing else for it, Avis reached for the plate of honeyed meat and vegetables first. "This is on every one of you if I don't like it." His tone a mocking growl as he pointed his fork at each member of his family. Then, once his plate was full, he uttered a frustrated snort and reached for his filled goblet, hoping to drown his taste buds in something palatable before he started on this nightmare.

But partway between the table and his lips, his nose caught the pungent smell that came from inside the goblet. It was wrong. *Horribly* wrong. It smelt practically … off.

"It is darida, Milord," Tilu said before he could ask. "The preferred beverage of the local pantheon …"

Oh, hell no! Avis shook his head with a very negative sound at the back of his throat and held the goblet out to her. "I draw the line at whatever *that's* supposed to be," he declared, wrinkling his nose at the incriminating brew. "Swap it out for ambrosia for me." Tilu took the goblet, held it a moment, then returned it to him. This time, everything about it was right, and Avis took a deep swallow of his favourite wine. He looked up at her with an appreciative smile and nodded once. "Much better."

CHAPTER THREE

As far as the food went it was *different*, and not in a good way. In fact, the only exception Avis would make to that had been the dessert of caramelised fruit balls coated in tiny seeds. He might have gone back for thirds on those. But the level of spice in everything else had him tossing and turning for hours on his mattress that night, unable to find a position that didn't aggravate his upset stomach. He counted every strip of gold enamelled timber in the overhead ceiling and played with strands of Clarise's hair to pass the time, but nothing would distract him from his cartwheeling stomach.

He was so over these food trials of Clarise's. She meant well, and he could understand her reasons for educating herself and the children, but as of that moment, he was *soooo* done with them. Let the rest of the family experiment to their hearts' content. He'd stick with good, old-fashioned, Mystallian food. Then at least, he'd be able to sleep at night.

Giving up on ever falling asleep, Avis shimmied out from under Clarise, using his hand to support the back of her head until he could replace his pec with a nearby pillow. He then leaned forward and kissed her brow. Perhaps a walk around the deck would help the meal go down. At this point, he was willing to try anything.

He rolled to his side and sat up with his feet on the floor beside his boots. With only one room on the ship, as soon as the meal concluded, the servants had shifted the dining setting into three sleep-ready mattresses for the evening. Another temporary addition had been the second doorway on the girls' side of the room, which allowed Clarise to craft a wafer-thin dividing wall with soundproofing properties to separate the two bedrooms. How the opaque tissue paper managed this, was a question he had no intention of asking. So long as it worked, which it did. There was no way he was going back to those early days of forced celibacy without a fight.

The bathroom was another piece of shifting wizardry. The curtain of tissue ran all the way to the bathroom door and melded around the demon steeds housed on the shelf. The seal between the two sides was complete, but as soon as either side needed to use the bathroom, a hand on one side of the bathroom door caused the curtain to slide silently along the shelf until it attached to the doorjamb on the other side. Whichever side of the door was touched on, the opposing one became hinged. And not once did the curtain lose its soundproofing. Avis loved it.

As was his habit, he slept on the side that faced their doorway. If danger was going to come at them through the open entryway, it'd have to go through him first. His days of hiding behind Clarise were also over. He bent forward to collect his boots and gnashed his teeth on the spiking burn that shot straight from his stomach to the back of his throat. *Fuck!* He'd had molten metal poured down his throat during his incarceration, and it hadn't hurt as much as this! Spice that bad should be viewed as a punishment, not a fucking preference!

Abandoning the boots, he arched his back and braced himself onto one hand, doing his best to alleviate his indigestion without making a sound. A few good, solid belches might have helped, but he didn't want to wake Clarise.

Never again, he promised himself, for the thousandth time since making the original decree. *Never, ever again.*

Once he thought he had a handle on the pain, he rolled forward to grab his boots, only to pause as the moon's reflection on the floor's gilded surface caught his eye. *Bad idea,* he thought to himself, his fingertips brushing over the top edge of his boots. If he went thumping around outside in them, he'd wake the whole family.

But he had to get out. The pain in his guts was killing him.

With nothing else for it, Avis slipped out of bed and quickly dressed. He wasn't about to walk around the ship butt-naked either. The cloak was the last piece of his uniform to be donned, and he tensed at what had to be the loudest click in history when the golden chain locked together around his neck. His eyes immediately went to Clarise, and he held his breath for a few seconds to see if she'd heard it, then relaxed when she didn't move. Despite the pain in his chest, a victorious grin tugged at his lips as he drew the covers over Clarise and kissed her hair, taking a moment to inhale her lavender fragrance. That always made him feel better.

Three steps across the cold, metallic floor made him pause in the doorway and toss a fleeting glance at the boots he'd left behind. It wasn't just the chill that grated on him. After multiple visits to Antenora (the Ninth Level of Hell, where he'd been frozen solid) it was more the principle of leaving the room inadequately dressed. The boots were part of the uniform and leaving them behind to walk around barefooted seemed ... *wrong.*

But his pride and whatever else was in play would just have to suck it up because no way in hell was he waking up his girls.

That decided, Avis stepped out onto the deck and took in a deep, salty breath. The motion stretched his ribs and aggravated his heartburn further, until he tipped his head back and opened his mouth, allowing some of the burning pain to escape his body in a bone-jarring burp.

Three more followed in rapid succession, and the relief after each was profound. He gnashed his teeth on the spicy aftertaste and subconsciously rubbed his chest through the doublet. *Stupid fucking Yarusian bullshit motherfucking dumbass ...*

His mental invective was interrupted by girlish laughter that wafted through the air from the back of the ship, and indigestion suddenly became the least of his concerns. "Columbine?" he mouthed, his body swinging automatically to the right. He didn't really need to ask; he knew his little girl's laughter anywhere. His heart leapt into his throat at the thought of her being so close to the open water without supervision, and he quickly made his way past the central room to where the deck had another throne and the stern observation platform. Columbine's laughter grew into a high-pitched squeal of delight, though he couldn't quite see her. He did, however, spot a brute squad guard hovering over the throne's fabric canopy with the smallest movements of its demonic wings, which put her location out past the safety of the throne. *Dammit!*

Peering hard through the arms and backrest of the throne, he spotted Columbine's pink, sleeveless nightgown on the observation platform behind the throne. She was perched on the ledge with her feet dangling over the side beside the serpent carved into the stern of the vessel, and Avis' heart flew into his mouth. There were no rails on either of the observation platforms, and she was right on the edge! One slip and she'd go overboard! His first instinct was to bellow at her for endangering herself like that, but he couldn't risk startling her. It didn't matter that she was an instantaneous shapeshifter who happened to have a brute squad guard lingering nearby. She was his little girl, and his protective instincts were on high alert. First things first, he had to get her back over this side of the throne where there were rails, and it was safe. Then he would yell at her for being so reckless. Laughter still tumbled from her lips as her hands clung to her sides and her feet kicked out as if they had a mind of their own.

Avis moved closer to his daughter, using the combination of his black uniform and night sky to mask his approach. Columbine's centipede-like governess cowered on the deck between himself and the throne, many of her lower limbs twisting together in an elaborate braid as she chittered in demonic concern; not that he was paying her any attention. Out of the corner of his eye, he noticed the massive dark shadows moving and swirling beneath the water's surface, and froze. *Fuuuuuck!*

Avis shot a glance at the three guards that were still perched overhead and noted how each of them had leaned forward as if preparing for the worst. He knew it hadn't been his imagination, but he still hoped that maybe it might've been. No such luck. They'd definitely been found, and for the brute squad to have moved at all, shit was about to get real.

A surge of water, not unlike the sound of a waterfall, drew his attention back to Columbine.

The dark shadow revealed itself, wrapped in a column of water like a sentient wave to maintain its integrity. Higher and higher it rose until it towered over his child. Its girth was wider than Avis could put his arms around, and the very top of it was folded over, like an adult bending forward to be on eye-level with a child. It was studying her.

Fucking Hell! Had it already identified her as a threat?

On the verge of panic, Avis' eyes widened and he instinctively turned his head to take in all of his surroundings at once. As such, he realised much to his horror that the shadows moving around the boat weren't from multiple beings. Their motion was too singularly fluid. It was but one creature, whose size dwarfed the ship. Easily. This thing was massive. The sound of Columbine's high-pitched squeal of laughter yanked his attention back to the platform. He found her rocking back on her buttocks, her little feet kicking straight out in front of her and her hands clapping happily as if she was having the time of her life. Avis, on the other hand, felt his blood pounding so hard in his ears and throat that he genuinely thought he was going to have a heart attack. But that could come later when everything had resolved itself. Until then, that monstrosity was not getting anywhere near his baby girl.

Shuffling forward as quickly as he could without giving his position away, he knew his top priority was to get Columbine to safety, or at the very least, insert himself between her and that … *thing* … and let the brute squad do their job. Attacking it mentally was his first instinct, but a being that immense had to be established in the pantheon. Gods hunted monsters like this for sport, and (talots aside) they just didn't grow to that size without an establishment field to guarantee their immortality. If Avis went on the offensive without knowing who or what it was capable of, its powerbase might be able to counter his attack and Columbine would be caught in the crossfire.

Just as he reached the throne and canopy, Columbine straightened up and clapped her hands twice more, then held them out flat toward the mass of shadow liquid. In return, it grew two thin tendrils roughly the same size and shape as his daughter's arms and repeated the motion, splashing against Columbine's hands when the two sets clapped together.

And Avis needed to pick his jaw up off the deck.

He knew that game! It was the same mindless, hand-clapping, knee-slapping game Columbine had taught him on the Akheron River months ago. He followed each move as the game progressed, holding his breath when they reached the point where he would typically pull her into his lap and tickle her.

His roar of denial came when the mass swelled and poured over the top of her in a column of water. But when it fell away, Columbine was giggling with her feet kicking out in front of her, as dry as when they had first started. It was a game. The whole damn thing had been part of a fucking game!

"Father!" Columbine called, having heard him … or felt him … or something. She twisted to face him; at the same time, her right hand waved at the dark, watery mass before her. "This is my friend, Lady Keket. She was really sad, but now she is happy. Lady Keket, this is my father, Lord Avis of Mystal."

Keket … Keket … Avis knew that name … from somewhere …

… and the way the mass hardened and swung savagely towards him, it knew him too. *Oh, shit.* "Columbine, go back to your mother!" He couldn't afford to have to say that twice.

Ordinarily, Columbine was the most obedient little girl in existence, who thrived on pleasing the people around her. But, just as he'd always feared, the emotional storm of Keket's unbridled rage and his choking panic for her safety were too much for the girl's sensitive nature to process. Instead of moving, her entire body shivered in a borderline convulsive manner, and her eyes glazed over. She was all but drooling. *SHIT!*

Thankfully, her guard moved for her. One moment she was sitting on the platform behind the serpentine carving and the next she was gone. A brute squad guard materialised on either side of Avis with the third hovering overhead. Their presence blocked his view sideways, but he heard Columbine's centipede governess scurry back to the safety of the main room. Which meant now, since Frash never had and never would count for anything in Avis' eyes, it was just the fighters on deck.

Game on.

Avis crouched to lower his centre of gravity and dug his toes into the deck. "You stay the fuck away from her," he snarled, never taking his eyes off the monstrosity that was morphing in front of his eyes. Grey fur formed around a tanned head that loomed out of the water and an elongated nose grew into a baboon's muzzle. When it curled its lips back in a feral snarl, its twin incisors were the same size as Avis himself. Her head was twice the size of their ship. And that was just her head.

A baboon's paw, roughly twice the length of Keket's fang (and not at all proportional to her head) broke the surface of the water and came straight at him. Its width across its knuckles was the same as his height, but as Avis watched its trajectory, he tried hard not to smile. For Columbine's sake, this needed to end with as little emotional outpouring as possible. Fortunately, Keket wasn't an established mindless monster that could throw his bending ability back in his face. She was a pantheon goddess with a working mind, and that changed everything. The best part was, he didn't even have to touch her to bring her to heel.

Some of the more brainless celestials thought ranged bending and shifting required eye contact. That if they hid their faces, somehow their minds were safe. Why they thought that, Avis had no idea. So long as a body part—any body part— could be seen, the mind behind it was accessible. After all, what did they think wiggled the fingers and toes, if not the mind connected to it? *Idiots.*

Though in this case, with Keket's head large enough to block out the moon, it wasn't as if she was trying to hide. "Enough!" Avis called, sending a mental command for the goddess to halt. The paw paused not two metres away from him. "This is not a fight you can win, Lady Keket," he declared, staring up at the colossal baboon.

NOT ALONE, ANYWAY, his subconscious added unhelpfully. Which was true. Away from his own powerbase, Avis could only affect one mind at a time like this. His attacks would be near-instantaneous as he moved from one mind to the next, but powerbases allowed established gods and goddesses to do some clever footwork as well. If he gave Keket the chance to call in reinforcements, he'd need to bring young Cora into the conflict as the only other ranged bender on the ship. In all fairness, his little tiger would probably relish the chance to flex her mental mastery but, whether she liked it or not, she was still just a kid, and he wouldn't make her a celestial murderer before she hit puberty. Not if he could avoid it.

The problem was, he couldn't hold Keket's mind forever. The bitch was a goddess inside her own realm, and with her powerbase behind her, she'd throw off his mental conditioning within hours of her release. Then the entire Yarusian pantheon would come after them with everything they had.

Avis sighed. This required diplomacy, but before he could negotiate, he needed to learn what his crimes were against this realm. He couldn't remember any of them, but that didn't make him innocent.

And so, he swept into Keket's mind for answers.

CHAPTER FOUR

After what seemed like days of sifting through Keket's memories, Avis pulled back to the edge of the ancient goddess' mind and released a slow, heavy breath. *Shit. Shit, shit, shit,* he thought, rubbing his hand across his mouth as he stared at Keket's view of himself, far below on the stern of the Yarusian vessel. Everything out there was frozen, including Keket's outstretched paw, still two metres from his body.

How in the realms was he going to dig himself out of this one?

When he'd first gone into Keket's memories, he'd hoped to find his transgressions against the Yarusians were minor; preferably some type of mortal misappropriation. Or maybe the theft of something they could spare. He'd once stolen an armful of nearly ripe peaches from Lady Xiwangmu for no other reason than because he could. It wasn't as if he needed the immortality or youthfulness they supplied. It had been like everything else he'd done during those years on the run. He'd thought he'd lost everything that mattered to him, so in his mind, he wanted everything else to suffer too.

Especially when, unlike most of the other realms he'd mindlessly rampaged through, Yaru didn't have a whole lot to offer him. Before he reconnected with his wife Clarise in Hell and swore himself to her and their children, he'd been a god of simple pleasures that began with wine and ended with women, and after his brief introduction to darida tonight, he knew he'd never have coveted Yarusian liquor. Remembering the stink of that repulsive brew, Avis grimaced and shook his head. No, way. There wasn't a level of desperation in existence that would've made him resort to darida for an alcoholic buzz. But they did have women, exotic ones at that, and he knew what he'd been like. A bender with ranged control that didn't have to take no for an answer. Back then, he'd thought it was more challenging when they tried to fight. Provided he hadn't forced himself onto any of the pantheon ladies, he'd believed restitution could be arranged.

And then he saw what they *were* holding him responsible for; the cataclysmic destruction of an entire celestial city and most of its neighbouring farmlands. Fifty thousand celestials and their homes … destroyed in a matter of hours. Wiped out after an offshore earthquake caused a tsunami to smash into the densely populated city. Apep, the snake anti-god of Yaru and twin brother of Ra, had fully admitted afterwards that his underground thrashing had caused the disaster, but instead of revelling in the carnage as was his due, he'd laid the blame firmly at Avis' feet. Apparently, his powerbase was all about preventing the sun from rising, and his thrall caused minor tremors and small, inconsequential earthquakes when (of course) he failed to stop the day from coming to pass. Catastrophic death and destruction within the celestial realm were not part of his thrall, and he was very quick to point out as much.

The pantheon was under the misconception that Avis had somehow collided with Apep with such force that the snake god had been folded in half, forcing the land above him to reciprocate. Not only did the disaster cost thousands of celestial lives, but the ground around the city was left so heavily salted from the Nun Sea's impact that the soil was rendered useless. Geb was still trying to clean up the mess, and more celestial bodies were being found with each passing day.

Avis rubbed his lips and scowled at the scene. The charge didn't make any sense. Apep had the waist measurement of a planet and Avis was the size of a man. How could any amount of ramming on his part have caused such a colossal creature to double over like that? Answer: Bullshit!

The whole thing stank of a demonic setup, especially since he honestly didn't remember any of it.

But, he needed to be sure.

Stepping away from Keket's mind, the Mystallian returned to his own body and turned his focus inward. Internalising, as benders called it. The way to see his past in exacting detail, but also have a meeting of the minds with images of people he'd met in his long life. He wasn't interested in the latter, just yet.

The easiest way to clear his conscience was to find out where he *had* been at the time. He'd already seen the exact point in time when Keket had been notified of the catastrophe, so all he had to do was find that point in his own memory and backtrack.

A few minutes later, Avis found himself sitting on his ass with his head in his hands. His eyes were closed, and his fingers speared through his hair. *FUCK!* He drummed the tips of his fingers against his scalp, willing himself to calm down. Frozen in time before him, was the memory of a single scale of Apep. The god was so enormous that even from this far away, that one scale filled Avis' entire vision.

He had caused this—just not the way the Yarusians thought. Physically, Avis couldn't have done shit to Apep, and that had been the whole basis of his claim of innocence. But what he hadn't taken into account was just how vicious and petty he'd been back then. At the time, he'd been running for his life with the Hellions hot on his heels. How they'd caught up with him was a long and complicated story that was completely immaterial. What had consumed him at the time was the fact that they had, and in the mortal realm, things were supposed to get out of the way of a god tear-assing through space. That was just how it worked.

But not when another celest happened to be in the mortal realm ... and in the way.

Before he'd realised it, he'd bounced off Apep at full speed and fallen flat on his back. At that point, the snake deity hadn't even noticed him. Why should he?

Avis could've just gotten up and kept running. It was what he should've done. Instead, as the sound of the hellions' blood-curdling howls rang in his ears, he'd lashed out at the god he'd felt was responsible for his delay. It wasn't as if he could miss something as big as Apep. In the length of time it took to scramble to his feet, Avis had reached into the snake god's mind and snapped it like a twig. *Then* he'd started to run again.

That one, solitary action which hadn't even taken half a second because of the blind rage he'd been in, had left Apep writhing in agony as his powerbase realigned his broken mind with that of the conniving evil god whom the mortals reviled.

And Avis hadn't even spared him a second glance. With the hellions closing in, the reflex action against Apep had been nothing more than an annoyed backhanded swat on his way through ...

... and the rest was precisely as the Yarusians believed.

Bottom line, it *was* his fault.

He needed the advice of his family. Although he hadn't spoken to any of them in years, he needed to move over into the other part of his mind where his imagination would give him working facsimiles of them.

Since he wasn't physically in his mind, Avis straightened his legs downwards as if the ground he'd been sitting on had lowered until he was fully upright. His eyes were still closed, and his hands were fisted at his side, but with a thought, he moved his consciousness from memory and into his imagination.

He opened his eyes, confirming the space around him was empty, awaiting creative instruction. From there he willed his throne room into existence. In an instant, white marble floors with gold striations came into being, along with metal and timber panels on the lower half of the walls. Each panel depicted a different member of the Life Court in the highest throes of their powerbase. No colour was added to the pantheon's depictions. They were subtle and poignant. Visitors to the room who couldn't meet the eyes of the Mystallians would be forced to look at the images and be reminded of precisely why they couldn't do it. Mystallians were powerful, inside their realm or out. There was no avoiding that power.

To his left, seven stairs led up to the dais where his throne was located. He wasn't as pretentious as some ruling gods. He had no desire to be so far above his people that they had to crane their necks to see him. This was his family, and for the most part, he wanted to be amongst them. They were strongest when they were together. When he sat on his throne, the seven steps gave him just enough height to be head and shoulders above the two-and-a-half-meter giant of Strength, and that was enough of a distinction for him.

Avis walked up the stairs like a man possessed and slowly circled his throne, pausing directly in front of it. His thumb hooked under his chin and drummed his fingers against the left side of his mouth. The grandeur of the throne still fitted his station, but something about it was off. Not the size. The measurements were just as he remembered them. Not the construction either. It held the perfect blend of soft fabrics, metals, precious gems and timbers. Yet something …

When he realised what was bothering him, he rolled his eyes and snorted out a sharp breath in disbelief. *Of course.* His lips twitched in amusement under his fingers, and he quickly made the required modification.

A moment later, he faced the middle arm of a double throne, where the second half mirrored the original. Not smaller. Not petite. Not a feminine replica to imply his beloved wife held a secondary status to his. Exactly the fucking same. His equal. His match. Happy with the adjustment, he turned, noting the stairs leading up to the dais and the dais itself had also doubled in width to allow them to step up and down together, side by side. Clarise was his queen in all things. She would never walk in his wake.

Avis stepped to his right and sat on his throne. Another modification had Clarise sitting to his left, just as his twin brother's wife Yasadan sat on Amaro's left in the Death Court. This was the future of Mystal's Life Court. Two minds ruling as one. He'd make this change for real once he returned home.

Provided they let me come back.

The unwanted thought sprang from nowhere, causing Avis to tense as a wave of uncertainty coursed through him like poison. If they didn't, he had no one to blame but himself. For years he'd convinced himself that every realm-damned thing that had happened since his exile was his pantheon's fault for exiling him. But now, he knew otherwise. If they hadn't kicked him out, they would have …

… died. Somehow, someway, they would've all died. Teon had barely been a fiftieth of Mystal's size, and that established realm had been utterly destroyed by six members of the Highborn Hellion Guard. Even the established pantheon perished. Just enough civilians were left alive to spread the word of that realm's demise and who had been behind it. Many thought the number was greatly exaggerated, the work of a bender sowing the seeds of discord. Six beings of any description shouldn't have been able to take out an entire established realm. Avis had been among those who thought the number was a hoax … until he'd seen the brute squad in action during the last few months. Their ability to be everywhere at once would've turned six warriors into six-plus-whatever-fucking-number-of-zeroes Belial and Beelzebub wanted them to be. When Beelzebub had marched on Mystal with hundreds of the golden bastards in tow, his family did the only thing they could to save themselves, hoping Avis' innate ability to safeguard his own life would protect him.

And for three years, it had. But then the hellions (led by his brother-by-marriage, the Archangel Uriel) finally ran his ass to ground and for the next two years he'd suffered every conceivable punishment the Nine Levels of Hell had to offer. As a result, he wasn't the same god anymore. He just wasn't. Looking back, he could see how out of control he'd been. His attitude adjustment had been a long time coming, but no one had ever had the balls to come after him until he earned Lord Belial's ire. But that, like everything else, was in the past. If he could convince his family of his changes, he'd never take their love or loyalty for granted again.

He looked down at the empty throne room and drew in a deep breath, releasing it slowly. This was his playground. His mind. If he didn't like where they took the conversation, he could change it. He glanced at Clarise on his left and lifted her gloved hand to his lips, savouring the lavender fragrance that always accompanied her. As much as he wanted her here with him, this first round of talks needed to be between him and his siblings.

"I love you," he whispered as he rose to his feet, gesturing for her to stay where she was. "But right now, I need to be my old, profanity-spewing self which I know you don't like, so I have to send you away for a little while." He knew he didn't have to explain himself, that this was just his imagination, but he couldn't bring himself to erase her without first gaining her permission. He held both of her armrests to corral her beneath him and bent forward to press his forehead to hers. "Is that alright with you, sweetheart?"

Clarise lifted her chin and kissed him lightly. "Of course, beloved. I trust you in all things."

A moment later she was gone, as if she'd never been there. *Just this once, sweetheart. I swear.* With that promise, Avis straightened and turned away from the empty thrones before he caved and brought her back. He took a deep, calming breath and cast his gaze over the empty room, refusing to dwell on the possibility that if the pantheon wouldn't take him back, this imaginary replica would be as close as he ever got to seeing them again.

Then he descended the stairs.

Needing their input almost as much as their company, Avis generated the three siblings of his pantheon that sat on his side of the realm. Griffith of Strength, Armina of War and Chance of Fortune. War and Strength appeared in front of him with their arms folded, but Luck was nowhere to be seen.

"Where's—ahh, shi—!"

A familiar weight landed on his back and shoulders before he could finish that curse, and while a gloved hand snaked around his neck, the other mussed up his hair as only his baby brother could. "Hey, ya' big lug!" Chance chimed, to the amusement of the other two snickering chuckleheads.

Chance had been doing this exact move for eons. Literally. This. Exact. Fucking. Move. It was so familiar that Avis' response to it ran on muscle memory. He reached over his shoulder for roughly the shoulder blade of his youngest brother's chokehold arm and, once he had a fistful of cloak and doublet, he rolled forward and twisted, forcibly dislodging the runt and hurling him towards the other two standing a short distance away. "Get off me, runt!"

The process was so predictable that as Chance flew through the air, Griffith reached out his left arm without moving any other part of his body and caught the little prick across the chest, then dropped him to his feet.

Avis looked at the three of them and bit his bottom lip, hard. Yes, it was only his imagination, but at that moment, they were so fucking real. After nearly six long years.

"What the fuck is that bleeding heart look for?" Armina demanded.

Avis missed this. He missed it so much he could cry ... if only his pride would let him. "Not one of you assholes is to have a realm-damned thing to say about this," he growled, and before anyone could ask, he went to his armoured sister and hauled her in for a crushing hug. He said nothing else as he pressed his face into her plated shoulder and held her close, waiting for her to return the hug; which he knew she would. Their family wasn't big on the whole mushy stuff in public, but any time any of them needed anything, it was given freely. Even this. As her arms curled around him, he wished it could be as real as it felt.

He breathed heavily, over and over, determined not to lose control. Not to cry. It was the one thing that had always been hammered into them. Never completely lose control. Never lose control at all, actually, but always hold on to some semblance of it at least. "I'm so sorry," he whispered into the black plate, knowing this was a pale example of what would happen when this was real.

"You fucked up big time, brother," Armina agreed, tightening her arms around his waist. She continued to hold him without saying anything else, for as long as he needed. Two other hands from different sources squeezed his shoulders in a show of unconditional support.

After a while, Avis clenched his eyes shut and sank his teeth into his bottom lip again. The allegation was true on a level they had yet to comprehend, but they soon would. He sighed and straightened up, still holding his sister's shoulder in a vice-like grip as he turned to face all three of them. "You have no idea," he replied. He looked at his two more aggressive siblings: Strength and War. "And once you do, I'm telling you now, you're not hitting me in retaliation." He stabbed his finger at Griffith as he spoke, then swung it to include Armina standing on his right. "Nor are you fucking skewering me either."

"What, no dire warnings for me?" Chance asked, laying a hand over his heart as if his feelings had been crushed. Had it not been for the way his molten gold eyes glittered mischievously, the little shit might have been believable.

Avis already regretted what he was about to say. "This is serious. My actions have caused the deaths of over fifty thousand Yarusian citizens, and now I have to get through their fucking territory without getting caught." It wasn't the Mystallian way to fudge blame or excuse it away. He'd done it. There was nothing to be gained by denying it.

All three of them widened their eyes in disbelief. Chance was the first to speak, and he did so after barking out a harsh laugh first. "Fuck me, bro'. Even I'm not that fucking lucky."

Yeah, you are, Avis mused to himself, but that wasn't the point.

"Do they know you're there?" Armina was all business, now that there was a threat to the family. She placed one gauntleted hand against her armoured hip while the other rubbed her jaw thoughtfully, her dark eyes never leaving Avis.

Avis nodded, forcing himself to meet War's gaze and accept the unspoken accusations within it. "One does, but I've got her mind in lock-down at the moment."

"Is she established?" Griffith asked.

If not for his personal discipline where pride was concerned, Avis would've broken eye contact and squirmed. Instead, he shifted his attention to the giant of a god and nodded. "It's Lady Keket."

"Fucking fuck! You sure know how to pick 'em, Avis!" Chance raked his gloved hand through his black hair and glared at Avis as if he was the greatest idiot to ever draw breath. "She's one of their fucking primordials!"

Avis knew that, *now.* Having gone through her mind, he knew Keket was one of eight original deities that made up the Ogdoad of Yaru. The gods and goddesses that resided in the Nun Sea were so formidable, even the Yarusian pantheon avoided them. "I know."

"Can you cause a distraction? Something that'll get them looking the other way long enough for you to escape?" Griffith suggested.

Avis gritted his teeth and shook his head. "I'd have to let Keket go to pull off something that big, and even then, it'd only buy me enough time to lean into my innate self-preservation and save no one else but me."

Chance's gaze narrowed suspiciously. "And exactly why's that such a problem? You *are* alone, aren't you?"

Uncertain how they'd take this part of the discussion, Avis released his hold on Armina's shoulder and rubbed his fingers across his palms. "Not anymore, no."

All three of them frowned. "Who in the realms have you got with you?" Armina demanded.

"Clarise and our girls."

Oh, how Avis would treasure this memory, even if it wasn't real. The stunned looks on their faces were absolutely priceless. "Clarise?" Griffith repeated.

"The wife you ...." Armina added but was abruptly cut off by Chance.

"Cora's with you too?" All sense of light-heartedness vanished as the words exploded from their youngest brother. In two quick steps, he was in Avis' face with more determination than Avis had seen in a long time, and he knew why. Chance had been the one to anoint Cora at birth in Avis' absence, making the girl almost as much his as Avis'. Despite his happy go lucky attitude, Chance was all about his kids, and their kids—and in a few cases, their kids' kids. He should've realised just how much his brother's separation from Cora within hours of her birth would've devastated him. "Is she. With. You?" Luck demanded, wrapping his fists into Avis' doublet and giving him a quick shake for emphasis.

Avis stared down at him without igniting his own fiery temper, even as War and Strength came forward to separate them. This really wasn't going to help. The runt had every right to be upset, and of course he would want to know everything Avis knew about Cora. The problem was, Avis had only just reacquainted himself with his little tiger about seven or eight months ago, and he had no intention of having this discussion more than once. The real Chance would be just as beside himself, and that was when he'd have this conversation.

Avis closed his eyes and reset the scene. This time, he made his siblings already aware of his wife and daughters and conditioned Chance not to bring up Cora again unless it helped resolve their current dilemma. With the new rules in place, he opened his eyes and began again.

"So, how do I do this?" he asked, moving his gaze from one sibling to the next. Questioning the real people would've been better, as they would have genuine insights rather than a rehash of his own knowledge, but at this point, he was out of options.

"You have four brute squad with you," Armina replied. "Use them."

"How?"

"Keket doesn't want to see her realm destroyed," Chance answered, correctly guessing where their sister was going. "Remind her of what happened to Teon."

"Her hatred of you will grow with her frustration, but in theory, she should put her realm before her vengeance," Griffith agreed.

"And once you've outlined her situation, let her go," Armina went on as if she'd never been interrupted. "The destruction of Teon at the hands of six Highborn Hellion Guards should be enough to remind her that at the very least, a large chunk of her realm will go down to your four, and what's left of the rest will be mopped up by Beelzebub when he turns up with the rest of them."

Avis raked his fingers through his hair. The one glaring flaw with her plan was the expectation of Beelzebub doing anything to help someone outside of Hell. He wouldn't, unless Lord Belial ordered it. Likewise, threatening Keket with the destruction of her realm when he knew the brute squad was only there in a defensive capacity seemed cowardly and didn't sit well with him. It wasn't the Mystallian way to bluff, because usually they didn't have to. And the part he hated most of all was the idea of hiding behind the brute squad, period. It went too close to the way he'd been forced to hide behind Clarise's skirts during the early hours of his parole from Hell's Nine Levels.

"Your only other alternative is to hand yourself over to the Yarusians and let Clarise bring the girls home without you," Armina concluded.

Avis shook his head, mentally ticking off the reasons why that wasn't a viable option. "I can't do that."

Griffith snorted, clearly unimpressed. "We know, brother. Your innate self-preservation ..."

"Has nothing to fucking do with it!" Avis roared, turning on the mountain of a god who'd spoken out of turn.

Most would've recoiled from any hint of aggression on Avis' part, but his younger brother merely folded his arms across his chest and arched a single eyebrow. The smallest of gestures, but it was enough. He knew they were only trying to help, and here he was, ripping their heads off for doing just that. For the next few seconds, Avis sawed his bottom lip through his teeth, willing himself to calm down. He refused to speak again until he had. "The main reason I can't do that is because if Cora goes beyond my ability to control her, she has an execution order over her head from the Highborn Hellions."

"FUCKING WHAT!"

Avis should've known he'd never get that gem out without Chance completely losing his shit. Luck had Avis' doublet fisted in his hands once more, only this time instead of shaking him, Chance lifted him forward onto his toes in a move that all but dared him to repeat what he'd just said. Griffith and Armina were already reaching forward to separate them again, but Avis was already over it. He could've brought Chance's image to heel through implied bending, but it was just as easy to roll the scene back a few seconds and add Cora's Highborn Hellion death sentence to their knowledge (which Chance wasn't allowed to react badly to) and start again.

"If I let Cora leave without me, the Highborn Hellions have issued an execution order on her," he repeated, though to his siblings, this was the first time they heard it. All three nodded, taking that unpleasant knowledge in their stride. "In fact, the brute squad guards we have with us are probably under orders to do it for me if I'm somehow incapacitated."

"Probably?"

Chance had caught onto the discrepancy. *Bastard.* Avis didn't feel like resetting the scene a third time in as many minutes. "A big part of my parole from Hell is that I have to stay in control of Cora at all times. If Cora ever gets beyond my control, I have to kill her and forfeit my freedom. All things considered, it's not that big a leap to assume if I'm not in a position to do it, they'll arrange to have her murdered for me. Either way, Cora dies, for no other reason than because she's more like us than them." Both of his brothers scowled, and Armina openly snarled, but at least Chance wasn't flipping out. "Exactly," Avis agreed, loathing how the Highborn Hellions could simply execute one of their own for behavioural issues. "I have to stay with her. If I thought offering myself up as a bargaining tool would get them all safely to Mystal, I'd do it in a heartbeat."

"Fuck me. You have changed," Chance said, running his eyes down the length of Avis and back to his eyes again. "I like this new you."

Avis sneered and flipped the runt off. He hadn't changed *that* much.

"Avis, blood-link to us. Let us bring you all home." Although the words were said as an order, Griffith's expression softened to the point of pleading. "I'll bring you home. Any of us will. Just … come home, brother."

And this … this right here … was what he missed most of all. Their ability to not give a damn about what he'd done or how many enemies he'd made, so long as he was safe and sound at home. He hoped with all his heart that the real versions of his siblings still felt this way about him. "I can't." His hand went up to cut off Griffith's argument before it began. "Chance is right. After everything that's happened, I have changed, and if I come home now, my thrall'll kick in and I'll go back to the way I was. I can't risk that." He shook his head with absolute conviction. "Not now that I've just found them again."

"You could send Clarise and Columbine through," Armina suggested. Ever the strategist, she was determined to salvage something of this.

Again, Avis shook his head. "I won't split up the family either. I promised myself and them that we'd all make it back to Mystal, one realm at a time. Together." *Or not at all,* he added, privately to himself.

"Then you have to use the brute squad. It's your only option."

He was beginning to see that. The real Armina would've probably come up with a dozen other more convoluted options that weren't even on the table to win this war, but Avis didn't have access to the real war goddess' intellect or her inter-realm connections.

Time to face reality.

* * *

CHAPTER FIVE

Avis returned to the physical realm in exactly the same space he'd left it. With Keket reaching out to pluck him off the deck and three of their four brute squad guards surrounding him. His grip on her mind continued, but he relinquished enough control for her to hear his words and understand them. He stepped to the side of the ship, ducking under the controlling arm of one of the two oversized paddles which the ship used as rudders and paused just outside the claws of her paw.

That momentary break of sightline allowed Keket to shove her paw half a metre closer, but then he regained control and locked her mind down again. He didn't need Columbine's ability to know how angry Keket was, but he hoped the maternal female that Columbine had been playing with was in there, somewhere. Some gods he knew would rather watch their realms burn just to enjoy the heatwave, but from what he'd just witnessed, Keket was behaving more like a goddess with nurturing instincts. He held both hands out to his sides as if he was harmless. Another half-truth neither of them would ever believe.

"The past cannot be undone, Lady Keket, and you have every right to hate me. No one's refuting that. Nor am I disputing the fact that your anger stems from the pain I've caused your realm, but that's also where your revenge will falter. You know what happened to Teon as well as I do, and at this moment, I have more than half the number of Highborn Hellion Guards standing with me that destroyed that entire realm." It galled him to imply that the same would happen here if Keket didn't yield, but if that's what it took to get them all safely out of the realm, he'd do it.

"Whether they're enough to end Yaru or not, I can't honestly say, but what I do know is the damage they're capable of will make your reasons for hating me seem inconsequential. This doesn't have to be the way of things." Avis paused, both to give himself a moment as well as her. "You and I, we're eternal. Our rage and our hunger for revenge can be just as eternal. Perhaps one day, you'll get the chance to explore that revenge. But not today. For the sake of your realm, you have to let me go."

Avis felt her mind struggle beneath his control, so great was her fury. "I know," he said, gritting his own teeth on the admission, though the baboon shaped goddess made no physical movement. "I'd want your hide for a wall hanging too if our roles were reversed." He drew a deep breath and released it slowly. "You don't have to like it, Lady Keket, and you're not going to. I get that, but we're … *I'm* not here to cause you any more trouble." He gestured at the brute squad, who continued to flank him. "They're not always going to be here to protect me, Lady Keket. In fact, they're not even really here for me. You must have heard about what I did to my wife before going on the run. The Highborn Hellions hate me, probably more than you do." His thumb jerked over his shoulder to the cabin behind him. "They're here for my little girl. My daughter. Columbine. The little one you were playing with just now. She means everything to them, even enough to defend a bastard like me."

He paused again, not because he had to, but because he wanted to give Keket real-time to process what he'd said. "We deliberately stayed away from the land in the hopes of avoiding everyone. This isn't an incursion. All I'm doing is taking my family home. That's it. If I ever set foot in your realm again after that, I'll be without the brute squad's protection, and you can come at me with everything you've got. I might even be inclined to stand still and let it happen."

The fact he never planned on crossing the Yarusian border once they left was something he kept to himself. Having said his piece, he waited another full minute before speaking again. "Okay. I'm going to let you go now, and you're not going to do anything stupid, are you?"

Of course, Keket said nothing, but everyone within the sound of his voice knew she had no choice. Even without the brute squad, he could easily lock her down again if she acted out.

Keket stiffened and sucked in a huge breath as her mind was returned to her. Her gaze sharpened as she refocused on Avis and breathed out a heavy snarl that blew over him like a gust of wind from the depths of a charnel house. He endured the stench without a single flinch, because as bad as it was, Hell had ground his face into much worse.

Then, ever so slowly, she withdrew her paw from the ship. *So far, so good.*

"You. Stay."

The guttural sounds were so deep he almost missed them. Power radiated from the primordial goddess almost as if she was in a position to barter or demand.

Yeah, right. Avis slowly shook his head, deciding not to antagonise her further by either rolling his eyes or snorting at her, much as he wanted to. "As I said, I'm taking my family home."

The goddess snarled again and slammed her paw at the water, covering the ship in a wide-arcing spray. Avis lunged forward and grabbed the gunwale as the swell struck the hull and tossed them about, but he managed to keep his footing ... *just.* "CUT IT OUT!" he shouted, locking his fingers around the rail and balancing his feet one ahead of the other and shoulder-width apart in case another wave struck. Saltwater stung his eyes, but not enough to blind him.

He saw the baboon's gaze shift from one brute squad guard to the next, but when she resettled on Avis, they glowed with hatred. "I mean it," Avis warned, icily, straightening where he stood, though he didn't release the railing. "Knock it the fuck off, Lady Keket."

Keket was so close to losing it. Even without seeing into her mind, Avis could tell by the way every muscle on her face bunched that she was seething. He was just about to retake her mind when Keket's gaze slid to Avis' left, and a glimmer of rational thought entered her eyes. "She. Stays."

This time Avis did snort, his chest convulsing derisively. There was never a question of which 'she' in his family Keket was referring to; not that it mattered. "Not a fucking chance," he declared harshly. "You want her, woman, you'll have to go through every realm-damned thing Mystal and Chaos can throw at you first." Adding Mystal to that decree might have been a stretch since his pantheon didn't know he'd reclaimed his family, but he knew the second they found out, they'd rally to protect his wife and kids at the very least. Blood meant everything to them, and they'd look after their own. It was perhaps the only thing the Mystallians and the Highborn Hellions had in common. Avis' hands tightened on the gunwale until his knuckles were white with the strain and his fingers had imprinted on the golden bar. "Columbine stays with me. Period."

The goddess screeched and flopped back into the water, disappearing beneath the inky surface. The guard floating over Avis' head suddenly disappeared as well. Probably to follow her. For a tense few seconds, everything was eerily quiet as Avis remained still, poised for … anything. He'd dealt with enough celestials in his long life to know he would never be permitted the last word inside another's realm.

Without warning, the entire ship was thrust above the general waterline and shot sideways on the crest of a wave. The movement was so fast that Avis's feet left the deck and he was flipped over the rail onto his back, looking up at the starry sky overhead. Only his grip on the railing prevented him from going flying off the starboard side. *Shit!* He should have taken the over-grown chimp down and kept her there, but he didn't think she'd do anything like this! He clung to the rail, his entire body flapping like a maritime flag, and there was not a damned thing he could do about it. Pressure mounted around his fingers as their speed increased and he knew the ape-faced bitch was trying to force him from the ship without technically touching him. All that prevented it was his weakening grip on the rail. He couldn't even pull himself back, or release one hand to try and flip himself over. Instinct demanded he tighten his grip, but he knew if he did so, he'd shatter the rail and be gone.

Dozens of thumb-width golden ropes suddenly appeared around his torso, covering from his underarms to the top of his hips. At least, he thought they were golden ropes until he realised they expanded and contracted with his breathing; anchoring him without harming him.

Avis lifted his head just enough to see the source of the vines over his left arm. One of the two brute squad guards had its tentacle arm pointed at him. Nothing else about it had changed. Its demonic wings remained locked in place, not so much as moving in the cyclonic conditions. Its other three arms were at its side, and its three legs stayed in place beneath it. Avis craned his neck to look at its feet … or rather, whatever constituted feet at the bottom of those tripod legs. Nothing had changed. Not even a claw or a suction cup or anything to signify how it was holding itself to the deck. It just did.

Damn, those fuckers were scary. Good thing these four were on his side.

Knowing he was secured, Avis readied himself for the whipping motion that would cause him to flip over the instant he released his left hand and let go. His body spun in a blur and as soon as he saw the hull of the ship, he snatched at the rail again. *Step one complete.* He was now facing the right way, even if one of his hands was twisted the wrong way. Step two was to fix that.

Locking the fingers of his right hand, Avis rotated his left so that both sets of knuckles were on top of the railing. *Okay.* Now, for step three; getting his ass back onto the deck. His cloak continued to whip around him, but it couldn't go anywhere. The golden clasp that held it around his neck had a higher chance of decapitating him than breaking. *Fucking overgrown, realm-damned, psychotic, flea-bitten, mangy, motherfucking monkey-bitch,* he swore, working one elbow over the rail, then the other. It hadn't escaped his notice that the brute squad guard wasn't in any way attempting to haul him back; it merely prevented him from being lost. Fortunately for his dwindling pride, (because it wasn't as if he could do anything but yell at them, and they wouldn't care) he had too much anger directed at the goddess under the hull to divide his focus.

With a lot of squirming, struggling and mental swearing, he managed to hook his toes over the rail and slide in behind the gunwale. The pressure of their movement pinned him against the hull, but he sought out his family's location through their familial links and found them still inside the cabin. He had no way of knowing their condition, but at least they were there. The fourth guard assigned to Columbine stood on the deck just past the enclosed room, and just like the other three, its poise was utterly neutral. Avis took that as a sign that all was well with the ladies of his family.

After what seemed like forever, Avis had had enough of cowering in the corner like a whipped cur. He twisted his feet into the hull where it met the deck and stretched himself out until he was able to hook his hands around the post that held the ship's tiller overhead. Then, inch by curse-filled inch, he pulled his body in behind the post. He needed the post for height. He needed the post to stand.

Sliding his feet into the deck, Avis used the pressure to drive himself upright, gnashing his teeth on the impact of his back against the post. The pain was intense, but inconsequential when compared to the pride he felt in being upright.

Having been alive for more eons than he cared to count, Avis was reminded of the times when Griffith had been a dick and thrown an uninhabited mortal planet at him; just to watch his older brother flex his celestial muscle and bring the rock to life. The initial impacts were always like this—crushing pressure that made it hard to breathe as he and the planet were hurtled through space—but he'd never let it beat him. Not then. Not now. He was a Mystallian, after all.

That sense of pride underwent a temporary setback when he looked down at himself and realised he was still tethered to the brute squad guard like an errant child. Pissed that he'd forgotten that fact, he lifted his slitted gaze to the guard, despising the way it could ignore his bending ability which would've otherwise corrected this oversight in an instant. And since being trapped in this hypersonic slipstream meant he couldn't shout out his demand either, he went for the only other thing he could.

He fought to lift his hand off his chest, just enough that when he stopped fighting the force of the wind, it would collide with the coils—especially when he rolled his wrist and curled his fingers into a fist to emphasise his point.

Unfortunately, it didn't quite go to plan, for the coils vanished right before contact and he punched himself soundly in the chest instead. The impact caused him to wince (and maybe even grunt a little if he were being honest with himself) and he shot a dirty look of disgust at the guard who now wholly mirrored his counterpart. *Stupid, realm-damned Highborn Hellion Guards and their bullshit speeds.*

Not wanting to be reminded of his folly, Avis twisted his body so that he no longer faced them. In doing so, he hitched his shoulder, allowing his cloak to catch the gale and whip across the starboard side with the pantheon sigil clearly visible; letting everyone who saw them know that a Mystallian stood on this deck.

After that, he just held on.

* * *

CHAPTER SIX

How long they travelled like that, Avis couldn't say, but he knew they were well into the following day. The sun had crested and was on its way down, which meant at least fourteen to sixteen hours had passed. Fortunately, being a celestial adult meant he could slow down his bodily functions to a crawl and still be able to conduct himself without humiliation. Food, drink, toileting and sleep could all be avoided for days ... even weeks, if necessary. It wouldn't win him any friends in the personality department as his body's objection to the lack of those necessities grew, but in a pinch, it could be done.

Unable to shield himself from Ra's sun or the incessant wind, the exposed skin of his head and neck burned, even more so than when he'd been riding through the air. Somehow, the water all around them made his sunburn worse. Or maybe that was Keket's doing. Being inside the powerbase of another celestial meant anything was possible. His back was still pressed against the tiller post and he'd managed to part his feet in the interim for maximum long-term comfort, but almost all of his attention was on the small cabin where Clarise and the girls were. He still only had his familial contact to go by and it wasn't enough to convince his overactive imagination that they were fine. All he knew for sure was they were alive, but not necessarily safe. They could be ... hurt ... bleeding ... dying even ... and he'd have no way of knowing. But he needed to know. For his sanity's sake, they had to be okay. They just had to be. He'd go insane if they weren't, and not even the threat of the Damned would dissuade him from the rampage that'd follow. Why would it, when he'd already be in his own personal hell for the rest of existence simply by living eternally without them?

By forcing himself to remember that none of the brute squad had moved since the assault began, he managed to pull his thoughts away from that dark place. Likewise, when it came to the servants, only Frash remained outside the room, and he knew that many touch and ranged shifters in one place almost guaranteed their safety. If anything, they were probably in better shape than he was.

However, dark hypotheticals began to worm their way into his thoughts. What if they weren't? What if they were moving too fast for Clarise to snare mass that she could later turn into sustenance for the girls? And what of Cora? She had tefsla in her system—a poison that prevented a shifter from shifting or being shifted. If this attack caught the sleeping child unawares, she could've been thrown from her bed and hurt before anyone got to her and there'd be nothing anyone could do.

Red haze crept into the corners of his vision. That better not be the case. His wife and his girls were his life, and if any of them had so much as a bruise because of Keket, every last Yarusian would pay fucking dearly for it. If it was the last thing he did. What he'd done in a moment of madness would become an all-out mental assault on every one of those copper-toned bastards, and he wouldn't stop until ...

Once again, Avis pulled himself up before he fell any further down that rabbit hole. Assuming the worst and acting on it without waiting for confirmation was what the old him would've done. Which was why most of the family went so far out of their way to ensure they had all the facts before they brought anything that he might not approve of to his attention.

But he wasn't that god anymore, and dammit, he could do this by himself.

Running his tongue across his lips, Avis tasted the thin layer of salt that clung to his skin and used its sharpness to keep his thoughts on track. At the end of the day, there was nothing to say his family were in any kind of trouble. Quite the opposite, in fact, since Columbine was still in the room and her personal guard stood on an angle between the doorway and the front deck that allowed it to see in all directions. Neither would be present if she were in any real danger.

This would all be over if Keket would just poke one fucking hair above the water where he could see it. *Monkey-assed, shapeshifting, motherfucking Chaotian fuck-faced whore who couldn't shift a fucking …*

As name-calling was a safer avenue for his volatile temper, he indulged himself for quite some time, until it occurred to him that the salt spray he hated so much was no longer battering his face. Nor, now that he thought about it, was the water battering against the hull. The latter had been constant background noise for so many hours that Avis had switched off to it. The sudden loss of it caused his ears to hum. Pressure still pinned him to the post, yet somehow, it no longer involved water. How was that even …? Because they were airborne! *Shit!*

As their short and unplanned flight lost momentum, Avis had just enough time to snap his arms around the tiller post before gravity plummeted them downwards.

With nothing else for it, he dropped one shoulder into the post and braced for the impact.

The crunch of the hull as it collided with something also smashed him into the tiller post with enough force to knock him to the deck. A bone-deep crack echoed in his ears as his back slammed against the unyielding surface. In the blur of pain that followed, it occurred to him that the sound could've been his own spine splintering. That would suck since spinal injuries took benders up to a week to walk off.

Then he looked up and saw the entire mast and all its rigging free-falling in his direction. *Fuck!* Not his spine at all! The mast of the fucking ship! His arms shot up and he twisted his head away, fully expecting to be buried under the mountain of timber and fabric. He even felt the cool breeze of a large object moving from left to right across his head and tensed further, but as the seconds ticked over, nothing actually … fell on him.

Already his battered body was knitting itself back together again as he lowered his arms and looked around, specifically for the missing mast and sail. From his prone position, neither were visible, but lifting his eyes he found one of the brute squad guards hovering in the air about ten metres above the deck and five off the starboard side. Its golden tentacles were extended down past the gunwale of the ship.

Putting the pieces together, Avis released a slow, deep breath and rolled onto his stomach. Then he pushed himself onto his knees and hooked his arms over the gunwale to haul himself upright. Confirmation came when he looked over the side of the ship and saw the mast and sail floating harmlessly in the water, both still tethered to the guard overhead. As much as it galled him to do so, Avis lifted his eyes to the guard again and tilted his head in an affirmative acknowledgement of the save. Had his reflexes been sharper, he could've caught the realm damned thing and tossed it overboard himself, but that was the least of his concerns.

A quick scan of their area told him they were still surrounded by water as far as the eye could see, however the ambience was different. Unlike Ra's killer orange sun, a softer, yellow sun shone demurely overhead, dropping the temperature to a much more comfortable level. He didn't even have to guard his eyes to look up at it. And the waters that lapped at the sides of the ship were a vibrant blue that danced and sparkled in the sunlight, rather than a silty brown. Wherever they were, they weren't in Yaru.

More importantly, he still had no idea how his wife and girls were!

Swivelling on his heel, Avis sprinted down the deck towards the boxed room. "CLARISE!" he bellowed desperately as he hooked his fingers into the entrance's architrave and swung into the open doorway, just as he had seen Cora do a thousand times before. But instead of sling-shotting into the middle of the room as he expected, he bounced off a wall of clear gel that filled the opening. He stumbled back, his eyes widening. "What the motherfucking fuck …?" he demanded, his over-stimulated mind automatically launching into attack mode.

"AVIS!" Clarise admonished just as harshly, from less than a handspan in front of him.

Although he couldn't see into the shadowed room, he could well imagine the icy look on her face as her hands snapped to her hips and her foot tapped in open disapproval. It was enough to make the violence that had erupted so instinctively inside him to shrivel into nothing. Both hands went up in apology as he tried to peer past the veil of shadow that hid the interior of the room from him. Then, as his eyes acclimatised, he found the two girls floating in the middle of the room along with the four demon steed statues. Where was their mother? No way had he imagined the sharp side of her tongue because he'd sworn out loud. Then he realised they weren't floating. The whole room was filled with a transparent, water-like substance that suspended them safely in the centre.

"Is everyone alright?" he asked instead, for as much as Clarise hated his use of profanity, he despised surprises of any description.

"Yes, beloved," Clarise answered, again from right in front of his face.

"Where are you?" He searched the room from one wall to the other and still only found the two girls and the demon steeds. Cora seemed to be having the time of her life. Dressed in her daywear, she twisted and rolled inside the liquid, sucking in deep breaths as if it were air and howling in delight. Then she did a short little jogging run that spun her in a tight half-circle until she was held upside down, laughing again at the absurdity.

"You should try this, Father!" she called, once she noticed him in the doorway.

Avis watched her chest rise and fall as she breathed. No air went in; no bubbles came out. She was breathing the liquid. Snorting, Avis shook his head, allowing the last of his apprehension to drain away now that he knew his family was safe. Cora may have enjoyed the constant sensation of drowning, but as far as he was concerned, the other eight levels of Hell had a better chance of freezing over before he'd ever try it. He didn't bother to ask how she was speaking through the substance. He'd given up trying to make sense of shifter bullshit a long time ago.

At least they were all safe for now. He'd deal with the rest shortly. "It's over, Clarise. Let me in," he said quietly.

Dark colours slowly infiltrated the clear gel as Cora was twisted right way up and both the girls and the demon steed statuettes were lowered carefully to the floor. The gel then withdrew from them and broke into five separate units, though only the mass in front of him took on the familiar pitch-black pigment. The other four became a variety of coffee-like tones, of which three became the missing servants. With his wife morphing out of the black gel right in front of him, Avis deduced the last, unmoving mass must have been the furniture. The shifters had quite literally used their bodies and everything else in the room to cushion the girls and the demon steeds.

Smart ...

... and it also explained why Clarise had gotten all bent out of shape at his swearing. She'd literally been right in front of his nose when he mouthed off. He looked down at her stern expression and hitched one shoulder in a silent half-apology.

"What in the realms happened?" she demanded, and Avis realised it wasn't his profanity that had her so cross, but because she still had no idea why things had gone so horribly wrong.

He wrapped his arms around her shoulders and drew her close, then dropped his face into her hair, smothering himself in her lavender scent to assure himself she was fine. Really fine. Those long hours where he'd only been able to identify her by familial location and not hold her close was the worst part of that whole ordeal. Clarise had forgiven him his past, and ever since then he'd never been away from her for more than three or four hours, and never without the immediate means to reach her; should he wish to. As Clarise wove her arms around his waist and twisted her head to hear his pounding heart, he took in several deep, calming breaths.

Then he bent down and captured her lips with his own, ignoring the drawn-out *'ewww'* that came from the peanut gallery better known as Cora.

"We aren't in Yaru anymore," he declared after he broke away, determined to keep his voice as calm and in control as possible. "Once she realised she couldn't get me because of the brute squad, Keket booted us out in the most expedient manner she could."

"Do you know where we are?" Clarise asked.

Avis didn't really want to answer that, because it would show him at a disadvantage. But the problem was, with so many realms butting up against each other, there was no way *to* know which direction Keket had pitched them in. The only thing he did know for certain was they had water under their hull and a bright sun overhead, so they weren't back in the Chaotic Ocean. It wasn't a huge help.

He licked his lips apprehensively.

And tasted a complete lack of salt.

Due to his celestial essence, Avis healed just as quickly as any other bender outside his powerbase, but that didn't extend to anything on him. Dirt and salt particles were still dirt and salt particles until they were washed away ... *or shifted away.*

His lips twisted into a wry smile before he dropped his eyes to confirm his pristine uniform. The light scent of pine crept between the layers of his uniform as if he'd just stepped out of the bath. He even had boots on his feet again. "Thanks, sweetheart," he whispered, feeling better already.

Clarise laid her hand against his cheek. "You really have no idea where we are, do you?" she asked intuitively, dusting her thumb across his cheekbone.

"Not exactly," he admitted, wishing it were otherwise. "But I know we haven't gone backwards. If anything, it's sideways." He knew he'd be able to rectify that just as soon as they crossed paths with anyone, but until then, they were floating blind. Refusing to look at the crushing disappointment in Clarise's eyes, Avis looked over her head to the girls. Cora stood with her feet apart and her hands on her hips as if she could take on the realm single-handedly and win. "Were you running in circles like a hamster the whole time we were on the move?" he asked if only to change the subject.

"What is a hamster?" Cora shot back, just as quickly.

Avis released his hold on Clarise and held his pointer fingers about a hand width apart. "Little furball roughly this big. Likes to spend its whole life eating, sleeping and running inside a wheel that goes nowhere."

"That sounds dumb."

"They don't think so, and if they're the ones having fun doing it, who cares?"

Cora twisted her lips thoughtfully. "So ... they own their space."

"They own their space," Avis agreed, with a slight inclination of his head. "More to the point, were you having fun doing all those flips?"

"Well ... yeah ..."

"Then what does it matter what anyone else thinks? If the object of the game was to enjoy yourself and you were, that's all there is to it. There's no right way to have fun. You either are, or you aren't."

"What if it was inappropriate?"

"One-word answer, tiger. Were. You. Having. Fun?"

"Yes."

"Then my previous statement stands. Stop when you're bored or stop if someone else is doing something that looks like more fun. Or stop because you feel like it. The point is, the space is yours, tiger, but only if you're willing to claim it."

Cora licked her lips and blinked slowly. Her gaze shifted down and to his right, and he knew she was looking at her mother for confirmation. Avis also looked down at Clarise still tucked into his side, practically willing her to agree with his logic regardless of how foreign it was to her. In Hell, the Highborn ladies were subservient to the men all day long. Cora's Mystallian view of trying to hold her own against the hellion lords was what caused her to be landed with a suspended death sentence from them in the first place. The irony was the bastards had thought it'd be a punishment for Avis to take Cora on. They really didn't know Mystallians well at all.

Clarise met Cora's eyes and breathed out a silent sigh. "Disrespect will still not be tolerated," she began, starting as all Highborn Hellions did, with the stick before the carrot. Another difference in a myriad of differences between Mystal and Chaos. In Mystal, the good stuff was emphasised first, so that by the time the downside came about, the individual was giddy with excitement and would agree to anything. "However, your father's words have merit. Your space is your own until we as your parents decide otherwise."

Not quite the angle Avis was going for, but he'd take it for now. "No one should influence what you like or dislike unless it encroaches on another family member's space. No one should influence your tastes. That is your space, tiger. Own it with pride."

Cora lifted her chin and tilted her head. "And if I think I might like what my cousins are doing? Even the boys?"

Avis knew this was the crux of her problem. The Highborn Hellions segregated the sexes, with the males claiming all the power. "Join in. It's that simple." Avis couldn't believe he was having this discussion again, but he'd have it as many times as necessary to get that view into her head. "Mystallians don't differentiate between sexes, Cora. We never have, and we never will. The women have to be tougher than the men, just to hold their own." Just saying the words wasn't going to be enough. He'd said them too many times already, and he could see the way her eyes glazed over that she was zoning him out.

Deciding on a different tactic, he asked with a sly smirk, "Unless you think your male cousins are more capable of making you do what they want than you are of defending your choices?" Gone was the glazed look. The muscles bunched around Cora's jaw and her eyes narrowed into glittering slits. Exactly the reaction he was pushing for. He cocked his eyebrow and offered her a lopsided smirk. "Then you'd better step up your game, young lady. Because if you allow them to push you around, they will."

"I was having fun," she declared, returning to the pose she held at the beginning of the conversation, where her shoulders were squared and her tiny, gloved fists rested against her hips.

Avis nodded in approval. "Then that's all that matters."

Satisfied he'd made his point; Avis shifted his focus to Columbine and frowned. Her knees were drawn to her chest, and her arms were wrapped tightly around her legs. Her unfocused gaze seemed locked on an empty spot on the floor between them, and her mouth was pressed into her knees. Being dressed in her Mystallian uniform meant he couldn't see her arms and legs to gauge how long she'd been curled in that cramped position, but he knew from experience that she'd hold that pose until she collapsed if someone didn't intercede.

He could easily slip into her mind to find out how long she'd been like that, but unfortunately, his adorable little princess would then know that he'd been poking around in her mind. She had no defence against it, but a ghost of his bending presence remained in her memory as surely as if he'd been there physically. The first time he'd seen a rendition of himself moving through her memories, it had thoroughly unnerved him and, if he were honest with himself, he didn't like it any better now. It was just … wrong. Weaker minds were never meant to know when a more powerful bender was reviewing their memories. Columbine's uniqueness just kept growing, and not necessarily in a good way.

"Clarise, would you mind taking Cora and the servants out onto the deck for a few minutes? I'd like a private word with Columbine."

"Of course, beloved."

* * *

CHAPTER SEVEN

Once the room was cleared, Avis moved over to Columbine, but instead of squatting down in front of her, he sat down properly on his ass and crossed his legs. She still had her legs drawn up to her chest with her mouth pressed painfully into her knees, and her arms wrapped tightly around her legs. He couldn't tell if her lack of rocking was a good thing or not.

After eyeing her for a few seconds and gauging her to be completely incognizant of his presence, he licked his lips. "Hey, princess." He barely breathed the words, and when she didn't react, he scooted close enough that their boots almost touched. "Can you hear me?"

She still didn't move, so he leaned forward and encircled her small frame with his arms without touching her. His mind was ready to go in hard and shut her down if he had to, but he was hoping it wouldn't come to that. Then he tightened the circle until his arms brushed lightly against hers.

The moment the contact was made, Columbine snapped back to the present with a surging gasp and Avis could almost feel the overwhelming misery that engulfed her. He immediately dragged her into his lap, hugging her tightly against his chest. "Shhhhhhh," he crooned, pressing her head under his chin and rocking her, much as he had seen his youngest brother do countless times before with his children. Now that he had one of his own, the absurd position that seemed to foster more blubbering than it cured finally made sense to him. Comforting his daughter when she hurt like this made sense. He lifted one hand to caress her face and neck, brushing away the tears that streamed down her face. "It's okay, princess. It's okay. No one's going to hurt you."

"Why was Lady Keket so mad? We did not do anything!" she wailed, clinging desperately to him.

Avis had to think for a minute about how to answer that. The last thing he wanted was for Columbine to know the specifics of his crimes—crimes which he hadn't fully explained to Clarise yet. "It wasn't about you, princess," he promised, starting with the safer ground of who *wasn't* to blame. "It will never be about you. Lady Keket adored you, just like everyone else does. In fact, when I stand on the last day of eternity, one of the memories I'm going to look back on with fondness is the image of you playing patty-cake with one of Yaru's oldest and more dangerous goddesses."

"But she was so mad!"

"At me," Avis insisted, quietly. "She was mad at me, baby. This was never about you."

"Why?"

Avis found himself licking his lips that had suddenly gone dry. "When … when your mother and I were apart … I did some … very bad things, princess. Some *really*, very bad things … and a lot of good people got hurt."

Columbine continued to sob, but then, through staggered breathing that ended in wheezing snuffles, she managed to bring her tears to a halt. One look at her tear-glazed eyes and Avis knew she'd unleash another torrent at the smallest provocation. "You were naughty?" she whimpered in shock.

Avis pressed his lips together and wiped her eyes with his glove, huffing out a humourless breath. *Understatement of the eon, right there.* "Yeah, princess. I was very, very naughty, and all those different gods and goddesses out there have every right to be angry with me."

"Why can you not just say you are sorry?"

Avis thought about what he had done. The women he'd forced himself upon … the pantheons he'd ripped through and the powerbases he'd upended. The carnage he'd caused at every turn and how determined he'd been to produce more. The death of the Yarusian city was just another entry in the long litany of his crimes.

He breathed out heavily and leaned forward to kiss her hair. Guilt had become a bitter master he couldn't outrun. "Sometimes, just saying you're sorry won't cut it, sweetheart. For what it's worth, I'm sorrier than I can ever say and I do wish I could take it all back." The back-pedalling went against his grain as a Mystallian, but in this instance, he meant every word of it. His voice broke at the thought of hurting her and their small family any more than he already had. "I went crazy back then, and I caused a lot of trouble. Now, I'm a wanted god out here, princess, by a lot of good celestials whom I wronged horribly. They're all going to be very angry if they find out I'm back in their realms again. But no matter what happens to me, I don't want you thinking you had anything to do with it. You didn't. This is on me. All me. Okay?"

Columbine blinked up at him, her glazed eyes tearing up again. "But I do not want them being mad at you, Father."

Avis sighed and cuddled her close again. "I don't want them being mad at me either, princess, but they will be, and they have every right to be. I'm not the same god when I'm with your mother, and back then I broke a lot of things …"

Columbine brightened and pulled away to stare up at his face. "If Mother and I fix their things, they will not hate you anymore."

Such a simple solution. Such an *adorably* simple solution. Avis closed his eyes and sighed, hating himself all the more. "Not these things, princess," he said repentantly as he stroked her hair. "And I think from here on, it would be better if you don't tell anyone I'm your father. At least, not until we get back to Mystal. Otherwise, they might do to us …" *what I did to them.* The words hung heavily in the silence as he contemplated the years he'd been on the run. At that moment he wished (even more than he'd wanted his freedom from the Nexus) that his family had directly handed him over to the Hellions instead of granting him the running start that kicked off his rampage. Clarise and his girls would've still been waiting for him when he left the Damned, and the rest of his downward spiral would never have happened.

Hindsight could be a real bitch.

"Was that why Cora did not like you?"

Cora and his treatment of their mother the day of her birth. Another booze-induced memory he wished he could erase. He bowed his head until his forehead rested on her hair, barely having the will to finish this conversation. "It goes really close, baby. But I think your sister and I have made our peace over that."

"She does not want to like you, but she does."

Avis suspected as much, but it was nice to have it confirmed by the one person who knew for sure. He pressed his lips to her hair again. "She's my daughter, princess. Just like you, so she has to forgive me eventually. It's the celests I'm not related to, that have no reason to forgive me. They want my blood, baby, and they want it very badly. And since I don't plan on handing myself over to them, we'll have to wait and see what happens. Either way, I won't let anything happen to you, or your sister or your mother. On that, you have my absolute word."

"*Ko wai koe, me aha koe kei roto Rangi-Tuarea, tangata ke,*" a brash male voice from outside called.

"Excuse you?" Clarise's crisp voice returned. Avis looked over his shoulder and saw Clarise step in to block the open doorway from the right with her back to him and Columbine.

Several things then occurred to Avis at the same time.

One: they were no longer alone. Two: there was a local out there, which meant three: he could now find out where they were. And four: Clarise had been right beside the open doorway the whole time and probably heard every word he'd said. *SHIT!* This was not how he'd wanted Clarise to find out about his rampage. He rose to his feet and placed Columbine on the ground behind him, warning her with a spread-fingered wave to stay behind him. He then moved up to Clarise's side, ready to drag her back into the room and mentally shred this newcomer if he recognised Clarise's uniform and went on the offensive.

"Ahhhh. Mystallian," the voice replied, still full of confidence. "Should have guessed that by the little white *kotiro* up on the observation deck. Well, then, my fair lady, welcome to Rangi-Tuarea. Realm of Oceanics."

...or not.

* * *

As Clarise stood outside the room, her mind churned with everything she'd overheard. She'd known her husband had gone insane with rage while they were apart, but it was still difficult to hear him speak of it. Rage, revenge and insanity were standard terms of everyday life in Hell, and she was all but inured to them. But it was different when the source was someone she cared about. She wanted more than anything to be able to stand at his side and not back down from anyone, but to do that, the two of them needed to sit down so that he could spell out exactly what he'd done. It wasn't a conversation she was looking forward to, but a unified front required an understanding of the stakes.

Her gaze swept towards where Cora stood on the observation deck at the bow of the ship with one of the four guards within arm's reach of her. The other two had taken up position on the corners of the flat cabin roof above her own head. The fourth still stood off just to her left. Their movement was the only warning she received before she heard, "*Who are you and what are you doing in Rangi-Tuarea, stranger?*" over her right shoulder.

Neither the demand nor being labelled a stranger pleased the visiting Highborn Hellion lady. It wasn't the language that posed a problem for her. She had studied many in her long life, as well as the pantheons that used them. It was the attitude behind it. Clarise had never been outside of Hell without at least one male member of her family chaperoning her, and they had always ensured she received the deference due to her station. Had the Lords of Hell (and by proxy every other hellion and demon travelling with them) heard such a belittling demand of her, the ramifications would have been … bloody. But they weren't here, because she was a Mystallian now and Mystallians didn't wait for anyone to fight their battles for them.

Her gaze snapped to the gunwale slightly ahead of the doorway between her and Cora where a young bipedal man with dark skin balanced effortlessly on the railing. He was short and well-built, with dark tattoos over every inch of exposed skin, even his ears and lips. His loincloth of reeded flora barely kept him decent, and the way he stood with his hands on his hips, it was as if he was waiting for her to compliment him on his physique.

"Excuse you?" she asked instead, as she stepped to her left to block the cabin doorway. He was heavyset, to be sure. Muscular, but quite short. The only reason Clarise had to look up at him was because the gunwale he stood on was that much higher than the deck under her feet. If they were on equal footing, he'd be substantially shorter than her.

"Ahhhh. Mystallian," he said, waving her icy tone away as if it were inconsequential. "Should have guessed that by the little white *girl* up on the observation deck. Well, then, my fair lady, welcome to Rangi-Tuarea. Realm of Oceanics."

That was a more appropriate greeting between pantheons. Inclining her head slightly in his direction, she offered a polite smile and said, "Well met, Son of Rangi-Tuarea …"

"Maui," he said, interrupting her.

Clarise paused, her lips pinching into a fine line of disapproval. His audacity bordered on overconfidence, almost as if he were compensating for something. A closer, more critical evaluation of him had her deducing that he most likely lacked experience in life. His youthful vigour, appearance and the fact she'd never seen so much as an image of him before all pointed towards his juvenescence. She brought her gaze back to his face. "Excuse you?" she repeated coolly.

Completely missing the second reprimand in as many minutes, the young man slapped himself on the chest and jumped down from the gunwale, putting himself almost a head shorter than Clarise—which in her current form said a lot. "I'm Maui." He paused and drew in another deep breath to inflate his chest proudly as if waiting for that name to mean something to her.

It didn't.

"Maui," Clarise repeated with a polite smile, if only to demonstrate how it was done. Until he identified himself as a member of the pantheon, Clarise refrained from giving him the title of 'Lord'. "I am Lady Clarise of Mystal." She heard a cautious movement in the cabin behind her and knew Avis was moving up to stand alongside the doorway so he could listen in on both sides of the conversation without giving his presence away. She adored his overprotective nature but didn't think she had much to fear from this child with an over-inflated ego. She gestured to Cora, who was still on the observation deck; though at some point she had turned to watch the proceedings. "And this is my daughter, Lady Cora."

Cora rolled her shoulders and dipped her head without ever taking her eyes off their visitor. The latter was something her father had taught her to do, most likely to keep her bending ability in play. "Maui," she said in acknowledgement, then straightened again.

Maui barely glanced at Cora before dismissing her with a bored eye roll, causing Clarise to add rudeness to his growing list of flaws. "Oh!" the small man exclaimed, throwing both hands in the air as if the obvious had only just occurred to him. "Here! Look at this!" He turned and grabbed the gunwale rail behind him with one hand, while the other clutched at something buried beneath the foliage on his hip. In no time at all, the single-hulled ship began to warp and change. "You're going to love this!" he promised over his shoulder, then grinned as the ship began to liquefy around them. "But you might want to hang onto something, Clarise."

Clarise did a great deal more than 'hang on', though she made no outward sign of it. She overlaid her own shapeshifting mastery to his enhanced hellion ability and kept enough of the ship intact to mimic his changes without endangering her family or staff. She also kept Avis and Columbine hidden in the altered room behind her, while Frash withdrew her connection to the oarsmen and returned to her singular hellion form up near Cora and her guard. Clarise clasped her hands serenely before her and waited for Maui to finish his feat of supposed magnificence. She hadn't missed his deliberate exclusion of her title, and she knew Avis hadn't either. His breathing beside her had taken on a growl of discontent.

When it was over, the ship had become a twin-hulled catamaran with two large decks and a massive three-sided sail overhead. Maui's likeness adorned the mainsail, apparently to remind them for the rest of their journey who had bequeathed them this wondrous gift. Cora and the servants stood hidden behind the mast on one of the lower floats, while Clarise and Maui were on the upper deck still in the doorway of a very spacious cabin. Clarise didn't think for a minute that his attempt at securing them privacy had been an accident.

"Awesome, yeah?" Maui asked, slapping his hands together as if daring her to refute it.

Clarise made a point of giving the ship another once-over as if to reaffirm her opinion of the workmanship. "Nicely done, young man," she agreed with an appreciative nod.

At that, Maui lost his proud swagger and openly scowled at her. "What makes you think I'm young?" he demanded.

Well, since you asked. "A man of experience would know to ask who they were dealing with before assuming they held the superior position." She kept her eyes on his face and smiled indulgently as she spoke because, in this instance, she meant no insult. He was young. There could be no question of that. Life experience had yet to shape him beyond a handful of decades. Maybe a century or two at best.

To give him an example of her own shifting capability, Clarise drew his attention to the sail above them and removed Maui's image from it, returning it to a simple but durable cloth. "However, the overall design of the ship is lovely and spacious, and I thank you for it."

Maui watched her modification, then dropped his gaze to glare at her. "You're a shifter," he said, practically accusing her of it.

"I am," she agreed, wondering where he would take this. The fact that he knew of Mystallians but hadn't recognised the four Highborn Hellion Guards with her was just as telling of his age in her eyes.

"I'm a shifter too!"

Her gaze softened, and she tried not to be condescending. "I can see that, handsome..."

The endearment was meant in a generalised manner to put him at ease, but she recognised the carnal look that entered his eyes, even as his lips pinched upwards on one side. She'd seen it often enough in Avis. "You think I'm handsome?" he asked, running his tongue over his lips suggestively.

Clarise refrained from uttering a sigh of resignation as she removed her left glove and pulled back her long sleeve to reveal one of her two marriage bracers. "I am afraid that will not be happening, young man."

At least he was old enough to recognise a celestial wedding bracer. His eyes widened at its presence and he stepped away from her as if stung. But then he paused and rubbed his bottom lip, frowning thoughtfully.

His next words completely floored Clarise.

"Is your husband still in Mystal?"

* * *

CHAPTER EIGHT

Avis stood alongside the curtained doorway, his hands clenching into tight fists. *Why you motherfucking, poaching little ass-wipe,* he fumed, even though the irony of the situation was not lost on him. Despite his own amorous history, if that boy said one more realm-damned word about making a move on Clarise, or so much as thought about brushing against her after this, he'd rip the cocky little shit to pieces. No question. He was already fairly certain he was going to anyway, but either of those would've guaranteed it.

Clarise also seemed to know where his mindset was, for she grew a third arm from beneath her cloak and reached back to intertwine her fingers with his. She made no movement of her body to indicate he was there, but her extra hand squeezed his and her thumb stroked his knuckles. He knew the meaning behind that gesture. She had this. Still, it pissed him off to be hiding in the shadows instead of stepping up and staking his claim.

"No, he is very close by," she replied, and again Avis felt her squeeze his hand for patience. After everything they'd been through, Avis was more inclined to squeeze the little bastard's neck until his fucking head popped off!

Lavender filled his senses, enough for him to get a hold of his murderous thoughts. Barely.

"Pity," he heard Maui snort, and his free hand clenched into an even tighter fist.

"If you do not mind me asking, Maui, which branch of the hellions does your blood originate from?" Clarise asked.

Maui snorted in disgust. "I'm no hellion," he snapped. "I can just change the shape of things."

The simplistic statement sent Avis' brain into a tailspin. *Wait ... what?* It took a moment to process the moronic comment, and once he had, he closed his eyes and covered them with his free hand. *Oh, for fuck's sake!* In the space of a day, they'd gone from meeting the oldest and most dangerous, to the youngest and most stupid. He shook his head in disbelief. *I'm not a celestial at all. I'm just a god. Of all the fucking idiots ...* Being a celest who could change the shape of others without a powerbase was the very definition of a hellion! Highborn Hellions also fit into that category, but since Clarise identified Maui as a hellion and not a member of her family, he accepted her judgement on the matter. But how could the kid not know he was hellion? Avis continued to shake his head. That boy needed to go back on his mother's tit if he didn't understand the basics of being a celest.

Unable to stay in the shadows any longer, Avis lowered his hand from his eyes, unwound his fingers from Clarise's and stepped in behind her. At his full height he was easily head and shoulders over her, and he used every bit of it to stake his claim. Both hands went around her waist and once he had his fingers knotted together, he pulled her back to his chest in a possessive manner that not even this idiot could misinterpret. Then he looked down at the newcomer. Way, waaay down. *Damn, and I thought Clarise was short.* The midget was marginally taller than his elbow. Way too short to be flirting with married women ... especially when their powerful husbands were within striking distance.

To the brat's credit, Avis' unexpected arrival did have him backing up a few steps.

"Maui, isn't it?" Avis asked over Clarise' head, in a way that implied the boy was on exceedingly dangerous ground.

Maui lifted his chin and squinted up at him, reminding Avis of every conversation he'd ever had with either Tal or Griffith—the two and a half metre giants of his family. *So, this is what it feels like to be on the other side of those conversations.*

"What of it?"

The boy was going to great lengths to lay on the bravado, but Avis had to admit Clarise's first impression was accurate; she could've handled this pipsqueak without his involvement. "Here's a piece of much-needed advice, kid. Don't go making passes at married women unless you know exactly what they're capable of and where their husbands are. A stunt like that'll get you killed faster than taking a dump on Belial's throne."

The elbow of Clarise's third arm slammed into Avis' abdomen with enough force to nearly rupture his spleen, and he locked his teeth together in a tight grimace to prevent any sound from escaping his lips. A hand width or two lower and he'd have been in real trouble. So, the ladies of the Hellion Highborn took offence to the mere thought of their patriarch's throne being desecrated like that. Or at least, Clarise did. *Duly noted.*

Ignorant of their silent interaction, Maui threw his head back and barked out a laugh. "Now who's the fool?" he taunted, flicking both sets of fingertips at them derisively.

Confused by his reaction, Avis turned his thoughts inward and spent the next few minutes replaying the warning through his memories to try and ascertain the source of Maui's amusement, only to come up empty. "I might not be the right one to ask that of, Maui," he admitted after returning to the physical realm, his brow creasing in annoyance. "I doubt you'll like my answer."

"Why is warning you to take care such a foolish notion in your eyes?' Clarise asked, snuggling comfortably against Avis' chest as if she hadn't just elbowed his guts through his teeth. Unified front to outsiders; she really was starting to get it.

"Because this is Rangi-Tuarea, and nothing can be killed here," Maui's words accompanied a shrug as if that should've been obvious.

Avis felt his right eye twitch. "Come again?" The statement was so mind-numbingly absurd that he could barely say the words. Without an establishment field, everything that lived had a potential expiration date. Even celests. "What in the realms do you mean nothing dies?"

Maui's smug grin was really wearing on Avis' last nerve. "Nothing can be killed here in Rangi-Tuarea. Except for me, everything lives forever."

Avis scrambled to make sense of that. Immortality without an establishment field was only possible by being descended from those who were already previously established. Even that was only a potential immortality because while you *could* live forever, you could also be killed by any other means, in which case, you died. The only way to guarantee true immortality was to become established. Constructs that were brought into being by either side had whatever lifespan their creators wanted for them and still ran the risk of being killed, and everything *mortal* died, period. It was right there in the title. How could a realm have NO death? And what exactly did he mean by *except for me?*

"Don't you eat things and use things that were once living?" Avis was completely baffled by the boy's gibberish, and he hated puzzles that made no sense. "For the realm's sake! How could you possibly live at all without having the things that came before you pass away?"

"Of course, we eat meat and use plants, but since they aren't alive like us, they don't die either."

The vein in Avis' temple began to pound unmercifully, and he swore by the Twin Notes that if this kid didn't start making sense soon, he would scream!

"How do you keep your whole realm immortal?" Clarise asked, far more civilly than Avis had planned to.

Maui snorted derisively, but since he didn't laugh outright, Avis let it go in favour of obtaining a rational answer. "We use incantations, of course," he said.

Ahhh – magic. Okay, that made a little more sense. "Who's your god of magic then?" Because in a realm like this, that had to be who was in charge. Magic also brought up another interesting point that had been bothering him. "Is that why you don't think you're a hellion? Because your shapeshifting is magically orientated?"

"He is a hellion," Clarise whispered, through a mouth she created at the back of her head to prevent Maui from eavesdropping. Paying them no attention, Maui twisted and reached into the reeded foliage on his left hip, removing a hooked bone of some description with a small coil of leather rope tied to it.

"This is what enables me to shapeshift," he declared, holding it up for them to see but ensuring they were in no position to take it from him. "It's my grandmother's."

Avis looked at the curved bone in his hand. He'd heard of stranger things being talismans. "So, your grandmother is the magical goddess of this realm, and she imbued that hook with magic?" he asked, confirming what he thought was obvious.

He didn't expect Maui to bark out another mocking laugh. "Don't be dumb," the pint-sized pipsqueak scorned, waving that stupid hook at them. "This *is* her. Her jawbone, to be exact. And with it, I get all her powers."

Ewww…fuck. Avis was officially creeped out. They were making weapons out of the bones of their elders? "Hold on," he frowned, as the two stories clashed. "How is your grandmother not dead if that's her jawbone?"

"Because she never lived here, of course. She was with my *papara.*"

"Who?"

"My father." He put the hook away. "Death happens all the time over there. I don't know why they never fixed that."

Avis scrambled to keep up. His mother was here in the Oceanics, and his father was … *still in Hell?* He needed to be sure. "So, where is your father?"

Maui shrugged, a little uncomfortable. "Not sure, really. I followed *kowhaea* once when I realised she was vanishing through the night. One second she was there, the next she wasn't. I hung onto her dress hem, and the next thing I knew, she was introducing me to my father." Maui patted his hip where his hook hung. "And he gave me this. With it, I can change anything I touch into anything else, including myself."

"That is indeed a powerful gift," Clarise said, picking up the conversation again.

Avis couldn't stand the loopy explanation anymore and went straight into the kid's mind. The limited spectrum of memories at the boy's disposal meant he'd either had his mind erased or was even younger than he seemed. Going all the way back to the beginning, Avis saw flashes of the boy's birth which confirmed the latter. A teenager. Sixteen or seventeen … maybe eighteen at best.

As Avis surfed through the limited memories, he began to understand what made the boy the way he was. Coming from the Nexus, Avis himself may have been abused as a child (and wished during those times he was dead), but no one had ever tried to discard him from the family like he was garbage. Maui was born premature, and in this pantheon it seemed that level of weakness was unacceptable. In a twisted way, he could almost make sense of that logic—if he were to believe a pantheon was only as strong as your weakest member; which he didn't. From personal experience, he knew the runts often turned into the worst and best kind of pit-bull. Chance was living proof of it. Maui's upbringing was different to Chance's though, in that while he may have gotten some help along the way, nothing was given to him freely. He had to fight for every realm damned thing he had, which was why he knew and had so little. He didn't know the right questions to ask or the right people who could answer them.

Avis watched as Maui—a young man of twelve or thirteen—crept back into his family home and reinserted himself into their lives. They recognised the familial connection that flowed between them, and while his brothers and sisters took him in, his mother needed much more convincing. The poor kid didn't help his cause when he was smart enough to realise the matriarch of the family vanished for hours in the early hours of the morning, only to reappear before the dawn. Determined to find out for himself what Taranga was doing, he attached himself to her hem so that when she blood-linked with her husband, he went along for the ride.

But the name Taranga called as she created her blood-link caused Avis' heart to freeze and his stomach to hit the floor all at once. Makeatutara. Master guardian of the fourth level of Hell, and very, very much established. Avis knew him and his love affair with poison and sharp blades all too well. A despicably nasty piece of work at the best of times that Avis couldn't see as a family man. And since Makeatutara remained in Hell while Maui and his siblings lived in Rangi-Tuarea (two realms away), he knew he wasn't wrong.

He cringed as the naive Maui went willingly to his knees before his father in reverence. *Run kid! Don't just sit there! RUN!* There was no way this was going to end well for the boy, and once again Avis wished for the power to change a past event. Taranga and Makeatutara spoke in lowered voices to one side, and just from their body language alone, Avis knew they were up to no good. The fourth level master guardian of Hell was incapable of acting any other way.

He almost winced when Makeatutara placed his clawed hands on Maui's shoulders and began reciting something in Oceanic. Maui's point of view swung upwards as he stared at his father in horror, and the knowledge of what Makeatutara had done suddenly became clear to Avis. It was supposed to have been an Oceanic blessing—the incantation that gave the boy immortality, just as Maui had claimed. But Makeatutara's wording turned it from an immortality blessing to a mortality curse. The bastard had just cursed his own son to be the first Oceanic to die!

Avis knew that was no fucking accident. Makeatutara didn't make mistakes like that. *None* of the master guardians of Hell made mistakes like that. No matter how much he supposedly apologised afterwards, it was all a fucking lie. No wonder the kid was living like every moment could be his last. Thanks to that bastard, it might very well be!

And that was when Maui had been presented with his 'grandmother's jawbone' as a magical compromise. With it, he was told he could shapeshift himself and anything he touched into anything he wanted. *Oh, you lying sack of crap!* Avis couldn't believe what he was hearing, but the way Maui handled the precious scrap of bone that held no magical ability whatsoever, it was clear the boy believed every word of it.

The boy's father was hellion. That made Maui hellion. Shifting themselves and anything they touched was their birthright, and Maui was being led to believe his power was unique because of a piece of useless fucking bone!

Glancing over other memories, Avis saw that up until three years ago, the realm of Rangi-Tuarea only had an hour of daylight each day. And of course, Maui's mother constantly bitched about her inability to cook their meals and eat them within that hour. Maui's brothers ignored her grumblings, but still thinking the sun still shone out of her ... backside, Maui hung off every word. One day, with the hope of impressing her, he coerced his brothers into helping him snare the sun while he took to it with the *magical* jawbone. The boy had no idea what he was doing, but through his actions, Avis did. With the jawbone in his hand, Maui had subconsciously hardened the bone to the point where it would harm the solar deity, and when he swung it, it hurt. Maui beat the sun into a permanent pulp which was why it now crawled across the sky and the days were now as long as any other realm. It was an interesting side story, one which Maui's people appreciated—even his mother. Too bad that didn't happen before the bitch arranged his death.

Avis pulled back from the young man's mind, more sympathetic than when he had first gone in. The kid was just making the best of a really fucked up situation. He of all people could relate to that. "He's Makeatutara's son," Avis said, for Clarise's sake.

"You know my father?" Maui asked as Clarise's eyes snapped to her husband.

Avis barely refrained from rolling his own, though he felt the upper right corner of his lips curl into a dark sneer. "You might say we've crossed paths."

Whether it was his condescending tone or what he'd said, Maui's gaze suddenly narrowed, and Avis felt himself being scrutinised. "You're Avis," he said. Surprisingly there was no hostility in that statement. If anything, the little huff that followed as he shook his head implied he should have made that connection sooner.

Avis was ready to toss Clarise to the safety of the cabin and turn Maui's mind into confetti, if he had to. His hands were already tightening around her waist. "That's *Lord* Avis to you, kid, and are we going to have a problem with that?"

Maui snorted and waved the idea away as ridiculous. "Not with me," he smirked, still shaking his head. "Your deranged antics got me out of a lot of trouble a few years ago."

Avis knew he was going to regret asking, but did anyway. "And how exactly did I do that?"

"My ancient ancestors weren't too happy with the thrashing I gave the sun, but after you came through and mentally tore up the place, I was the last thing they cared about."

Three years ago. Just a few months before he was incarcerated. *Okay.* "So, what are your plans now?"

The boy gave a half shrug. "Haven't decided. I only came over because I saw your ship getting tossed right out of Yaru and I wanted to meet whoever had managed to get them so riled up. For the most part, they're pretty placid, so I knew it had to be someone big. I should've guessed it was you."

"He genuinely has not decided what to do about us," Clarise whispered through her second mouth.

Avis eyed the boy carefully. His base instinct told him to put a stranglehold on Maui's mind and force his compliance for the rest of their time in Rangi-Tuarea; leaving nothing to chance. That's what the old Avis would've done in a heartbeat. But seeing for himself the hell the boy had been through already, he decided to cut him a break. "Would you be interested in a deal?" he asked instead.

Maui tilted his head and folded his arms as if he had no clue how easily Avis could force his hand. "You've got my attention, trouble-maker." He blinked and dropped his arms to his hips, emitting a loud, boyish laugh. "*Kai a te ahi!* Never thought I'd ever get to call someone else that for a change."

Avis clicked his tongue against the roof of his mouth a few times to prevent himself from taking the little shit's head off. "Former," he said, once he had his rising temper under control. "My only objective now is to take my wife and children home."

Maui looked up at Avis. Then he dropped his gaze to Clarise and turned to probably look at Cora on the lower deck out the front. "You have more than one *kotiro* running around here?" he asked, bringing his attention back to Avis and Clarise.

Kotiro: girl. Amongst other things, Avis picked up the basics of the Oceanic language during his time in Maui's mind. He turned and beckoned Columbine to his side but kept her tucked safely behind his leg and under his cape. "Two in total," he said, as Columbine waved shyly at Maui.

Maui looked down at her and grinned at her. "Well, aren't you a cute little thing?"

A growl reverberated through Avis' chest as he pushed Columbine back behind his leg and lifted himself to his full, intimidating height.

Maui screwed his face up as if he'd tasted something foul. "Really, man? Ewwww … no! She's just a kid." Unfortunately, his innocence went up in smoke when he dropped one hand on his hip and rubbed the other across his chin thoughtfully. "Now if in a decade or two, your deal was to consist of a possible …"

Clarise cut him off with a succinct, "That will not be discussed at this time," before Avis could take matters into his own hands. "The deal I believe my husband spoke of was information, in exchange for safe passage." The hand of her third arm stroked his ribs under his cloak, and lavender wafted from her in waves, removing the distinct red tinge that was fast swallowing up his vision.

"What kind of information?"

"The kind you should've had if your parents weren't complete assho …"

"*A better understanding* of the realms around you, and your place in them," Clarise sharply overrode, adding a light squeeze to Avis' ribs to silence him. "Unfortunately, sweetheart, not everything in your life is as you have been told."

Maui drummed his fingers against his tattooed lips, his eyes shifting between the two of them. Then, he pulled his hand away from his chin and held it out to Clarise. "I'll get you as far as I can, but if anyone discovers us, you're on your own." He looked down at her unmoving hand and arched an eyebrow. "Well?"

Clarise slid her hand across his and locked her fingers around his wrist. Then she bowed forward, to which Maui leaned forward and pressed his forehead to hers. Avis stiffened at the apparent intimacy, but when the pair released each other a few seconds later and Maui stepped away, he realised it was merely the Oceanic way of sealing a deal.

"I suggest you stay inside as much as possible," Maui said, and Avis had no doubt it was to him he was speaking. The native then went to the nearest rigging and scurried up into the sail with the same speed and ease of running across the deck. Taking a deep breath of the ocean spray, he hung off the top of the mast as if he were king of the realm, and at that moment, he might well have been. "Things may get a little … bumpy."

* * *

CHAPTER NINE

For the next week and a half, Avis refused to sleep. Putting it mildly, he didn't trust Maui as far as he could toss the little prick. What started out as an hourly check of the boy's mind for his motives then devolved into an ongoing supervision that had Avis sweeping through his thoughts every few seconds. *Now? How about now? What about now?* It still would've been a lot easier to just create a mandate of obedience in Maui's head and make it stick for the foreseeable future, but noooo, he'd been stupid enough to mention that option to Clarise. Now, after she insisted he not to make the situation between himself and the Oceanics any worse than it already was by being pre-emptive, he was stuck doing this stupid responsive dance.

It sucked.

From the lower deck, his eyes followed Maui as he ran across the boom and shinnied up the mast. Another brief sweep of his surface thoughts told Avis they hadn't changed in the last few seconds, but how was he to know exactly when the decision to betray someone would be made? Avis watched with a tight scowl as Maui ducked in behind the sail, and when he didn't immediately reappear on the other side, the Mystallian patriarch assumed the worst. "Bastard," he swore, storming to the front of the deck in anticipation of shredding Maui's mind the moment he caught sight of him again.

Just as he reached the corner of the lower cabin, a black-gloved hand shot into his path and spread across his chest with enough strength to pull him up. "Enough, Avis," Clarise said, stepping around the corner to face him. The gold in her eyes hardened into jagged peaks of displeasure, and her fingertips pushed into his ribs, reminding him of their presence. "You need to stop."

Avis stared down at her hand then followed her arm back to her face; his own creasing in confusion. *He* needed to stop? How was *he* in the wrong when right now, at this moment, when Maui could be contacting someone to harm her and the girls? Just the thought of it had his eyes snapping back to the rigging overhead, even as his right hand curled around her fingers. "I'm fine," he said dismissively, attempting to step around her.

Clarise braced herself against him. "Avis, no," she said, determined to stand her ground.

Avis blinked, then frowned down at her. How could she not see Maui for the threat he was? And worse, why was he suddenly the problem here?

"Beloved, we have four Highborn Hellion guards here with us, as well as four touch shifters, two ranged shifters and another ranged bender apart from yourself. Do you really think anything could happen to us in the next few hours, that we cannot take care of without you?"

As her words slowly filtered through his sleep-deprived brain, Avis' frown of confusion intensified. "Where exactly do you think I'm going?" he finally asked.

"To bed," Clarise stated, with the snap of command.

Avis' mouth immediately flew open to argue, but Clarise placed the fingers of her other hand across his lips to silence him. "You have not slept since Keket attacked us, beloved. Nor have you eaten. If your plan is to stay awake and safeguard us until we reach Olympus sometime in the next few months, I see a fundamental flaw in your execution."

Avis stepped away from her, not to retreat but to give himself some space to speak where her lavender fragrance wouldn't sway him. "This is Maui ..." he argued.

"Exactly," Clarise countered, holding her position at the corner. "He is but a child living under the pretence of being a man, and you are treating him as if he is a threat capable of besting all of us single-handedly. If anything, now is when you should be making the most of the situation by getting some much-needed rest, before someone or something with real power arrives to challenge us. That is when we will need you."

Avis looked up into the rigging again, refusing to admit she was right. He pursed his lips and worked his jaw from side to side because, realms dammit, he still didn't trust Maui.

"Avis," she chided from right in front of him; placing a hand against his cheek and spooking him in the process. He hadn't heard her move. "It will be alright."

"You can't guarantee that ..."

"I can," she insisted. "And you know I can. We have enough power on this catamaran to destroy half the realm, and if necessary I can and will have Uriel here within seconds to deal with the other half. Nothing is going to happen to us while you get some sleep."

The thought of Uriel saving them did not sit well with the Mystallian. "I hate your brother."

"Going by the way he tortured you for two years, I would say the feeling is entirely mutual, beloved. Nevertheless, he will protect us, should it come to that."

Avis shifted his weight to the left and leaned his shoulder into the cabin wall; his arms folded stubbornly across his chest. "It doesn't matter," he stated resolutely. "I can't go to sleep. Even if I wanted to, which I don't, the bender in me won't switch off."

He expected a huge argument. One that he had every intention of winning. Instead, a broad, indulgent smile spread across Clarise's face and she slipped her hands around his neck, drawing him down into a warm embrace. For the life of him, he couldn't figure out why. Especially when he'd just told her he wasn't going to ...

"Do you trust me?" she whispered softly in his ear.

"Of course." The response was automatic.

Using their bodies as cover, she loosened her hold and dropped one hand between them. She curled her thumb and fingers as if she were holding something small and cylindrical. Then, as Avis continued to watch, mass poured out of her little finger until a shot glass filled with cloudy liquid took form. Avis didn't like where he thought this was going, especially when she pushed the glass into his left hand and firmly curled his fingers around it. "The cabin upstairs has a Mystallian mattress already made up for you, beloved," she said, rising up onto her tiptoes and adding the necessary height to kiss him lightly on the cheek. "No one is going to force you to sleep, but that drink will give you the same eight hours that one of your sleeper holds does."

Avis glared at the drink, then at her. "If no one's forcing me, why do I feel forced?" he grumbled, scowling darkly.

Clarise smiled again. "Because it's for your own good, and you know you need it." Her hand brushed his cheek. "And because you already know what you are going to do, regardless of the choice you've been given."

Avis looked down at her serene face, wishing he had a legitimate counterargument for that. But he didn't because in just a matter of months, his beloved wife had become almost as adept at manipulating him as the runt himself. She'd known better than to say he had no choice, as that would make the bender in him roar in defiance and he'd have thrown the shot glass overboard and stomped off. No, every word out of Clarise's mouth had reinforced the notion that he was still the one in charge. His choice about what he needed to do. His space.

Avis' chest heaved, feeling more cornered by the second.

"Trust me, beloved. Nothing will happen while you rest." She stroked one side of his neck. "I love you."

Avis *really* didn't want to do this. Almost as much as he hadn't wanted to eat that Damned meatball a few months ago. He dragged his bottom lip through his teeth without saying a word. Everything in him demanded he ignore her manipulations. After all, just because she *said* she could handle it, didn't mean she *actually* could. What if she just *thought* she could handle it.

What if, while he was sleeping, they were attacked? Sure, the brute squad would step in, but they were the only real fighters on the ship. Cora may have had the instincts of a warrior (after all, she'd carved him up back when they'd first met) but she'd also known at the time that he was established and beyond her ability to kill. There was a massive difference between that and actually going to war where murder was a very real probability. He didn't want that kind of blood on Cora's hands. Not until she was much older.

And the servants were flat-out useless in a fight. *Though, if Trush managed to get herself killed ...*

"Avis."

A growl built up in Avis' throat before he could stop it.

"Everything will be fine, beloved. You need to go and get some sleep. Now. For everyone's sake."

Avis growled some more but said nothing else as he stalked around her and went up the ladder to the second level cabin. He didn't want to acknowledge her words, even if there was a very, very slim possibility that she might've been right.

As promised, the cabin had been prepared with a king-sized bed, multiple pillows and a pair of wooden side tables. A doorway on Clarise's side of the bed led to the bathroom. Frustrated beyond belief, he strode up and down the gap between his side of the bed and the wall, turning at the side table and at the foot of the bed respectively. He didn't want to do this, and he wasn't in the habit of doing things he didn't want to do. It was that simple. He placed the shot glass on the side table during one of his many passes, but that only served as a visual reminder of what Clarise wanted him to do, every time he walked towards it.

He made nine more passes of the side table before his hand found the clasp of his cloak and he twisted it, allowing the chain and fabric to slide from his shoulders to the floor. On his next pass, he scooped it up and hooked it over the peg on the wall—not because he was a servant, but because if he had to get up in a hurry to protect his family, he didn't want to be tripping over it on the floor. A few more passes of the side table had him pulling one glove off, then the other. Both were dropped unceremoniously beside the drink. Another pass had his belt looped over the same peg that held his cloak.

Avis really didn't want to do this. *So why the fuck am I?* The Mystallian didn't have to think long for an answer. *Because Clarise wants me to.* He continued his pacing.

ALWAYS GONNA FUCKING KOWTOW TO EVERY FUCKED-UP FUCKING BULLSHIT THING SHE FUCKING WANTS?

The question his subconscious posed brought his pacing to an abrupt halt. *Would he?* Almost as quickly as he'd asked himself the question, he knew the answer. *Probably.* The admission made him huff in annoyance as he dropped his weight to the edge of the bed and ran a weary hand through his hair. Which just plain sucked. With his elbows braced against his knees, Avis stared at the timber floor between his boots. He was bone tired. He couldn't deny that. Being on constant alert for so long made that unavoidable. Huffing again, he dragged one boot off, then the other. Then he dropped his weight back across the bed with his feet still on the floor. *What in the realms am I doing?* he wondered, staring up at the timber ceiling. He had no chance of going to sleep. Not with Maui out there. Even now, that little bastard could be calling in the heavy hitters of his pantheon.

He rolled up into a sitting position with every intention of storming back onto the deck. Then he paused and braced his arms against the mattress. Everything in him demanded he go and reassert his authority, but Clarise had made it clear she wanted him to stay, and logically he knew she was right. He was being stupid. His eyes found the shot glass, then snapped away. There had to be a way he could make himself go to sleep and still be able to wake himself up in a hurry if it became necessary. Maybe he could relax all by himself and drift off. He'd just said he was tired, right?

Deciding on that as the better plan, Avis stretched himself the right way along the bed and wrapped his arms around one of the many pillows as his head found another. He rolled to his right side and found the shot glass front and centre of his vision, taunting him.

So, he did what all adult supreme gods did when faced with something they didn't like. He rolled over and put his back to it. So there.

With one pillow hooked under his chin, Avis closed his eyes, willing himself to go to sleep. *Sleep … sleep … sleep … sleep … sleep … sleep … sleep … sleep … sleep … sleep … sleep … sleep … sleep … sleep … sleep, for fuck's sake!*

Frustrated, he opened his eyes and stared at the far wall. It was never going to happen. He was too on edge.

There was only one thing left to do. Not wanting to admit the inevitable, he shut his eyes again and rolled over, reaching blindly for the shot glass. It was precisely where he'd left it, and once he had his fingers wrapped around it, he lifted himself onto one elbow; still refusing to open his eyes. If he didn't look, he didn't have to visibly acknowledge the defeat. He tossed the drink down, then threw the empty shot glass as far from him as possible in disgust.

The sound of glass shattering against the far wall was the last thing he remembered.

* * *

"Paranoid SOB, isn't he?" Maui asked, having learned in the previous week and a half not to swear in front of Clarise or the girls.

Clarise heard him land on the deck beside her but never moved her attention from the open doorway of the cabin, or her unconscious husband within. She'd known he would eventually settle down and do what he needed to do, but the process never seemed to get any easier for him. "He has made many enemies, and his fear is not for himself, but for us."

"I know. It's actually one of the main reasons I decided to help you out."

Surprised, Clarise turned to look at the youth, who lifted one shoulder in a sheepish shrug.

"I've heard the rumours about him. If even half of what I've heard is true, he's got more than enough power to cut and run, leaving you and the little ladies to fend for yourselves. Yet he hasn't. In fact, he's wiping himself out just to make sure you three are safe. It's … weird." As much as Clarise valued his honesty, his next words weren't nearly as endearing. "I don't appreciate being called a child who's pretending to be a man."

Schooling her expression, Clarise slid her hands behind her back and clasped them at the wrists as she had seen Avis do many a time. Insulting the young godling had never been her intention, though in her defence, he shouldn't have been eavesdropping either. "Maui, you are a little over a decade older than those two young ladies over there." Clarise lowered her gaze to where Cora was playing with her sister on the lower deck in front of them, knowing Maui's eyes followed suit.

"So?"

Clarise swallowed a knowing smile, for his petulant response only served to reiterate her point. The way Maui used single-syllable words like 'so' as a catch-all to hide behind was not the behaviour of a seasoned adult. "So … Avis and I are billions of eons old. That is over eighteen zeroes to our age. We literally have more zeroes in our age than you do years."

Maui hunched his shoulders and looked down and away from her. "I don't see what that has to do with anything," he muttered resentfully.

Clarise did not need her innate ability for this one. "Oh, I think you do, young man."

Maui hooked his right hand against his hip, his fingers idly tracing the woven rope of his hook buried within the rustling reeds. "Well, I suppose that's an improvement on 'a child pretending to be a man' … *marginally.*"

Maui added that last word with a sarcastic sneer, causing Clarise to chuckle. "Sweetheart, if you think you hold the monopoly on sulking and long-term grudge holding, I would truly suggest you think again." Without meaning to, her eyes drifted to her sleeping husband; the undisputed reigning champion of both categories.

Maui followed her gaze and barked out a laugh, already over his tantrum. "Very true."

"Maui, if you do not mind me asking, why do *you* think your father cursed you to die?" With Avis behaving little better than a cornered savage ever since they'd entered Rangi-Tuarea, this was Clarise's first chance to bring the matter up. Avis had almost given himself an aneurysm when the boy had declared himself a non-hellion shifter, and that was before he'd gone over a week without sleep. She couldn't trust his responses now. Likewise, she hadn't wanted to try and speak to Maui in quiet tones alone, because that would've caused an entirely different meltdown from her exhausted husband.

"It was an accident," Maui said, with another defensive shrug.

Avis had told her that Makeatutara had absolutely done it on purpose, but now wasn't the time to correct that. "How difficult a mistake is that to make?" she asked in its place.

Maui released his hook and ran his hands down his thighs. "It's never been done before," he admitted with a surly scowl. "The blessings we receive from our elders is how our immortality works. All it took to turn it around was three words in the wrong order." His scowl deepened and his eyes snapped to her defiantly as he dug his hook out again and waved it at her. "But he didn't mean it. He wouldn't have given me my hook if he wasn't sorry …"

Clarise held up one placating hand to stem his tirade. "I do not recall saying anything to the contrary," she said, in a calm, deadpan way that closely mimicked her father's powerful monotone. She tilted her head to give the illusion of an afterthought. "Perhaps it is your own mind that bears this confliction?"

"No," Maui declared, shaking his head, holding his hook so tightly his knuckles were turning white. "My father loves me. He—He just made a mistake."

The unconditional love of a child for their parents.

An ache built inside Clarise's chest as she watched the young man defend his father's deplorable actions because he wanted to believe in the elder hellion. She had left her own bastard son to be raised in Hell by his father, but that was the least despicable thing she'd done that day. At two years old, Charon already had the look of an ancient and withered Mystallian. That alone was bad enough where her family was concerned, but to have the Mystallian propensity for emotional outbursts as well would have been his ruin. Execution orders for behavioural issues were a thing amongst the Highborn of Hell, and Clarise had known she wasn't going to be there to protect him. So, she'd done the only thing she could to safeguard his future. She'd lobotomised the part of his brain that housed his emotions.

Now, in moments like this, the guilt of that decision was crushing.

"I hope that is true." As much as she meant the sentiment, she knew otherwise. Makeatutara had no interest in children, unless they were part of the Damned. But a deceptively worded truth on her part was less hurtful than an honest one. She refused to be responsible for the loss of another child's love; however misplaced it was.

* * *

CHAPTER TEN

Avis had no concept of the time when he first woke up. The sun had moved, but either it had gone backwards, the boat had turned around, or at least three-quarters of a day had passed. Despite the woollen feel to his mouth that seemed to reach the back of his eyes, he was pretty sure he knew which one of those it was. *Eight hours, my ass.*

He rolled to his side and lifted himself off the mattress, planting his bare feet on the floor. His tongue licked every surface inside his mouth, trying to rid himself of the horrible aftertaste. In his exceedingly long life, he'd been knocked out more than a few times, but never once had he woken up feeling as if he'd swallowed half the stuffing of his pillow. Clarise would have to work on that if she ever wanted him to drink another one of her knock-out shots.

Remembering the events leading up to his sleep, Avis' head snapped up and he surged to his feet. He threw open his familial link and located Clarise and the girls outside. Clarise was easy enough to identify since she didn't have the youthfulness of the other two, and the girls were together on the front deck. Bottom line: they were okay. They were still all together on the boat, and they were all okay.

He released a breath he hadn't realised he was holding. *Okay. Okay, okay.* Maybe he *had* been a little over the top in his paranoia.

He rubbed the back of his neck as he considered that possibility, grimacing on the dried sweat and salt crystals that dragged across his skin. He really needed a bath. Running his fingers through his hair emphasised the salt-laced greasy feel, and he didn't want to know how badly he stank. For a second, he wondered why Clarise hadn't rectified his condition (given how meticulous she was about maintaining propriety in front of company) but put it down to how badly his foul mood would've probably taken it.

With nothing else for it, Avis made his way around the bed and into the bathroom to take care of the matter himself.

Like the choice of bedroom furniture, this room had about as much in common with the Oceanic culture as he did. A Mystallian toilet and sink were on the right, exactly where Avis expected to see them. However, because of the confined space, there was no deep bath on the left for Avis to sink into. No, in this regard, Clarise had been creative. On the opposite wall to the toilet and sink, about a third of a metre above his head was a multi-holed slit spanning the width of the wall. Steam wafted off the water that constantly poured through the holes with enough force to create a gap between the water and the wall, not unlike a powerful waterfall. It fell to the ground and disappeared through another grid of fine holes at the base of the same wall without ever spilling into the cabin below. A never-ending flow of comfortably hot, clean water. Clarise had developed and fine-tuned the construct back in Yaru, and while it wasn't the same as a bath (hard to totally relax and switch off while standing upright), he could appreciate the water cascading over his shoulders when he dunked his head beneath the spray.

Making quick work of his doublet and leggings, Avis stepped partially into the water with his mouth open to catch some of the water. He swished it around his mouth and spat it out again, repeating the process twice more to remove most of the wadding sensation. Then he stepped all the way into the water.

Having the heat pound into his muscles felt wonderful. He closed his eyes and pressed his forehead into the bathroom wall, just enjoying the feel of it against his skin.

… until a pair of petite hands danced lightly across his lower back and ass, and he came alert with a start. He whirled around, knowing precisely where he had to look to meet Clarise's eyes. At least, it'd better have been Clarise's eyes!

"Clarise," he wheezed, when his dark-haired, golden-eyed beauty filled his vision as readily as her familial presence filled his core essence. Her gaze was molten and sultry, and it took him a second to realise she was as naked as he was.

"Feeling better, my love?" she asked, stepping forward to press herself against him; her tongue tracing light circles around his right nipple while her hands slid up the insides of his thighs.

As his eyes rolled back into his head and his shoulders hit the back wall, some tiny part of his logical brain caught sight of where the bathroom door should have been. Emphasis on 'should have been', because all he saw was a solid wall with no way in or out. About as impenetrable and probably (knowing his wife) as soundproof as a celestial shifter could make it. Trapped … all alone … with the most beautiful naked woman in all existence fondling him …

Getting his primary head back in the game, he straightened and slipped his hands under her backside, then lifted her onto his hips. "Oh, I'm getting there," he promised, as he turned into the water spray and pinned her to the wall. Their lips locked together as he slipped deep inside her. "Definitely getting there," he whispered, beginning a steady rhythm that had Clarise's head tip back and to the side, exposing the long length of her neck. He licked and kissed the line from her ear to her neck, sucking and biting at the flesh as he continued to thrust into her. The hot water that flowed over his shoulders and down his back and legs only added to the ecstasy of the moment …

… and maybe this water out of the wall concept wasn't such a bad idea after all.

* * *

An hour or two later, Avis left the bathroom in a recreated doublet and leggings, feeling better than he had in a long time. His clothes were as clean as he was, and after padding across the timber floor, he sat on the edge of the bed and slid his feet into his boots. Even they were polished to a high sheen; however that was more likely Tilu's handiwork than his wife's.

He paused when he felt the bed sink from Clarise's side and smirked to himself, though he pretended not to notice her crawling across the bed towards him. Her arms encompassed him from behind, and her lips danced across the back of his neck, causing all the hairs in the area to stand at attention. "Are you hungry?" she breathed against his ear.

Avis' lips broke into a provocative grin and without a word he twisted at the waist and wrapped his arms around her, hauling her bodily across his lap. Halfway through the grab he realised she was already fully dressed, but that wasn't too much of a deterrent for him. Little was when it came to this woman. "Depends entirely on what you're offering, sweetheart," he purred, nibbling on her earlobe. And, of course, that was when his traitorous stomach chose to growl in defiance of him.

Clarise chuckled and pushed him to arm's length. "We have all of eternity for that, beloved. When you are dressed and ready, Frash and Tilu have prepared lunch for you on the upper deck, and you have been avoiding the girls since we arrived here. You need to spend some time with them, especially young Columbine."

That drove all thoughts of carnal pleasure from his mind. "What about Columbine?" he asked, stiffening where he sat.

"She cries a lot when no one is looking and tries to keep to herself down on the floats, though her sister is forcing her to engage in play to keep her distracted from whatever is upsetting her. She is miserable and it is bringing down everyone on the catamaran. No amount of comfort from me seems to help and short of removing her tear ducts, I am at a loss as to how to proceed."

Keket. Fuck! His vigilance of Maui had become so all-consuming that he still hadn't dealt with the fallout of what happened between himself, Keket and Columbine. He quickly removed Clarise from his lap and rose to his feet, already reaching for his belt. "I'll deal with Columbine first," he declared, sliding the belt around his hips and buckling it into place. He barely heard the creak of the bed to indicate Clarise was now standing behind him; not that it mattered. He was too busy kicking himself for not fixing the situation with Columbine. That should have been his priority! She was such a sweet, sensitive kid, and the memory of Keket's fury must've been tearing her apart. He shoved his hands into his gloves, still berating himself. How could he be so stupid? But as he reached back for his cloak, his hand was intercepted at the wrist by both of Clarise's.

"No," she said as if she were laying down the law. He turned his head to look at her; a single eyebrow raised questioningly. 'No' wasn't a word he heard very often. Clarise tightened her grip and refused to budge. "Avis, you need to eat first. Columbine's predicament will not change in the short time it takes you to gain the nourishment your body requires."

Avis thought about arguing with her, but then he realised he could smash out both objectives at once and still keep her happy. Benders were clever like that. "Fine," he agreed, perhaps a little too readily. "If you keep Cora away from the top deck, I'll deal with Columbine after I've had something to eat." Technically, it wasn't a lie. He had a plan.

Clarise's gaze narrowed at him, but after a moment's contemplation, she nodded and released his wrist. "Very well."

He did his best to keep his expression neutral as he took his cloak and rolled his wrists to spread it across his back and shoulders with the two gold chains laying over his collarbones. Another twist latched the chains together, holding it in place.

"Very handsome," Clarise praised.

Avis snorted. "Always," he said, and hooked his finger into her gold chain, pulling her in for a parting kiss. He manoeuvred himself around her as they kissed and broke apart once he was on the other side of her. "To be continued," he promised, swatting her lightly on the backside before he turned and made his way outside.

"COLUMBINE!" he called. Although he couldn't see her, he knew she was somewhere on the front left float; mainly because Cora was lying on her belly with her head over the bow on that side and her legs bent at the knees with her boots kicking idly in the air. Through their familial links, he knew both girls were together. At the sound of his bellow, the older of his daughters immediately rolled to her left and lifted herself onto one elbow to look at him. Columbine's head also popped up over the deck's edge beside her sister.

"Father?" she asked, morosely. Even with the distance between them, Avis could see the sparkle that normally glittered in her eyes had been replaced by a sheen of unshed tears and her features were pale and withdrawn.

Fuck! Breathing through the emotional sucker-punch that accompanied his appraisal, Avis raised a hand and curled his fingers beckoningly. "You're not in trouble, princess, but you and I need to talk while I have some lunch." He beckoned her once more. "Come here."

He waited just long enough to see her climb up the two steps to stand alongside her sister before he turned and made his own way to the ladder at the front of the cabin. From there, he hauled himself to the topmost deck in three quick steps. Spread out before him was a picnic rug covered with a variety of Mystallian foods, not dissimilar to the meals they'd had on the Acheron River. Which was good. During his crankiness, he might've mentioned once or twice what he thought about their recent meal choices. A new addition to the setting was a massive cushion where he usually sat. The only problem was, with Columbine on her way, he needed two.

Avis weighed up his options and slid his gaze to the pair of servants lingering nearby. "Frash," he said, never knowing one from the other but expecting the named servant to answer.

Which she did. "Milord?"

Avis stabbed a finger at the empty space on the opposite side of the rug to him. "I want a second cushion where Columbine usually sits. Make yourself useful, woman."

As Columbine's head crested the deck, Frash moved to where Avis had pointed and melted into a gelatinous puddle which then reformed into a large, plump cushion. She'd have probably preferred to craft one out of something else, but time didn't allow for that.

And Avis wasn't the least bit upset by the inconvenience, since he didn't like

Frash. Like … at all. "Sit down, princess," he said in a much gentler voice, reaching forward to claim a fresh strawberry, which he then dipped in a tub of whipped cream and popped into his open mouth. The small item was something he could swallow with ease, covering his promise to Clarise to eat 'before' his chat with Columbine. He hadn't said how much he would eat. "You hungry?" he asked, watching her as she crossed the deck and took her seat opposite him.

"No, Father," she replied dully. Her eyes met his just long enough to convey that message before she looked to her left where Tilu stood.

As far as standing her ground was concerned, it was a tiny step in the right direction, so he focused on that positive and not her inability to maintain it. "Well, alright then," he said, licking his lips free of cream. "I guess we can jump straight to the main event." And before Columbine could react, Avis' consciousness leapt across the void between them and swept into her mind, knowing the outside realm would freeze the moment he did so.

CHAPTER ELEVEN

It had been Avis' intent to ignore the glass-like cascade of memory on the left that did nothing but give him a headache and go straight for where the two of them could hash out their differences inside her imagination. But the instant he crossed the threshold into her mind, he realised just how badly he'd underestimated the situation. The unhappiness she seemed to exude in the physical realm had nothing on the melancholy that permeated her mind, and tears of despair welled in his eyes before he could stop them. A deep orange, yellow and tan tint was everywhere, coating everything including himself in that misery. The weight of it brought about a bone-deep ache and he knew if it wasn't for his Mystallian stubbornness to fixate on the problem at hand, he'd truly contemplate suicide. Him: a god with everything. But right now, it was as if he had nothing; *was* nothing. Several times during his incarceration in Hell he'd been dunked in the river of Melancholy, and even that had nothing on this.

He stood on the divide between her memories and her imagination, her past and her possible futures with his fisted hands pushing the knuckles of his forefingers into his eyes as he breathed through the hopelessness. He was useless to her like this but he couldn't break free.

FOR FUCK'S SAKE, GET A FUCKING GRIP, AVIS!

By the Twin Notes, he was trying to, but the sorrow was so overpowering! He'd have run himself through with his own sword if he had the means!

How long he stood there like that, barely breathing through the debilitating heartache, he had no idea. Hours? Days? Months? Years? Time had no meaning in a place that didn't function like that. But all at once, it eased.

"Father?" Daring a peek over his clenched fists, Avis saw his princess approach him. "Why are you here?" The closer her image came, the more those realm-awful tones receded until she stood directly in front of him, clearing the area entirely.

His relief was just as palpable. "Hey, princess," he rasped, lowering his hands to his sides. He went down on one knee in front of her, taking a moment to gather his own thoughts and remind himself of why he was here. "As I said, you and I need to talk." Moving slowly so as not to startle her, he reached out and hooked her under the arms, lifting her into the air and settling her on his hip. He took a moment to cuddle her close, if only to convince himself that they were both safe. "Those colours of yours are certainly intense, aren't they?" he asked, looking at the perimeter of amber shades in the distance.

Columbine rolled her head into his shoulder. "They were hurting you," she whispered.

It wasn't something he could in good conscience deny. "Yeah, they were. I've never felt anything like what I feel when I come into your mind, princess, and that was the worst. It's like everything is magnified to ridiculous levels."

"Mag…nified?"

Avis scrambled for a parallel that she'd understand. "Ahhh—It's like how your eyes can only see so far as a Mystallian, but when you want to see something a long way away, as a shifter you can change your eyes to see it." He was quite proud of that analogy.

"I have felt you in here before, father. You and Cora."

Swallowing hard, Avis lifted her out from under his chin and pressed his lips into her hair. "I know, princess, but it's probably not a good idea to tell anyone else that."

"Why?"

"It's … not something you're supposed to be able to do, baby." On the long list of things she wasn't supposed to do, that one barely scratched the surface, but it was as good a starting point as any.

"Is this … you being here … a bender thing?"

Avis snorted and lightly smiled. A bender thing. How very … *shifter* of her. "It is, princess. We are currently inside your mind." He used one hand to gesture at the crystal montage of her memories. "Those are your memories over there. In time, when your bending manif …"—he swallowed and changed his wording— "When you get a bit older and your bending ability comes to you, you'll be able to go in there by yourself and look at everything for as long as you want without taking up any time in the real realm. That's the least of what you'll be able to do as a ranged bender, princes." He stroked her hair and smiled. "But until then, only one bender at a time can come in here to visit you like this."

Columbine turned her head. Whether it was away from him or towards something else, he couldn't be certain, until she sighed and said, "You should not be here, Father."

Avis bristled at her dismissal. He couldn't help himself. "Why would you say that?" he asked, determined to keep the bite from his words but knowing he hadn't entirely succeeded.

She looked back at him, her dark eyes glistening on the verge of tears. "This place hurts you, father. All the time. Just like it does Cora."

As much as he wanted to roar and bellow and declare himself capable of handling anything his baby girl could throw at him, he knew that was crap. He'd been utterly incapacitated by the depth of her misery, and if she left it'd probably overwhelm him again. "How does it work?" he asked, lifting his eyes to the colours tinting everything but their immediate area. "And what did you do to pull them back from us, princess?" Because in his mind, if she explained it now, it'd be in terms of a four-and-a-half-year-old that even he couldn't screw up. Then he could deal with it himself and not rely on her to bail his ass out.

Columbine's bottom lip rolled into a full pout. "I do not know. I felt you being sad, and I heard the mean voice using naughty words, so I came looking. You were standing so still, and I knew it was not because you wanted to. The colours had you, and I wanted them to stop." She gave a little shrug. "So, they did." She swallowed again. "You need to go, father …"

They were back to this again? "No." He tightened his grip on her as if they were still in the physical realm. She began to squirm and when he wouldn't let her go, she shifted into dust and materialised a short distance away.

Not happening! Avis flexed his mental muscle and brought her right back into his arms, this time locking down what she thought was her shifting ability. "Here's something about having a more powerful bender in your mind, princess," he said, as she gasped at her sudden return to his arms and surged against him. "It may be your mind, but once I'm in here, I call the shots." He gripped her tightly, being careful not to force her mind into compliance in case his manipulation somehow disrupted the control over the melancholy. "Knock it off, princess. This is going to play out exactly how I want it to, and I need you to be a good girl and let me help you."

It didn't take Columbine long to stop struggling. "I am so tired, father," she said softly against his chest.

The admission was so heartfelt Avis had to gnash his teeth to keep his own rising emotions at bay. "I know, baby," he crooned, rubbing his cheek against her hair.

"It is so hard to keep it all in here. To not let any of it out. Cora says ..."

Avis stilled, lifting only his eyes to stare at an empty point in front of him. If it killed him, he was determined to not to show any outward reaction to the news that Cora had somehow influenced this. His lips may have been pinched together so tightly they ached, but he silenced the growl that burbled to life deep in his chest and he curled his toes into his boots to avoid fisting his hands. It should've been enough to fool anyone except Columbine, who rolled her shoulders forward and refused to say more. The orange-yellow-tan closed in on them and Avis realised he didn't have a lot of time.

Hooking her chin with his fingers, he forced Columbine's consciousness to look up at him. "What did Cora say, princess? Tell me the truth. All of it." Knowing he'd said that harsher than he'd intended, he dropped his voice and whispered, "It's okay, baby. I just want to know."

Though shuddering breaths wracked her whole body, she finally admitted, "She said she hates it when I feel too much. That it is my problem, not hers, and that if I do not keep them inside me, she will make me sorry." Columbine's eyes welled in tears. "But I am already sorry, father. And I try ... I try really hard ..."

Dammit, Cora! "Ssshhh-shh-shh," he crooned as he rubbed the pad of his thumb across her lips while making a mental note to tear Cora a new asshole when he got out of here for bullying her sister like this. "I know you do, princess, but sometimes the best way forward is to just go forward and deal with what you're avoiding. It'll be okay. You won't be alone, baby. I'll be right here with you. Always." He lifted his hand to touch her forehead. "Here," he said, reiterating the oath he'd made to her the second time they'd met. His hand then dipped to her chest; specifically, her heart. "And here. Always. Just like I promised." He pressed his forehead to hers. "Remember?"

As he'd hoped, the colour in their immediate area shifted to a sapphire blue and the heaviness seemed to lift. Blue, he decided, was a good colour in here. Orange-yellow-tans … sucked. "If I'm right, you can't get past what happened in Yaru. So, that's where we're going to start."

Columbine whimpered and hid her face against his throat. "I do not want to."

Avis did everything in his power to project the love and support he felt for her. "I know, princess, but you can do this. I'm right here. Just as you protected me, I'll protect you. Believe me, baby, you can't let this one moment destroy you. You're better than that. You're a celestial … and you're my daughter." Willing to risk the chance that those ominous colours had infiltrated her imagination, Avis left the entrance of her mind and teleported them both to the one environment where he controlled everything. "I want you to bring up an image of that night, princess."

Could he have done it for her? Absolutely, but then what would that achieve? She'd still have those insane emotional colours to deal with, and if he did the mental legwork for her, she'd learn nothing. "Go on, princess. Show me you can. Make me proud."

Avis could feel her heart hammering through her uniform, though the space around them shifted until they were standing on what he assumed was the deck of their Yarusian ship during that fateful night. If they were, he was already noticing a few anomalies within the setting; such as how much darker she'd made the night. The original had stars shining overhead, which was how he'd been able to see in the half-light. By contrast, the dark fog Columbine had created was so thick he could barely see through it except for when lightning danced across the sky with thunder close on its heels. The ground beneath him lifted, shifted and dropped, and he quickly spread his feet and bent his knees for balance.

This wasn't right. The weather before he and Keket had locked horns had been blissfully perfect.

Leaning into his own control, he stilled the churning ocean and lit up the night sky enough so that he could see. The return of the stars showed him he was standing just behind the rear throne of the vessel. Diviten fussed to his right and above them hovered Columbine's brute squad guard. The whole scene was tinged with that realm-damned orange-yellow-tan which Avis knew no amount of bending on his part would fix. He had to get Columbine's mental stability under control first.

Not the easiest thing, when he peered through the throne's canopy and found Keket's huge living wave crashing down on the observation deck; rage and hatred pouring off her every movement. A second Columbine figure in a bright pink nightgown clung to the snake carving beneath the onslaught as Keket's living wave continued to bombard her. But as if saturating her wasn't enough, Keket struck the wave with lightning each time it poured over her, ensuring her skin crackled with bursts of painful electricity. Being so close, the charge jolted through Avis as well, with enough force to make him flinch.

From within his arms, Columbine's consciousness bowed her head in acceptance of the situation as her due.

That was when Avis realised exactly what he was looking at, and holy hell did he want to swear all over again! In that instant he killed the lightning strikes and brought the whole scene to a frozen standstill, giving her imagination exactly zero choice in the matter. Self-flagellation to appease someone who wasn't even in attendance was insane.

"Columbine," he growled, looking down at the girl in his arms. With his thoughts, he forced her to lift her chin and look up at him. He was too pissed right now to be subtle. "If I go back through your memories, princess, am I going to find out you've been doing this to yourself this whole time?"

Columbine stared up at him, then burst into tears. "K-Ke-Kek-et w-was s-s-so m-m-mad ..." she blubbered, and Avis could feel the sea around him attempting to churn up. He refused to let it.

"Princess, you need to cut this out. Right now. Keket was never mad at you. This was never about you. You'd be breaking her heart if she knew you were doing this to yourself because of her." Holding everything around them at bay, Avis turned the throne around so that it was facing the observation deck instead of the central room and sat down on it with Columbine's consciousness still in his arms. He gave her enough room to make herself comfortable on his lap, but she wasn't going anywhere until they had this bullshit straightened out once and for all.

She twisted into his chest and cried some more, to which he rubbed his chin against her hair and glared at the looming tint that continued to invade the scene. This would be so much easier if her emotions yielded to him as fast as her mind could.

"Cry if you must, princess, but we aren't leaving here until you accept none of this was your fault, and I really don't care how long it takes."

Subconsciously, he knew that wasn't true. Unlike most other celestials who had centuries, if not a few millennia under their belt, he couldn't risk spending years or even months dealing with this. Not while Columbine was still physically a child. The longer he kept the two of them in her imagination, the more she would understand without maturing a minute beyond her physical age and the sooner her mother would figure out exactly what he'd done.

But a few days to sort this shit out wouldn't hurt anyone.

Avis waited until she cried herself out, not liking how long it took. Several times when he'd thought she was done; she'd started all over again as if she'd just given herself a stimulation wave. The fifth time had him deciding enough was enough and rather than letting things run their course, he observed her body language for any sign of fatigue. The second there was a slight reduction in her sobs, he moved in and prevented her from resetting herself.

The result was a period of whimpers and shudders with no new waterworks, and even that ended in short order. Avis gave her a few more seconds of silent coddling, just to be sure she was thoroughly spent. "Okay, baby," he crooned, nuzzling her hair to gain her attention. "Now, I need you to turn around and watch what really happened that night. Not this fu … messed up version of it.”

"I-I was there …”

"No, you weren't,” he insisted. "Not really, princess. You saw that night through the feelings of everyone around you instead of your own perspective. You saw my fear for you and Keket's rage at me.” He rubbed her hair, willing her to understand the difference. "It's all gotten so jumbled up inside that pretty little head of yours that you think everything that night was your fault. Believe me, princess, none of it was. Keket was never mad at you. For Mystal's sake, you were playing patty-cake with her! I've lived a long time, princess, and I don't think anything will ever top watching a primordial goddess playing patty-cake.”

"Should … we not have been?” Columbine seemed confused.

Avis closed his eyes for a moment and shook his head, a small chuckle working its way through his chest. When he opened them again, she was still staring up at him. "That's not what I meant, baby. It's not a matter of what should have been done. It's more … well … when you get older … *a lot* older, a lot of things tend to get overlooked. One minute a star will come into being and as far as we're concerned, the next has it crumbling into a black hole, taking everything in its gravitational pull with it.” Columbine frowned at the big words and he shook his head dismissively. "It's not important.” He hooked her fringe over her ear and pushed on. "What is important, is that when whole galaxies come and go without meaning a thing to us, taking the time to play patty-cake with a child that's not our own doesn't happen very often.”

He could see she was about to say something, but since nothing productive could possibly come from her at that point, he shushed her again. Then he shifted his weight to sit sideways on the throne with his knee braced against the throne arm. This way, she could watch what was going on but still have the security of having her cheek pressed against his chest. "Just watch, princess. We'll do this as many times as we have to until you accept it wasn't your fault.”

Avis was true to his word. After he replayed the scene exactly as he remembered it, he reset it and played it again, and again, and again. And again, and again, and again for good measure. With each replay, Columbine settled that little bit more into his arms and slowly, the orange-yellow-tan around them began to fade.

When he felt she was ready to take the reins, he froze the whole setting and pressed his lips to her hair in a light nudge. "Alright, princess. Your turn.”

Columbine stiffened and pushed her tiny hands into his chest. He gave her just enough distance to let her kneel on his lap, bringing those beautiful big black eyes on the same level as his. Then he smiled warmly to assuage her fears. "You can do it, baby,” he assured her, stroking her arm with one hand encouragingly. "Just play that scene out, exactly as it happened. I don't want you to add anything that wasn't there. Not one bit of colour that implied any of this is your fault. Do you understand me?”

Columbine looked to his right, staring out at the frozen scene and sucked in her bottom lip. Her breathing was still hitched, but not panicked. Not yet, anyway.

Avis kept going. For her sake, he had to. "I know you were scared. I was scared for you, and Keket was very mad at me. That's the order of the colours. I do not want to see any of Keket's anger aimed at you. That's called embellishing, and I don't want to see it. Play it, just as it was." His fingers prodded her gently in the ribs. "Go on."

Lowering herself to his lap, Columbine curled back into his chest and peered out at the scene with one eye. For a moment, he thought he was going to have to intercede when nothing else changed, but then, ever so slowly, the scene reset itself. Avis eyed the intruding colour tint as much as the scene itself, finding it the more concerning of the two.

She remained encompassed in his arms the whole time she followed his instructions, all under his watchful eye. Any deviation from the memory had him nudging it back on course without her knowing. Over, and over, and over they sat through the scene until she could play the whole damned thing without needing his input. The process was slow, but it was getting there. With each pass, the colours he hated so much dimmed as her confidence grew.

Hours after they began, she started to fuss on his lap. "Again," he said, for what seemed like the thousandth time. They would see this all the way through if it killed him.

He was surprised when she tensed her shoulders in refusal and buried her face into his doublet, fisting her tiny hands into the fabric.

It was the first hint of defiance he'd ever seen from her, and as much as he loathed the need to invalidate that stance, he knew he had to for her sake. Rolling his shoulders forward, he created a tiny gap between them that allowed his hand to capture her chin and draw her out. "Don't you go hiding on me, young lady," he murmured, gently extracting her face from his chest and guiding it back to the scene.

"But, Father ..."

"No. You have to do this all the way through, just the way I want to see it. Neither one of us is going anywhere until you can do it three times in a row. I told you, I don't care how long it takes."

It killed the control freak in him to let her do this by herself. It really did. So many times she went so close to getting it right that part of him wanted to say, 'fuck it, that's close enough'. But he knew if he left so much as a hint of what she thought before, she'd be dragging it back out and by the end of the week, they'd have to start all over again.

They replayed the scene hundreds more times, but eventually, she made the three runs without his influence and was rewarded with lots of cuddles and crooning sounds of approval. Avis rubbed his cheek and chin across her hair, watching the last of the orange-yellow-tan disappear with great satisfaction. A bluish-peach tone took its place, and blue was definitely a good colour. The peach, he wasn't so sure about, but blue had proven itself. He nuzzled her hair some more. "You want me to get out of here, princess? We can get back to our lunch now if you want."

Columbine pulled back and smiled at him. "Yes, please."

Frustrated by the repetitiveness of their previous task, Avis' pointer finger fell across her lips before he could stop himself. Then he brought his head down so that they were on the same eye level. "It's just 'yes', princess. Mystallians don't grovel to anyone."

She blinked at him in confusion and he lifted his eyes, searching the canopy overhead for patience. "I know, sweetheart. It's going to be a hard habit to break, but by the time we get back to Mystal, you must be able to speak without giving anyone any ground over you. Thanking someone is fine. It means you appreciated their efforts without lessening your standing in anyone's eyes. But *please*?" He felt his whole face screw up as if he'd sucked on the sourest lemon in existence and shuddered. "That's begging, princess, and we just don't do that. Ask for what you want by all means, but do it putting your feet firmly on the ground and standing strong. The person you're asking the favour of may then lay out conditions for that favour, which you can either accept or walk away from. But at no point, and I mean at no point, baby, do you shuffle backwards from what you want by grovelling, either with words or actions. Okay?"

Columbine nibbled on her lower lip, but at least she maintained eye contact with him. It was a good start and he appreciated her effort. "I know, I know," he conceded with a lopsided smile. "You were punished for not saying 'please' in Hell, but we aren't there anymore. Nor are we likely to go back there any time soon. We're going to my home, and the rules are very different there. I also know it's going to take time." He hooked her fringe over her ear again, using the move to lay his hand across the nape of her neck. "Fortunately, we have plenty of that. Just tell me you understand what I said. We'll work on making you more comfortable with it at a later point."

Columbine nodded. "I understand, Father."

Avis grinned and pulled her forward to kiss her forehead. "Good girl." He rose to his feet, and after one last quick cuddle, he put her down and stepped away. "On that note, princess, I'll see you back in the physical realm."

With that, he winked and left her mind.

CHAPTER TWELVE

Belial sat back in his Upper Realms throne and eyed his bending counterpart from across the Table of Divinity. All of the Known and Unknown Realms lay on the grand table between them, but the supreme demon only had eyes for the stunned look on Theodrick's face. It was absolutely priceless.

A deep rumble burbled from the pit of Belial's stomach, turning slowly but surely into a chest-heaving chuckle. "Did you forget she was the Weaver?" he asked condescendingly.

Theodrick's eyes snapped to his, and his face darkened dangerously. "Fuck it up your fucking ass, you horn-headed motherfucking piece of shit!" he swore, sulkily folding his arms across his chest like a proverbial two-year-old.

There was nothing else the Bender could say in his defence when they both knew the score. As shocking a revelation as it had been at the time, Columbine's innocent declaration had once again proven herself to be the third member of their triumvirate: the stabilising force between mind and body. She was to become their heart.

She wasn't there yet, but to have a third-party conversation inside the mind of another pillar and assume that conversation wouldn't be overheard was asinine. Even the Weaver held that much power within herself.

Belial turned his attention to the far left-hand side of the table. With all the celestials making their homes in the Known Realms, both he and Theodrick had positioned their thrones in such a way that they could oversee that half of the table without much strain, leaving the Unknown half to its own devices. It had always been that way, ever since the two notes of existence were sung that brought them all into being. Order, Chaos, and the two pillars that mastered them.

Now, change was in the air. Beyond the far edge of the table, where nothing had previously existed, colours were starting to seep into being. They were subtle at first; like shadows moving just out of sight. Then came the tones, which deepened ever so slightly to imply something was evolving. Belial had noticed it the moment it began, but it took the addition of twinkling lights to catch Theodrick's eye.

"That ... motherfucking, piece of gaudy shit had better fucking not be her realm-damned, bastard of a fucking throne ..." Order had snarled in disgust at the time.

Belial had to admit it was certainly going to be ... different. Already tiny pinpricks of starlight glittered through the swirl of soft colours as they moved through the space like a gaseous breeze, and although it hadn't taken any formalised shape yet, Belial could already see the delicacy that suited his granddaughter's youthful femininity.

By contrast, Theodrick's throne was cut from a single diamond. Sharp, jarring angles that never changed, mirroring the bender's inflexibility and determination to control every aspect of his existence down to the last molecule.

Belial's own throne was just as imposing. The Damned constantly groaned beneath his weight, and his enjoyment at making any or all of them scream whenever the whim took him was its own statement piece. They were the masters of their domains. Everyone feared them.

But would they fear Columbine, as was her due? Belial eyed the girlish substance of her throne and shook his head. He just couldn't see it.

As always, time would tell.

* * *

After Avis returned to the physical realm, he reached down and claimed another strawberry as if he hadn't just spent nearly two full days inside Columbine's subconscious. He popped it into his mouth and chewed slowly, watching her eye the spread between them. "Dig in, princess," he said with a magnanimous wave at the food as if she needed his permission. "There's plenty here for both of us."

Columbine glanced up at him, then ran her tongue over her lips before claiming a substantial slice of quiche that required both hands to balance. Watching her bite down on it, Avis' stomach growled in approval.

"I think you've got the right idea there, princess," he admitted, and after swallowing the strawberry with ease, he went for an enormous, triple-decker club sandwich that had so many layers to it, it was bigger than both his hands combined. Edible skewers at various intervals held it all together. Doing his best to contain it all, he crushed it down between his fingers and bit into it, relishing the variety of familiar flavours. Among other things, Clarise had also been right about how hungry he was. He was starving.

The pair ate heartily, Avis washing down his meal with ambrosia while Columbine drank several glasses of sugared fruit juice. He observed her eating habits, noting with satisfaction that by the end of the meal she wasn't constantly gauging his reaction to her choices and was helping herself to whatever she liked. In Hell, she might have had to wait for permission to touch anything, but that wasn't how Mystallians operated. His family were firm believers in 'You snooze, you lose'.

Whether it was her tiny size; the fact that he hadn't eaten in a long time; or a combination of the two, Avis knew despite his own ongoing hunger, exactly when Columbine had had enough. She straightened where she sat and clasped her hands together in her lap, waiting to be excused.

"Princess, are you full?" he asked innocently, knowing she'd never speak first.

"Yes, Father."

Avis nodded and tilted his head in the general direction of the ladder. "Then off you go, baby. I'll be down shortly."

Columbine needed no other encouragement. She popped to her feet without a word and rushed to the ladder; clearly wanting some alone time to process everything they'd shared. He couldn't blame her for that. It had been a long two days, mentally speaking.

"Who the fuck said you could move?" he snarled, as Columbine's cushion began to melt along the edges. The edges immediately firmed again and Avis resumed his meal. He had no use for Frash as an extra cushion now that Columbine was gone, but if keeping the bitch in that mundane form annoyed her, well … that suited him just fine.

He took his time finishing his meal, working out his own next move with each thoughtful bite. Cora couldn't be allowed to get away with bullying Columbine, but if he landed on her as hard as his first instinct demanded, he'd potentially destroy everything he'd spent the last few months building between them.

But what other choice did he have? *Hmmm, maybe I'm overthinking this.* Cora wasn't Columbine, so he didn't have to treat her with kid gloves in any way, and she'd never know he was making adjustments to her mind on the fly. She'd be oblivious to his mental commands but still forced to obey them.

That realisation made things a whole lot easier for him. Of course, he'd make it a mental command! There was nothing wrong with that. He just needed to work out the perfect wording. Something that would make allowances for a situation where Cora needed to bully her sister for her own good. A perfect example of that would be during his fight with Keket. Columbine had shut down entirely, putting herself at great risk of being hurt. Had her brute squad guard not been on hand to whisk her away to safety, she'd have needed someone like Cora to bully her into moving. Thankfully, he knew how protective Cora was of her little sister. He'd seen it firsthand. But it needed to be in Columbine's best interest; not just a matter of 'because'. That was the key.

He swallowed the last bite of a caramel tartlet and reached for his goblet of ambrosia. Taking a small sip, he slid his tongue through the familiar wine thoughtfully. Perhaps in time, when Columbine had learned to stand up for herself, he could remove the command from Cora and permit their relationship to evolve naturally. Despite the necessity now, the thought of permanently leaving such a restrictive order in place didn't sit well with him.

With the goblet still in his hand, he rose abruptly to his feet and made his way to the ladder Columbine had used a short time ago. However, instead of climbing down, he covered the mouth of the goblet with his free hand, stepped off the ledge and landed on the deck below as if he were walking down a set of oversized stairs. A further two steps forward had him at the edge of the second deck, and a third put him down on the same level as Cora. This wasn't the time for subtlety.

Cora gasped when his boots impacted the deck behind her and she both rolled over and sat up on the same move. "Father, what …?"

Avis gave her no warning. **You will only bully Columbine if it is to Columbine's benefit.** Nice and simple. He didn't care what her reasons were. There was nothing that could justify the internalised crap he'd witnessed in Columbine's mind. He stalked forward to stand over her, his free hand pressed into a loose fist against his hip. His pointer finger came away from the goblet of ambrosia to identify exactly who he was speaking to. "If you *ever* tell Columbine to keep her sadness to herself again, *you'll* be a lot sadder by the time I'm through with you. You understand me, tiger?"

Cora's eyes rounded briefly at the threat, but then they became slitted. "Why the hell should I feel sad just because she is?" she argued, scrambling to her feet to match his stance with an angry one of her own. "I've got enough crap of my own to deal with."

"Because you're her older sister. Instead of telling her to keep it to herself, you should've been figuring out who caused it and gone after them."

"And just how the fuck do you suggest I should '*go after you*', Father?" Cora's words were filled with icy venom. "When we both know I can't do shit to you."

Avis was more interested in the statement itself than the swearing (which from his side of the family came second nature). The hand he had on his hip loosened and he shifted his weight to one leg; a physical representation of how the conversation was moving away from an accusation and into a discussion. "So, you knew I was the source?"

Cora went to roll her eyes but caught herself at the last second and chose to blink deliberately at him, which meant she was learning … *slowly*. "It didn't take a genius to figure out. You're hated all over the Known Realms and she's been like that ever since we were booted out of Yaru." Staring at him like he was the realm's greatest moron, she made a show of holding up both her pointer fingers shoulder-width apart, then brought the two together in front of her to emphasise the simplicity of her deduction.

The muscles in Avis' jaw jumped and red crept into the fringes of his vision, but to avoid biting her head off (or worse), he deliberately raised his goblet to his lips and took a deep mouthful of his drink. He swallowed more than the wine before he spoke again. "So, you didn't check her memories yourself to be sure?"

Cora snorted in disgust. "As if I'm ever going to set foot in her mind again. I don't know who did what to it, but fuck that. I like my sanity right where it is."

And that was when it all clicked together for Avis. As Columbine had said, Cora had gone into her sister's mind at some point and hit that same colour palette that'd put him on his ass. As a Mystallian, she'd hated the entanglement and had reacted to it by verbally telling her sister to keep her feelings to herself, which Columbine then took to heart. In small doses, Columbine had been able to manage the suppression on her own, but when they became overwhelming, it could've seriously hurt her.

Cora hadn't made the sneer a true mental command. It would've been the first thing he hit when he went into Columbine's mind if she had. No, this was a verbal push and shove between siblings that Columbine shouldn't have obsessed over.

Mulling this over, he drained the last of the ambrosia, then tossed the goblet high into the air, easily sending it soaring above the third deck. On its downward trajectory, a tendril shot out over the edge of the third deck, wrapped itself around the goblet stem and whipped both back out of sight; reminding Avis of a frog capturing its dinner. At least someone up there was paying attention, and it pleased him to think it was Tilu; whether she had done the deed or not. He looked back at Cora, breathing out slowly and heavily through his nose. "I don't appreciate you telling Columbine she has to keep her emotions to herself."

Cora's scowl turned nasty. "Why not? They're not mine. They're hers."

Unable to help himself, Avis took a step into her space and poked her in the shoulder with one finger. "Because she's your little sister, you little twerp, and her heartache is *supposed* to affect you." He waved his hand back towards the rest of the ship to incorporate Columbine, though his eyes never left Cora. "She may choose to deal with it herself, but you're older. It's your job to get into her space and give her the support she needs when she's hurting. Not kick her in the guts when she's down and make her feel even worse."

He gave her a few seconds to digest that, before pushing on. "She can't help the way she is, and you know that better than all of us." That was a guess on his part, but an educated one. Siblings, for the most part, shared a bond that transcended all others. "While we're stuck in such tight quarters, you can't avoid her. So, the best way to bring about an end to your misery is to help her get to the end of hers." Realising exactly who he was talking to, his temper got the better of him. "For Mystal's sake, you're supposed to have an adult head on your shoulders, tiger. Use it. I shouldn't have to be telling you this."

He watched her body tense with each word until she turned her head away from him to gaze at some distant point on his right. From her profile, he hoped she had her lips pinched together because she was thinking about what he said. "You get me?" He'd go into her head and make sure of it if he had to.

Just as he was about to give her a mental nudge, her shoulders relaxed and she nodded. "Yeah, I hear you."

He too, relaxed. "Good." He turned on his heel and took a step away, but then paused and looked back over his shoulder at her. "Oh, and tiger?"

"Yeah?"

"You asked the wrong question. It's not *'how the fuck do you suggest I should go after you?'* once you figured out I was the problem. What you should've asked is, *'What's the best way I can help her?'* Because if you'd have asked yourself that one, you'd have known to come and tell me what was going on. I won't always notice everything with you two, especially once we get back to Mystal, but she's your sister and you'll always be more attuned to her inner workings than I'll ever be. Columbine should never have been left to deal with that by herself for days."

He shook his head, more pissed at himself than her for that. "Mystallians don't operate that way. Never have, never will. We work as one." Not expecting anything of it, he raised a clenched fist to signify the unity his family held. "Mystal. Always." What he would've given to have her come forward and knock fists with him as was the Mystallian custom, but he knew Cora wouldn't, especially not for his gratification. This was something she'd either do on her own or not. He certainly hoped it wouldn't be the latter.

CHAPTER THIRTEEN

For the next two weeks, Avis eyed Maui with open suspicion that bordered on hostility. He didn't go back to thinking of him as a threat (that was beyond stupid and just went to show how wrecked he'd been), but more like an annoying cockroach that he wasn't allowed to step on. The boy had done nothing new to earn that ire, but he had it in spades, nonetheless. Not only because the little prick had made that initial pass at Clarise, but every time he thought of Maui sequestering Columbine in a romantic sense, the blood vessels in his temples threatened to rupture. *Over my dead body, you little fucker, and I can't fucking die.* The same wouldn't be said for Maui if he so much as thought something that disgusting again, and Avis made a point of checking … regularly.

Clarise seemed just as determined to push Avis through his dislike of their host. One evening, long after the girls had retired and the two were alone in their room, she broached the subject of inviting Maui to their family meals. "It is the least we can do since he is taking us through his realm at great risk to himself," Clarise argued when he flat-out refused to entertain the notion.

In his mind, there were three levels to the catamaran, and since Maui had turned up all by himself when they'd first met, the kid was obviously used to eating alone and wouldn't have a problem with that arrangement. They didn't have to dine together.

Clarise thought otherwise and played the one card guaranteed to finish the argument in her favour. "I see," she'd said in a sultry voice, putting Avis on notice for what was possibly coming next. "And since you went without sex with me for a very long time before we met, by your logic you must also be comfortable with not having sex with me and wish to forego it in the near future. Is that not correct?"

Avis had never been so tempted to throttle and make out with a woman at the same time before. He even went as far as to take her delicate neck in both hands, but instead of squeezing, he pulled her to him and kissed her passionately. "One of these days, that threat's not going to work on me," he said, once he was done plundering her mouth with his tongue. He pressed his forehead to hers so he could stare her in the eyes.

The gold of Clarise's eyes practically glittered. "And what do you suppose will happen on that day?" she asked in a husky whisper.

"On that day, I'll be putting this beautiful body of yours over my knee and spanking some much-needed sense into you. The sex card is not to be used lightly, and certainly not on an idiot kid like him."

Her hands cupped his ass and she squeezed almost painfully. "What if we take it the other way?" she murmured, pushing into his hold to rub herself across his body the way a cat would.

Avis' breath caught in his throat as his entire body tensed. "Now you're cheating."

Although one set of hands still massaged his ass-cheeks, a second set went between his legs just to show him how much she *could* cheat. "But is it working?" she purred, knowing damn-well it was.

Finding the inner strength from somewhere, Avis walked her backwards, not stopping as the mattress collected the back of her knees and she fell across the bed. Avis went down with her and used his weight to pin her in place.

Over the next hour, he showed her precisely how well it worked.

"It really means that much to you?" he asked, as they lay on their sides with her back spooned into his chest. His hand was draped across her middle, his fingers lightly dancing around the soft flesh around her belly button. He had his head propped up on his other hand to watch what he was doing.

Clarise rolled over to face him, putting some distance between them. He didn't like that and tried to pull her back against him, but she pushed both hands against his pecs. "Maui has yet to get anything out of our arrangement, Avis, and he is the one risking the wrath of his whole pantheon by helping us. We have agreed to give him knowledge but to date, all he has received from you is open hostility. Sharing a meal with him would go a long way towards making peace."

"Just one meal?" Avis asked, hopefully. The condemning, flat-palmed slap against his chest answered him more effectively than words.

Loathing the impasse, Avis scowled and rolled away from her. He sat up with his feet on the floor, his eyes boring into the timber wall as his hands slowly fisted into the sheets on either side of him. "I just don't get how can you ignore the fact that he said he wants to sleep with Columbine," he growled, shaking his head at her indifference when the very thought still made him murderous. "Not to mention his pass at you."

He felt Clarise on her knees behind him and wasn't surprised when her arms came around his shoulders with her lips pressing into the back of his head. "He said that nearly three weeks ago, and we both know nothing is going to come of either suggestion. He is just a baby, my love, and children are renowned for saying inappropriate things at the worst possible times in an effort to sound clever and grown-up. You cannot fault his behaviour since. He has even gone to the trouble of showing the girls how to fish and sail to keep them occupied. In fact, when Cora openly laughed at his insistence that he was not of hellion stock, he did not lift a single retaliatory finger against her. No, he went up into the rigging and sulked for hours."

She nuzzled his hair. "He sulked, beloved. We both know that is the behaviour of a child, and I think nearly three weeks of being excluded is long enough to expunge what he said in a moment of childish stupidity."

Avis didn't like it. Three weeks. Three years. Three eons. He never let go of a slight; especially when it came from outside the family.

Her lips travelled down his neck and out over his right shoulder, where she could meet his eyes with large, rounded, puppy-dog ones of her own. "Do it for me?" she asked, her breath barely a whisper.

Avis would walk naked through hellfire for her. But he still couldn't bring himself to say the words. Instead, he closed his eyes and inclined his head twice, knowing she would take that as a hellion acquiescence.

She nibbled an appreciative line to his throat. "Thank you."

PUSSY-WHIPPED MOTHERFUCKER.

Avis breathed out heavily, unable to argue with the subconscious deduction.

He managed to claw back some control at the following meal though, by making sure the seating arrangements were to his liking. That is, he had Clarise sitting opposite him at the far end of an extended table in the larger of the two enclosed rooms on the lowest deck. The girls sat to his right with their backs to the wall, and Maui sat opposite them with his back to the open doorway. There was no room behind the girls for the servants, but as shifters, they could serve both sides of the table while standing on either side of Maui.

The boy watched apprehensively as the two servants towered over him like demonic guards and only seemed to relax once they stepped back. The look Clarise shot Avis told him she knew exactly what he was up to, at which point he raised his goblet of ambrosia and smirked at her over the lip. He'd fulfilled his agreement. The boy was there, wasn't he?

Close to a week later, Maui surprised Avis with a Rangi-Taurean meal. The aroma had Avis salivating as soon as he and Clarise walked into the room, but a quick search of Maui's recent memories dimmed the Mystallian's culinary excitement. The brat had been ... busy. "I don't do new foods," he declared, as he ushered the girls in behind his seat to take their own places against the wall.

Some of Maui's excitement dwindled. "But it's really good," he argued, pointing at the parcels of woven leaves in the middle of the table. "It's not spicy like that Yarusian stuff that you said turned your stomach. You'll like it ..."

"I've heard that before." Avis was already done with the conversation.

"Well, I would certainly like to try some ... what are they called, Maui?" Clarise asked with a polite smile, gesturing for one of the servants to dish her up a helping of whatever was buried beneath the leaves as the other helped her into her seat.

"It's baked fish, pork, rice and vegetables, cooked hangi-style." Maui gestured to each, but when a servant moved to open the parcels, the young godling snatched up the knife sitting on the table in front of him and sprang to his feet. "I've got it," he insisted, already cutting through the leaves of the nearest package to expose the pork within.

It did smell wonderful. Avis drew in a deep breath and held it, delighting in the way it danced across his senses. He hadn't realised he'd closed his eyes until the scent of the pork grew stronger and he jerked his head back to see Maui offering him a large slab of the frayed meat. Maui's lips were parted in a cocky grin and his eyes went from Avis' to the meat on the end of his blade and back up to the Mystallian again; as if waiting for permission to plate it. "You sure I can't tempt you, old man?"

Avis smelt none of the spice that had upset his stomach so badly. If anything, it had the same aromatic flavours he was used to back home, with one or two slight variations. He stared at the surface of the meat, searching for any lurking spice. When he found none, he gestured with a flick of his left index finger for it to be put on his plate.

The meal was actually quite palatable. The wood-flavoured meat melted in Avis' mouth and the soft root vegetables reminded him of roast vegetables he'd had at home. Maui seemed very pleased with himself and as much as it galled him, Avis had to admit the little shit had done well.

Throughout the meal, Avis would've had to be blind to not notice the way Clarise pinned him with a stern look, then pointedly moved her gaze to where Maui sat. That wasn't to say he didn't try to ignore her, but the truth was, he had fallen down on his half of their deal. The boy was trying, and it was time he stepped up and met the little pain-in-the-ass halfway.

As always, after everyone had had their fill, Maui was the first to leave. Wanting to clear the debt (at least from his side) Avis rose and followed him outside. He was surprised to find the deck directly outside the room empty, but having followed Maui around for over a week and a half, Avis thought he knew which direction he'd have taken off in.

Making his way around to the bow, Avis found the boy leaning his elbow against the rail in the far-left hand corner. His head was tilted back and he stared at both the sails and the starry night beyond, his features clouded in a thoughtful expression.

More out of curiosity than any real desire to know, Avis glanced up into the sails to see what had him so engrossed. When nothing jumped out, he returned his attention to the young man who was now eyeing him suspiciously. "What brings you out here, old man?"

"I told you when we first met that your understanding of things sucked, and we agreed the trade-off for your assistance was to rectify that. I figure now's as good a time as any to uphold our end of the agreement."

For the longest time, Maui searched Avis' face for something. "Okay," he drawled, licking his lips and bobbing his head cautiously. "I suppose I do have a couple of questions for you."

Avis hadn't planned on turning this into a Q and A session but decided it would make things easier if he used the questions to gauge how much the boy knew. Whether he chose to answer them would, of course, always be at his discretion.

The older celestial stepped up to the rail alongside Maui. "What's your first question?"

"What's the significance of the black animal hide you all insist on wearing?"

What the fuck did that have to do with anything? Frowning darkly, Avis crossed his arms and turned his attention to the water. "You know it's the Mystallian uniform."

"Yeah, but why?"

Without turning his head, Avis slid his narrowed gaze to the boy and found he'd rolled around so that his back and elbows were resting against the bamboo handrail and his feet were crossed at the ankles on an angle to his body. He appeared at ease, though the look in his young eyes said otherwise. "And, more to the point, what'd Cora do to not be allowed to wear it?"

That made the question a lot more pertinent. Maui had noticed the minor fissures within the family and wanted to understand them. "Why do you care?" Avis wasn't about to explain everything, but Maui's motives would be the deciding factor in how much he learned.

Maui lifted one shoulder in a shrug. "Call it one outsider recognising the plight of another, and I like her spunk. What'd she do to warrant being ostracised from the rest of you?"

It really was none of Maui's business what happened inside the Mystallian pantheon, but something in Avis kicked up at the thought of anyone thinking Cora's current predicament was his fault. "She hasn't done anything wrong in my eyes," he snapped irritably. "When she's ready, she only has to let us know and her outfit will be changed to acknowledge her Mystallian heritage. The call is hers to make. No one else's."

Maui nodded as he mulled that over. "I figured she must've taken after you."

For a second, Avis thought he meant she shared his stubborn streak, but even Maui wouldn't be that suicidal. Releasing his breath in a slow, steady stream, he used Clarise's trick of mentally counting to ten to keep a lid on his temper. "What makes you say that?" he asked, once the hint of red had left his vision.

"Well, if she took after her mother, she'd be a shifter, and she hasn't shifted anything the whole time I've known her." He rolled his right-hand palm up between them. "And you just said someone else would have to give her the uniform, so I guess she's like you. A bender."

Avis snorted. "Under normal conditions, she'd shift your ass into any ream-damned thing she wanted." No need to tip their hand and let Maui know Cora was in fact, both. There might come a time when she'd need to bend him and the less he knew about that capability, the better.

Maui tilted his head to the left and rubbed that side of his jaw. "And the conditions right now aren't normal?"

Perceptive prick. Avis paused before answering that. "Her mother's family poisoned her with something that prevents her from shapeshifting. Long story," he swiftly added, when Maui flicked himself to his feet, suddenly very interested in the conversation. "And no, I'm not going into it. Suffice to say, she's stuck as she is until the poison runs its course."

"And how long's that going to take?"

Avis had never actually asked that question. He'd been in such a fucking hurry to leave Hell that it'd never occurred to him to ask anyone how long would the tefsla remain in her system. Was it years? Decades? Centuries? Surely it couldn't be millennia. Could it?

Watching his face carefully, Maui's expression grew incredulous. "You never asked, did you?"

"It's not my area of expertise."

Maui abruptly burst out laughing. "That has to be one of the dumbest things I've ever heard you say, old man!" He laughed so hard tears began to form in his eyes. "For the realm's sake, if it *was* your area of expertise, you wouldn't be asking anyway! The whole point of asking is to learn something ... *outside your area of expertise.*"

Avis' reaction was as instantaneous as it was automatic. It didn't matter that Maui was right. No one made fun of him, and no one ... *no one* fucking laughed at him! The hints of red that normally crept around the edges of his vision when he was angry blasted across his eyes, blinding him to everything else but the source of the mockery. *You arrogant motherfucking ...*

Avis launched himself at the boy, both mentally and physically. Mental fire erupted behind Maui's eyes moments before Avis crash tackled him to the ground. Maui had to be destroyed! At this point, nothing else would satisfy him. He straddled Maui's upper body and began wailing on his face. Maui writhed in agony under the Mystallian three times his size and struggled beneath the crushing blows Avis rained down on him. The first strike broke his cheek and nose. The second shattered his jaw. Maui's hands swung wildly beneath the barrage, desperate to fend off his attacker. As if distance mattered to a ranged bender. The physical stuff just felt good. Maui's thrashing fingers hooked the chain of Avis' cloak and the boy's fingernails slid across his throat, causing four burning lines that barely registered with the enraged god. Still, it registered. Avis grabbed the offending wrist and twisted it, crushing it with ease. Then, still holding the shattered limb, brought the back of his clenched fist into the side of Maui's already destroyed cheekbone.

END THIS FUCKING FUCKER!

Gladly!

Avis ramped up his bending burn and Maui's muscles arched him off the deck, his mouth wide with silent screams.

"What are you doing, Father?"

The quiet, almost shy question that came from somewhere behind him froze Avis in his tracks faster than if he'd been tossed into the heart of Hell's Antenora. The icy sense of dread that replaced the red in his vision was just as numbing. *Shit! Shit ... shit ... shit ...* He didn't turn to see who was behind him. He didn't need to. Without the mental burn to sustain his silence, Maui's broken lips opened to scream.

Silence! Avis couldn't make that mental command quick enough or loud enough. The fact that Maui was still alive at all was a testament to his shifting bloodline. With his face barely recognisable and his mind in ashes, he'd be dead if he were a bender. Avis pulled himself back to his haunches, shifting his shoulders slightly to use both his greater mass and the presence of his cloak to hide the evidence of his brutality.

"Princess." His voice sounded as if he was gargling rocks and he still refused to look at her. Not when he knew Maui's blood was probably splattered all over his face. "What are you doing out here?"

"Why are you hurting Maui, Father?"

Fuck! His rage had triggered her empathy and she'd come out to see why. Avis ran his tongue over his lips and froze all over again when he tasted a solid, metallic smear of Maui's blood. *Crap!* His eyes jerked down to what was left of Maui's face, searching for any tell-tale teeth marks. Had he really bitten the boy in a fit of rage? No, surely not. He'd have remembered that ... wouldn't he? He couldn't tell, because there wasn't enough skin left on Maui's face to tell either way. The kid was a mess.

Thankfully, it was nothing a shifter couldn't shake off. The problem was, he needed a working mind to do that.

Avis didn't think twice about what he had to do next. Not with Columbine right behind him asking questions he didn't want to answer. Without a word, he dove straight into what was left of Maui's mind. He had two good starting points for recreating memories out of the ashes. His voyeurism over the last few weeks meant those twenty-ish days were easy to replace. He'd also seen the memories involving Makeatutara's supposed 'accidental' cursing and how Maui had been compensated with the 'shapeshifting' bone. It was more than enough.

Avis then gave the solidified memories a power boost that sent them sifting through the ashes for any correlating fragments to attach to. Each memory fanned out in all directions, rebuilding every other memory around it, which in turn rebuilt many others. Since time in the physical realm stood still, Avis was on no real clock in here. Many benders who had to spend years ... centuries ... even millennia inside the mind of another often commandeered the subject's imagination to keep themselves in touch with what waited for them outside. Sometimes, just recreating a family meal for an hour or so was enough to keep an individual grounded. Other times, more in-depth interactions were required. None of these memories were allowed to stay, of course. Once the activity concluded, it was wiped away as if it had never been.

In Maui's case, the seventeen years of knowledge took exactly ninety-one hours to rebuild.

It was a long four days.

CHAPTER FOURTEEN

When Avis pulled out of Maui's mind, the boy had most of his early childhood memories back, along with the most recent decade. More than enough to get by on, for sure. Only a bender would get his or her nose out of joint over a little amnesia. Shifters, like mortals, forgot things all the time and were never any the wiser.

He knew Columbine was still right behind him but didn't turn to acknowledge her. Not yet. Maui's body was in the midst of reshaping itself back into his natural form, which meant the boy was in there. Avis leaned forward, closing the distance between them to a hand's width. "I'll give you back your voice when you can use it without screaming like a little bitch," he whispered, hoping Columbine hadn't heightened her hearing to eavesdrop.

Once Maui no longer looked like he'd been used as a chew toy for an enraged talot, Avis calmly rose to his feet and stepped off the younger god. "We were just … settling a few differences, princess," he assured her, not quite turning to face her. Maui clawing his throat wasn't what made him keep his face in the shadows since most of that had already healed. No, it was the blood which still coated his face that he didn't want Columbine to see. "Shouldn't you be getting ready for bed?"

"You were very angry, Father. Glowing angry, and you scared Maui."

Avis' first instinct was to puff out his chest in pride for that had been his overall goal at the time. But then he realised what she'd admitted to within Maui's hearing and his eyes widened in panic. *Glowing angry*. Had Maui healed enough to make sense of her empathic ramblings? The unresponsiveness of Maui's prone body said otherwise, but he couldn't risk it. He ran a mental hand through Maui's memories and erased the last few seconds.

"Princess, you've been told not to talk about that in front of people."

He hadn't meant to make that sound so disciplinary, but she needed to be more careful. It was far too dangerous to blurt things out like that in front of others.

"You are not going to hurt Maui anymore, are you, Father?"

Avis took his time answering that as he stared down at the boy, watching his left eye reinflate in its socket. "Not at the moment, princess," he answered, refusing to lie to her. Tomorrow was another matter that had yet to be decided. He tilted his head to glance at her over his shoulder in such a way that his cloak and the shadows of the night still hid his face from her. "Why don't you go and write up your diary entry for the day and then have Diviten get you ready for bed, baby? Once I'm done here, I'll come and tuck you in. Alright?"

"Yes, Father."

"Good girl. Off you go." Avis held his position as she turned and happily skipped across the deck to the ladder. She paused on the first rung and gave him a shy wave, then scampered up to the second floor. A moment later she disappeared around the far side of the cabin where she shared a room with her sister.

Once she was out of sight and he was free to move again, his attention returned to Maui, where all sense of civility deserted him. "Don't you ever, *ever* laugh at me again, you little prick. And I mean fucking ever! I've killed godlings a lot older and a lot more powerful than you for a hell of a lot less. If anything, you need to thank that little girl, because if it wasn't for her, your death curse would've already come to pass right here and now."

Coincidentally, Maui chose that moment to come to life with a gasp and he rolled onto his stomach. His arm swung high and wide, hooking at the wrist over the bamboo rail. His other hand clawed at the deck and he dragged himself into a sideways sitting position, staring up at Avis over his arm in horror. Credit where it was due, no tears formed in Maui's eyes. Nor had he broken down and blubbered at his near-death experience. Most did in his position, yet the boy was somehow holding his own. He panted heavily and sweat covered every inch of his body, but eventually, he released his hold on the rail and pulled himself forward to rest both elbows on his knees with his head bowed. His breathing continued to deepen until a single, lung-filling sigh escaped his lips. Then he straightened up and leaned back against the gunwale, his eyes sliding to where Avis loomed over him. Since his surface thoughts were no longer clouded by pain, Avis returned his voice to him.

"How did you do that?" the boy demanded, in a hushed, accusatory tone.

The statement was too ambiguous for Avis to answer with specifics, but rather than delve into his mind to see what he meant, Avis decided to generalise his reply. "It's why you don't fuck with Mystallians." Whatever had the boy rattled, telling him it was a given ability across the entire Mystallian pantheon added to their intimidation factor.

"But I couldn't shift you off me ..."

Ahh. The kid had anticipated his mind burn, but not his shifting invulnerability. Unfortunately, Avis was the only member of the family that had Clarise's blood running through his veins, making him immune to almost every other shifter in existence. *Oh, well.* "Keep that in mind."

Yes, he could've corrected Maui's misunderstanding, but how was that going to benefit either him or Mystal?

Maui rolled away from Avis, using the motion to lift himself onto his knees. His hands curled around the side rail and after taking a moment to steady himself, he slowly dragged himself upright. Somewhat. His chest doubled over the rail and his arms locked into the bamboo so tightly it began to crack. "Owww," he complained, staring straight down at the water beneath the floats as if he was going to be sick. "Damn, and I thought Tu could blow up over nothing ..." He twisted his head and glared at Avis over his shoulder, still panting heavily. "You've got some serious issues, man."

"And a lot serious fucking muscle to back them up," Avis shot back just as fast. "So don't piss me off again, Maui, unless you really want to learn how bad it can get. Trust me, you're getting more warning than anyone else to date, so don't waste it."

"Mmm," Maui murmured through pursed lips, then wheezed a few times before he tested the strength of his arms and pushed himself onto his feet. Both hands remained on the rail for stability. "I'm beginning to see that."

"For your sake, I hope so."

It was another ten minutes before Maui recovered fully and was back to his old, exasperating self. Which was about a day and a half sooner than he should have been. Avis watched his 'miraculous' recovery with growing suspicion. By the end, it was as if his mind had never been burnt at all; something no one shook off in minutes. Even the unestablished kids back home didn't snap back from a mental thrashing that fast, and not only were they more familiar with bending fire, but none of them had been taken to the brink of death. Something wasn't right here, and Avis hated surprises.

"So, Cora's been poisoned, and that's why she can't shapeshift," the boy reiterated taking the exact same pose he had when the conversation started, with his feet crossed at the ankle and both elbows braced on the rail. He lifted his chin at Avis and grinned smugly. "That right there is how I know I'm not a Hellion."

Knowing who Maui's father was and how ridiculous that made his statement, Avis folded his arms and rested his hip against the rail beside him. "Do tell," he drawled in annoyance, looking forward to what stupidity the youngster was about to spout this time.

"My shapeshifting doesn't rely on me, so poisoning me can't lock me into a shape. I just grab the bone, and it lets me change shape."

"And if you lose the bone?"

Maui shrugged again, though Avis noticed a light shudder sweep through him. "Then I'm stuck in whatever form I'm in at that time. But only because I've lost the way to change. Not because I'm locked in."

Oh, you can't be that stupid. Avis had to close his eyes. This level of absurdity shouldn't be allowed to breathe. He drew in two deep breaths and released each slowly, determined to see the ridiculous conversation through. If he made it all the way through just once, his part of their deal was done and he'd never have to revisit it.

When he thought he had his temper under control, he opened his eyes and speared Maui with a telling look. "Alright, junior. Let's run with that for a second. You see those two as being mutually exclusive. You're stuck, without being locked in. Just how exactly have you managed to delude yourself into thinking they're not the same thing?"

"My grandmother's jawbone is full of magic."

The muscle under Avis' left eye ticked as uncontrollably as the one in his jaw. "If we're going to get to the end of this conversation without me trying to kill you again, you need to stop calling it your grandmother's jawbone, kid. Just call it a hook. It's a *hook*."

Maui shrugged one shoulder as if it didn't bother him either way.

"Have you ever tried to shapeshift without it?"

"What's the point?" Maui asked, testily. "I can't."

Avis felt his lips curl into a cruel grin. "Humour me, Maui. Put the hook down and try." By the Twin Notes of all creation, it was going to be fun watching the shocked look on his stupid face when he learned he could shift just as easily without that damned scrap of bone.

Maui huffed, adding to Avis' delight, but he nevertheless removed the hook from his belt. Making a show of things, he elaborately tied its leather line to the rail, hooked it over one of the supports, then stepped away with a gracious roll of both hands to prove he had in fact, distanced himself from it.

Avis rubbed his thumb and forefingers together, barely able to contain his glee. *This is going to be great!* "Now, try changing into … a turtle."

Uncertainty swept across Maui's face as he licked his lips and took in a nervous deep breath. The focus in his eyes became razor-sharp, but as the seconds ticked by, he didn't change. He huffed and puffed from exertion, then closed his eyes, clenching his hands into tight fists. So much effort went into it, that his entire body started to shake.

Then, he snapped his eyes open and glared wildly at Avis. "See?" he snarled; his tone full of venom. "I told you I couldn't do it!"

Avis couldn't understand why. Maui knew how to shapeshift. With the hook, he did it as easily as Clarise, so it wasn't the fundamentals of shapeshifting he was struggling with. But the boy was genuinely struggling. His young body shook like a leaf and his chest heaved as if he'd run to the other side of the realm and back. "You did go through the same motions as if you held the hook, didn't you?" The question was rhetorical, but he had to be sure.

Maui looked insulted as sweat ran in rivulets down his brow and cheekbones. "Of course," he snapped, wiping it away impatiently.

And that was when it hit Avis with all the finesse of a solar collision. The shakes. The inability to do what should've come naturally to him. The irrational, short, sharp snaps for responses afterwards, and now the sweats.

Avis closed his eyes and covered them with one hand as a groan of disbelief escaped his lips. By following his directive, the boy had inadvertently gone to war with his powerbase and his thrall was kicking his ass.

"What?" Maui demanded with a savage growl.

"You're fucking seventeen! That's what!" Who in their right mind lets a seventeen-year-old kid get established? It explained everything Maui had been able to do and not do in one fell swoop, but it was beyond asinine! In some pantheons, seventeen wasn't even old enough to drink hard liquor or have sex, let alone manage a realm-wide powerbase! "You told the mortals about the powers of the hook, didn't you?"

"Of course!" Maui rubbed his upper arms and shoulders and continued to shiver. His eyes were riveted to his hook as if that piece of bone held all the answers.

Avis stepped between the two. "And so now they now believe your power comes from that stupid piece of fucking bone!" He threw the words out as an accusation because, in his mind, it was.

"What are you talking about?" Maui demanded, using his forearms to wipe the sweat from his face, though he shook so badly he hit himself several times in the process.

"You've just shot yourself in the foot, and you don't even know it." He stared at Maui; whose muscles would soon cramp until his bones broke. Avis had seen it happen before. "Congratulations on your establishment, you moron," he said, though his tone and name-calling implied the exact reverse.

"What in the realm are you on about?"

"Establishment is the peak of our power. With it, we can become anything the mortals want to believe, but if you're stupid enough to have them believe in these crippling limitations, you devolve instead of evolve."

Maui right leg gave out, driving him to his side on the deck, his face contorting in pain. "Make sense …"

Avis had to give himself a moment to edit out all the cursing he longed to hurl at the naive twit. "You've become what the mortals believe," he said again in accusation. "It's now become your reality." Stepping aside, he gathered up the hook by its line and swung it loosely across his body, watching as Maui's eyes followed its every movement. "How badly do you want this?" he asked, knowing Maui would slaughter everyone he held dear to get his hands on the scrap of bone.

Maui's hands flexed involuntarily and he dragged himself towards the source of his relief. Then, realising what he was doing, he dug deep and willed himself to stop. Another wave of pain was his reward and he dropped his head, pressing it into the deck. "It's ... not ... that ... bad," he lied between shallow breaths.

Deciding he'd suffered enough (and knowing how much worse it would get if he continued to ignore it) Avis untied the line and threw the hook to the deck between Maui's hands. "Take it," he ordered.

Maui snatched up the piece of bone and over the next few seconds he shifted into dozens of different living things, all of which had different masses. Avis had wondered about that. He'd only ever seen that speed in Columbine, but even she took time when it came to gathering and losing mass. Likewise, what was with the changing into living things only? Shifters could become anything at all—even dust. Had his father told him another lie to hamper his ability or had he truly not tried to change into an inert object? Either way, it was weird.

After nearly a minute of constant shifting, Maui returned to his natural form; on his knees with the hook clutched in both hands, panting with relief. "What in the realms ...?" he demanded, turning to the one person who in his eyes must have held all the answers.

Avis folded his arms across his chest and stared down at him. "That is what happens when you tell mortals about your abilities, then try to fight what they believe. It's stupid."

"So, you knew that would happen?"

Avis nodded as if it should have been obvious. "Once I knew you were established, yeah. You shouldn't be anywhere near an establishment field for thousands of years at least. Especially not without the support of your pantheon. You're lucky to know which way your dick's pointing at your age."

"How did this happen?"

"Because you told the mortals of your shifting ability, and in the process, you got some of the critical details wrong. Once they believed you, those incorrect details became fact." Seeing the confusion in his eyes, Avis searched for an example he would understand. "Say you were born with two perfectly normal legs and spent the first twenty years of your life running wherever the hell your heart desires. Everything's going great for you until you fall and break both your legs at the knees. With me so far?" He waited for Maui's head to bob before continuing. "And if you managed to drag yourself into a hole, you'd recover in a week or two. But if the mortals found you in the meantime, and you were stupid enough to tell them you were a fallen god, they would worship you as a fallen god with two broken legs ... *and you'd never walk again!*"

Avis hadn't meant to shout that last part at Maui, but the lost look on the boy's face made Avis want to punch him all over again.

"*What?*"

"Yeah," Avis said, with a curt nod. "Not only can you *not* shapeshift without your hook, but your thrall'll also kick you in the balls every time you try to fight it. But look. The shakes have already left most of your body. You'll be fine in just a few more seconds."

Maui looked down at his right hand, then clenched it into a fist. Just as Avis had said, when he opened it a few seconds later, it was as steady as a rock.

"And now you know what it feels like to fight your establishment thrall. The realm's belief in you won't release its hold that easily."

"I'm never doing that again," Maui declared, rubbing his hands down his sides.

"Only a fool fights his or her thrall more than once."

The filthy look Maui shot him would've killed a lesser celestial. "If you've got any more great ideas like that up your sleeve, keep them to yourself."

Avis snorted derisively for two reasons. One, as mad as the kid was, he'd learned not to antagonise a Mystallian by throwing out an 'or else', and two, Avis knew very well if he wanted to do anything else to the brat, Maui wouldn't be able to do shit about it. He moved on to a more prudent topic. "So, what else do the mortals know about you?" Even as he said it, Avis suddenly had a sinking feeling he knew. *Oh, you can't have …!* Unable to keep his expression neutral, he snarled, "For the love of all that's fucking celestial, tell me they don't know that your father cursed you to die."

"As if I'm going to lie about something like that," Maui shot back, and Avis wanted to throttle him all over again.

"Kid! For fuck's sake! What the fuck is wrong with you? You never tell the fucking mortals shit like that! It all but guarantees the fucking outcome!" He couldn't help himself. Yes, he might've wanted to kill the kid just a short while ago himself, but that was one celestial to another! Maui hadn't even seen out his second decade, and he was already established! He'd heard of some fucked up shit in his time, but to be established as someone who was going to die was the exact opposite of what an establishment field was supposed to do! If Avis had been mortal, he'd be having a stroke right about now. He was sure of it. Blood pounded in his temples and he whirled and punched the gunwale off the deck, wishing it was Maui that was sailing off toward the horizon as opposed to the stupid piece of cross-lashed timber. "You … *fucking idiot!*" he roared.

"What in the realm's wrong with you?" Maui demanded.

"Didn't you hear a realm-damned word I just said? If you hadn't told them, your establishment would have protected you from the death curse! Now, instead, you're fucking guaranteed to die!"

"AVIS!" Clarise admonished from overhead.

Avis cringed at the reprimand. He'd been so wrapped up in his rant that he failed to notice how loud he'd become, or the attention his profanity-filled bellowing would draw. He whirled on his heel and looked up at his wife standing on the bedroom deck above them with her hands resting on her hips; a look of sheer condemnation on her face. If she'd been in her demonic form, he had no doubt that her tail would've been whipping furiously around her ankles. "Sweetheart, did you not hear what he just said?" As he spoke, Avis gestured wildly at Maui still standing at his side.

"I assure you, the entire catamaran has heard your opinion on what he just said," Clarise replied, crisply.

Knowing she meant the girls; Avis raked the fingers of one hand through his hair until his hand cupped the nape of his neck and looked off to one side.

"…and I would appreciate it if you could refrain from making such outbursts again."

By the time Avis lifted his eyes to the upper deck again, Clarise had already gone. *Shit*. Picturing what that must've looked like to the only witness, Avis' gaze narrowed and his lips tightened. "Not one realm-damned word, brat," he warned through gritted teeth as he slid his gaze to the boy.

Maui's expression was stone-cold sober. Only the twinkle in his eyes gave away his inner amusement. "Wouldn't dream of it, old man."

CHAPTER FIFTEEN

Before his temper got the better of him again, Avis stormed to the ladder and stalked up the rungs without using his fisted hands. After months of being on the water, he'd learned how to maintain his balance using only his feet.

"Do not expect me to apologise for getting angry at him," he warned, seeing Clarise poised at the bottom of the second ladder with her right hand and foot balanced on the rungs.

"Of course not." She lifted her eyes to the rungs above her head and started to climb upwards. "Join me, my love."

Avis watched as she climbed high and disappeared over the edge of the upper deck without a backwards glance at him. Part of him was elated that she'd finally found the inner strength to make demands of a man without Hell's infernal grovelling, but another wasn't so pleased to be the subject of her first male command. He glanced down at Maui, who continued to roll his hook between his hands as if assuring himself he still had it. Thrall was a bitch like that and fighting it was just plain stupid.

Avis went to the ladder and scaled it with ease. As his eyes crested the deck, he found Clarise standing at the rear of the platform with her back to him and her shoulders squared. She had her hands clasped behind her back and her feet were shoulder-width apart. He'd taken that pose many a time while waiting to lower the boom on someone and he wasn't about to capitulate to it himself. Striding across the deck, he stood at her side and matched her stance with a similar one of his own.

It took a few seconds of uneasy silence between them before Avis broke first. "Maui's a fool."

"Ignorance is not stupidity, Avis. It is merely ignorance." Her eyes slid across to him as she spoke, then returned to the ocean.

He knew because he'd glanced sideways at her first and hadn't gotten to the 'looking away' part yet. "It was still a really stupid thing to do."

"And where, in your scale of foolishness, does Cora's assumption that she could bend your mind to her will sit? Maui is barely a decade older than she is, beloved, and as I have reiterated many, many times to you, children will make mistakes. It is one of the few advantages of being a child."

It pissed him off to admit Cora's idiotic theory had been just as brainless. He mumbled a heated curse under his breath and shook his head in frustration. "Their mistakes aren't comparable," he argued, finally getting his thoughts in order. "That idiot's stupidity has made him a walking corpse."

Clarise suddenly turned to face him; her hands placed firmly on her hips. "The outcome of which is completely beyond your ability to control. If you were being even remotely honest with yourself, you would admit that that is what truly irks you the most in this situation."

Oh, Avis *really* didn't want to go there, even if she was right. He folded his arms tightly across his chest and ground his lips together, biting back the nasty retort that flew to his tongue. Tension soared within him as her eyes softened in sympathy. The last realm-damned thing he wanted was for her to feel sorry for him in any way.

He almost resisted her touch against his cheek, until the heavy scent of lavender filled his nose and he released his breath in a long, heartfelt sigh. "It's not right, Clarise. If he leaves the realm, the curse follows him and he dies. Now, if he stays here, his own powerbase will kill him just as surely. He's made himself a walking corpse, and his thrall's made sure he doesn't care." Focusing on the spot where he guessed Maui was if there weren't two decks between them, he frowned and clenched his fists against his ribs. "It's not right."

"I see a lot of Chance's exuberance in Maui," Clarise said, forcing her hand through the bend of his left elbow, despite his right fist blocking her way. She pressed her ear against his bicep and moulded herself into his side.

"Chance was that stupid once," Avis confessed without meaning to. He felt her head roll against his arm until her eyes stared up at him and knew no amount of wishful thinking on his part would allow him to take that back. The indifference of the ocean around them was easier to deal with, so he lifted his gaze and focused on that. "Back when we all first esc ... when we first left the Nexus. He was just a kid. We all were, I suppose, but he saw the mortals he came across as the friends he never had, and despite our best efforts, his innate luck would give him the freedom to keep going back to them. It only took them a few decades to realise he was divine, and after that, they turned him into their slave. They believed he was at their beck and call to make their wildest fantasies come true, and so he was."

Clarise stilled at his side. "What happened next?"

The muscles of Avis' jaw twitched and tension rippled through him as he processed the pros and cons of telling her. "This was all long before Mystal was established. We hadn't even finalised the borders yet, let alone attuned ourselves to the realm. As a result, the handful of mortals that 'worshipped' Chance had to keep him within five metres of them to ensure his loyalty. They achieved this by leashing him like a dog to be passed around any time someone wanted anything."

He sank his teeth into the flesh inside his cheek, using the stab of pain to keep himself focused. "When he didn't come back for months and stopped answering our blood-links, we went looking for him. Chasidah waited in the celestial realm with Blagden while the rest of us tracked him down." Visions of what they'd encountered that day flashed through his mind, and he suddenly felt nauseous. His stomach knotted and he dragged a dry tongue over his lips in an unsuccessful attempt to moisten them.

"The mortals were feral, sweetheart, and they turned Chance into a freak. A-A ... genie ... or something I think they called him. And the costume they made him wear ... it was ..." The lump that wedged in his throat made it hard to breathe, though he forced himself to continue.

"Clarise, it was ridiculous and horrible, and when he saw us, he was so happy to be a chained slave. Amaro and I, we were stunned speechless, and Griffith had to wrestle Tal to the ground to hold him back. Armina was the only one of us with a clear enough head to think of a workable solution on the fly. Instead of flipping out like us, she approached Chance with a huge smile that she'd never used before and her arms raised as if in a congratulatory hug. Thankfully, the mortals had turned all of Chance's luckiness away from himself and focused it all solely on them. Even his innate luck would've seen right through her. As it was, he never saw the ambush until the touch contact was made and he lay unconscious in Armina's arms. In my haste to break their connection with Chance, I—might've ripped off the arm of the mortal he was chained to. Armina then passed Chance to Griffith, who blood-linked with Chasidah and got him out of there."

Avis saw Clarise's arched eyebrow and added, "Despite his powerbase of Strength, Griffith's a gentle giant and he would've felt bad about the amount of blood he knew we were about to shed. The rest of us … we insisted on it. Hungered for it. We were so incredibly blinded by hate. That was the first and last time Amaro lost his temper. We spent months slaughtering every last one of those little f…" He barely caught himself but left the description as a pregnant pause. "…along with everyone else on that miserable, mudball of a planet. Then Tal punted the world into the nearest star. The impact made the sun lose its heat and change colour, which in turn froze the surrounding planets and destabilised their orbits. The entire system to this day has remained a barren wasteland of orbiting rocks to serve as a reminder for us to not let our kids go too far unsupervised. I won't let anything live there. Ever. For the next few years, we held off finishing our borders while we took turns nursing Chance through his ongoing thrall withdrawal. It's not an experience I recommend to anyone. After that, I made sure everyone touched base with the family at least once a day to prevent it from ever happening again."

"Which is why you are so dogmatic about everyone attending the evening meals," Clarise said, nodding as that part of the mystery explained itself.

Avis knew none of the other pantheons had such a strict 'touch base' policy which he insisted upon. Decades, even millennia could go by before some gods caught up with their families. The mere thought of that uncertainty gave him hives. "Or at very least, someone has to know exactly where they are if asked."

Clarise snuggled into Avis' side, and despite his earlier bout of temper, he uncrossed his arms and draped one across her shoulders, drawing her against him.

"You all showed great restraint, killing only one solar system of mortals for enslaving your brother," she murmured.

Avis grunted in agreement. If he and his siblings hadn't been so worried sick about Chance, that entire galaxy—and quite probably several around it—would have perished. It was their first experience with long term thrall withdrawal, and it had been brutal.

"Now I understand your dislike for being in Maui's presence. I never realised how much he reminded you of your youngest brother."

Avis curled his lip into a sneer. Personally, he didn't see it that way at all, though he supposed an argument for vague similarities could be made in a pinch. "It doesn't matter. Maui's worshippers are also the Oceanic worshippers. They're all one and the same, and the pantheon will fight tooth and nail to preserve their mortal powerbase. They may not care about Maui, but they care about themselves. It's almost impossible to wipe out a whole pantheon from inside their own realm."

Almost being the operative word. His father-by-marriage had sicc'd half a dozen of his brute squad on Teon, destroying the realm and almost everyone in it. A handful of shattered survivors lived to tell the tale. But that was the one and only exception to the rule, and no sane god dwelled on that anomaly for long. Security came with the belief that nothing could topple a pantheon from within its own borders.

Clarise's arms snaked around his waist and squeezed. "If all of that happened while you were still setting up your borders, how do you explain what happened to Blagden?"

Avis rubbed his chin against her hair, breathing in more of that lavender fragrance to keep himself centred. "What do you mean?"

"I heard you telling the girls how Blagden became the god of sickness and disease because he approached the mortals while he was ailing and without having them under total control. Why would he do that if he saw what befell his younger brother?"

"Because he only saw the aftermath, sweetheart. He was with Chasidah when we first found Chance, and he's the next youngest to the runt. In our stupidity, the rest of us decided not to tell him or Chasidah what we'd seen. Blagden loved his little brother and was probably the closest out of all of us to him. It was hard enough for him to watch Chance go through semi-permanent thrall withdrawals, without adding the humiliation of how he'd been treated by the mortals to that mix. And since we didn't want him and Chasidah to know, I-I put a mental command in place that prevented either of them from going into the runt's mind to see what happened." He closed his eyes against that memory and sucked in a deep breath, holding it for several long seconds. It was one of his many regrets, and why it gutted him to see Blagden living away from Crohen and only visiting family once a day for the required meal. He knew deep down he was responsible for it.

"You did what you thought was right at the time, beloved. No one unestablished truly knows what the future holds."

"That's what I keep telling myself, but it doesn't change the outcome. If I'd have let him see what happened, Blagden would've known better than to go looking for his establishment before we were ready. Chasidah, in her own way was just as naive, but her innate ability warned her against it, so she stayed close to us."

"Avis, I'm so s…"

Avis clamped his hand over her mouth before she could finish that, holding her head against his chest. "Don't ever feel sorry for us," he insisted, hating the way the conversation had somehow turned into platitudes and commiserations. It's why he wasn't the kind to talk things through like this; least of all his feelings. Make your stand and take a hard line to it. The end. Condolences aimed at them implied they were at a disadvantage. That they were weak.

They weren't.

The molten gold in Clarise's eyes sharpened right before she opened her mouth wide against his palm and sank two rows of needle-like fangs through the leather glove into his hand.

Avis gasped and released her head, shoving her half a step away from him while stepping in the other direction himself. The combination of her triumphant expression blended with a mouthful of blooded piranha teeth in a Mystallian body was very disconcerting.

"What'd you do that for?" he snapped as he shook out the bitten hand, staring at her in astonishment. He could tell the dozens of minuscule pinpricks had already healed over, and the glove's soft interior had rubbed away the coagulated blood, but that wasn't the point. She'd bitten him, and not in a playful way. He was more annoyed than anything now.

Shifting her teeth back to Mystallian normality, Clarise ran her tongue across their surface to clean them. "I have become quite adept at reading your moods, beloved, and your thoughts were turning too dark for my liking." She glanced down at the hand she'd injured and back up to his face. "Shock has a way of detracting from inner darkness, or so I have been told."

Avis wasn't sure how he felt about that. Any of it. Clarise was now reading his emotional state as easily as Columbine could, and she was willing to be proactive about keeping him focused on her and not his ego.

Actually, that last part didn't seem so bad, now that he'd articulated it inside his head. He looked down at the glove and ran his thumb over the tiny puncture holes still visible in the leather, not so impressed with that part.

Through the top of his vision, he saw Clarise close the gap between them until she stood right in front of him. Her hands slid over his shoulders and he felt her fingers lock together behind his neck, but he still didn't look up. "I know you hate surprises," she purred, using the tips of her fingers to massage his neck. "However, I am not fond of your dark moods either, so perhaps we should consider this middle ground to be a good thing and move on from it."

That was fair. He wasn't a fan of his temper either. With a small, agreeable smile, he slid his arms around her waist and interlaced his fingers across the small of her back. She, in turn, pressed her ear to his chest and the two held each other for a long time.

"I assume that fiasco with Chance was why you and your siblings chose the blackest of black leathers and fabrics for the Mystallian uniform instead of something more colourful?" she asked, breaking the silence.

"It might have had something to do with it," he answered with begrudging honesty.

"And have you thought about what you are going to say to your family to get them to change your powerbase thrall?"

Avis looked down at her sharply. *Where in the realms had that come from?* With her ear still against his chest, he watched her molten gold eyes blink up at him inquisitively, and his lips dried out all over again for an entirely different reason. It was on the tip of his tongue to say, yes, of course, he'd 'thought' about it. He'd spent whole days thinking about it, in fact. But thinking about it and having a viable solution were two very different things. He pressed his lips together and twisted them to one side. After everything they'd been through, it never occurred to him to engage her in a verbal two-step. "Every time I play it through my head, it sounds like grovelling—even to me. I've got no idea how I'm going to convince them to help without appearing needy."

Clarise angled her head so that her chin jutted into his chest and he saw her whole face. "Is it so bad to sound needy if you do truly need them? Personally, I would have thought that was the very definition of needy—to be in need. You want to go home, almost more than you want to take your next breath, and you need their assistance to get there. They love you. They must, for they were willing to incite Father's wrath to give you that running start you spoke of. Strength is not just about who is the strongest. At times, it is also measured by having the courage to bend your knee and supplicate when you must."

Avis tensed. Ignoring the two years he'd been one of the Damned, he'd rather eat the entire contents of a manure cart than yield to anyone, but three of Clarise's fingers appeared across his mouth before he could speak. "Do not say what I can read so easily on your face. You know I am right, beloved. This is your family. Not everything is about barking orders and expecting compliance. Knowing when to lean on each other is not a sign of weakness. It is also a sign of great strength."

Could Avis have stopped her from having her say just as easily as she had stopped him? Yes. Did he like the subject matter at hand? Not particularly. But he loved the fact that she was taking a stand, knowing he didn't agree with her. Once he was sure she was done, he covered her silencing fingers with his hand and pressed them further into his lips as if to kiss them, then pulled both their hands away so he could speak. "It's not that I don't hear you, sweetheart, but you need to understand they'd castrate me on sight if I begged. Not only that, I'd hand them the blunt butter knife to do it. Begging doesn't work for us. It just doesn't."

Her eyes lost none of their molten appeal. "And in your mind, is there no middle-ground between begging and commanding? Something that may, perhaps, vaguely resemble *asking*?"

If she were anyone else, her sass would've rubbed him the wrong way. As it was, he'd already come to the same conclusion. "And that's exactly where I'm at, sweetheart," he sighed, cuddling her close and drawing in more of her lavender fragrance. "I'm trying to work out how to word it so it doesn't come across as grovelling yet still asks for their help. It's a really fine line."

He was about to say more when a series of hand slaps on timber worked their way up the ladder rungs towards them until Maui poked his head over the edge. "Oh, good. You two aren't having make-up sex," he said, without coming to join them on the deck. "I need you both to go down and secure your kids with the servants and demon steeds on the lowest deck. *Hohoro*."

Hohoro. Quickly. Clarise and Avis looked at each other, then back at the young godling. "Why? What has happened?" Clarise asked, moments before Avis could.

Maui rolled his hand towards the catamaran's bow. "That's what I was checking out before Avis and I got into it." He lifted his hand and arched his fingers to point further out to sea. "We're almost at the border, and the only chance I've got of sneaking you past the *taniwha* patrolling out there is to drop us into the mortal realms and avoid them altogether."

Avis had seen the *taniwha* in Maui's mind. A race of medium to large serpentine creatures in a variety of colours, depending on their primary environment. Some looked like sea dragons that swam through the oceans. Others had wings and flew through the skies. Others still blended almost seamlessly into the forests. When he'd come across the image of one turning into a shark and another shifting into a lifeless log, he'd deduced they were either constructs of the established realm or basic shapeshifting demons in servitude of the pantheon. Violent, yes, but from what he could gather, they were primarily border guardians, protecting the realm they called home.

When Keket tossed them out of Yaru, he hadn't realised how lucky they'd been to land in the Oceanic realm without garnering the attention of those supposedly dangerous creatures. Avis labelled them 'supposedly' dangerous because the taniwha had been explicitly tasked with looking out for him (Maui had seen the orders being passed with his own eyes) yet they'd failed to do so. The old taunt of 'You had one job' sprang to mind. Had they been Mystallian border guardians, Armina would've slaughtered them all and started again. But then, they wouldn't have failed her in the first place.

Maui may not have known why the Rangi-Tuareans hated Avis so much, but Avis did. This realm, he remembered. He'd just left Asgard and, pissed that the celebration there had been cut short by the sons of his best friend's idiot blood-brother, he'd found pleasure between the legs of Tawhirimatea's daughters. That was why the hellions had almost caught up with him back when he'd first collided with Apep. If he'd known he was only two realms away from Chaos, he wouldn't have taken the time to entertain himself with so many of them. As he had with Clarise back in the day, he'd used guile and innuendo to seduce each of them in turn, and when that hadn't worked, he'd gone for their minds and simply taken what he wanted. And just like his father-by-marriage, Tawhirimatea must have figured it out after the fact. It wasn't the worst of his crimes in the Known Realms, but now that he was a father himself, he could see how heinous it was from Tawhirimatea's perspective. He glanced down at Clarise and gave her a light squeeze, more to reassure himself that she was still with him, regardless of his past.

"The taniwha are Rangi-Tuarea's border guards, are they not?" she asked, already moving towards the ladder with Avis at her side.

Clarise's knowledge on the matter surprised him. It hadn't been something they'd discussed yet.

Maui nodded and jutted his chin towards the approaching border. "That's them," he said, releasing his hands. With a small jump, he slapped the arches of his feet against the ladder's side rails and slid down the timber to land with a bump at the bottom. "They're mostly sea dragons, though they can become other things any time they want. Lots of teeth and a fiery breath that'd challenge Hell itself for the hottest fire. Mean, vicious killers when crossed, and your boy there is at the top of their dietary wishlist."

Avis wasn't about to get into an argument over which realm was the most thermogenic, mainly because Hell won hands down and everyone with a scintilla of intellect knew that. So, he and Clarise hooked an arm around the other's waist and stepped off the deck to land in unison beside the boy instead.

"How do you plan on getting this catamaran into the mortal realm?" Clarise asked, as Maui scrambled for the second ladder and disappeared over the edge.

"I have to get us airborne!" he shouted back at them. "I'll be riding the seas hard and driving the *drua* out onto a wave crest with enough force that when the water drops out beneath us, we'll land in the mortal realm and not the celestial ocean. It's going to get rough, and the smaller and lighter I make the *drua*, the better my chances are of getting us there."

That sounded dangerous, and Avis didn't like it. He'd had his fill of being on water-based vessels as they were thrown through the air and had no desire to be on another.But Clarise was already leading them to the far side of the second deck where the girls' room was located. "What if we use the demon steeds?" he asked, then shook his head in denial of his own suggestion. "Never mind. Tawhirimatea will have his children looking out for us, and once they sense the presence of Hellfire, it'll be all over."

Maui had been running towards the stern where the tiller was tied to maintain their current bearing, but at Avis' admission, he skidded to a halt and swung around to face them. "Really?" he demanded; his eyes wide with shock. "Tawhirimatea's the one you made an enemy of? The warrior who single-handedly beat into submission almost every one of his brothers, and even went blow for blow with our war god Tu? He drove Tangoroa and all his children into the sea and destroyed every one of Tane's forests. Rongo and Haumiatiketike had to hide beneath their mother just to survive his wrath, and that's the god you've got hunting you down?" When he realised Avis wasn't joking, he *hmphed* and shook his head. "Damn!" he finally laughed, slapping one thigh. "You really know how to pick your enemies, old man."

Avis bristled, automatically putting himself between Maui and Clarise. "Is that going to be a deal-breaker?" he asked.

Maui snorted and waved him off as if he was being ridiculous. "No." He turned and made his way to the tiller, effectively putting his back to both a ranged bender *and* a ranged shifter. A stupid move, unless he honestly thought he had nothing to hide. "It just means we're going to have to be extra careful. Once we hit the mortal realm, what the wind doesn't hear, the clouds will see, and they all report back to their father. This just got a whole lot harder than I first thought." He untied the tiller and wrapped the line around his wrist. "Go and see to the girls. I'll tighten things up to make us as small and light as I can. If I'm right, we have about half an hour before things get really nasty."

"Why are you doing this for us, Maui?" Clarise asked.

Maui looked directly at her, then sliced his eyes to Avis and became as solemn as the Mystallian had ever seen him. "You may not like me very much, old man, but in your own weird way, you've always been honest with me. Even when you've openly hated me, you haven't pretended to be anything but what you are, and I can respect that." He flicked a finger at Clarise. "Plus you're standing by your family. So if it kills me, I'm going to get you all over that border."

At that moment, Avis *almost* regretted beating him to a pulp.

CHAPTER SIXTEEN

A few minutes later, Avis and his family had gathered inside the lower cabin with their servants. (Though if there was only one room left on the catamaran, could it really be called 'the lower cabin' anymore?) He didn't waste too much time worrying about that, mainly because he was too busy losing his ever-loving mind over what his wife had just 'volunteered' him for.

"Sweetheart, you must be joking," he snarled, unable to stop himself, though he managed to hold back the profanity by the skin of his teeth. Having Columbine perched on his right hip with her right hand hooked around his neck and her left fisting his cloak had a lot to do with that. Her dark eyes went wide at the heat in his voice, but he wasn't letting this go. Initially, he hadn't had a problem with his wife's plan. Putting the girls and the demon steed statuettes back inside her gelatinous bubble for safety was perfectly reasonable. The part that absolutely pissed him off was her assumption that he'd be going into that safety bubble with them.

Just the thought of being encased like a helpless infant had his temper soaring. "No way!" *Not gonna fucking happen.*

The gold in Clarise's eyes sharpened just as aggressively, and although the rest of her maintained its serene demeanour, Avis knew battle lines were being drawn. Her hand went to Cora's shoulder, and she gently but forcefully pushed the child to one side to clear the way between Avis and her. In doing so, he saw the derisive look on Cora's face: one he'd seen too many times when he'd gone toe to toe with his more robust siblings and either Chance or Chasidah had worn it in the background. *Now you're gonna get it.*

"Avis, would you permit Diviten to take Columbine for a moment so that we may discuss this matter outside?"

In Avis' mind, there was nothing to discuss. Not a damned thing. He'd made his call, and by the Twin Notes, he was never backing down from it. Never! Diviten shuffled to within arm's reach of Avis but stopped short when he twisted his head to scowl at her murderously, which meant unlike Frash, this hellion servant had some sense of self-preservation.

Clarise, on the other hand, had no such qualms. Nor should she. But that didn't stop him from eyeing her approach with the same level of wariness he would show any other dangerous creature. She walked down his left side, pausing just long enough to cup her hand under his bent elbow. "Avis," she said, squeezing ever so slightly. "I really would like to talk to you outside, beloved. *Now.*" With that, she released his arm and kept going towards the open doorway behind him. Seconds later she was gone, leaving no doubt that she expected him to follow. A single brute squad guard followed her out.

Like countless men before him, Avis was torn between standing his ground on principle or keeping his wife happy (which in turn would benefit him in the bedroom that night). The Mystallian in him insisted he hold firm if only to prove she couldn't push him around, but she'd also had the last word. That annoyed him almost as much as her expectation of his compliance. Either way, she was going to win.

At least if he went outside, he could have his say. Maybe salvage *something* from this. Hating how easily Clarise painted him into a corner, he huffed in irritation and cuddled Columbine closer. "I'll be right back, princess," he promised, as she wrapped both arms around his neck and hugged him in tightly in return. He kissed her hair, then pulled back to look into her beautiful big black eyes. "Don't go anywhere, 'kay?"

Columbine giggled. The joy she radiated at his attention was infectious and he found himself grinning despite his sour mood. He looked over her head at where Diviten hovered and lifted his chin in silent permission for her to approach. The servant was at his side in a heartbeat; her many arms outstretched in anticipation.

Avis kissed Columbine's hair one last time, then passed her over to her governess and followed his wife outside.

The shift in his mood as he crossed that threshold was as dramatic as the temperature change, though he held his tongue until one of the other servants shifted a thin, opaque film across the doorway to grant him and his wife a little privacy.

Clarise stood at the mainsail mast, facing him. The gold in her eyes was now completely jagged and her cloak whipped around her knees, her hands resting angrily on her hips.

Avis wasn't about to let her get in the first word. "I assure you, there's nothing to discuss, Clarise," he declared, widening his feet to match her aggressive stance with one of his own. "I'll be Damned all over again before I go willingly into that floating ..." —he gestured wildly at the cabin behind him— "... whatever the hell that was. It's not going to happen, Clarise. Not now. Not ever! No way!"

For the first time since he'd met her, Clarise lifted her chin and met his infuriated gaze head-on. "Maui has already said it will get rough," she argued, pointing out the obvious.

Avis was incensed. "So, what? I can handle that idiot's idea of rough!"

"And had we not been married; I would then be in a position to shift away any damage you incurred due to your foolishness. But that is not a luxury we have anymore, which means we need to safeguard the one form you have ..."

"Stop treating me like a child!"

"Then stop acting like one and listen to reason."

Red flashed across Avis' vision and he sucked in a savage breath. But before he could exhale and truly explode at her, something akin to horror swept across Clarise's face, and her whole demeanour changed. Her eyes dropped to his knees, her shoulders slumped submissively and, without warning or invitation, she closed the distance between them. Not once did she look up at him as she slid her arms around his waist in a tight hug and pressed her cheek into his chest.

Bewildered by the sudden change in tactics, Avis held his breath and straightened to his full height to put his nose well above her head, wanting nothing to do with her or the lavender scent she brought with her at that moment. He also lifted his arms to be level with his shoulders, refusing to encourage her mitigating cuddle in any way. Now that they were married, her mind was beyond his reach so he couldn't command her to step away. Nor could he speak the request without wasting valuable air. Physical was out as well since he refused to push her away, and any backwards movement on his part would be seen as a retreat. Which meant he was stuck.

At the end of three minutes, his lungs burned with need and he finally gasped, then panted, and immediately felt better with the inhalation of her fragrance. The lavender that was so thick he could taste it. Clarise never said a word, though her death grip on his lower ribs lessened once he dropped his arms and hooked his hands together in the middle of her back. "If you were anyone else, sweetheart ..." he growled, lowering his head to breathe in more of her soothing scent.

After a moment of peaceful silence between them had passed, Clarise bowed her head against his chest. "I should not have lost my temper and provoked you," she whispered softly.

Well, at least she hadn't apologised. Or worse, begged his forgiveness.

Still a little confused by the abrupt turnaround, Avis snorted and rubbed the back of her head. "If that's your idea of losing your temper, sweetheart, I'm going to have to educate you on the finer points of a verbal throw down. That was barely a warmup."

He'd hoped Clarise would appreciate his attempt at humour, but her forehead remained fixed to his chest and even when he slid his fingers under her chin and exerted pressure to guide her face to his, she still refused to look at him. "Hey," he crooned, liking this even less than the argument they'd *almost* had. When she still wouldn't move except to look further downwards, he reached around his back and took her wrists in both hands, gently prying them apart. Then he stepped back, using his hold to keep her at arms' length. His head dipped until they were on the same eye level. "Look at me, sweetheart."

At that she did, and Avis' heart broke at the unspent tears welling in her eyes. More than anything in the realm, he wanted to wrap her in his arms and tell her it was fine, but it was more important for her to know she hadn't done anything wrong in the first place.

He released her wrists and took her face in both hands, running the thumbs across her cheekbones to wipe away the excess moisture. "Don't ever regret standing up to me, sweetheart. Not ever." He paused again, staring at her intently, willing her to understand how serious he was. "You. Did. Good. Okay? I'll be the first to admit, no one's ever called me a brat and lived to talk about it before, but you'll always be my one exception. Always. You're going to have to get used to the fact that Mystallians argue all the time. It's what we do, and you need to be comfortable enough inside your own skin to have your say without fear of reprimand, sweetheart. You're one of us now."

When she didn't cringe, he wrinkled his nose and shook his head a little. "I won't pretend I'm not still a little pissed at what you said, but I'm way too happy that you stood your ground and took the fight to me to let that bother me. It's a huge step for you, baby, and I won't have you regretting it. Not with me, and not with anyone else." He stepped forward and kissed her lightly, then pressed his forehead to hers. "Tell me you understand what I'm saying, sweetheart."

"I have always taken the fight to you, beloved. But this time I did not express the perfectly valid reasons behind my decisions in such a way that you would understand and agree to them. Instead, I chose to say something that I knew would upset you ..."

"Good for you! How else do you think we win arguments we don't think we'll win any other way? More often than not, logic hardly ever comes into it. If you see a weakness, you're supposed to exploit it." Clarise stared at him with quiet resolution building in her eyes. Avis could see it, and he kissed her again with more passion. "I love you," he said, once the kiss was over. "No amount of arguing between us will ever change that."

She smiled at him genuinely at that, the gold in her eyes returning to their molten state. "What I should have said is—using your birthright to assist someone you love is neither a sign of strength nor weakness. When you love someone so much, any injury you can prevent and do not is intolerable. For example, if you saw an assassin sneaking up on me, even though you know I am a Highborn Hellion shifter, would you not use your bending abilities to protect me anyway?"

As usual, she was right about her logic talking him around to her point of view, but since he didn't want to agree with her rationale just yet, he changed tact. "If Cuschler tried, I'd not only render him a drooling idiot, I'd break every bone in his body afterwards for good measure."

And it worked … to a certain degree. Her lips twitched in amusement and he scored one for his side.

"And if the assassin in question did not happen to be your twin's firstborn?" she asked, playfully.

"As the Mystallian God of Assassination, it'd be a sad day for both his ego and his powerbase if a rogue killer operated in our realm without him knowing. And I'd still hand him his a—his backside for allowing you to potentially get hurt." Clarise chuckled despite his near slip, and Avis folded her back into his arms. "So, what made you so mad that you went for my ego instead of applying your usual logic?"

As Clarise slid her arms around his waist and sighed deeply against his chest, Avis wondered if he'd brought the issue up too soon. While it was a distinct possibility, Mystallians weren't the kind to let things fester until they 'magically' worked out. His people sorted their shit out there and then, and moved on.

"Adults in Hell do not disagree in front of the children. Not like that. The children must believe everything they are told by us is from a unified perspective."

As Avis' mind scrambled to process that, he blinked slowly in surprise. Of all the things she could've said, speaking of a lack of harmony between them in front of the girls when they were by definition half hellion was not the answer he was expecting. "But demons fight all the time …"

"Not the hellions nor the Hellion Highborn. Not in front of the children. In Chaos, things are tumultuous enough as it is, without adding the uncertainty of knowing your elders are incapable of agreeing."

Avis tried to nod in agreement, but he just couldn't bring himself to do it. It was too ridiculous on too many levels. Shielding a child from everything until they were an adult went against everything he ever believed. How in the realms were they supposed to cope with friction if it wasn't around them from the very beginning? "So what happens when a child stops being a child and sees adults arguing for the first time?"

"They are shown that the children are to be protected at all costs, and as young adults, it is their duty and honour to continue that process."

"And ... they don't feel like they've been lied to their whole lives?" Avis thought about trying that mentality in Mystal and shuddered at the visual. The cornerstone of being Mystallian was knowing exactly where you stood at all times, which was impossible if the adults around you pretended to agree on everything without really meaning to. The screams of teenaged outrage when they learned of the treachery would shatter every marble tile in the palace.

Clarise seemed to see nothing wrong with it. "Of course not. They feel privileged to be part of a family that protects its own. It's empowering to know others will see to your well-being on your behalf ..." Clarise stopped because Avis had bitten his bottom lip to keep from saying what he was thinking. She frowned and slapped him in the stomach. "I am being serious, Avis!"

"I know. I know, I know," he said, trying to swallow back his astonishment as he rubbed her back to placate her. "It's just ... wow." *How can our cultures be so freakishly different?*

"Avis, you and I ... we cannot argue in front of the children ever again."

Well, *that* broke him out of his daze.

"What?" he asked icily.

Clarise lifted her chin to look him in the eye, unmoved by the sudden bite in his tone. "It should not be a hardship for you, beloved. You already show a unified front to everyone not connected to the pantheon, regardless of the dynamics behind the ..."

"That's different." Avis pulled away from her and crossed his arms over his chest, then scissor-sliced them through the air in a negatory fashion before adding, "Friction within the pantheon gets sorted out at the time of the issue, regardless of who it's between. We don't hide this stuff from the kids and we certainly don't second-guess what each other really means."

"Not even if I were to ask for it?"

Avis raked his hand through his hair and ended the motion with a firm massage of the back of his neck. His gut reaction was a resounding *NO!* Not speaking his mind in front of everyone, children included, was about as foreign to him as swearing was to Clarise. Fortunately for his ego, his calmer, follow-up response mirrored his initial reactive one. He shook his head, long before he started to speak. "No. I'm not giving you that one, sweetheart."

"Avis ..."

Avis quickly raised one hand. "Hold on. You had your say. Now, it's my turn." He waited just long enough to confirm she wouldn't interrupt, then kept going. "I've been in and around foul language my whole life and it's completely ingrained in me, yet to keep you and Columbine happy, I've been working on my censorship around you two. That's reasonable. But hiding a stand behind closed doors and pretending to be okay with something I'm not, is taking things to a level that I'm not prepared to do. Lines in the sand and standing by them is crucial to us and asking me to change that is like asking you to start swearing fluently."

Clarise seemed to mull that over. "What if you were to subtly gesture for me to leave the room with you?"

Avis choked at the ridiculousness. "Have you even met me, sweetheart?" he asked, rolling both hands down the length of himself. "At what point have I ever been remotely subtle about anything?"

Even Clarise had to smile at that. "True," she agreed.

"Besides, you crossed the line first when you told the girls what I was going to do, without running it past me first."

At that, Clarise's eyes narrowed sharply. "Excuse me?" she asked, in a way that was by no means an apology.

Avis had to make her understand. "By declaring my actions to the children without first consulting me, you took my space away from me *right in front of them* and made it your own. Whether you meant to or not, sweetheart, that's exactly what you did. Now, don't get me wrong. I don't care if you want to try that, but you have to be ready for me to call you on it when I don't agree. That's the price for making that assumption."

Clarise's eyes widened and she raised her hand to her throat. "I did not make that connection to your mantra," she admitted.

Avis' stance softened. "I know, sweetheart. 'Owning the space' is a big deal to us, and it's got a lot of moving parts. As I said, I'm not complaining that you did it. In fact, if I'd agreed with it, we wouldn't have argued in the first place. But you have to be ready for me to voice my dissention if I don't happen to agree, because you better believe I will. Very loudly."

Clarise took a moment to gather herself. "Very well, beloved. However, in this particular instance, I did have more than just your safety in mind when I made that statement, and I wish you had consulted me before declining my suggestion outright."

Aaaand......we're back to this. Avis pursed his lips and folded his arms again. "What else?"

That may have come out a little harsher than he intended, though Clarise wasn't fazed. She stepped forward and put her hands on his forearms, applying enough downward pressure to pull them apart. "Stop being so defensive with me, Avis. I am well aware of how much you prefer to make your stand as opposed to accepting the aid of those who love you and don't want to see you come to harm. You would rather accept the consequences of your stubbornness, even if it means you end up getting sick ... or hurt ..." —Clarise's golden eyes sharpened into peaks of jagged intensity and she sent him a pointed look— "... *or nearly starve to death.*"

Avis bristled; hard. Months ago, when they'd first started this journey on the Acheron River, they'd nearly lost Columbine to starvation because of her insane decision to avoid eating altogether instead of voicing her displeasure at eating the only food source available to them at the time. Avis had barely caught on to that, and the alternative still had him waking up in a cold sweat. "That's not ... It's not the same thing!"

"Of course it is, beloved. At least, it is to her. Columbine is young and is learning by your example; just as she was always taught to do. She watches everything you do, and whether you realise it or not, she will do her utmost to emulate you. It is not her fault that she does not have her sister's intellect to make the adult decisions that you and I can."

Avis raised both hands and locked them behind his head, lifting his eyes to the cloudy night overhead. He didn't want this! He hadn't asked for it! He didn't need to ask for help! He would if he had to, but he knew he didn't have to. Countless eons had proven his innate ability to survive on his own.

He felt Clarise's hand on his chest at the same time as her fragrance assaulted his senses. "It all comes down to what type of parent you want to be for them, beloved. You can be the strong, unyielding one, if you wish. The one who shows that strength and pride are the most important aspects of a person, to the detriment of those you love. Or, you can show that little girl she means so much to you that you would swallow your pride and join her in the safety bubble, just so she can learn that it is alright to accept help from others." Her head canted to one side. "And it would not hurt that your presence will appease her innate concerns about your well-being as well."

Avis closed his eyes and dipped his head down and away from her, breathing out a long, heavy huff of defeat. He wasn't amused by Clarise's light chuckle, though he did like the way she wrapped her arms around him again. "Parenting does get easier, my love. I promise. These first steps of change will always be the hardest for a dedicated bachelor as yourself to accept."

"I fucking hate this, Clarise," he growled, deliberately using the profanity to see if she would dare make something of it.

Her expression cooled but didn't quite turn to ice. "You may wish to curtail that sentiment before you go back inside. If Columbine feels your resentment and frustration towards her, she will almost certainly start to cry."

Avis huffed again and looked over her head to the sealed doorway, knowing she spoke the truth. Again. Columbine was probably already upset by his emotional state. *But to pretend to be something I'm not?* Avis scratched the tip of his glove finger against his bottom lip. How was he ever supposed to get his head around that?

"You are the master of minds, my love," Clarise said as if reading his. She twisted to one side and freed her left hand. From somewhere (more than likely the deck they stood on) she gathered enough mass through her body to create a filled goblet in that hand, which she then pressed into his chest. "Focus your thoughts around your love of this drink and keep them away from what you know will upset Columbine."

Avis scowled down at her. "I'm not going to pretend to be okay with this…"

"No one is asking you to. But there is a difference between being irked and being outraged. It is all a matter of perspective, beloved."

Avis stared into her eyes for what seemed like an eternity, before he lowered them to the goblet and removed it from her grip. He didn't need the physical representation of the alcohol to shift his thoughts as she suggested. A quick trip into the plethora of his own alcohol-infused memories would've been sufficient for that, but since the liquor was right here in front of him …

He lifted it to his lips and took a generous swig, making a point of savouring the taste as it rolled across his tongue and down his throat. Yes, tending to a goblet of good ambrosia was one of his favourite pastimes. With warmth flowing out from his stomach, he sighed and skolled the rest, then passed her back the empty goblet. "Alright, let's do this," he said, rolling his head and shoulders in resignation.

CHAPTER SEVENTEEN

Avis led the way back into the cabin and, without a word of explanation, went over to where Diviten held Columbine and reclaimed possession of his precious child. The moment he had, Columbine wrapped herself around him, hooking her heels over his hips and her arms in a chokehold around his neck. He smiled to himself and cuddled her close in return; one wrist and forearm supporting her backside and the other around her back. It was insane just how much he loved his family, but he did. He had to. Nothing else in the Known Realms would ever make him do what he was about to otherwise.

With Columbine safely in his arms and both her mother and sister in the same room as them, his grim mood flipped on its ass until he was practically bursting with happiness. From over Columbine's shoulder, he saw Cora's head canting to one side curiously and shot her a surreptitious wink to prove all was well, then slipped easily into Columbine's mind.

Specifically, her imagination.

Here, everything had the tinge of sapphire blue; a colour he was more than happy to be bathed in. He wanted them both to be comfortable, so he recreated the sitting room that he and Clarise had shared in Hell; complete with the pair of high back velvet chairs partially facing the open fireplace.

He knew Columbine would probably be even more comfortable in his bedroom since that was where they'd gotten to know each other during his convalescence, but that was also a line he was never going to cross again; not now that he was at full health. Just thinking about the impropriety that came of them being alone together in a master bedroom had his stomach churning in disgust. "Columbine?" he called, spinning the larger of the two velvet-lined chairs around to better survey the room. He sat down and semi-relaxed into the padded seating; his eyes scanning the room. "Come on, princess. I know you know I'm here. Don't keep me waiting."

An image of Columbine materialised halfway between himself and the hallway door, her expression a mixture of confusion and delight. "Father?"

A huge smile parted Avis' lips as he leaned forward and clapped his hands together, beckoning her to him with the tips of his fingers. "Come here, baby. I want to talk to you."

Columbine swept across the room and up into his arms without hesitation, pressing her head firmly into his throat. One hand hooked around his neck while the other went up under his arm in a lopsided hug. Sitting back in the chair, Avis dropped a kiss on her hair and held her close. Because of where they were, there was no longer any rush. "Are you okay, princess?" he asked after a while, stroking her long, dark hair.

He felt her nod against his throat. "Yes, Father."

"Okay, then. Just like last time, there's something very important that I need to talk to you about, and you need to be a big girl and listen to me, okay?" It dawned on Avis just how many times he was using the word 'okay' with her and mentally ordered himself to stop. Being so unsure about how to be a good role-model left a sour taste in his mouth, but the truth was, he'd never had to be one before.

Columbine pulled away and sat up straight with a worried look on her face. The move caused hints of white to creep into the surrounding overtone of blue, and Avis was starting to get a sense of what that meant as trepidation crawled through him. "Did I do something wrong?" she asked.

"Not intentionally, princess." Her brow scrunched into a confused frown, and he cursed himself for not choosing a simpler word. "You didn't mean to, baby, but yes ... yes, you did."

Cue the streaks of that fucking orange-yellow-tan bullshit colour he hated so much. He gnashed his teeth as it bombarded his chest, causing his whole body to clench. "Knock it off, princess," he said as levelly as he could, though she still wilted in his hands. He tapped two fingers against her backside to break her out of her funk. "Sit up straight and make it go away, like you did before." It galled him that he couldn't do it for her, but that was the way of this colour palette thing. It had to be her. He tapped her again. "Go on."

Columbine's breath was hesitant, but eventually, she settled down and the colours around them became a muted pale blue. For now, it was close enough. "This is about you being a little girl, and how little girls need time to learn how to be big girls ..." Realising how disastrously that sentence came out if viewed in a perverted way, he straightened up himself and shook his head. "... I-I mean, you're too young to know everything you'll need to know ..." *Oh, for fuck's sake! That's just as bad!*

Avis closed his eyes and released a slow, cleansing breath. How in the realms did his siblings have any kind of educational conversation with their kids without sticking both feet halfway down their throats? *Because you're the only one with your mind in the fucking gutter, moron! She's a naive five-year-old girl. You can do this.*

As Chance always said, 'third time's the charm'.

He opened his eyes and forced an unwilling smile upon his lips. "Let's try that again. As you know, I'm a lot older than you, princess. In fact, I've been alive a very, very long time, compared to most things. You get that, right?"

"Yes, Father."

Alright, that was a good starting point. "And you understand how it took me all that time to learn what I know now?"

Columbine's expression grew wary. "Yes, Father."

Avis didn't want her to be apprehensive either. He stroked her hair softly, using the motion to encourage her to relax. "It's okay, princess. What I'm trying to say is, I've learned what I can and can't do over eons of trial and error. That's a very, very long time and you're not old enough to know how to make the right choices yet. Not only that, but every celestial is different." He curled his fingers and combed them through her hair as he spoke, gently massaging her scalp.

"You especially are very different. Even as old as I am, I can't even pretend to do what you can, and I'm not going to try. But likewise, you shouldn't try to be me either. I don't want you to be like me. I want you to be you. The problem is, you don't know where your limits are yet, and you need to stop pretending you do. You're too little to know what's safe and what's not. Not yet. It's that simple, princess. And until you do, you need to let me and your mother make those decisions for you."

He could see her thinking about that and nodded encouragingly. "That's right, baby. There will come a time when you'll be old enough to make your choices, but you're not there yet, and your mother made a good argument about not showing you other options for you to learn from. So, even though I don't *want* to go along with what's about to happen, and I don't *need* to go along with it, I'm going to let it happen anyway to show you what I want from you." He paused for emphasis and brushed the back of his fingers against her cheek. "When we go back out into the physical realm, your mother's going to fill up the room so that you, me and your sister are kept safe during this next stage of our journey."

Columbine's eyes widened, but he placed a silencing finger across her lips. "Sssshhhh, it's okay. I don't mind. Not this time. I've never shown you how to accept help from others, and if this is what I have to do to make you understand that this is what I want from you, so be it. I'll keep you safe, and your mother will keep all of us safe. But I really need you to take notice of what's happening and why, because this isn't comfortable for me and I can't promise I'll do it again any time soon." He moved the finger to her cheek and cupped her face in his palm. "That's how much you and your sister mean to me."

Columbine threw her arms around his neck and clung to him tightly. "I love you too, Father."

He cuddled her, then rose to his feet. "Then, I'll see you outside in the physical realm." And with that, he withdrew from her mind, finding her in exactly the same position in the physical realm with her legs hooked around his hips and her arms locked around his neck. His lips curled in a possessive smile, and he tensed his body in an all-over hug meant just for her. Then he met Clarise's gaze and nodded his consent for her to begin.

* * *

Avis had never been on a sinking ship, but he was willing to bet the last thoughts of those doomed men and women were not unlike what he was having at that moment. Clarise and the four servants all melted into a gelatinous liquid which filled the room to his ankles with ease. Then came the slow and uncomfortable process of watching that line of clear gel rise as Clarise added mass from outside. Like standing in quicksand, it slowly crept up his boot to his knee and poured over the boot's collar until the mild chill around his calves and feet made him wriggle his toes.

It then covered his hips, holding him in place. While he still could, he shifted his weight between his feet, trying to get himself acclimated to the strange sensation. It was thicker than water; more like partially set plaster. He lifted one heel a fraction, just to remind himself he could. His grip on Columbine tightened as the cool gelatinous substance seeped into his glove, and he fought the desire to hold her out of the way.

Then it climbed to his pec and Columbine's waist. He felt the resistance of it against his chest as he breathed and tried not to think of how this was going to end. He'd be fine. It would all be fine. Cora, he noticed, was already fully submerged and pulling derogatory faces at him from inside the comfort of the gel. If he hadn't seen in her surface thoughts that she was doing it to distract him, he might've taken exception to her rudeness. As it was, he chuckled uncomfortably.

At least, he did until the gel nudged his chin and the reality of what he was about to do set in. He was deliberately going to drown himself. Knowing for an absolute fact that he wasn't going to die didn't ease his escalating heart rate in the least. Drowning was still drowning, and he'd had plenty of experience with that sensation during the two years of his incarceration.

When it touched his upper lip, Avis knew his shallow breathing bordered on hyperventilation. This was insane! He lifted his heels off the ground and stretched his neck to try and rise above the gel. Why in the realms had he agreed to this?

As if on cue, Columbine's head pushed against his ear, and he knew this had to be scaring her as much as it would any other Mystallian. He had to be strong. For her. He had to do this. Taking one last deep lungful of air, he closed his eyes and dropped back onto his heels, forcing the gel over his eyelids.

And then he locked every muscle in his body into place and waited for the inevitable panic to set in. He wouldn't be able to help it. He'd been drowned too many times, only to be brought back because his establishment prevented him from dying. He knew the sensation well.

However, as the oxygen ran out, a sense of inner peace came over him. Not just peace. Love … Trust … Safety …

Avis opened his eyes and watched the liquid climb over his head to the ceiling, acknowledging the cool kiss of the substance that surrounded his body but not the fear of it. *There,* he thought to himself, once the gel filled his lungs and oxygenated his body. The tension in him eased, and the rhythm of his breathing became relaxed and constant. That hadn't been nearly as bad as he thought it would be.

He released the death grip he had on Columbine, hoping he hadn't hurt her in his time of … uneasiness. Now that it was done, he couldn't wait to get home and tell his siblings about this. They'd lose their fucking minds! He was actually breathing through Clarise's gel like a fucking fish! Sucking in as deeply as he could, he felt the ripples against his face and breathed out a maniacal laugh. It was the weirdest sort of crazy!

Cora grinned at him from across the room and with a broad smile of his own, he nodded slowly in unspoken agreement.

Columbine pushed against his shoulders with both hands until she could see his face. "Do you feel better now, Father?"

He snorted and said, "I'm fine, princess," pleased to note that his voice worked just as well as theirs within the gel. He rounded his lips and breathed against the gel, chuckling at the way it flexed and wobbled against his cheeks.

After a few minutes, he felt the first of countless soft nudges and bumps that indicated Maui was getting ready to drop them all into the mortal realm and braced himself accordingly.

The jarring impacts intensified as he expected, but instead of being done and dusted in a matter of seconds, the pounding around him continued until he was certain that at least a full hour had passed. Then, he knew something was wrong. Not his usual 'something is always wrong' feeling. This time, it was serious. It shouldn't have taken Maui this long to drive the catamaran into the mortal realm, which meant the boy was battling his pantheon on Avis' behalf. Alone.

Fuck that shit.

Avis squared his shoulders, having no intention of hiding now that they'd lost the element of surprise. Both Cora and Columbine had drifted off to sleep some time ago, and it was a simple process to extricate himself from Columbine's grasp and leave her floating in the gel.

He turned away from her and edged towards the door. If Tawhirimatea wanted a piece of him, he was going to be reminded just what the Mystallian Life patriarch was capable of firsthand.

"Where are you going, beloved?" Clarise's voice thrummed against his eardrum as if she were in her Mystallian form, whispering in his ear.

"This is taking too long," he answered, pushing further into the gel with the expectation that Clarise would clear him a path now that his arms were empty and it was no longer necessary for him to be an object lesson for Columbine. "Something's wrong."

Contrary to what he'd expected, the density of the gel increased around him, making it harder for him to move. "Wha ...?"

"Beloved, no. We must remain in here. Maui has said ..."

Oh, Hell, NO! Avis wasn't about to let himself be trapped by anyone! Not even Clarise! *I will not be told where I can and can't fucking go!* To prove it, he focused everything into pushing himself through the gel. But the harder he fought, the thicker the gel became. What started as an average step went to half steps, then quarters as he met more and more resistance. Still, he struggled on, using the jarring impacts from outside to jostle himself closer to his goals. His eyes never moved from the doorway, and when he was close enough to touch it, he reached out. The gelatinous density responded by doubling down again, then tripling, limiting his hand's movement to mere millimetres. "LET ME GO, CLARISE!" he shouted.

"Avis, you need to stop. Your presence on the deck will only make matters worse for him."

"No! I can end this!" Hadn't he already proven that when he took out a Yarusian primordial inside her own realm without even breaking a sweat? If Tawhirimatea needed the same lesson hammered home, he'd be happy to comply! "Let me out!"

Gnashing his teeth, he fought against the resistance until his thoughts fragmented from exertion and stars began to wink in front of his eyes. His fingertips scraped against the door's architrave as if the length of the room were between his eyes and his hand, but still he fought on. His perspective had gone to crap, and out of nowhere it suddenly dawned on him why. *Sleeper hold!* Once he thought the words, he realised all too late that his own lesson in Mystallian anatomy had come back to bite him in the ass. Clarise was applying pressure to the carotids in his neck to put him down!

NO! CLARisse....! Fog closed in, narrowing his field of vision to a tunnel effect that grew ever smaller and more distant until it winked out entirely.

* * *

Clarise's heart broke into a thousand pieces as her beloved husband slumped unconscious inside her gel. She hadn't wanted to subdue him like that, but he'd been precariously close to breaking free, and that she couldn't allow. As a wanted fugitive, the only way for Avis to ensure both their safety and the safety of their host was if he stayed out of sight.

Nearly two hours ago, it had become apparent that something more than a troublesome crossing was taking place outside. The catamaran was being pounded brutally from multiple directions. Wanting to know what was going on without alerting Avis, she'd slipped a clear tendril out to where Maui stood at the stern with one hand controlling the tiller and the other wrapped around the mainsheet, battling to keep the catamaran upright and on top of the water. His face was flushed with excitement as he used his full body weight to secure the whipping sail.

Clarise inflated the tip of the tendril and shaped it into a ghostly clear balloon of her face. "Do you require assistance?" she asked, bracing herself as the ship slid sideways along the interior wall of one wave and out through the overhead foam. Maui shook his head free of the spray, blinking his eyes clear in the process.

"No!" he shouted, laughing maniacally. He bent his knees and shifted his weight forward, just as the catamaran shot up onto one float and pirouetted a full three-sixty on its stern. "Keep that idiot you married out of sight! Right now, Tawhirimatea and Tangoroa are battling it out, and if we keep our heads down, we'll slip right through the fringes of their fight before they realise we're gone!"

Winds ripped through the sails and the dangerous-looking grey-green sky lit up with lightning. The ocean retaliated with huge swells and crashing waves, but Maui lifted his chin and yowled at the top of his lungs as if he was having the time of his life. "Go on! Get out of here, Clarise! Take care of your family! I've got this!"

Clarise knew as soon as Avis learned of the conflict, he would be charging out onto the deck to add his mental muscle to the fray. So, she did everything in her power to keep the gel around him at a constant pressure, shouldering most of the heavier blows herself. There was no question in her mind that Avis could have ended the conflict sooner, but Maui needed to live here after they were gone. Regardless of the number of enemies the youngster had made in his life, what remained of his mortal life would be measured in moments if the Rangi-Tuareans discovered he had protected Avis instead of handing him over.

Maui had gone a long way out on a limb for them, and she wouldn't repay that kindness with cruelty.

She only hoped her husband would forgive her for her apparent betrayal. In her gelatinous form, she caressed his sleeping face and placed numerous feather kisses on his lips and closed eyelids, willing him to understand. Yes, there was a vicious battle going on outside, but it simply did not involve them. It was between two sibling deities of this realm that already hated each other and for the sake of everyone involved, it needed to stay that way.

The catamaran took many more hours of heavy pounding while Clarise and their servants repaired and reinforced it on the fly until the battering punishment ended in a forward shunt that defied logic.

Unlike the way they were expelled from Yaru, the sudden motion had them skipping across the water's surface for a few seconds.

Until their momentum ran out.

Then, nothing.

Everything was still.

Not willing to risk physically going outside in case of an ambush, Clarise shut off all her simplistic Mystallian senses, which in turn opened up her essence to every piece of sensory information within a hundred-metre radius of herself at the same time.

As she expected, the catamaran had come to a floating halt in a large mass of water that reeked of saline saturation much stronger than the oceans of the Rangi-Tuareans. Also, the air had an icy, electrified feel to it akin to static and the sky overhead was dark and sprinkled with stars. The only hint of rolling thunder and lightning flashes were in the distance behind the catamaran and beyond her hundred-metre range. Maui stood at the helm, staring back at the storm with a huge, beaming smile plastered across his face. His white-knuckled grip on the tiller and mainsheet eased and ever so slowly, despite his constant shivering, he began to laugh. It started deep in the pit of his stomach, but as it rolled through his body, he put his hands on his hips and lifted his head to the sky, bellowing with laughter.

They'd done it. They were beyond Rangi-Tuarea. Which meant they were in the mortal realm of Asgard. Had Clarise been in her Mystallian form, she'd have sighed with relief. Of all the realms around them, Asgard had to be one of the safest realms for them to be in, given her husband's history with the Asgardian king.

Clarise had taken a bit of a gamble, using Columbine as an excuse for keeping Avis inside the cabin. As a master shapeshifter in her own right, Columbine could have easily joined them in their gelatinous form and remained perfectly safe, but she was also a Highborn Lady with empathic abilities. Clarise had counted on their daughter ascertaining Avis' agitated state and choosing to remain Mystallian to give him something tangible to hang onto.

That was what it meant to be a Highborn Hellion Lady: to aid the lords, without drawing attention to oneself. A lady's place was to remain in the shadows of the lords and observe. Then, if necessary, intervene without being caught. Basically, the exact opposite of Mystallian women, to which Columbine had played her part perfectly.

Sensing Maui was on his way towards the cabin, Clarise slid her essence into the mass around her husband and shifted herself into her Mystallian form with her hands hooked under his knees and behind his shoulders. Following her lead, Gingen and Diviten did likewise with their wards while Frash and Tilu emptied the room of excess gel by shifting it to saltwater and allowing gravity to flush it out the open doorway.

Clarise grew a tendril from the wrist that supported Avis' shoulders and manoeuvred the tip of it to sit under his nose. While she may not have been able to alter him physically, so long as his kind maintained a plethora of corporeal weaknesses, she would always have options; such as coating the tip of that tendril in ammonia. She'd learned how sensitive the hairs inside a Mystallian's nose were to strong fragrances and believed the pungent aroma would rouse her husband. "Time to wake up, my love," she whispered, angling his body upright so he could hit the ground running.

It didn't take nearly as long as she thought it would.

Surging forward, he propelled himself three quick steps and shot his arms out to his sides in anticipation of a fight. But then he must have internalised the last thing he remembered, for his boots locked against the floor and a layer of positively dark iciness fell across his demeanour as he slowly turned to face her. "You took me out of play," he snarled through gritted teeth and narrowed eyes, daring her to deny it.

"I did," she agreed, studying his face for any clue of what would happen next. Ideally, she would've rather had this conversation in private in case it turned violent, but with Maui outside, the girls asleep in the room with them and a member of the brute squad standing in each corner, this was as private as she could hope for. At least Frash and Tilu had created an opaque, soundproof screen with their bodies to give them some semblance of privacy.

Avis stalked back into her space, looking every bit the Mystallian patriarch as he loomed over her. His eyes glittered with rage. Instinct demanded she break eye contact and accept his discipline as was her due, but she tightened her hands into a double fist behind her back and forced herself to meet his eyes. For several long, tense seconds, the two stared at each other. His body continued to shake with barely leashed fury. She didn't need to be a bender to see the internal struggle he was having with her betrayal. It was clear with every thunderous crease on his face. The monster he had once been was fighting for supremacy, and she had no way of knowing which one would win. She doubted if he did either. His fisted hands lifted to her shoulders and she braced for their impact. It came in the form of flattened fingers which he slid around her cheeks; effectively cupping her head in his hands. She continued to meet his eyes and didn't try to resist, willing him to feel her undying love for him.

He tilted her head sharply to the right, exposing the left side of her neck. But instead of striking her, his lips dropped onto hers and his tongue shot between her teeth, urgently plundering the space within.

Shock rushed through her. This was not what she'd been expecting. Her hands fell apart and gripped his elbows, uncertain if she wanted to push him away or encourage the toe-curling kiss. Not that Avis was giving her a choice. He twisted his head from one side to the other, determined to claim every part of her mouth.

When he finally let her go, Clarise was breathless and Avis was grinning down at her. "That's my queen," he purred in approval. But then he completely undermined his praise by swatting her backside, hard. "Don't do it again."

More shock flooded her system. The burn of his handprint on her skin hurt and her first instinct was to either numb the sting or remove its cause entirely. Then, as she took a moment to bask in the praise that went with it, a small smile of pride crossed her features and she decided she'd do neither. The knowledge that she had taken on her husband at his worst was extremely vindicating and she found herself wanting to keep the handprint as long as it would naturally last (and maybe a little longer), wearing it as a badge of honour.

Still wearing a soft smile, she lifted her chin and looked directly into his eyes. "Then do not make me," she returned, showing no hint of remorse.

Avis threw his head back and laughed, then wrapped his arms around her and kissed her once again.

CHAPTER EIGHTEEN

"Really?"

At the sound of Maui's voice, Clarise jerked her lips away from Avis' and spun inside the circle of his arms like a reprimanded teenager, causing Avis to snort mischievously. He'd seen the boy approach halfway through the kiss and had no intention of stopping. If anything, he'd intensified it just for show; because he could. To emphasise that Clarise was his, and his alone. Grinning like the cat that got the cream, Avis banded his arms around Clarise and pulled her back against his chest.

"Maui," she panted, as the young godling stood in the doorway with his hands on his hips and a look of disgust on his face. As if that stance meant shit to Avis.

"For the love of realm! I'm out there, busting my b—backside to get you lot across the border safely, and you're in here making out? What are you, a pair of celestial rabbits?"

"Jealous?" Avis asked slyly. He couldn't resist.

"Yes!" Maui snapped as he stormed inside. "You could at least wait until I'm back in Rangi-Tuarea before having another make-out session."

Avis heard the unspoken part of that sentence but still needed to confirm it for his peace of mind. "So, we're in Asgard?"

"Midgard," Maui corrected, though in order to avoid looking at the Mystallians, he focused on the opaque wall that seemed to divide the room in half. "Are the girls on the other side of this?" he asked, lightly drumming the screen with the tips of his fingers.

"They are still asleep," Clarise confirmed.

Since Maui was the one with all the information, Avis slipped inside his mind and sought out the point in the youngster's memories where Maui took the helm and told him and Clarise to go inside with the girls. He sped through the boring part where Maui had worked to get the catamaran airborne but pulled up once he realised the mass of misty streaks that surrounded the vessel was Ao-Takawe, the fastest of Tawhirimatea's cloudy children.

Avis stroked his chin as Ao-Takawe contacted his brother Maranai, and in less time than it took Avis to blink, Tawhirimatea appeared before them. Maui cursed under his breath, but Avis could see he already had an alternative plan and applauded the boy's quick thinking. Maui deliberately heaved on the mainsail with all his might, causing the catamaran to pirouette up onto the tip of one float at the crest of a wave and drove it beneath the ocean, knowing full well Tuaraki and Ao-Takawe would not be able to resist giving chase. The north wind and the hurricane clouds pierced the water with a howl of excitement before Tawhirimatea could pull either of them back. The water surged at their incursion, not only to expel the two airborne intruders but to take the fight to their father who lingered overhead.

The two mighty deities met in a horrendous crash that sent the catamaran spinning. Maui fought to keep the vessel upright as the immortal armies of both sides sprang to the defence of their respective lieges. The taniwha poured through from the celestial plane to aid both sides, leaving the way clear for Maui to power through, provided he could keep the catamaran in one piece.

That became less and less likely as chunks were ripped from the vessel and lost to the ocean, but he wasn't about to give up. Contrary to their first agreement where Maui had said he would drop them all at the first hint of discovery, it seemed the young man was determined to see this through.

At some point, the ghostly head of Clarise appeared in front of Maui to ask him if he needed any help. Combining that brief conversation with his own memories at the time, Avis was finally able to make peace with what she'd done. He may not have liked it, but he understood her misconceptions. After all, Maui would only be in danger if he remained in Rangi-Tuarea.

During the last hour of his waking memory where he'd done nothing but carry Columbine, Avis had decided to take him with them.

In his own mind, he had it all figured out. If they made it back to Mystal, he could set Maui up somewhere along the Pandess coast where he could fish and sail and have as many hangis as his crazy little heart desired. Alternatively, if they had to start again in the Unknown Realms, Avis would set things in motion that gave him a safe home where he could live out eternity. Either way, the youngster's residence would be complete with servants, women and a full-time contingent of guards to maintain his safety. (The latter being discreetly placed of course. While he didn't want Maui to feel like a prisoner, he needed to avoid a repeat of where the fool went unchaperoned into the mortal realm and got himself stupidly established.) Then, under Clarise's guidance, the young godling could learn how to shapeshift properly as a hellion in his own right and they could finally ditch that fucking useless bone that his father gave him. *Win-win.*

Having what he came for, Avis returned to the physical realm. "It seems I owe you a debt of gratitude," he said. The words tasted like broken glass on his tongue.

Maui cocked an eyebrow at him, then folded his arms and rested his shoulder on the opaque wall, chuckling quietly to himself. "Well, I bet that hurt to say."

Avis closed his eyes and grimaced. "You'll never know," he promised.

"Well, if it's any consolation, you don't owe me as much as you think."

With his curiosity piqued, Avis opened his eyes again. "Oh?"

Maui shrugged. "Tangoroa figured out you were on the catamaran, and while you're not his favourite person, his hatred for Tawhirimatea proved too much for him to ignore. He gave us that last nudge over the border as a final, double fingered salute to the brother that drove him and his children into the sea."

Avis' mind swirled with the information. *Brother ... turned on brother ... for an* outsider? Not just *any* outsider, but one who had physically and mentally screwed over the pantheon! By the realms, such a thing was so alien to him he had to reword it several times inside his mind just to accept it as being remotely possible. No one in Mystal would ever do such a thing. They just wouldn't. Their loyalty to the house was absolute! They would always stand as one to defend each other and each other's decisions.

And that brought his thoughts back to Maui. "Maui, about you going back to the Oceanics ..."

Clarise turned in his arms to see his face as he spoke, and he knew from the way Maui arched his eyebrow again that he also had the boy's undivided attention. "What about it?"

"I think you should come with us." Avis knew he had the power to make it a mental command, and would if he had to, but hopefully Maui would see the wisdom of his plan and come along willingly. "You'll be safe with us, and you'll never want for anything again." Avis had never offered that to another before and doubted he'd ever do it again.

But instead of embracing the idea, Maui's expression sobered and he took a large backwards step towards the doorway. "Why would I want to do that?" he asked, his expression morphing into a suspicious frown.

Stunned by his resistance, Avis' eyebrows shot up into his hairline. "Maui, you can't seriously mean to go back there!" he barked, even though the quick brush with the lad's mind told him that was exactly what he planned to do. "They're going to kill you!"

"Avis," Clarise chided.

Avis dropped his eyes to her, at the same time throwing his hand out in Maui's direction. "Don't 'Avis' me, Clarise! He can't go back there! He just can't! They'll kill him for sure! I know I would!"

Indulgence filled Clarise's soft smile, and she lifted her hand, placing it tenderly against his cheek. "You cannot keep every stray you pick up, beloved."

Avis pulled away with a jerk. "I'm hardly doing that! Maui risked his life for us, and I'm not about to let him die for it."

* * *

Maui watched the married couple argue like—an old married couple, as he slowly eased himself out of Avis' line of sight. His hand slid down to his grandmother's jawbone and once it was firmly secured in his hand, he willed himself to become a flying cockroach. Something small, but incredibly agile and quick. He knew all about Avis' mental abilities. How the Mystallians didn't need to touch things to force their way into people's minds and make them do things, even outside their realm. He'd heard various members of his pantheon curse that ability and knew to be wary of it.

He also knew his best chance of escape was now, while the fool was distracted with his wife. Like the Mystallian, Maui had no intention of abandoning his family. Stirring trouble for them was one thing and being tricky was what he did for fun, but abandoning them altogether? That just wasn't his style.

But something was horribly wrong with his shapeshifting. It wasn't instantaneous. It was slow ... and sluggish ... like the hellion servants that became whatever Avis and his family needed them to be. At this rate, Avis would catch on before he'd escaped for sure!

As his body sank into a puddle of *glop* (What other word was there for what most of his body had become?), his vision shifted into that of a flying cockroach. Relief flooded his system as he looked over each of his six limbs, ran his front feet over his antennae and spread his wings to confirm that yes, he had become a flying cockroach. But what was with all that glop on the floor? That had never happened before! He rose into the air and stared hard at the back of Clarise's head as if she held all the answers. Because when it came to shifting, chances were, she did. It didn't hurt his high opinion of her shifting when she discreetly grew a third hand out of her cloak and waved him towards the door.

She was right. The big oaf would only be distracted for so long, and regardless of how much he liked the Mystallian family, it was time to leave. Now—while he still could. Getting his mind overhauled by the Mystallian patriarch had never been part of their bargain.

Still confused by the strange shifting process, Maui flew through the open doorway whilst the Mystallians continued to disagree. The sooner he got back to Rangi-Tuarea, the faster his shapeshifting would behave the way it was supposed to. At least, he hoped that would be the case, and it couldn't happen fast enough.

* * *

When Avis realised Maui was gone, he whirled on his heel to go after him, but both of Clarise's arms curled around his right elbow, holding him still. "Let him go, beloved," she cooed.

"But they'll kill him!" Avis looked down at her, his voice a mixture of horror and concern.

Clarise disagreed. "He may temporarily suffer for assisting us, but once he's been disciplined, he should be fine. Honestly, Avis. Do you really think you could bring yourself to actually murder one of your own for making a bad decision before he reached the end of his second decade?"

Avis looked back at the open doorway. The longer he was caught up in this discussion, the less likely he was to catch Maui before he got too far away. "Maybe," he admitted, not wanting to hurt her feelings but knowing his temper would swing that needle so hard towards an overwhelming *yes* that the weight of a planet couldn't have moved it any faster.

"Well, he does not. Tawhirimatea may be angry with him for a time, but Maui is their trickster god and the pantheon must have accepted his antics as part of his establishment field a while ago. His family will protect him."

"Until he dies."

Clarise smiled. "All things die, Avis. Even gods sometimes."

"But he doesn't have to, sweetheart. If he came with us, I'd keep him safe."

"As safe as he was last night when you almost killed him in a fit of temper?"

Crap. He'd hoped she hadn't seen that. "It's not the point ..." Avis refused to be drawn into an argument that did nothing but keep him distracted. He jerked his arm away from her and darted from the cabin, but when he reached the rear gunwale, all he could see in every direction was water. His eyes skimmed the surface, looking for anything out of the ordinary. Outside his realm, Maui's power behaved just like any other hellion's, and he could become anything living or dead. Even the seafoam floating in small clusters on the surface was searched for surface thoughts.

Nothing. Maui was gone.

Avis swore and slapped the gunwale, more frustrated with himself than the missing godling. This—this right here was why people like him didn't wait to see if someone was willing to comply. If he'd taken control of Maui when he had the chance, the boy would've been none the wiser and he'd be safe to boot. *Damn that kid ... and damn me for giving a realm-damned damn!*

* * *

As the *drua* drifted further away, a pigmy mantis shrimp broke the surface just enough for one of its stalked eyes to peer above the waterline. Between the chilling breeze above and the icy water below, the tiny shrimp shivered uncontrollably. The level of cold in this realm was ridiculous! Who in their right mind chose to live here?

Not that he was about to allow the temperature to force him into giving up his freedom either. That had never been part of the plan. But he had to give it to Avis; the stubborn son of a bitch didn't give up easily. Maui quickly pulled his eye back underwater when the Mystallian's scrutinising sweep of the water had him slowly swinging his head in the Rangi-Tuarean's direction. The crustacean held his position, willing himself to block out the cold as he counted to twenty. To quote the asshole of a god he was now hiding from, he was *fucking freezing*!

At the end of the count (which he had to restart twice after the cold made him lose what number he was up to) he floated upwards and risked another cautious look topside. The sooner he could get back to the warmth of Rangi-Tuarea, the better.

He watched as Avis continued to search the water, willing the obstinate bastard to abandon the hunt. *Give up, damn you,* he swore, still shivering. *Just let me go.*

It was another few minutes before Avis finally straightened to his full height and slapped the railing in frustration.

Yes! I win! Maui flexed his legs in victory as the Mystallian turned sharply on his heel and stalked back inside the cabin.

Happy with that knowledge, the young man sank a short distance below the waves and shifted into a large sailfish. Again, the shifting process took far too long and the cold made his fins ice up, but imagining how warm he'd be if he was on one of the beaches back home somehow allowed him to thaw out enough to manoeuvre himself in the water until he was pointed at the Rangi-Tuarea/Asgard border.

Good luck, you temperamental old boar, he sent as a parting thought, then shot off towards home. *You're going to need it.*

CHAPTER NINETEEN

Good luck, brat, wherever the fuck you are, Avis thought to himself as he turned and stormed back towards the cabin. *Because you're damn sure gonna need it, and I'm not coming back for your fucking funeral.*

But there was no point dwelling on it. Maui had chosen his preordained coffin over common sense, and he had a much bigger problem to deal with. One that had slipped his memory until he felt the chill of Asgard's winter and remembered the circumstances of the last time he'd felt it. There was no question that he and Odin were solid. He doubted if anything could undermine that friendship, but the same could not be said about him and Lord Loki. After everything that he'd been through in recent years, it had slipped his mind just how upset Lord Loki had been when Avis murdered one of the trickster god's unestablished sons.

Well, not him—directly, of course. Officially, it was Narvi's own twin brother that tore the mouthy little prick to pieces in the middle of Odin's celebratory feast in his grandson's honour. But every celestial in the room knew Avis had been the one to make him do it. As always, Odin understood his reasons and stood by him as a friend, but when Loki lost his shit and demanded retribution (both for the death of one son and the mind-fuck of the other), the All-Father thought it best if Avis left Asgard and stayed away for a few decades until the trickster god calmed down.

To date, it hadn't even been one. It hadn't even been half of one. The frustration of being chased from his best friend's feasting hall at the peak of its festivity was why Avis had taken his time with so many of Tawhirimatea's daughters … which in turn allowed the hellions to finally catch up with him.

Bottom line, it might be a bit soon for him to show his face in Asgard.

Huffing out a sharp breath of annoyance at what that meant for him and his family, Avis saw the puff of warm air and realised none of his girls were wearing appropriate cold-weather gear. Technically he wasn't either, but after what he'd been through in Hell, he doubted if any shift in temperature would ever bother him again.

As he entered the cabin, he noticed two of the guards had already taken up stations at either end of the cabin roof with their headpieces rotating constantly in search of danger. *Good.* Despite their insane speeds, he hadn't liked the idea of all four of them being cramped inside the room instead of out here on lookout. It felt wrong.

Clarise didn't appear to be showing any signs of discomfort in the cold either, though as a shifter, that was hardly surprising. She could constantly reset her internal temperature at will, *if* her insides were even still Mystallian. His beloved wife was clever like that. "Sweetheart, am I correct in assuming the girls' governesses have got their side of the room heated to keep the girls warm since they're asleep and can't do it for themselves?" Heads would roll if they hadn't. Literally.

"Yes, my love. Diviten and Gingen are aware of the Mystallian comfort limits and would have taken appropriate measures to ensure their wards' well-being."

He nodded in approval, accepting Clarise's word as an end to the matter. "Excellent. When they wake up, would you mind putting a discreet fur lining inside

Cora's clothes, much like what you've done for yourself? Until she gets her shifting back, she's not going to be able to do it for herself, and she's too much like me to admit she's cold when no one else is reacting to it."

"Of course," Clarise replied, crossing the room to sidle up against him with her head resting against his ribs. "But our current circumstances are only temporary, are they not? Once Lord Odin learns of our presence, we should be perfectly comfortable inside the Asgardian palace."

Avis stilled with his eyes fixed on the dividing wall over her head, but through his peripheral vision, he saw her twist her head and narrow her eyes into slits of suspicion. "Unless you have done something to jeopardise that."

"I wouldn't *technically* say I jeopardised it ... exactly ..." he hedged.

Clarise broke all contact and stepped around in front of him with her hands on her hips; her expression as frosty as the environment outside. When that didn't elicit an immediate response from him, the fine line of her right eyebrow rose in silent warning.

"Look, the truth is I'm not exactly sure where I sit with the Asgardians in general," he admitted, but when her eyes flared and she sucked in an explosive breath, his hands went up with his fingers flared to ward off whatever she was going to say. "I was justified," he insisted, earning him a short reprieve in the form of her cautious exhalation. He folded one arm across his chest to act as a ledge for his other elbow and scratched his eyebrows with his thumb and middle finger in a de-stressing massage that covered a large portion of his eyes. "For the most part."

"What happened?"

At least she hadn't outright accused him of anything, yet. He growled lightly under his breath at the cowardice he was showing by hiding his eyes and lowered his hand to look at her. "There was a ... situation in Asgard. A frost giant by the name of Hrungnir, who couldn't handle his mead, ran his mouth at an Asgardian feast in his honour. He claimed he would kill everyone in the room and carry the Halls of Valhalla on his shoulders to his homeland Jotunheim."

Avis had hoped she'd jump on the bait he dangled before her because they both knew his temper was dark enough to react violently to such a threat. If she had, he could then claw back some credibility by saying he hadn't reacted to that part at all. Just because Hrungnir's insults had been aimed at the Asgardians and not him was beside the point. Odin had been mad enough for both of them.

But no, Clarise didn't bite. She maintained her position with her back as straight as an arrow and her hands still on her hips, waiting for him to continue.

Seeking out a momentary reprieve from that glare, Avis took advantage of his height and looked over her head to the wall on the other side of the room. "Lord Thor came in on the tail end of Hrungnir's boasting and lost it. Even as drunk as he was, Hrungnir knew he was in trouble, but before Lord Thor could kill him on principle, Hrungnir threw out a death-challenge."

"If Lord Thor was the superior warrior, why would Hrungnir challenge him?"

Relieved she was talking to him again, if only to ask questions, Avis met her eyes. "Because the next time they met, Hrungnir wouldn't be drunk, and he'd have his weapons on him. As a guest of Odin's, Hrungnir had nothing but his mouth at the feast. Lord Thor didn't care and would've crushed his skull with Mjolnir there and then, but with the challenge laid out, nothing would happen until the two met on the border between Asgard and Jotunheim a few days later." Avis held up one finger, not to stave off her questions, but to emphasise his next point. "It wasn't a contest. Just one blow from Mjolnir killed Hrungnir, but Lord Thor was right in front of Hrungnir when the giant keeled over dead. The brash idiot got trapped under the carcass."

"Any particular reason why Lord Thor didn't simply shapeshift out from under the dead giant?"

It was a fair question. As one of the Aesir, Thor, like his father before him, could trace his line back to demonic shifters. "The most important reason of all, sweetheart. Establishment and subsequent thrall. Word of Lord Thor's victory spread to the mortal realm almost as soon as it happened and by the time the other Asgardians got to him, it was believed Lord Thor couldn't free himself, and the gods didn't have the strength between them to free him either."

"Who in the realms would tell their mortals a story like that?" Almost as soon as she said the words, realisation flashed across her face and Avis sneered in total agreement.

"Mm-hmmm," he hummed. "Once again, Lord Loki for the win." He released a light raspberry and shook his head. "I tell you, sweetheart, there's no way I'd put up with his cra…" —Avis caught himself and amended it to— "…his rubbish if we were back in Mystal. I really wouldn't. The first time he even thought about pulling something like that, I'd make him think he was a rat and stuff him in a locked shoe chest with no air holes for a few eons."

Clarise's expression soured. "You are getting off-topic," she warned.

Damn. He was hoping she hadn't noticed. "Yeah, well, Odin wanted me to reach out to Griffith for help since he'd still have his full strength and wouldn't be knee-capped by Lord Loki's prank. He didn't like it when I told him I hadn't spoken to my family in years and wasn't about to start then, not even for him." He frowned at her condescending expression. "What? I was still sore at them since they didn't stand by me against your father."

"But they did," Clarise corrected.

"I know that *now*," he snapped irritably. "But back then, I was just mad. Like, all the time. I blamed everyone else but me for what happened." Her condescension was replaced with a look of parental disapproval, and that judgement brought out the worst in him. The faintest wisps of red crept into the edges of his vision as he shook his head. "Don't say it, Clarise, or I swear I'll start using profanity. It's not who I am now, but I won't lie about who I was back then either."

He paused to see if she'd cross that line anyway, and relaxed when she didn't. "Anyway, the mortals didn't know about Lord Magni, Lord Thor's three-year-old son. Since he had no establishment, he had no thrall, and the kid was Asgard's answer to Griffith. He broke away from his governesses at the palace and spent two days getting to his father's side on foot. I was part of the search party that went looking for him. No one in a million years thought he'd actually make it to his father. But he did, and just as Odin and I tracked him to the border, we saw him lift the dead giant over his head and toss the body far into Jotunheim. Odin and Lord Thor were ecstatic, and on top of their praises, they gave Lord Magni Hrungnir's horse, Golden Mane." He rubbed his hands together, then parted them casually. "The kid was a shifter, so riding a frost giant's beast that big didn't bother him for long. And the celebratory feast we had that night made the one that Hrungnir took part in seem like a snack. Everyone wanted to hear Lord Magni's story, and Lord Thor was happy to relay it … over … and over … and over."

Now, they were getting to the troubling part of his tale. In hindsight, Avis was starting to see a pattern between his heavy drinking and his tendency to behave badly. "The party went for days. Weeks, even. People who didn't normally come to the feasts turned up to take part." He closed his eyes for a moment. "Including some of the unestablished kids."

Avis could almost feel the tension in the room surge in anticipation of what he was about to say next. "Lord Loki had two of his sons in attendance. Twin boys. Lords Narvi and Vali. They were basically good kids, but with a skinful under their belts, they got mouthy. Real mouthy. Lord Narvi in particular. I could ignore it so long as they were insulting everyone else, but then Lord Narvi turned that sass on me, and he had plenty to say." Avis' teeth ground together at the memory until a muscle twitched under his right eye. He met Clarise's gaze, all but daring her to speak right then. "I warned him, Clarise. By the Twin Notes of all creation, I warned him more than I've ever warned anyone else to shut his mouth, but he just … kept … pushing, and my patience finally ran out."

"What did you do?"

"Lord Narvi's mother realised I'd reached breaking point and tried to block my line of sight on him by flipping a table to hide them both, but by that stage, it was already too late. I was going to get him, and even as I stood up to do it, Odin and Lord Thor tried to hold me back. Lord Loki killing himself laughing on the sidelines didn't help matters one bit. I remember someone trying to cover my eyes with something, and in a fit of rage, I went for the nearest person I could find to attack Lord Narvi on my behalf before that happened. Lord Narvi's twin brother, Lord Vali." It was painful to acknowledge the hurt in Clarise's eyes, but he forced himself to keep going. "I made Lord Vali shift himself into a wolf with the mental command to tear his brother to pieces. Lord Narvi didn't survive."

Clarise rubbed her forearms as if to stave off the cold. They both knew it had nothing to do with the temperature. "You murdered a baby."

It was a vile accusation, but not one Avis could refute. "He was a young man, old enough to drink, but yes, ultimately I killed one of Lord Loki's unestablished sons. Lord Loki wanted my hide after that, and things blew up from there. Odin seemed more annoyed than outraged, and since Lord Loki was only his blood brother and not real kin, my old friend sided with me. Before any more blood was drawn, Odin's youngest son, Lord Baldur got in the middle of everything and started to calm it all down."

Thinking of how easily he'd done that, Avis shook his head. "That kid's got an impressive career in front of him as a negotiator, I'll tell you. He was actually pulling it off. Odin met my eyes while the boy worked his magic on the crowd and in his surface thoughts I saw him telling me to leave and come back in a few decades when the dust had settled. So I did. Today's the first day I've set foot back in Asgard since."

"Do you think Lord Odin blames you for the discord?"

"I don't think Odin cares either way, to be honest. If he wanted to hold me accountable for the killing, I wouldn't have left his feasting hall. The only thing I can see him having a problem with is the fact that I came back too soon. All that happened just a few months before your family caught up with me."

"Just a moment," Clarise said, her brow scrunching in confusion. "I thought you once told me that your nephew Strahan branded you with some kind of magical ward to prevent you from entering the celestial realm."

Avis subconsciously rubbed his thumb over the spot under his chin where the painful brand had been. "He did, but Odin's a god of magic in his own right. While I was here, he intercepted me in Midgard and used his magic to push back the power of the brand in order to take me to Asgard."

"I was not aware Lord Odin was innately magical."

"He wasn't … isn't. That's why he couldn't get rid of the brand totally for me. He could only negate it while we were both within his realm." But thinking about which Asgardian *did* have the innate magical ability, Avis' smile grew. "Lord Baldur's their innate mage. He just hasn't developed it beyond a few basic tricks yet because he's always trying to put out fires inside a pantheon full of blooded warriors. That neutrality is why his parents are so protective of him, no question. Lady Frigg even made a deal with nature …"

Clarise straightened, her eyes widening with realisation. "Oh, I remember that. It was two or three centuries ago, was it not? She invoked a promise from every plant and animal in the realm to do her son no harm."

Highly doubting that she realised she'd interrupted him and loving her all the more for it, Avis pinched his lips together to contain his delight and nodded. It certainly wouldn't have happened twelve months ago. "And it worked, sweetheart. I saw it with my own eyes. The kid's completely invulnerable to everything anyone can throw at him. His parents even set up displays to show it off, permitting anyone of any size to try and hurt him with a weapon. It all just bounces off."

"Rocks and forged weapons would not fit into the living or former living category."

"True, but Lord Baldur's fatalistic nightmares had such a prophetic nature to them that his father neutralised the threat of standard weapons long before Lady Frigg even thought of adding living things to the equation." Avis pulled himself up, realising he had subconsciously diverted the subject again. Staring hard at the dividing wall, he raised his hand and placed it flat on the solid surface, reminding himself of what was at stake.

"I'd let Odin know I was here if I was on my own because at the end of the day Lord Loki's huffing and puffing doesn't mean anything to me. But you and the girls aren't established, and at the very least, that mother-f…" —he sucked his upper lip between his teeth and dragged it through, curling his flattened hand into a fist against the wall in the process— "…that particular god'll be looking for an eye for an eye where his dead son is concerned. Be Damned all over again before I give him either one of our girls to murder in cold blood."

"No," Clarise agreed. "While I grieve for his loss, I will not permit him to mitigate it by killing one of ours, which means we must continue to be discreet in our travels."

Because he'd already been playing with the idea for a while now, Avis was way ahead of her. "I was thinking since we're already in the mortal realm, we should stay down here and travel as we did in the Chaotic Ocean, setting up the night house somewhere in space away from the sapient mortals. Maybe in the middle of one of their suns or something."

Clarise stared hard at his chest as she drummed the tops of her fingers together in a fingertip applause of contemplation. "This is not Chaos, beloved," she said, finally lifting her eyes to his. "Whilst we were travelling through my homeland, we were fully aware that Father knew where we were at all times and had chosen to turn a blind eye to us. It is not the same situation here. If we do anything to stand out in one place too long, we will draw the pantheon's attention."

Which quashed the use of the overnight house, but not necessarily the demon steeds ...

As it dawned on him where she was going with this, his eyes widened in horror. "You want us to mingle with the Asgardian mortals?"

"We mingled with the Damned on the Akheron River, did we not?"

Avis wasn't impressed. "Firstly, they were deceased souls in eternal torment. They knew their places at the bottom of the heap. Mortals before their physical expiration date have an entirely different outlook on things, and it's one of self-gratification. Secondly, I'll only be able to tag them one at a time. Even if I bounce from one to the next, to get any serious numbers done, I'll be internalising for weeks every time we stop ..."

"Not if we blended in instead of conquering them."

Avis hated that idea even more. "Why in the realms would we want to do that?"

Clarise put both hands against his chest, then drifted them up to his shoulders and hooked them behind his neck. "Since we are counting our reasons, I can think of two," she said, smiling up at him as her fingers massaged the muscles at the base of his skull. "One, the less we stand out, the less likely the Asgardians will learn of our presence. Two, it would be incredibly educational for the girls to experience the Asgardian way of life."

Avis groaned and tilted his head back to stare at the ceiling. They were back to this again. He thought he'd put the kibosh on this schooling crap weeks ago.

His next inhalation brought a lungful of lavender with it, and he knew it wasn't a coincidence. "Clarise ..." he grumbled, wanting to argue this out even as his body took the lead and his arms banded around her shoulders, holding her against him. He leaned down and kissed her forehead, then pressed his forehead to hers and whispered, "You're playing dirty again."

Her smile broadened without denying it. "I am certain the journey through Midgard will not be as bad as you are envisioning, beloved. At the very least, the Asgardian palate is to your liking. It must be. You have mentioned many of Odin's feasts, and I doubt you would have returned after the first one if they had served you a beverage like darida."

Avis felt his stomach roil at the mere mention of the Yarusian brew that had more in common with stale urine, in his opinion.

Clarise's hand found his cheek, refocusing his attention on her. "They may not be as cultured as we are, but I am certain we will make the best of it."

"My other concern with staying permanently in the mortal realm is just how easy it is to get turned around down here. Bearings in the celestial realm are easier to maintain because there's usually only one sun. In the mortal realm, every single galaxy has hundreds of billions of them."

Clarise slid her hands down his arms and turned around to face the far wall. She moved her left hand over to hold his right hand in both of hers and turned his glove palm up. "What if I created something similar to the glowing bead that gave us the direction sense you require?"

Avis looked over her head to where she held his hand. "What sort of something do you have in mind?" The last thing he wanted was a thousand glowing beads that had his hand looking as if a firefly possi had taken up residence.

Clarise ran her fingers over the glove, settling on the space between the cuff and his wrist. "I was thinking of an embossed arrow just here on the inside of your glove. One that doesn't stand out at all, unless you already knew it was there."

"And the purpose of this arrow?" He couldn't see how a single arrow would help.

"By having it constantly point towards Mystal, you will have your bearing, beloved." To prove her point, she turned her own wrist over and crafted a tiny embossed arrow, half the size of a pin, to appear on the cuff of her own glove. "See?" she asked, twisting her hand from left to right and showing him how the arrow remained on a constant heading.

Avis was impressed, but he still saw a potential problem. "And what about up and down? We need three dimensions in the mortal realm, sweetheart. Not two."

Clarise lifted her arm, and despite being a two-dimensional image, the arrow appeared to bank forward until only the back of the fletching was visible. "Like that?" she asked, smugly.

Avis chuckled and cupping her chin with his hand, he twisted her head to give her a quick kiss on the lips. Then he rolled his hand over and lay it across her palm. "My turn," he declared.

Moments later, he stepped away from her, his gaze fixed on the embossed arrow on his glove. The tip and tail quivered, pivoting on a central point as if it were alive. Just as she had done, he twisted his arm from side to side, fascinated by the way it maintained the same alignment as Clarise's had towards the front of the catamaran. He even turned in a tight circle, his eyes glued to the arrow to see if it would move. It didn't. "And you're sure that's the way back to Mystal?" he asked, lifting his right hand to point in the same direction of the arrow. It wasn't that he doubted her integrity, just her knowledge of Mystal's actual location within the Known Realms.

"Yes, my love. No matter where you are, that mark will always point you towards home, as long as you continue to have it."

He looked up at her and grinned. "I could've used this six years ago. You know that, right?"

Clarise crossed the room and folded herself back into his arms. "Need I remind you just who was responsible for our separation back then?"

Avis snorted and refrained from answering. He'd walked into that one.

CHAPTER TWENTY

Three hours later, the girls were up and having breakfast. An hour after that, Avis and his party were airborne, hovering over the small Rangi-Tuarean vessel while Clarise broke it down to its smallest molecules to avoid discovery; and a further five hours of intense riding put them tens of thousands of mortal galaxies closer to Mystal.

Just as he had in the Chaotic Ocean, Avis took his cue from the glowing bead on his glove to keep track of time, and when the bead fell in line with his middle finger, he pulled them up and selected a random planet covered in oceanic waters and frozen greenery as the place to have their lunch.

Scoring Clarise's smile of approval wasn't entirely necessary, but he couldn't deny the shaft of intense pleasure it gave him as he led them down through the planet's atmosphere. The black of space slowly shifted into dark indigo which then softened into a light azure, the farther they descended. He knew in mortal terms, entering a planetary atmosphere at this speed should have burnt them to a crisp, but the atmosphere played by the same rules as everything else in the mortal realm did. That is unless something was actively trying to harm them, it did everything in its power not to. This included temporarily rewriting what it considered the norm.

The surface thoughts of the girls as he glanced over his shoulder at them would amuse him for years to come. He couldn't remember the last time he saw anyone looking at the mortal realm's amenability with such wide-eyed wonder, and he knew neither of them could wrap their minds around it. For him, it was simple. The rules of reality were different here, and he was about to give them a crash course in those differences. Cora at least.

Once they were a hundred or so metres above the waterline, he levelled out their flight path and skimmed across the ocean surface. The water hissed and evaporated as it came into contact with the demon steeds' hellfire, creating vast clouds of steam in their wake like a reverse bow wave. The girls' combined shrieks of laughter brought another smile to his face, for that was exactly the reaction he was hoping for.

In the far distance, he spotted land and further slowed their party to under several thousand kilometres an hour. As they got closer, he noticed the crags that lined the shore were pillars of sheer stone climbing hundreds of metres into the sky. Tufts of weeds clung to the cracks, and what he'd thought would be a sandy beach turned out to be a coastline of bleached rocks; some as large as him.

In other words, nothing they could land on.

Not one to give up easily, Avis followed the rugged coastline until a suitable beach leading back into the snow-covered woodlands caught his eye. While that would work, he remembered the ocean's reaction to hellfire and didn't want the snow to evaporate and a wildfire blow up the moment they landed. So he drew them all to a complete halt, hovering a body-length above the sandy shore. "Sweetheart, is there any chance you can turn the demon steeds into wingless mystallions with hides the colour of dirt before we land?"

"Of course," Clarise answered, nodding sharply to confirm that fact. But then she frowned and tilted her head to one side. "Though I am curious as to why you would find that necessary."

A year ago, she'd have never questioned his decision, assuming he as her husband was all-knowing, and by asking him to explain himself, she was somehow showing a lack of trust in him. Avis couldn't help but grin in delight. "Hellfire and the mortal realm don't normally mix, sweetheart. Hellfire burns and melts anything mortal it touches—even the suns. With us being right on top of it, the mortal realm will probably drop that damage to melted hoof-prints that have the steeds sinking up to their knees, but we still don't want that level of attention. I know from experience that the Midgardians ride horses with coats ranging from creams to browns to blacks, much like Armina's army. We're not going to stay long, but just in case we run across any locals, it'll be easier if they don't look like winged mounts of living hellfire." Oh, how it galled him to admit they were hiding amongst the mortals.

Clarise either realised it was still a sore subject to be avoided or she'd already gleaned what she wanted to know because she turned to view the girls riding behind them. One after the other, the demon steeds lost their wings and fiery appearance and dropped down to the beach as if they'd just cleared a hurdle.

Once again, Avis was astounded by the complacency of the demon steeds. They had literally just had their entire structure reworked without warning, and not so much as a hint of reaction to it. No rearing, neighing … nothing. No way in the realms would she ever get that level of compliance from the mystallion herd. Even if he took the shift from fire to flesh out of the equation, forcing them into an inferior, wingless shape would've had the herd totally losing their shit *forever*, and he wouldn't blame them.

By contrast, the modified demon steeds waited patiently for them to dismount, then wandered over to the nearby snowfields where they scraped their hooves through the snow to reach the minimal grasslands beneath, as if they'd been eating grass their entire lives.

"Same goes for you four," he said, making eye contact with each of the servants. "Shift into a Mystallian form. Over half of the mortals in Midgard have a Mystallian appearance."

"And the other half?" Cora asked from directly behind him, genuinely curious.

Avis looked over his shoulder at her so she could see he wasn't annoyed in the least by her interjection. "They're a variety of races and capabilities. Dwarves, elves, giants and basic shifters. You name it. It comes from having a mix of benders and shifters within the Asgardian pantheon."

He saw the way Clarise eyed the guard nearest her and could almost hear her thoughts on the matter before she spoke. "The Highborn Hellion Guards do not shift like other Highborn Hellions, beloved. Nor are they capable of being shifted by us. They are able to adapt to whatever weapon they require, but their form is always maintained for intimidation purposes."

And they do a fucking good job of it, Avis thought, very privately to himself, following her gaze to the guard whose presence had become so familiar that he had to remind himself just how terrifying they were.

"However, due to their speed, they can stay in hiding and still be with us in the blink of an eye, should we need protecting," Clarise went on, ignorant of his internal monologue. She then turned to look at him. "Do you concur, beloved?"

Avis bit his tongue for a moment rather than answer. He'd just finished complimenting her for making a stand, and she had to go and spoil it by saying something like that. He would've preferred that she simply made her stand, and if he had a problem with it, he would voice it himself. It wasn't up to her to seek out his approval. "Yes, I agree," he said, once he was sure he could keep his words civil.

Clarise made a dismissive gesture with both hands, and a heartbeat later there was no sign of the Highborn Hellion Guard. Avis looked all around for them, from the wooded land behind the demon steeds to the open ocean and even up in the air. Nothing. Damn, Armina would positively kill for that level of speed to be incorporated into her army.

A tiny hand hooked through his elbow and tugged, causing him to look down at whichever of their daughter's had him by the arm. "Father," Cora said, her tone implying she was about to ask a question as much as the pressure of her hand in the crook of his elbow. The latter was a complete violation of adult/child Hellion Highborn protocols, but every day his tiger was returning to her Mystallian roots and he grinned down at her.

"What's up, tiger?"

Cora frowned and licked her lips apprehensively. "Father, why'd all the fireballs and mass balls get out of our way this morning?"

Fireballs and mass balls? It took Avis a few minutes of internalisation to make sense of her illogical question, but when he did, he chuckled deeply and squatted down in front of her. "They're called suns and planets, tiger. Not fireballs and mass balls. The mortal realm is full of them."

"But why'd they get out of our way?"

Avis noticed Columbine edge closer to also hear his explanation of this phenomenon and waved her forward with his fingertips. "It's what they're supposed to do," he said, once both girls were standing in front of him. His eyes bounced between the two, gauging their reactions for understanding.

"But why?" Cora insisted.

"Because we're celestial, and the mortal realm accepts our right of way in all things." He continued to shift his gaze between them, ensuring he had their full attention. This was important. "It's why when you are in the mortal realm, it's both dangerous and liberating at the same time."

Columbine winced at the unknown word, forcing Avis to rephrase his last sentence. "Liberating means freeing, princess. You can do anything you want down here, but the catch is, if you aren't careful, down here can bite you back just as hard." Realising he'd jumped too far into the lesson, Avis returned to the start of the conversation. He glanced at Cora. "As you said, the suns and the planets got out of our way. That's because we were coming through, and the mortal realm as a whole will never cause us harm. In the time it takes us to ride past, everything has moved and moved back so quickly that nothing is any the wiser."

"So, nothing in the mortal realm can hurt us, Father?" Columbine asked.

Avis sighed because this was where they covered the 'dangerous' part. He stared hard at Columbine, willing her to understand. "For the most part it won't, princess.

But you two need to be careful, because yes, in certain ways the mortal realm can hurt you." He looked at Cora then, for of the two, she would be the one to challenge this and lose. "In fact, it can hurt you a lot. Like, kill you. It all comes down to something called intent." Back to Columbine. "Intent is when you want to do something on purpose. So while the planets and suns get out of your way, a mortal is able to punch you and stab you if their intention is to hurt you."

"So wait, a great big freaking sun'll get out of our way, but some idiot nobody gets a free shot at us just because he or she wants to? That's messed up!"

Cora had caught on quickly, just as Avis knew she would. He chuckled at her very visual interpretation. "It's called belief, tiger, and it's at the foundation of everything we are. If they believe they can land a punch, that belief mitigates ..." a quick look at Columbine's worried frown had him searching for another word. "... ahh ... neutralises ..." That was just as big. *C'mon Avis! Think of a smaller word!* "... ummm ..."

"It cancels it out," Cora supplied for him snappishly, still irked by the revelation.

Avis shot her a grateful look and carried on. "Yes, that. Their belief *cancels out* what would otherwise happen, and they can hit you as hard as they like."

"By the Twin Notes, they'd better make it count against me," Cora sneered, her tone taking on a distinct hellion edge to it. "Because if I get back up, they won't."

Avis flicked his pointer finger at her in approval. "Exactly. No one will blame you for making them pay for it after the event, but you have to survive the attack first, and that's where being careful comes into its own. The fact that I'll wipe out a hundred galaxies in every direction soon afterwards won't bring you back from the dead if they manage to kill you. If you see it coming, you can counter it with your will. But if they get the drop on you, you will go down. Hard." His eyes returned to Columbine. "And while we are here, we can't tell the mortals that we're divine. Not even a little bit. Do you understand me?"

Columbine nodded obediently. "Yes, Father."

Cora wasn't so easily swayed. "Why not?"

Avis couldn't help but think of Chance all those eons ago and decided then and there that he wasn't having this conversation in real-time. One; because Columbine would do as she was told regardless and two; Cora wouldn't believe him until she saw it for herself. Also knowing he wouldn't be able to explain what happened to Chance without a whole lot of profanity entering his voice might have factored into it too.

So he went into Cora's mind. Specifically, her imagination.

"Alright, tiger. Front and centre!" he barked, using his mental control to bring his elder daughter's consciousness to him. She appeared almost immediately, right where he directed. He placed one hand on her shoulder and turned her around so he stood at her back. "Allow me to show you why you don't let mortals know you're celestial until you've got the little bastards under control." He created a landscape much like the one they'd found Chance on, only instead of the Mystallian luck god being at their mercy, Avis substituted a second image of Cora. He sped things up and skipped out chunks of miscellaneous information so that she could watch a years' worth of Chance's de-evolution in a matter of an hour. His teeth ground together on certain scenes that were stark reminders of what the runt had gone through.

Having no clue this was a modified scene from her Uncle's reality, Cora hissed and lunged against her father's hands as a chained slave collar was locked around her image's neck, but Avis held her firmly in place. "It gets worse," he assured her.

Although he hadn't been there personally for any of this, he'd seen it all unfold in his youngest brother's memories after the fact. Five of Chance's older siblings had regrouped in the runt's mind to witness every minute of this debacle for themselves and to reiterate why it must NEVER be allowed to happen again. They also agreed that Chance didn't need to remember any of this. As the eldest and most powerful of those present, it was left to Avis to cast a blanket across the memory, going from where the mortals first changed Chance into that hideous costume and ending with their sister's touch-knockout. While the other four chose to retain the memory, Chance would be saved from himself.

The runt knew he was missing the memory but had just enough leading into it to know his siblings were protecting him and never pushed for the specifics. Ironically, one of the two Nexus children to not know a thing about what happened, was the very one it happened to.

Bringing himself back to the present, Avis froze the current scene before him just prior to where he and his siblings came upon Chance, locking the image of Cora in place with that idiot costume and grinning like the happiest lunatic in existence. Cora whipped around and looked up at him. "They can do this to us?" she snarled, her eyes wide with both rage and horror.

"They can. Especially the feral ones. It's why you've got to be so careful, tiger. If they work out you're divine, they can take control of you so long as you stay within five metres of them. And when they figure *that* part out ..." He lifted his hand and rolled his fingers open towards the frozen scene. "They get all the power that's meant to be *your* birthright." He let his hand fall. "I told you all this on the Akheron River."

"But you didn't say it was could be like this!"

"That's because we were still getting to know each other, and I didn't want to rush your bending." He stepped out from behind her and walked over to the immobile genie version of her. "Take a good, hard look, tiger," he said, circling behind the image, sliding the fingers of his right hand across her shoulders. "For this will be your fate if you let mortals figure out you're divine without having attunement over them first."

"That's fucked up!"

"Yes, it is, which is why you need to be careful." He returned to her consciousness, once again placing his hands on her shoulders from behind so as not to impede her vision. "This is just an example of what could happen if they know you're divine." He emptied the scene until all they stood on was a square of ground in a barren space. "Now, watch what happens when they don't know you're divine and *still* believe they can kill you." With another thought, he rebuilt the scene to include the same six mortals as before, but this time, he had the image of Cora approach them as an equal. They laughed and joked with her for a few minutes, just long enough for Cora's consciousness to relax under his palms, and then he had one of them throw out an anti-feminine slur that implied the only good woman was a raped one; present company included.

He hadn't liked the image he presented, but he had to get Cora good and mad. Mad enough to not think, and he succeeded better than he ever intended.

Cora's consciousness went absolutely berserk. Spittle flew from her opened mouth, exposing rows of razor-sharp fangs and her eyes ignited with hellfire, letting him know that she was fast approaching demonic blood rage. Avis immediately froze the scene and doubled down on his control of her consciousness to keep her from completely losing it. He wasn't concerned with the rage itself. That would abate just as soon as the image of Cora tore her antagonist to pieces. He had to hold her still so that even in the midst of her rage, she would see what came next.

Releasing the scene, they both watched as the image of Cora grew her demonic talons and slashed through the mortal's throat, decapitating him in that single movement. He was dead before he hit the ground.

The satisfaction that swept through her consciousness was what he had anticipated, but he kept her watching as her image threw her head back and laughed in hellish delight. That one move took her focus away from his colleagues, who reacted to the killing of their comrade by drawing their swords and hacking her Mystallian form to pieces; faster than her shifting could regenerate.

Cora's consciousness was mortified. "How in the realms are they doing that? I'm celestial!"

Avis would've laughed at her outrage if the situation weren't so serious. He froze the scene once more and allowed her to stomp around, if only to vent her frustration. "They did it because they wanted you dead and they believed they could kill you. And since your body wasn't set up with the means to stop them, it happened. Now, do you understand?"

"What if I'd seen them, or reinforced my body beforehand or something?"

Avis smirked, knowing it didn't reach his eyes. "Don't play dumb. You know if you see them coming, you own them. You're a celestial. They're not."

Cora looked over the frozen scene, and Avis could tell from the way she paused on different aspects that the lesson was sinking in. "This isn't the first time you've mentioned attunement," she said, turning back to him with a look in her eyes that went far beyond her years. "You and mother have alluded to it plenty of times, but no one's actually said what it is or how we come by it."

"It's how you get bulk control of a realm. You're naturally attuned to whatever realm you're born in but leaving that realm and going to another means you have to leave behind your old attunement and work on getting the new one. Columbine for example, is attuned to Chaos, and she's going to have to start all over again when we get back to Mystal, whereas you'll be going back to yours once we get there." Believing a visual depiction would help her understand this, he created a single land and water mass to represent the celestial realm, and a layer of neighbouring galaxies under it for the mortal realm. "Here," he said, rolling his hands to draw her towards the image. "Pretend this normal space up here is the celestial realm, and the starry one beneath it represents the mortals."

Cora eyed the image carefully. "Okay."

"For attunement to work, there must be a defined border in place, first and foremost." He drew a golden ring around the outside of the layers. "And before you think it's that easy, it takes upwards of a thousand years to set up properly, if you want a half-decent realm. The bigger the realm, the longer it takes."

"How long did it take you to set up Mystal?"

Avis hadn't thought about that in a long time. "We were greedy," he admitted with a chuckle. "Every time we thought about stopping, we'd decide to go bigger and add a few more thousand galaxies. There were eight of us marking out that border, but it still took us close to seven hundred centuries to complete."

"Seventy thousand years!" Cora shouted, translating the figure into its basest form.

Avis shrugged, not even trying to remove the grin from his face. "Give or take." He created a glowing dot in the middle of the celestial realm, just in front of her face. "Pretend that dot's you," he said, just in case she hadn't figured that part out.

The pinched look of disgust she wore as she rolled her head in his direction had him chuckling evilly. "Pay attention, twerp," he said, nudging her shoulder with his elbow. "Your very presence will eventually permeate down into the mortal realm below, like this."

Technically, there was no 'above' or 'below' where the celestial and mortal realms were concerned. They more or less took up the same space, but no god worth his salt would put his home realm on the same level as the mortal realm he controlled. As he spoke, Avis allowed the illumination of the dot to seep down into the mortal realm at a much faster rate than actually happened until it filled the space within the golden ring. "You see all that glowing space now?" he asked rhetorically. "Everything that glows is now yours to command."

"How will I know when it's done?"

Avis cast his mind back to that moment when his essence locked onto the attunement. The rush of power that swept over him and his siblings was unforgettable. "You'll know," he promised on the tail end of a heartfelt sigh. "Once we get back to Mystal, you'll see what I mean. You were born in Mystal, so your natural attunement is there."

"And then I can do whatever I like in the mortal realm?"

That brought Avis up hard. Memories of Blagden before and after his establishment reminded him in extreme detail the horror of that line of thinking. "That was where your Uncle Blagden screwed up, tiger. He wasn't well but didn't want to be left behind when the rest of us decided to make our move. After so long, if we'd only waited a few more days ..."

He gritted his teeth and shook his head, acknowledging one of the few great regrets he had back then. "Blagden's thrall locked him in because he didn't put in place exactly what he wanted from his attunement beforehand. Like you, we thought once we were attuned, we were done. The reality is, it's a blank book that allows you to make all the rules you want the mortal realm to play by, no matter how ridiculous. If you don't have at least some of the rules sorted out before you descend, having the attunement makes little difference."

"Why would anyone want to risk that?"

"Because it's in our essence to rule. It's not just our destiny, tiger. It's what it means to be a god. We can no more deny it than you can deny there is Highborn Hellion in your ancestry."

"So, I don't get a choice?"

"You can choose to be common if you wish," he said, though the words tasted like acid on his tongue and he really hoped in time she wouldn't force him to make her see sense in that regard. "But you will be treated as such, and once your family's achieved power, it's not that easy to walk away from."

"That's what makes us immortal, isn't it? Where the commoners die out in fifty or sixty thousand years, we're immortal because we yearn to rule. We're driven to it."

Now she was getting it. He bobbed his head in agreement. "Yeah, tiger. Taking orders from others doesn't sit well with the likes of you and me. We prefer to be the ones barking them."

Cora looked up at him and her brazen smirk all but confirmed it.

"Since we're in here, do you want to learn how to use your bending properly?"

Cora's face lit up in excitement. "Oh, Hell, yeah!"

CHAPTER TWENTY-ONE

Laughing at her impatience, Avis reset the scene, this time putting a see-through version of himself in front of a crowd of equally transparent assailants. The assailants had weapons drawn and were in the midst of attacking him. "Ready?" he asked, looking to his left where Cora stood in eager anticipation of the show.

"Definitely."

"See if you can keep up." And with that, he animated the scene and immediately a string of light leapt from his eyes to the nearest person. In that instant, everything froze except the internal workings of the supposed 'brain' of the person Avis tagged, where a little version of himself ran around setting fire to everything. Once he was satisfied with the level of damage, he withdrew from that person (in the form of a retreating light) back into himself and moved his eyes to the next, barely giving the antagonists in the scene a second or two to react. He then launched into the mind of another, where he placed a mental command for the male to impale himself on his own sword.

Over and over, he attacked them in this fashion to cement in Cora's mind what he was doing. In just a few seconds of physical time, Avis had subdued every mind in his vicinity, with none of them being any the wiser. At the conclusion of the final target, the light that represented his mind returned to his body and he waited for each of them to either carry out their implanted command or fall to the ground in a drooling heap.

It was always an impressive show after the fact.

"This is how it works if the people you're up against are either mortal, demonic, lower tier than you, unestablished, or outside their realms," he said, making sure she understood the difference. "If the celest is inside their own realm, it won't matter where they sit in relation to you, power wise. The second you leave their minds, if what you've done goes against their establishment field, their powerbases will automatically kick in and try to overcome the damage and set them to rights. It's the same as when a shifter shifts someone into something else inside their realm. You can hold them there, but only as long as you're willing to do so. Were we in Mystal and you tried to turn me into a chair, it would last for a few minutes because my powerbase would turn me inside out in an effort to shift me back into what the people worship." He pretended to scowl down at her and added, "And I wouldn't want to be you, half a second later."

As soon as he made the shifting reference, Cora understood what he meant. Nevertheless, she giggled at his supposed threat and crossed her eyes over her nose to taunt him. Avis snorted and mussed up her hair. "Brat," he rumbled affectionately.

"So, when do I get a go?" she asked, rubbing her hands eagerly.

"Right now," he answered, resetting the scene, this time without his image. Better to practice in here, where she could hone her skills under his guidance, than the physical realm, where things could go horribly wrong. He gave her head a little push so she'd fill the vacant spot where his image had been.

For the next few hours, Avis had her practicing her bending abilities on random people he created for her to dominate. Not just to destroy, but to control. Bending was all about control. He started by teaching her the difference between learning from another person's memories and stealing that knowledge outright. The latter was by far the easiest, and when dealing with mortals and celests who didn't matter, it was the most natural way for a bender to go. From the outside, both choices were instantaneous. Whether the bender spent an instant stealing the knowledge or years learning it the hard way, it all amounted to the same thing to everyone else. Cora loved the knowledge theft. To her, it made perfect sense to use that one above the other.

But as she was about to learn, things weren't so clear-cut with connected celestials. Benders were especially sensitive to lost knowledge. Even unestablished shifters outside their realms figured it out over time, depending on how soon they went to draw on knowledge they should have had. Either way, it didn't end well for the thief if their identity was ever discovered.

To prove this point, Avis started to modify each reset scene so that it edged ever closer to resembling the Well of Hell. His little tiger was having so much fun with her new-found thieving ability that she hadn't noticed the changes.

Then with the background in place, he created an image of his brother-by-marriage Uriel. An established celestial inside his realm of establishment.

Without missing a beat, Cora lunged into the archangel's mind and ransacked it for knowledge. As this was an object lesson, Avis kept the replica's knowledge just above what Cora would know to tempt her into stealing it. Which she did. And Uriel retaliated with the full force of his shifting and archangel powerbase, tearing Cora's consciousness to shreds.

Avis froze the scene right before Uriel could land the killing blow. "And that right there, young lady, is why you need to learn the other way to gather knowledge."

Cora's tattered consciousness crawled out from under her frozen uncle, her entire body shaking in both pain and terror. "You did that on purpose!" she shouted at him through tears of humiliation and agony.

"I selected him as a test for you, yes." Avis kept his expression unrepentant. "But you were the one who thought you could take on a superior ranged shifter without repercussions. Now, shake it off, tiger. You only think you're hurt. Pretend you're back in the physical realm without any tefsla in your system and pull yourself back together again. Right now, you're embarrassing yourself."

With that, Cora's pained expression hardened and her shredded flesh rolled back up onto her shattered bones, moulding the broken body parts back into one cohesive unit. A stimulation wave a few seconds later finalised the repair and she was once again whole and unharmed. Eventually, she would discover the mind was a place where things including herself could be reset instantly, but that was a lesson for another day. "You suck," she snapped at him sulkily.

"And you needed to learn," Avis countered, again without remorse. "This is why we've got a secondary way of gathering information. One that allows us to glean it from a target source without removing it from them, because most celests take great offense to having their hard-earned knowledge stolen."

Cora's look of disgust was classic. "So I have to sit there and learn it at their stupid speed?"

"In your case, I'd say you could probably skip through things as they click faster for you. But don't skip too much, or you'll miss relevant things."

"So I can be in their minds, watching what they learned as they learned it, and they won't be any the wiser, no matter how long I'm in there?"

"That's right. You can be in here," —he tapped the side of her consciousness' head to represent her personal internalisation, then jerked his chin towards Uriel's frozen form— "Or over there in his mind for as long as you want." He paused for a moment, because what he needed to say next went against everything he personally felt as a Mystallian god. "Cora, while we're in Asgard, I need you to *not* steal the mortals' knowledge."

Cora's face creased in confusion. "Why the hell not?"

"Because we're trying not to get the pantheon's attention, and when a mortal loses their knowledge, the first thing they do is seek out a divine rationale for it. When that doesn't work, they pray for divine intervention for a swift recovery. Either way, our cover is blown. Do you understand?"

"So, you don't want me to steal the memories of the mortals, not because we're worried about them as such, but because of who they may bring in on it afterwards?"

"Exactly."

"You know, this trip would've been a whole lot easier if you hadn't made an enemy of every fucking pantheon out there, Father."

Avis bristled at her cutting tone, but Cora hooked her hands on her hips and stood her ground. "Just saying."

"Well, I did, so build yourself a bridge and get the fuck over it." He didn't need Cora to remind him of his failings. With a magnanimous wave of his right hand, he cleared the scene, no longer in the mood to do this. "But that's enough training for now. I'll see you outside in the physical realm." He was about to leave when he realised she'd probably mess around some more with her new abilities after he left. "Oh, one other thing before I go. I don't want you playing around with this in your imagination while I'm not here to oversee it, tiger."

"Why not?" she asked, confirming that was exactly what she planned to do.

"Because this is your imagination. It'll do exactly what you want it to and not represent reality. Without me here to keep it all in check, you'll keep changing the parameters of what happens until you've got it completely wrong." To hammer home his point, he brought up that final image of Uriel standing over Cora, as seen through his eyes. "Two minutes ago, you thought you could beat him, and without me in your imagination to keep it real, you would've. Over and over again, and every time you'd have patted yourself on the back for a job well done until you had yourself convinced that you could take on the real Uriel and win just as easily." He gestured again to the image and looked down at Cora's mollified face at his side. "Need I say more?"

"Gotcha," she murmured.

"Then let's get out of here. I don't know about you, but I'm starving."

* * *

Avis returned to the physical realm, extremely proud of Cora despite her brainless swipe at his past. In less than a day, he'd watched her grow from barely being able to send out mental commands to being fully capable of mind-raping and destroying any target mind she chose at will. And with that last lesson about the importance of choosing targets based on their ability to retaliate still so fresh in her mind, she'd have something to think about over lunch. There wasn't any point in stealing knowledge if she wasn't going to live long enough to use it.

The look on Clarise's face suggested she suspected what he'd done, to which he smiled without responding. He wouldn't lie if she asked, but if she couldn't bring herself to ask the question, she'd never know for sure. That was the Mystallian way.

"Did you accomplish what you set out to teach her?"

See? That wasn't so hard, was it? Still on his haunches in front of the girls, Avis glanced at Cora and shot her a crafty wink. "For now," he admitted, as Cora matched his secretive smirk and tried to look anywhere but at her mother. Clarise would've pitched a fit if she knew just how long they'd been gone. But before he could think of something to change the subject, the scent of freshly cooked chicken lathered in herb butter interrupted his train of thought and his head swung to where the servants were busily preparing their lunch on a blanket nearby.

His stomach growled and his mouth salivated all at once.

"I assume Asgardian food meets with your approval, my love?"

Avis didn't bother answering what they both knew was true. Instead, he hooked Columbine under the arms again and rose to his full height, settling her on his hip with his right arm banded around her waist. His left hand went behind Cora's back to guide her over to the lunch blanket.

"You carry her a great deal, beloved," Clarise said, her tone not quite reproachful but definitely bordering on it.

Not knowing why that would be such a problem, Avis looked over Columbine's head to where his wife walked at his side. "So?"

"You are spoiling her."

Avis still didn't see the problem. His girls were his to spoil any way he saw fit, and if he wanted to enjoy the way Columbine snuggled up to him as he carried her; no one was going to stop him. But rather than repeat his previous answer, he shrugged as if he didn't care and led them over to the blanket, depositing Columbine on the nearest cushion. Thankfully, Clarise let the subject go, but he could see in her eyes as they took up their cushions on opposite sides of the blanket that she still wasn't overly impressed.

Cora took the cushion to his right and the meal came and went with minimal fuss. Each course had Avis introducing them to some of his personal favourites and delighted in the way they reacted so positively to them.

Once he finished the last mouthful of ambrosia, he placed the empty goblet on the blanket and rose to his feet, dusting his hands against his leggings. "I'm going to go for a walk to stretch my legs before we head out again." He walked around behind Cora to stand at Clarise's side and held out a hand to her invitingly. "Care to join me, sweetheart?"

Clarise smiled and slid her hand into his, allowing him to help her to her feet.

"We'll be back shortly," he said to both girls as Clarise cast a stimulation wave to rid herself of sand. "If you choose to wander, don't go far, and make sure you take at least one of the servants—*and one of the guards*—with you." The latter was said loudly enough to include the missing brute squad, wherever they were watching from. He knew they already had their orders not to let anything happen to the family, but he wanted to remind them of it anyway.

"Yes, father," both girls replied, though of the two, Columbine was the more believable.

Avis looked pointedly at Gingen, Cora's governess, who dipped her head at the unspoken command. Cora would be watched.

Satisfied, Avis dropped his arm across Clarise's shoulder and stepped out towards the boulders at the far end of the beach.

As soon as they were out of sight, Clarise said, "You really should not be carrying Columbine around as much as you do."

"Why not?"

"She will grow to expect it all the time, and then you will be carrying her for the rest of existence."

Avis thought about carrying Columbine as a teen or young woman and snorted at the absurdity. "You worry too much, sweetheart," he said, rolling her left shoulder around in front of him so he could plant a kiss against her hair. "She's not going to be little forever, and I'm just making the most of this time while she is."

"No doubt she is also enjoying her time with you as well," Clarise agreed, moving away from him just enough to slide her fingers through his.

For the next half an hour or so, Avis and Clarise strolled hand in hand down the sandy beach, simply taking the time to appreciate the peace of being together alone. He loved his girls more than he'd ever thought possible, but sometimes just knowing they weren't right under his feet gave him a moment to breathe for himself. She was right. The girls had four hellion servants, and at least two, probably three of the brute squad guards, so what could possibly go wrong?

One thing Avis could never be accused of was not having an overactive imagination, especially after two years of being incarcerated in Hell as one of the Damned. And since he was stupid enough to ask himself that question, he was now visualising just how horribly wrong everything could have gone in his absence. Every step away from them brought another possibility even worse than the one before it and with it, a deeper wave of dread.

Clarise seemed to sense the shift in him because she turned them back towards the lunch site without asking. "It would seem I am not the only one who worries too much," she mused, disentangling her fingers from his. Before he could ask what she was doing, she slipped her arm around his waist and rested the side of her head against his pec. "They will be fine, beloved."

Avis draped his arm across her shoulders and squeezed. "They'd better be." The words may have sounded more ominous than he meant them, but he honestly didn't know what he'd do if they weren't. What was he thinking, letting them out of his sight? What if the Asgardians found them and descended? Loki could be killing his girls this very second, and the only way he'd know was when their familial link winked out and it would be too late! What a fucking idiot he was to leave them alone! Or worse, what if the Midgardians had found them? He couldn't bear it if he came upon them the way they'd found Chance all those eons ago. It would destroy him. Or what if it was a blend of both? What if Loki was there, making the mortals enslave them?

The mere thought of something so calamitous had him wanting to sprint back to the girls, and not even the lavender fragrance of his wife could deter him from imagining the worst. "Avis, I swear they will be fine. You need to learn to relax, or you are going to give yourself a mortal heart attack."

Avis ignored the insult of suffering any kind of mortal affliction. "But what if they're not, Clarise? We're here and they're there. We have no way of knowing for sure ..."

Clarise pulled around in front of him and stopped with her hands pressed against his chest, forcing him to either stop or run over the top of her to get back to the girls. The choice wasn't as clear cut for him as it probably should've been.

"Avis, enough. The presence of Highborn Hellion Guard, the four hellion servants and the girls' own ranged abilities disagrees with your assessment. We *do* know for sure they are fine." She slid her hands up his chest and around his throat, spearing the hair around his ears with her fingers. "Everything is just fine," she promised, rubbing her fingertips across the back of his head in a soft massage.

Avis was just as determined to resist her ministrations. "But we can't know that for sure, can we? The Asgardians are all powerful here. What if Odin uses his magic? What if ..."

"Teon had four innate magic users within their pantheon and a powerbase structured around invincibility to protect them all, and none of that saved them in the end. The Highborn Hellion Guard are unstoppable in all realms, and we have four of them, protecting the four of us. We could not be any safer." She then pulled him down for a long kiss, determined to break through his fixation.

Avis tried to convince himself of her logic. He really did. At times, he almost thought he had. But then another possibility, worse than its predecessors, sparked to life inside him. Finally, he jerked his head away from her. "I can't, sweetheart. I can't relax while you and the girls are so vulnerable and away from my protection. None of you are established, and it scares the cr—the life out of me that I could wake up one day, and you're gone. Forever." Just the thought of it had him looking down the length of the beach, willing the girls to come into view.

Clarise pinched his chin between her thumb and forefinger and tilted his head so he was looking down at her. "Does that mean I have your word that once we are established, you will no longer behave so irrationally about our safety?"

He was about to say, 'Yes, Of course!' and follow that statement with all the relevant body gestures to convey his stance, until he remembered who he was talking to. Then his assurance dwindled as the truth dawned on him and his upper lip curled into a half-sneer of frustrated annoyance. "Probably not." The admission pissed him off.

"Good."

Ahh—what?

Her response startled him, but the dazzling smile she wore right before she kissed him again removed any chance he had of dwelling on it. One of his arms closed around her shoulders while the other snaked around her waist, securing her to him. He could never get enough of this woman.

Eventually, Clarise sucked his tongue between her teeth and nipped it to break them apart. "Yes, good," she repeated, determined to make her reasons understood. "Because no parent worthy of the title ever completely stops worrying about their children."

Which brought his mind full circle to the girls being left on the beach. "We need to get back to them," he said, not quite willing to say 'I' in case that came across as a weakness on his part.

Clarise's smile was indulgent as she hooked her hand through his elbow. "Very well."

CHAPTER TWENTY-TWO

As Avis and Clarise rounded the last boulder that separated them from the girls, Avis' heart leapt straight into his mouth. Four strange men were clustered in a loose semi-circle around his girls, with two women standing behind them. One of the two men directly in front of the girls had knelt down beside his companion, making him more difficult to spot, but being twice to three times the size of the one still standing meant nothing would hide his immense bulk for long.

No words were being exchanged as a series of soft, hauntingly sweet notes drifted on the ocean breeze towards them. "Uhhh—very well done," the man on one knee finally said in Asgardian once the tune died away. "You must have done this before, sweetling."

Through the legs of the standing men, Avis saw Columbine lower a thin reed whistle.

"Like I said, my sister doesn't talk much," Cora answered, in fluent Asgardian. "But she's an accomplished skald who picks things up very quickly."

The man who stood alongside the kneeler hooked the thumb of his right hand into his sword belt and eyed Cora suspiciously. "As do you," he said, probably picking up on her advanced speech.

Avis wasted no more time trying to play catch-up. He launched into the mind of the nearest warrior to him (the one standing with his back to Avis) with every intention of reducing him to a physical shell. But as soon as he crossed the threshold, he recognised Tilu's consciousness and skidded to a halt. *Well, alright then,* he thought, making his way through her recent memories until he reached the part where he and Clarise had left. *I'm guessing that makes Frash the other warrior on Columbine's side.* It was quick thinking on the part of the two servants, somehow knowing two children and four serving women would be harassed by the mortal males, whereas two strong, male bodyguards would be taken more seriously.

He skipped over the parts where the girls played on the beach and started watching in real time how the two men had approached them from the dense, snow-covered woodlands. Tilu had viewed their approach as a potential threat and followed her sister's lead, shifting from a 'helpless' female servant into a fully armed male bodyguard.

The encroachers never deviated, though they did slow down long enough to cast an admiring look at the four 'horses' that grazed on the frozen grasslands. The smaller of the two even went as far as to attempt to stroke the neck of the nearest steed, though it stepped aside and issued an irritated snort of warning.

"Hey! Get away from them!" Cora bellowed from across the beach, more loudly than was naturally possible.

Both men had the instincts of fighters, immediately going for their swords as they swung in her direction. Then, seeing it was only a girl-child who addressed them, they looked at each other and chuckled, releasing the hilts of their swords. The smaller one shouted something back as they approached, though to Tilu it was nothing more than jumbled nonsense.

Avis pulled back from Tilu's mind and rebounded straight into the smaller of the two outsiders still standing in front of his girls. The mental command of **'if you**

wish to address us, you will do so using our titles' appeared in the forefront of the man's mind like a curtain, ready to dominate every decision he was ever going to have. Avis recognised Cora's handiwork, but ignored it for now in favour of learning more about these men. A quick perusal of his past identified him as Arrik the Chosen, the ruling Jarl of the district. The huge man kneeling at his side was his younger brother, Geir.

Avis skimmed through Arrik's history at high speed. From what he saw, neither brother had had an easy life. Having had their Jarl status stripped from them as children, the two had fought long and hard to have it returned to them, taking back over twice as much land as what had originally been stolen. Both were very accomplished warriors, though Geir was the more brutal of the pair. More relevant to Avis, they were both married with large families (in Geir's case, a gaggle of no less than nine girls for the brute to fuss over) so they knew how to behave around women and children. That was probably their only saving grace. Too many men who lived for nothing but the raid would've tried to kill the guards and taken the women, children and horses for themselves.

And in truth, Arrik had considered it. He wouldn't be an Asgardian if he hadn't. But he was also the intelligent one of the pair, and the odds of this seemingly under-guarded party just appearing on a beach not half a *rost* from his *herred* without any kind of sea vessel to assist them made him very wary. Especially when he could've sworn he saw four women and two girls on the beach, and now it was two warriors and two women. He'd suspected some level of magic, and until he got to the bottom of it, he was going to be on his best behaviour.

Which was lucky for him.

Geir it seemed, had always followed his brother's lead, and when it became clear they weren't going to just take everything by force, the big brute started a conversation with the girls by gently asking their names.

Cora tilted her head, and a moment later, answered, "I'm Lady Cora, and this is my sister, Lady Columbine," in perfect Asgardian.

"And these are your servants?" Arrik asked, his point of view shifting more to the pair of warriors who stood silently on either side of the girls than the two women behind them.

Avis froze the scene and took a moment to bask in the cleverness of his older daughter. *Nicely done, tiger,* for Arrik's ability to speak now and Geir's congratulatory words previously had meant she hadn't stolen the language outright from either warrior. That had been his initial concern, but thankfully, she'd heeded his warning against it. No doubt he was going to hear about it next time they were alone, given how long she'd been poking around in their minds to get their language down so perfectly. A month or so at least. Maybe two. He restarted the memory.

"They are," Cora answered, although Avis had already forgotten what the question was.

Arrik looked back at the girls. "And where are your parents, child?"

Cora's whole demeanour changed and she peered up at him icily. "Call me child just one more time," she challenged, placing her left hand on her hip, her expression bearing an eerie similarity to her mother's when Clarise was pissed.

"Are you not a child, sweetling?" Geir asked, attempting to defuse the situation with flattery.

"Depends," Cora replied, not permitting herself to be swayed in the slightest. "Are either of you two likely to answer to '*boy*'?"

The two men looked at each other in surprise. Then Arrik cleared his throat. "Very well. Where are your parents, *Cora*?" He used her name to prove he had been listening.

"*Lady* Cora. And my sister is *Lady* Columbine. **If you wish to address us, you will do so using our titles.** I'll accept nothing less."

So that's what that was all about. Avis twisted his lips to one side, torn between his growing pride in her handiwork and the need to marginally correct it now that he understood the context. The 'us' could relate to anyone with a title, making the command a little ambiguous.

Then again, what did he care if the Jarl showed appropriate manners to everyone for the rest of his life?

"Lady Cora, where would we find your parents?"

"They're nearby," she answered, as if he were the realm's greatest idiot for assuming she'd admit how alone they were.

Arrik very, very slowly ran his tongue over his cracked lips to moisten them and it was clear from his thunderous thoughts that he wasn't accustomed to being spoken to this way at all. "Very well, *Lady* Cora. I am Jarl Arrik Arisson and this is my brother Geir Arisson."

"The Chosen of Thor," Cora said, appearing to take more interest in the older brother now that he'd identified himself. "I've heard of you."

Avis laughed long and loud at Cora's natural flair for bending and knowledge adaptation. Regardless of which brother she had latched onto for information, it was clear she'd done a hell of a lot more than just learn the Asgardian language. She'd done her research and probably knew more about this community of mortals than he did.

Geir, it seemed, was more interested in Columbine. As Arrik watched on, the big man knelt down before the younger girl and smiled warmly. "You are a pretty little thing, Lady Columbine," he said, though the gleam in his eyes was more sympathetic than admiring.

Columbine tilted her head, her tiny dark eyes darting between the man and her sister.

Cora then said something which Arrik couldn't interpret, to which Columbine smiled and rolled her shoulders shyly.

"What language is that?" Arrik asked.

"None you would've heard before. My sister's gift is music. Mine is languages."

Nice. The mortal wasn't to know they were visiting celestials, and that her ability to learn any language came from her bending: a gift her sister didn't share. He made a mental note to teach Columbine the Asgardian language just as soon as he was done here.

Arrik tried to make the most of Cora's information. His point of view moved across to Tilu (whom he thought was male) arrowing in on the location of all her various weapons. Like her sister, Tilu had created a veritable arsenal. "So your guards can't understand a word I'm saying?" His thoughts were as ominous as his tone.

Both Frash and Tilu stiffened and shifted their weights forward semi-aggressively. "They all read body language just fine," Cora answered, elusively referring to the real bodyguards hidden nearby as much as the four hellion servants with them.

"And you like music, sweetling," Geir said, reaching inside his fur vest.

At that point, Avis stopped looking through the memories and went back to the one where Arrik thought he'd seen four women on the beach. "No, you didn't," he mused to himself as he plucked that memory out and replaced it with one of two men and two women, then went forward and blanketed Arrik's later questioning thought. Everything else he left as it was including his confusion about their means of arrival. After all, a healthy dose of WTF never hurt anyone.

Avis pulled out of Arrik's mind and moved onto Geir. A quick glimpse at the man's past added flavour to what he'd already seen in Arrik's mind. Something he'd missed in Arrik was the fact both men had been virgins up until twelve years ago. At twenty-five and thirty-six, that was almost unheard of amongst mortal males, but that also went to show just how dedicated they were to winning back their birthrights. With almost two dozen legitimate kids between them now, being the region's Jarl and Jarl's warrior brother had obviously allowed them to make up for lost time. Geir was also definitely the brute of the pair. Where Arrik was surgical in his strikes, Geir preferred to bathe in the blood of his enemies.

But Geir felt sorry for Columbine and his 'pretty' comment had been offered out of pity rather than honesty, finding her dark locks the most horrible choice of hair colour. Having matching eyes was just too sad for words. He felt his low opinion of her was confirmed when she acted so shyly to his compliment, as if no one had ever offered them before because she was so ugly. Such a sweet little soul in such an unsightly wrapper.

Of course, Avis knew all about the Asgardians' biased bullshit towards black hair, often connecting it to malevolent spirits and general bad character. The first few years he'd spent in that pantheon's company had often put him at loggerheads with different members of the Aesir, who thought their narrow-minded opinions of him could be voiced because he was the non-shifting outsider. The Vanir were smart enough to say nothing of what they were thinking, which meant Avis only had to take half of the Asgardian pantheon to task. Odin appreciated a formidable warrior when he faced one, and in short order, they went from being bitter enemies to the closest of drinking allies.

As mad as he'd been when the Aesir dumped on him for his appearance, it was nothing compared to how furious he was at the thought of these pathetic fucking mortals looking down on his precious little princess like that. His baby was beautiful, and if he had to lay waste to the whole fucking planet to make them see that ...!

The only ... *only* thing that stopped him from completely obliterating Geir's mind was the way the mortal's heart bled for his baby girl and how determined he was to make her feel better about herself, if only for a few minutes. His compassion earned him a *temporary* reprieve.

When the sister mentioned her love for music, Geir pulled out a short reed pipe the length of his forearm with a dozen holes down the front and held it still just long enough to guarantee he had Columbine's attention. Then he lifted it to his mouth and played a series of notes one after the other in a simplified melody Avis recognised as an Asgardian nursery rhyme. Geir watched Columbine as he played the tune twice more, noting the way her fingers flexed in mimicry of his own. "Would you like to try?" he asked, knowing she wouldn't understand his words but saying them anyway as he held out the pipe to her.

Columbine took the pipe and with her fingers covering the relevant holes to play the first note, gave it a cursory blow. The sound was horrendously off-key, but as Geir reached to take it back, she pulled away and tried again. It still wasn't perfect, but it was much closer. "Try again," Geir said, rolling his fingers encouragingly.

The third time was closer still, and by the fourth, she had it. Then, she began to truly play. What started as Geir's simplistic nursery rhyme quickly morphed into a haunting melody that only the most accomplished of musicians could match. Geir looked up at his brother, seeing shock also mirrored in the older man's expression.

"Uhhh—very well done," he'd said, for something needed to be. After swallowing heavily, he added, "You must have done this before, sweeting."

Still on her feet, Cora placed her hand on Columbine's shoulder. "Like I said, my sister doesn't talk much, but she's an accomplished skald who picks things up very quickly."

"As do you," Arrik said, bringing Avis up to date with the conversation.

Avis left Geir's mind and returned to the physical realm. His right foot had moved a grand total of two finger widths in the time it took to see into all three minds. As his boot landed heavily in the frozen sand with a crunch, he proceeded forward with Clarise at his side. "Warriors," he called, by way of greeting.

Geir jumped to his feet and Arrik turned, both once again going for their swords. This time, their hands stayed on their hilts, because neither of them had made it this far by being stupid. Frash and Tilu bowed their heads forward. "Milord, milady," they both said in unison.

Arrik seemed happier to be dealing with genuine adults over a girl-child with an adult level of understanding. "From where do you originate, stranger?" he asked, straightening to his full height.

"Farther than you've ever been," Avis replied, as he and Clarise joined the small gathering. It was no accident that he put himself between the strangers and his daughters; nor that of the two sides, it was the men who were forced to step away. Clarise remained on Avis' left, keeping both men within line of sight.

"Evidently, or you would not have abandoned your children in what most would consider an unfriendly environment."

Avis' eyes narrowed and the muscles bunched along his jaw. *You arrogant little fucker!* he fumed. Raising a hand, he rolled his wrist forward and pointed his splayed fingers at the ground between them. If nothing came of it, it would look as if he were angrily shutting down the conversation, though since the demon steeds and servants registered intent, he was sincerely hoping the other more combative hellions in their vicinity would as well.

He wasn't disappointed.

Both men gasped and leapt back a full body length as hundreds of thousands of arrows from what appeared to be just as many directions suddenly speared the ground between them. In just a few seconds, they were so densely packed together that Avis could've easily stepped up onto them and walked across the platform they created. He showed no reaction to the militant display and was pleased when Clarise didn't either, as if they both expected it.

With a curse he was glad the women couldn't understand, the men drew their swords and swung their backs into each other, protecting each other's flank. Both had their knees bent in anticipation of battle, their eyes scanning the nearby terrain. "How many men do you have out there watching us?" Geir snarled, no longer the charming father-figure.

"Enough to assure you that my children were *never* in any danger." The truth without specifics. Over the last six months, he'd learned how to speak 'Clarise'.

"This is not an invasion, Jarl Arrik," Clarise added in fluent Asgardian. "We are visitors passing through and will be gone shortly, never to be seen again in your lifetime."

Avis tried really hard to not react to Clarise's inclusion to the conversation, though inside he was having his own WTF moment. To his knowledge, she'd never been outside the Well of Hell, so when in the realms had she learned to speak Asgardian? Worse, she *had* understood their cursing. He stared at her for so long that she squeezed his elbow and shook her head ever so slightly, drawing him out of his daze.

With no other hostilities presenting themselves, Arrik straightened up and cautiously sheathed his sword, shooting Geir a look to do likewise. After a few seconds of relative peace, Arrik said, "If you swear to leave your army out here, I will welcome you into my home for a true celebratory respite."

"You have our word, our army will remain out here, provided our servants, our guards and our horses stay with us," Clarise answered, just as respectfully. Hearing exactly how she worded that, Avis glanced down at her again, this time fighting to keep the sly grin from curling at the corners of his lips. All hail his beautiful queen of misdirection. He hid it behind a kiss to her hair, then lifted his head and looked back at Arrik, silently giving his beloved wife the floor.

"That is entirely acceptable ... Lady ...?"

"Lady Clarise, and my husband, Lord Avis."

The transition from a total freak out to an invitation to dinner was a little too conspicuous for Avis' dubious nature, and a cursory look over Arrik's thoughts revealed the mortal's intent was two-fold. Midgardians believed in offering hospitality to travellers in the hopes of gaining that hospitality themselves in time to come, but that hospitality usually spread to include everyone in the travelling party. Ever the battle strategist, Arrik was deliberately attempting to separate this family of strangers from what he perceived to be their powerful army and in the process win them over with his generosity before another Jarl could. Failing to do that, his backup plan was to hold them all hostage until terms of the army's surrender could be agreed upon. The latter was definitely a last resort, as the Jarl and his family were popular with their people, and Arrik didn't want the type of bad karma that came from being an ungracious host.

Avis huffed. The dumb shit had no idea how bad the fucking karma would be if he tried that.

"We are actually celebrating the return of Sol as this is the first day she has graced us with her presence after being eaten by Hati yesterday. Geir and I were game hunting when we came upon you."

"With only your swords and daggers?" Avis asked, arching an eyebrow sceptically.

Geir twisted his lips in irritation as he thumbed over his shoulder. "The rest of our kit is back at the edge of the forest."

Arrik gestured towards the four horses grazing nearby. "We didn't want to accidentally harm such beautiful specimens if we could avoid it."

"You should see them at their best. They're on fire then." Avis chuckled at the double meaning that he knew would be lost on the men. But instead of laughing with him, Clarise pressed her forehead against his upper arm and Cora openly groaned in the background. Well, he'd thought it was funny. "Go back and gather your supplies, gentlemen. We'll meet you at the forest's edge in a few minutes." The statement which left no room for negotiation, was perhaps the closest Avis had ever gone to having a meeting of the minds with mortals, and the need to do so doused his good mood considerably.

The men could've argued, but self-preservation instincts ran high in this pair and they seemed to sense now was not the time to assert themselves. With a curt nod, they backtracked to the edge of the woods, where they started gathering up their supplies.

It gave Avis the chance to address Clarise's multi-lingual capability. "When did you learn Asgardian?" he asked, turning to face her.

Clarise met his gaze unwaveringly. "I have spent my whole life in preparation for my eventual marriage. All places. All cultures. All expectations. I would hardly be the epitome of a perfect wife, if I was presented to my husband-to-be without fully comprehending his language and expectations of me, would I?"

Avis couldn't fault that, though he was having a hard time wrapping his mind around the colossal waste of time and energy that every Highborn Hellion lady undertook as the norm. To have to memorise every culture, and every language from every celestial realm ... just so they could impress one person from one realm at some unknown point in the future. And because they couldn't even internalise for a quick review when it was warranted, they'd have to keep studying it. Over, and over again. It was just so fucking stupid!

Not wanting her to read too much into his silence, Avis stepped away from her and hooked Columbine under the arms, lifting her back onto his hip. He hadn't noticed she still had Geir's reed pipe in her hands until its hard, bevelled edges scraped his chest. "I liked what you played," he said, giving her a light squeeze.

But instead of smiling shyly and going all coy as he expected, Columbine sighed and dropped her head onto his shoulder.

"What's wrong, princess?"

"Cora said Geir said I was pretty, but his colour was all wrong when he said it."

Having been inside Geir's head, Avis had a very real sense of where this was going. "What do you mean?" he asked, hoping he was wrong.

Columbine shifted the pipe to her left hand and hooked her right around his neck. "When you say I am pretty, your colour is a dark blue and it makes me happy. His was ... light purple, and I did not like it at all."

Avis breathed out deeply and kissed her hair. How in the realms was he going to explain this? He glanced at Cora and inspiration struck him. "Alright. Imagine if Cora spent a whole day shape shifting what she thought would be the perfect present for you, and when she gave it to you, you didn't like it at all. I know you've been raised to be honest above all else, but would you really hurt your sister's feelings by telling her you hated it?"

Her eyes rounded and began to glisten with unshed tears. "So, he did *not* think I was pretty?"

Avis had never wanted to throttle a mortal so much in his life! "He was an idiot, princess, and you don't have to care what he thinks. In fact, I'd rather you didn't. He thought you had a beautiful soul, and that's high praise coming from one of them."

Columbine wiped her eyes on his shoulder, then looked past him to where the men were. "Silly mortals. We do not have souls," she said.

Avis chuckled at the apt description and twisted to cast a dirty look at the man himself. "Mortals are always silly," he agreed, using his free hand to both stroke her hair and hold her head against his shoulder. "That's why I don't want you to pay any attention to them, at all. If they say something that annoys you, you step on them and then they're not there to annoy you anymore. Okay, baby?"

Columbine closed her eyes and rolled her face into his neck, though her surface thoughts revealed she wasn't quite onboard with the whole 'stepping on them' part. Not to worry. She'd get there soon enough. All celestials did.

Believing nothing more needed to be said on the matter, he looked across at Clarise and said, "I'm going to internalise with Columbine and teach her the Asgardian language."

One of Clarise's eyebrows arched sharply. "Would it not be more prudent to simply take the knowledge from either of those two?" she asked, her eyes sliding to the men who were now starting to fidget uncomfortably under the intense scrutiny.

Avis glanced briefly at the men again and shook his head, reminding himself that she hadn't been present for the conversation he'd had with Cora about this. Besides, there was a more important reason why he didn't 'simply take their knowledge', as she'd so eloquently put it. "If I do that, Columbine will get a complete understanding of every word in their vocabulary." One side of his lips curled upward in wry amusement, and covering Columbine's exposed ear, he asked in a lowered voice, "Do either of them look like blushing virgins to you, sweetheart?"

"I see." She sighed and clasped her hands before her. "Do not be gone long, beloved."

It was on the tip of his tongue to remind her that internalisation was by its very nature instantaneous to everyone else, but that would sound far too patronising. So he went the safer route of kissing Clarise on the cheek. "Be right back."

He went into Columbine's imagination and recreated their go-to space for her education: the sitting room from his and Clarise's old hellion apartment. He crossed the room and sat down in one of the two comfortable lounge chairs in front of the roaring fire. "Where are you, princess?" he called. Columbine manifested in his lap with her right arm hooked around his neck and her head on his right shoulder, just as she was in the physical realm. The boldness of the move pleased him.

"I am here," she said, snuggling closer to him.

"Yes, you certainly are." He stroked her hair and smiled. "I know you're only little, princess, but I don't like the idea of the Asgardians thinking less of you because you can't speak their language. So we're going to fix that right now." He created a timber bookstand between his knees at just the right reading height. "First, I need you to imagine a book right here, with all the Mystallian words you know in it." It was on the tip of his tongue to have her make it alphabetical for future reference when he remembered her memory was instantaneous and the order wouldn't matter. Besides, he didn't want to waste any time explaining what the word 'alphabetical' meant.

It was a sad indictment of her age that when the book appeared a heartbeat later, it was barely half the thickness of his little finger. "Okay," he said, swallowing back his disappointment before she had a negative reaction to it. He reached forward and opened the book to the first page. "I'm going to read out the Mystallian word you know, and then say the Asgardian word that means the same thing. Once we've done that, you and I will start building sentences until you're talking normally in Asgardian. Okay?"

Columbine nodded. "Yes, Father."

"Good girl. Here we go …"

CHAPTER TWENTY-THREE

Just as he had with Cora, Avis left Columbine's mind and returned to the physical realm with an immense sense of accomplishment and satisfaction. His little princess had been a natural, accepting everything he'd said and going with the flow until it all clicked inside her tiny mind. What he'd originally thought would take at least a day or two, in fact only took sixteen hours.

"Sorted," he said in Asgardian, shifting Columbine's weight to better view his wife.

"I can speak Asgardian, Mother," Columbine added in the realm's native tongue, confirming his claim. It seemed he wasn't the only one who was immensely proud of her achievement.

"That is very good, dear," Clarise answered with an indulgent smile. "Do you wish to also educate the servants? They do not know the Asgardian language either."

Avis didn't have the heart to tell her he'd already found that out for himself. So, without a word, he slipped into the mind of the nearest servant. The instructions he gave each of them in turn were nowhere near as gentle as he'd been with Columbine. He gave them a similar imagined book on the basics to memorise, but then hammered home their mistakes with ever increasing pain until they stopped making them. Frash especially. He left her until last, knowing his temper would be at its worst by then. It would've been so much easier if they'd just had a drop of bending blood in them. Just one drop of common, bending essence. Then he could have gathered them altogether and done it once instead of repeating the process four fucking times!

Clarise must have guessed his mood by the time he was finished, for without a word from him to say he was done, she slipped her hands through his left elbow and rested her head against his upper arm in silent support.

Avis allowed the scent of her lavender and the love of his family to wash away his vile temper. Meanwhile, Cora let out a thumb and forefinger whistle which brought the demon steeds trotting over to them. She took the reins of the nearest one and slid up onto its back without any help from anyone. Avis gave Clarise a squeeze and stepped away from her to deposit Columbine on the back of another. Clarise went and settled herself onto the third. He ran his eyes over them all one last time, then gathered up the reins of the remaining demon steed and mounted, tightening his grip on the reins to prevent Hotspot from prancing too far forward. (Avis still had no way of differentiating the hellfire beasts from each other at the best of times, so 'Hotspot' was still the designation he gave whichever one he happened to be riding.)

"Do you four know how to ski?" he asked of the servants. Even though they had the strength to walk through neck deep snow as if it didn't exist, that would tip their hand just as fast as the natural form of the demon steeds.

Before he could explain his reasons, a set of wooden skis appeared on the ground beside each of the four servants. They quickly stepped into the centre of each thin wooden plank and held themselves still. The leather straps of the skis took on a life of their own by working their way up their booted feet to secure them in place. Since the skis had been created from range, Avis glanced at his wife. Of the two ladies that still had access to their shifting, he doubted Columbine had ever skied a day in her life. He watched the way Clarise observed the servants and knew his instincts hadn't let him down.

"Move your feet and adapt to the movement," she commanded, as only a Highborn Hellion could. "I will not tolerate you making fools of yourselves before these mortals."

The servants offered no argument and shuffled their feet. Each movement was compensated somehow until they were able to lift their feet and hop from one side to the other with an unnatural level of expertise. *Fucking shifters,* Avis grizzled, good-humouredly. True, he'd learned that skillset even faster back when he'd first found the need to, but that was because he'd stolen the knowledge from some hapless celestial commoner and made it his own, not because of his own merits.

Once they were situated, Avis moved the party forward. As was their custom, the girls rode directly behind them, while Diviten and Gingen took up positions on either side of the girls, leaving Frash and Tilu at the rear. The brute squad remained in hiding.

He led the way to where the men were waiting. Arrik pinched his lips together and lifted his chin at their approach; his eyes locked onto Avis. "It's been a long time since anyone's deliberately made me look up at them, Lord Avis," he growled indignantly.

Red poured into Avis' vision, but a random thought popped into his head before he could retaliate.

KILL HIM, AND HIS SOUL WILL BE ESCORTED TO VALHALLA BY ODIN'S VALKYRIES BECAUSE OF THE NUMEROUS VICTORIES HE HAS ACHIEVED AS A MORTAL WARRIOR. IS THAT WHAT YOU WANT?

Fuck!

Where that thought came from, Avis had no idea, but the point it made was ridiculously valid. Arrik was branded with a birthmark of Thor's Mjolnir across his back and his fighting prowess was known clear across this world. If ever a mortal was going to have his soul escorted to Odin's Hall of Heroes it'd be this worthless piece of shit, and while they sang his praises, his execution at Avis' hands would be all too quickly revealed to the very people he and his family were trying to hide from.

Okay, back to basics … **Anyone under your command, including yourself, who fails to treat Lady Clarise, Lady Cora, Lady Columbine or Lord Avis with the utmost level of respect is to be disciplined most harshly … without being killed.**

While commoners and average warriors wouldn't end up in the Halls of Valhalla after they died, they'd still end up with Hel in Hel. From there, it'd be a coin toss as to whether that icy bitch would notify her father Loki of Avis' presence, depending on how close she was to her deceased half-brother. Despite the seriousness of the situation, he tried not to find it funny that his very next thought was, *Either way, she's a lot closer to him now.* Because unlike other pantheons, the Asgardians not only relied on golden apples to keep themselves immortal, they also had it built into their attunement that their essence wouldn't disappear like other celestials when they died. Instead, it was believed that when Asgardian celestials passed away, they would go on existing alongside their mortal counterparts as denizens of Hel. Doubly stupid, if you asked him. Going from being all-powerful to a trapped slave was the worst possible way to see out the rest of existence.

Arrik immediately dipped his head. "My apologies, m'lord. That was uncalled for."

Geir baulked at his brother's reverence. "What are you doing?" he asked, frowning so deeply his eyebrows touched over his nose. "He's nothing spec—"

His words were cut off as Arrik whirled on his heel and drove his fist into his brother's jaw with enough force to knock him to the ground. "You will address Lord Avis as m'lord, and the Jarl ladies with him as m'lady, and ensure everyone else does as well. Fail me on this, and you and any other heathen will be flogged and branded accordingly." He moved to stand over his prone brother, his fists still clenched. "Understood, *bacrauf?*" *Asshole.*

Clarise sniffed sharply at the use of profanity and Avis kicked himself for forgetting that part. Raising his left hand in her direction, he flared his fingers in both apology and for her continued forbearance, then looked at Arrik's angry back. **You will never swear again in front of Lady Clarise or Lady Columbine again. You will react to others who do so as if the individual had not used Lord and Lady when addressing us.**

Without attunement, Avis could only change the minds of one person at a time, but to make it easier on Arrik, he also implanted the same series of commands in Geir's mind. How long he and his family stayed would be the deciding factor as to whether or not he'd bother with the rest of the region's jarl class or leave it for the ruling brothers to wrangle the lower classes into submission.

"Understood," the younger brother replied, dipping his head in acknowledgement. "It will not happen again, brother."

Arrik stepped back and allowed Geir to clamber to his feet with a nod of acceptance. "This way to our herred, m'lord," he said, taking Hotspot's reins near where they attached to the bit and pointing out the worn path through the trees.

As they travelled on, Avis finally noticed the time difference between the world around them and the glowing bead on the cuff of his glove. The sun was already beginning its descent past the distant mountains, yet the bead sat between his middle and pointer finger, indicating it was roughly an hour after midday in Mystal. This was the opposite of Yaru, where the sun had been beating on their backs for more than seventeen hours a day. Sol was only just starting to reclaim her chariot of daylight, and as such, the sun shone for an hour or two at best.

He glanced back over his shoulder at his daughters, both of whom were wide awake and taking in the wintry landscape with growing fascination. He supposed he couldn't really blame them. The closest thing either of them might have come to a woodland in winter was the rim of Antenora, or the Ninth Level of Hell, and there hadn't been small animals darting across the snow or huge trees that seemed to defy the icy terrain by maintaining their greenery. This place had life.

Remembering how much fun there was to be had in these conditions, Avis cast a quick glance at Clarise. She met his eyes with a twinkle in her own and smiled, but whether she meant to or not, she gave the smallest, *tiniest* headshake which Avis took as a 'no'. Well, as a 'no for now', anyway. He had every intention of introducing the girls to the concept of a snowball fight before they left this world. His lips curled in anticipation of their reaction. Cora would especially love it.

Fifteen minutes later, the sun had disappeared completely, and the party was being led through the darkness by lit torches that the mortals carried with them. Over the rhythmic crunch of the horse's hooves in the snow, Avis heard the movement of other animals that trailed them in the shadows and grinned at the occasional *erk* as something came too close to the travelling Mystallians and paid for it with their lives. The brute squad missed nothing.

In the distance Avis both heard the festive sounds of the settlement and smelt the savoury warmth of cooked foods therein. They might have only just finished lunch, but the delightful fragrance had Avis licking his lips again.

Hunuvatr was a very fruitful herred indeed.

Not giving their guides any forewarning, Avis raised his right hand and pulled the party to a halt. Arrik and his brother swung towards them; surprise written all over their faces.

"I assume your mead hall is just past those trees?" Avis asked with a jut of his chin in that direction, more for the girls' sake than his own. He'd spent many a century inside Odin's mead halls, including Valhalla itself, and he knew all the signs. When the men nodded, he went on. "Then at least one of you should go ahead and let your people know that it's not in their best interest to disrespect us." Again, he wasn't making the concession for the people of Arrik's herred. Personally, he didn't care if Arrik lined up every one of them up and slaughtered them all as bloodily as he could. His concern began and ended with Columbine, and after everything she'd endured on the Akheron River, he'd do everything in his power to protect her from that level of emotional backlash.

"Good idea," Arrik said, and with a quick look at Geir to get his brother's attention, he flicked his head towards the settlement. Geir nodded without a word and skied ahead until only the glowing light of his torch could be seen through the trees. "You picked an auspicious time to visit, m'lord," Arrik said as he tightened his hand on Hotspot's reins and slowly skied forward. "The return of Sol is perhaps the greatest celebration in either season."

Thought so. Avis smirked to himself as he glanced uselessly at the darkness around them. Sol was ordinarily a very punctual goddess, and only ever let the Asgardians down when the great wolf Hati overtook her chariot and swallowed her for a single day each year. Every time she fought for her freedom and escaped the following day, which then started the hunt for her all over again. Eventually, she'd be eaten for good at the beginning of Ragnarok, but for now, her temporary loss served as a reminder of that eventual fate.

"I know," Avis said, for the celestials of Asgard didn't like the darkness of her absence any more than the mortals did and his best friend celebrated her return with gusto. And, on a more personal note, Avis liked the young charioteer as well. Her tenacity to never give up even in the belly of the beast reminded him of the women back home. He glanced over his shoulder at Cora and mentally compared the two, acknowledging one fundamental difference between them. Sol constantly ran from her adversary, whereas Cora, even at this young age, would haul her chariot to a halt and launch herself straight at Hati, taking the fight to the wolf. That was what made her a Mystallian ... and his daughter.

A smile of pride creased his lips, which only deepened into a humorous chuckle when Cora noticed him staring at her and mouthed a peevish 'what?' at him.

Turned as he was, Avis missed the moment when they broke through the crowded woodlands and stepped out onto a snow-covered field, but he quickly swivelled back and swept his eyes over the new terrain. Stone fences cordoned off the fields, though no animals grazed due to the cold. They were probably holed up in any one of the longhouses scattered all over the terrain. But the longhouses were utterly dwarfed by an enormous structure that had more in common with an upended boat hull in the middle of the township. It was at least eighty or ninety metres long, and well over forty wide. Four different doors faced them, each with an awning to prevent snow from entering the opening.

Currently, people were pouring out of all four openings in anticipation of their arrival. Geir stood at the closest door with a well-dressed woman on either side of him. Both women were taller than average, though one had platinum blonde hair and a decorative eyepatch, while the other wore her red hair in a tight braid. In the arms of the second was a squirming infant. But for the fact the woman also bore a slight belly-curve to indicate another child was on the way, Avis wouldn't have paid her any attention at all. Children of various ages lined the wall behind them, all talking amongst themselves with their eyes shifting towards the visitors and away again. Like everyone else in that small group, the blonde woman's poise made her jarl class, and initially Avis assumed that she was Geir's wife until it dawned on him that she stood marginally ahead of Geir. A quick brush through her surface thoughts confirmed she was in fact the wife of Arrik and was none too thrilled by the unexpected arrival of new guests.

As soon as they were within a few metres, Arrik left Avis' side and went to his wife, taking just long enough to remove his skis before giving her a brief kiss on the cheek. Then he turned and raised his hand towards the visiting Mystallians. "Ingun, my wife. These are our honoured guests. Lord Avis." Avis raised an eyebrow without saying a word (not like he owed these mortals anything). "His wife, Lady Clarise." From his peripheral vision, Avis saw Clarise smile and nod ever so slightly. "And their children, Lady Cora and Lady Columbine."

"Geir tells me they are of high jarl ranking," Ingun said, after acknowledging each of them with a curt nod of her own.

Before she could say anything else, Avis implanted the same series of mental commands in her that he had in her husband and brother-by-marriage. "One of the highest," Avis agreed, with a tight pinch of his lips that bordered on a scowl.

Ingun smiled to show she meant no ill-will and lowered her head in reverence. "Of course, m'lord. You and your esteemed family are more than welcome in our home."

"Your menfolk mentioned they were in the process of hunting when they came upon us," Clarise said, injecting herself into the conversation. Avis found her wearing the same indulgent smile she wore when speaking to the children and did his best to mimic it. "Since we stopped them mid-hunt and they have returned empty handed, it would hardly be fitting for us to come to your table without a contribution of our own." She twisted at the hips and made a grand wave towards the back of their party. Avis also turned, more out of curiosity than anything else. As far as he knew, they had no contribution to speak of.

Diviten and Gingen were just as he'd last seen them, standing on their skis alongside their mounted wards. However, Frash and Tilu (still in the guise of muscular men) each carried the carcass of a freshly killed elk across their shoulders which they annoyingly managed to maintain while balanced on their skis.

Fucking shapeshifting shitheads, he huffed, though of the two irritants, it was more the pathetic offering of elk meat that annoyed him the most. He'd rather turn up with nothing at all than put the Mystallian name to the pair of stingy carcasses that were either immature bulls or adult does at best. Pathetic. The lack of even one decent bull was embarrassing enough, but to know both 'men' were hellions that could've shifted either beast into a much bigger contribution and chose not to was just damned insulting.

He was about to say as much too, when a series of audible *oohs* and *ahhs* came from the crowd on either side of the jarls, reminding him he wasn't dealing with celestials. From a mortal perspective, he supposed carrying the two hundred and fifty kilo carcasses across a single set of shoulders might've been seen as impressive.

"See?" he heard Geir whisper, though his excitement made the whisper more of a shout. Frash and Tilu moved forwards on their skis until they stood on either side of Avis and Clarise. Then, as one, they hoisted a shoulder and dipped the other, dropping both carcasses between the two groups with a hefty impact that shook the ground. Avis still felt it was a pitiful offering, though several mortals ran forward to take charge of the beasts. "This is going to be a great Sol celebration."

Three grown men struggled to lift each of the elk, but once they had, they carried them towards the far end of the mead hall.

In the meantime, the four hellion servants manually removed their skis, then rose to their full height and rested them against their shoulders with the tips being buried in the snow at their booted feet. Arrik immediately searched the line of villagers to his right. "Eiris!" he shouted, causing a middle-aged man with reddish hair and beard to gasp in surprise. "Show those men where their lord's horses can be stabled and their skis stowed, then bring them inside. Anyone who can carry an elk across the backwoods in mid-winter by themselves has earned a spot at the high table." That caused a heavy cheer of agreement from those around them, while Eiris rushed forward and took the skis from the two female servants before returning to Tilu's side.

All eyes went to Avis and his family, who had yet to dismount. Arrik gestured towards the main doorway. "There is warmth and a good meal waiting for us inside, m'lord."

Avis glanced at Clarise and grinned. "I also plan to make use of your bath-house at some point," he said. Without taking his eyes from his beloved wife, he slid from Hotspot's back on her side and held out his hand for her to join him on the ground. Clarise slipped her hand into his and dismounted with all the airs and graces of her Highborn Hellion upbringing. Lavender filled his senses and before he could stop himself, he raised her right hand to his lips and kissed her knuckles as he passed his reins behind him to Tilu with the other. He had no way of physically knowing which was which, but Frash had long ago figured out it was better to let her sister deal with him while she remained closer to Clarise; which was probably for the best.

"Of course," Arrik agreed, breaking through Avis' thoughts. "But first, let us get out of the cold. The bath-house will be maintained for the duration of our celebrations, so it will be at your disposal whenever you wish."

"I would have thought you of all people would have had enough of excessive heat for one century, beloved," Clarise said with a cryptic chuckle, knowing her words would pass over the heads of the ignorant mortals around them but remind him of his two-year incarceration in the Nine Levels of Hell.

Avis chuckled himself and drew her into his arms, stooping slightly to nuzzle the hair around her left ear. "But this time, I get to decide when I've had enough, and that makes all the difference to me."

Clarise reached over her shoulder and speared her fingers through his hair to hold his head still, then turned and offered him a quick peck on the lips. "As always, beloved."

Unashamed of his love, Avis nevertheless straightened and looked back to where the girls still sat on their demon steeds. "Let's go, you two," he said, curling two fingers beckoningly. "The sooner we're inside, the sooner we warm up."

The girls quickly slid to the ground, passed their reins to their respective governesses and moved forward to stand with their parents. The governesses then passed the reins to Frash and Tilu, who turned and followed Eiris with all four demon steeds in the same direction as the other men had taken the elk carcasses. Columbine lingered behind Avis' right leg while Cora strode into the foreground and lifted her chin to stare straight at the Jarl's family to get the measure of them. Of the two, Avis approved more of Cora's stance, and released Clarise to slide his hands under Columbine's arms, lifting her up onto his left hip where she'd hopefully find it easier to look at the mortals …

… and in the process, he deliberately ignored the way Clarise smirked and shook her head at him.

Arrik turned and led everyone back into the large mead hall. The temperature shift as Avis passed the threshold of the doorway was intense, especially since he still had on his heavy-weather gear. Hands fell across his shoulders from behind, startling him. But as he went to swing around, Clarise slipped her hand through his elbow and held him in place. "Let Diviten take your heavy furs, beloved," she said, giving him the pointed reminder that he wasn't actually wearing two sets of clothing. The furs had been incorporated into his uniform while his attention was elsewhere, and the only way he was going to be free of their sweltering mass was if he allowed a trusted touch shifter to perform a little subterfuge.

He looked back over his broad shoulders to where Diviten stood with her hands still outstretched and dipped his head once in consent. Diviten's nimble fingers took the collar of his cloak and made it look as if she were peeling back a double layer of thick black fur to reveal the standard Mystallian uniform underneath. Even the fur in his boots and gloves had returned to standard leather, thanks to a brush of her hand and a touch of her booted toe against the back of his boots. A very duplicitous piece of shifting which Avis almost applauded.

When Diviten was done, she folded the heavy fur over one arm and bowed again, stepping to the left of the Mystallian patriarch to repeat the process with Columbine.

"I would prefer to keep our servants with us, Lord Arrik," Clarise said, having shed her own heavy weather clothing. "Do you have anyone trustworthy who could take our furs to wherever we shall be spending the night?"

"Of course," Ingun answered, on behalf of her husband. "Yr," she called. A large, older woman with long grey braids and a weather-worn face shuffled forward. "Take the furs to our longhouse and prepare bedding for our guests." The woman bobbed her head, then gathered up the specified furs and withdrew from the mead hall, all without saying a single word to anyone. "Yr is a mute who has served my family since before I was born," Ingun said with a shrug, answering the question Avis was sure no one cared enough to ask. "Her loyalty is absolute."

"Why are you wearing brown?"

The young voice from nowhere had Avis looking down and to his left where a boy, maybe a year or two older than Cora, was talking to her as if he had the right to. His attire made him one of the jarl children, but rather than knock him on his ass for his impertinence, Avis waited to see how Cora would handle this.

"Why do you care?" his little tiger shot back.

"Because it makes you different to them."

"Your point?" Cora parted her feet and squared her shoulders as she spoke, her small fists sitting loosely against her hips in a blatant dare for him to make anything else of it.

The youngster opened his mouth to speak again but was quickly gagged from behind by an older girl who looked as if she hadn't quite reached puberty. "Hush, Bjorn," she scolded. "They are *faoir's* guests, and unless you want to miss the start of the festivities and tend a sore rear at the same time, you will hold your tongue."

Avis pressed his lips into a tight smirk at the way Cora lifted her chin and snorted in victory. In doing so, she noticed his scrutiny from above and he added a quick wink of endorsement. *That's right, tiger. These are mortals and you don't take shit from any of them, ever. Own them. All. Day. Long.*

CHAPTER TWENTY-FOUR

Having either missed the interaction between their children or choosing to ignore it, Arrik and Ingun led the way past a series of timber tables that were covered in carved bowls of food and wooden utensils. They wouldn't have appeared lesser, except the three tables at the head of the hall were covered in durable tablecloths with metalwork plates and cutlery. Two chairs in the centre of the jarl tables had high backs and intricately carved armrests. *So, where are you going to sit, mortal?* Avis wondered, having already claimed the pair of thrones in his own mind.

Clarise squeezed his elbow again. "If you take their chieftain seats, you will have to bend every person in the room into being alright with that, beloved," she whispered in Mystallian. She made a point of casting her gaze around the room as she spoke. "I think there might be as many as two and a half thousand people here."

"I'm not going to sit in a lesser seat," he growled under his breath. The very suggestion was beyond reprehensible.

The gold in Clarise's eyes softened. "We can easily recreate seating which will surpass the splendour of those two chairs once we're situated. Need I remind you of the reason we are not announcing our presence to the Asgardians themselves?"

Avis scowled thunderously and sank his teeth into the side of his mouth until he tasted blood. He wasn't the same god he'd been back then. He almost regretted having to kill Loki's son; just not enough to forfeit one of his own daughters to balance that blood-debt. Translation: he had to accept the compromise or risk the lives of his girls. *Fucking, motherfucking fuck.*

Columbine rolled her head into his throat and tightened her grip on his neck and he knew in that instant he'd do whatever it took to safeguard them. Whatever it took. And as he tilted his own head to rub his cheek against her glossy ebony hair, somehow he felt more at peace with the necessity.

Arrik and Ingun led them to the jarl tables, gesturing to the chairs specifically to the right of the jarl himself for them to sit at. Seats that were meant for Geir and his family … if the put-out reaction of the big guy's wife was anything to go by. So they weren't to receive the top two seats, but they were going to receive the next best thing. It still stuck in his craw that he and his family would have to take a secondary place to a mortal, but for his girls' sakes, he would.

A dozen or so manned firepits lined the centre of the room. These both cooked the meal and kept the mead hall toasty warm. The combined scents of braised steak, mustard seeds, garlic infused baked vegetables, fresh breads and veal stew had Avis licking his lips despite his simmering mood. Slaves stirred large stew pots that hung over the fire by heavy chains from the rafters. The simple attire of the slaves and their down-trodden attitude made them easy to identify amongst the freemen, and he hoped Columbine wouldn't grow curious about why they felt so miserable. Slavery wasn't something he wanted to explain to her … like, ever.

Geir and his family claimed the next set of seats to Clarise's right, who in turn pushed others around the table until the lowest ranked mortals had to find another place to sit at the timber tables. When that space was filled, seating moved onto stools, then cushions, until finally a rug was provided for the nameless peons at the bottom of their mortal pecking order.

Cora and Columbine sat between him and Clarise, where he could keep an eye on them. This would not be the case when they returned to Mystal, but while they were in an environment he couldn't ultimately control, he wanted to keep them close, where it was safer. Columbine sat next to him; Cora alongside her mother. Two seats between Geir's family and the next were left for Frash and Tilu, when they returned. Avis watched as slaves carrying urns made their way around the table, filling up horns as they went. Arrik and his family held up horns to be filled without thinking … even the youngest of children who were years younger than his girls.

Clarise accepted a horn of fruit wine and after sampling it, smiled warmly in appreciation and began a conversation with the red headed wife of Geir. Avis heard something about babies or pregnancy or some such and immediately zoned out.

As promised, Diviten and Gingen shifted the seats in gradual increments until Avis and his family sat on high-back thrones of their own. He still wasn't happy with the original downgrade, but since the fault for their low profile was his, he forced himself not to dwell on it.

Seeking something to distract him, his peripheral vision snagged on a subtle shaking motion low and behind his family's chairs. He wouldn't have noticed it at all, except the ornamentation on it glinted in the firelight, drawing his eye. Taking a deep breath, he stretched his spine upwards and arched back into the chair, casting a casual look down the backs of his family. There, between Cora and her mother down at seat level, he spied a drinking horn being shaken discreetly.

His gaze narrowed. *Really* …

When he'd told Cora she couldn't have any alcohol until she could handle it, he'd meant she couldn't have celestial alcohol. Mortal liquor was barely water with a fun after-buzz in comparison, and Cora could've swallowed every drop in the room without missing a beat. But it was clear from her actions that she hadn't made that distinction and was seeking to circumvent his call as discreetly as she could. That was the part that pissed him off the most; the deceptiveness of it. Mystallians didn't fucking sneak. If she wanted the wine so badly, she should've either argued her reasons for it, or simply shut up and accepted the fact that she wasn't going to get it.

His scowl deepened when a diligent slave filled her horn, and ignoring everything else that was going on around him, he leaned forward onto his elbows and drummed his fingers against his own drinking horn. He watched Cora out of the corner of his eye, refusing to give her any warning that he was onto her by turning his head.

It wasn't that he *couldn't* get inside her head and force her to comply with his wishes, but this was her mistake to make. She'd chosen to make it, and if she went through with it, she'd bear the painful repercussions of it.

He watched as she brought the horn to her lips; his fingers stilling. *Don't do it, young lady,* he thought to himself. *Don't you dare.*

In defiance of the warning he never said aloud, she went to tip the horn, only to have her tiny nostrils flare and her eyes fly open and she jerked away from the horn as if it reeked. Her brows scrunched in confusion and she cautiously brought it back to give it another tentative sniff.

A single-word surface thought then blasted through her mind as her eyes shot to her left.

MOTHER!

Wondering what Clarise had done, Avis pried a little deeper and found the wine had been shifted into an extremely bitter concoction that would've turned the stomach of a trash golem if it had been forced to drink it. Nasty, and one he whole-heartedly approved of.

Cora screwed up her nose in a disgusted pout. "So not fair," she grumbled unhappily, dropping the arm that held the drink to the table but holding it in such a way it didn't spill everywhere.

Clarise interrupted her conversation with the red-headed wife of Geir just long enough to say, "Your father told you no alcohol until you were able to cope with it and you should have adhered to that ruling." Not once did she break eye contact with Geir's wife as she spoke.

"But it's not even real wine," Cora mumbled under her breath in Mystallian. "It's mortal garbage, for Hell's sake."

"And that should've been your opening argument instead of trying to sneak it past us like a worthless slae-el," Avis chimed in, a long way from happy himself. "You try that stunt again, and I'll kick your tail so hard between your teeth that you'll be spitting out pieces of leather for a month. You understand me, tiger?"

Cora stared at the heavily laden table before them, rubbing her pursed lips together in a conversation she refused to have aloud. Avis chose to stay out of her surface thoughts for that one, mainly because he didn't want to lose his temper and really hurt her, should she be mentally calling him every name under the sun. Which was why, when she finally twisted her head towards him and met his eyes, her next question took him by surprise. "Which part was worse? The fact that I went after the wine even though you told me 'no', or the way I tried to sneak it past you?"

"More the latter," he admitted. "Mystallians don't prowl around in the shadows. We go after what we want … in a frontal charge. Observe." He looked over his shoulder to where Diviten and Gingen loitered. "Either one of you," he said, tapping his finger against the horn to get their attention. He didn't know one from the other in their natural forms (let alone these Mystallianised shapes they currently wore) but when one stepped up behind his chair, he held up his horn. "Do something about this slop they call wine."

Without a word, the servant took the horn, held it, then passed it back to him with a reverent dip of her head. Already the familiar scent of ambrosia filled his nose as he lifted the goblet to his lips and took a sampling sip. "Much better," he said, nodding at the female happily.

"Am I allowed to do that?" Cora asked.

Avis huffed and took a much deeper swallow of his ambrosia. "Not now," he answered flatly.

He fully expected to hear her favourite 'it's not fair' catchphrase whenever she didn't get her own way, but instead Cora went back to glaring at the table as if it was somehow to blame.

"The way I see it, you have two choices, tiger," he declared, deciding to throw her a bone—Mystallian style. "You either drink what's in that horn because it's your fault it's there, or you can go without any kind of drink except water for the rest of the night. Those are your choices. You either fix the mistake you made or wear the consequences of making it."

Avis watched the myriad of emotions flicker through her expression as she mulled over those options. Personally, he'd have gone with option two and forfeited the drink for a single night, but he knew his tiger was just stubborn enough to go for the first option and spend the rest of the night hurling in a bucket somewhere instead.

He saw the moment her eyes took on a steely, single-minded focus that she was going to go for it. And in a single, fluid motion, she brought the horn to her lips and threw her head back, rapidly swallowing mouthful after mouthful of the coarse liquid until there was only air left in the horn. Then she pitched forward and slammed the horn down on the table with enough force to crush it flat against the solid timber surface.

Avis quickly swept through the surface thoughts of every Midgardian around them, pausing just long enough to purge the memory of anyone who happened to notice the feat of celestial strength, though there was little he could do about the crushed horn itself. Then he looked back at Cora.

Her head was still tilted to the side away from her mother and her eyes were closed but not scrunched, as if she were fighting what Avis felt was the inevitable next step of this process. Her body was stiff with every muscle locked into place.

Then, ever so slowly, she relaxed, opened her eyes and stared at him in rock-solid triumph. "Done," she declared, though the word came out more like a pant.

Avis acknowledged her success with a growing smile. "You must have a cast-iron stomach, tiger," he mused.

"So, do I get to try the Asgardian wine now?"

Avis looked over her head and gestured for the nearest wine bearing slave to come forward. "I hope it was worth it, tiger," he said, doubting that would be the case. No matter how good the wine tasted, (and in his opinion it wasn't that great) sitting on a base of sour sludge that had to be coating the upper half of her digestive tract would destroy any enjoyment the flavour would otherwise bring.

As the slave sidled up beside them, Cora held up her perfectly restored horn in expectation of the liquor and Avis frowned, wondering who had repaired it for her. It couldn't have been the servants. They needed touch. Nor could it be Clarise, since she was chatting to Geir's wife. That left Columbine. He felt confident in his assumption, especially when he cocked an eyebrow at her and she immediately burst into childish giggles. Her laughter was infectious and he found himself chuckling quietly with her.

Frash and Tilu chose that moment to join them, though they sat on the other side of Geir and his family as honoured guests in their own right. The women easily slotted into the masculine conversation of the men around them, belching over meat bones, drinking heavily from their horns and sharing supposed tales of their various deeds. They didn't even bat an eye when some of the mortal females slipped suggestively into their laps. Avis had to remind himself that it was all an elaborate sham designed to help their master and mistresses blend in with the locals.

As time moved on, the jarl children approached Cora and Columbine with curiosity in their surface thoughts. Avis pretended not to notice, though a quick scan of those interested in Columbine had him vetting the ones who saw her eye and hair colour as repulsive. As tempted as he was to lay waste to their minds (Clarise wanted them all to blend in, and having children intermittently keel over brain dead was the exact opposite of that) they simply decided against coming over and went back to their seats.

Cora could be her own gauge, and he was curious how she'd handle these inferior creatures. Initially, it had been the mid-ranged ones that approached his red-headed tigress, but as their simplistic viewpoints of dolls and play bored her, she sent them away with the same mental dismissal that he'd used on Columbine's 'admirers'. Avis took another swig of his ambrosia to hide his smile. She was such a quick study.

That then brought two of the older boys over: Kori and Gris. Kori had recently hit puberty, if the new arm ring around the boy's right bicep and slew of black tattoos down his left arm were anything to go by. Personally, Avis found tattoos abhorrent. Adding art to clothing and other non-descript items was fine, but to change the pigment of one's own skin by choice went too close to a shifter's mindset for his liking.

Gris was a year or two behind his older brother, and everything Kori wasn't. Where Kori was broad in the shoulders, Gris was lanky. Kori had hair so white he'd be lost in the snow, whereas Gris' locks were fiery red. In fact, the only similarities between the boys were their interest in Cora's apparent adult comprehension and their deportment. Both knew they were the sons of the herred's ruling Jarl and carried themselves accordingly.

"You have a very clever young girl there in Lady Cora," Arrik said, drawing Avis' attention away from the boys.

"Yes," the Mystallian agreed, not particularly interested in the mortal's high praise for his daughter.

"May I ask what draws you through our lands at the peak of winter? Most people choose to travel when the weather is more favourable, especially when children are involved."

"Our agenda is time-critical."

"It must be, for you and your army to be moving with your wife and children at this treacherous time of year." With an almost wry smile, the jarl went onto ask, "So, are you running towards your enemies, or away from them?"

Avis' vision narrowed into a thin slit of red haze and he ever so slowly turned his head to give the mortal his full attention. Celestials in the thousands had perished for assuming less.

* * *

Clarise, who at the time had been listening to Thornor speak of the difficulties of her current pregnancy, immediately held up a finger to silence the woman and swung her head towards her husband. There were a thousand ways he could have handled the jarl's question, and very few of them ended on a positive note. The very best case would be if he laughed it off as a joke and bent the jarl into never bringing it up again. The worst would be if his temper ignited over the assumption that the Mystallian military ran from anything. Unfortunately, she knew which was more likely, especially when the muscles lining his neck and face became corded and the look in his eyes before he turned ever so slowly towards the jarl was one of pure murder.

"Tilu," she called, knowing she had milliseconds to intercede before Avis erupted and this whole festival ended in a bloodbath. "I am certain Jarl Arrik and his herred would much rather see a wrestling match between you and Frash then listen to our numerous exploits." *"Keep it bipedally mortal,"* she added to each of them, vibrating their eardrums without needing to say the words aloud. The two 'men' paused: one with a leg of meat between his/her teeth, the other drinking from a freshly filled horn. As one, they emptied their hands by silently passing the items to their neighbours and rose to their feet; much to the bellowing cheers and applause of the crowd.

While Clarise spoke to the servants, she pushed her right hand under the table beside her knee. Drawing mass in from the floor under her boots, she extended her hand at the wrist and snaked it across the underside of the table above the girls' legs until her long fingers brushed against her husband's larger knee.

Enraged as he was, Avis drew in a sharp breath and bucked at what he probably assumed was a covert attack. But after his hand shot under the table to snatch at hers, he recognised the long, delicate feel of her fingers and his anger immediately abated. The added triple dose of lavender she affixed to her glove didn't hurt matters either. When he turned to look at her, his eyes had lost their murderous intensity and his lips slowly curled in a relaxed smile. He was back. Releasing a breath she wasn't aware she'd been holding; she smiled in return at the way he rubbed his thumb across her knuckles reverently. "They are merely curious, my love," she whispered in Mystallian, pursing her lips in an air kiss to keep him firmly side-tracked. "He meant no insult."

Frash and Tilu quickly cleared the line of jarl tables, while others moved the tables and stools to make as much space as possible for the pair. Ideally, the wrestling match would have taken place in the centre of the hall where the Jarl and his family had a clear view of the rough-housing. However, since the stone firepits that were carved into the ground and the steel pots filled with veal stew and chained to the rafters overhead couldn't be moved by mortal means, the combat would take place down one side of the firepits. A lull fell over the hall as the two demonesses came before Avis and Clarise and bowed at the waist, then turned and canted their heads at Arrik and Ingun. Even the poets that were scattered throughout the room fell silent as everyone eagerly anticipated the brawl. The two combatants turned to face one another. They each raised a single finger to their foreheads in salute of the other's fighting prowess, then dropped the hand and lowered their weight into a wrestler's stance. "Begin!" Arrik bellowed, over the cacophony of the crowd.

Fortunately for everyone's sakes, Frash and Tilu ignored Arrik's shout and waited for Avis' consent before moving. Upon receiving it in the form of a sharp nod, they let out a masculine roar and launched at each other.

The show was more for the mortals around them and as such, Clarise lost interest in what she saw as a mediocre display very quickly. It seemed she wasn't the only one.

"What is that smell?" Ingun asked over the roar of the crowds, having leaned forward to look past her husband at them.

"Lavender," Avis answered, accepting the situation and becoming more sociable now that Clarise's hand was in his and her scent kept him firmly grounded. The heat in his eyes as he continued to stare at her over their children's heads would forever melt her heart. "It's my wife's preferred fragrance."

"And in tight quarters such as these, the scent is sometimes quite powerful," Clarise added, before it occurred to her beloved husband that its strength had been for his benefit.

"It's certainly different," Ingun said, taking another deep sniff. Her face creased thoughtfully. "Some type of floral-pine smell." She sniffed a third time and smiled. "I think I like it. Where did you get it?"

That was a difficult question to answer truthfully. Like all Asgardian worlds, this one spent most of its year in weather too cold to grow the mid-region plant naturally. In that moment, Clarise realised she could give her mortal host something far more valuable than a pair of elk carcasses. Something no other mortal on this world, or any other in this realm would ever procure. And the best part ... it still meant nothing to her.

"Gingen," she called, looking over her shoulder to the servant shadowing them. Gingen straightened attentively. "Go to where our equipment is being stored and bring me one of my potted lavender plants." The request from a mortal perspective was simple enough, and fortunately she knew the governess would be able to read between the lines. *Pretend to go to where our equipment is being stored and add the necessary mass to any unneeded living thing you find along the way. Once you have shifted it into a potted lavender shrub, bring it to me.* The original source of life wasn't limited to either plant or animal. The only prerequisite was 'living', as life was the one thing shifters couldn't create. They could puppet-master a mass and give it a clockwork illusion of life (like they did with constructs), but outside an establishment field like the one her husband had, they couldn't bring to life something that wasn't already living.

"Yes, milady," Gingen answered with a formal bow at the waist.

"You carry these fragrant plants with you?" Thornor cut in, surprise lacing her every word.

"They are a reminder of home," Clarise replied, without necessarily answering the question she was asked. She saw the mischievous gleam in her husband's eyes and batted her own at him innocently.

"*Faoir* says you can play the pipe," a young girl-child said, somewhere in between herself and Avis. Just like that, the spell between them was broken and Avis dropped his eyes to the unfolding scene just as she did. Like Cora, Columbine had drawn the attention of two of the jarl children and she had at some point rotated in her chair to face her admirers. The closet one was a girl a year or so older than Columbine with amber eyes and blonde hair. In her hands was a worn rebec (sized for a child) and a matching bow. "Do you know how to play other things, like this?"

Clarise felt Avis tense and immediately squeezed his hand in reassurance. Their eyes met, and she smiled with a discreet nod. Columbine had this. There was no question in Clarise's mind. The rebec the child was offering their daughter was too similar in design to a violin, which was her father's favourite source of music aside from the screams of the Damned.

"Yes, I know how to play the rebec," Columbine replied, as she took the instrument and placed the base of it between her knees with its neck flush against her sternum. "My grandfather likes an instrument like this very much and he often asks me to play for him." With the fingers of one hand poised over the neck strings in anticipation of her first note, Columbine held out her other hand for the bow. As soon as she had it, she rolled the horsehair towards the body of the rebec and ran the bow across the strings with practiced ease.

People were suddenly torn between the obvious display of violence from Frash and Tilu and the musical mastery of Columbine. The skalds in particular edged ever closer to the jarl table to witness the child playing with more enthusiasm and ability than all of them combined.

Clarise's smile broadened and she used her eyes to draw Avis' attention to the skalds around them. Not that impressing a group of mortals was anything for a celestial to brag about, but Columbine was a very gifted musician, even for them. In just a few notes, Avis' head was also bobbing in time with the beat and his fingers tapped out the tune against Clarise's palm. So long as nothing else provoked him, the beast within him was at ease.

Gingen returned shortly with a small, potted shrub of lavender in her hands. Clarise removed her hand from Avis' grip and waved the servant over. She made a show of inspecting it for flaws, though in actual fact, she was shifting its composition to withstand the colder climate. In deference to the ruling pantheon, she also limited its ability to grow beyond the pot it was currently housed in. That is, the plant would grow, stalks could be broken off, but once the plant broke contact with the soil, it would stop growing. It could never be transplanted or spread like a weed. This one potted shrub would be the beginning and end of lavender in Asgard unless the ruling pantheon decided otherwise. In time, if the jarls realised the significance of the gift and combined with Columbine's musical talent, Cora's advanced intellect and the strength of their 'bodyguards', they would probably realise they had been in the presence of celestials. Those mythical legends would then spread, and since they hadn't identified themselves as belonging to another pantheon, the Asgardians would rightfully take all of the credit for their visit. It would never clear their debt as far as the loss of Loki's son was concerned, but every little bit helped. She just had to make sure Avis shrouded their faces with non-descript shadows and removed their names from the mortals' memories before they left.

Knowing she had Ingun's undivided attention, Clarise handed the potted shrub back to Gingen. "Take this to Jarl Ingun."

Again, the governess bowed and shuffled through the crowd of youngsters to the ruling jarl and his wife. Arrik seemed surprised by the gift, but Ingun took immediate possession of it and ran her fingers through the flower spikes, breathing in the burst of fragrance. Her eyes closed as she savoured the scent. "Thank you," she said, her eyes taking on a dreamy look once she opened them a few seconds later. "I will always treasure this."

"I am certain you will," Clarise agreed.

CHAPTER TWENTY-FIVE

Over the next few hours, Avis kept a close eye on the glowing bead of his left glove. It wasn't that time moved differently on this world. It was just at a different point daylight-wise. The girls had long since left the table and gone in two separate directions with the children who they most affiliated with. Avis wasn't concerned. Not when he had Frash and Tilu follow the girls. The two governesses specifically tasked with the well-being of the girls were quite put-out when they were made to stay with Avis and Clarise, but it wasn't the ladies in servitude that these mortals respected. It was strength. Or rather, a show of strength. He had no doubt that the brute squad were right where they needed to be to keep everyone safe, but the mortals didn't know that. What they saw was a young pair of children with apparently no means of protection. That assumption would absolutely get them killed, which in turn would bring the visiting Asgardian pantheon into the fray. Better for everyone's sake to look the part and keep everybody happy.

Frash and Tilu had thought quickly enough to become men, and it was those males that the mortals respected. Avis also kept tabs on the girls through his familial link. He assumed of the two, the one jerking and weaving all over the place was Cora, since he could picture those motions coinciding with a wrestling match. That made the other link Columbine's. If so, she'd gone to a place not far away from the mead hall and stayed there.

Within minutes, panic began to rear its ugly head as horrific possibilities involving his precious child and the older boys of this village occurred to him. Worse, once he'd thought of it, he couldn't convince himself of another scenario where Columbine could be taken somewhere away from the mead hall and be forced to keep still. Bile rose to the back of his throat until he couldn't ignore it anymore and he shot to his feet, waving for Clarise to stay where she was. It would only take one of them to either confirm Columbine was fine, or lay waste to every fucker in the herred if she wasn't. A quick word of assurance was all he spared her before he charged out of the mead hall in search of Columbine, using their familial link as a celestial homing beacon.

Fear's grip stopped him from noticing the cold. Standard Mystallian leathers were no match for an Asgardian winter (even a mortal one) but right now he had more important matters to take care of. Columbine's link drew him across the frozen ground to a set of twelve stone steps which led up to another longhouse situated higher than any of those in the herred. It wasn't difficult to guess which family lived here.

Ignoring the risk that someone might notice, Avis pushed off the ground with one foot and landed well past the top step on the other. Columbine's well-being and what he would do if she wasn't in perfect condition consumed him.

Snow was banked high on either side of the pathway almost to Avis' shoulder, and the slush on the path itself was ankle deep, showing signs of regular clearing. Mortals would have had to be careful about where their feet fell in order to not break their neck, but Avis was a celestial on a mission and the slush avoided him accordingly. His hand found the door handle and with a quick twist, he stepped over the threshold and down into the longhouse proper. His first thought was to leave the door ajar as a testament to his irritation, but he knew the jarl's longhouse was the most comfortable in the herred, and as such, his family would be staying here for the night. Regardless of his concerns for Columbine, he wasn't about to explain to Clarise his reasons for allowing a metre of snow piled throughout the longhouse.

Giving the door a quick reverse mule kick that had it shutting with a bang, he stalked down the long room. Another much smaller firepit warmed the central building, and on the right, he saw several weaving looms; two with half-finished fabrics still attached to them. Clothes hung over a line against the wall and a single long table, large enough to fit the entire jarl family and any guests they might be entertaining. Avis blew past all of these and only pulled up when he reached an opening to the right that must have led to another wing of the longhouse. His eyes quickly scanned the beds further down the main section of the longhouse, but his familial link with Columbine pointed him down the side wing.

Not wasting another moment, he ducked down the smaller wing which turned out to be a stable—of sorts. Unlike the stables in Mystal, this one consisted of a single large space where all the animals congregated to keep warm. His anxiety soared as he remembered his own alternative uses for a well strawed stable. In fact, the only reason he wasn't losing his ever-loving mind was because Columbine was only five and not even her paternal grandfather had been that sick in the head. Still, Asgardians hid nothing from their children, not even sex, and he couldn't completely rid himself of the notion that they might choose to 'experiment' when they thought no one was looking. The mere thought of it had his fists and teeth clenching so tightly that his jaw started to ache, and his fingers lost sensation. *Motherfuckers …!*

He stalked through the room, zeroing in on his precious child. A torch balanced in a bracket beside the doorway was all the lighting the room had, but it was enough for Avis to adapt to. That, and he heard children's laughter in the left-hand corner of the room which butted up against the main longhouse. As he worked his way through the packed animals, he took solace in the fact that the laughter was childishly innocent.

Okay. Maybe … just maybe … I might've possibly allowed my overactive imagination to potentially get the better of me. He ran his tongue over his parched lips to try and moisten them. *Maybe.*

Using a horse as cover, Avis peered over the beast's back to a penned area in the corner. There he found Columbine, along with many of the herred's younger children. Standing directly behind her was either Frash or Tilu, with his/her arms folded and an indifferent expression on her masculine face. In his frenzy, he'd forgotten he'd sent the servants to shadow the girls.

When she spotted him, she unfolded her arms and bowed her head forward respectfully. *Tilu*, he decided, nodding in return. He couldn't say it was done in approval. Had he been an enemy instead of Columbine's father, he could've gone on the offensive before she reacted—and run afoul of at least one of the brute squad. They were in here too, somewhere. *Shit.* If he'd have remembered either of those facts two minutes ago, he might not have freaked out so badly.

YEAH, KEEP FUCKING TELLING YOUR DUMBASS SELF THAT, YOU FUCKING PARANOID FUCKWIT.

Since when had his subconscious developed a sense of humour?

Avis huffed and rolled his eyes. Apparently, very recently.

A quick glance at the gathered children told him most of them were younger than Columbine and none of them were more than a year or two older. Clearly they weren't engaging in his greatest fear. Instead, they were passing dozens of baby animals to his precious little girl, who cooed over every single one of them. The latest was a greyish ball of fluff that yipped and yelped at being separated from its mother. At least it had, until Columbine cuddled it close to her chest; at which point it settled instantly and even went as far as to lick her on the chin.

"The animals like you, m'lady," a feminine voice from outside the pen said. Avis looked sharply in that direction and found a beefy mortal woman in her mid-fifties leaning against the side wall with her arms and ankles crossed. Her hair was wrapped in a messy bun that had a hand-width of messier plait poking out the bottom, and her face was smeared with what Avis hoped was dirt. She made no effort to approach the children, and for that, Avis found her presence acceptable. That, and he checked her mind and learned she was in charge of all the young animals, especially those with no mother.

"I like them too," Columbine replied, rubbing her cheek against the puppy's fur and nuzzling its neck. Almost casually, her eyes lifted and slid across to him and she beamed shyly while rubbing her cheek against the puppy's plush fur.

It was so realm-damned adorable that Avis almost shivered at its intensity. He should've known he couldn't sneak up on her. Even without a familial link, Columbine would have pinged the approach of his aura. There were no words to describe how proud and scared he was for her at that moment. If anyone figured out she was a celestial empath …

Avis forced himself to smile back at her. "You just be careful, princess," he said, leaning against the horse's back to better view the area. "We still have a long way to go, and most mothers can be very dangerous when they're separated from their young." He knew that from experience.

"Not these ones, m'lord," the older woman assured him.

Irked by her contradiction, Avis' vision narrowed and he slid his gaze towards the woman.

She immediately gasped and stepped away from both him and the pen, stammering, "Th-the mothers of th-these ones are used to their young being handled, m'lord. P-please … I-I meant no disrespect."

Avis ignored her blubbering and returned his gaze to Columbine. "I'm holding you to that, woman," he said, making sure his words and his body language portrayed two different things by smiling warmly at his little girl and even going as far as to add a dash of false amusement to his tone. "You're going to stay right here and ensure none of these animals do any harm to my daughter. When I come to collect her, she must not bear so much as a scratch or a bruise." Not wanting Columbine to understand the next part, he switched up his choice of wording and added in an ominous monotone, "Failure to do so will constitute a catastrophic eradication of your entire lineage, as if your earliest ancestor had never been conceived. If you believe nothing else in your pitiful existence, believe that."

He made a point of looking at Tilu, who dipped her head in understanding. She then eyeballed the mortal woman and hooked her left thumb in the sword belt alongside the sword, drumming her fingers threateningly on the hilt. Credit to the mortal woman – she went even paler than he thought possible. "I-I un-understand, m'lord," she stammered, her eyes wide in terror.

I doubt it, Avis thought to himself, though outwardly, he said, "Good," as if all was right in the realm. And maybe he was in a better mood, since it occurred to him that by having another 'Midgardian' warrior fulfil the threat instead of doing it himself, he would not be the last thing they saw before they died. The difference this made was significant, for it would mean Hel would need to dive beyond the moment-of-death image that all mortals carried with them into the afterlife to learn of his involvement, and the odds of that happening when she dealt with billions upon billions of dead at any given time were slim to none.

As he went to step away, Columbine clambered to her feet without releasing her hold on the squirming animal and moved towards the frightened woman. "Why are you so scared?" she asked, tilting her head to view the taller woman. Her free hand reached out to touch the mortal's forearm in comfort.

"Leave her alone, princess," Avis barked, before she could undo all his threats with her natural kind-heartedness. Columbine's hand jerked away from the woman's arm as if stung and looked across at him in confusion. He immediately cursed the sharpness of his tongue and tried in a more soothing tone, "It's okay, princess. Sometimes people just get scared …" —he met the woman's eyes and added— "… and sometimes those fears are justified. It's just the way of things."

When he looked back, Columbine's brows arched up and disappeared into her hairline and her lips curled into the cutest little pout of consternation that Avis had ever seen. He in turn arched his own eyebrow in a parental way, though he couldn't quite keep the grin from his lips. "I mean it, young lady," he said, switching to Mystallian. "You leave her alone. Just like you did with the Damned on the Akheron River."

It wrecked him to see her expression crumple with that memory and, with another heated curse at himself for not being more careful, he ducked under the neck of the horse and stepped over the small barrier that separated the young younger animals from the older ones. Children scurried out of his way as he waded through them to Columbine, and once he reached her, he scooped her into his arms and settled her on his hip while mindful of the puppy she still held along her left forearm. Twisting on his heels, he used his head and neck to block most of her view of the woman. "She's scared because she needs to be careful, and being afraid will make her be very careful. If you make her feel better, she won't be so careful, and then what she's afraid of will happen. You don't want that, do you, princess?"

Columbine straightened in his arms to look over his shoulder at the woman, then sadly shook her head. "No, Father."

"Good girl." He kissed her forehead and gave her a firm cuddle to try and cheer her up. From out of nowhere, the desire to rub the head of the little long-haired furball consumed him and he scratched the pooch's head behind the ears. Columbine's reactive giggle made the act worthwhile, and deciding to end on a high note, he placed her back on the ground amongst the gathered children. "Everything'll be fine, princess. You just focus on having fun with the baby animals and leave the rest to me. Okay?"

"Okay."

He smiled and lightly mussed her hair. But then—as he straightened and knew for certain Columbine wasn't looking—his smile vanished and he levelled a lethal scowl at the mortal woman to reinforce his previous threat. The way she fell to her knees with a whimper, it was safe to say she got the message.

Pleased with himself, he turned and made his way through the stable and into the longhouse proper.

A few minutes later, he was back at Clarise's side. The girls' chairs had been removed while he was gone, and both his and Clarise's seats had been merged into a single, extended throne built to fit them both. Avis grinned as he slipped into his seat without Clarise noticing his return and after waiting a few seconds to confirm she hadn't, he suddenly wrapped his arms around her waist and hauled her sideways into his lap.

Clarise, who was in mid-conversation with Geir's wife, gasped at the unexpected manhandling and in a blur her eyes ignited in hellfire and fingers became into razor-sharp claws that buried themselves to the first knuckle through flesh and bone alike of his left shoulder and upper right arm. He couldn't deny the ten points of unexpected agony hurt like a bitch, but after everything he'd been through, that level of intense pinpoint pain could almost be mistaken for demonic foreplay. "I'm back," he said through gritted teeth, as recognition flashed across her face. She immediately retracted her fingers and doused the hellfire, returning her eyes to his preferred Mystallian state.

"Avis, you scared me," she scolded, her hands gently massaging his bleeding flesh through his doublet. He caught his breath as the chill of an icy gel coated his wounds, but no sooner had it been applied then the area went numb and he relaxed fully. She also kept his uniform pristine instead of blood soaked to prevent the mortals from seeing the severity of her retaliation. His wounds were already starting to heal and would be gone within a few minutes, and he grinned in delight at her fussing. "You should never sneak up on a Highborn …" He pulled her into a deep kiss, cutting her off before she could say precisely what she was in a moment of distraction. Not that Asgardians believed in Hell or the Highborn Hellions that ruled there, but they did have their own version of Hel, and the word was too similar for the cross reference not to be made. At the same time, he lifted her legs and planted her feet on her seat to stop anyone else from claiming it.

Not knowing precisely what had taken place between them, many laughed and cheered at the love they so openly shared, raising a toast to their ongoing health and happiness. Only Geir's wife, a woman by the name of Thornor, had to have the image of Clarise's hellfire eyes removed from her memory. Everyone else was either looking away, or too drunk to see it for what it was. "I love you, sweetheart," Avis whispered against his wife's lips, as the revelry around them intensified. "Don't ever, ever doubt it."

The concern in Clarise's eyes melted away and a soft, blissful smile crossed her lips. "I love you too, Avis."

From then on, the pair only had eyes for each other.

That was hours ago.

Now, his eyes kept flicking back to the bead on his glove that indicated the girls should've been in bed already. Cora was still as active as she'd been when he went to check on Columbine, and Columbine hadn't moved from the baby animal pen. Frash and Tilu wouldn't necessarily know of the specifics of their nightly routine, and he and Clarise had the girls' governesses here in the mead hall with them. Eventually, Clarise noticed his distraction and pushed herself out of his lap. "I will fetch Cora if it suits you to see to Columbine," she said, pretending to right her clothing. "Then we should regroup at the Jarl's longhouse, since it has the best accommodations in the herred. Do you agree, beloved?"

Thrilled that she was making decisions like a Mystallian, Avis nevertheless felt a sudden ripple of discomfort crawl across his skin. "How about you go after Columbine, and I'll take care of Cora?" he suggested instead. The last thing he wanted was Clarise to see what Cora was doing when the cheeky little shit had been up to her eyeballs in mud and snow, wrestling with the older boys ever since she'd gotten bored with the feast.

Clarise's expression remained pleasantly demure. "That would have been preferable, beloved, however you mentioned earlier that you were holding the barn wench responsible for Columbine's well-being. You cannot evaluate that, if I am the one to fetch her."

Clearly Avis hadn't thought that threat all the way through, and rubbing his thumbs against his fingers, he scrambled for an alternative that wouldn't undermine everything he'd achieved with Cora. "Well, why don't you stay here and enjoy the festivities for a little while longer, and I'll go and see to both girls," he said, as he rose to stand beside her. No one could ever accuse him of being subtle.

Between his added height and her growing scepticism, Clarise's head pulled back in a perfect imitation of a striking cobra. "And just why would I do that?" she asked, her tone cautionary at best.

Looking down into her soft (not molten) gold eyes, Avis considered his options and realised in short order he had none. He could never lie to her, and he had no truth at hand that could be worked to imply a lie. With a heavy sigh, he said, "Because I know exactly what Cora's been up to the last few hours, and I know you're not going to like it."

That golden pliancy hardened into jagged peaks. No other part of her changed, which made her calm stance that much more intimidating. It reminded him too much of her father. "And what would that be, my love?"

Avis carefully folded her into his arms and dared a quick kiss against her tight brow. "She's been rough-housing with the older boys, sweetheart, Mystallian-style. Nothing intimate, and no weapons. Just plain old, hand-to-hand stuff that you won't see as ladylike."

"And how precisely have you been made aware of this? With the one exception of checking on Columbine, you have not left my side all evening ..."

Avis bent his head forward to make the conversation semi-private. Not that it mattered. Between the over-indulgence of alcohol and the mindless revelry it caused, very few were paying attention to the foreign language anyway. "I've been watching her movements through our familial link. Nothing specific, but the jerking motions and moments outside indicate an ongoing wrestling match."

"With a familial glow as the only point of reference, there are other actions that could explain those motions ..."

"Cora's not like Columbine, sweetheart. She's a born fighter. After everything she witnessed in her young life, if any of those boys even thought about bedding her, she'd literally tear them to pieces ... and then make a point of eating those pieces right in front of the others as a warning to the rest."

"And she has her guards with her," Clarise agreed, relenting ever so slightly.

"Plural," Avis agreed, reminding her of the brute squad fighters they had tailing everyone from the shadows. He kissed her brow again, and since this time he didn't feel any tightness to the skin to indicate irritation, he twisted his head and moved in on her lips. Her mouth readily opened for him, and as their tongues duelled, he felt her arms unfold and her hands slide over his shoulders, locking together behind his neck. *Much better.*

When she pulled away and stared up at him, her smile was soft, and she uttered a tiny, wistful sigh. "For the record, my love, do not think for one moment your handsomeness has negated the trouble you are in for not disclosing Cora's activities to me when you knew I would not approve of them."

Avis chuckled and cuddled her close, resting his chin on the crown of her head. He could listen to that idea of a reprimand all day. "Did you want to stay here and enjoy the festivities while I go and see to the girls?" Now that she had all the facts, the choice would be hers.

He felt her shake her head against his chest. "No. I will come with you to collect Columbine. Diviten will stay with me and prepare her for bed, and while that is happening, Gingen will accompany you to see to Cora's presentability before bringing her into the long house." She pulled her head away from his chest and lifted her eyes to his. "If that pleases you."

Avis forced himself to smile. *So close.* She went so close to behaving like a Mystallian, and then she had to go and let her Highborn Hellion upbringing rear its ugly head right at the end. Still, it was a drastic improvement on last year and she didn't seem too pissed that he'd held out on her regarding Cora.

He breathed deeply and released a heavy sigh, then bowed his head to be on eye-level with her once more. His hands worked their way up to her shoulders, where his thumbs began small, rotating circles from her shoulders to just under her ears and back again. "Baby, what pleased me more than anything else in the Known Realms just now was when you gave me your honest opinion. When I asked you to do something, you told me 'no' and then laid out your own plan. That right there makes me so happy. You are your own person, and I revere your individuality. I've been telling you for months that you're my voice of reason when I have none, and for you to be effective, I need you to be vocal and honest. Don't spare my feelings, because once my temper's lit, I certainly won't be sparing yours, sweetheart."

Clarise smiled and her eyes returned to their molten state. "Then we should both go and see to our children."

CHAPTER TWENTY-SIX

Having already travelled this path once, Avis led Clarise up to the Jarl longhouse. In a blur of demonic motion, one of the governesses appeared ahead of them and opened the inward swinging doors with a silent bow in anticipation of their passing. Most of the children were already asleep on raised platforms covered in animal furs that lined the far end of the room, which also raised the problem of where Avis and his family would sleep. He wasn't happy with the idea of his children sharing pallets with these mortals, especially when he'd promised himself after they left the Akheron River that they'd never again be forced to sleep in compromising conditions. His eyes found the only real bed in the room: the one belonging to Arrik and Ingun at the furthest point of the room. *That will do.* At their age, he and Clarise could go at least a week without sleep and still function adequately. That's not to say the arrangement wouldn't put a serious crimp on his plans with his beloved wife, but for the sake of the girls, he'd go without sex for one night.

Avis led them into the side room where the animals congregated and sure enough, Columbine was the only child left inside the small pen. She was surrounded by baby animals, each vying for her undivided attention with yips, yowls, shrill screeches and impatient head-butts, and she shifted her focus from one to the next as quickly as her hands could move without breaking out her Highborn Hellion abilities. Thankfully, she'd remembered to remain a Mystallian and not sprout a dozen or so arms like a Mystallian squid.

At first glance, she appeared fine, but that didn't exactly mean a whole lot. Not when she could take it upon herself to maintain her physique regardless of injury. Clarise knew him so well. He wouldn't be satisfied until he'd seen the step-by-step progression of the night with his own eyes, and to do that, he needed to get into the mind of a witness. Preferably not his little princess, since she would know he was there. That left either the servant or the Midgardian woman.

Avis chose the mortal wench, and was pleased to see she'd taken his threat very seriously. From the moment he'd left the barn, she had dedicated herself to Columbine's well-being, as she should. Every animal's movement was scrutinised, and due to her diligence, Columbine had spent the time unmarred by the creatures who flocked to her for attention. They seemed to gain a sense of safety in his little girl's presence and clamoured for more.

One by one, the other children had put themselves to bed, until only Columbine remained.

Avis withdrew from the woman's mind and made his way towards the knee-high fence. The look of relief and terror that washed over her as he made his presence known was profound. "She ain't hurt, m'lord," the mortal insisted, gesturing with both hands at Columbine to prove her claim.

"I can see that," Avis agreed, lifting his leg to step over the fence. Columbine looked up at the familiar sound of his voice and smiled wearily. That tiny smile ate him up every time and he found himself smacking his lips in an air-kiss that had her giggling in delight.

"I was beginnin' to think you'd forgotten 'bout her, m'lord," the woman grinned, as she slapped her meaty hands against her thighs as if that would somehow remove the stench of animals that clung to her like a second skin. "But by the by, if y' don' mind me askin', where 'bouts do you folks call home?"

Relief seemed to have made the woman light-headed enough to be loose-lipped; not something Avis wanted to encourage. "What makes you want to ask?"

Perhaps he should have said, *what makes you so stupid as to ask,* for the mortal shrugged and gestured off-handedly at Columbine. "I was just talkin' to the little lady there an' she was tellin' me how she's never seen anything as pretty as a gyrfalcon chick or a lapphund pup before." Something must have twigged, for her eyes widened and she cleared her throat, rubbing the back of her neck. "Don't mean to be nosy an' feel free to say it's none of my business …"

"It is," Clarise cut in. The two single-syllable words were spoken with such an undertone of icy menace that the woman gasped and backed away from them until her shoulders struck the back wall of the room. Her shoulders dragged down the wall until she sat in a crouched position with her knees pressed into her chest, her eyes returning to their fearful state.

Avis looked across at his wife's cold gaze and smirked. So, she didn't like meddlesome mortals any more than he did. *Sweet!* "Alright, princess," he called in Mystallian, clapping his hands once to gain Columbine's attention, though in truth her eyes had never left him. "Put the animals down. It's time for bed."

To her credit, she did put the creatures down … albeit one at a time. And for every creature she released, a dozen more clambered into her lap in a bid to take its place and she didn't seem to be particularly interested in discouraging them. His heart soared at her first act of Mystallian rebelliousness, for 'dragging one's feet' was almost a prerequisite for kids back home who were being made to do something they didn't want to do. It was practically expected of them.

Not wanting Clarise to react badly to her first display of unhellion-like behaviour, he held out his left hand towards his wife with his fingers tutting the air, hoping she would take it as a sign to not interfere. This was a good thing in his eyes. He went over to where Columbine sat and crouched on his haunches in front of her. "We have a long way to go in the morning, princess, and it's well past your bedtime. You need your sleep, so you won't get hurt while we're riding. If your infatua—if your *love* of young animals is still this strong by the time we get home, I'll arrange for you to have your own touch farm with more young animals than you'll ever know what to do with …"

Columbine's eyes widened and sparkled in delight. "Really?" she asked, biting her bottom lip in an attempt to rein in her excitement.

Avis grinned and clapped again, then rolled his fingers inwards to beckon her to him. "Really," he promised with all his heart as he parted his hands invitingly. If only all the problems of Pandess could be solved so easily. The creation of a petting zoo in Pandess would be laughably easy for Griffith's boys of construction.

Columbine struggled to her feet and stumbled sleepily through the animals towards him. As she fell into his outstretched arms and wrapped her own around his neck, the stench of so many animals filled his nostrils to the point of gagging. Was that really urine he could smell on her? *Ewww* … Still, he closed his arms around her waist and lifted her into the air to escape the horde of small animals, hoping against hope that the stink wouldn't be transferred to him. "But first, you need a bath, young lady. Or a stimulation wave at the very least. By the Twin Notes, you reek."

"Diviten will see to that," Clarise declared, as Avis twisted on one heel and made his way back to his wife's side, effectively turning his back on the farming wench who still cowered in the back corner. The mortal had served her purpose, and he had no further use for her. Diviten (he assumed, since the other servant didn't move) had already stepped to Clarise's side with her arms outstretched, ready to fulfil her duty.

Columbine stifled a yawn against his shoulder, though her young arms tensed around his neck defiantly. *Daddy's girl.* The term that he'd heard Chance use with his chest puffed in pride had always seemed so silly to him, but he couldn't deny the sudden thrill it gave him now. Columbine was definitely his little princess. He would've given almost anything to keep the moment between them going, but he really did need to fetch Cora. "Let me go, princess," he murmured quietly rubbing his cheek against ear. "I'll be back with Cora before you go to sleep."

"Promise?" she asked, rolling a sleepy eye in his general direction.

Avis knew there was every chance she'd be asleep before he got back, so he kissed her forehead and said, "Promise ... even if I have to wake you up just to say goodnight."

Columbine's lips parted into a weary smile and her arms loosened their hold just enough that he was able to pass her over to Diviten. "Love you, Father."

"Love you too, baby." Avis went to step away from them all, when something occurred to him and he turned back to his wife. "Keep in mind she's a tired Mystallian, sweetheart. Not a tired Highborn Hellion." He really wanted to underscore that point, even as he gave Columbine's dark tresses a parting pet.

Clarise followed his actions with her eyes and nodded in understanding. "So long as that momentary defiance of us is the extent of her bad behaviour, there will be no repercussions, beloved."

Again, not quite what he was going for, but it'd do for now. "I'll be back soon. The girls can have Arik and Ingun's bed at the head of the longhouse, and once they've had enough sleep, we'll head out again."

Again, Clarise nodded. "I too thought that was the most viable plan, my love. Next time, we'll select a smaller longhouse with less foot traffic and shift in two comfortable beds. One for us, and one for the girls."

"We'll need to make that three beds, sweetheart," Avis corrected.

"Oh?"

"In their Mystallian forms, Cora thrashes worse than Tal in her sleep and if you put them both in the same bed, Columbine'll get hurt."

The gold in Clarise's eyes thickened as she let out a slow, tight breath. "I see."

Avis titched and leaned down to give Clarise another quick peck on the lips. "Don't be like that," he chided.

Instead of mellowing and accepting his kiss, Clarise pushed him away and looked up at him. "It is difficult to be any other way, beloved. A Highborn Hellion losing control of their physical form is both abhorrent and an embarrassment to our bloodline."

Avis hadn't made that correlation, nevertheless he raised his hand to her cheek and dusted her cheekbone with his thumb. "She hasn't got her shifting mastery at the moment, remember, sweetheart?"

Clarise took in a sharp breath to say something, but Avis wasn't quite ready to hear her arguments. "Hang on a second, sweetheart. This is really important. Most kids her age only have to deal with one side of the power scale and they master that one ability with ease. Cora's been left with trying to figure out how to balance both when she's never had any real bending experience before I came back. If a temporary loss of physical control at night allows her to come to grips faster with her bending, couldn't you just turn a blind eye to it? For her sake?"

He stared at her long and hard, willing her to see the logic of what he was saying. As such, he saw the moment she relented and kissed her deeply in gratitude. "Be back soon," he promised with a boyish grin afterwards, stepping away from his family. He flicked his cloak as he turned his back on them. "Gingen. With me."

Because Cora's familial link had her on the other side of the herred, Avis passed the mead hall and continued on until he reached a structure that had two of its sides open to the weather and three very large, bricked fire pits packed with hot coals. But unlike the mead hall, these pits weren't for food. Not if the huge hoppers that rose above the coal fires into the ceiling or the oil or water filled slack tubs were on either side of the fire pit were anything to go by. Large bellows leaned tip down against a well-used anvil, and tongs and hammers lined the walls, all of varying size and density.

As if that wasn't enough of a clue, hundreds of other tools and weapons hung from every available space in various stages of assembly. He heard the muffled sounds of cheers and jeers through the back of the workshop and sensing Cora was also back there, he quickly headed in that direction.

Despite the many twists and turns it took to get past the weaponsmith's equipment, he came to what some would consider a door, though in his mind that description was a generous one. The slats of worn timber that were all bolted together had a hand-width gap around three sides and the bottom third of the door had deteriorated into nothing. A single hinge at the top right-hand corner was all that kept it upright and there were no handles.

Avis pushed the door, and was immediately confronted by a deafening blend of approving roars and drunken curses. And not just the prepubescent boys that Cora had socialised with in the mead hall either. Men of all ages crowded the space. Each holding horns of either beer and mead which sloshed at their every move as they shouted and shook their free fists. The crowd right in front of Avis had to be at least three people deep.

"EAT SHIT, COCKSUCKER!" bellowed a young female voice he'd recognise anywhere for the rest of his life. While he chose to use profanity around her for flavour, that statement took things to the next level and it was clear she'd learned it from the men around her at some point.

Avis closed his eyes and pinched the bridge of his nose. At the very least, her mother was going to lose her ever-loving mind if she ever found out about this.

The sound of bodies scrambling in front of him had him snapping his eyes open, just in time to see a large, ungainly mass come sailing through the air in his direction. He instinctively put up a hand to block it, but a blur of motion had it change course mid-pitch and land in a heap to Avis' right. Having already played out this exact scene once before in Yaru, Avis didn't worry about internalising to confirm who'd saved him or how.

He looked down at the mangled face of a well-built man in his late twenties who appeared to be suffering from multiple broken bones. The fact that he still had a head at all meant Cora had gone easy on him. The fool gurgled on his own blood as he tried to roll to his side and stand again, but after a moment his energy gave out and he collapsed in an unconscious heap.

Some of the noise around them continued, but an eerie silence permeated from Avis' location. When he slowly looked around, he noted many sets of eyes were on him; Cora's included. The servant he deemed as Frash bowed his/her head forward respectfully from her place behind Cora and held that submissive position for several seconds before straightening. "Milord," she said into the growing silence.

At least Cora was unharmed. Her bright hair was a little mussed and her face and hands were dusted in dirt, ash and the blood of others, but overall she seemed fine.

Everything had stilled in anticipation of his next move, which gave him the chance to take in the immense size of the room. It was twice, perhaps three times the size of the mead hall. He'd never seen its like in Asgard. Men crowded the immediate space around him and he recognised a fighting atmosphere when he walked into one. Perhaps that was what this room was for, though it didn't make a whole lot of sense. Most Norsemen trained out in the open during fair weather and hunkered down during the winter. They had no need for a designated training hall like this—unless it was specifically to keep their skills up during winter. If that was the case, Arrik was indeed a smart man, for he would have a fully honed fighting force the second the thaw permitted him to travel.

Avis stepped forward, and the men around him shuffled backwards to give him room. Cora fidgeted a little, still hyped up from her win; such as it was. Knocking a mortal on his ass wasn't exactly noteworthy. She rolled her shoulders and cricked her neck in both directions, then ran her hands down the sides of her leather pants.

"Warriors," he called, once he reached Cora's side and placed a possessive hand on her shoulder. "This contest is over."

Many grumbled about the sudden conclusion of their entertainment, but a handful were drunk enough to take it upon themselves to argue the point directly with Avis. "'ere," one particular spokesman drawled. "Who'd y' think y' are, *bacraut* …" To emphasise what he thought was Avis' unworthiness, the idiot attempted to hit him with wild sucker punch that never made it halfway before a large hand encased it mid-swing.

Avis made no reaction to the interception, except to follow the muscular arm to Frash's deadly scowl. "Your orders, milord?" she asked in Asgardian, never once looking away from the target of her wrath.

Avis dropped his eyes to Cora, whose ruthless expression mirrored Frash's. In that instant he remembered he didn't have to worry about her childish sensibilities. Mentally speaking, Cora was as much an adult as the men around them, and he knew if he didn't deal sufficiently with the situation, she'd most likely do it for him.

"Crush the hand into pulp," he commanded in ice-cold Asgardian, never once taking his eyes off Cora's face.

Something akin to vindictiveness flashed in her eyes as the mortal's scream mingled with the rending of flesh and splintering bones. "You liked that, tiger?" he asked, concerned for the first time about her hellion heritage. She'd still be welcomed into Mystal with open arms regardless, but they had no use for a demonic torturer.

In his peripheral vision, men scattered and fled down a dozen or so trap doors that he hadn't been able to see when he first came in. Underground tunnels certainly went a long way to explain how they were able to regroup for training purposes when the whole herred was supposed to be in lock-down during winter.

"Hell, yeah," Cora replied, flashing a ruthless grin at the man whose right arm now ended in a bleeding stump of pulverised flesh and bone. Her eyes came back to his and there wasn't a hint of regret anywhere in them. "You weren't one of the contestants, Father. That was an unprovoked, coward's punch and losing the hand meant he got exactly what was coming to him."

Avis visibly relaxed. Vengeance, he could work with. As she went to move away from him, he tightened his grip on her shoulder, holding her still.

The added pressure had Cora's eyes widening in surprise. "What?" she asked, truly confused.

Avis's eyebrows dipped into a dark frown that blocked some of his vision. "Eat. Shit. Cocksucker." He separated the words, emphasising his growing displeasure by applying more pressure to her shoulder with each one. "For Mystal's sake, are you fucking insane, tiger?"

Cora squirmed and somehow managed to slide free of his grasp. "They said worse to me," she argued with sharp cutting gestures, deliberately putting herself just outside his reach. That only made him want to hunt down and butcher every male in the herred. It did nothing to alleviate the trouble she was in, and she still didn't see why.

"It's not what you said, tiger! It's how loudly you said it! What were you thinking, screaming that at the top of your lungs when anyone could've walked in on it! What if it'd been your mother instead of me? What if it'd been one of your hellish uncles?" He clenched his fists, infuriated by her blasé attitude. "Do you honestly think who said what first would make a lick of difference whatsoever to their reaction? You know better than anyone that the Highborn Hellions don't screw around when it comes to punishing their ladies! Your mother would've flayed you alive!"

"But I'm not Highborn Hellion anymore, am I? They threw me out."

The savagery of her words masked a deep-seated hurt that kneecapped Avis' tirade. How could he argue with it? He stepped forward and took hold of her shoulder once more, then knelt down in front of her. "Tiger, their loss is our gain. Don't ever doubt that. But whether you like it or not, your mother is still a Highborn Hellion, and she *will* discipline you according to the rules she was raised with."

"That's not fair!"

No, it wasn't. But it was what it was. "When I say your mother would've flayed you alive for swearing, tiger, I meant it literally."

Cora pinched her lips together as acceptance took up residency in her eyes. "Don't ask me to apologise for kicking their asses."

"Wasn't planning on it," he answered, rising to his feet. "You got lucky this time, tiger. Learn from it, because next time I'm tied up with Columbine it'll be your mother who comes to fetch you, and let's just say by the time she's done with you, you won't be in any state to apologise to her either."

Having said his piece, it occurred to him that without any of the mortal minds to peruse, he had no way of knowing which of these underground tunnels led back to the Jarl's longhouse. That was annoying, for it meant they'd have to either realm-step, or go back outside. Realm-stepping would put them momentarily in the celestial realm of Asgard, where it was a thousand times colder than in the mortal realm. If the situation was life or death, he might have considered it, but a short run through mortal snow that would get out of his way didn't warrant it.

Avis rose and twisted on his heel to stand at Cora's side, looking straight at Gingen. "Shift cold weather linings into Lady Cora's clothes and then get ready to carry her back to Jarl Arrik's longhouse." Not waiting for the governess to acknowledge the command, Avis dropped his gaze to Cora and said, "Your mother knows you've been wrestling with the older boys. That's the extent of it. Don't embellish, and definitely don't brag. She's already not happy with either one of us about it."

Cora snorted, and her surface thoughts told him why. Never had a Lord ever expressed concern for the trouble he was in with a Lady. She didn't think less of him for it though, which was a good thing. To her, it was just weird. *Get used to it, tiger,* he thought to himself as he moved his attention to both female servants. Unlike the demon lords, Mystallian men took the moods of their women very seriously. He turned his attention to the two servants. "And neither of you is to speak a word of it either. Lady Cora's behaviour as a Mystallian is not up for discussion in any way unless Lady Clarise asks first, and you will not give her cause tb ask. Am I clear?"

"Yes, milord," Gingen said, bowing her head and rounding her shoulders obediently.

Frash merely dipped her head in acknowledgement, much like the brute squad would.

Avis *really* didn't like her.

As Gingen came forward and gathered her ward into her arms, Avis approved of the thick fur that sprouted under the cuffs of Cora's gloves and around her neck under the doublet. It was a short trip across the herred, and the fur lining would be enough to keep her warm. However, as he stepped towards the barely-there door that led back into the blacksmith's workshop, Frash blocked his way with her arm. "Forgive me, milord," she said with her head bowed, even though her masculine arm still barred his way. "But would you not also require warmer clothing before travelling outside?"

Even if he had, the boiling of his blood at the reversal of her supposed apology and her unmitigated gall would've maintained him through the frozen wastelands of Antenora itself. "As usual, you assume far too fucking much," he snarled, taking the woman's masculine arm by the wrist and thrusting it aside with a great deal of force. Everything about her had him wanting to murder her in cold blood and by the realms, he was *sooo* looking forward to the day when her services would no longer be required.

Knowing Cora and Gingen would follow in his wake, (and not giving a fuck what Frash did) he stormed through the weaponsmith's forge and out into the bleak winter weather. The snow had picked up in the few minutes since he'd been inside, but he pushed through the elements, mentally daring them to do their worst. Thanks to Frash, he was now furious enough to explode.

CHAPTER TWENTY-SEVEN

"Lord Avis!" He barely heard the words over the howling wind a few minutes later, but once he registered them, he paused and turned towards the mead hall. He'd been so wrapped up in his own rage that he hadn't even realised he was alongside it. Still, there was no mistaking the figure that struggled through the thick snow to catch up with him.

Arrik overtook Avis and twisted around to face him so that his back was to the wind and he blocked the Mystallian's way. Snow clung to the fur of the jarl's hood, matching the ice in his eyes. "Herjolf was one of my most promising warriors!" The words were snarled through gritted teeth, as if his acrimony meant a damned thing to Avis.

Absolutely not in the mood for mortal posturing of any sort, Avis backhanded the man's mind well past the three and a half decades of life that the mortal had lived. Arrik dropped to the ground; his eyes unseeing and his shallow breaths drew in more snow than they did air. Avis looked down at him. Left as he was, he'd be dead in a few minutes from asphyxiation and although that would probably be favourable to the empty husk of a life he would now live, Avis needed him alive. At least for the next few weeks.

Hooking his foot under the man's shoulder, Avis flipped him onto his back. Then he squatted down beside the mindless man. **"When you do finally die,"** he sneered, branding the mental command onto the mortal's very soul. **"Tell Loki … Avis says hello."**

Feeling a little better now that he'd lashed out at something, Avis straightened and stepped over the fallen Norse leader as if he were nothing more than a part of the pathway and went on his way. Even without a mind, Arrik could potentially live a full lifetime, especially if his people cared for him as much as he claimed. Sticking it to Loki after that would be the icing on the cake.

"Father, STOP!"

Surprised more than anything else, Avis did just that.

He turned to find Cora had broken free of Gingen's hold and was kneeling at the side of the fallen jarl leader. Her gloved hands were on his exposed cheeks as if she could stave off the cold and mental damage by sheer willpower alone. Avis didn't have time for her fussing, and as he stepped towards the jarl's longhouse, he rolled his right hand at her to follow him. "Come on, Cora. Your mother's waiting for us …"

"But Arrik didn't do anything wrong."

Not used to being argued with once he'd made his final ruling, Avis stopped again and slowly rotated to face her. In doing so, he saw Gingen rush up behind her and slide her hands under her ward's arms with every intention of lifting her into the air again. It would've worked too, except a second later the woman's head flew back and her whole body stiffened as if she'd been struck by lightning. With a wide-eyed gasp, she released Cora and fell flat on her back in the snow. "Touch me again with the intent of forcing me against my will, and I will *seriously* fuck you up," Cora promised, giving her governess a positively vicious glare as the demoness rolled sideways to her hands and knees, shuddering profusely.

"Cora ..." Avis warned, breaking her stare down with her governess.

Maintaining her hold on Arrik's face, she locked gazes with her father and stubbornly shook her head. "No. He's done nothing wrong, Father. It's not fair to leave him here like this."

So much for his marginally better mood. "Knock it off, tiger. You're riding the high that comes with victory, but in this case it's a shallow one. Mortals mean nothing to us." Pointing at Arrik's prone form as a perfect example of why, he added, "Never did. Don't now. Never will."

"But his people need him."

"And I should care why, exactly?" The snarky comeback may have been just that as he said it, but now that it was out there, Avis honestly wanted to hear her response. If her reasoning convinced him, he might even consider her request. This was no longer about Arrik, but something far more important. A clear rationale was invaluable when it came to negotiating anything (not that he needed it in his position, but Cora had a lot of people above her on the food chain who couldn't be bent to her will), and if he could teach her how to utilise that skill by dangling the extinguished mind of one mortal as a reward, it would be time well spent.

"I'll come willingly with you to wherever Mother and Columbine are."

Avis snorted and folded his arms, unimpressed. "You're going to have to do better than that, tiger. Willingly or otherwise, you're going back to the longhouse with me just as soon as I decide this conversation is over. What else have you got?"

Cora broke eye contact with him and skirted her eyes over the snowy ground before them. Her lips puckered a little and her teeth chewed on her lower lip. Clearly, she had nothing.

"Then we're going," Avis declared, turning back towards the longhouse. He raised one hand to his shoulder and dropped it forward in a universal gesture. "Let's go, tiger."

"Wait! What if ..."

Avis looked over his shoulder at her. "Yeah?"

"What if I give you my word I won't tell anyone what you did to mother just after I was born?"

Well, this just got a whole lot more interesting. Turning once more, he placed his gloved hands on his hips and cocked an eyebrow. "Everyone who matters already knows what I did to your mother ..."

"Not the exact specifics."

A muscle under Avis' left eye twitched. "What exactly are you saying, tiger?"

"I'm sure they all know you raped her in a drunken stupor, but I'm willing to bet you didn't give them a blow-by-blow accounting of exactly what you said and did at the time."

She had him there. It was one thing to throw around the word 'rape', and another to get handed a detailed accounting. He raised his right hand and rubbed his lips. Threats ordinarily enraged him, and he usually dealt with them the same way he dealt with the mortal Arrik, but he'd been the one who'd started this. He'd told her to give him a good reason to save Arrik, and in chess terms, she'd just put him in check. Potentially checkmate.

"You do realise that that particular promise could get you anything in existence as far as I'm concerned. I'd give you a galaxy of mortals just like him to play with when we get home. Or ten. Or a hundred. Billions upon billions of planets, each one containing billions of mortals that you can do anything you like with. It's yours for the taking. Are you sure you want to waste such a valuable promise on this one mortal that's not even yours?"

Cora didn't even hesitate. "Yes."

Avis walked back to stand over her and the fallen mortal leader. "Own the words, Cora. Make it a boon." He was never going to be blackmailed with this again.

"Give Arrik back every facet of his mind and don't arrange to have it taken again, and I'll never communicate in any way the specifics of what you did to mother in my nursery the day I was born." Her voice never faltered as she laid down the terms of her agreement.

Inwardly, Avis was thrilled. She was smart enough to cover her intent with precise wording. Had she left his side of their deal at 'put his mind back', he'd have done just that and then destroyed it again straight afterwards as an object lesson for the future. Many celests used verbal trickery to get what they wanted out of a boon and when one mortal's mind was all that was at stake, this would've been the perfect time to teach her that lesson.

Except she didn't need to be taught at all. His little tiger had a smart head on her tiny shoulders. "Very well, tiger. I accept your terms."

Avis lowered his eyes to the fallen warrior and slipped into his mind. As expected, he found a wasteland of ash in every direction. Nothing was left that the mortal could build on. Centralising himself, Avis tapped his ancient power and slowly reversed what had been a momentary process, building it one second, then one minute, all the way up to one year at a time. This was such a colossal waste on a mortal. It really was. Not to mention time-consuming. Had Cora not slipped in the 'every facet' aspect to their deal, he would've repaired maybe half to three-quarters of the mortal's mind, hitting all the major points in his life but not caring about the insignificant details. Cora's wording meant he had to make sure every second of his life was back the way it had been. It took him over a week to complete, and every time he felt frustrated by the ridiculousness of it, he remembered what he would gain. No one would ever learn of what he'd done to Clarise from Cora. This one act would forever seal her lips.

That was how boons worked. They weren't just a gentlemen's agreement between beings to be ignored when it became inconvenient. So long as at least one of the participants had celestial blood, it was binding. Many of the Known Realms' more stupid situations had come about because of boons, and only a fool entered into one without understanding all the costs involved. Unspecified boons were for the desperate or insane and were to be avoided at all costs. Nothing was worth owing someone else anything they wanted.

In time, he was certain Cora was going to look back on this decision and regret it with every fibre of her being. Especially since he planned to remind her about it every chance he got ...

Avis pulled himself up hard on that thought, knowing he was talking out of his ass. The old Avis might've gone down that road, but that wasn't him anymore. Like her sister, Cora was his baby and her confidence had taken a cruel enough beating thanks to his wife's bullshit family without him adding to it. So, no, he wouldn't tear her down over her nonsense stand. He'd boost her up for choosing to make one. It was the least he could do as her father.

Once he was satisfied that everything was as it was meant to be, Avis' next task was to remove his uncompleted celestial command. As a mental vegetable, Arrik's kin would've wrapped him in cotton wool and he'd have lived a long, if not fulfilling life. Now, there was every chance the useless prick could get himself killed at any moment and Avis didn't want his taunt getting back to Loki before he and his family were safely in the next realm. He also had to rework the last minute or two of Arrik's memory so that it coincided with what the physical realm portrayed, without revealing his true power. That is, a mortal reason instead of a divine one to put him on his back in the snow with Cora kneeling over him.

The solution was ridiculously easy. Arrik was already full of his own importance, so having him think he'd attempted to get physical with Avis instead of merely getting in the Mystallian's way was an easy switch. Then he had Frash intercept the blow, much like she had in the fighting arena. His subsequent order was, "Drop him on his ass."

A quick, circular twist of her arm had Arrik flipped over onto his back in the snow, and since there was no actual blow, there would be no follow-up contusions. After that, he had Cora run to Arrik's defence while he and Frash loomed overhead, and here they were. Sorted.

He played it through from the beginning, just to make sure there were no mistakes. Normally, he didn't take this much care of anyone, but a boon meant he had to uphold his end, even if Cora was going to seriously regret hers.

Happy with the result, he returned to the physical realm.

Cora immediately took Arrik's hands and hauled him to his feet. "Are you okay?" she asked, staring up at him in concern.

Squaring his feet for balance, Arrik opened his mouth to answer, then lifted his gaze to Frash and across to Avis. "Who *are* you people?" he demanded in wonder.

"Like my wife said, we're just passing through." Having completed his part of their boon, Avis wanted nothing more to do with the jarl, but Cora seemed hesitant about leaving his side. That was more concerning to him. Did she doubt his work? "Cora, you good?"

Cora slipped her hand into Arrik's limp one and squeezed it. "Yeah, I'm good." She grinned up at the dazed mortal and said, "Seeya 'round, Arrik." With a parting bob of her head, she withdrew her hand and charged across the ground to overtake her father. Just as it had been with the mortal planets and suns, the snow which ran in some places up to her hip parted and reformed behind her as her tiny legs ate up the distance with ease.

Shocked by her apparent dismissal of Arrik after she'd sacrificed her one enormous bargaining chip for him, Avis couldn't help but bounce his attention between the pair in confusion. Then he realised he was being left behind, and Cora had no clue where she was going. "Cora, wait up," he called, and picked up the pace. When he caught up with her, he hooked a hand over her shoulder, deliberately slowing her down. "Didn't you want to make him a pet or something?" If Arrik's welfare was more important to her than the whole galaxy of mortals he'd offered her, he couldn't understand why she was letting him go now. Anyone else would've put an ownership collar or branded him or claimed him somehow.

"No," Cora scoffed. The rest of her answer confused him all the more. "I don't even like the conceited prick."

Okay, enough is enough. Refusing to take another step without making sense of this, he hauled her to a complete stop. "Then why in the realms ...?"

"Because he didn't deserve what you did to him, Father. He was a leader looking out for his people, and we haven't exactly been broadcasting where we sit in the grand scheme of things. Without that information, he didn't deserve what you did to him at all."

Avis stared at her and, seeing the sincerity in her eyes and surface thoughts, forced himself to suck in a deep, angry breath and hold it. Then he lifted his gaze to the peaceful night sky overhead for patience, unable to believe what he was hearing. *Of all the idiotic ...!* The unfathomable stupidity behind that ridiculous statement was almost too fucking dumb to comprehend. "What the fuck were you thinking?" The words exploded out of his mouth before he could stop them, not that he regretted them for a second. When he'd agreed to the boon, he'd assumed she had a good reason for making it. This was about as far from that as it could possibly be.

Cora's expression soured. "What?" she shot back, just as aggressively.

Avis clenched his hands into tight fists to stop himself from shaking some much-needed sense into her. "You had the ultimate bargaining chip where I was concerned, and you threw it away because a worthless mortal wasn't being treated fairly? I've got news for you, tiger! Ninety-nine-point-nine percent of every-fucking-thing in existence doesn't play fair! How could you be so bloody stupid?" He was genuinely shouting by this time, and he didn't care that he was speaking Mystallian. If Cora expected life to be fair, she was in for an eternity of disappointment. Her own childhood to date should have shown her just how unfair things were in reality.

Cora immediately bristled. "I don't give a flying fuck if every other bastard in existence is fair or not!" she shouted back. "You're my father! If you can't set the example of the way it's supposed to be around me, then what fucking chance has anything else got?"

Whatever Avis was going to say next lodged in his throat along with his next breath, and the two stared long and hard at each other. For several tense seconds, the icy wind and snow whipped around them, but Avis felt none of it. His heart and his head were having too hard a time coming to terms with what she'd said. Finally, unable to stomach the silence any longer, he licked his lips and said quietly, "I've never played fair, tiger."

Cora snorted in derision. "You think I don't know that? I was less than two hours old when you showed me just how unfairly you like to play things, Father."

Her answer perplexed him. "Then what do you want from me?"

Instead of answering straight away, Cora broke eye contact with him and looked over the herred, stopping every now and again as inconsequential things caught her interest. "What I want ..." she said in almost a whisper, unconsciously scratching her left forearm. But then she must have realised what she was doing, for her hand stilled and fell to her side, and her eyes snapped back to him, skewering him where he stood. "What I want is for you to show me that I mean enough to you that you're willing to embrace what matters to me. Yes, I'm well aware of how unfair life is. My entire childhood to date is a compendium on the subject. But that doesn't mean I have to put up with it, and I won't if I can help it. If you don't understand that, then you'll never understand me."

Avis tilted his head to one side. "You want me to be tolerant of other people?" he asked, in clarification.

Cora nodded. "If they've done nothing wrong, yeah."

"Tiger, you do realise … if they're in my way, they're already doing something wrong as far as I'm concerned."

That was perhaps the wrong thing to say. He didn't even need to go into her surface thoughts to see why her eyes glazed over until they matched the empty frigidity of their surroundings. Her next words confirmed it anyway. "That's what I thought you'd say," she said numbly, turning away from him in more ways than one.

Refusing to let that be the end of it, Avis dropped his hand on her shoulder, holding her in place. "Wait a minute, tiger. You don't get to drop that on me and then walk away like we're done. You wanted to hash this out, so consider this us hashing it out. We're either talking about it right here and now, or I'm moving this conversation to where you can't avoid me."

Her head twisted just enough to look at him wearily over her shoulder. "Is there any point, Father?"

Avis whirled her around and held her in place, refusing to have such an important discussion with her back to him. "Yes, there's a point," he insisted, going down on one knee in front of her. "I've been the way I am for a really long time and you can't say I'm not trying to change. But what you're asking of me is impossible. I will NEVER treat commoners or mortals like that Arrik" —he stabbed a finger at the named mortal— "as equals. I barely see other pantheons as my equal."

"Who said anything about being equals, Father?" Cora asked, rolling her shoulder in an attempt to dislodge his hand. The slickness of the melted snow on their clothes made it difficult to maintain his grip, but he refused to let her go. "Knocking a servant down for speaking out of turn or destroying a mortal for the same crime is not something I have a problem with. It's not about equality. It's about respecting boundaries. You can't hide stuff from people, then hurt them because you've successfully hidden it from them." She paused, just long enough to search his face for something. Whatever it was, based on the dejection that swept across her features, she didn't find it. "And you're never going to get it, are you?"

Avis opened his mouth but was at a loss as to what to say. He wouldn't lie to her, but he desperately wanted one of Clarise's twisted answers that would satisfy her, nonetheless.

Cora's expression didn't change as she dropped her shoulder beneath his grip and somehow managed to pull herself free. "Don't worry about it Father," she said with a downhearted shake of her head. Her right hand waved him off. "It's not important."

But it was. Everything from the slight slump of her shoulders to the tiny, despondent sigh she huffed as she turned away from him screamed as much.

He was making a complete hash of this, and he needed help.

Avis turned his thoughts inwards and launched into his imagination. There, he wasted no time in recreating all seven of his siblings, wanting everyone's input. He created a window that they could all see through, and replayed what had transpired between him and Cora on the other side. Chasidah was already covering her eyes with her right hand and shaking her head. Chance waited until the part where Avis had told Cora that anyone in his way was already a problem before he joined Chasidah. By the time the scene had run its course, they were all looking at him like he was an idiot. Even Blagden, who had no kids. "So how do I fix this?" he asked, gesturing to the window. "And what'd I say that was so wrong anyway?"

"Cora was throwing you a bone, you bonehead," Chance answered, before anyone else could.

"And not only did you entirely miss the point where you should've picked it up, you kicked it back at her so hard you embedded it in her skull," Armina concluded.

Tal, the two and a half metre giant of Destruction from the Dark Court, snarled and folded his arms in disgust. "What the fuck is wrong with you, brother? She obviously needs you, and you're kicking sand in her face."

"Tal," Amaro cautioned. That one word from Death was enough to silence Destruction, though he still scowled openly in displeasure.

Since it seemed only his side of the realm that had anything useful to say, Avis impatiently dismissed his siblings from the Dark Court. "So how do I fix this?" he asked again of the remaining three.

"Cora looks tired," Griffith said, bending low to stare out the window where the scene had been frozen.

"Oh, come on! How in the realms could you possibly know that?" Avis bellowed, because he'd only shown them from where he'd dropped Arrik in the snow, not five minutes earlier. Certainly not enough time to deduce that, even if he was right.

"Well, duh—because we've all had kids and we know the look from a realm away." Chance's look of condescension as he said that was quickly replicated by the other two. "You can see around her eyes just how tired she is."

Avis rewound the scene to where Cora knelt at Arrik's side. "Where?" he argued, seeing nothing but a stubborn child who wasn't getting her own way.

Armina expanded the image to zoom in on Cora's face. "Here, and here," she said, pointing to the slight glaze of her niece's eyes and the added creases under her eyelids. "If you keep her up another hour or so, this section under here will start to darken, and when it gets too dark, you'll know you're alive because every word out of her mouth is going to make you want to kill her."

"Well, she'll become more difficult to deal with, the longer she's up," Chance said, ever the diplomat.

"Just put her to bed, brother," Griffith said, rising to his full height. "And in the morning, go into her imagination and don't come out until you've got this shit sorted out. You made her feel like she didn't matter to you, and now you have to fix it."

"Dammit, that wasn't what I meant ..."

"But it's what she heard," Chance said, losing all sense of humour. "And I could seriously kick your ass for letting her feel that way even for a second. You bend over backwards to do whatever Columbine needs you to do, and I think half the time you've forgotten you have *two* daughters."

Avis' gaze narrowed, sharply. "Watch it," he growled in warning.

"Or what?" Chance curled his upper lip into a snarl as he parted his feet and slammed his hands on his hips, showing without words that he had no intention of backing off. Not when it came to Cora.

"Personally, I wouldn't wait till morning," Armina said, stepping between the two of them before things got ugly. "I'm all for putting her to bed right now, but I'd only wait an hour or two for her to fall into a deep sleep. Once she's there, I'd be going in to sort this mess out."

"And what do I say?"

"Tell her the truth," Griffith replied as if the answer should've been obvious. "It's a work in progress. One that you're going to need her help with since you suck so abysmally at it."

Avis flipped his middle finger at his younger brother, and by extension the other two.

"You do," Armina agreed, while Chance nodded curtly. "But if she can see you're genuinely willing to try and meet her halfway, it'll be a good start."

Okay. Bed. Wait an hour. Then go in and talk to her. He could do that. Repeating the order until it was almost a mantra, Avis cleared his imagination and returned to the physical realm where he could put it into practice.

CHAPTER TWENTY-EIGHT

The journey across the herred was made in total silence. Avis couldn't stop thinking about Cora's half of their conversation, and her look of disappointment right before she iced up and turned her back on him, shredded him beyond words. She wanted him to be fair. No, she needed him to be fair. For her. A lot of people had asked many things of him in his long life, but 'being fair' had never been one of them. He wasn't even sure how to start ... or where to start. How did one go about being fair when 'fair' was a matter of perspective? For Mystal's sake, kids that didn't want to eat their vegetables considered that necessity 'unfair'.

Frash reached the door first and opened it for them with a bow, though Avis ignored her as he always did. He hadn't realised how cold he'd become until the congested warmth of the longhouse struck him in the face and prickled his skin beneath his leathers. Clarise rose from where she'd been sitting on the edge of the jarl's bed at the far end, no doubt keeping a close vigil on Columbine as the girl slept. She smiled warmly at them, though it quickly faded when she took in their sombre expressions. "Is everything alright?" she asked, shifting her gaze from one to the other and back again.

Avis unconsciously looked to his left where he'd assumed he'd find the jarl's children still sleeping on their various furs. The fact that every pallet was empty was a surprise, but not one he particularly cared about. "Not really," he answered with a heavy heart. He was about to say more, when his vision filled with a light so bright he thought he'd go blind. He didn't even have time to raise his arms when two thick bands snapped around his waist and he was hoisted to the left in a blur of movement that left him breathless.

The light was instantly followed by an explosion so deafening it rocked the longhouse and left his ears ringing. The pain caused by both sent his head pounding, but worst of all was Clarise's heartfelt scream of denial. No matter what his physical condition, he'd recognise that terrible sound anywhere and the uncertainty of why she had sent his heart hammering against his chest in panic.

Cora!

Until he knew she was safe, he fought to regain his sight and hearing though of the two, sight was by far the more important one if they were under attack. He and Zeus had tussled enough times over the eons for him to know a lightning bolt strike when he was in the presence of one, which meant somehow, their cover had been blown. The Asgardian thunder god was here and blinded as he was, he was damn-near helpless.

Shapes and then images returned to him in short order, and what he saw had him surging against the four arms of the brute squad guard who held him in place against the far-left wall of the room. Clarise was also struggling within the confines of a brute squad guard, her face glistening with tears and her arms outstretched towards where he and Cora had been standing.

NO!

Avis' heart flew into his throat as he shot his gaze towards the space near the door, fully expecting to see a scorch mark on the floor to signify the death of their child. Halfway between Clarise and where he'd been with Cora stood the giant trickster/fire god alongside the powerful god of thunder. *FUCK! Loki!* The thought was fleeting as Avis searched for Cora.

There. Right where he and Cora had been standing, was the charred outline of a lightning strike victim etched into the floor. The realisation of what that had to represent sent Avis into a frenzy. He twisted and thrashed, screaming death threats and profanity that would have done his father proud. The brute squad guard never once released its hold, and as Belial's elite, its mind remained beyond Avis' ability to break. More coiled bands appeared, restraining his hands, elbows and knees, while another thicker band of rolled leather whipped across his mouth and locked his teeth apart to silence him. However, this only made him more determined to break free and truly go berserk.

Pinned against the golden armoured behemoth as he was, he couldn't avoid the sharp prong that penetrated the flesh below the base of his skull, nor stop the substance that was then injected into him.

Whatever it was, his spiralling thoughts immediately stabilised then sharpened; his anxiety reducing to a point where he could function again. The forced return of logic made him realise one other important detail about the charred mark that had him losing his mind so badly. The outline of the body who had perished was far too large to be Cora. Their daughter may have had the mind of an adult, but she was still stuck in the body of a five-year-old and killing her in this fashion would've rendered the charred mark of her passing as a much smaller outline.

So, it's not Cora. Okay. Okay ... okay. Not being Cora meant he could breathe again because that put the death as one of the servants. Given Clarise's reaction, it was more likely Frash which, if anything, made him a little happier. He'd planned to kill her himself as soon as they were back in Mystal, and if the thunder god beat him to it, he would no longer be on Clarise's shit-list for her death. *Win-win.*

Avis planted his boots on the floor and shifted his weight so he no longer needed the support of the brute squad guard behind him. The guard immediately released him and stood at the ready to his left, but he still didn't know where Cora was. The room continued to sizzle with unspent electricity as he searched the area for her. He needed to see her, to know for sure she was okay. It was the only way to allay his fears.

He found her standing in the shadow of the weaving loom that he'd noticed near the door when he first entered the longhouse. Gingen lingered behind her, fidgeting nervously, while a brute squad guard stood to her left with its arms crossed over its iridescent golden body, its domed headpiece spinning in constant appraisal of its surroundings. Cora remained stock still, her mouth slightly ajar as she continued to stare at him. He skimmed over her surface thoughts and saw how his loss of control over what he'd thought was her death had shocked her. Like him, she'd been ripped from the point of danger long before the lightning bolt landed and was still trying to make sense of everything. "I'm okay," he mouthed. Already knowing the answer to his next question thanks to his perusal of her mind, he asked, "You?" to which she closed her mouth and nodded.

"You are a fool for returning, Mystallian," Thor's voice boomed, drawing his attention to the god of storms. "The wergild that lies at your feet is higher than you could ever repay."

Avis looked back at the Asgardians. Very rarely had these two ever seen eye to eye on anything, yet here they stood. Shoulder to … well, waist. With their red hair and beards, anyone would think they were family, but their blood connection was strained at best. Loki had shared blood with Odin before Thor was born so technically, there may have been a teaspoon of shared blood between them. At Thor's side was Arrik, kneeling with his head bowed to the floor as any good slave or mortal pet should be.

And that was when the pieces all fell into place. The birthmark of Mjolnir that covered Arrik's back was no birthing coincidence! Nor was the moniker that the rest of the mortals around him had labelled him with. This mortal *had* been branded with Thor's personal mark because he *was* the chosen of Thor, which meant everything this mortal undertook went directly to the thunder god himself, including Avis' implanted taunt at Loki. It may have been removed a minute or two later, but in those two minutes, he might as well have shouted it at the storm god.

But even the Asgardians needed time to travel, and there wasn't a fireball's chance in Antenora that his mental insult had been the catalyst for their arrival. No, they'd probably been on the move ever since Arrik heard Avis' name during their introductions hours ago.

None of which changed a realm-damned thing right now. Avis lifted his eyes to the giant standing beside Thor. "I gave Lord Narvi more warning than he deserved …"

"Don't you dare speak of my son, you worthless cur!" Loki bellowed, his cry shaking the rafters. "You murdered him!"

Avis wasn't denying that, but what he couldn't understand was why Thor stood at Loki's side. Their history was tumultuous at best and there was no reason for him to accompany the trickster, which meant he was missing something. So, he did what he always did when someone knew something he wanted to know and didn't. He remedied it.

Blowing through the memories of his best friend's son, he found where Thor had marked Arrik as his chosen just before the mortal's birth, and realised he'd gone too far back in the storm god's memories. He needed more recent ones. The ones that happened after Narvi's death.

He backtracked until he came across Baldur's beloved ship the *Hringhorni* being set alight and sent out to sea to burn. Laying atop the central platform were two wrapped bodies. Avis' eyes widened. It was an Asgardian funeral. Most celests ceased to be once they died, but because Asgardian celests acted more like mortals after death, the rules about their lifeless bodies mirrored that mortality.

Wait a minute! Vali had eaten Narvi, which meant there shouldn't have been any bodies left to burn—let alone two. And why would they burn Baldur's ship anyway? On top of that, these memories were too recent. Months, maybe a year at best. Long after the feast where Narvi had died. Avis returned to the beginning of the ceremony, curious to learn who else had been killed since his last visit.

The last person he expected Odin and Frigg to tearfully name as the pyre torches were lit was Baldur and his equally young wife Nanna. What the ever-loving, fucking hell happened? Baldur was the favourite son of his best friend and he was supposed to be invulnerable to all manner of weaponry! He'd seen it himself. With his own eyes! How was he dead now? *HOW?*

The only possibility he could think of was one that he'd have never considered five years ago. As Mystal's supreme god of Life, he was also almost indomitable, but if anything happened to Clarise and her body remained lifeless for all to see, he knew without a doubt that he'd want to crawl onto her funeral pyre and burn with her. Maybe that's what happened here. Nanna wasn't invulnerable the way Baldur was. She was his weakness.

Backing things up a few days, he watched Nanna grieve. Avis had never seen the usually serene woman so mindless with grief. She wailed and thrashed inconsolably, throwing furniture around the room and clawing at herself, calling for the return of her beloved Baldur; who never answered. The image stunned Avis. Baldur had never, *ever* ignored his wife. Thor charged across the room and wrapped his sister-by-marriage up in a tackle that lifted her off her feet and the two fell across her bed but still, she shrieked and struggled. Eir arrived soon afterwards, and between the two of them, they forced Nanna to drink a steaming concoction that the healer brought with her. As the fight slowly ebbed away from Nanna, both Thor and Eir whispered words of condolence as they laid her properly in the bed and covered her with furs. Thor promised her retribution.

By the Twin Notes, was it possible that the invulnerable Baldur had been killed first?

Avis skimmed through Thor's memories in search of the storm god's last interaction with his quiet brother. As expected, it was in Valhalla, where Baldur stood before his esteemed father with a bored look on his face. Avis could well understand his boredom. He had witnessed this very turn of events a dozen times and watching everything bounce off the young god's bare chest did grow tedious. Not so for the Asgardians. Every spear and rock that rebounded created a cacophony of drunken shouts and cheers from the onlookers.

Until one didn't rebound.

A spear shaft penetrated the flesh of his ribs and jutted out the other side; coated in his blood. For the briefest moment, a shocked look came over Baldur as he stared down at the instrument of his imminent death, and then he collapsed. Lifelessly. Thor's perspective became a blur of images as he cleared the table he'd been sitting behind and rushed to his fallen brother, shoving everyone else out of his way. But it was too late. Avis had seen enough death to know Baldur was gone. But who the fuck had killed him? Baldur was a good kid and had a great future ahead of him as the Asgardian god of magic. Everyone loved Baldur! Even he—an outsider with no dog in this fight—had a soft spot for the kid, and dammit, someone was going to pay for breaking the heart of his best friend!

He went back to just before Baldur's death and slowed the imagery right down, following the trajectory of the spear back to its source. The spear first appeared in Thor's memory in mid-flight, so Avis knew that wouldn't give him the answers he sought. Fortunately, he was able to garner the information he needed from other memories around that one. Specifically, one where Thor had casually looked around the room during a conversation with his wife Sif. Avis froze the image at where the spear first appeared, then ever so slowly crept the visual backwards as he imagined the flight path through the crowd.

At the back of the room, Thor and Baldur's blind brother Hodr sat on a stool near the open doorway. As always, he refrained from joining in the revelry in case he was jostled and listened to the festivities instead. Poor, blind Hodr. Loki had a lot to answer for there as well since the bastard had thought it was funny to condemn the poor kid (who'd done nothing to him) to an eternity of blindness by manipulating Hodr's establishment field. It wasn't the first time Avis had wanted to hand the mischievous fire god his ass, even if his best friend and the father of Loki's victim had thought the 'trick' was hilarious.

Which was why he was so surprised to see Loki squatting down beside Hodr, talking to him as discreetly as a giant who towered over everyone in the room could.

Then, Avis' blood ran cold.

In Loki's right hand was the spear. *The* spear! The spear that killed Baldur! Loki had murdered his own blood-nephew! Why the fuck had Odin not found the deepest hole to bury the bastard alive in? Avis' past rage at Loki had nothing on the fury that coursed through his veins now. Unlike that mouthy brat Narvi, Baldur had never done anything to anyone and certainly didn't deserve to die like that.

Time restarted the moment he removed himself from Thor's mind, and the first thing he did was level a mental blow at Loki. Setting the giant's mind on fire was a joy, but he wanted Loki to remember why he was so pissed at him, so the fire was for pain, not the eradication of his memory. Loki's leg muscles flexed as if the fire were physical and he blindly leapt away from Avis, rolling across the ground in a ball of pain.

Avis also threw a mental punch at Thor as an afterthought, mainly to stop the brutish fighter from getting a blow in first.

Unlike his step-uncle, the Asgardian thunder god merely stumbled back two steps and dropped Mjolnir.

"I don't have a grief with you, Lord Thor," Avis insisted, as the Asgardian froze in his hunched position, then unfolded himself with slow, graceful menace. His eyes were aglow with lightning and a flex of his fingers had the mighty hammer returning to his hand.

"Perhaps not, Lord Avis. But you and I are certainly amiss."

Avis' eyes jerked back to Loki. Standing directly in front of the giant's prone form with a raven on each shoulder and a wolf on either side, was the one-eyed man Avis had called 'friend' for most of his adult life. "Odin," he breathed, relaxing just a little. With the All-Father present, Thor and Loki were less likely to act out and things might not have to end in bloodshed. "Look, if there's still bad blood between us over Lord Narvi, I'll leave with my family and wait until I hear from you …"

"Your deeds have precipitated others that will never be forgiven. From my realm, you will be driven. But childless you will also be, for then you will feel my agony."

Avis frowned, unable to comprehend what his friend was saying. To the left of the Asgardians, Clarise turned and gathered Columbine protectively into her arms, and Avis' fingers itched to do likewise with Cora. Columbine stirred and hooked one arm around her mother's neck; her legs exposed from the knee down from where her nightgown had bunched. Her face was partially hidden in her mother's hair, but through her locks, he saw her right hand rub at her eyes wearily. On either side of them stood a brute squad guard; their demonic gold wings bouncing on non-existent air-currents, their headpieces spinning constantly. At least they were okay for now. Avis needed to find out what in the realms was going on.

Refocusing on the man he called friend, the Mystallian patriarch swept into Odin's mind. One way or the other, he had to get to the bottom of this and because of Thor, he knew when to look. Nevertheless, it gutted him to watch the death of Baldur from the All-Father's viewpoint. The helplessness and despair that clung to his friend's recent loss were horrendous, and unlike Thor, Odin had seen it all. But it hadn't been Loki who threw the spear and killed Baldur. No, that would be too upfront for the cowardly shithead. Instead, Loki had cajoled Baldur's blind brother into delivering the killing strike.

Why in the fuck was that bastard still free? If anyone … friend, family … *anyone* so much as *tried* to cost him the lives of one of his girls, there'd be nowhere that person could hide from his rage. *Nowhere!*

To confound matters to Avis, Odin ordered the immediate death of his blind son Hodr but left Loki alone because his trickery in the matter was somehow to be commended. *What kind of ass-about horseshit logic was that?* Yes, if he'd been in his friend's place, he'd have probably killed Hodr in a fit of rage too, but that would've been a quick, reactive death that he might've regretted later. In contrast, what he'd then do to the brains behind that stunt would be a lesson in torture that'd make the Master Guardians of Hell sit up and take notice.

Of course, once Odin and Frigg managed to put down a mead tankard for longer than ten seconds, Loki was brought to them to explain himself, but unbelievably, the bastard turned everything around and blamed it all on him! Oh, sure, he started with the usual, "Life is about risk, and when you made him invulnerable, you took away the realm's right to natural selection. I was merely balancing the scales," but that acknowledgement put Loki right in Odin's sights. Realising he needed to deflect the blame, the trickster then snapped, "Baldur defended Lord Avis when that bastard murdered my son right in front of me! An eye for an eye is our way. If you want to blame someone, blame him for starting all this by first murdering my son!"

Shock flooded Avis, though it was quickly followed by rage. How dare that fucker turn this back on him to get out of his own punishment! Narvi had been warned! Multiple times! The drunken brat just hadn't listened!

But what came next absolutely floored Avis.

Odin rose from his throne and walked down the dais to stand alongside the bound Loki with a longsword in his hand. Avis expected to see Odin bury at least half a metre of steel into the trickster's ribs, but instead, the sword was used to set Loki free.

"Agreed," his ancient friend replied, using a tone that meant he was making a proclamation. "Had Lord Avis not taken your son, you would not have made my Baldur bleed. A life for a life has always been our way. For his crimes against us, Avis will pay."

Avis staggered backwards away from the memory until shock robbed him of the ability to stand. His entire body suddenly ached with horror and disbelief. Odin was one of his closest friends. Millions of eons had gone into their friendship, and it was just … over? For a crime he'd had nothing to do with? He'd been suffering in Hell as one of the Damned when Loki made his move against Baldur. How could Odin possibly hold him responsible for that?

Too heartsick to return to the physical realm yet, Avis went over into Odin's imagination. He couldn't think rationally, but he knew he wanted to be alone, so he refrained from summoning his friend—*former* friend to explain himself. In short order, the numbness of shock faded and was replaced by rage. He needed something to destroy. Not just hurt. Destroy. Loki was the obvious choice, but seeing him right now only served to remind Avis of his anguish and he dismissed the image as soon as it appeared. Nondescript things. That's what he needed. Things he could vent at mindlessly. He created an endless array of objects to destroy, and he attacked them with gusto. He kicked, punched and smashed his way through them, howling his rage until his lungs burned and his voice was lost. Then he created more things to take his pain out on. How long he went on like that, he couldn't say, but eventually, when his arms ached and his legs threatened to collapse, Avis cleared the scene and dropped to his knees with his head bowed and his eyes closed.

And there, in a place where nothing could bear witness to his loss of control, Avis felt the tears slide down his cheeks and drip from his chin.

It took a long time for him to accept the inevitability of his lost friendship. A *really* long time. Odin hated him, almost as much as he would've hated Odin if he'd felt the Asgardian was to blame for the death of one of his girls. He took a deep breath and released it, removing all trace of his breakdown as he rose to his feet. Once upright, he rolled his shoulders and cracked his neck in both directions, much as Cora had done. *So be it.*

He returned to the physical realm with more understanding of the danger than when he went in, and it must have shown in his eyes, for Odin's remaining eye narrowed accusingly. "Like what you see in there, *nidingr*?"

Nidingr. Vile villain. That hurt more than he wanted to admit. Yes, he'd been called worse plenty of times, but not by someone he once considered a friend. "No," he answered, truthfully. "It astounds me how you continue to make excuses for that overgrown ice cube, which makes me wonder just which of you really rules Asgard."

Another flash of bright light obscured his vision, but this time he was ready for it. He closed his eyes and slapped his hands over his ears, not resisting in the least when he felt the dual bands snap across his chest and yank him out of the way. Damn, he loved having the brute squad at his back.

"How dare you, you insolent cur!" Odin bellowed, loud enough to be heard over the ringing in his ears.

When Avis opened his eyes, he found himself standing alongside Clarise and Columbine at the far end of the longhouse. Not where he wanted to be when Cora was all alone at the other end of the room! "Cora!" he shouted in reflex, his hand instinctively reaching for her as if by will alone he could bring her to him. In hindsight that was perhaps the dumbest thing he could've done since it caused all three Asgardians to turn towards the weaving loom near the front door. He clenched his outstretched fist and punched himself in the thigh. *SHIT!*

But despite his moment of stupidity, he couldn't be prouder of the way his little tiger stood her ground. Her chin went up and her shoulders squared as she stared all three of them down. Her surface thoughts when he looked were nowhere near as confident as she portrayed, but since Asgard had no ranged benders, her false bravado was damned impressive. Loki in particular, twisted his stance into one of admiration as he continued to observe her.

Avis looked between his child and the three grown men, weighing up his options. If he dropped them now while their backs were to him, Cora would view it with the same disdain she had when the mortal had tried to sucker-punch him. But on the upside; she'd live long enough to have that opinion. Now that he knew the Asgardians were holding him responsible for the deaths of two of their youths (three if they counted Nanna, who'd obviously committed suicide if she was burnt alongside her husband) he also knew they'd never stop until his girls were just as dead. The Asgardians believed in an eye for an eye, which he understood all too well. Mystal believed in that too, though they added a kick in the teeth for good measure.

Taking the risk of being grabbed in the celestial realm, Avis braced himself for the icy wasteland of Asgard's peak winter (that almost matched Antenora) and stepped both forward and up. Most pantheons believed in a simple above and below style separation, however, the Asgardians' entire realm had been shaped into a tree called Yggdrasil. The frigidity of the Asgardian winter slammed into him the moment he entered the celestial realm and he used his forward momentum to take another quick step to leave before he was frozen solid. Without the right cold-weather gear, becoming frozen in place took a few seconds of exposure at best.

In comparison, Antenora did it almost instantly.

His second step dropped him back into the mortal realm, right in front of Cora. His back was to her as he faced the Asgardians; his size alone blocking her from their view. "I'm here, t-tiger," he said without turning to look at her, hoping his announcement would bolster her confidence and that she wouldn't notice the slight chatter of his teeth. Already, the warmth of the longhouse brought feeling back to his numbed fingers and his clothes began to thaw out; allowing his cloak to fall loosely against his knees where it had previously been snap-frozen into a board.

"Not for long," Thor growled, readying to throw another lightning bolt.

With a strange look on his face, Loki stepped in front of Thor in much the same fashion as he himself had stepped in front of Cora. "No," the giant said, his gaze never wavering from Avis' stomach as if the bastard could see right through him to his daughter. "You might hit the girl."

Outraged, Thor struck Loki with Mjolnir, knocking the first giant back to where Avis and the brute squad guard had been standing when Frash was killed. "What?" the storm god roared, unable to believe what he was seeing or hearing.

Loki clambered to his feet and dusted his thighs unrepentantly. "I like her spirit. She'll make a good replacement for Narvi."

Avis' left hand immediately went down and back, searching for and finally latching onto Cora in both protection and possession. His other hand fisted at his side. "Not gonna fucking happen," he declared, his temper clawing the inside of his skull for release. He shifted his focus to Odin. "I don't regret what happened to Lord Narvi for an instant, and I take no responsibility for the loss of Lord Baldur." His chin jerked towards Loki. "If you want to give that idiot a pass for murdering him like you do everything else, that's your choice. But no realm-damned way are you getting my girls in compensation for his actions." Avis shook his head to emphasise that. "No way."

"The price of our loss is not yours to set. Only I decide what will clear your debt. An eye for an eye is what I desire, for you to avoid my righteous ire." Odin's bearded chin lifted as he prepared to make his decree. "Loki has made his claim, and I will do the same. Your younger daughter will die this day. For your crimes, she will pay."

As he spoke, more Asgardians arrived, filling the large room. Specifically, Odin's Valkyries. Armed female warriors that matched Armina's elite in grit and power. Avis' eyes moved from one to the next, lingering on the two that flanked Odin's wolves. Captains Brynhildr and Svava stood with their swords drawn, ready to do whatever Odin commanded.

"No, she won't," Avis argued with a snarl. He wanted to say and do so much more, but when he glanced to where Clarise carried Columbine to see how they were holding up, he saw the tight set to Columbine's lips and the streaks of angry tears that poured down his little princess' face. The sight made it all the harder to control his own rising temper. How dare the Asgardians make his little girl cry! This had to end, and not the way Odin wanted.

"Lady Cora." Loki's booming voice took on a lyrical undertone in an apparent attempt to draw her out. Avis' hand tightened, just as determined to not let that happen. Loki was a tricky shifter and currently, Cora couldn't shift. History had proven Loki wasn't above mesmerising a non-shifter like the snake he was to get what he wanted. "Come here, child. I won't hurt you."

"Damn right, you won't." But even as he said it, he felt his grip on Cora slip and heard her step away. His head jerked in her direction. "No!" He couldn't allow her to play any part in whatever Loki was planning, but with so much danger present, he couldn't risk taking his eyes off the Asgardians for long either. "Cora, get back here!" he hissed, trying and failing to keep her behind him.

"Why should I trust you?" she demanded.

Avis stopped dead in his tracks, mortified that Cora would say such a thing. They might not have had the best start and were currently having a few issues, but he'd genuinely thought they were past this stage.

Then he realised she wasn't talking to him. She was eyeballing Loki; not that that was any better. She was supposed to be a five-year-old girl, and children of that age didn't stand up to frost giants with all the attitude of a pissed off warrior.

Worse, when he swept through her surface thoughts, he found she was genuinely curious. For fuck's sake, surely their relationship hadn't taken such a hit that she was willing to become an Asgardian ... had it? Ten seconds ago, he'd have bent her mind to his will and forced her to return to his side, but that was before her surface thoughts drew a line in the sand between them. Cora wasn't a regular child. She had the mind of an adult, and that adult had *chosen* to step away from him—to listen to Loki. Even if it killed him, he had to respect that space.

Don't do this, tiger! he wanted to shout, his eyes moving constantly between the two. By the Twin Notes of all creation, he didn't know what he'd do if she chose Loki over him, but it wouldn't be good.

Loki smiled, with all the charm and danger of a realm-damned basilisk. "Such a smart girl," he cooed, kneeling on one knee to be closer in height to her. Avis gnashed his teeth and clenched his fists, but so long as Loki made no physical move toward her and was incapable of a mental one, he'd let Cora hear what he had to say. "I can't help but notice, sweet Lady Cora, that you are the only red-headed

Mystallian I have ever heard of. I wonder, do you think there might be a reason for that, sweetling?"

Where the fuck are you going with this? Avis wondered with a snarl. It was no secret Mystal only had a handful of redheads, but that wasn't why Belial had chosen the hair colour for her. There was a loose myth that redheads were nothing but trouble, and given how anti-Highborn Hellion she'd behaved, Belial had forced her to bear her rich red locks as a 'punishment'.

"Not particularly," Cora answered, polishing a single tooth with her tongue as if the subject or the condescension (or both in her case) annoyed her.

"You should." Loki's voice took on a resonating tone that belied the danger. "Because you and I both know you don't belong with these people. Not even a little bit." He moved his eyes to Avis and curled his lip into a sneer. "Their kind are too pristine for us. Too stuck up." His eyes returned to Cora. "Getting down and dirty is what people like you and me do for fun. You have never worn their uniform because deep down, you knew it wasn't a good fit for you. Look inside yourself, my sweetling, and know I speak the truth. You have the spirit of an Asgardian warrior, and your place is here with us." Ever so slowly, he uncurled a hand at her, inviting her to join him. "Come, Lady Cora. Show these fools where your loyalty lies. Show them all, where you truly belong."

"Show you all where I truly belong," Cora repeated in agreement, taking two steps forward and two to the right to stand directly in front of her father.

Before Avis could enter her mind to see what she meant by that, her tan clothes darkened into the deep obsidian he knew so well, complete with the all-important gleaming gold Mystallian sigil in the middle of her cloak. She held her right hand up to her shoulder and clenched the fist. "Mystal," she declared, without looking backwards, to which Avis reached forward and knocked his fist against hers.

"Mystal," he agreed, barely able to hear his voice over the pounding of blood in his ears. After all this time, she'd finally chosen to be Mystallian! *YESSSSSSSSS!!!*

CHAPTER TWENTY-NINE

The room erupted into chaos at that point. Loki roared his disapproval. Thor's wild shouting joined in. On an unspoken command, the Valkyrie drew their swords and charged at Avis and Cora, only be sent straight back in the direction they came by two barely discernible golden blurs. Another group of figures appeared at Avis' side, though the wafting lavender fragrance and the familial link that connected them all kept him from retaliating. In a single, fluid motion, Avis swept Cora into his arms and repositioned her on to his left hip to free his right arm. Then he hooked his right hand around Clarise's right shoulder, knowing Columbine was still being nursed in her arms and pulled them all together. On the other side of them were the other two golden blurs.

"Lord Odin! Pull your Valkyrie back before they get wiped out!" *Lord Odin.* Avis hadn't called Odin that in so long it sounded strange on his lips, but now wasn't the time to be sentimental. He had nothing against the Valkyrie and under normal circumstances, they were a force to be reckoned with, but not when they were up against Belial's brute squad. Too many of them were already dead or dying. "You can't win this! You have to know you can't!"

Odin raised his hand, and the conflict stopped just as abruptly as it had exploded. The four brute squad guards materialised in a boxed formation around the Mystallians and their remaining three hellion servants. Despite the death and the carnage that had occurred in just those few seconds, no blood was present on their limbs or wings. They were as immaculate as always. Odin ground his teeth in fury. "There will come a time, Mystallian," he promised, his one eye narrowing hatefully. "When you will not have these vile monstrosities to protect you." His gaze travelled from one guard to the next as he spoke, then settled back on Avis. "And on that day, no matter how much you scheme and plan, we will secure that which is our due."

"Isn't Baldur still in Hel with Hel?" Avis snapped in return. "Instead of huffing and puffing at me, get off your f—fat ass and go get him." *And then we can put this shit behind us and Loki can go fuck himself!* Clarise still winced at his profanity, but it was better than what he started to say, and they had bigger problems than his choice of language.

Watching Odin, Avis saw in his surface thoughts that he was already working out who to send to the death goddess as an emissary. Baldur had been their best negotiator by far, but he wasn't their only one. Hermod, Baldur's older brother, was the first to make the shortlist. Avis barely refrained from rolling his eyes. Why the hell hadn't he thought of doing this before? Not that it mattered. The fact that Odin was considering it now gave him a small measure of hope that things weren't as over between them as they had been moments earlier.

Avis flicked his eyebrows to indicate that while they might finally be on the same page, he was still too angry at his former friend to smile. Maybe things would go back to the way they were at some point, but that day was in the far distant future. Odin had threatened the lives of his girls and Avis wasn't the forgiving type either.

"No! She'll learn to be mine! I claim her as Narvi's replacement!" Loki bellowed again.

"Your temper is annoying, and my patience wanes. Mystal is the home her heart claims."

"I don't care! He will not leave Asgard without repaying his debt to me!"

"Agreed," Thor growled, equally as furious as Loki and being just as unable to act on it. "He must be made to pay for Baldur."

Avis had heard enough. Under the deadly glares and vicious taunts of the Asgardians, he gave the charred outline in the middle of the room a final, parting look, then moved his family (and by proxy the three remaining servants and the four guards) towards the opening on the right-hand side of the longhouse that led into the stable. The Valkyrie followed them, shuffling forward in such a way that kept both feet on the ground and their swords held in both hands over one shoulder in anticipation of Odin's order to attack again. The women were fearless, but also obedient. They wouldn't attack without Odin's say-so.

The animals did not appreciate being surrounded by so much angry divinity. They barked and howled. They whinnied, clucked and squealed. Those with wings flew across the ceiling rafters in a rage. Those without wings lashed out at whatever was nearest to them, kicking and clawing and biting at each other. The racket was intense.

In fact, the only animals that weren't acting out, were the four horses hitched at the furthest point of the room. They stood with their ears forward and nickered darkly in hellish excitement. Fortunately, the Asgardians hadn't looked too hard at the animals housed within the stable. If they had, they might've realised these four were disguised demon steeds and eliminated them to reduce the Mystallians' movement rate to a crawl.

Avis tilted Clarise's shoulder towards him so he could whisper in her ear. "Asgard is in the peak of winter. As soon as we get up there, we're going to need a shield to separate us from them and keep out the cold." It pissed him off to know they had to abandon the relative warmth of the mortal realm in favour of the frozen winter of the celestial one, but now that they'd been discovered, any of Asgard's attuned celestials could upend reality on a whim and make his girls' situation a fatal one. They had to get back to where the rules of existence were more rigid, even if that rigidity was in the midst of a bitter winter.

Clarise slid her slitted gaze across to him to acknowledge what he'd said without tipping their hand. In doing so, he felt the leather and fabric of his uniform swell to accommodate the thick fur lining she'd added. Still perched on their hips, both girls must've felt the shift and realised what it meant, for Cora's uniform and Columbine's simple nightgown shifted into full-body cold-weather gear. Thankfully, between their black uniforms, the swaying motion of their cloaks and the flickering shadows caused by the wall-mounted torches, Avis was confident that the Asgardians hadn't noticed; even if he had broken into an uncomfortable sweat.

Avis released Clarise and lifted his thumb and middle finger to his lips, emitting the high-pitched note which should've brought forth the demon steeds' fiery wings. As he'd hoped, the outer shell of the beasts exploded into their natural form of living hellfire, complete with wings. The hay under their hooves ignited at once—and was extinguished almost as quickly.

Neither knowing nor caring who had stopped the fire, Avis deposited Cora onto the back of the second demon steed from the left and claimed the outside steed for himself. It was becoming second nature by now for him to put the girls in a central place of safety while he took the more dangerous position on the outside. Not that any of the Asgardians were going to get through the brute squad to threaten either of them, but it was good practice for when they were on their own. Clarise then mounted the next demon steed beside Cora with Columbine still in her arms, while Tilu gathered up the reins of the fourth demon steed.

Columbine had her face pressed tightly into her mother's neck, and it was clear from the way her tiny fists were clenched behind her mother's head and her whole body shuddered that she was understandably distraught over the loss of Frash. The thought of her so heartbroken pissed him off all over again and he turned his savagery towards the Asgardians around them. *Fuckers,* he swore, lashing out at a random Valkyrie and eradicating hundreds of centuries of memory from her in the blink of an eye. Just … because.

The woman blinked and frowned, all without lowering her weapon. Her surface thoughts showed that in a single sweep of the room, she had deemed Avis and his family to be the present threat to Asgard; despite the friendship that she knew existed between her lord and the Mystallian patriarch. A heartbeat later, she resumed her battle stance alongside her sisters and shuffled forward in perfect sync with them.

As tempting as it was to add a few hundred eons to that figure, Avis knew wouldn't change the outcome. Valkyrie were constructs; crafted by Odin (who, despite his rulership, wasn't an established Life God) to do his bidding. As a bender, he could drop-kick her mind all the way back to the first day of her creation, and she'd still fight just as she was. That's not to say it wasn't tempting as all fuck (especially as mad as he was right now), but he had other priorities.

THE GIRLS HAVE NEVER REALM-STEPPED.

Shit! Realm-stepping was supposed to be second nature to all celestials. Even the youngest of Mystallian children were taught that each step wasn't a matter of moving in three dimensions, but four. The added *oomph* of going up into the celestial realm and down into the mortal one was no different from stepping forwards, backwards, side to side or jumping up and down. But the girls had been raised in Hell, where their every movement was monitored by the men. They wouldn't have been trusted to know how to realm-step, and without his guidance, Cora would be left behind when everyone else left.

Like fuck. Avis had not just won the ultimate prize only to lose it on a technicality. Cora was Mystallian, and Mystallians stood together. Or, in this case, found safer ground together. Without giving it a thought, he shifted both his reins into his right hand and leaned forward over Hotspot's neck, taking up Cora's right rein in his other hand. There was no doubt that Cora would only need to be shown this once. He was just annoyed that she needed to be shown at all. *Stupid Highborn Hellions.*

At least, for once, he wasn't alone in his anger. The gold in Clarise's eyes had hardened into jagged peaks of deep fury as she took in each Asgardian around them, almost as if she couldn't decide which one to unleash on. *That one. No, that one. No … that one over there.* Having such a target-rich environment could do that to people who weren't used to battle. Even Tilu wore a brutal expression that promised a realm of intense suffering. Given that Thor had murdered her sister not five minutes ago in the other room, he understood why, but out of everyone, he seemed to be the only one with a modicum of rational thought in the angry atmosphere. He wasn't sure why that was, but he knew this was not the place to draw battle lines. Not when the Asgardians could control reality just as soon as they remembered to apply it. He needed to get them all into the celestial realm. There was little doubt that the Asgardians would follow them, and a really big part of him didn't care. In anticipation of the fight, he tightened his grip on his reins and snorted like a bull. *Bring it.*

* * *

Cora looked at her father out of the corner of her eye and frowned. *Dammit, shorthorns! Get a grip on your anger before Father figures it out! He's already starting to!*

What in the name of the realms do you think *I am trying to do?* Columbine shouted back uncharacteristically, her tiny fists clenching even tighter behind their mother's neck. *It is everywhere in here, and I do not like it!*

It's only everywhere because you're the one projecting it everywhere! Cora roared in return. *Now shut it the fuck down, before we all kill each other!*

Columbine jerked her head to the side where she could glare at her sister through red-rimmed eyes and her tear-stained hair. *You swore!*

You made me! she counted. *They may have started it, but you're making it a thousand times worse with your damned blowback!* Blowback. An apt description for the way Columbine's innate power operated at full capacity, and Cora was impressed she'd thought of it all by herself. From now on, that would be how she described the annoying feature.

Like her father had done moments ago, Cora put both reins in her left hand and discreetly stretched her right towards her mother and younger sister. She wasn't quite long enough in the arm to reach, so she folded the bones of her hand into a single, boneless tentacle, and thrust it at her sister's shin. With more shifting, she parted the leather of Columbine's boot and pressed the tentacle against her sister's bare skin.

And was immediately inundated with a wall of raw fury so intense she couldn't see straight. Her teeth sharpened until they practically begged to be sunk into the neck of an Asgardian. No, not just an Asgardian. Her head snapped to their father, believing he made just as tempting a target. In fact, they all did. Her mother hadn't allowed her to be a Mystallian! She hadn't even given her the rights every other Mystallian woman enjoyed *freely*! And the servants! They were always forcing their ways onto her, like they had the right to! Even the demon steeds, for ... well ... they just did! They all needed to die! Everything needed ...

Knowing the blowback rage was feeding off the way she felt about random crap, Cora dug deep into her Mystallian pride and snapped her bared teeth together, forcing herself to stare at the fiery mane of her demon steed and avoid all other distractions. *When I kill something, you faceless fucking blowback, it'll be because I. FUCKING. CHOOSE. TO. DO. IT!*

Breathing grew difficult for her, but she still refused to let Columbine go, believing the more fury she could bleed out of her irate sister; the quicker

Columbine could get herself under control and shut this shit down once and for all. *And then I'm gonna kick your fucking*—No! *No, I'm not! Fuck it! Fuuuuck!* Cora hissed long and hard in frustration. How do you fight something, when offering any level of resistance is in itself a fight? Finding a viable workaround had never been this difficult in Hell, but then, neither of them had ever been permitted into the Nine Levels, so Columbine had never tasted true rage before either. Not like this anyway. It was almost palpable, even before Columbine's innate power fed into it. How in the realms was their mother holding her own? She'd been nursing the scrawny little pain-in-the-ass ever since the Asgardians turned up and she seemed as indomitable as ever. How was she not losing her mind?

"Cora!" her father barked. Cora snapped her head up to see him staring at her but wisely kept her mouth shut. "Watch what I'm doing!"

Fuck you!

Cora was certain she hadn't voiced that, but the way her father's head jerked towards her and his eyes flared, then shrank back into thin slits, she knew he'd heard it anyway. *Great.*

She watched him closely, observing the way he directed both demon steeds to simultaneously step forward and up, phasing through the veil that separated the mortal realm from the celestial one …

…and straight into the worst fucking blizzard she'd ever had the misfortune to be caught in! *Holy fucking frost-balls of a frozen realm-damned yeti!* Even through the furs, the cold penetrated her to the very bone!

Again, Cora struggled with the emotions that she knew weren't entirely of her own making as she doubled, then tripled the layers of insulation in her uniform. Had their father really come up here in nothing more than a single layer of leather and fabric? Moron! No wonder he was stuttering like a bird when he came back. *What kind of stupid lunatic …?*

THE KIND THAT WAS DETERMINED TO PROTECT YOU FROM DANGER; REGARDLESS OF THE COST TO HIMSELF, her subconscious was quick to point out. Cora screwed her face up and lightly slapped her right thigh in frustration. She knew that. She did. His complete flip-out at the thought of losing her had been proof enough. He had plenty to be accountable for, but endangering himself to protect her wasn't one of them. If anything, that should've been commended, and if it weren't for her sister's projecting, she wouldn't have swiped at him at all. *Fucking hell!* Anger was an insidious bastard of an emotion once it took on a life of its own.

Cora looked to her right where her father had been and couldn't see a realm-damned thing through the blizzard. The pelting snow stung her eyes and hurt her face and ears, and without a second thought, she crafted a complex face shield with breathing vents and a thick, stretchable head sock that protected her exposed head and neck. Shifting herself back into her hellion form wouldn't have helped since that was even less capable of handling the cold than her father's form; not that she'd ever tell him that.

A tiny window in the face shield was supposed to fix the problem of snow-blindness, but unfortunately, the heat of her eyes and forehead against the elements had the window fogging up in no time. *Okay, let's try this again,* she thought, as it suddenly occurred to her that focusing on a neutral problem prevented her from falling deeper into the quagmire of her sister's anger. Since one window didn't work, logic demanded she try two, one in front of the other, with a buffer to prevent fogging. Still not enough. The original problem of snow-blindness hadn't been solved. Worse, she could hear the Asgardians roaring over the blizzard nearby. Determined not to be blind-sided by them (literally), she quickly cycled through hundreds of visual spectra, searching for one that could pick up any small flecks of colour to the exclusion of white and settling on a monochrome skin which she applied to the external window of her visor.

The difference was like night and day. She could see her father with his left arm raised and his head ducked low and to the right, using his hand and cloak collar in a pathetic attempt to shield himself from the elements. *Snow's kicking your ass, huh?* she mused, even as she took control of the snow whipping around his head and reshaped it into a replica of her own headgear.

His reaction to her surprise gift pissed her off all over again; for instead of being grateful, he gasped and dropped his reins, his fingers immediately clawing, then patting every surface of the face shield and head sock. What did he think it was going to do? Poison him? Bite his face off? It was just a headpiece, for fuck's sake. He should at least say 'thank you'.

Her top lip curled to expose one of her many fangs, once again fighting to rein in a temper that wasn't hers. They were in enemy territory and something had just encompassed her father's whole head without warning. With no idea who had done what, wanting it and his assailant identified as friend or foe was totally reasonable.

For the love of the Well, get a grip, shorthorns! She wasn't sure how much longer she could hold back the desire to maim everything in her vicinity or die trying.

Let me go, if it is too much for you, was Columbine's snarky reply.

Cora's temper spiked and as she hissed into the fabric of her head sock, she squeezed Columbine's leg so tightly she cut off the circulation and at the very least bruised the bone. Maybe even cracked it. Through their touch connection, Cora knew the exact moment when Columbine opened her mouth to squeal, and stopped the sound from ever reaching her lips. She then numbed and repaired the damaged flesh, wiggling her tentacle from side to side as if to rub it better. *Sorry ... sorry ...shh-shh-shh ...You're okay ...* Cora recanted, desperately hoping their mother hadn't noticed. Violence was high on everyone's agenda, and drawing that level of unwanted attention to herself was not in her best interest.

That hurt! Columbine snarled.

Well, your temper's making me mad. Come on, shorthorns. Rein it in. Cora was about to say more when it dawned on her that this was entirely the wrong approach. Instead of putting all of the emphasis on Columbine to fix the situation, they needed to work through this together like they used to in Hell. *What if I gave you a sedative? Would this all stop if you were asleep, shorthorns?* She'd have to come up with a really creative lie for why she'd done it, and somehow weave in the truth to get it past her mother, but that was 'Future Cora's' problem. 'Current Cora' had enough of her own.

How would I know? was Columbine's snappish reply. *Argh!! It is too much! I cannot block it out!*

* * *

Avis had never been so close to wringing someone's neck as when he realised the thing that materialised around his head was a heavy-duty cold-weather headpiece, complete with some type of bronze/silver lens that allowed him to see much more clearly than he had before. One of his girls had bailed him out, but that wasn't what enraged him. They should've given him a fucking heads-up before pulling that shit on him in enemy territory! Not only that, but when he turned towards all three of them and saw Cora wearing exactly the same piece of equipment, he was also reminded that her shifting had come back. Exactly when had that come about? More to the point, how long had the little shit been playing him for a fool? He swept through her surface thoughts, allowing that to be the deciding factor. If he found so much as a flicker of amusement there, he'd completely lose his shit at her.

But what he found took the fight right out of him.

What if I gave you a sedative? Would this all stop if you were asleep, shorthorns?

With everything that was going on, he'd forgotten all about Columbine's accursed sensitivity to everyone else's emotions! She must've been going out of her mind with so much unfamiliar rage coursing through her! He knew the second he saw Cora's surface thought about sedation that it wasn't going to work. He knew, because both he and Clarise had tried that with both bending and shifting while they were back on the Akheron River and it had only made things worse.

Through trial and error, he'd learned the best solution was to surround Columbine with a more preferred emotion. Back when the Damned had become too much for her to bear, a strong cuddle and whispered words of love and comfort went a long way towards making her feel better. In his own head, he rationalised it with the belief that touching her physically added more weight than a hundred or even a thousand emotions in the distance. Clarise was in the perfect position to offer her that support, but her eyes had taken on that multi-eyed fly look she did when she was building them accommodations, and the skin of her face and lips took on the impervious blue-white tones of the frost giants. She was supporting Columbine physically, just not in the way their little princess needed right then.

He could hear the Asgardians in the distance, and felt himself grow angry at their presence. It was their fault she was in this state and he didn't want them anywhere near her. For a second, he wondered why they hadn't stepped up into the celestial realm with them, then realised they probably had, only to be displaced however far back by four extremely competent golden guards.

Avis couldn't see exactly what Clarise was up to, but that wasn't important. She was her own person. He nudged his demon steed around the front of Cora's; forcing hers to step away. *Asshole*, her surface thoughts swore, but she was smart enough not to voice it. Much like she had when she'd told him to fuck off earlier in anger. His initial instinct had been to backhand her right off her demon steed, but he forced himself to remember she hadn't learned how to vet her surface thoughts the way she could her voice yet, and until that happened, he had to give them a pass. As annoying as that was.

When her demon steed backed away, he caught sight of the fleshy tether and followed it back to Cora. Well, that explained how she planned on administering the sedative she'd wanted to use before.

Believing the more touch-based emotional support Columbine could be offered, the better, he didn't try to sever it.

Clarise definitely saw him coming. Her head may not have moved, but as he reached forward and slid his hands under Columbine's armpits with every intention of taking her core weight, Clarise reached over her shoulders and pulled apart Columbine's hands. Columbine twitched and flexed as he lifted her off her mother and nestled her against his chest. Her tiny body was so tense for a moment he'd thought she'd partially frozen. But when he swept through her surface thoughts, all he found was rage. "Ssshhh, it's okay baby," he said, though between the face shield and the raging storm, he didn't know if she'd heard a word of it. "It's going to be okay."

"Make it stop, Father!" Columbine demanded savagely, bunching the padding of his doublet in her clenched fists and sobbing into the thick fabric. "They are all so angry!"

"Sssshhh, I know, baby," Avis crooned, petting her as best he could through their cold-weather gear. He fought his own surging temper as he spoke, determined to stop his rage from making the problem worse. *Calm … calm … calm. Don't lose it. Don't try to think about how much this situation's hurting her … and especially don't think about destroying every last motherfucking Asgardian for causing her …*

He heard the soft, un-Mystallian growl ripple against the fur on his neck and forced himself away from those thoughts by lifting his chin and trusting her with his exposed throat. Trust was an emotion, wasn't it? Trust and love. At this stage, it was all he had to work with. "Stay with me, princess," he said, rubbing his padded throat against her hooded head. "You're stronger than this. Better than this. Don't let it win. Don't let them win." Mystallian pride. That, he could convey all day.

As he spoke, he continued to stroke her head and back through the thick padding of his gloves and her clothes. She shivered against him, and he could practically feel the rage coming off her in waves. "You can do this, baby," he insisted, though even as he said it, he lifted his eyes to the starless night sky overhead and wondered how himself. It was going to take a month or two of hard riding to traverse the length of Asgard and Columbine was already nearing her breaking point after only a few minutes. He was furious with his former friend for putting her in this situation, and angry with himself for not having a viable solution. They had no shortcuts. None. Belial had made it clear his family were off-limits, which meant the only blood-links that might help them were all in Mystal. He couldn't risk reaching out to them and making contact with his powerbase and subsequent thrall. If he thought they were in trouble now, having him turn back into the uncaring bastard he'd been before would be the last straw. No one else would help. He'd burnt every other bridge, and now his little girl was going to pay for it. *Princess, I'm so sorry …* He wished he had another way. Any other way. This was going to be a true test of torture for all of them.

Looking up as he was, Avis saw something cutting through the night sky towards them. It was large and clear, like a giant glass bowl, and as it descended over them, it cut off the blizzard that howled around them. Just in case it was an elaborate Asgardian trap, Avis shot out a mental barb and found no mind within it, which both pleased and irritated him in equal measure. A target he could vent at would've been really useful right about now.

As soon as it touched down, all sound outside the dome was eliminated and the snow on their side melted into a carpet of Mystallian grass that rippled across the ground under their demon steeds' fiery hooves. His skin prickled in the new-found warmth.

One of the brute squad guards materialised on the outside of the newly formed barrier right in front of him. To anyone else, the guard looked as it always did, with its arms crossed and its weight evenly distributed between its three legs, but Avis knew what to look for and saw that its knees were slightly bent and its wings patted the air in anticipation of combat. Beyond it, Avis saw the shadowed masses emerging out of the snow as the Asgardians rushed towards them. Loki and Thor led the charge. It was strange to see so many dangerous warriors pouring into view with their mouths open in a battle cry and not hear a sound from them. Stranger still, to know with absolute certainty that their ferocious charge amounted to absolutely nothing to him. He could turn his back on them, should he choose to, for all the threat factor they offered.

Right or wrong, Avis assumed the brute squad had kept the Asgardians back until a hard line had been created to give them a defined border to protect. In hindsight, the Asgardians had probably tried to realm-step right alongside the Mystallians, only to have the brute squad intercept them and vanish before he realised they were even there. The constant game of stepping in and being shoved out would certainly explain where the remaining two guards had gone.

The more often he witnessed the brute squad's capability, the more convinced he became that it really did only take six of them to destroy Teon.

First things first, they had to get out of their cold-weather gear. Already, he felt the sweat soaking into the furs that surrounded him. He took the faceplate in one hand and heaved it forward, tearing it like paper from his head. "Gingen, get Columbine out of these hot furs," he ordered, more concerned about her than himself. The servant bobbed her head and rushed forward, but Avis made it clear by tensing his other arm across his little girl's back that he had no intention of handing her over. He wanted Gingen to reach up; which she did.

As Columbine's furs melted into her regular uniform, he felt his own doing likewise and arched an eyebrow in surprise. With Frash dead, he didn't think any of the other servants would be dumb enough to step up and take her place on his shit-list by assuming to do things to him without first asking. Facing the rest of the party the way he was, he quickly deduced by their locations that it hadn't been a servant. None of them were in touch-contact with him. Columbine was still clutching him, but her mindset made that level of focus impossible. While it might have been Clarise, it was Cora he'd found staring at him.

Well, he assumed she was. Her own uniform had returned to normal, but she maintained the strange silver/bronze eye shield that hid her eyes from view. She raised her right hand, holding her ring and middle finger to her palm with her thumb, while her pointer finger and little finger stayed fully extended. The universal sign of a shifter who was pleased with either themselves or the work they'd done. Usually both. *Cheeky shit.* Before he could say as much, her head straightened to allow her to look past him to the dome wall not two body-lengths away from them.

Avis followed her line of sight, but without her fancy eyewear, all he saw was snow.

"Can you believe he actually thought I'd go with him?" she snarled incredulously. "He honestly thought I'd be okay with me paying for what you did!" It was only then that Avis noticed her jagged teeth and grimaced.

"Get your anger under control, tiger," he warned. "It's affecting Columbine."

Cora's jaw fell open as her head whipped around to face him. Her surface thoughts were full of expletives and disbelief, causing him to frown darkly at her.

"You know she's an empath that absorbs the emotional state of others," he growled, then checked himself. *Nice thoughts. Happy thoughts.* Fuck, that was so much easier said than done when he was this mad. *Happy, happy, happy.* He breathed out a huff and slid his gaze to the dome, then back to Cora. His hand continued to pet Columbine's raven locks. "The only chance we've got of blocking *them* out is if we surround her with the love and support of the family."

Cora also looked at the dome, though unlike him, she saw those on the other side. "Fine," she said, also on a huff. Then, in complete contrast, she barked out an evil laugh and turned back to him. "Oh, Father, you have got to see this," she said, already creating a second lens across his eyes. "Loki's getting his absolute butt handed to him. It's brilliant."

Avis would put *a war* on hold to watch that.

Sure enough, the silver lens revealed the mischievous fire god lying flat on his back about three metres away from the dome. Froth and spittle collected around his lips like a lunatic. Then he opened his mouth and screamed at the sky. In a blur of movement, he rolled to his hands and knees and smashed his doubled fists into the ground.

Two ground-shaking punches later, he'd gouged out a huge boulder which he then hurled at the dome, only to have it cast straight back in his face with enough force to knock him ass-over-tit backwards into the other Asgardian warriors.

Avis threw his head back and howled in laughter. That had to be the funniest thing he'd seen in forever, and its timing couldn't be better. He latched onto that euphoria with both metaphorical hands and added it to the love he felt for his family.

"I could watch that all night," Cora guffawed, slapping her hands together.

'Night' was the operative word for Avis. The girls should've been asleep hours ago. Mindful of the tether, he lifted his left leg and dropped to the ground on Cora's side of Hotspot. "Come on, tiger. It's time you two were in bed."

Cora looked down at them both and sobered. "What are we going to do about her, Father?" she asked, dropping down beside him. Her attention was still on Columbine, who remained in a tight ball in his arms. "She can't keep doing this. It'll kill us all."

Avis sighed and lifted his supporting arm to kiss Columbine's dark hair, having no answer to that. Not when she was one hundred percent right. Columbine was an integral part of their family and her loss would forever destroy them all. Him at least. "We'll do what we have to," he answered, knowing how pathetic that sounded but having nothing else to offer.

Cora pursed her lips. "This sucks."

"Yeah," Avis drawled in agreement. "It does."

Rather than spinning around and getting himself all tangled up in Cora's tether, Avis walked around his older daughter and turned inward at the last minute to face the same direction she was. In doing so, he saw that Clarise had finished the house and was finalising the stables for the demon steeds. He, of course, had had his back to it the whole time and was looking at the border. Because ... why not?

"Ready when you are, sweetheart," he said, lifting his gaze to Clarise, who was the only one of their family still mounted. It pleased him to see her features had once again become Mystallian.

Columbine constantly shifted from growling into his throat to whimpering against it, and it shredded his heart to know she was being inundated with everyone's rage, only to regret how angry it made her. No amount of sympathetic rubbing by him was going to fully alleviate it.

Hopefully, once they got inside, exhaustion would hit her and she'd sleep through the next few hours of this. Tomorrow was going to be hell.

CHAPTER THIRTY

Once they were behind closed doors, Avis sent Cora off with Gingen to have a bath and be put to bed. He had her retract the tentacle before they went, and was forced to breathe through his rising temper as it rolled back to her side and became her left arm once more. *You and I are going to have a long talk about that, just as soon as we're out of Asgard,* he promised, knowing this leg of the trip would take a couple of months but needing something to appease his temper. It wasn't in his nature to put an ass-ripping on hold like that, but for Columbine's sake, he would keep the family as anger-free as he could.

Which reminded him ...

Clarise stood at her end of the table with her hands pressed into either side of the corner. With Cora gone and Columbine barely functioning, Clarise's eyes were closed and she twisted her head from side to side as if she were dealing with some of her own issues. He guessed the biggest one was the loss of Frash. "Sweetheart," he crooned softly as he approached her. "For what it's worth, I'm sorry you'll miss her so much."

"You hated her," Clarise snarled, snapping her head up to glare at him.

Whoa! What the...? The rage that leapt across the table at him was almost palpable, and on pure instinct he swivelled his hips to put Columbine protectively behind him. His free hand came up with his fingers flared to show he had nothing to hide. "Easy, beautiful. I'm on your side, remember?"

The jagged gold in her eyes softened and she went back to looking at the table edge. "I am sorry, beloved," she said, curling her gloved fingers into the table veneer. "This entire situation has me on edge, and I cannot seem to control myself."

Well, at least she hadn't compounded the matter by adding 'Please, forgive me'. That would only make him more pissed than he already was. Avis relaxed and went to stand behind her, using his free hand to rub the back of her neck. "It's been a rough night for all of us," he agreed.

"Frash is dead," Clarise stated, turning just enough to stare up at him. The edges of her eyes watered, though she refused to let the tears fall. Avis sighed and rolled his arm to draw her into his chest alongside Columbine.

"Sweetheart, Frash was dead the moment she started dictating my actions back in the Well. You knew that. She's been living on borrowed time for months ..."

"Your intentions in this matter are irrelevant. You were not the one who killed her." She went to pull away, but he tensed his arm and nuzzled her hair, hinting without saying that he wanted her to stay put. It was enough to take the fight out of her, though her head lifted and shot a filthy look at the front doors. "He was. Thor had no right to take my servant from me."

Avis opened his mouth, then paused with a frown. Something wasn't right here. His beloved wife was the epitome of Highborn Hellion upbringing. From birth, she'd been trained to let nothing faze her. Not a damned thing. He had no doubt in the realm that she loved him with every fibre of her being, but she had still maintained her decorum when she'd been forced to abandon him to the Walk to heal. She'd left with her head high and her shoulders square and never once looked back. Yet, as she said, the loss of a servant (a personal one, granted, but a servant nonetheless) had left her barely able to control herself.

Not knowing what else to do, Avis dropped his lips to hers and kissed her. Deeply. He didn't care if Columbine saw the intimate gesture. It would give her something else to focus on. Besides, Clarise had used the move to snap him out of a bad mood or two in the past, so theoretically, the reverse should occur.

At first she squirmed, but all too quickly her struggles ceased and the tension left her lips. "I love you," he whispered once it ended. He stared her in the eye, willing her to accept that pledge.

It was a huge relief to see the gold in her eyes returned to their molten state. "I love you too, Avis," she promised, resting her forehead against his pec. "But I will never forgive Thor for what he has done this day."

He kissed the top of her head and twisted her away from the table, effectively putting her back to the main doors, and by extension the Asgardians as a whole outside. He herded her towards their apartment. "I won't hold you to that, should you change your mind tomorrow," he said, as Tilu opened the apartment doors for them and bowed. "But for now, why don't you let Tilu draw you a nice hot bath? Then, once you're relaxed and clean, sleep may yet take its course. We're back on the Akheron River as far as Columbine's empathy is concerned, and we can't afford to make any mistakes because we're tired and irritable."

He kept his tone as light as he could while slipping in that crucial piece of information, and was pleased by the way her eyes widened and shot across to Columbine that his message had been received. Perhaps this had been what Belial was preparing them for when he'd kept them so fucking long on the Akheron River. Agony and anger were both emotional states, though the former had very strong ties to the physical aspect which was why Columbine probably had an easier time coping with them.

The only thing he knew for sure was when it came to his bastard father-by-marriage, no one *ever* knew anything for sure. Releasing a small huff of frustration, Avis leaned down and kissed Clarise lightly on the lips. "I'm going to try and put Columbine down. I'll be back shortly, okay?"

Clarise pursed her lips together but nodded in agreement anyway. "Very well," she answered somewhat begrudgingly, then she leaned across and kissed Columbine on the cheek. "I will see you in the morning, sweetheart," she promised, though tension rippled across her face and neck and when she looked up at him, the gold had become glacial once more. Without another word to either of them, she whirled on her heel and strode across the room, following Tilu into the bedroom.

Avis stood in the main doorway with his head cocked, watching her go. Something really weird was going on here, and not knowing what it was, was seriously pissing him off. *No—no it isn't … breathe, stupid. Happy thoughts.*

He released a cleansing breath and cuddled Columbine close, focusing on his love for her and all of their family. In the back of his mind, he knew they were never going to make it a day or two, let alone a couple of months. He had a better chance of taking over Hell. But what other choice did they have except to try?

Despising the ominous sense of defeat that came with those thoughts, Avis turned and walked to Columbine's apartment. He carried Columbine through her sitting room and into her bedroom, where he found Cora already in the bed. Both governesses lingered near the ensuite door.

"What are you doing in here, tiger?" he asked, as Cora flipped back the comforter to reveal she was clean and dressed in her nightgown. Avis ran his eyes over her, unimpressed. Since it'd only been a couple of minutes since they'd all been in the dining room, the only way she could've pulled this off was with a stimulation wave.

Cora looked up at him and patted the empty space in the bed beside her. "I'll keep her company," she said adamantly.

Avis snorted haughtily and shook his head. "Not a chance in hell, tiger. Even if I was going to say yes, you thrash in your sleep almost as badly as your Uncle Tal. Or haven't you noticed the destroyed state of your beds every morning?"

Cora's gaze narrowed, and maintaining that dirty look, she pulled herself up onto one arm and liquefied her body; elongating it into an armour-plated body with tri-taloned hands. Her eyes melted into empty, oversized smouldering sockets and large leather wings sprouted from her shoulders. Her Highborn Hellion look was completed when a pair of multi-tipped antlers sprouted from her head and the tip of a long, thin tail poked out from under the comforter. "Now, I won't," she rumbled in her deep infernal voice. She sat up properly to free her bracing arm and reached both hands out for Columbine. "Give her to me, Father. We both know we're not going to get through this if you and mother don't brainstorm and figure something out."

Avis had only seen Cora's natural form once when he'd first been released from the Damned, and the sight of it now after all this time put him on the back foot. But she made sense. Even if it was just for an hour or so, freeing himself up to discuss the matter with Clarise and hopefully finding a solution would be time well spent. Then he could come back and send Cora to her own bed … if either of them were still awake.

"Alright, tiger," he said, kneeling into the mattress. He leaned forward and eased Columbine out of his arms, coaxing her with soft caressing until her full weight was transferred to her sister. The smouldering smoke that wafted from Cora's eye ridges expanded to seep through the empty holes of her nasal cavity and she tensed, curling her wings around Columbine for maximum contact.

"Go," she snarled, the demand made all the more unnerving by her manner of speech.

Under any other circumstances, Avis would've chipped her for the tone, but not tonight. As he straightened and pulled away from the bed, Cora wriggled her ass down the bed and lay back so that her horns wouldn't collide with the headboard. Columbine lay on her chest, still cocooned by her sister's wings. "Go," Cora hissed more quietly.

In a move Avis had seen his youngest brother do more times than he could count, he raised two fingers to his pursed lips and turned them towards his children in silent farewell. Then he withdrew from the bedroom; his thoughts in a whirl. This was a total clusterfuck. *What* was he supposed to go and discuss with Clarise? There was literally nothing *to* discuss. They were screwed. He nibbled on the stitching of his right glove thumb as he strode through the sitting room, his mind doing another sweep of the house to pinpoint each member of his family. It seemed Clarise had taken him up on his suggestion and was already asleep, if the stillness of her link was anything to go by. The girls behind him were just as still, though he doubted either one of them would be asleep this quickly. Well, maybe Columbine, if they were all lucky.

He went out into the dining hall and began pacing the length of the table. There had to be a way out of this. There had to be! He just couldn't see it! After his second lap, weariness gnawed at his muscles and he hooked his foot around the front leg of his chair, pulling it around to face him. On the next lap, he sat down with a huff and allowed his whole body to relax, lifting his eyes to the ceiling overhead. Parenting was ridiculously draining. Where he could normally go days without rest, right then he felt every second of his age. Finding no answers on the ceiling, he dropped his chin to his chest and stared unseeingly at the two sets of double doors that housed his family. Twenty minutes ago, he'd been ready to take on every Asgardian in the realm, and sleep had been the last thing on his mind. Yet, as his eyes rolled from one set of doors to the other and back again, he found it harder and harder to keep them open.

Realising how close he was to falling asleep, he stiffened with a start and drove most of his weight into his left elbow, determined not to succumb to it. He had a perfectly good bed just two rooms away, with a beautiful wife waiting for him to snuggle up to. He just had to get there. *Starting ... now.* He exhaled with every intention of surging to his feet, but the release of his breath had the opposite effect. It was as if the breath itself was what had been keeping him upright, and its loss caused the elbow supporting his weight to slide out from under him and he sagged over the arm of the chair, unconscious.

* * *

Odin waited until every Asgardian warrior had left the longhouse in pursuit of the Mystallian family before unclenching his fists and shifting sensation back into them. Physically, his warriors stood no chance of apprehending his former friend so long as the coward hid behind Belial's brute squad. Why the hellion ruler was helping that *nidingr*, Odin had no idea. Nor did he care. A physical confrontation wasn't what he had in mind anyway. Not now. If Avis thought he was going to escape the wrath of the Asgardians, he was about to learn no one ever did.

He walked to the far end of the longhouse, casting his eye over the messed sheets of the only bed in the room. At his sides plodded his wolfen companions. He sat on the edge of the mattress and ran his hand over the nearest pillow; the one that still had the indentation of a child's head in it. "I would say this is not personal, child, but that would be a lie. Your father is responsible for the loss of my son, and for that, you must also die."

He found what he was looking for, caught in the threads of the pillow. A single strand of obsidian celestial hair. Odin held it up to the light and smiled an ugly smile. "And thus we have an eye for an eye." With his other hand, he reached into a pocket and retrieved the finger bone of Baldur's that he'd been carrying with him ever since his son had perished, and wrapped the strand of hair around it. Seidr, or blood magic was normally the domain of females, but Odin, in true omnipotent fashion, refused to permit a power within his realm that he didn't master. When none of the hags would teach him the rituals, he'd gone to Mirmir, the oldest being still alive in the Asgardian realm. Older than any of the pantheon could remember, Mirmir agreed to give him the knowledge he sought, along with other valuable insights, in exchange for his eye.

Odin agreed to the price and learned more that day about seidr magic than even the hags knew.

He took a dagger and carved runes into the bone, muttering quietly under his breath. Then, at a pivotal point, he raised that same dagger and plunged it deep into his own chest, twisting it at the handle to force his ribs and heart wall apart. As a shifter, he could have bypassed the pain, but pain was an essential part of making the curse work. It was what imbued his hatred into the object he carried, especially when he thrust it into the open wound alongside the blade, ensuring every part of it was coated in the blood and rage from his heart. His chanting continued, despite the light-headedness that the injury caused him. It continued as he pulled the blood-soaked talisman from his chest, and it continued after he shape-shifted the wound closed. The cursed item pulsed a crimson glow in his hands, throbbing with ancient power. On and on he droned, flooding it with enough of the murkier side of seidr magic that not a particle of the girl's celestial essence would be spared once the curse landed.

It continued right up until he rose to his feet and walked the length of the longhouse to the open fire pits near the door. At this point, his wolves and his ravens kept their distance, because they knew better. Seidr curses were ordinarily dangerous, but Mirmir showed him how to have a blood curse bypass a celestial's physical and mental capability and latch directly to their essence. And once attached, there was no escape.

Placing the talisman on a firestone, Odin raised another and crushed the two together, grinding them until it looked like a mess of wet paste and white flecks smeared across the stones. Then he threw both rocks into the fire; for the incineration of the talisman was what would send the curse on its way.

Once it landed, the curse and the child would be one, never to be parted until death finally took her. And because of the level of seidr magic involved, her death would be slow and horrendous; nothing less than Avis deserved. Let him watch his precious child die horribly. Then maybe ... maybe he would understand.

The T'lormn disease, as it was known around Asgard, was fatal to mortals and celestials alike, and very few knew it was a curse conjured with ancient blood magic. To everyone else, it was merely a vile disease that struck indiscriminately. "Let us away," he called to his animal companions. "Without delay. The spell is cast and cannot be denied. He will pay at last, for those who have died."

Let Avis think he had won. Odin knew otherwise.

* * *

CHAPTER THIRTY-ONE

By design, very little surprised the Almighty of Heaven inside his own borders, and it was a well-known fact that he took a heavy hand to anything unwise enough to fall into the previously non-existent category. His warrior angels were also included in this number, so when a large house and matching stable appeared on a bed of grass under a protective dome just outside his pearlescent walls, they tensed in anticipation of his order to have both the building and its inhabitants destroyed.

He would've given it too, had his powerbase not identified the family who appeared inside a few seconds later. Then it no longer mattered how they came to be there. They were. After all this time, the Mystallians were finally in Heaven.

It had been almost as long since the Almighty had manifested beyond the all-seeing entity that ruled from afar, but these guests were worthy of a personal visit. Materialising outside the dome, he cast his gaze between the three Highborn Hellion guards who held their positions around the house then stepped towards the dome. An armoured hand, belonging to one of his more trusted angels fell across his chest, holding him back. "M'lord, we cannot allow you to go in there," the angel said, and although his body language was filled with regret, the hand blocking his way remained firm: for all of three seconds.

The glittering ashes of the suddenly deceased angel drifted across the clouds to where the others had gathered. The Almighty said nothing else as he looked from one to the next to see if anyone else would be unwise enough to bar his way. They all bowed their heads and stepped away respectfully.

Satisfied that his point had been made, the Almighty stepped forward, passing through the outer perimeter that separated cloud from grass as if it wasn't there. He leaned heavily into his powerbase as he approached the house, for although he'd taken offence to his angel's obstruction, he wasn't a fool where these hellish guards were concerned. The accord between him and Lord Belial would last only as long as it lasted. That wariness was confirmed when two of the three guards maintained their posts on the roof, whilst the third became his permanent shadow. *So be it.*

The Almighty opened the front doors with a thought, long before he reached the stoop, and walked inside.

There he found a large dining room that took up the whole front width of the house. It seemed ludicrously oversized for a family of four but Mystallians were renowned for their pretentious architecture. He himself preferred a much simpler approach to life; allowing divinity to speak for itself.

Speaking of the Mystallians; Avis, the leader of that pantheon, lay collapsed as if drugged in his seat at the head of the table. The Almighty walked down the side of the table and stood at the Mystallian's side. His smile was huge as he knelt down beside the sleeping god. "At last," he purred, cupping Avis' head in both hands and gently lifting it to see the younger god's face with his own eyes. Then he pressed his forehead to Avis'. "You're finally here."

Having waited so long, the Almighty wasn't interested in learning about Avis' life in little bits and pieces. Since Griffith's wife was one of the many constructs that he'd given life to, he'd never completely lost control of her and saw through her eyes on a minute-by-minute basis what the Mystallians were like and how they lived their lives. He even knew of the stories she'd told them about the realm of her creation, in a valiant effort to have them at least visit Heaven. Stories of strength and power that should've at least made them curious. He ruled a small realm that bowed to no one. He took no prisoners. Well ... that wasn't entirely true. He permitted slavery and used it against whole generations for disciplinary purposes, which he supposed amounted to the same thing. But he rarely showed mercy and he made those who challenged him in any way regret it. Depending on his mood, a lot more than just the individual involved paid that price.

That was why his angels had backed away from him outside when he'd looked at them. They'd fully expected their deaths to follow their fallen comrade's for being in his vicinity, and before he realised his visitors were Mystallian, they may very well have.

Mystallians respected strength. The stories of his exploits should have swayed them, yet not even Griffith's marriage to Heshbon, or the eventual birth of their triplets, could coax the Mystallian of Strength to set foot in Heaven. They all hated him, and he'd never understood why.

Until now.

The Almighty did more than just *see* Avis' past. He learned everything there ever was to the Mystallian patriarch, including why he felt the things he did. The stories of Heaven's exploits had begun long before Heshbon entered the picture. Through his friendship with Heaven's neighbours, Avis had been given a very detailed accounting of the style of god he was, and it wasn't flattering. Especially, when the end result had Avis and the others privately putting him on par with Theodrick in cruelty and brutality.

With wide eyes, the Almighty released Avis' head and fell heavily onto his backside.

They're comparing me to HIM?

Slowly making his way to his feet, the Almighty backed away from Avis until his shoulders bumped against the front wall of the house; his mind still reeling with that revelation. Every one of the former Nexus children saw him as another Theodrick! The last person in all the realms that he ever wanted to emulate in any way!

At that moment, he made a profound decision that would forever change the way Heaven operated. He was going to take a good ... long ... *honest* look at himself in the very near future, and chances were, he wouldn't like what he saw when he did.

Wishing to be alone, the Almighty tapped his powerbase and vanished in a flash of divine light.

CHAPTER THIRTY-TWO

"AVIS!"

Recognising Clarise's cry, Avis launched to his feet before his eyes were opened and collided heavily with the corner of something hard and unyielding at approximately hip height. *What the fuck …?* His legs were already ramming whatever blocked his way, even as his hands shoved the obstacle aside. A quick recount through his most recent memories helped his addled brain put the pieces together, reminding him that he'd somehow fallen asleep at the dinner table. "CLARISE!" he bellowed back, willing to tear apart whatever he had to, to reach her.

He rushed towards the double doors of their apartment, his mind supplying him with countless terrible reasons for why she'd cried out for him in fear, each worse than the last. He couldn't risk realm-stepping away from the safety of the dome to shave off important seconds. Not with the Asgardians waiting to snatch him up in the mortal realm. He'd never make it back.

The doors to the bedroom flew open just as he reached them and Clarise collided with his chest. His arms snapped around her shoulders and he lifted her off the ground, while hers clamped around his waist. The two spun in a tight circle, hugging each other tightly.

"Avis, you never came to bed last night and you said you would," she said accusingly, once they stopped spinning. "You scared me, beloved. I could not find you through our familial link and I was left to believe the Asgardians must have taken you."

Avis didn't answer straight away. As she only wore her jade green shoestring negligee and her hair was hanging loose, he buried his face into her exposed neck, using both her presence and the very real scent of her lavender perfume to calm his fright. In those few seconds of uncertainty, he'd almost convinced himself that the Asgardians had somehow managed to breach the dome and were doing … unspeakable things to her. But they hadn't. She was right here in his arms. Whole and okay. *Okay … okay … Wait, what was that she said about the familial links?*

He jerked away from her and swung back towards Columbine's apartment: the last place he'd seen their girls. Sure enough, instead of two distinct familial pings inside, everything in the whole fucking place glowed and he couldn't define a single realm-damned thing! It was like trying to find a candle flame in the middle of a hellfire blaze!

Fearing some level of mystical attack from his former friend, trepidation bordering on panic ripped through him again and he charged towards Columbine's apartment. Clarise's soft footsteps put her less than a step behind him. *Childless you will also be …* "CORA!" he roared.

The door to Columbine's sitting room shattered inwards in an explosion of timber shards when the latch didn't open fast enough for him and he smashed straight through it without ever slowing down. The doors at the other end of the room fell open before they arrived, probably courtesy of Clarise. Not that he gave a rat's ass about the fucking doors. He barrelled into the room, the doors banging against the walls on either side as he slid in sideways, ready to combat whatever he found.

His eyes went to the bed and found Cora in her hellion form already standing beside it in a fighter's stance. The claws of her tri-taloned toes dug into the ground for added traction and her wings stretched both high and wide, each with its claw-tip extended and dripping a green slime that was no doubt toxic. Pure hellfire burned in her empty eye sockets and nasal cavity. Her hands were stretched with her fingers curled; her knuckle-length claws elongated into half-metre razor-sharp talons in anticipation of a brawl. Through the gaps of her wings and the antler tips (which also seemed to have sharpened) Avis saw the darker crown of Columbine's head moments before she lifted herself high enough to peer at him.

Each side recognised the other and much of the tension fell away. "Are you alright, Cora?" Avis demanded, utterly ignoring the pair of governesses that chittered in terror in the corner. The presence of Columbine's brute squad guard at ease near the headboard said she was, but he wanted to hear her say the words.

"What the actual fuck, Father?" Cora snarled, immediately doubling over at the waist. She pressed the heel of one hand against her knee and rested the other on her side. Several deep pants later, she lifted her chin to glare at him. "You scared the ever-loving shit out of me."

"Leave Cora to me," Avis immediately said, throwing an arm out to the left to ward off his wife's reaction to the perfectly legitimate use of profanity. He then gestured at Columbine, who could now be seen clearly on the mattress behind her sister. "If you could check on Columbine?"

It was never his intention to ever give Clarise a direct order, but wording it as a question which she could refuse if she chose to was an acceptable compromise. From the way both girls reacted, he was confident that Columbine was just as okay, but distracting Clarise with their younger daughter would leave their tiger and her very Mystallian fright-based outrage for him to deal with.

"Ditto, tiger," he said, as he crossed the room and placed his hands on her shoulders, pulling her up straight so he could run his eyes over her whole body. "Are you sure you're alright?" He had no idea what her limitations were in this form. None at all. But there didn't seem to be anything wrong. He knelt before her, still holding her shoulders. "Do a full stimulation wave, tiger. Head to toe. Tell me if anything isn't right. Anything at all. No matter how trivial."

"Father, what's wrong?" Nevertheless, she did as she was told. He could feel the ripple of her leathery plates underneath his hands as the wave passed over her shoulders. To him, there was still no difference.

"Anything?" he asked, ignoring her question for the moment. His eyes searched her face for any hint of an underlying problem.

"Father, I'm fine. I swear. What's going on?"

What indeed. Maybe it was nothing … but it didn't *feel* like nothing. "C'mere," he said, and without a word of explanation, he rose and hooked Cora under the arms, settling her on his hip with one arm supporting her back under her wings the way he'd done so often with Columbine. Cora must've sensed his caginess, for she didn't fuss at the manhandling that was normally reserved for Columbine, but she did retract those vicious talons back into small claws.

Clarise was already nursing Columbine in much the same fashion on the other side of the bed.

The sight of them both standing so at peace drew much of his angst from him, and it almost broke his heart to be the one to destroy it. This fright had been the icing on the cake for Avis. He wasn't playing around anymore. "Clarise, you three have to get out of here. I'm not just talking about this building, but Asgard itself. Your father only stopped us from getting help from your side of the family, knowing very well I can't reach out to mine for help because I'll get drawn back into my thrall. But there's nothing stopping you from reaching Chance or one of the others, and then the three of you can …"

Clarise stiffened. "We are not separating," she declared, the look on her face daring him to suggest otherwise again. "You promised me."

Avis winced as if slapped, but he was determined to see this through; even if he did have to bite the inside of his cheek hard enough to draw blood. He'd have given anything to let her first real stand in front of witnesses count for something, but the truth was they were flat out of options. "Baby, you have to believe there's nothing I wouldn't do to keep us together," he argued. "But not at Columbine's expense. You saw what happened to her last night. What happened to all of us. And that was just within a few minutes. We're at least two months away from the other side of Asgard, and you can't ask her to go through …" Having mentioned Columbine by name, he glanced down at her hiding amongst her mother's dark hair and couldn't help but notice the way her lips were struggling to hold back an amused smile. "What's so funny, princess?"

Clarise shifted her weight so she could look at their daughter as well.

"The angry people are not out there anymore, Father," she giggled, rolling her shoulders as if someone was tickling her.

There was no doubt in her answer. None. Avis looked at the two sets of open doors, then back to her. "W-what do you mean, they aren't out there anymore?"

"They are not out there, Father, but there are others. Many, many others. And they are puzzled, like you are now. There is so much love here and everyone is happy. Even Uncle Uriel." The smile on her face was huge and her eyes gleamed with unshed tears of sheer elation. "So happy," she sighed, snuggling into her mother's neck. Tears finally broke and slid down her cheeks, that had gone red from smiling too much. Clarise's lips parted into a huge smile and she rubbed her cheek against Columbine's hair as if sharing in that happiness.

Avis didn't trust it. The sudden happiness was too fake, given where they were. His former friend coveted trickery over courage and following that thought, his overactive imagination began to fill in unwanted reasons for the deception. Mainly, the image of Columbine being so overjoyed that she trotted out to the dome when no one was looking and straight into the jaws of death. That thought and others like it caused a tightening in his chest until he growled and shook his head irritably. Odin had no idea about Columbine's empathy. He'd have had no reason to plan a work-around for something he knew nothing about.

So what was he up to? Nothing Avis could think of explained the purpose of overloading the familial connections, and he *hated* not knowing what other people were planning. All he did know was Odin had to be digging really deep to come after them if this was blindsiding even him.

He looked up at Clarise and saw a similarly suspicious look in her eyes.

Without a word of explanation, he walked around the bed and deposited Cora on the floor beside her mother. "Stay here," he said, addressing all three of them. "I'm going to go outside and take a look."

Soft sunlight bathed him as he stepped out from the stoop a short time later. He lifted his hand to shade his eyes as he looked through the one-way dome overhead, trying to make sense of the weather. Inside the dome was the comfortable environment Clarise had created for them, but outside should've been buried in Asgard's vile midwinter. Higher and higher he looked, searching for a sun that couldn't be found. When that proved fruitless, he dropped his gaze to the ground between his feet in search of a shadow. From there, he knew he could correlate the sun's location. Or, at least, that had been his plan. But nothing had a shadow. Not him, not even the blades of grass when he used the edge of his boot to bend them over. The radiance that soaked into everything had no singular source. It was everywhere – much like the familial screw-up.

Okay.

For the first time since he woke up, an inkling of a possibility so ridiculous he thought he was losing his mind began to take root in his head. All of Asgard was at the peak of its winter. Sleet and snowstorms made movement ridiculously difficult and were probably why he and his family had been able to enjoy the mortals' hospitality for several hours before Thor and Loki found them. With the hatred his former friend and the rest of the Asgardians felt for him, they'd have eaten their way through the snow to get at them if they had to.

But that was last night. Right now, Columbine felt none of their rage and hatred, and the sky looked nothing like an Asgardian winter. Could they have been moved? And if so, how? Not just how, but where? Where in the realms were they? His head refused to completely abandon the trickery aspect for which the Asgardians were renowned, but with the facts as they stood, he was no longer as confident as he had been.

He walked out to the dome wall and placed a hand on the surface, peering through the clear wall. Instead of a screen of sleet and snow, a carpet of low-lying fog rolled out across the ground at the same short height as the grass inside the dome. It went out to the very fringes of his vision where it merged with the rich, blue sky overhead.

Frustrated that the view had no answers, he turned on his heel to face the house … and froze.

A wall, standing so high it towered many storeys over the top of the house and stretching endlessly in both directions shimmered in iridescent pastels. His heart hammered out of control as flashes of a similarly imposing wall flashed across his mind's eye. The height and grandeur were too close to the one he and his siblings had been forced to scale all those eons ago to be a coincidence. But it wasn't exactly the same. Theodrick's crystal border was flawless and terrifying. The pastels that swirled through this one made it seem—as Columbine would say—pretty. Like looking at the inside of a wet oyster shell.

And with that mental description, Avis realised what he was looking at and his insides began to ice over. His gaze narrowed hatefully and he gritted his teeth so hard his jaw twitched. It wasn't a wall of iridescent pastels. The wall was fucking pearlescent and it stretched as far as the eye could see in both directions. *No way. No fucking way!* Up his eyes travelled. Up, and up, until he found a line of bird-winged warriors in battle armour lining the very top of the wall.

Angels!

Snarling openly at so many wank-less wonders in one place, Avis resisted the urge to go on the offensive there and then and slaughter as many of them as he could. It was insanely tempting, but in the end reason dictated there were too many. Hundreds, maybe thousands lined that wall, each only an arm-length from the next. He'd never get them all, especially if the survivors retaliated by taking to the air and swarming him from all sides. Then what would they do to his family?

One thought kept bouncing around in his head as he cautiously made his way back to the house, waiting for any of them to make the first move. *Heaven. We are in fucking Heaven. HOW?* He still had no conclusive answer when he returned to Columbine's sitting room and found Clarise had moved the girls to the comfortable seating near the fireplace. She sat on one of the two lounge chairs with Columbine perched on her lap. Cora stood impatiently beside the chair. All three were dressed in their Mystallian uniforms.

"You're not going to believe this, but I don't think we're in Asgard anymore," he said, still reeling in shock himself as he crossed the room towards them.

"Excuse me?" Clarise demanded as she surged to her feet; her eyes widening.

Cora's mouth fell open, temporarily mimicking a goldfish. "How?" she demanded, which to Avis was the question of the eon.

Because Odin hated the angels as much as he did. More, if anything. Where Avis simply killed them and moved on, Odin (true to his demonic ancestry) was far more creative with their demise. If they were lucky, Thor and the others got to them first and they were ended quickly. *So how did we get here?* If what he'd seen outside was real, they were in Heaven. And not just in Heaven, but far enough that they sat at the base of the pearlescent wall and nowhere near the Asgardian border. Even if there had been an Asgardian willing to risk the ire of Odin by helping them to escape, the power required for that assist should've ended at the Asgardian border.

Then, somehow, the angels had to pick them up in almost exactly the same fashion and move them here. And the best, most ridiculous part of this lunacy was, those same angels then managed to perfectly replicate the dome-enclosed Mystallian house and stable that they'd never seen before. As insane as that was, the alternative was even more insane. So crazy, in fact, that he couldn't even bring himself to think it.

Predictably, Cora rushed forward towards the front doors to see for herself.

Avis stepped to his right to intercept her. His arm snaked around her waist and he hoisted her off her feet. "No one's going outside just yet," he declared as he walked back to Clarise, repositioning Cora so she sat on his hip again. The punch of frustration he felt against his back was almost amusing. "Unless Odin's utterly outdone himself with his illusionary powers, we're really not in Asgard anymore." Thinking about it, trickery was still the most likely scenario, but that didn't explain Columbine's empathic connection with these people. Illusions would only affect what they were crafted to deceive, and Odin didn't know about Columbine's innate ability. If they were still in Asgard, the Asgardians' anger would smash through the illusion like a fist through a pane of glass. His free hand pointed towards the rear of the house. "The pearlescent wall of Heaven is right back there."

Although he'd never seen it personally, he'd heard enough stories about this place from his friends to recognise it from their descriptions. Heaven was one of the oldest realms in existence and Avis didn't trust the home nest of those parasitic bastards as far as he could spit it. Unlike most realms where the borders butted up to each other, he'd heard how Heaven had set its walls back far enough to allow travellers to pass through without going into Heaven proper. No one would ever be able to convince him that it wasn't to draw the enemy into the space that was controlled by Heaven, giving those winged fuckers the advantage before the outer wall was ever breached.

On the plus side, if it wasn't Asgard, at least the angels wouldn't be trying to kill his family. No, in this realm, the hatred went the other way. Avis would've happily ripped the wings off every one of them if he had the time.

"What will we do?" Clarise was clearly out of her element. She wasn't the only one.

"Right now, I'm more interested in how in the realms we got here. If this is all real, we're months away from where we should be. So who moved us, how, and why?"

"Does it really matter?" Cora asked in return. When he twisted his lips to one side and frowned at her, she dropped her gaze to his chin, but at least she managed to keep her thoughts coming. "I mean, if we're really out of Asgard, someone back there did us a favour. Why do we have to care who it was?"

Avis licked his lips. The idea of accepting aid without questioning the motives and capabilities behind it was both dangerous and very Highborn Hellion Lady of her. "Because the 'how' has longer reaching repercussions. People don't do things for nothing, tiger. There's always an angle, and in this case, a power issue. Whoever helped us could come back one day and demand full payment for that aid."

"In which case, we tell them what they can go do with themselves," Cora argued. "I mean, we didn't agree to anything, so it's not like there's a boon being held over our heads."

That was a very good point. "The last thing I remember was sitting down at the dining table after leaving you two in Columbine's bedroom." Knowing that wasn't quite right, he rectified it to, "Actually, the last, *last* thing I remember right before I fell asleep, was checking on all three of you and found you all unmoving." His eyes widened. "Clarise, what if we didn't fall asleep at all? What if we were all put to sleep and then moved?"

He didn't appreciate the way his wife's expression morphed into a blend of ridicule and indulgence. "So now you wish to believe someone in Asgard is capable of slipping past not one but four Highborn Hellion Guards and knocking out one of the most powerful ranged benders and three of the more powerful ranged shifters without any of us noticing. Then, while we all slept, that same individual was able to relocate our whole party *and* the domicile I constructed for us into a neighbouring realm without any interference from either Odin or the Almighty?"

And that's why Avis didn't want to even consider it. Yet here they were. Squaring his shoulders, he said defensively, "I'm open to alternative suggestions."

Cora squirmed on his hip. "The way I see it, it still doesn't matter." Avis stabbed his fingers sharply into her sides. "Don't be like that, Father. I'm serious. It's probably like that situation with the Rangi-Tuarean brothers and there was an Asgardian power-play against Odin while he was distracted. And since the whole lot of them are behind us now, who gives a fu—I mean, why should we even care?"

Nice catch. "Because I want to know," Avis snapped, peevishly. He didn't like the idea of Cora making so much sense when his sensibilities had been pricked. "I mean, even if it was an Asgardian power-play, that person's power would have ended at the border of Asgard. We're in Heaven. *Way* into Heaven. So far in, I couldn't even see the Asgardian border when I was looking for it. Someone either moved the whole dome with us or rebuilt it here and moved us into it." The gold of Columbine's personal guard nearby caught his eye, and remembering their ridiculous speed, he looked at Clarise. "Sweetheart, is it possible for the guards to do more than just guard if they're ordered to?"

"What do you mean?"

"Say we did get booted out of Asgard by someone making a play for Odin's throne. Would the guards have then been able to move us here and then rebuild this home for us using their stupid speed?"

"I have only ever seen them behave as warriors, beloved. I doubt they have the cognitive capability to build anything as intricate as this abode so meticulously."

Avis did his best to not react to the way she elevated her work and kneecapped the capabilities of the brute squad guards in a single turn of phrase. But one thing was for sure: she'd better not accuse him of being prideful in the near future or he'd be reminding her of this conversation.

"Maybe the nice people here built it for us, Father?" Columbine suggested innocently.

A blend of horror and repulsion shuddered through him before he could stop it, though he managed to force his lips into a semblance of a smile for her sake. "I know you like these people, princess, but you might as well know now, I don't. These people and I have a history—the kind where I really don't like them. Not even a little bit. And don't get me started on what I think of their precious *Almighty.*"

Columbine's happy smile fell away. "I do not understand, Father."

Avis sighed, doing everything in his power to not roll his eyes. "No, I don't suppose you would," he admitted, shaking his head.

Clarise bent forward and scooped Columbine into her arms, placing her on her left hip in a mirror image of Avis and Cora. "Perhaps we should see what they want, beloved?" she suggested, stepping to his right. Avis was fully aware that this was done to keep the adults on the outside and the children protected between them.

"Perhaps we should," he agreed, following her out the door.

* * *

In a place both a long way away, and not that far at all, Belial raised his right hand off the arm of his upper realm throne and stroked his chin. *That was too close.* Having the untrained Pillar of Emotion surrounded by so much anger with no means of escape was the very epitome of a perfect storm. He drew his gaze away from Heaven's spot on the Table of Divinity before him just long enough to meet the eyes of his champion standing at his side and slowly nod once in approval. When speed was critical, only one thing in the realms was faster than his champion on a mission, and no one had seen the *Maestro* since the original Twin Notes were sung.

Beelzebub returned his pillar's stoic nod, then straightened to assume his regular, imperturbable pose at his liege's side.

CHAPTER THIRTY-THREE

Avis led his family past the corner of the house and paused, giving them the chance to adapt to Heaven's pearlescent wall and the presence of so many armoured angels standing along the top. Surprisingly, when he looked up at those winged shitheads himself, he realised a different kind of angel was interspersed with the warriors, at a rate of about twenty to one. These new ones wore their hair loose, while long, seamless fabric curved around their bodies and under their arms, hugging them in all the right places.

Columbine gasped and straightened in her mother's arms. "Uncle Uriel!" she called, waving at the left side of the wall.

Avis tried not to groan as he followed her line of sight. That particular brother-by-marriage was one of the last people he ever wanted to cross paths with ... especially while the bastard was inside yet *another* powerbase. Soon, the day would come when he and Uriel would meet on neutral territory (Mystal was too much to hope for) and on that day there'd finally be a reckoning for all the abuse he'd taken at his brother-by-marriage's hands.

His eyes skimmed the line of warrior angels, until in the far, far distance, he thought he might have caught sight of Uriel's orange feathered wings amidst the white plumage.

"It is Uriel," Clarise confirmed with a smile, also looking in that direction.

He could only assume she'd done some telescopic thing with her vision to see that far in her Mystallian form, which meant he had no chance to pretend they were mistaken. *Great.* "Do you want to drop the dome then, sweetheart? We might as well get this meet and greet over with."

"Uncle Uriel!" Columbine called again once the dome was lowered, waving furiously to gain the archangel's attention.

The crown prince of Hell spread his feathered wings and leapt from the wall, gliding across the non-existent currents between them until he righted himself two or three arm's lengths from Avis and landed on the carpet of cloud. Columbine squirmed and eventually dissipated from her mother's grasp, rematerialising with her arms around Uriel's neck and her legs banded around his waist in a tight hug. "I have missed you so much, Uncle Uriel! It has been almost a whole year!"

Avis' estimate was closer to seven months, give or take a few days, but he wasn't about to contradict her.

Uriel baulked at the unHellion-like move but recovered quickly. "I—have missed you too, little one," he chuckled with a musical tone to his voice as he closed his arms, and wings around her. He squeezed lightly, then loosened his grip enough to look at her. "However, you seem very ... excitable ..."

"She should be," Cora interjected, stretching her neck and spine to add enough height to meet Uriel's eyes. "We're finally out of Asgard, and that place was really getting on everyone's last nerve. Especially hers."

Uriel said nothing as he drew Columbine into another hug, but when his chin went over her shoulder (and his face was out of her line of sight), a flicker of hellfire entered his normally bright blue eyes and he frowned disapprovingly at Cora.

The unspoken reprimand for butting in caused an instantaneous response in Cora. Gone was all the confidence Avis had been fanning to life and in its place was the broken girl he'd first met. Her shoulders slumped forward subserviently and her gaze went down and away as Highborn Hellion custom demanded. Not only that, but her surface thoughts were filled with apologetic grovelling.

Avis wanted to scream! "Torment your own fucking family!" he snarled, forgetting all about Clarise's presence as he repositioned himself so that Cora could no longer see the manipulative prick. **Ignore your Uncle Uriel, tiger. He's an asshole**. He interwove the two mental commands so that Cora wouldn't automatically treat every 'he' she came across as an asshole. It pleased him to know that she would forever think of Uriel this way, at least until he countered it. Which, considering the way he felt about his brother-by-marriage right now, would be some time past the future date of nevermore. The Highborn Hellions had lost any right to bully her when they cast her out of their ranks. Now she was firmly in the Mystallian camp by her own decree, and no one pushed them around or made them feel bad because they had something to say.

Ever so slowly, Cora began to unwind from her near foetal position until her head snuggled against the side of his neck for comfort. A protective growl worked its way through his throat as he rubbed his cheek across her hair (the reverberation of which seemed to settle her further), while glaring daggers over his shoulder at his brother-by-marriage.

"I believe I was," Uriel sang, rolling his gaze lazily to Avis. "Although we prefer to call it adequate discipline. From memory, you are also well acquainted with that concept, are you not, Avis?" Just like he had in Hell, every word out of his mouth had a double meaning that was meant to go over the ladies' heads and target him directly. His next sentence was no better. "If not, I will be more than happy to arrange a revision …" He flicked the tips of wings tauntingly and grinned.

Red flooded Avis' vision and he launched at Uriel's mind. Fuck waiting until they were on neutral territory!

But instead of punching through into Uriel's mental perimeter as he fully expected to do, Avis rebounded against an invisible shield and was forced to return to his own body. Shock flooded his system and he stared at Uriel in disbelief. *No way*. No fucking way did Heaven have thralls in place that protected a non-bender from someone like him!

It wasn't that they couldn't, but for a thrall like that to be in place, the pantheon would've had to inform its mortals that there were other pantheons in existence that they needed protecting from. To his knowledge, none of the other pantheons ever had. Yet something was clearly protecting the prick and he didn't know what. It was just one more thing that he was on the back foot about, and he was getting really tired of it.

"Uriel, stop it," Clarise said, placing her hand on her husband's bicep to make a unified stand as a Mystallian.

Uriel turned his head just enough to stare wide-eyed at his sister.

"Mystallians are not Highborn Hellions," she went on, ignoring his astonishment. "… and Cora has made the only decision available to her after the High Court of Hell made its ruling and exiled her. To expect Hell's level of discipline to be maintained when she is no longer welcome under that pantheon's banner is both exceedingly narrow-minded and beneath you. She is Mystallian, and I would appreciate it if you would treat her as such."

Regardless of how outraged he'd been at not being able to devastate Uriel's mind, Avis suddenly wanted to whoop and dance in victory. The gobsmacked look on his brother-by-marriage's face would be his favourite memory for a very long time! *Sic' him, sweetheart*, he cheered, no longer wanting to destroy Uriel from the inside. Not when it was so much more gratifying to watch his wife verbally eviscerate him, and that wouldn't have happened if Uriel had had no mind left to react with.

Uriel quickly schooled his expression, his gaze shifting from one Mystallian to the next of the three in front of him. "I see," he sang, though how he was able to put so much venom in just two words while maintaining a lyrical undertone was beyond Avis.

Movement rippled along the wall and Avis looked up just in time to see the number of angels swell. Not the warriors, though. The newcomers were more of those plainly dressed ones with the golden rope coils; taking the ratio of their armoured brethren to about four to one. And the warriors moved aside and even took to the air to give them room.

The additional numbers and the way they stared down at Avis in displeasure had him on edge. It didn't help when he swept over the mind of the nearest slip-wearing one and bounced off the same mental barricade that he'd encountered around Uriel's mind.

Motherfuckers! But okay, if that's the way they want to play ...

He might've been at a severe disadvantage without his ranged bending, but that didn't put him completely out of the game. The billions of centuries he'd spent at His sister of war's side had taught him how to fight. Anticipating the need to drop Cora behind him and go into an all-out brawl, he shifted his weight onto the balls of his feet—only to realise it wasn't him the angels were focused on.

No, all eyes were fixed on Uriel, until the archangel was forced to acknowledge them by twisting his head to look up at the wall behind him. Side on as he was, Avis saw the way he lifted his chin to them, mashing his lips together into a tight line of displeasure. His breathing deepened as he petted Columbine's hair, his eyes cutting from Avis to the angels overhead and back again. When the frequency of all three actions increased, Avis noticed the blue in his eyes was beginning to glitter with flecks of hellfire that winked in and out of existence.

"Columbine," Avis said, his voice dropping to a low, soothing monotone to avoid scaring her, even if his own heart rate had increased dramatically. "Go back to your mother, baby. Something about your Uncle Uriel is a little bit ... off at the moment." *And I'm a little bit bad-tempered.*

Columbine still had her legs wrapped around the archangel's waist when she pushed against his collarbones to look at his face. "Is this where you live, Uncle Uriel?" she asked, ignoring her father's instruction. "When you are not in Hell?" She tilted her head to see past him. "Is it nice in there?"

Uriel didn't answer her straight away, but when he did, it wasn't with words. The flickering hellfire in his eyes returned to a solid icy-blue and his entire posture relaxed. His hand went to the back of her head and he gently but forcibly pulled her forward while at the same time lowering his own until their foreheads rested against each other.

For a long moment, they stayed that way; neither saying anything.

"I love you, Uncle Uriel," Columbine whispered, loudly enough that Avis could still hear her.

"I know, little one. I know," the Archangel finally sang, back to his old self. He pulled away from the close contact and turned so she could have a better view of Heaven's pearlescent wall. His hand continued to pet her long hair. "As to your previous question, yes, this is where I live some of the time when I am not in Hell and yes, it is very nice. Would you like to come and see my cloud some time?"

"Oh, yes." Columbine nodded enthusiastically. "I would like that very much, Uncle Uriel. Um, but who are they?" she asked, as only a child could.

Uriel didn't even bother to look. "They are angels, little one," he replied, still in song. "Emissaries of Heaven."

A snarl of disgust made it past Avis' lips before he could catch it. *Emissaries indeed!* Invading parasitic leeches was more like it.

Uriel ignored him completely. "The ones in armour, like myself, are the Sixth Choir, better known as Heaven's Might. They are Heaven's military."

"And the other ones?"

That took Uriel a little longer to answer. "They are ... the virtues. The Fifth Choir. They ... *correct* the way people think and feel."

Avis lifted his own gaze to the plain-clothed angels. *They* were the ones that were trying to make the crown prince of all Hell forget his hatred? He remembered back to the strange conversation he and Uriel had once had regarding Heaven, specifically their policy of forced forgiveness, and wondered if these were the ones his ... *delightful* brother-by-marriage had been talking about. Perhaps that was why the militant angels gave them room. He of all people should've known that soft and sweet and delicate looking did not in any way equate to harmless and ignorable in the celestial realm.

Still ... making an angry demon forget his anger? And Crown Prince Uriel, no less. That was a trick Avis wanted to see.

"Why are they all looking at you?"

"They do not like how ... upset I am at your father."

"Why are you always so angry at him?"

Uriel looked over the top of Columbine's head to shoot Avis a withering look and, even without his surface thoughts, Avis heard his unspoken meaning loud and clear. *Intercede, Mystallian, before I tell her exactly why I hate you.*

"Princess, you know there's a lot of people out there who are very angry with me," Avis said, in as neutral a tone as possible. Columbine turned in Uriel's arms to look at him. "Your Uncle Uriel is Heaven's Archangel of Vengeance. It's his powerbase here. He can't help hating me on behalf of all the people I've wronged." It wasn't quite an outright lie, but it was close enough to it. Already, the muscles around Uriel's eyes began twitching, fighting whatever it was that kept him civilised.

Columbine rolled her bottom lip into a pout. "But, Father ..."

Avis shook his head. "No. That's enough for now, princess. You need to let your Uncle Uriel go and return to your mother. Right now, young lady. Off you go." He was ready to make it a mental command if she didn't comply. That was how serious he was about getting some distance between those two before Uriel kicked off again. Something about him was definitely off. "I'm not asking."

Columbine breathed out in a heavy sigh and looked down at the ground between them. "Yes, Father," she answered dutifully.

The hellion submission grated on his nerves, though if he prioritised what he hated about this situation, that was at the bottom of a very long list. She gave her uncle a parting hug, then disappeared from his grip and reappeared on her feet at her mother's side. Clarise immediately swept her up into her arms and held her tightly. "Do not do that again, Columbine," she scolded, pressing Columbine's head into her shoulder as if to assure herself that Columbine was whole and well and within the protective ring of her arms. "Stay with me until your father or I say otherwise. No matter what. No more running off."

"Yes, Mother."

The sudden change in Uriel was phenomenal. Without Columbine in his arms to keep him distracted, his eyes exploded into hellfire and in a blur of movement, he had his sword drawn and was advancing on Avis. "There have been many ... *many* attempts to cleanse me of my hatred towards you," he snarled, somehow managing to keep a harmonic tone to his hellish roar. "But I swear as the Almighty is my witness, it will never happen! I will never allow it!"

Avis' eyes widened. Even in the darkest pits of Hell, the Chaotic crown prince had always maintained a level of aloofness that fell second only to his father. An overriding superiority born of the knowledge that everyone else was inferior. Yet right now, the mere mention of being forced to lose his hatred had his teeth sharpening demonically. Columbine squealed and clung to her mother's neck in fear, and angels from both of the choirs overhead leapt into the air and speared towards the out-of-control-angel with incredible speeds. Not as fast as the Highborn Hellion Guard, who materialised between Avis and the Archangel to create a protective barrier for the former.

Uriel was caught and restrained by the angelic warriors, who were marginally faster than the virtues that followed. The archangel threw his weight forward against them, spitting his defiance. "I will never stop hating you! *Never!* You hear me? I will have my vengeance! None of you can stop me! None of you!"

Through the gaps in the brute squad's arms and wings, Avis stared at the out-of-control hellion prince in shock. Everything he knew about Uriel said this was all wrong. Captured as he was, Uriel could have calmly shapeshifted his way to freedom and destroyed those who had dared to hold him in the process, not kick and thrash wildly in their grip with all the finesse of a savage animal. This wasn't the same Uriel who took great relish in draining every drop of blood from Avis' inverted body and drinking it right in front of him, only to peel away sections of Avis' exposed skin afterwards for a makeshift napkin. What was wrong with ...

Thrall!

By the realms, Uriel was caught up in his secondary thrall. Avis gaped as Uriel continued to buck and struggle helplessly against those he called kin. *What in the realms have Heaven's mortals done to you?*

"I hear you, if he does not, brother," a female angel with long, honey-blonde hair sang as she landed beside the Hellion born archangel. Her white fabric slip was held in place by a gilded rope of twisted gold around the top edge that knotted over her sternum just enough to keep her decent. Small crystal flowers decorated the knot, along with a single multi-faceted crystal gem the size of Avis' thumb and forefinger round beneath the bouquet.

Something about that golden rope and gem combination seemed very familiar to Avis, but not even a decade of internalising and ghosting through the last few million years of memories gave him the answer he was looking for. In the end, he rationalised that wherever he'd seen it before, it had to be some small, inconsequential matter in his far-distant past.

The female cupped her hand under Uriel's elbow. The moment the contact was made, the archangel stiffened and sucked in a sharp breath. The hellfire in his eyes went out and his teeth returned to normal by that touch alone. The woman smiled patiently. "Come along, Uriel. Your heart is far from at peace. Let us help you find your way again."

Uriel didn't fold completely, but Avis could already see the physical differences in his brother-by-marriage from the woman's touch without needing to delve into the mental ones. His eyes lost their usual vibrancy as a dull, grey murkiness began to cloud them. More of that fog was added when another, much larger and stronger male in a matching slip threaded his hand through the restraining warriors to clamp it on Uriel's other shoulder as if he and Uriel were the closest friends in the realm. The archangel rocked on his feet. One of the warriors pried Uriel's fingers from the hilt of his flame sword and stepped away with it, and Uriel was powerless to stop them. "Yield, brother. Come away from the source of your wickedness and find peace in the house of the Almighty. You need help, brother. Let us guide you."

Not knowing what else to do, Avis stepped to Clarise's side and hooked his hand around the back of her neck. His heart shattered at the tears that silently streamed down her face and without saying anything, he gently but forcibly twisted her into his chest, then used his cloak to shield all three of his girls from Uriel's ultimate defeat.

Just in time.

A third hand on the back of Uriel's neck finished him off. His muscles sagged and his eyes glazed over completely. "Come away, Uriel," that third one sang, and this time, with their hands still holding him, the archangel allowed himself to be taken up and over the pearlescent walls.

CHAPTER THIRTY-FOUR

"Avis," Clarise sobbed into his chest, long after Uriel was taken away. "They forced him …"

Avis tightened his grip on all three of them and pressed his lips to Clarise's hair. "He was in thrall, sweetheart. That wasn't the brother you knew, and the second he leaves this realm, he's going to be mortified by what just happened here. If I had to guess, being an archangel of vengeance and failing to extract that vengeance causes him to lose it. Armina has the same problem when I tell her she can't go to war." He lifted his head and rubbed his chin across Clarise's head, willing her to understand that none of this was her brother's fault. "More often than not, she has to be taken down hard by the rest of us as well." He never thought in a billion eons he'd ever feel sorry for that fucker, but family life had obviously mellowed him. That or being forced into an unwilling submission was something else he could closely relate to. Either way … "He's one of them now and by his own admission, this isn't the first time they've tried to break him. If I was still throwing out guesses, I'd say it doesn't stick because he's also the heir to Hell, and that part of him keeps bouncing back the second they let him go." He ran his tongue across his lips and added, "I'm going to have to avoid Uriel while we're in Heaven. He's a raving lunatic here."

"Some would say you bring out that trait in everyone, Lord Avis of Mystal."

Avis looked up and across to his left, just as an angel drifted down off the wall to stand before him. He wore a similar slip to the other virtues, but unlike the white fabric of his colleagues, this one's slip was all gold, blending into the rope coil that held the slip in place. More notably, it wasn't two wings that carried him across the air, but six. The warriors and even the virtues that remained on the ground rolled their shoulders and bowed in reverence; stepping away to make room for him. He smiled at each of them and nodded.

"And who might you be?" Avis asked, seeing no reason to be polite.

The angel *titched* lightly, though it might have been an amused chuckle. It was hard to tell when music followed every sound here. "I am Raphael, choirmaster of the Fifth Choir," he sang.

Avis ran his eyes down the length of the newcomer, taking in every facet of him before returning his attention to his face. "So, the six wings make you the choir*master*?"

Still smiling, Raphael shook his head. "No, m'lord. The six wings mean I also belong to the First Choir of healers, known as Seraphim. You might say in my long life, I've worn many hats and I've learned to multitask." He took a moment to mimic Avis' on the spot appraisal and when he was done, he took half a step back and placed his hands together in a loose prayer. "You have journeyed a long way, my friends, and in your short stay, you have already influenced our father for the better. Welcome to Heaven."

"You don't get to declare us friends, choirmaster," Avis shot back cuttingly, not believing for a second that his family's presence alone could change anything for the better. Especially not when *he* was with them. Having the brute squad between his family and this strange, lying creature made him feel a lot more comfortable. "We're a long way from it."

Raphael's smile lost some of its radiance, though it didn't abandon him completely. "Perhaps I spoke in hope instead of fact," he replied in concession. "We've been waiting a very long time for one of Mystal's original Elder Court to come and visit us. Some of us had almost given up hope that you ever would." He looked over his shoulder at the pearlescent wall and when he turned back, the brilliance of his smile returned, along with a sparkle in his eyes. "But not the Almighty. He never gave up hope that you would visit."

Instead of feeling valued, Avis's instincts ran closer to cynicism. Mystal's original elder court, indeed. That was a very specific group of siblings. The more his dirty scowl shifted from Raphael to the pearlescent wall behind the choirmaster and back again, the darker his thoughts grew. Heaven's accursed Almighty had been waiting for one for the original Nexus Mystallians to cross his path, why?

"I know what you're thinking."

The absurdity of the choirmaster's words was as surprising as the interruption itself. Avis was the second most powerful bender in existence and nobody ... *nobody* outside the Nexus could ever read his mind. Unable to fold his arms in contempt with his family still in his embrace, Avis shifted his weight to one leg, squared his shoulders and cocked his head in a show of mockery. *"Really?"* he sneered.

Warmth creased Raphael's eyes in the corners. "Well, perhaps I should have said 'I can *guess* what you are thinking, based on what you are feeling'. For that, I do know. It comes off you in waves of colour. Frustration. Anger. Love. Fea..." Raphael stopped abruptly and jerked his head as if he were listening to something—or someone behind him. A few seconds later, he dipped his head in acknowledgement and returned his attention to Avis, though this time his smile was a little more forced. "I meant, of course, to say how ... *concerned* you obviously are for your family's well-being, which is in itself highly commendable. Worrying over loved ones should be at the top of every decent family man's emotional palette. But, as I was saying, emotions and the effects they have on people are as visible to the Fifth Choir as colours are to you, m'lord, and I *am* their choirmaster." As he spoke, his eyes slid from one member of Avis' family to the next until his gaze alighted on Columbine and he offered her an endearing smile. "Though I must admit, this is the first time even I have ever heard of someone having that quality innately. It is a great honour to meet you, Lady ...?" He left the question on an up-note for Columbine to fill in her missing name.

Columbine giggled instead and hid shyly behind her mother's hair.

Avis never thought he would be so grateful for the Highborn Hellion way of not answering shit without parental permission, but the last thing he ever wanted was for this angelic choirmaster to be able to identify Columbine by name. It was bad enough that he'd already ascertained her natural empathic ability and knew she was his daughter. Those two pieces of information alone were dangerous, for it also meant he knew she wasn't limited to any one realm when using it. "You just keep your realm-damned distance from my family," he growled in warning, shuffling his feet until all three of his ladies were behind him. The filthy glare he sent the angel over his shoulder was to let him know he wasn't playing on that score.

"Possessive, controlling, condescending *and* abusive," Raphael sang, with a tsk of benign displeasure. "I see the apple doesn't fall far from the tree, even if it did roll a few realms away."

Avis was sure there was an insult in there somewhere, though he failed to see how a fruit tree of all things was supposed to achieve this. "I'm warning you ..."

Raphael smiled indulgently, "I know. You are very serious about keeping your family safe, and I applaud you for that. The Almighty does too."

"You can take your applause and shove it up your ..." The four fingers of Clarise's left hand fell lightly across Avis' lips before he could finish that sentence. His eyes shot to her in surprise.

"Allow me, my love," she whispered. "I might be the better one to speak for us, at this juncture."

In the past, Avis would've ripped the arm off anyone who dared to try and silence him in such a blatant manner in front of outsiders, but if Clarise wanted to have her say, she would always be his one exception. With her perfume filling his senses and her soft gold eyes staring up at him imploringly, he kissed the inside of her fingers and nodded his consent.

"I—did not see that coming," Raphael admitted, staring between the two of them with his mouth hanging slightly ajar in surprise. But then he beamed so happily that a light glow outlined his entire shape. "Congratulations on your transition, Lord Avis."

Clarise removed her hand from Avis' lips and planted it on her hip as she stepped to one side and looked directly at the choirmaster. Columbine, still on her other arm, was kept behind Avis' shoulder. "On what transition, exactly?" she asked, making her own direct stand as a Mystallian.

Raphael didn't seem concerned. Not if the way he continued to look at them as if they were prized students who'd finally passed a secret grade was anything to go by. "Capitulation to a loved one is a sign of strength and should never be viewed as a backwards step." He lifted his eyes to Avis. "Yet, for the longest time, that was exactly how you saw it, wasn't it m'lord?"

Just because he wasn't wrong, didn't mean Avis had to like it.

"Our presence within your realm does not give you the right to treat us as children," Clarise warned, proving she'd heard the same condescension that he had.

The choirmaster smiled and dipped his head at her. "My sincerest apologies, m'lady. When you've lived as long as I have, it's difficult not to see the youth in everyone."

"What'd you do to the familial links?" Cora asked, entering the conversation with an entirely new, but no less relevant topic. Since Avis wanted the answer to that one as well, he didn't silence her. "Everywhere we look while using them—it's like being in the middle of a fire."

The ocean of indulgence within Raphael's smile had Avis wanting to punch him in the face. "That is not my doing, little one. The Almighty is all around us and he bathes us all in his love."

"Love means nothing to a familial link," Clarise said, moments before Avis could say more or less the same thing ... sort of.

"We are all his children," the angel insisted, opening his arms with his palms turned upright. "And we all live under the light of his love."

Avis closed his eyes and shook his head in disgust. This was why he didn't waste his time on words with angels. They turned everything back to their beloved Almighty. "Whatever," he mumbled under his breath. Whoever the Almighty was, or however he'd set up his establishment field and subsequent thrall, one thing Avis knew for certain; the bastard was no kin of his.

Raphael opened his mouth to say something, then snapped it shut and looked over his shoulder once more. The look in his eyes became pleading, but eventually, he uttered a despondent sigh and dipped his head in submission. "As you wish, m'lord," he murmured.

When he met the eyes of Avis and his family, the smile had been wiped off his face and in its place was a mask of serene neutrality. "You will find safety here, Lord Avis. You and your precious family will always be welcome here. Take as long, or as little time as you need to cross our realm. Should you desire true answers to your questions, the Almighty has said he will personally see to your answers, but he won't impose. All you need do is gain the attention of any one of our brothers or sisters on the wall, and we will ferry you directly to him."

Repulsion flooded Avis like ice water. Trust an *angel* of all things to *carry* him over the wall … to their leader? What in the realms was this fucking idiot on?

"We will be close, should you need us. Until then, rest, relax, and know that you are safe in the arms of the Almighty." Raphael pressed his hands together in prayer once more and bowed at the waist to the Mystallian family. When he straightened, he flared his six wings and leapt into the air, soaring high over the wall and those that lined it and disappearing in seconds. The other angels followed him, settling once again on the rim of the wall.

"That was weird," Cora stated.

"Yeah, it was," Avis agreed. He still didn't trust them. That Raphael one in particular. Something about him tugged at Avis' subconscious, but for the life of him, he couldn't place how or why.

"I couldn't get inside his head, Father."

"What?"

"I wanted to know what he was so smug about, but I couldn't get in. I bounced off the edge of his mind … just like I do with yours."

Wait, is that what it feels like when someone fails to get inside a superior bender's head? As a child he'd known better than to even think about trying to invade his parents' minds, and once they were out of the Nexus, there was no one he couldn't mentally dominate. So he'd never felt the blockade sensation before. Was it possible that this 'Almighty' had incorporated a realm-wide bending shield into his establishment field that not only protected him and his angels from people like Avis, but it also hid him behind a familial link that implied he was everywhere? That was a lot for one entity to think of before establishment locked everything down. If he was as excited to meet the original Mystallian siblings as Raphael claimed, he had to have known who and what he was inviting in. Maybe it was revenge for something in their far distant past that none of them remembered.

"Be on your guard, everyone. Make sure every feeling you have is your own." He looked up at the plain-clothed Fifth Choir angels that still dotted the wall and added, "Those ones can do more than read emotions. They can also force them, and that is not okay."

* * *

Cora was more concerned with her father than the angels overhead at that point. She watched every movement of his facial features with growing apprehension, gauging the level of his irritation by way of the little muscles twitches along his jaw and around his eyes. He didn't like knowing something else could force an emotional shift in him, and things that bothered him almost always morphed into making him angry. Those two went hand in hand, and the way his eyes moved from one angel to the next as if he expected such an attack to happen at any second spoke volumes to his growing agitation.

This was exactly what she'd always feared but secretly hoped he'd prove her wrong on. He'd been the one to teach her that celestials fell into two types: shifters and benders. All this time he'd loved and protected Columbine because he'd thought her control of emotions began and ended with herself. Cora knew otherwise. There'd been times during their time in the bowels of Hell, when Columbine's heightened emotional state had rubbed off on her. Not often, but often enough for Cora to identify the source as 'not me' and then narrow it down who it was. Up until two minutes ago, Cora had always thought Columbine had no clue she was doing it, but that 'happy-whammy' she just hit Uriel with showed she was at least partially aware of what she was doing. A few times during the journey Columbine had pulled their father out of a dark funk with what appeared to be a cuddle and a promise of love, but Cora had seen it for what it was.

Between their father's distrust of emotional powers and Columbine's growing familiarity with them, Cora's heart began to race. *Shorthorns, I need you to stay close to me for a while,* she sent, using their private mind-speak. This method of mental communication hadn't worked with anyone else, nor could any shifter or bender eavesdrop on it. Over the years, Cora had tried to mind speak with others. But no matter how much she pushed her thoughts at different people, the only one who could ever read her surface thoughts was her father, and that was if he happened to be looking. Even then, it wasn't real communication. He just saw whatever was in the forefront of her mind; not what she wanted him to hear. This trick of speaking with their minds seemed to be a gift between herself and Columbine only. *We'll shift in a tunnel between our bedrooms like we did in the Well.*

Columbine remained pressed against their mother's throat. *Why?*

Cora ran the tip of her tongue around her lips to moisten them. *Just … trust me on this for a little while, shorthorns.*

Why?

How in the realms was that trusting her? *Because.* It was a sucky answer, but it covered all the necessary points.

Why do you not like the angels?

What?

Why do you not like the angels? You and Father both have the same light orange in your colours. It is … what Father calls icky.

It's called suspicion, shorthorns. It means Father doesn't trust the angels.

And who do you not trust?

Damn it. She'd heard the exclusion. Cora subconsciously glanced at their father and away, determined not to give her sister any hint of the target of her distrust. It wasn't that she didn't *want* to trust him per se. They'd come a long way in that regard since he'd come back into their lives. She just didn't ... *trust*-trust him. Not now that his hostility towards those who were established in a field that came naturally to Columbine was clear. *It doesn't matter, shorthorns. Just ... stay close to me for a while. Okay?* The last thing she wanted to do was to have Columbine spiral into another emotional tailspin when her worst fear might never eventuate. Better that things stay as normal as possible between them while she kept an eye on them both from the sidelines.

O...kay.

* * *

Having no clue of the private conversation between their two daughters, Avis and Clarise returned their family to the dining room of the house, placing each child in their respective seats in front of a fully prepared breakfast. "How do you wish to proceed, beloved?" Clarise asked, still standing alongside Columbine with one hand on her shoulder.

Avis ran his tongue across his teeth behind his closed lips. "I definitely don't trust those plain-clothed parasites. They have the power to turn your brother, the crown prince of Hell, into an emotionless puppet. The only time I've ever seen anything like that was when Tal got out of hand once in the middle of Crohen and Amaro was over in Pandess with me. Cuschler blood-linked his father and I went back with him for added muscle, but by the time we arrived, Paz had already leaned so heavily into her powerbase that Tal was passed out in a snoring heap on the floor with a peaceful smile plastered on his face. He woke up the following day and honestly couldn't remember why he'd been so mad."

"Which one's she again?" Cora asked.

Avis thought the 'peaceful' inference should have made the answer obvious. "Your cousin Paz, my twin brother's daughter of Peace." The answer was simple, and as soon as he finished, he looked across the table at Clarise. "But that's the extent of what she can do. If she gets hold of you, she can bring a sense of peace inside you. It's not the same as this. How do we trust anything we're feeling, if they can change all of it at will?"

"By comparing it to what we felt before we arrived here. If you start singing the Almighty's praises, I am going to assume they have influenced you."

Avis scowled at her from his place beside Cora. "Not funny," he insisted, pressing on the nerve at the base of Cora's neck as the little shit started to snicker. Cora yelped out a laugh and squirmed in her seat, but his fingers followed her movement and retained their hold no matter how low she ducked and writhed; if only to show her he could. Provided of course, she didn't shift.

"No, you are correct," Clarise agreed, even if the twinkle in her eyes said otherwise. "This is a serious situation, though I do not believe it is as bad as you think, my love."

Avis' eyebrows arched sharply. "You don't?"

"Perhaps it is because I am a shifter and we have always been raised to be wary around benders, but personally, I do not see much of a difference between making someone act out because of an emotional adjustment as opposed to one that is achieved via a mental command."

Avis hated the logic she portrayed. To an outsider, those two may have born some semblance of similarity, but to him they were polar opposites. Mainly because one he controlled, and one he didn't. Night versus day.

"If the emotions they instil are for the benefit of the individual, is it necessarily a bad thing?" she went on.

"That means you have to trust the individual to not be malicious," Avis answered, shaking his head. "I don't do trust on that scale … especially not with them."

"That is more a loss of control issue than an emotional one, beloved."

Avis snapped his teeth and ground them against the expletives that came so readily to mind. He'd never hidden the fact that control was a big part of his makeup, so why was she beating him over the head with it now? He was the eldest son of Order itself, for Mystal's sake! Of course, he had to maintain control! He gestured haphazardly at the meal between them, letting go of Cora's neck in the process. "Maybe having breakfast will put us all in a better mood," he said, moving to his seat.

The servants fussed around them, reheating and chilling the various foods to bring them back to optimal edibility.

As they ate, he noticed Cora wasn't eating anywhere near as much as she usually did, and he ran his mental fingers through her surface thoughts. *Shorthorns*, **don't go anywhere without running it past me first.** *You hear me?*

The mental command itself was sloppy, but Avis still smiled at the way she circled the wagons around her little sister and turned his attention to his meal. It was good that Cora saw the angels for the threat they were just as much as he did. If the girls stuck together, that would free him up to make sure the Fifth Choir kept their distance. The first time Avis had heard Cora's nickname for Columbine, he'd almost taken her head off for what he'd thought was an ongoing slur between the two of them. But later he came to realise it was a true term of endearment, for 'shorthorns' also meant non-aggressive, meaning Cora would always have her sister's back because Columbine was too sweet to start anything herself. That might not have been an ideal situation for the average Mystallian, but once Avis made it known he'd thrown his hat into that protective ring as well, he doubted anyone would be giving his princess any trouble for not being so competitive.

The feeling of family unity gave him back his appetite and he began to eat in earnest.

After breakfast, Clarise and Avis decided to move their journey along. The family sat astride their demon steeds while Clarise broke the home down, just as she had hundreds of times before in Chaos. The servants took their places behind the family, and of course, the four brute squad guards created a square of protection around them all.

When it was done, Avis waved his hand forward and the party took to the air.

Curious to see what might have been on the other side of that wall, Avis took them higher than the angels along the wall. Other warriors quickly swept in to form a different type of wall, but not before Avis got a glimpse of what he was looking for. He couldn't say what he'd expected to find over there, but a bottomless sky with wispy clouds and a smattering of angels going about their business was quite a letdown. Angels, he supposed, were like birds, and birds preferred the air and perches to a solid ground. He looked back at the ground only a few storeys beneath his party and frowned, then shrugged. The strip of solid cloud that travellers like him walked on outside the pearlescent walls, was only there to *give* wingless travellers like him a strip of cloud to walk on. Yet another layer of security for Heaven that he hadn't thought of before. Keeping everything aerial was an interesting way of dissuading non-flyers from invading, that's for sure.

Having seen what he wanted, Avis focused on the way forward, though that didn't stop him from glancing to his left now and again to see if maybe something other than cloudy skies and angels existed over there.

Eleven drawn-out hours of riding later (the twelfth being swallowed up by a lunch break in the middle), left the answer a resounding 'no'. It was just … sky over there. Blue skies with angels either flying in between the clouds or walking across the fluffy surfaces.

Avis learned another annoying thing about Heaven soon after they landed for the evening. They didn't have a night. None whatsoever. It wasn't blazing daylight like in Yaru that would cook even a god to a crisp, but it was still annoyingly well-lit.

After the evening meal, the girls were made ready for bed while Avis and Clarise remained at the dining table. Avis reached forward to pick up his goblet of ambrosia, then swirled the burgundy drink until it rose in waves almost to the lip. The symmetry of the liquid's movement seemed to ease his mind, somehow. Or distract it.

He almost leapt out of his skin when Clarise's hands slid across his shoulders and tightened on the cords of his neck. The ambrosia splashed across his gloved hand and he bit back a dark curse at both the mess and his lapse in concentration. "We are safe," she murmured, as he deposited the goblet on the table with a heavy-handed thump and raised his clean hand to cover one of hers.

"I know," he admitted after a long time, though it gave him no joy.

"So what is it that truly bothers you about this place?"

Avis opened his mouth to answer, but before the words formulated, she tightened her grip on his shoulders and added, "And do not waste our time telling me it is the way the angels invade every other established realm. Something else about this has been bothering you all day. Something personal."

Avis let out his breath in a small huff. "That's exactly what's bothering me, sweetheart. I can't put my finger on it." He pursed his lips in frustration and shook his head. "Especially that choirmaster. Raphy-whatever his name is." He lifted his right hand away from the goblet and pinched his fingertips together in front of his face. "It's like it's right there, shouting at me, and I just. Can't. *See it.*" The growl that escaped him did nothing to ease matters.

"Perhaps you have met before?"

Right, like I hadn't thought of that myself. Avis shook his head to clear the snark from his thoughts. "I went a long way back through my memories while we were riding today, trying to find him. He's not there. As far as I can tell, our paths have never crossed before this morning and it's …" —*pissing me off*— "… annoying me, like a lot." He twisted his head into her hand and pressed his lips against her palm. "I'm sorry if it's bothering you."

She smiled and bent down to kiss him lightly on the cheek. "Well, the children are currently with their governesses, getting ready for bed. If it means so much to you that you would rather sit here all night pondering over it, I shall bid you a good evening and retire myself." As she spoke, she traced one finger from his left shoulder to his elbow and back up again, then outlined the helix of his left ear. "Goodnight, Avis," she breathed softly into that ear, then turned and sashayed towards their apartment.

She made it a grand total of four steps before he launched out of his seat and caught up with her in two, scooping her into his arms and continuing onto the privacy of their apartment, leaving Tilu with the clean-up.

Goodnight, indeed.

CHAPTER THIRTY-FIVE

Avis awoke the following morning feeling both relaxed and sexually sated. The latter happened quite often, but it had been a while since the former had occurred. Not wanting to break the mood, he lay still, content to watch his wife sleep snuggled against his chest. It was hard to believe just how much his life could change in one short decade. Back then, he'd have woken up either amidst a throng of women who only clung to him for his power, or alone, and would've found nothing wrong with that. Now, there'd be everything wrong with it.

For over an hour he indulged himself this way, dedicating to memory every single detail he'd already memorised a thousand times before and enjoying the soft lavender fragrance that accompanied her presence. If he had to die right then, provided his girls were safe, he'd do so with a smile on his lips.

And, of course, right on cue, his brain had to ask, *what if they weren't?* He didn't actually believe anything had happened to them since last night, but the more he tried to ignore the idea, the more insistent it became. *Go and check. Just to be on the safe side. Then you'll know for sure.*

It was more irritating than worrisome, but he knew he wouldn't be able to return to his peaceful, mental meanderings until that thought had been put to rest.

Reaching over his head for one of the many pillows stacked there, he spent the next few minutes extracting himself from under Clarise's head, carefully substituting the pillow for his pec without waking her. If everything was fine with the girls, he'd be right back and Clarise would never have to know he was gone.

Avis rolled to his feet, regretting not having a handy robe that he could toss on and tie around his waist whilst moving around his own set of apartments the way the rest of his family did. In the past, it was either his full uniform or nothing, and he hadn't cared who saw him in the nude as he strode around inside his own personal wing. But now, that space consisted of his children in the next set of rooms over, and that wasn't a line he was ever going to cross. *Ever.* Which meant he had to dress in his full uniform.

As he grabbed up his leggings and prepared to don them, he paused and looked at the bedroom doors. *Or get someone else in the next room with touch shapeshifting to do it for me in a tenth of the time.* It wasn't as if every one of his girls hadn't made use of that shifting ability a dozen times before, so why shouldn't he?

Grinning at his cleverness, Avis gathered up his uniform in its entirety and made his way into the sitting room. "Tilu," he whispered after quietly shutting the doors behind him, knowing the named servant would hear him even if she was at rest.

Tilu rose from where she'd been curled in her hellion form on the hearth tiles in front of the roaring fire, and immediately shifted into her Mystallian form with her hands clasped and her head bowed forward. "M'lord," she said.

Avis held out the clothes. "I wish to check on the girls." He added nothing else, allowing that one sentence to imply what he wanted of her.

Tilu's head bowed lower and then she straightened and approached him. One hand touched the nearest boot, which then melted into the other. Every piece of clothing folded into the mix until it was all liquefied, at which point she rolled her hands towards Avis. The mass stretched out and engulfed Avis' left hand, morphing into his uniform glove. It continued to crawl up his arm and stretch out across his chest to the other arm, darkening and shifting back into his doublet. Seconds later he was fully dressed with boots on his feet and his cloak spread across his shoulders. Avis rolled his gloved hands and curled his fingers, then looked up at Tilu and smiled, nodding in appreciation.

Tilu lowered her head, both to hide the way she was smiling shyly in return and to bow in acknowledgement of his unspoken praise as she twisted and stepped out of his way.

Despite his love of the bender's way, Avis had to admit, the Hellions were certainly ... *efficient*. It would've taken him at least two or three minutes to get dressed manually, even if he had help from the Mystallian servants, and that wasn't including the small-talk that the servants often engaged in.

Avis made his way through the room and passed through the double doors that led into the dining room. Inside his own head, he had almost convinced himself that there was nothing to worry about, but still he needed to be sure ...

... and that was when he took in the state of the dining room.

At first he froze; his head scrambling to make sense of what his eyes were telling him. Not only were Cora's apartment doors swinging wide open, but so too were the front doors. Which meant either Cora was outside, or something from outside had come in and gone into her apartment.

Icy dread filled his veins as he bolted down the length of the dining hall and shot into her rooms. His instinct was to shout out her name, but if she was in any kind of trouble, that shout would've alerted her attacker to his presence.

Avis took in the scene of her sitting room at a glance and mid-sprint he rolled his mind inwards to give himself time to properly process what he'd seen. Gingen was scurrying across the floor as quickly as her centipede form could take her, bumping into both the table and the wall in her haste to avoid ... something.

That was not important. Nor was the servant.

More concerning to Avis; the bedroom doors had been completely ripped off their hinges. In fact, timber chunks heavily bolted into the hinges were all that remained of them. Avis was just about to lose his mind when his attention snagged the shattered edge of the timber chunks—specifically, the bent angle of the timber fibres. They weren't angled towards Cora's bedroom. They were bent in the direction of her sitting room. And all of the timber shards lay scattered across the floor between him and the door frame.

So, no one had broken in. For whatever reason, Cora had smashed through her own doors from inside the bedroom, and due to the soundproofing that Clarise had incorporated throughout the house, he hadn't heard a damned thing from thirty metres away.

He made a mental note to have Clarise modify the structural soundproofing so that it was a one-way kind where he could still hear what was going on under his own roof; even if no one else could. This shit was not happening again.

Convinced that Cora had been the instigator and not the victim, Avis returned to the physical realm and skidded to a halt. Then he did an about-face and charged back into the dining room. He might not have understood why she'd done it yet, but just knowing she had made him feel a little better about the situation.

He also promised himself that if she didn't have what he considered a good reason for doing this, his boot and her ass (both mentally and physically) were about to share a very repetitive difference of opinion.

He raced across the dining hall and went outside onto the stoop ...

... and stopped dead in his tracks for the second time in almost as many seconds.

There, in the middle of the lawn, Avis found not one, but both of his children dressed in their Mystallian uniforms. Cora stood between him and her sister with her back to the house, but and the way her legs were braced apart and her arms were folded across her chest, she was on sentry duty. *Wait ... Columbine instigated this?* She must have, since she was on her knees in the grass, rubbing her hands across the heads, necks, bellies and wings of—*what the fuck are they?*

Creatures easily matching the size of Tal or Griffith lay on the grass all around her. Dozens of them. Unlike his huge brothers, each of these things had two pairs of wings and no fewer than four faces on their singular head. With the numbers that surrounded Columbine, he could see examples of the four faces that allowed them to look in all directions. One was a lion, another was an ox, the third was a Mystallian and the last was an eagle. Each face had one limb central to the eyes that corresponded with the face above it. The lion's chest had a huge forepaw. The ox had a muscular leg that ended in a hoof. The Mystallian had an arm with a working hand and the eagle's foot had four large talons, each the size of Columbine's head. Instead of legs, they seemed to have two solid brass pins that ended in gleaming hooves, though how they could possibly walk without a knee to bend was beyond him. Not that he cared about that. They looked dangerous. He'd always known claws and talons were perilous, but in recent years he'd learned hooves could be just as detrimental to one's health if their possessor was so inclined. And the intelligence he saw in the Mystallian eyes meant these things weren't monsters. They were sapient. *Bastards!*

Determined to learn everything about the situation, Avis went into Cora's mind first. He blurred past everything in her memory in reverse order until he found the starting point. Snippets from Cora's point of view where she ran backwards from the front door after it banged against the side walls and then closed. More snippets where Cora hurtled backwards over the dining table and ran backwards into her sitting room with the doors shutting in her face. Some level of confrontation with Gingen had the servant rushing to the mantle and extending a tentacle to Cora's throat. Cora's hand came into view as it threw a blanket over the back of a high-backed chair on her way back into the bedroom. Then her vision shifted into a dozen different spectra and Columbine materialised in front of her. The two danced around until Cora leapt backwards onto the bed and Columbine came forward to fill Cora's vision. Then an exploded mass came back together in the form of a swollen Uriel, who then shrank back to normal ...

Wait ... what?

Avis pulled up suddenly and returned to the Uriel memory, this time watching the sequence of events flow in the right direction. He recognised the opening scene from yesterday, where Cora had been in his arms and Uriel had shredded her confidence with his bullshit silent eyebrow stunt. Only this time, it was Cora who roared her displeasure at him, and somehow that scathing reprimand made Uriel swell up like a puffer fish until he finally exploded.

Avis didn't need to see the fogged edges of the memory to know this was an internalisation—probably a dream. From a bender's point of view, the two were very closely linked, though the more bizarre imagery came from dreams. His own head might have been telling him to hurry up and get to the point of gathering information, but time outside was no longer an issue, so he went back and watched the absurd memory play out again. And again. And maybe a few more times for good measure. It was positively hilarious!

At the conclusion of his final pass, the foggy dreamscape broke when something jerked on her right hand. Avis watched as she grimaced and fought to open her eyes, only to have Columbine's face completely fill her blurred vision. Avis watched as Cora blinked and pushed her sister out to arm's length, struggling to right her orientation. "What ... what's going on, shorthorns?" And then her senses snapped into place and she launched herself to her knees, one hand snatching at Columbine's wrist to haul her behind her for safety if necessary, the other already shifting her fingernails into hand-length talons in anticipation of a fight.

Avis snorted and folded his arms, knowing exactly who she'd inherited that level of heightened self-preservation from.

"Are you alright?" she asked, when it was clear there was no one in the room that needed eviscerating.

"I want to go outside," Columbine said, still holding Cora's restraining wrist in both of her hands and tugging impatiently. "Come outside with me, Cora. Please? They are waiting for us."

Cora reared back in disbelief, heaving her hand free. Her talons reverted into fingernails and she took her sister's shoulders in both hands, giving her a severe shake. "Are you out of your freaking mind?"

Well, at least one of them was thinking, Avis thought to himself, though he couldn't believe of the two, it was Columbine who'd broken the rules. Worse, she'd begged like a commoner for her sister to go outside with her. Both actions had Avis mentally counting to ten ... several times over.

Still being held by her sister, Columbine looked longingly towards the doors. "But they are out there, Cora. They want to be with me, and I want to be with them ..."

"Shorthorns, I don't give a rat's—*no!*" Columbine had already dropped her shoulders (somehow shifting her way free of Cora's grip) and fled towards the doors, forcing Cora to jump to her feet and leap over the top of her. Avis watched through her perspective as she twisted in mid-air to land in front of the closed doors with her arms outstretched to either side in denial.

Again, Avis froze the scene, this time drumming his fingers thoughtfully against his chin. If the doors to the sitting room were still shut and neither governess who'd been resting in the sitting rooms were alerted, how in the realms had Columbine gotten into Cora's bedroom in the first place? And, just as tellingly, why wasn't that a question Cora was asking? Avis smelled a rat.

Backing up the scene, he searched the backgrounds from when Cora woke up, looking for any hint of how Columbine had come to be in the room. Yet nothing seemed out of place. Not even Columbine's guard, who stood to one side with its huge double arms folded and its wings as close to at ease as those creatures could be. Its headpiece kept spinning, but to be honest, he'd be more worried if it ever stopped.

Still not knowing how Columbine and the guard managed to get into the room undetected, Avis restarted the memory where he'd left off and felt more than saw Cora fold her arms decisively. "Forget it, shorthorns. You're not going anywhere. Period!"

Now Avis openly cursed the sound-proofing his wife had painstakingly installed in the walls. All these memories were less than an hour old, which meant he'd been awake watching Clarise and playing with her hair the whole time this fiasco was taking place! If he'd had any inkling it was going on he'd have been in here to sort it all out before either one of them got it into their heads to go outside.

Columbine was already in her uniform. "But you said all I had to do was tell you where I was going," she argued, stepping first to her left, then her right in a feeble attempt to get past her older sister.

"And I meant it," Cora shot straight back, shifting her weight from side to side to block her every move. "You're absolutely not going out there. No way. Father'll skin us both alive! You for doing it, and me for letting you."

She had that right. He was furious.

Columbine's eyebrows arched and her bottom lip trembled, but then a flash of steel entered her eyes and she suddenly vanished.

"No!" Cora snarled, and with her thoughts on full display, Avis could see she'd deduced Columbine had dissipated into a clear, gaseous form that left Cora unable to get a mental lock on her. The guard had also disappeared. This was exactly why he'd called the mental command a sloppy one. Columbine had filled the criteria just by saying what she planned. It hadn't stopped her from carrying those plans out.

The next few seconds were filled with a variety of colour shifts as Cora cycled through dozens of different visual options. "Bitch," she swore, when none of the different spectra revealed her sister. Without wasting any more time, she braced herself and charged at her bedroom doors, hitting them on the full.

Gingen launched upright from her place beside the sitting room fire as the door latch shattered and flew a few body-lengths to skid across the carpeted floor, along with the rest of the door fragments. Cora tore through the room, grabbing a blanket from over the back of the chair that faced the fire. "Mistress, you must stop!"

Cora ignored her, right up until something like a tentacle encircled the bare skin of her throat. Not enough to choke her or pull her off her feet, but just enough for the contact to be made. Cora's fingers automatically went for the restraint, but already her vision began to swim and she went from sprinting to staggering in just a few stumbled steps.

"I cannot permit you to leave, mistress," Gingen declared with absolute authority.

Realising what he was witnessing, Avis let out a vicious howl of outrage. *Fucking shape-shifting assholes!* He'd made no secret of his plan to murder Frash for doing this very same act, and now he learned the governesses were secretly applying that crap to his girls behind his back? *No. Fucking. Way!*

Determined to see where this went (and mete out punishment accordingly) Avis' growl quickly turned into a cheer of victory when Cora's vision cleared just as quickly as it had blurred, indicating she'd countered whatever Gingen had done. The red tinge that coated his vision whenever his own temper was triggered quickly poured across his daughter's sight as she swivelled on her heel to face the centipede hellion. He could only guess the murderous expression on Cora's face at that moment, if the way the governess abandoned the tentacle and slithered pleadingly on her belly was anything to go by. "For the last time, **back the fuck off, bitch!**" The latter half was sent as a mental command which had Gingen scurrying backwards, tripping over everything in her haste to get away … from basically everything.

Cora wasted no more time on Gingen. She rushed towards the door leading into the dining hall, using the blanket she'd snagged to shift her nightgown into her uniform. The front doors were still closed, but they both knew Columbine would've passed through the gaps without notice and Cora needed to make up as much time as she could. So instead of going around the table, she charged straight at the bulky piece of furniture and dove over its polished surface, using her hands on the far edge to flip her feet past her head so that she would land upright and her momentum kept her running.

Nimble little monkey. But of course, Avis already knew that. She'd shown him numerous times just how acrobatic she could be.

As Cora body-slammed into the front doors and slid out onto the stoop, they hit the sides of the house and bounced back again. That explained why they'd been slightly ajar when he came out.

Columbine was already in the middle of the lawn, kneeling in the grass amongst those … whatever they damn-well were.

Avis took in as much detail as he could about the strange creatures, up to and including the point where Cora attempted to search one of their minds for answers and hit the same brick wall he had with Uriel. Avis's growl of frustration matched that of his elder daughter. They were both getting extremely fed up with how everything in Heaven defied the natural order of things! It was utter bullshit!

Cora shook her head, probably in disgust, and her point of view went from one side of the perimeter to the other. There, on the outer edge where the grass butted up to the low-lying fog (or rather, the clouds, this being Heaven and all) he caught sight of Columbine's brute squad guard. Avis stopped the memory and went back to where the guard stood. With its ridiculous speed, it could've easily put itself in the middle of the group if it needed to, but why in the realms was it way the hell over there? It was almost as if it was giving its charge and these creatures a modicum of privacy.

Realising how stupid that was, Avis rolled his eyes in disgust. Now he was being paranoid *and* ridiculous.

The creatures closest to Columbine had their heads on the ground, staring up at her in wistful adoration. Those further back rested on their elbows with the same doe-eyed look in their eyes. Others still sat with their torsos angled into the one limb that braced them off the ground. None of them were standing upright. Avis noted that Columbine's hands moved from one to the next, stretching and shrinking her arms as necessary to reach the ones at the very back. Those she reached past lifted themselves to rub their heads and throats against her arms like a cat. And speaking of 'cat', every single one of those lion faces was purring. They seemed to be as enthralled with Columbine as she was with them.

Avis didn't like it, though he could well understand why Cora felt more inclined to stand guard instead of dragging Columbine back to the safety of the house. No one appeared to be in any danger thus far, and any discipline that needed to be handed down as a result of this would come from either him or Clarise.

For once, their young tiger was in the clear.

The thought amused him, but not for long. Columbine may have been his darling little girl, but she knew she wasn't supposed to be out here by herself, especially in the midst of company like this without his or Clarise's permission. He dragged his thumbnail across his lower lip, then flicked it between his teeth. As her father, he also knew what he had to do to prevent it from happening again, but by the Twin Notes, he'd rather cut off his own arm. Columbine's natural desire to please had meant he hadn't needed to discipline her before today, and he really wasn't looking forward to doing it now.

Still, it had to be done. Columbine had crossed the line and broken the rules. At the very least, offering her a free pass for something he'd have landed all over Cora for wasn't fair to his tiger, and that girl had made it very clear how she felt about favouritism.

But, maybe these creatures had drawn her out, somehow. Could that have been what happened? Seeing that as a viable option that offered him a way out, Avis latched onto it with both hands. Yes, yes it could. In fact, it was more than just possible. If they had some level of establishment, maybe … maybe they were like the sirens in Olympus or something. Well, not *exactly* like them, obviously. The house was soundproofed, so no amount of singing out here was going to draw Columbine to them, but maybe they used something else? Something like—maybe a special scent. He'd never heard of a particular pheromone drawing a Mystallian out against their will, but before he'd met Zeus, he hadn't heard of a songstress doing it either and this was his first time in Heaven. It'd be the last time too, if he had his way.

Regardless of his thoughts, the only person who had the answers he sought was Columbine, and to get them, he had to confront her consciousness and the colours she controlled.

There was no way around it.

CHAPTER THIRTY-SIX

Withdrawing from Cora's mind, Avis rebounded off his physical form and relaunched himself at his younger daughter. In the space of a heartbeat, he went from a well organised, logical thought process to the mind-numbing pictorial overload of Columbine. Everything in her recent memories was saturated in rich deep blue, which Avis knew represented innocent love. It was one of the few colours he could identify. He hoped he never had to learn what the difference was between this childlike version of love and the more lustful version that may or may not come when she reached maturity. He was pretty sure he'd geld anyone who forged that type of bond with his princess, but this rich blue, he could work with.

Just as he had with Cora, Avis sought out the beginning of where Columbine thought it was a good idea to go outside. Which meant he had to go back further than when she'd woken her sister up. Unlike watching Cora's memories play out, Avis was able to 'jump' scenes, reaching back for a different image that overlapped with the current one. As such, he found himself in Columbine's dream, where three huge, four-legged creatures towered over his little girl. They had the head, wings and forefeet of an eagle, and the body, rear legs and tail of a lion. Avis' eyes widened at the sight of the creatures that were at least half as big again as his own mystallion back home and he shook his head.

"No way," he murmured, still shaking his head, even as he froze the scene and stared at the beasts that were practically a myth even in celestial circles. "No fucking way."

Through his companionship with Zeus, Avis had seen eight of these spectacular creatures from a relatively safe distance. The specifics were too exact to be second-rate constructs, though many had tried. True gryps were impressive, and many pantheons wanted to pretend that they had such magnificent creatures at their beck and call. By far, the easiest way to achieve this was to 'create' them through a combination of construct and worship, though anyone who had ever interacted with the originals knew these recreations were shallow copies at best because they were never perfect. Not like this. As an example, one pantheon forgot to give them wings. Another gave them a lion's forepaws instead of an eagle's taloned feet. Another still used a peacock's head instead of an eagle's. It was as if they were being prevented from matching the original.

Unlike those losers, these images were perfect. From their jewelled eyes to their wicked claws, nothing about them implied a lesser creature. Everyone who was anyone had heard the legends regarding them. They were almost as terrifying in battle as the brute squad and a billion times rarer. Their wings and claws could cut through anything. Anything at all. Legend had it not even shifters could stand up to them in battle. Any who tried were torn to pieces regardless of what form they took, and died before they could shift into anything else. Benders were obviously in no better position. The one and only time Avis had ever tried to force his mental dominance onto one of Apollo's eight true gryps in the hopes of stealing it, the winged behemoth had thrown out its wings and screeched in outrage, then flown across the room at *him*. Literally. Like it had somehow known he'd tried! Jumping to and from the mortal realm in the hopes of losing it did nothing. It didn't stop chasing him until Avis blood-linked with Amaro and got the hell out of Olympus altogether. Years later, Zeus had sent word through his grandson Yitzak (who was also Chance's grandson and Mystal's established god of the Drink) that the true gryps had given up the chase and Avis could return whenever he wanted. He'd heard from other Olympians that it took Zeus almost as long to stop laughing. Bastard.

He took Zeus up on his offer, though he made a huge point of staying far, far away from Apollo's stables.

And now his little girl was dreaming about meeting them? A creature she had no way of knowing about? It had to be a trick. It had to be. Some sort of influence that these beasts were able to conjure up.

Having his theory grow more credible by the second, Avis watched the scene roll forward. The icing on the cake for Avis was when the true gryps' images began to have a meaningful conversation with her. None of them used their beaks to speak, but their words echoed throughout her memory in a tell-tale shout. That right there proved the lie. True gryps couldn't talk. They weren't even sapient. They were incredible beasts of war and legend, but that was it.

So something was tricking Columbine into thinking they were having this lovely conversation as if she was their best friend, and his foolish, foolish little princess was swallowing it hook, line and sinker. They told her how much they wanted to meet her. How badly they wanted her to go outside. To be with them.

They wanted it so much that Columbine wanted it too.

Avis froze the scene and dragged all his fingers through his hair, clenching them into a double fist behind his head. *So, that's how you fucking did it,* he swore, knowing Columbine would never have undertaken this venture by herself. Somehow, these realm-damned things were able to push their desires into her so strongly that even from outside the house, they were able to influence her emotions. But they still weren't *real* true gryps. The creatures that were fawning all over her outside looked nothing like them. These were just impressive images to lure her out to them!

Determined to see this through, Avis squared his shoulders and folded his arms across his chest, allowing the scene to carry on. Just like the creatures outside, these ones dipped their heads and dropped their shoulders to the ground, exposing the soft fur of their underbellies for her to rub like a dog. Yet more proof of the absolute crap of the scene. Columbine giggled and reached both arms over the barrel-sized chest of the nearest one, dragging her fingers across its short fur. Another nudged her from behind with its head. Not hard, but hard enough that she turned and rubbed its head as well. More of the damned creatures arrived, each wanting their turn at being touched by his baby and turning almost mindless by the blissful contact. *Come outside,* they all pleaded. *Please. We need you. We love you.*

O…*kay.* Avis tweaked his working theory about how they drew Columbine out. It wasn't just her own deep-seated desire to go outside. These bastards had played on her fundamental desire to please. An emotional double whammy that she couldn't resist.

From the loss of fog around the edges, Columbine's point of view had her sitting up in bed. Dark orange blended with rich blue as her young heart pounded with the need to be outside with her new friends. Only one thing took precedence.

Shorthorns, you don't go anywhere without running it past me first.

The mental command hung at the forefront of Columbine's mind, causing Avis to almost fall to his knees in relief. If Cora hadn't had the forethought to do this last night, Columbine probably would've gone straight outside, with no one being any the wiser.

In his mind, the creatures interacting with Columbine went beyond vile in nature. They had to be. Their modus operandi was too similar to Zeus' sirens, only more insidious because they could invade someone's dreams to do so. For that alone, he was going to kill them. Whatever they were … however they were connected to Heaven, he didn't care. The second they went after his girls like this; their lives were forfeit.

Columbine looked at her bedroom doors, then rose to her feet and slipped out of her nightgown. Avis deliberately averted his eyes to the ceiling at the top of her view until the flesh tones in his peripheral vision went away, indicating Columbine was no longer looking down at herself. Even during internalisation, witnessing a blood member of the family in a state of undress was not acceptable to him.

The next thing to enter Columbine's vision was her uniform, which she shifted into mist and drew the cloud of fog to her. Unlike the way Tilu took seconds to mould his uniform around him, Columbine's uniform snapped into place the moment the fog made contact with her outstretched hand. Over time, Avis had learned the two differences in her shifting. The instantaneous side of things only worked with the mass she had already assimilated. That was, anything she needed to add or take away was done at the same rate as any other shifter, but once it was part of her, it was hers to do whatever she liked with immediately.

Avis' gaze narrowed. Now came the interesting part: how she'd gotten into Cora's room without alerting either of their governesses. His arm and shoulder muscles tensed in expectation as Columbine didn't even attempt to use her doors. Instead, she rushed straight into her ensuite, passing the tub and toilet in her haste to reach the dividing wall. *O—kay.*

In a blur, Columbine's perspective changed to include everything in all directions as her mass dropped to the floor and poured smoothly into a hole the width of his thumb hidden in the shadows of the skirting board.

Whoa! Avis froze the scene and blinked heavily, not because he'd discerned her escape route, but because he was experiencing for himself what Clarise had described numerous times. She'd said a shifter's senses blew out whenever they lost physical access to those senses, but he hadn't expected it to look and feel like this! She saw everything! She tasted *everything!* She even heard everything going on between the two sets of apartments! Cora snoring in the room next door. The fires crackling in each of their fireplaces. She could scent everything through the walls, though the creatures' pronounced musky scents outside intertwined with Clarise's sweet perfume. Even his own preferred pine fragrance from the room next door merged with the burning timbers in the fire. But the visual was by far the most convoluted. Every single visual spectrum overlaid the next, from heat to skeletal, giving more clarity to an object than mere colour or shape. It was too much! Avis could spend a week going through everything she took in at that moment!

Avis skipped over the next few seconds, picking it back up after she'd reformed into a little Mystallian girl.

Cora was sprawled out asleep in the bed in front of her. Although they still hadn't discussed the return of her shifting ability, it thrilled him to see her stay as a Mystallian whenever she could.

Not so delightful was the way Columbine rushed to Cora's side and grabbed her outstretched hand, jerking on it in an effort to wake her sister up.

Avis hissed and winced, covering first his eyes and then his mouth at such a stupid, stupid move. No one should ever wake a more powerful bender by making touch contact. It was just too dangerous! Depending on where in their dreams that bender was, they could come out swinging and the weaker mind might forever be destroyed.

He made yet another mental note to sit down and explain this in explicit detail to Columbine, the first chance he got. Fortunately for both his girls, Cora recognised her sister and, when cognitive thought kicked in, so too did her protective instincts.

The rest played out just as it had in Cora's memory, though Columbine's remained full of all the conversations that the creatures were throwing at her. Nothing about the way they communicated indicated a hidden agenda. If anything, it corroborated what he and Cora had surmised. They were simply that desperate to be with her.

Now that he had all the facts, the plan as he saw it was a simple one. He'd return to the physical realm, get the girls to go back inside, and then he and these feathered fuckers would ... *discuss* in no uncertain terms why this unsanctioned interaction with his daughter was never going to happen again. He'd use the brute squad if he had to. With no bending to speak of and being so far from his powerbase, he knew he was at a huge disadvantage, but he was banking on losing the first round. Theoretically, that would bring the brute squad in to defend him, and if he was hurt badly enough, they might even have to kill them. Then he would heal, and they wouldn't. In the words of Armina, "Checkmate."

Happy with his strategy, it occurred to him that Columbine's consciousness had yet to make an appearance. Not believing for a second that she didn't know he was here , he searched his immediate area to no effect. Perhaps, like all children who knew they were in trouble, she was making herself scarce. If so, smart girl.

Avis returned to his physical body and stalked out on the lawn, the heavy clip of his boots drawing everyone's attention.

Cora swung around and sighed in relief. Columbine on the other hand, was frightened. But the creatures around Columbine? Every one of them donned a warrior's fierce expression and, in a fraction of a heartbeat, went from laying down and subdued, to upright and aggressive. Columbine was pushed further and further away from him as each of these things stepped in front of her, using their wings to guide her back. Every weapon they had was on display. Their lips curled back to expose rows of teeth that sharpened and tripled in length. So did their claws and talons. The hooves stomped at the empty air and ignited, and from out of nowhere their Mystallian hands brandished a longsword which they all rolled with the ease of a master. Even the feathers of their wings flared as if each of them was a weapon of some sort.

And finally ... finally! The brute squad guards moved. One instant he was alone on the lawn, and the next he had one flanking him on either side and the third one hovering overhead. The fourth was still on the outside boundary, though it moved closer to Columbine.

"Cora, get back inside," Avis commanded, never taking his focus from the creatures that dared to stand between him and his little girl.

Cora glanced between the two rival parties, then scurried past him without a word. He heard one of her boots hit the stoop and the other a second later pass the threshold of the front doors. "You picked the wrong family to fuck with," he growled, low enough that Columbine wouldn't hear his curse but loud enough to have his meaning understood.

"Abso-fucking-lutely."

Avis froze at the bastardised word that was both childlike feminine and familiar. His eyes dropped to his side, where Cora's mass had already shifted into a pool of silver molasses that stretched itself into a long, tapering object about one and a half metres in length. The width was roughly that of his hand, though it wasn't until the piece sliding into his hand became a steel coloured hilt with a pommel on the end that he realised what Cora had turned herself into.

This was not what he'd meant when he'd sent her to the safety of the house! Adding yet another lecture to his ever-increasing to-do list, Avis lifted the newly created sword and rolled it across his body, testing it for both balance and fit. "Mystallian steel, right?" he murmured, hoping Cora had remembered to become the type of sword he'd introduced her to back in Hell and not one of those more useless ones that everyone else carried.

What he'd thought was a decorative eye in the steel pommel winked cheekily at him, reminding him that he was still holding one of his daughter's as a weapon. He scowled darkly, not liking that fact at all. Yes, she was a shifter that was clearly capable of becoming a sword, but she was also his unestablished daughter. What if she got broken during this battle? Would that hurt her? Would she die? He wasn't a shifter, and as a bender he couldn't get past the mental nightmare of knowing he'd be swinging his daughter through his enemies as a weapon. Just the thought of it had him shuddering inwardly in horror.

But short of going fist to sword, he didn't have a choice ...

... *or did he?*

The creatures were clearly protective of Columbine, which meant the only person in jeopardy was him, and he was truly immortal. With that realisation, Avis turned and pitched the sword back into the house, embedding it to the hilt in one of Columbine's closed bedroom doors. "Stay there!" he roared, pointing warningly at the sword that was already melting out of the door and reshaping into Cora's Mystallian form. He meant it too. No matter what these bastards did to him, he'd survive. That was in no way guaranteed where she was concerned and he wasn't prepared to risk it.

"No!" she shouted in hurt outrage. "I can help!"

Stop.

Avis felt that demand through the depth of his bones.

And suddenly, the confrontational atmosphere evaporated, drawing Avis away from Cora and back to the creatures on the lawn. On an unspoken command, they made a path down the centre as they each turned and stepped aside, dipping their massive heads forward and lowering their wings to the ground in reverence. Columbine ran down the gap by herself, and once she was between him and the creatures, she swung around to face them with her arms open protectively. "My family is not to be hurt," she declared, her young shoulders lifting and falling with the strength of her conviction. "I will never speak to any of you again if you do."

The creatures looked at each other in alarm and immediately dropped to their central arm, crawling across the ground towards her while emitting squeaks and whimpers in a blatant effort to appease her.

What was more telling was the way her designated brute squad guard (who never should've left Columbine's side in his opinion) casually strolled around the gathered creatures to rejoin its ward by standing behind and to the left of her, instead of in front of her protectively. Avis had no idea what to make of that on a multitude of levels, but he knew he didn't like it.

He had no way of knowing he wasn't alone.

CHAPTER THIRTY-SEVEN

"You fucked-up, fucking lying motherfucking bastard!" Theodrick roared, throwing himself to his feet on his side of the upper realm's Table of Divinity. If his throne hadn't been so securely locked in place, Belial had no doubt it would have gone flying. Rage poured off his counterpart so thick his eyes had gone completely bloodshot and his hands landed on the edge of the table between them. "You fucking promised me every last motherfucking one of those winged pecker-headed assholes was fucking DEAD!"

"I promised you I had taken care of them," Belial countered, remembering his wording choice at the time perfectly. "And you have known about the survivors since Apollo found that abandoned clutch of eggs …"

Theodrick banged his side of the table again. "I don't give a rat's ass about those fucking brainless retards that that fuckwit idiot has." He pointed at the table— specifically the spot where their granddaughter stood alongside Heaven's Second Choir, or cherubim as they preferred to call themselves now. "Those fuckers know!"

"Some of the original pryde needed to be saved," Belial argued, keeping his voice in its regular monotone. "I made an arrangement with YHWH, and he took in twenty-six survivors. They were lost without their Eechee and Eechen, but YHWH set about establishing them in Heaven. They will never repledge to Columbine, and once their thrall was in place, they were kept both clutchless and within the borders of Heaven. Very few outsiders visit YHWH, and those that do have no idea why his cherubim guards are so very good at what they do. The cherubim may still feel their connection to the Weaver, but they won't leave Heaven to follow her. Their thrall will keep them where they are. I give you my absolute word, Bender. Of the thirty-eight true gryps still left in all the Known Realms, none of them are breeding or a threat to your precious crystalline gardens."

"I fucking hate you," Theodrick growled, allowing every nuance of his rage to shine through right before he vanished from the upper realm in disgust.

For several moments, Belial stared at the empty throne of his bending counterpart to see if the fool would return.

When he didn't, the Shifter's eyes drifted almost leisurely to the other half of the Table of Existence where the Unknown Realms lay, and ever so slowly, his lips parted into a wicked smile that exposed his extended canines.

* * *

With the situation semi-resolved, Avis went from protective to parental in the space of a heartbeat. He could no longer delude himself into thinking these creatures had strong-armed Columbine into leaving the safety of the house. No, she was the one in control; and had been all along.

Knowing what that meant, he drew himself up tall and squared his shoulders, sliding his hands behind his back to clasp together under his cloak. "Columbine," he called, his tone laced with disapproval.

With her back still to him, Columbine visibly flinched, and slowly … cautiously peered over her shoulder at him. "Yes, Father?" she asked, her eyes wide and her eyebrows disappearing into her fringe.

Oh, yes, she was in trouble and she knew it. Avis made himself frown for good measure. Two fingers of his right hand crooked beckoningly while the other hand remained in the small of his back. He took no pleasure in the way she cringed, and braced himself for what was about to happen. He'd have landed on Cora with both feet for sneaking out like this, and he refused on principle to live by the same double standards that his own mother had applied when it came to protecting the runt from their father.

Columbine's bottom lip wavered and tears banked in her eyes, though she did hesitantly move towards him. "Uh-uh," he tutted, waving those two fingers from side to side. "I don't want to hear how sorry you are—and I'm *definitely* not having this discussion out here in front of them," he added, when she opened her mouth to speak. His eyes went to the creatures that were still capitulating to her, knowing how fast they'd go back into their war-mode if they saw what he was about to do.

Columbine wasn't the first Mystallian child to have dangerous beasts at her beck and call. Back in the day, Strahan had been forced to secure his tigers before Tal could apply any discipline to the boy, because Tal didn't take kindly to being bitten and clawed by his son's overprotective pets, and the tigers didn't take kindly to … well … dying.

Knowing how much worse it would be if he had to fight his way through these … *things*, Avis reached down and slid his hands under Columbine's arms, lifting her into the air. As he settled her onto his hip, he glanced at the brute squad guards who surrounded him and said, "None of them get into the house. I mean, none at all. They all stay out here." He turned on his heel and headed back into the house, not bothering to wait for a response.

The creatures howled and bellowed, screamed and screeched their distress at being separated from Columbine, but Avis didn't care. He had the only thing in this situation that mattered to him. The doors closed behind him without his assistance. He didn't care how that happened either.

Cora scowled at him from in front of Columbine's doors, and it was a look he was happy to match. It was always a lot easier to be mad at her. With a snap of his thumb and middle finger, he thumped his pointer finger against the table edge directly in front of him. "Park it," he barked, then deposited Columbine alongside the spot he'd poked.

The difference between the sisters could not be any more extreme. Where Columbine looked absolutely devastated and on the brink of tears, Cora stalked forward, slapped her hands on the other side of the table in disgust and swivelled her hips in another display of acrobatics that had her legs swing out and around until her feet were alongside her sister. A single shove forward brought her the rest of the way over.

"You wouldn't let me help!" Cora snapped out the accusation, probably to try and get her defence in before he could start.

"Damn right, I wouldn't! Like it or not, tiger, I'm established and you're not, which means I would've survived whatever they threw at me. What in the realms were you thinking coming back out there after I told you to go inside?" Yes, it was definitely easier to rail at Cora. She *made* it easier by arguing back. Case in point …

"I was *thinking* that you were standing out there without a weapon, just begging to be splattered," came her snarky reply, while Columbine buried her face in her palms and sobbed. As usual, Columbine's tears tore him up, but now wasn't the time to lose focus. He ground his teeth against the sensation, then bit deeply into his cheek, using the pain to keep himself from caving. Cora also took a deep, stabilising breath and kept going. "And I was *thinking* that I didn't see why I should let that situation continue when I had the means to tip the scales back in our favour."

"And what happens when your blade breaks on the backs of those indestructible creatures?" She opened her mouth to speak, but Avis roared over the top of her, "You don't know a damned thing for sure about those things, tiger! If I've never seen them before, I can guarantee you haven't either and neither of us has any idea if Mystallian steel will penetrate their hides! What if it doesn't? What if that broken blade represents your neck? Wouldn't that mean you're dead?"

"No, actually, it wouldn't," Cora shot back, with such conviction that Avis decided to hear her out. "Shifter mass doesn't correlate like that. A chipped blade is just that. A chipped blade. It has no bearing on us except for the loss of mass and essence, which we can reabsorb at any time. Only when my neck is a Mystallian neck, do I run the risk of dying from having it broken."

That took a lot of the sting out of his fury towards her. He might not have known what she was doing but she had, and she wanted to make a show of Mystallian unity to those that threatened her family. It was a move he could relate to. A lot.

Taking a half step back, he folded his arms across his chest and stared down at her. "Alright," he finally conceded. "So you weren't in any real danger. Fine. Moving on to the next point. When I tell you to get your tail back into the house, young lady, I don't care if I know all the relevant facts or not, you get your tail back into the house and keep it there. You knew very well I meant …"

"I wasn't about to leave you out there by yourself, Father. Bending and shifting against them was useless, and Columbine's just as useless when she gets scared." In a quieter voice through one side of her lips, he heard her say, "Sorry, shorthorns, but you are." Then she picked her volume back up. "Not only that, but the way the brute squad were acting all goofy, I wasn't sure if they were going to be of any help either."

So she'd noticed the brute squad's strange behaviour as well. It wasn't just him. He looked over his shoulder at Columbine's guard, who stood stoically inside the doorway, wishing he could get to the bottom of that but knowing he probably never would. They were supposed to be indomitable and uncompromising, yet the presence of these new creatures had the elite warriors of Hell *walking* all the way around them instead of using their speed to carve a path through the middle of them. Almost as if there was an understanding of sorts between them and one knew not to push the boundaries of the other; as stupid as that sounded.

"While I appreciate the show of support, tiger, I haven't been around this long by not being able to handle myself," he said, stepping closer to them so he could poke her in the chest for emphasis. "When I tell you to do something, you follow the spirit of what I mean, not the literal interpretation of it that gives you an out. Do you hear me?" Sulky silence met his demand, sparking his temper. "Cora," he growled darkly in warning.

"Not a fireball's chance in the Ninth Level of Hell, Father," she replied, screwing her nose up and shaking her head indignantly. Avis' chest swelled with the tirade he was about to unleash. "If I agreed to that, you'd hold it over my head for the rest of eternity."

Avis snapped his attention to an empty spot over her head as red poured through his vision, and through a heavy breath he started mentally counting to ten. Thankfully, it cleared away by seven, which meant he could re-engage her civilly. "Cora, I'm really not in the mood for this," he warned, dropping his gaze back to the older of the two sisters. "What you just did was both hare-brained and dangerous and it scared the sh—stuffing out of me. I'm not used to having to look out for members of the family, and I'm definitely not used to having my orders thrown back in my face like that. I've never had to worry about the other kids your age before. Ever. Your aunts and uncles took care of them. All I had to do was oversee the family as a whole. That's not even close to the case where you and your sister are concerned."

His focus slid to Columbine to include her in this. "Your safety is my direct responsibility, and until the pair of you are established, you have to do as you're told. You just do. I can't protect either one of you if I'm constantly looking over my shoulder to see if you're behaving." Columbine sank a little lower and her bottom lip quivered once more.

Refusing to let it sway him, he looked back at his older daughter. "I'd rather have you mad at me for all eternity because I put a mental command in place that allowed you to live that long, than lose you over the next few years because you bit off more than you can chew. Do you understand me?"

Cora licked her lips and looked across at Columbine, then back at him and nodded. "Yeah," she said, before he could chip her about not answering with words. "That's fair."

"Good." He gestured to her rooms. "Now, go and tighten up that mental command you gave Gingen half an hour ago. I'm not saying she didn't deserve every second of it, but she'll be utterly useless as a servant if she's forever backing away from everything she ever comes across."

Cora snorted and shot a disgusted look over her shoulder at the double doors of her apartment. "Fine," she huffed, then slid off the table and went into her room as instructed.

Once the doors were closed behind her, he silently turned his attention to Columbine. He'd seen through his peripheral vision that she'd started to cry, but as he focused on her without saying a word, the heart-wrenching sobs slowly ebbed away into tiny hiccups, as if she knew it was her turn to face him. The ache in his chest was almost physical as he continued to stare at her, not knowing where to start.

Then, deciding he didn't like the way he was towering over her, he put his right arm alongside her left thigh and slid her around the table's polished edge until she sat in front of his chair, whereupon sat down so they could be on the same eye level. "What am I going to do with you?" he asked, staring into those huge black eyes, rimmed with tears and shaking his head ever so slowly.

"But they were friendly, Father," she insisted, her shoulders shivering from the effort to keep her emotions in check.

"They were dangerous," Avis countered. "Didn't you see the way they went for me and your sister?"

"You scared them."

A derogatory sound burst from Avis' lips before he could catch it; not that he particularly wanted to. "Princess, little girls like you get scared," he said, hooking one finger under her chin to prevent her from turning away. His other hand swept to the front doors. "Things like that don't get scared. They get homicidal." Her brow scrunched, and he realised he'd once again used a multi-syllable word, huffed under his breath. "They kill things, baby. A lot of things. It's what they do. It's what they live for." He used his raised hand to stroke her hair. "You think the best of everything, princess, and while I love that in you, it scares me to death when you act on it without asking and put yourself in danger."

"But you are a *life* god," Columbine said, ever so softly. She sniffed and blinked, and from one second to the next her tears were gone, thank the Twin Notes. Those things really did kill him.

The fact she was speaking at all, Avis took as another win. He nodded in agreement. "Which just goes to show how badly it scares me. There are things out there, princess. Things that will do whatever they have to, to trick you into trusting them. Things that will pretend to be your friend. Things that will actually want to hurt you, and you won't know until it's too late. And I don't know what I'd do if that ever happened, but I promise you, it won't be good." Just the thought of something along those lines had Avis feeling a tad murderous himself, so he understood he was just one homicidal maniac recognising the capability in another.

"But they love me," Columbine's voice rose a fraction.

Avis placed his hands on her shoulders and began working his thumbs in small circles. "I know it seems that way, princess ..."

"But they did, Father. I know it. I felt it."

That might have been the case, but it wasn't where he wanted this discussion to go. "But what if it was a lie?"

She tilted her head to one side, her face awash with confusion. "It was not..."

"But what if it was?" Avis asked again. "Not only did you choose to go out there, you took your sister into danger as well. Even if they weren't going to hurt you, you had no way of knowing what they were going to be like around your sister. What if they attacked her?"

"I-I would have stopped them, just like I did when they were going to hurt you."

Avis breathed out again. "Princess, the threat of never speaking to someone again isn't that bad in the grand scheme of things. Most things will flat-out laugh at you." He cupped his hand under her chin, making sure she understood how serious he was. "And dragging your sister out there without telling me or your mother was very, very naughty."

Did it make him feel like a heel, knowing the mental command from Cora left her with no choice in the matter? Maybe a little, but mental commands were how benders operated. So long as he agreed with the reason for their existence in his daughter, Columbine would have to learn to adapt to them and still stay on the right side of things. "You understand that, right?"

Tears sprang from her eyes and poured down her cheeks as she went to nod into his palm, but then she paused and said weakly, "Yes, Father."

Steeling himself for what came next, Avis ground his teeth until they locked together, at which point he applied enough pressure to make his jaw twitch. "Then this should not come as a surprise to you." He pushed his chair out from the table and drew himself to the very edge of the seat, so his lap wasn't encumbered by the arms of the chair. Then, he pulled Columbine into his lap and rolled her over so she was face down across his knees and pushed her cloak out of the way, using that arm to hold her there. "I really hope you learn from this, princess," he said, as he raised his right hand to his shoulder.

CHAPTER THIRTY-EIGHT

Nine was the number of times his hand rained firm swats against her upturned backside. Each caused her to cry out and squirm as it was meant to, and with each, his heart splintered further. But he had to do this. He'd already roared at Cora for her part in this debacle, and what kind of a parent would he be if he landed on the helper, and let the instigator go unpunished? Once he was done, he righted her so she was standing on the same side as the apartments and gave her a light push towards her rooms. "Go."

He watched as she tore into her apartment howling and noticed through the gap in the door that Cora was already in there with her arms outstretched, waiting for her. That damned hole between their rooms. He was going to have to do something about that, though right now it was hardly a priority. After the doors banged shut, he released all the tension he'd accrued in his back and shoulders and slumped into his chair. Still sitting on the edge as he was, his shoulders hit the back of the chair first and knocked his head forward until his chin collided with his chest and his arms draped over the chair arms. From there, he didn't want to move. He felt like a piece of shit, so a shit posture suited his mood perfectly.

His choice of discipline had been the way of the Chaotians, and it didn't sit well with him at all. That is, physical pain. Sooner or later, he was going to have to use mental discipline with her before they crossed paths with his family, and he wasn't looking forward to that either. Despite her apparent strength, she seemed so fragile when it came to matters of the mind, and the last thing he wanted was for her to shatter like a glass orb because he came in too strong. But how was he supposed to gauge that? If he came in softly and slowly increased his blows until she gave the right reaction, he could end up punishing her for an hour by the time he reached the point he should have started with. Likewise, if he guessed a starting point and got it wrong, he could really hurt her. How was he supposed to know? It wasn't like his imagination could give him any solutions either. At the end of the day, that would still just be a guess, and he was never going to resort to guesswork where his girls' safety and wellbeing were concerned.

He rolled his right hand to look at his palm accusingly, then pulled the glove off with his teeth and thumbed the flesh underneath. It didn't hurt, but the pressure of the contact reinforced the wrung-out feeling he'd experienced every time his hand fell. In the past, he'd often heard his siblings say how the hardest thing they'd ever had to do was discipline one of their own, and he'd never understood why. As children, they'd all witnessed the others take a beating or worse, and at the time their only thought had been, "Thank the Twin Notes that wasn't me." That understanding now hit him between the eyes with all the finesse of one of Griffith's fists. As a former member of the Damned, he was perhaps the only individual in existence who could honestly say he would rather go through the combined wrath of all Nine Levels of Hell than have to do that again.

It had also taught him that, contrary to popular belief, the need to discipline wasn't just a learning tool for the child involved. It was one for him as a parent too. The heartache that came from needing to do it served as a stern reminder to not let things ever get to that point again.

As his thoughts wandered, he went back over what he'd seen in Columbine's mind and compared it to his own somewhat brief experience with Apollo's true gryps. He folded one arm across his chest and drummed the fingers of the other hand against his lips, lifting his eyes to where the wall met the ceiling over the table. True gryps were one of the few creatures to his knowledge (the brute squad being another) that could tell both benders and shifters to fuck off. In fact, not only were they blatantly immune, they also had the wherewithal to react to a failed attack. The part about the shifters he learned much later, over drinks with Zeus. The bastard had laughed so long and loud at how Avis had been handed his ass by the ferocious beast that he nearly ruptured something. But then he'd gone on to begrudgingly admit that as a shifter, he was just as inadequate against them. If that were all true, then there was a distinct possibility that all of those things out there were true gryps. *No.* He shook his head adamantly. It can't be. There were too many of them here. Dozens. At least two to three times as many as Apollo had.

And they didn't even *look* like true gryps.

And these ones were smart.

Maybe they were established? The way they defied the celestial norm, they had to be under some level of divine influence. *Wow, if they are original and somehow managed to get themselves established, that'd change the whole game.* Heaven's mortal worshippers only had to believe that this pack of true gryps looked like … whatever they were now, and it would've happened. It would also explain their advanced intellect. In fact, it explained everything.

Avis breathed out slowly between his fingers. One phrase in particular kept bouncing around in his brain. It was entirely probable that Heaven had dozens of true gryps. Heaven literally had dozens of fucking true gryps.

Once again, a familiar set of gloved hands slid across his shoulders and pinched the muscles at the base of his neck. "The only aspect missing from your horrendous deportment is the crossing of your boots on the table, my love," Clarise purred, working her fingers into the muscles across his neck with meticulous precision. Given her tiny height and how slouched he was against the high back seat, Avis knew there was no way she could reach both his shoulders from either side of the chair *and* see what she was doing, and he really should've known better than to roll his head back to see what she was doing. Nevertheless, he did just that and found her arms and neck stretched out to ludicrously impossible proportions over and around the back of the chair. Her head was the most disconcerting of the three; sitting at the top of an elongated neck that had more in common with a giraffe.

He immediately closed his eyes, wishing he could erase that sight from his memory. "Don't tempt me, sweetheart," he grumbled.

Despite the fact her hands never moved, he felt her forehead press up against his and kept his eyes closed, refusing to picture what she must've looked like to achieve that.

"Will you tell me what has you in such an unpleasant mood?" she asked.

"How much of that did you see?"

"When I came out, I saw you in a pose of a petulant teenager. Since you have your glove off, I assume your right hand had something to do with your unsavoury mood. Other than that, I have no idea, beloved, which is why I would like you to enlighten me." Though his eyes were closed, he felt her head slide to the left until her lips nibbled his earlobe. "Do not make me say please," she whispered with a hint of attempted fun in her tone.

Avis wasn't at all amused, but he still couldn't find the energy to open his eyes to scowl at her. "Only if I have your word you won't add your discipline to my own," he replied without missing a beat. While he might have felt terrible for spanking Columbine, he knew from personal experience that his wife had no problem using her demonic tail as a disciplinary tool with the girls; and that thing was essentially a bullwhip. It was something he never wanted to witness again.

He felt her hands leave his shoulders at the same time as her forehead left his and knew this was either going to go really well, or really terribly. The way he was feeling at that moment, he didn't have a preference.

Her weight slipped into his lap and she relaxed down his right side, allowing her head to rest on his collarbone, alongside his throat. Her hand curled over his opposite shoulder and for a long time, the two sat in that awkward position. "It will get easier, my love," she promised, tilting her forehead to rub against his cheek.

At that, Avis did crack his right eye open. "What will?" he asked, watching her out the corner of that eye suspiciously.

She pulled her head back far enough that she came into focus and smiled tenderly. "When you are ready, you will tell me what Columbine did to warrant her first spanking."

Both of Avis' eyes shot open and he pulled himself upright. "How ...?"

Clarise chuckled and made herself more comfortable against him now that he was supporting himself again, brushing the back of her fingernails across his opposite cheek. "You have no difficulty disciplining Cora when the need arises, but Columbine has you wrapped around her little finger." He sucked in a breath of denial, but she shushed him with both the sound and a firm finger against his lips. The soft creases in the corners of her eyes made their molten state all the more indulgent. "She does, beloved. Anyone with eyes and a heart can see it. This is not a complaint on my part. Merely an observation. You are troubled, and by your own words of caution, it has to do with a behaviour modification of one of our children. The loss of your right glove and your sullen mood has made the deduction of 'which child received what' a relatively simple one for me."

Avis huffed unhappily, even as he pulled himself (and by proxy, her) back onto the chair properly and returned his glove to his right hand. "It all started with what originally looked like the biggest pack of true gryps I've ever seen getting into Columbine's head," he said, deciding to lay it all out for her.

* * *

"Go."

Tears streamed down her face as Columbine left her father and ran for the safety of her room, practically falling into her sister's outstretched arms. She wrapped her own arms around Cora's neck and howled against her sister's throat, barely able to breathe through the pain that thrummed across her backside and the misery that shredded her from the inside. Her father had spanked her! Worse, he was hurting badly as a result of having to do it. The pain they both felt was all her fault!

"Awww, c'mon, shorthorns," Cora crooned as she cuddled her close, tears now pouring down her face as well. "Knock it off. You're making me cry too."

But no matter how hard she tried, the flood of negative emotions continued to inundate her, drowning her in them.

"Okay, then. I guess we're doing it this way," Cora declared, with a confidence Columbine could see she didn't really have and with no other warning, the older of the two twisted to one side and swept her forearm behind Columbine's knees, lifting her into the air. "Diviten, get the bedroom doors."

Columbine buried her face in her hands. "I-I'm sorr—ry," she wept, knowing from the way her sister's colours had sharpened that the physical contact was causing her undue emotional pain.

"Just shut-up, shorthorns. You'll be in bed soon enough."

True to her word, Cora carried her the short distance between the two rooms, pausing just long enough for Diviten to draw back the quilt before lowering her to the mattress. Columbine clenched her eyes shut and tried without success to muffle her sobs. As her weight pressed into the plush mattress, pain shot through her tender backside and she yelped, rolling away from Cora automatically.

"Hey, easy … easy …" Cora crooned, sliding in behind her to support her back and shoulders with her upper torso but keeping her lower half off the bed and away from Columbine's backside. "I don't get it, shorthorns. It was just a simple spanking, and a light one at that. You and I have both taken way worse every time we blinked the wrong way back in the Well." Cora's arms slid around her waist and she rested her forehead against the back of Columbine's head. "What's made this one so bad?"

"Father … d-didn't … want … t-to do … it," Columbine stuttered, through sobs. "And … I-I m-m-made him."

"Ah, shit." The words were whispered so quietly into the back of her neck that Columbine almost missed it. But she hadn't and she stiffened at the unacceptable use of profanity. Cora clicked her tongue and held her close. "No, don't be getting your tail in a twist," she crooned almost musically against her neck. "You weren't meant to hear that. It's not your fault, but your emotional reading of others can be a real pain in the butt at times. Especially when we all keep forgetting how sensitive you are. Anyone else getting their tail kicked for whatever reason wouldn't give a rat's … backside about how the person who was doing it felt. Only you, you soft hearted scallye. But that's okay. **You just need to heal yourself now,** shorthorns."

Because her sister spoke in the same neutral monotone that their grandfather used, Columbine relaxed, almost to the point of melting into Cora's supportive embrace. The pain from her father's spanking dimmed until it faded completely into a distant memory. Of course it didn't hurt anymore. She was a shifter, and physical pain could be overcome … so … easily …

Realisation struck Columbine with all the finesse of a rockslide and her eyes shot open. She had just shifted away from a punishment! Something she had never done before, because it had been beaten into them from birth that to do so was to invite a worse discipline, with the added threat of tefsla!

Gasping in horror, Columbine began to struggle.

Cora immediately pivoted and threw a leg over hers, pinning her lower half to the bed. "Shhhh-shh-shh," she crooned. One arm held her shoulders against Cora's chest while the other stroked her hair out of her face, and just like that, she didn't want to fight anymore. *That's right.* **Just relax***, shorthorns. This is no different to what you did for me last year. If anything, it's a whole lot less from your viewpoint and I won't let you take the blame for it. This is my call. They don't realise it, but any time they lay into you like that, you're taking twice the amount of punishment than you should be, and Father would flip out like a mo-fo if he knew. I might not be able to take the emotional stuff away from you, but I can sure as hell make you ease off on the physical stuff so you can sort out the rest at your own pace. And I will.*

Columbine closed her eyes, twisting her face into the mattress. Her sister had used bending to force her to heal herself. If she'd had a choice, she'd prefer to deal with physical pain as that only hurt one person; herself. Without the pain of the spanking to keep her distracted, the ache in her heart became unbearable. She had hurt and continued to hurt her father, and it destroyed her on so many levels.

Don't start crying again, Cora warned.

I cannot … help it, even her thoughts were broken as her body convulsed with sobs. *Mother is … with him … and … he still … hurts.*

Cora sobbed too deeply to use words. *A-And remember when we were on the Akheron River and we had the Damned all around us?*

Too heartbroken to figure out where she was going with this, Columbine nodded.

Remember that game we started to play towards the end? The one where you would pick just one person's emotions and use those colours as a shield to block out everyone else when you had to?

Columbine's left hand snaked out from under Cora's grip and snagged one of the many pillows from the top of her bed. She drew it across the mattress and covered her head, wanting nothing more to do with her sister's plan. It was bad enough that the physical discipline had been removed, and now she was trying to ease the emotional one?

Cora wasn't impressed.

How exactly is hiding your head gonna change anything? We're mind speaking, stupid.

The familiar taunt had Columbine's bottom lip rolling into a pout. *I am* not *stupid.*

Then stop acting like it and focus … on … me. Just like you did on the Akheron River.

But you are always so mad at everything. I do not like focusing on you.

Then pick Mother! Pick Diviten! I don't really care who the hell you pick, shorthorns! Just get your focus off Father! Right now, he's your problem …

See? You are such a bully!

Oh, I'm about ten seconds from showing you what a real bully I can be …!

You are so mean! Columbine squirmed under her sister's hold, finding it as tight as before. She was just about to shift into a gaseous form when a light chuckle breathed across the back of her head.

There, see? I told you, you could do it.

In that moment, Columbine realised her sister had goaded her into doing exactly what she wanted, and she allowed herself to slump against the mattress in defeat.

Cora wasn't finished. *It's not your job to feel for everyone else. Let 'em feel for themselves. They've been doing it all their lives and long before you turned up.*

It is not the same, and you know it. I do not get to pick and choose which feelings of theirs I feel, any more than they pick for themselves. And those I care about mean the most to me.

I'm not arguing that. But one day, you'll learn to do what you have to, to get above this. You have to. After that raft ride on the Akheron River, you've been getting stronger. I know you can do this. You just have to keep practising, shorthorns.

Columbine's fists tightened into the sheets and pillows; her face scrunching up in the darkness. *I do not want to. What I have already scares Father. I do not want to scare him even more.*

Tough nuts, shorthorns. It's innate. You don't get a say in it. Either you take control of it, or it will continue to control you. That's just the way power works for us.

Columbine huffed miserably into her mattress, knowing she was right. At least, in part. She had gotten much stronger since her time on the Akheron River. In the beginning, everything about that river upset her and whenever Cora wasn't doing her best to distract her, she would spend hours staring at the horizon, wishing for an end to their pain. But by the end, it was only the worst of things that made her cry with them. The pain of the Damned was still all around her, but she'd learned how to separate herself from it ... to a small degree. The problem was, she'd only learned to cope with the emotional backlash from physical pain. There were so many other mean emotions to take into consideration. The anger of Lady Keket and the fear her Father had felt when he couldn't see them had left her not wanting to eat for ages (though her mother and sister made sure she did), and she'd fared no better against the Rangi-Tuareans at the end or even the Asgardians. Anger was by far the worst, because it was extra mean and horrible and she didn't like it. It made people say and do things that hurt others on purpose.

Cora gave her torso a quick squeeze. *Now that you're focused on me, why don't you try and go to sleep for a little bit, shorthorns? I'll stay right here, unless Mother or Father want me for something.*

For quite some time, Columbine lay there swaddled in her sister's love. It was more than just the body that covered hers. It was her colour. Rich, deep blue ... and it was all for her. This was so different from the way things had been between them in Hell that she didn't ever want it to end. There was no doubt in her mind that this change had come about since the return of their father, and it only raised the pedestal he stood on in her eyes.

Eventually, one question drifted across her sleepy mind.

Without opening her eyes, Columbine quietly asked, "What is a mo-fo?"

CHAPTER THIRTY-NINE

When Avis finished his story, Clarise pushed away from him and twisted on his lap to face the front doors. "We need to get to the bottom of this immediately, beloved," she said, lowering her feet to the floor and tapping his forearm to remind him that at some point during his explanation he'd wrapped his arms securely around her waist and now he needed to let go.

Avis wasn't sure what she had in mind, but whatever it was, he'd back her play. Always. As such, he loosened his hold and helped her to stand (much as he had with Columbine, though the reasons were radically different), then rose to his feet behind her. By the time he had, she'd cast a stimulation wave over herself to correct any flaws in her appearance, then slipped her hand into his and smiled up at him.

Still unsure of her plan, Avis' smile was more guarded. "Whenever you're ready, sweetheart," he said, not wanting her to know he still didn't have a fucking clue.

If she had any inkling of his ignorance, she didn't let it show. Her hand squeezed his for reassurance as she led him to the front doors, opening them with ranged shifting before they arrived to make their entrance appear that much more impressive. They both stepped out onto the stoop in unison; Avis shortening his stride to match hers.

Having expected to see the disorderly pack of animals scattered across his lawn, Avis was surprised to find them back past the lawn/cloud boundary and in a militant half circle two rows deep. The first row lay across the ground facing him, propped up by their central limb. The second row stood with a leg pin on either side of its counterpart's thighs. And in front of the very middle of the half circle stood a Mystallian boy around eleven or twelve with short, ebony hair and dark eyes full of warmth. He wore a slip not unlike the virtues, only his didn't carry the gem encrusted gold rope. It was just a simple slip.

The boy beamed happily and clasped his hands before him, shivering in excitement as Avis and Clarise crossed the lawn towards him. Once they reached half way, he bent his arms at the elbow and tapped his double fist against his lips until he eventually started nibbling on the thumbnails. Then, he started jiggling from one foot to the other.

From the corner of his eye, Avis saw Clarise's eyes slide to him and her lips twitched in amusement, which had him raising a cautious eyebrow at her.

"He reminds me of someone I know," she whispered, still smirking to herself.

What Avis would have given right then to read even her surface thoughts ...! Still, he'd get to the bottom of who the kid reminded her of and why she found it so funny.

The boy's excitement grew until he bounced up and down on his toes and the dimples in his cheeks threatened to cave in his head. "Hi," he managed to squeak, waving at the approaching adults.

"Hello to you too, young man," Clarise said by way of greeting, once they reached the border. She offered him the fingers of her right hand.

He proved he knew the etiquette of the Highborn Hellions because he stepped forward and took her outstretched hand in one of his, then bowed slightly and pressed his lips against her knuckles. "Welcome to Heaven, both of you." He popped upright again almost immediately; his hand still clutching Clarise's fingers as he looked over at Avis and bit his bottom lip. This time, he actually giggled. "I still can't believe you're actually here!"

Avis eyed the boy warily. The only way he could confirm what was going on inside his head was if he could get in there, and lo and behold, the moment he tried, he rebounded harder than a broken catapult restraint. *Motherfucking, fuck!* He'd been in Heaven for all of a day and he was already done with the place. Their blanket immunity to his bending was seriously pissing him off!

"I am Lady Clarise, and this is my husband, Lord Avis." She paused, waiting for the boy to either respond, or at the very least let go of her hand. When he didn't seem inclined to do either, her fingers flexed and she cleared her throat, slightly hitching one eyebrow. "And your name is ...?"

The boy looked at her curiously, then his eyes widened. "Oh—*Oh!* I'm YHWH!" He dropped her hand and threw his arms open as if expecting a hug.

For a second or two he stood like a complete moron with his arms outstretched, but when it became apparent that neither Clarise nor Avis had any intention of hugging him, he dropped one hand to his side and drew the other to the middle of his chest, offering them another tight wave. "Um ... hi!" Again, those dark eyes fell on Avis.

Don't expect to use or hear the title of Lord when speaking to YHWH.

"This is ... like ... wow!" The boy sawed his bottom lip through his teeth and jiggled on the spot again. "You're finally here!"

Another idiot kid. Terrific, Avis thought to himself. Since when had he been such a magnet for these annoying little brats? Apparently, since he'd gained two children of his own to take care of. Unimpressed with YHWH's behaviour so far, Avis shifted his attention to the twin rows of beasts behind the boy. He couldn't believe these were the same creatures that had fawned all over Columbine. Their military poise was exceptional. Not a feather moved, even to indicate they were breathing.

"YHWH," Clarise spoke his name using all the undertones of a disapproving parent.

"Huh?" YHWH blinked and refocused on her. "Uh, what?"

It seemed the boy had the same attention-span of a gnat that every other kid back home had. Clarise rolled her raised hand towards the double row of creatures. "How much do you know about them, dear?"

The boy turned to his right and ran his eye to the far edge of the double row, sobering instantly. "I know quite a bit," he admitted. Still facing Clarise and Avis, he stepped backwards until he stood between a pair of standing creatures and raised a hand to caress the metallic pin of the nearest one. "They were all lost and needed somewhere safe to live, so they were given refuge here." His hand then stilled and his eyes found Clarise first, then Avis. "But they've never behaved the way they did this morning. I mean like ... ever. Ever-ever. They actually abandoned their posts to come here on their own, and they were talking non-stop to your daughter. They've never said a word to anyone else outside their choir. Not even to me. Never ever. But they were talking to her." Some of his enthusiasm returned along with his beaming smile. "Isn't that awesome? I didn't think they'd ever be whole again, but in those few minutes, they were."

"That is actually why we came out here, sweetheart, though I must admit I wasn't prepared to find a specific someone capable of answering those questions."

The boy shrugged. "Like I said, I know lots of stuff. But whatever's going on between them and Columbine is eluding even me."

Avis' hackles went straight up. "Who told you her name?" he growled icily.

YHWH raised his hands palm out and patted the air. "Calm down, Avis. No one's hurting her. Like I said, I know lots of stuff." Lowering his hands to his sides, he added, "I suppose you could compare me to Culkin in that regard."

Culkin. Chasidah's husband in the Death Court and the Mystallian god of Knowledge. His thrall allowed him to know whatever anyone entering the realm knew up to that point. The future was the domain of Culkin's beloved wife and Avis' younger sister. This kid certainly knew his pantheons.

"So, you are established," Clarise said, putting the pieces together as quickly as he had.

YHWH nodded. "Uh-huh, and I hear and see everything that happens inside Heaven. Both mortally and celestially."

Avis flicked a finger at the half-circle of creatures. "So, are they true gryps, or do they just put out dream illusions to that effect?" He considered a thousand ways to word that question, ranging from 'what are they?' to 'how do you control them?', but in the end, he decided to go for the most obvious question to rule out any misconceptions. Provided of course, YHWH answered honestly, though Clarise would know if he lied.

YHWH stilled and released a guilt-ridden sigh. "They were," he admitted with difficulty. "But they were being hunted to extinction. Changing everything about them was the only way to save them." In the silence that followed, the beast YHWH touched curled its nearest wing around his shoulders, while the other reached over with its Mystallian hand and squeezed his forearm in comfort. It was a touching scene, if YHWH hadn't just admitted they were twenty-six of the most dangerous things in existence. "It was the only way to save them," he reiterated softly.

Avis knew it wasn't them he was trying to convince. "And you have no idea why they are so fixated on Columbine?"

YHWH glanced between the two of them and shook his head. "I don't think they understand why either, only that they are." He stroked the marginal coverts of the wing. "But they do feel it very strongly. Strongly enough in fact, to abandon their posts and come here to make a nuisance of themselves. I swear I did not see that coming and I can't apologise enough for it. It was never my intention ..."

"Do they have a name or designation?" Avis didn't care what the kid's intentions were and had zero interest in his simpering.

YHWH looked at Avis, then nodded. "They're the cherubim. The Second Choir. They're ..." —whatever he was about to say, he amended it to— "... *Heaven's* last line of defence."

"You call them cherubim?" Clarise repeated, for the word clearly meant more to her than it did to Avis. He caressed the back of her hand with his thumb, showing his support for whatever she said without saying it aloud. "As in, the Hatti word for griffin?"

Avis' thumb stilled and his jaw hit the ground. *Griffin* was one of the many alternative names that the various pantheons used to call their false gryps creations. "You're hiding them in plain sight?" he all but screamed at the boy.

YHWH smiled. "Many things are hidden in plain sight, Avis. That is the beauty of doing so. They needed to keep something of what they were – even if it was just the bastardised name of the Hatti constructs that were made to replicate them."

Avis pinched his lips together and shook his head. "You're certainly well-versed in the meaning of 'irony', YHWH."

An indecipherable expression flashed across YHWH's face. "You have no idea, Avis." Having made that cryptic statement, YWH closed his eyes and drew a deep, cleansing breath which he released while rolling both hands down his chest and forward in an emptying gesture.

Avis wasn't sure what that was supposed to do, but when YHWH opened his eyes again, the sparkle that had been missing since the conversation turned to the … *cherubim* had returned. Avis decided to push on. "It's an interesting thrall your mortals have thrown them into," he said, digging a little deeper into their origins. "But taking them from beasts of war to sentient guardians is a bit risky, isn't it?"

"They were never beasts of war," YHWH contradicted in his strongest voice yet. "The legends about them are truer than most realise. There was a time when their intellect rivalled our own, but after their annihilation, the few that managed to survive did so without their parents' guidance. They became little better than animals, acting on the whims of their pantheon masters. It was one of the fastest and saddest devolutions I have ever had the misfortune to bear witness to."

"Really?" Avis said, blinking away his surprise. In all his years, he'd never heard *that* story before. He eyed the line-up of true gryps with new eyes. "So which are these? The animal breed or the earlier, smarter ones?"

"These were members of the original pryde."

"Then why don't they talk? To us? To you?"

"After everything they've been through, I … it was never forced upon them." YHWH's gaze sharpened. "You need to understand, brother, they lost everything when they lost their pryde. Even the will to live. Forcing an establishment field and subsequent thrall upon them was the only way to bring them back from the brink of suicide."

Avis' response was so automatic that the sneer escaped his lips before he realised it. "Don't you ever call me 'brother', you little prick. We're not family."

Clarise nudged Avis' side with her elbow and frowned at him, to which Avis squared his shoulders and shrugged unrepentantly. It was a single word of swearing, and he'd never made a secret of what he thought of angels and the way they called each other 'brother' and 'sister'. Only his seven siblings in Mystal had that right.

YHWH flinched as if slapped, and he looked down and away in an apparent unspoken apology. "Perhaps you'll feel differently in time."

"Don't bet anything you value on it." Then he realised what else YHWH had said. "Wait … suicide? The survivors suicided? Were they really that dependent on each other?"

"They're that dependent on their leaders, Avis. They pledged their entire existences to their leaders, and once those two leaders were slain, it was all over for the whole pryde." YHWH's hands continued to stroke the wings around him. "From what I understand, none of the others lived long enough to raise the young they produced on the run. The nests were abandoned as soon as the eggs were laid." He pinched his lips together, as if just talking about it distressed him. "Most of them were broken up and eaten as a delicacy before they were ever hatched."

Which explained their exceedingly limited numbers now. Avis raked the fingers of his free hand through his hair. Not an hour ago, he'd had the same impression of true gryps that everyone else did. That is, they were fantastic beasts of war that any pantheon was lucky to have in its arsenal. It never occurred to him to think that they might've once been so much more.

"Are they safe to be around?" Clarise asked.

YHWH looked at her quizzically.

"They are fascinated with my children, YHWH. With all due respect to their disastrous history and their connections to you, if they harm one hair on my children's heads, their endangered status will be immediately amended to one of total extinction."

YHWH's eyes creased and he chuckled deeply at her. "We are family, little sister, and it's been decreed that you will all travel through the realm of Heaven unharmed. If anything, from the way the Second Choir has been behaving towards Columbine, I would say you have an added layer of protection that's been extended to no other."

"She might," Avis argued, remembering all too well the vicious stand-off between his side and the true gryps less than an hour ago. "But they don't seem to have any problem turning on the rest of us." It was on the tip of his tongue to add, 'And we're not family, dammit!', but YHWH got in first.

"I did see that." YHWH stepped away from the wings and moved his gaze to the nearest true gryps on his left. He paused just long enough to glare pointedly at each member before moving onto the next. He then repeated the process to those on his right. As each member of the choir fell afoul of that blistering stare, their heads hung repentantly. When he brought his attention back to Avis and Clarise, there was an age to his eyes that belied the youthfulness. "I can absolutely assure you; it will not happen again."

"Thank you," Clarise said, with a dip of her head to indicate her time with YHWH was coming to a close. "We would appreciate that."

"Clarise," YHWH called, as hand-in-hand, the two Mystallians turned back towards the house.

Clarise paused and looked back at him over her shoulder. "Yes?"

"Might I make one small request of you?"

"You may ask," Clarise answered, before Avis could; which was probably for the best. "Whether we honour that request will of course be at our discretion."

"Of course. May I …" —his dark eyes shifted between Clarise and Avis, pleadingly— "… may I ride with you as you journey through Heaven?"

"Could we stop you?" Avis asked. It was a fair question in his mind, though it may have come out as a derogatory sneer. What was the point of asking permission for something you could simply take because you were in your home realm? Stupid.

YHWH grinned and shrugged childishly. "I could ride outside your square of protection, sure, but I really, really want to ride with you inside it. I promise I'll be on my best behaviour ..." As he spoke, he drew a cross over his heart and offered them a huge smile that exposed all his teeth; his eyebrows sliding up under his fringe in a display of mock-innocence.

Avis assumed the 'X' represented a weapon's target; something he would absolutely take YHWH up on if Clarise allowed this and the brat fucked it up.

"How would you keep up with us?" Clarise asked, squeezing Avis' hand once more. "Meaning you no disrespect, our party will be airborne and you have no wings to speak of, YHWH."

YHWH tuned and looked over his shoulder at the creature standing behind him. "Any of the cherubim would gladly carry me, if it meant being that much closer to Columbine," he said. "And the rest will act as an escort on either side."

Not trusting himself to say 'no' politely and definitely not wanting Clarise to agree to this crap without first discussing it with him, Avis decided to cut the conversation short. "We'll think about it," he said, giving Clarise's hand a firm squeeze to indicate he wanted to leave. Subtlety had never been one of his strongest suits.

"Of course," YHWH agreed, beaming from ear to ear. "Take all the time you need. I'll be right here."

As he and Clarise went back inside, Avis glanced over his shoulder. The dumb fuck was still grinning and waving at them, even as the doors shut between them, blocking him out. The second they were alone; Avis released her hand and erupted. "Not just no, Clarise, but *hell no!*" he exploded, throwing both hands over his head and slamming them down to slap against his thighs.

"Avis ..." Clarise chided, but he wouldn't hear it.

"No!' he reiterated, shaking his head while waving has hand at the front doors. "No way in all the realms combined is that ... whatever the f ..." —he barely caught himself, but amended his wording to— "... whatever he is ... getting inside our inner circle. I don't care who says what! No way!"

"He has never lied to us, Avis. You know I would know if he did. He truly believes he is able to maintain control of the true ... of the *cherubim* and keep our family safe. If that is the case, why would we not want him at our side to guarantee our safety?"

The snarl that escaped Avis' lips was more beast than man. "Isn't that what the brute squad are here for?" Which brought up another valid point in Avis' mind. "And what's going on with them, anyway? They danced all around those true gryps, instead of sticking with Columbine, almost as if they were too scared to get in between them!"

"You know that is not the case, Avis," Clarise admonished. "The Highborn Hellion Guard fear no one. They are literally incapable of it."

"Then what?" he bellowed, wanting some semblance of this mess to make sense.

"Avis, you need to calm down!" Clarise lifted her voice just enough to be heard over the top of him, and despite the pent-up rage that coursed through his body, something in him registered the sharpness of her tone along with the unspoken threat that accompanied it.

Not wanting to shout at her anymore, he turned and stormed to the far end of the table where he usually sat. Every step was made with a furious stomp that echoed around the room, but if he thought getting some distance from her would lessen his foul mood, he found the exact opposite to be true. Nothing about this realm made any sense to him. Even in Asgard, he'd known where he stood and that position had been one of an enemy. This … this … whatever Heaven was doing to him, was driving him crazy. 'You're all welcome, but you can't use any of your powers.' 'We trust you like a friend, but we have beings that can make you feel what we want you to feel.' 'We are all one big happy family … but we have the biggest fucking pack of true gryps at our disposal to fuck with you if you don't behave.' Not to mention he still wanted to personally declare war on every motherfucking angel in the realm! This place had gone as far as to set up a situation where he was forced to spank Columbine, for Mystal's sake! Something he didn't think he would ever have to do!

The illogic behind blaming everything on Heaven didn't bother him in the least. As far as he was concerned, every accusation was justified!

Avis stalked to the side wall of the house adjacent to the front doors, and, with a heated curse that was sure to cost him in the bedroom, threw his clenched fist through the thick marble brick, driving it all the way to his shoulder.

It was as if the whole fucking realm was conspiring against him, trying to send him mad. Worse, it was working! It didn't surprise him to see that Clarise had stayed near the front doors. He wouldn't want to be anywhere near him right now either!

But as he tensed his arm and heaved it free, a thick plume of rose scented smoke and dust exploded out at him; so overwhelming he immediately gagged. Barely able to breathe through it, let alone see, he pushed one hand against the wall and gasped. The ghastly burn of the fragrance shot all the way to the bottom of his lungs and deep into his stomach. His eyes watered and he doubled over in a coughing fit, still holding himself against the wall. Each exhalation forced him to breathe in more of the obnoxious substance on the intake, until he finally found the wherewithal to use the sleeve of his non-supporting arm to mask the overpowering scent.

Then he coughed and hacked and snorted some more.

The conscious effort it took to draw enough air through the fabric of his sleeve cleared most of the burn from his lungs. Begrudgingly, he also had to admit it destroyed his vile mood just as thoroughly. It was difficult to maintain an unhealthy rage when the luxury of breathing was so rudely taken away.

As his breath eased back into a natural rhythm and he no longer felt as if he were sucking in ground glass, he straightened up ever so slowly and pulled his face away from his sleeve, turning towards Clarise with deliberate menace. "Not. Nice," he scowled, knowing damn well that she'd done that on purpose. After all, a floral-scented, explosive marble dust right where he happened to punch the wall in frustration? *Really?*

Clarise kept her face completely neutral, though he knew she had to be laughing her ass off on the inside. "I do not recall forcing you to punch that wall," she reminded him, her hands clasped imperially before her. "In fact, I specifically said you need to calm down. You are the one who chose to do the exact opposite of my suggestion." Her hands broke apart and she rolled her right one in his direction.

"The repercussions of choosing that alternative action are entirely of your own making."

Avis ground a clenched fist into his hip and twisted his lips to one side. Twelve months ago, Clarise wouldn't have said so much as 'boo' to contradict him. Six months ago, she found the inner strength to stand up to him and not back down. Now … this obnoxious powder trap had all the markings of a Mystallian bitch slap. More and more, she was becoming the queen he knew she could be.

But that didn't stop him from wanting to put her over his knee just like he had Columbine and showing her that things like this weren't okay where he was concerned. "You've made your point, sweetheart. Now, get it off me," he growled, holding his hands down and away from his body at a forty-five-degree angle as if he were dripping wet.

An instant later, the scent of rose was no more, and his uniform was back to its usual pristine state.

"We still need to discuss YHWH," she said, tilting her head to see if he had changed his mind in that regard.

Well, guess what? He hadn't. "There's nothing to discuss," he stated, folding his arms over his chest with his feet shoulder-width apart. "He's not welcome. The end."

"Avis …"

"No." Avis shook his head to emphasise that decision. "I'm done talking about it, Clarise. He can ride beside us, outside our square of guards. That's it."

"You would forbid even that, if it were within your capability."

No shit. Avis had thought that was pretty obvious, but since she'd voiced it, he figured he might as well hammer the point home. "See? We are getting somewhere after all. The answer's still no."

Clarise's surly expression said the exact opposite. "Avis …"

But Avis shook his head and walked down the side of the table that led to the apartments; the side that also put the entire dining suite between them. Again, no coincidence. "I said no, Clarise, and I mean no. Not him. I don't know what his game is, but whatever it is, I sure as hell don't trust him. I've no idea why he wants to pretend to be a Mystallian kid, but it's clear he's a lot older than he looks. I don't know of anyone who's heard that story about the true gryps going all suicidal at the loss of their leaders, let alone claim to have been around when it happened."

Clarise took one step towards the table. "He's already admitted to being established, Avis. As such, it is entirely possible that his establishment thrall is similar to Chance's and he cannot help but portray himself as an immature youth. We learned yesterday that there are nine choirs to Heaven, but so far we have only been introduced to six. He could very well be a member of one of those other three."

"And what would their powers be, that I would feel any better about having them anywhere near us, sweetheart? Just one of those choirs can make you feel whatever they want, and he's already admitted to being Heaven's equivalent of Culkin."

Clarise took another step that would've had her abdomen colliding with the table, if she didn't shift into a cloud of dust that drifted across the table's surface to reform into her Mystallian shape on his side a few seconds later. It took everything he had not to automatically step away from her when she appeared right in front of him. He loved her with every breath he took, but it was going to need to be a lot bigger reason than this before he'd concede actual ground to her in the middle of an argument. Mystallians rarely ever backed off from anything.

"That only adds to his credibility, beloved."

Avis frowned in confusion. "How do you figure?" The words escaped his lips before he could catch them, and his frown deepened with personal recrimination. Hadn't he just said the subject was closed? Multiple times? Why were they still talking about it?

With a disarming smile that he was sure was meant to suck all the agitation from him, she leaned into his chest and slid her arms around his waist. Her chin pressed into his sternum as she looked up at him adoringly. "He has already admitted that he can hear and see everything that happens within Heaven's boundaries, beloved. If he had any kind of an alternative agenda, letting us know of that powerful capability up front would have been extremely counter-productive."

"Or a failed attempt at intimidating us," Avis countered, breathing in her perfume and sighing ever so slightly at the unwelcome comfort it gave him.

Her cheek rubbed against his chest. "This is his home realm, beloved. If he truly intended to cause us difficulty, he already has all the knowledge about us he needs to achieve that. For whatever reason, he wants to reach us on a personal level."

"Maybe that's his game," Avis argued.

"Or maybe he has no game at all. Avis, be reasonable ..."

"I *am* being reasonable," Avis insisted. "I've already said he can ride alongside us—outside the brute squad's perimeter."

"Have you not thought about how upset it will make Columbine to be so close to her new friends yet unable to interact with them?"

Avis huffed and looked away from her. "She'll get over it."

CHAPTER FORTY

"… I'm still shocked that the cherubim are talking so openly with you," YHWH laughed, as he urged the cherubim he was riding to close the gap between himself and Columbine. Not that it took much. "They've never talked to anyone outside the Second Choir before. Not even me."

"But you can hear them?" Columbine asked, glancing up and across at him just long enough to acknowledge him before returning her attention to the open sky ahead.

"Oh, I can hear them, sweet pea. I can also direct them too, when it's necessary. But they've never talked to me the way they're talking to you. They're so alive! Even now, they're arguing over which one I'll be riding tomorrow and be that much closer to you."

Columbine giggled and looked over to where the choir flew parallel to them. "I know. It is so silly."

"Not to them." He tilted his chin towards her and his tone became serious. "You mean something to them, sweetie. Something very, very special that I still can't get my head around. It's both fascinating and, if I'm being honest, a little scary."

"Why scary?"

YHWH grimaced. "It's one of my many jobs to know everything that's going on inside of Heaven, but you are what even the celestial realm would call an enigma." He looked at her confused expression and winked with a broadening smile. "That's a puzzle that's yet to be solved."

"But I am not a puzzle. I am a little girl."

YHWH lowered his gaze to the cherubim he rode and chuckled quietly to himself. "Maybe you're both, sweet pea."

Clarise (who had been riding directly behind Columbine for several hours now) watched the interaction between the two of them with a growing smile of her own. It had taken four days of Columbine staring miserably at YHWH and the cherubim flying outside their perimeter before Avis had capitulated and permitted the boy and *one* cherubim to join them. She glanced briefly at her husband's deadpan stare and sighed. *Why do you have to be like this?* she wondered. *Why must everything be a 'me or them' situation with you?*

For the life of her, Clarise couldn't fathom it, no matter how hard she tried. They were safe here. Not only did they have the Almighty's blessing to journey through the realm, they also had one of his primary angels and his entire Second Choir acting as an escort. But Avis neither relaxed nor enjoyed the temporary reprieve. No, he chose to sink further and further into himself instead. It didn't help that with his bending, he could internalise for months between one instant and the next, further adding to his mental decline. It was almost as if he preferred the danger of the other realms, as insane as that was.

After their first meeting with YHWH, Clarise had spent the whole day watching Avis grow so tense with hatred that she'd worried he'd hurt himself. Every time is eyes skirted to YHWH (which they did constantly), his teeth ground together and tensed even more. But YHWH's behaviour was exemplary, so there was nothing for

Avis to vent his bad temper at. She endured it that first day, and once the girls were in bed that evening, she sat him down on their bed and demanded that he explain himself.

"You just don't see it, do you?" he'd snapped, which had perplexed Clarise.

"See what?" she'd asked in return.

He hadn't answered; muttering a dark curse under his breath as he rose to his feet and stalked into the ensuite, dismissively waving either her or the conversation or both aside.

Of course, she'd followed him. It may not have been the Highborn Hellion thing to do, but she'd learned it was very much the Mystallian thing. After a period of back-and-forth where he'd stripped and entered the tub, he finally admitted the whole realm put him on edge, especially YHWH and Choirmaster Raphael. They continued to discuss the matter while he soaked and she massaged the tension out of his stressed muscles. Again, he brought up the feeling in Heaven that he couldn't quite put his finger on, and how he hadn't liked that either.

Since he hadn't been able to quantify that feeling beyond his original statement, Clarise had attempted to move him past that opinion and back to hers with platitudes pointing out the benefits of the realm. How they were safe. How they could relax. How they weren't being hunted here.

Rather than allowing common sense to resolve his issues for him, Avis had shut down and refused to speak of it again, no matter how much she tried to coax him into sharing his thoughts with her. In doing so, he'd crossed the one line he vowed no Mystallian would ever cross. He'd bottled it up; and like any sealed canister under pressure, that dark simmer had swelled to destructive levels.

Last night, after two nights of watching him retreat to the ensuite instead of coming to bed, Clarise had finally managed to re-engage him by reversing their roles and becoming the 'Mystallian' in their relationship. That is, she sat on his side of the bed and when he strode past her towards the ensuite, she popped to her feet and barred his way with one hand against his chest. He drew to a halt without looking at her. "There are less than five metres between where YHWH is currently riding and where the rest of the family would like to see him ride. So unless you give me a very good reason right now ... one I can get behind ... I *will* be permitting YHWH to ride inside the Highborn Hellion Guards' safety perimeter tomorrow."

At the very least, she had expected him to snarl since the challenge had been laid out and his Mystallian ego should've been pricked. She searched his eyes, looking for the spark of pride that usually resided there. When had it gone out?

His shoulders sagged, then his facial features softened in an unwelcome way as he stared down at her restraining hand. "Do whatever you want," he said dismissively, never once looking at her as he brushed past her hand and continued on into the ensuite. "I don't care."

Clarise remained where she stood for a few moments, stunned by his level of despondency. Avis cared about everything! He always had an opinion, whether it was warranted or not.

After everything they'd been through, if he thought she was going to leave it at that, he really had no idea who he'd married. Clarise drew in a deep breath and followed him into the ensuite.

"Avis, I have had enough of this nonsense!" She caught him by the elbow and whirled him around, barely resisting the urge to shake him. The anger and resentment he'd shown up till now had been bad enough, but this despondency was intolerable. "What is wrong with you?"

"Because of course, the problem has to be with me, doesn't it?" he replied, quite without heat. "It couldn't possibly be either you or YHWH, could it?"

Clarise baulked at his statement, then reached up with her hands and cupped his face. "Avis, what has happened to you? I am not a bender, and I cannot see what you are thinking. If you have had a lengthy conversation inside your head without me, I am already on the back foot here, defending words I have never said. Talk to me, beloved. As you say so often to Columbine, use your words. Please!"

She had expected his temper to ignite over her use of hellion manners, but all he did was close his eyes and run his tongue over his parched lips. The pulse on the side of his neck hammered as if he'd spent the last three days running on foot and his breathing was incredibly shallow.

"Just ... leave it alone, Clarise. I'll be fine," he lied. "Why don't you go back to bed." When he opened his eyes, she saw a level of glassy emptiness that she'd never seen before. Not even when she'd rescued him from the Damned. "I'm going to go and have a bath."

Clarise tossed up the pros and cons of following his suggestion. She hated the idea of leaving him like this, but giving him the time to have a bath would also give her a chance to process what little she'd gleaned from their conversation and maybe try and make sense of it. She didn't have his ability to internalise, which meant real time had to go into her reflections.

Before she left, she needed to give him something positive to think about, in case he went back inside his own head. She pulled him down to her lips and kissed him deeply, pushing everything she felt about him into that one act. She refused to stop until his lips softened against hers, if only a little. Then she pulled away and pressed her forehead to his. "If the problem you have with YHWH riding with us is the fact that he would be riding behind us where you cannot see him, why not let him take the lead with Columbine at his side? The path we are travelling is a straight one with the pearlescent wall on our left, so it is not as if they could take a wrong turn without us noticing. You will then hear everything they talk about and see every move they make. You will still be in total control of the situation." She hoped the infusion of control would help bring about his old self. "Just ... think about it while you have your bath, and we can discuss it when you come out. Alright?"

She felt him nod very marginally against her forehead, and wanted to cry. This was not like him at all. "Very well, then, my love. I will be right outside. Do not keep me waiting long." She kissed his lips lightly once more, then drew away from him and returned to their bed.

Crawling across the mattress, she allowed Tilu to draw the sheets up around her before dismissing the servant with a silent wave. She honestly couldn't comprehend her husband's strange behaviour. The hospitality Heaven had shown them was impeccable and it had to be preferable to that of the realms they had passed through so far. It made such a nice change to not be on the constant lookout for danger.

With nothing else to occupy her time, she did what she'd done the last two nights and permitted her thoughts to drift towards the son she'd left behind in Hell. As always when Charon came to mind, she drew her knees up towards her chest in a subconscious effort to comfort herself. She missed him so much, and couldn't help but wonder what he was doing at that moment. One thing she knew he wouldn't be doing, was wondering about her. Not after she had effectively lobotomised him, separating him from all his emotions before she'd left. She hadn't wanted to do it, but he was so young and it was the only way she could guarantee his safety in a realm that reacted violently to unsavoury behaviour in its upper class. By the time he learned how to give himself back the missing parts of his brain, years would have passed and he simply wouldn't want to.

But try as she might, she couldn't bring herself to regret her temporary union with Charon's father. He'd been there when Avis wasn't, and he'd supported her in all things. In a time when she'd thought she'd never see her abusive husband again, her father's military commander had shown her great gentleness and compassion. Emotionally, she'd been spiralling downwards ever since she returned to Hell with Cora, knowing she was pregnant with Columbine. Avis knew that part. He'd put his hand up and accepted full responsibility for it. But he didn't know about Charon.

Clarise cupped her hands together and created a tiny replica of her young son that fitted in the palms of her hands. She aged him a little. He'd be three by now. His language skills would have improved enormously in that time. Tears welled in her eyes as her thumbs caressed the tiny form, wishing she could cuddle the real Charon and tell him everything was going to be alright. The heartache that spread across her chest was almost unbearable.

"Fine," Avis said from the ensuite doorway, startling her. With a flash of guilt, she quickly clapped her hands together, absorbing the replication of her son into her flesh before he could see it.

Dressed in only his robe (a new addition since their arrival in Heavn), Avis walked across the room towards her, but pulled up halfway and stared at her, running his eyes across her body and back to her face. His eyebrows pinched together in concern.

Clarise blinked, using the motion to reabsorb the moisture in her eyes. Under such heavy scrutiny, he'd notice if she cast a full stimulation wave to rid herself of any imperfections. "I am fine, Avis," she said, relying on his catch-all phrase to answer the question he hadn't asked. "Merely lost in thought." The truth, without specifics. She was becoming good at that. Forcing herself to meet his gaze without flinching, she lifted the corners of her lips in what she hoped would come across as a serene smile. "What was it you were saying?"

The look in Avis' eyes right before they dulled again said he didn't believe her for a second. "I said, YHWH can ride ahead of us with Columbine. That's what you wanted to hear, wasn't it?"

Clarise nodded in stoic agreement, refusing to say or do anything else that may upset him. "Of course. I shall let him know first thing in the morning."

Avis broke eye contact with her and shook his head, cutting her off. "I'll do it. You might as well get some sleep, Clarise. I'll be gone awhile." And without a backwards glance, he crossed the room still dressed in his robe and let himself out, closing the doors behind him.

Unable to comprehend what just happened, Clarise stared at the closed doors, then slapped the sheets on either side of her feet in frustration. What in the realms was wrong with him? Hadn't she just found the perfect solution to suit his needs, and then offered to tell YHWH so that he wouldn't have to deal with the young man personally? How could that have possibly been the wrong thing to do? Did he want to disagree with her? Was that it? Determined not to chase after him, Clarise remained seated in the bed, waiting for him to return.

Sleep was the furthest thing from her mind, but as the minutes turned into hours, she had to accept the fact that he wasn't coming back. Confusion and hurt rained upon her until she could bear it no more and she tossed the quilt aside and rose to her feet. Seconds later, she was pacing the floor in frustration.

What it was about YHWH and Heaven that brought out this attitude in her husband? Was it because he hated surrendering control to another? Well, yes, that went without question, but every realm they ever passed through had forced him to take a secondary position to the pantheon that ruled there, and to date he'd never been like this.

Perhaps it was the presence of the true gryps? YHWH had all but admitted Heaven's Almighty had taken them in only to save them; not to use them. What began as an act of mercy only later became a strategic war advantage for the realm, and even then, the Almighty of Heaven hadn't been boastful of his acquisition. No, they'd been hidden behind the façade of a celestial construct to avoid notice. The intensity of Avis' hatred made no sense, and if it made no sense, then it wasn't entirely true. But there had been no lie in the words he shouted at her. None whatsoever. So what part of his rant merely touched the truth? Was it his hate? Clarise shook her head. No, he definitely felt that. But perhaps that hate was part of a bigger issue.

She paused mid-step, drumming the fingers of her right hand against her thigh.

That had a ring of truth to it. YHWH was but a cog in the machine that was Heaven, and since her husband couldn't rage at the Almighty directly, it was entirely plausible that he had settled on the nearest physical aspect of Heaven he could find. A man-child with a lot of eons under his belt who had been nothing but the most gracious of hosts. Had their roles been reversed and YHWH had been behaving so atrociously while a guest of Mystal, Clarise had no doubt that her husband would not be so gracious towards such an ungrateful visitor.

But was that all this was?

With no clear answer coming to her, Clarise summoned Tilu to draw her a bath. She had no need for its cleansing ability, but she'd found the soaking warmth soothing in this form. After removing her nightgown, she stepped into the water and sat down until it covered her shoulders, dismissing Tilu once more. Her fingers spread out to caress the marble tiles on either side of where she sat. If Avis were here, over half his chest would be exposed to the elements. Their heights would only be the same if she were sitting on his lap.

She wanted that. She wanted him in the bath with her. She missed him. She missed *them*. Her hands crossed over her breasts and she rubbed her upper arms and shoulders, trying without succeeding to pretend those hands were Avis'. Technically, she could alter them to match his, but what would be the point? They still wouldn't be his, and that was what she wanted so badly it hurt.

But he was too angry to see that, and she couldn't make him see sense. At least, not before they had to leave shortly. It would be a different story come tonight. Avis was her man, and if he refused once more to listen to reason, she'd either use force to make him, or he'd be sleeping outside on the lawn. The house, and everything in it, was hers.

Hopefully, it wouldn't come to that. Yes, her husband was one of the most stubborn males in existence, but in the past, he had listened to her when it mattered, and regardless of his current mood, she had to believe he'd listen again.

At the end of her very long bath, she used shifting to dry and dress herself in her uniform. The slow and arduous process of rubbing a towel across every centimetre of her skin, then donning one piece of clothing at a time was not something she cared to do when she was alone. It was such a waste when shifting achieved the same result using a fraction of the time and energy.

In seconds, she emerged from the bedroom, ready for the day.

Three steps into the sitting room, she found Avis seated in a high-backed chair before the fire, with his bare legs crossed at the knee and nursing a goblet of ambrosia. Unaware of her presence, he stared sightlessly into the flames, lifting the goblet to his lips on occasion when he seemed to remember he had it.

"Avis?"

Avis jerked, his head swinging towards the sound of her voice even as ambrosia spilled across the back of his hand. The fullness of the goblet meant it had either only just been refilled, or he hadn't really been drinking it. "Clarise." His tone was upbeat and he almost smiled at her, but then his whole demeanour collapsed and he turned his attention back to the fire. "That time already?"

The mood switch added to her confusion. "Avis, why are you being like this?"

Avis stiffened and shook his head. "What does it matter anyway?"

"Avis, please! Whatever you …"

She went to step forward with her hands outstretched, but he slapped his free hand against the arm of the chair and swung on her sharply. "Spare me, alright? I don't want to hear it." He turned his attention back to the fire. "I really don't," he added, almost to himself, then lifted the drink to his lips and swallowed one mouthful after the next until he emptied the goblet.

Clarise looked at her hands clasped before her. "Will you at least permit me to cleanse and dress you?"

Through the top of her peripheral vision, she saw his left shoulder flick upwards in a half-hearted shrug. "Whatever."

Accepting the consent (such as it was), Clarise removed all dirt and sweat from his skin and hair, then added the tapestry on the wall to the mass of his robe to create his more substantial uniform. "We should have breakfast with the children before we go."

Avis' expression tightened until a muscle jumped along his jaw as he tossed the empty goblet into the fireplace and solemnly rose to his feet. He paused for a moment to watch the explosive chemical reaction between the flames and the ambrosia traces, then turned without further acknowledging Clarise and made his way out of the apartment.

Clarise sighed and followed in his wake.

Breakfast had been a brief affair. It was as if the children could sense the discord in the air and were keeping their heads down. While she knew this was true of Columbine, it just went to show how obvious it had been that even Cora sensed it. Determined to break the sombre mood, Clarise turned to Columbine and said, "Your father has agreed to allow YHWH and one of the cherubim to join us, girls."

Given that this news was to end Columbine's four-day misery, Clarise had hoped for more than the small, almost forced smile that Columbine offered them both. "Thank you, Father."

Avis growled his response, and a few minutes later they were all outside, waiting for her to break down the house. YHWH rode on the back of the cherubim, though it was difficult to say what part was its front and what was its back, when it had four fronts. The one facing upwards was the eagle, and he sat abreast of it with its huge talons curled around his torso like a safety harness.

As they flew, YHWH began chatting to Columbine. She hadn't been very responsive at first, but partway through the morning, something changed and her whole demeanour shifted until she matched YHWH's youthful excitement. Not for the first time, she wished she had Avis' ability to see into Columbine's memories to learn just what YHWH had done to bring a real smile to their little girl's face for the first time in days.

Clarise glanced to her left where Avis rode in brooding silence and sighed again. Just one more day. Less than one. Ten-ish hours. The stubborn male may not have known about her oath to get to the bottom of his mood swings that evening, but he was going to find out just as soon as the girls were asleep.

CHAPTER FORTY-ONE

Around the middle of the day, Clarise watched as Avis let out a shrill whistle and raised a hand, rolling it forward for them all to land for lunch. As this was the first meal YHWH had joined them in, she wasn't surprised when Avis organised the seating so that the boy was on one side of the blanket, Avis and Clarise were adjacent to him, and the girls sat opposite their guest. If it had been his intention to make the angel feel as unwelcome as Maui had felt, he failed miserably because this arrangement put everyone in front of YHWH and the young man made the most of it, chatting up a storm. He even had Cora snorting at a funny story or two, despite her best efforts to mimic her sullen father.

During his conversation, YHWH built his club sandwich exactly as Avis had, right down to the single string of mayonnaise with a dot of spicy brown mustard in the middle of the line. Then he squashed it down, mirroring Avis' technique of holding it securely in both hands before lifting it to his mouth. As he bit into it and the multitude of flavours registered, he rolled his eyes and moaned in delight.

"Have you never eaten a club sandwich before?' Clarise asked, unable to believe such happiness could be derived from one sandwich.

"Not in a *really* long time," he admitted, licking his lips before taking another bite. "I'd almost forgotten how good they were." He looked to his right at Avis and smiled as if they shared a secret, but all Avis did was stare blankly into the contents of his own sandwich before taking a silent bite of it.

"Where do you sleep at night, YHWH?" Columbine asked, bringing Clarise back to the discussion.

"Columbine," she admonished, for that information was private.

YHWH raised a soft hand at Clarise in a gesture of consent. "It's alright, Clarise," he said, his eyes creasing warmly, even as he turned back to Columbine. "As it turns out, sweet pea, I don't sleep."

"Why not?" Cora demanded; in true Mystallian fashion.

YHWH rolled his left shoulder in a half-hearted shrug that reminded Clarise too much of the type children offered to avoid answering directly. "I got into the habit a long time ago of not sleeping unless I really had to, and now that I'm established, my thrall stops me from ever needing to sleep again."

"Why?"

"Because that's the way thrall works. When you become established, you also become whatever the mortals who are worshipping you expect you to be. None of Heaven's mortals expects me to be able to do my part and sleep at the same time."

Clarise may not have heard a specific lie in that answer, but she got the distinct impression YHWH deliberately applied Cora's question of 'why' to the latter part of his explanation, rather than the former. Something in his past had kept him awake at night. Was that something a memory of a past event, or fear of what the future held? Or both? Though Avis never spoke of his own past in any great detail, the snippets she had gleaned from him painted a very bad childhood, and it seemed, he wasn't alone in that. For YHWH to be so scared in his youth that sleep was a luxury he couldn't afford, something truly terrible must have happened. A kidnapping or a murder or something that left him forever scarred. Clarise was beginning to wonder if she were in the minority when it came to decent celestial upbringings.

Whether he meant them to or not, YHWH's casual words of hardship endeared him all the more to her.

"Would you care to join us for an evening meal?" Clarise wasn't sure what made her blurt out the offer, but the way Avis's eyes darted to her, then dulled and went back to his sandwich, she realised the enormity of that mistake.

"Uhhh … I don't think that'd be such a good idea," YHWH stammered, casting a telling look between the two of them. "Thanks, all the same."

The rest of the first course was eaten in absolute silence. YHWH copied every portion Avis ate, grinning happily after each bite. She doubted if he was doing it to deliberately antagonise her husband, but she could tell from Avis' posture that it was happening anyway.

Towards the end of the meal, the remnants were taken away by the servants and replaced with treats and sweets for dessert. Avis said nothing during this change of courses, and once it was done, he reached for a caramel tartlet with a dollop of cream. So, of course, YHWH reached for one as well.

Clarise, please don't react, the words drifted through Clarise's thoughts like a light breeze, but she knew instinctively who was doing the communicating. It had all the nuances of YHWH.

She had impaled two pieces of caramelised pineapple on a wooden skewer when the words came to her and she paused; not knowing what to make of them.

Avis' eyes immediately cut to her, and although she could see the question banked behind them, he merely stared at her.

Clarise forced herself back into motion by tapping the skewer against the edge of the bowl to shake off the excess caramel. "I am fine, Avis," she said with a tight smile. "I was merely … lost in my thoughts."

Still saying nothing, Avis redirected his attention to his lunch once more.

HOW ARE YOU DOING THIS? she made the thought as loud as she could, not certain if the young man would hear her response.

As it turned out, he could. *There is no need to shout, little sister. This is how the cherubim communicate with each other. They will not speak to me, but I have learned how to utilise this means of communication to reach them and others discreetly when necessary.*

Thinking back, Avis had said as much on that second morning. Somehow, the true gryps had been able to communicate with Columbine without using words, or even vocal sounds. He'd described it as 'words that appeared inside Columbine's mind'. Until that moment, she hadn't fully understood just how literal he'd been at the time. However, now that she did, she wasn't happy with the deceptive nature of the mental speech. It went too close to whispering behind a raised hand for her to ever be comfortable with.

I won't speak long, YHWH sent, as if reading her thoughts on the matter. And for all she knew, he could. If Heaven had angels that could alter moods, it wasn't a stretch to think other angels could read her thoughts like a bender. *You are in desperate need of information, Clarise. And time is of the essence.*

How are you even doing this? she demanded for the second time, popping one of the two caramelised pineapple cubes into her mouth to keep Avis from guessing she was having a conversation behind his back.

As I said, it's the mental speech of the true gryps. They call it telepathy. It enables them to communicate with each other from within the same realm, no matter what form they're in or how far away they are from each other.

Never in all her countless eons, had Clarise ever been so grateful as she was at that moment for her strict upbringing; for it allowed her to subconsciously stop her entire body from reacting in any way to YHWH's blasé admission. The mental speech hadn't been a thrall capability at all, but a natural one of the true gryps, so they could communicate … *regardless of shape or distance from each other?*

Despite her every effort, Avis' eyes bored into her, as if he could tell something was amiss.

To avoid his gaze, she reached forward for a glass of iced fruit juice … only to have Avis' hand close around her wrist and hold her still. "Clarise, what's wrong?"

He had the audacity to ask her that when she'd posed that very question to him countless times in the last few days and received nothing but a cold shoulder for her troubles? Irritation bubbled inside her, but rather than speak her mind, she drew in a deep breath and plastered a neutral smile on her lips. "As I said, I am fine, Avis. There is nothing for you to concern yourself with." Perhaps, once they aired things that night and she was finally able to understand his moods, she would inform him of this latest revelation about true gryps. It would be a more pleasant subject if things between them became too heated.

Avis released her hand and pulled back to his side of the blanket, staring intently at the dishes in front of him as if they had all the answers to the questions he couldn't bring himself to ask.

YHWH looked between the two of them, and Clarise caught a glimpse of the young man's true age as he frowned and ever so slowly shook his head in parental disapproval.

But Clarise was still processing what YHWH had said about the true gryps to pay it any real attention. He'd said this was the natural speech of true gryps. Not the cherubim. True gryps. As in pre-establishment. The creatures that were already so rare and so powerful that they'd become legends just by existing, possessed something akin to bending in the way they communicated. Something they called 'telep…athy'. Worse, according to YHWH, they needed it because they were also shifters. Shape shifting creatures of mass destruction with the ability to communicate mind to mind in order to coordinate their attacks without anyone being any the wiser. It was almost too much to believe.

This is precisely what I was talking about, YHWH sent in reproach. *You're going to lose him for good if you aren't careful, little sister.*

Clarise's gaze slid to YHWH, her left eyebrow hitching a fraction. *Excuse me?*

Avis is already on edge because of his inability to see my thoughts, let alone force my hand when he feels the need, and now he no longer believes he has your support either. By defending me at every turn, he thinks you are taking my side against him. You're not helping matters when at night your thoughts turn to the son you left behind. The son you refuse to speak of, but mourn over. Avis loves you with every fibre of his being and he's picking up on all the misery you're projecting. Without his bending to inform him of your reasons, he's assuming it's all because of him and his unyielding hatred of all things to do with my realm. His insecurities run deep, little sister, and after years of internalised self-doubt and recriminations on his part and nothing from you but a single kiss this morning to contradict it, he's got himself convinced that you've finally figured out you're better off without him. Not only that, but he believes your affections are now with me and that sooner rather than later, you're going to leave him for me. He's just bracing himself for when that happens.

"WHAT?" The screech flew from Clarise's lips and her head swung towards Avis in a combination of shock and outrage. *He thinks I am leaving him?*

Avis straightened and looked back at her; a dark, worried frown on his face. "Are you ...?"

"No, I most assuredly *am not!*" Clarise's voice was almost a shout as she threw herself to her feet, stepping both away from the rug and to the right behind YHWH in a single motion.

Be gentle, Clarise. YHWH warned, concerned that she'd taken his news so badly.

Clarise gritted her teeth as she stared down at the young man looking up at her beseechingly. *YHWH ... sweetheart ... I may be forever in your debt for bringing this to my attention, but right now you need to mind your own business. This is between me and my husband.*

YHWH visibly sighed. *As you wish, little sister. Just remember, the vast majority of this misunderstanding stems from your unwillingness to tell him about Charon and the negative emotions his memory invokes in you. Do not make the mistake of assigning all the blame to him.*

YHWH's words were like a bucket of ice water to her anger, and with it, she felt tears well in her eyes. For all his bravado, Avis without his bending was as fragile as spun glass in matters of the heart and she'd known that. It was one of the main reasons why she hadn't spoken of Charon before now and why she'd thought giving him space and time to sort himself out was the right approach for him. Never in a million eons had it ever occurred to her that he thought she was ending their marriage after only a week of friction (and regardless of how long he'd internalised their predicament, in the physical realm, it had indeed been less than a week). It would take a lot more than that. Like an extramarital affair that produced a bastard.

"ENOUGH!" Avis leapt to his feet, his temper igniting over the sight of her tears. Both Cora and Columbine leapt away from the rug; Cora automatically shoving Columbine behind her for protection. "Don't tell me nothing's wrong, Clarise!" He shot YHWH an accusing glare even as he pushed himself between the two, corralling Clarise behind him with his arms. "What've you done, you little bastard?"

YHWH simply looked up at him and raised an eyebrow.

Still reeling from the shock of it all, Clarise interlaced both sets of fingers through one of Avis' and squeezed. "It's not him, Avis. It's you and I. We need to talk, right now. In private. I was mistaken about this being able to wait until tonight."

The shattered look that suddenly replaced Avis' anger confirmed everything YHWH had told her and it broke her heart to think he thought this was the start of their eventual divorce. His tongue slid across his parched lips and he swallowed heavily. Through two layers of leather gloves she could feel his pulse hammer in sequence with the pounding artery in his neck.

"Girls ... stay with the brute squad."

His tone was missing its usual air of command, and unable to bear the weight of their discord any longer, Clarise tightened her grip on his hand and hauled him a short distance away. From there, she created a large, soundproofed room the same size as their sitting room with four solid opaque walls and an equally solid ceiling overhead. She didn't worry about changing the soft, cloud-lined floor into carpet, but illuminated the dark space with a series of lit wall sconces.

"Clarise, I …"

Clarise turned and placed a silencing finger over his lips. "No. You must listen to me, Avis of Mystal. The only reason I did not say my piece out there and put your mind at ease sooner, was because I do not want the girls to be privy to this discussion, or any other that does not see us as a unified front." She pulled her other hand free and placed both against his face, holding him still. "You must—*hear*—the words I am saying to you, beloved." She paused, just long enough to ensure she had his undivided attention. "There. Is. Nothing, between YHWH and I. Nothing at all. There never has been, and there never will be. He is merely a well-mannered young man whose conduct is a credit to his Lord Almighty. Now and again, he has hinted at his enormous workload, yet he is still willing to personally escort us through the realm. Not only that, but he has been incredibly accommodating of your rudeness and condescension inside his own realm. What I have for YHWH and his Almighty is respect and gratitude. Nothing more."

Taken off-guard, Avis stumbled backwards half a step. "But—but I … you …"

Clarise shook her head and moved into his space again. "No buts, Avis." She removed her left glove to expose one of her marriage bracers and held it up between them for him to see. "I married *you*, beloved." A long finger tapped against the rearing mystallion that stood opposite her father's rearing demon steed, signifying the union of the two pantheons. "That is not a dove and it never will be. The blood that shares my veins is yours. Yours. Not YHWH's. Not anyone else's. Yours. You are the love of my life, Avis. Do you understand what I am saying to you?"

Avis looked from her face to the exposed marriage bracer and back again. Over and over his eyes moved between the two, until he removed his own glove and placed his matching bracer over hers. "Then … why'd you turn on me? Every time I voiced an opinion about YHWH, or the angels, or Heaven in general, you threw it right back in my face, defending them as if they were Mystallians. And you've been crying every night since you met YHWH. I've seen it. I'd ask you what was wrong, and you'd looked me straight in the eye and you'd lie to my face. You lied, Clarise. I know you did. What was I supposed to think? What am I still supposed to think?"

Clarise covered her mouth with her gloved hand. Being happily married to Avis was all she'd ever wanted, but as convinced as he was that their marriage was over, she knew the secret she carried would destroy it so categorically that there'd be no return. Tears she could no longer hide poured down her face until she couldn't bear to look at him anymore. Her mass collapsed into a gelatinous blob that quickly shot across the room and reformed back into her Mystallian shape; albeit kneeling with her head slightly bowed.

Avis gasped and lunged forward. His hands reached for her; the fear in his eyes escalating to terror. But before he could formulate a word, she doubled over and pressed her forehead to the clouded ground like a Hellion servant. "It is not you who is unworthy of being in this marriage, Avis. It is me. I have shamed you, then compounded that shame by hiding the truth from you; forcing you to doubt yourself when you had nothing to fear."

She heard Avis' rapid approach until he slid the last two body-lengths across the clouds on his knees towards her. "No!" he shouted, his voice thick with emotion as he took her shoulders and hauled her back into a sitting position where they could see each other's eyes. When she refused to lift her head, he fisted her hair from behind and gently forced her look at him. Tears were in his eyes too, but he didn't seem to care. His grip tightened and he shook her a little, just as determined to be heard as she had been. "I won't have this, Clarise. Never. I don't care what you did or what you think you did. I don't. Nothing *ever* puts you on your face to anyone. Not even me. Don't ever do it again, or I'll-I'll …"

Clarise couldn't see him through her tears and her voice was broken with sobs. "B-But I … I have shamed you."

"For the realm's sake, I don't care!" When her whole body trembled, he released her hair and dragged her into a tight hug with her head tucked under his throat. "I don't. When it comes to you, I have no pride, Clarise. Don't you understand that? And if I don't have any pride, then there's no shame to be had. Not between us." He petted one side of her face and squeezed her with the other hand, dragging his chin across the top of her head in a third caress. A light growl preceded his next words. "For fuck's sake, sweetheart. All this time you've had this stupid notion rattling inside that beautiful head of yours, and it's made me think … well, it doesn't matter what it made me think. The whole damned thing's been for nothing."

"But I have a son not of your lineage that was born after our marriage," she blurted against his chest, then fell silent awaiting his explosion.

Surely, he couldn't ignore that!

* * *

At first, Avis didn't know how to react. He merely stared at the clouded carpet between them and the far wall, stunned by her revelation. He'd made thousands of guesses as to what her big secret could be, but none of them involved her sharing herself with another man with enough frequency to bear a child. It took him a minute to swallow the lump that found its way to his throat. "Does … does your family know?"

He surprised himself with his lack of concern for his own feelings, knowing only too well what the Highborn Hellions would do to her should they discover her infidelity. He was even more surprised when she nodded silently against his chest.

Not wanting to screw this up again, when he turned his thoughts inwards, he ensured all of his siblings were free to be sincere. (Looking back, he knew during his downward spiral, he'd modified them to the point where they simply agreed with his deductions like puppets. Stupid.) Once he showed them what had happened, he asked them for their opinion. Their *honest* opinion. Armina was the first to point out the obvious, to which they all agreed. The only conclusion that fitted all the facts had him right at the heart of it. *Still* not Clarise's fault.

Returning to the physical realm, he slid his hands under her knees, and with the other still behind her back, he lifted her into the air, rising himself. She had a son. A son who wasn't his and wasn't with them. After everything he'd done to her, did she really think this was a deal breaker for him? Obviously. The way she curled herself into a ball in his arms and buried her face in her hands, she must've thought he'd leave her. The irony of which was insane. After their separation, he'd gone on a three-year rampage, both aggressive and sexual. And unlike her, not all of his partners had been willing. Very few, in fact.

Realising how close they'd come to losing it all, Avis ground his teeth together and held her tightly against him, promising himself that he was never going to ignore his Mystallian roots again. Next time if he so much as thought there was a problem in the air, he'd man up and call her on it. Right there and then. No more of this bullshit guesswork that nearly destroyed their marriage. "Baby, can you give us something comfortable to sit on together? A stretch couch or a daybed or something like that. I don't care what."

He felt her head twist to free her face and a minute later, a three-seater lounge grew out of the clouds. "Thanks." He carried her to the newly formed piece of furniture and sat down at one end of it, wanting his arm to be supported by the arm of the seat. After all, they could be here a while, because neither of them were leaving until they were both back on the same page. No matter how long it took.

"Clarise," he said, once he was comfortable and she'd settled into his lap. He nuzzled her hair, then pushed her away just far enough that he could see her face. His fingers brushed her fringe back over her ear. "I will always hear what you have to say, sweetheart, but not from the floor, and never on your face like a servant. *Never* from down there ..."

"But ... I am a whore ..."

Avis' temper detonated before he could stop it, and the hand that had been stroking her face dropped and clamped across her mouth. "*Never* say that again," he warned, red mist crowding his vision. Just the thought of those words being affiliated with her made him want to shake her so hard her teeth rattled. "I'll kill anyone who hears those words from your lips and put you over my knee as if you were one of the girls! I swear I will!" Clarise looked down at his restraining hand with a dulled look of defeat in her eyes. *No!* His chest heaved, but he fought to get himself back under control. Too much was unravelling too fast. They were both worn so painfully raw that they were overanalysing and overreacting to everything.

With his thumb still over her lips, he hooked his fingers under her chin and lifted her face to him again. "I love you," he said, willing her to accept that pledge as a starting point for them to build on. "I still love you. I will always love you. Do you understand? If you had to find comfort in the arms of another because of the way I treated you back then, that's on me. My failing. Not yours. If you believe nothing else, believe that, sweetheart. Because it's the truth."

The tip of her pink tongue peeked through her lips and she ran it around the surface, moistening them. "You ... will not challenge his father?"

Why? Do you still have feelings for him? The thought flashed across his mind before he could stop it, along with the desire to stomp back to Hell and rip her lover to pieces for touching what was his. No one would've challenged it, since he'd be within his rights as her husband after all. But then he circled back to the fact that if he'd done the right thing by Clarise back in Mystal, the newcomer would never have been in the picture. If he wanted to beat the shit out of someone for causing this, he needed a mirror first.

He sighed, wishing yet again he could go back in time and kick his own ass. Then he relaxed into the back of the lounge, cuddling her close and tucking her head between his jaw and his shoulder. "Start at the beginning, sweetheart, which was probably just after you left Mystal, if I'm not mistaken."

He felt the cool breath on his throat as she inhaled deeply. "After our ... encounter ..." Avis winced at her terminology. "... I could not bear to be in the presence of another male outside our family ... and as I grew bigger with Columbine my fear went on to include all males, including those of the Hellion Highborn. I withdrew completely into the ladies' chambers, refusing to come out— even for meals. I shifted the rock walls of my rooms into barely enough sustenance for Columbine."

She paused, no doubt to gauge his reaction, so he rubbed his chin against her head, saying without words that she had his unwavering support. "Without my immediate protection, Cora suffered many punishments during those first months before her sister was born. She evolved quickly, refusing to ever be weak and helpless again. The cognitive capability she must have possessed to push herself that far that fast should have been a clue to her unique bending and shifting blend, but in my diminished state I failed to notice. She grew horns and battle armour within weeks, and combat pincers within a month. All of which were torn off her, yet she replaced them as soon as she was able. At some point, Father decided enough was enough and had his wife, Lady Erishkigal order us out of the ladies' chambers and into others, where both men and women congregated."

She paused again, as if the memory was a painful one. Avis continued to caress her, having nothing else to offer that wouldn't interrupt her. "The thought of people being so close to me terrified me, and with Cora securely in my arms, I turned the only opening of our chambers into a solid wall to keep everyone out. In my mind, no male was ever going to cause us harm again."

Avis stared at the far wall, determined not to cry and succeeding by the barest of margins. He'd never thought about this. What life for her would be like after he'd forced himself upon her. She had returned home, pregnant and broken, to a family with more rules and expectations than the Nexus. Instead of wanting this unknown male who touched what didn't belong to him dead, he should've offered him an unspecified boon for stepping up and putting his precious wife back together again.

Clarise went on, oblivious to her husband's discomfort. "Soon afterwards, Father broke down my barrier and informed me I was to have a male bodyguard who, with the exception of certain aspects of a lady's life, would be with me at all times. That was when Beelzebub arrived."

Avis' eyes widened. *Beelzebub?* His rival for Clarise's affections had been Beelzebub? An image of the powerful hellion commander blasted through his mind's eye.

"He is ..."

"I know exactly who he is, sweetheart," Avis said with a heavy swallow, not nearly as confident about destroying her former lover as he had been moments ago. "Your father's second in command, militarily speaking. One of Hell's heaviest hitters and commander of the hellion brute squad."

Clarise nodded against his throat. "I have known him my whole life, but that did not stop me from being terrified of him. Of everyone. I deliberately kept myself between him and Cora, never taking my senses off him for a moment—even in sleep. What was worse—he was under father's orders to remain at my side, regardless of how miserable it made us both."

"When did he finally sleep with you?" Avis had tried to ask that question gently. By the Twin Notes of all creation, he tried.

Nevertheless, the fingers of Clarise's free hand picked at the edge of his cloak. Her other hand was tucked behind his back. "A-About seven months after Columbine was born. It started with harmless conversations ... then about a month later I allowed him to rub oil into my wings when I was too spent to cast a stimulation wave. He was incredibly gentle with me ... the way you were in the conservatorium. I knew he was only following father's orders, but I couldn't resist. I wanted to prove to myself that two beings could mate more than once without it turning into ... what happened with us. I wanted to know that so very, very much. I do not expect you to understand or forgive ..."

"Clarise." That one word silenced her, and the look she cast him after she pulled away from his chest had his heart tying in knots. She still thought he'd see her as something tainted. *As if!* He manoeuvred her legs so that she straddled his thighs and they were on the same eye-height. Then he framed her face with his hands, dusting her cheekbones reverently. "Sweetheart, *I* broke you. *Me.* But even if I hadn't, there's not a thing you could do that I wouldn't forgive you for. Do you hear me? Not a thing! I wouldn't care if you had a thousand kids out there. After all the forgiveness you've shown me, I would *never* be the one to walk away from us. Ever. I thought you were the one leaving me."

Tears streamed silently down Clarise's face and rolled over his hands to splash on his chest. "I was so afraid after the way you behaved with Maui for merely showing an interest that you would turn me away ..." she wept, unable to control herself.

Avis pressed his lips to her forehead. Then he kissed her closed eyes and her cheekbones, following the wet trail of her tears to her lips where he kissed her long and hard. "I'm going to growl at anyone who makes a pass at you, sweetheart, whether or not it's reciprocated." The words were whispered lovingly against her lips. "Let's get that straight. Anyone with a ... with a working piece of male anatomy is going to want you, but so long as that's as far as it goes, they'll get to walk away afterwards—though maybe with a limp or two and a few years of ashed memories."

With a predatory grin, he wrapped one arm around her shoulders and twisted her to his right. She gasped as gravity pulled her into the cushions, but he rolled with her, positioning himself so that his other forearm crashed against the far arm of the couch, taking both the brunt of their fall and keeping his weight poised over the top of her. His eyes feasted on the sudden rise and fall of her chest as she panted and his right hand tugged at the hem of her doublet until he was able to burrow beneath the fabric for some skin on skin contact. He knew there was a reason he hadn't put that glove back on. "From this day forward, the only one who gets to enjoy this playground is me."

"Avis ... everyone is just outside ..."

Her words of warning had the completely opposite effect on him, for what had started as a harmless exploration of the body he had denied himself for too long ignited into an overwhelming inferno of desire. If she hadn't really wanted to do this, she'd have stopped it—flat. "Exactly," he purred, nibbling a line between her earlobe and her throat as his thumbnail flicked her nipple and he pressed his weight between her legs. "Which means they're not in here. Give me this, sweetheart. I need it. I need you." He rocked his hips in a mock thrust. "I need *us* really badly."

Her uniform became a gelatinous mass that fell away from the couch as her arms slid around his neck. His uniform quickly followed suit. Her expression, when he looked was just as voracious. "As do I, my love. By all the realms combined; as do I."

CHAPTER FORTY-TWO

It was some time before they emerged from the room, but when they did so, Clarise cleaned away all external presence of their lovemaking and returned their uniforms to pristine condition. Hand in hand they strolled from the dissipating room. Only their broad smiles and the love in their eyes gave any indication that their talk had consisted of anything more than mere words.

"Add another one, YHWH!" Cora ordered, dragging Avis' attention away from the woman who walked at his side.

At some point since they'd gone into the silent room, the brute squad had extended their perimeter to give the party more room to move. As such, YHWH's cherubim lay with its lion head facing Columbine, who was using the soft pelt of its torso as a makeshift pillow to lean against. The beast purred and kept trying to lay its huge paw over her possessively, to which she laughed and shifted out of its way. "Stop it. I cannot see," she scolded with a giggle.

See what? Avis wondered, though he noticed how the rest of the cherubim prowled outside of the highborn guard, without actually putting the guard between themselves and Columbine. From what he could tell, they were in four groups, pacing in four very straight lines that kept Columbine within their sight at all times. He could well imagine how thrilled they would've been to be pushed back, and he was a little peeved he'd missed it.

A flash of fire caught his eye and he immediately jerked his head towards it. In the middle of the brute squad's perimeter, Cora had no fewer than eight fist-sized fireballs rotating through her hands in a large singular arc that went high over her head. Her attention was on the higher fireballs, rather than those she tossed between her hands.

"You sure?" YHWH asked, in his hand a ninth fist-sized ball that had yet to be ignited.

"Toss it, dammit!" Cora snapped back, her brow creasing impatiently. "I've got this!"

YHWH looked back at Columbine's widened eyes and winked, causing her to giggle again. "Sheathe your claws, tiger. Here it comes." As he spoke, he tossed the ball underhanded into her left hand just ahead of the one that was falling from above. The ball burst into flames upon contact with her glove, and without missing a beat, she shoved it towards her other hand and slowly corrected the spacing between all nine, her hands constantly moving to keep them all airborne. "Yeah!" she crowed with pride. "Piece of cake!"

Avis felt conflicted. On one hand, YHWH had kept the girls busy while he and Clarise reconnected, but another more possessive part of him bristled at the way YHWH had drawn on his pet name for her. That was *his* nickname for her. YHWH never had and never would earn the right to use it.

Clarise must have sensed his irritation, for she squeezed his hand and wrapped her other arm around his bicep, practically willing him to ignore it. She had a point. Things for them were in a really good place at the moment, and if he roared, there was a chance it'd all be ruined. *Still ... not cool, YHWH.*

"Mother! Father! Check this out!"

"I see …. *oomph!*" A very familiar hip-high weight collected Avis around the legs and thighs. He dropped his hand and looked down, though he didn't need the eye contact to know the feel of Columbine's arms or the way her tiny chin dug into his thigh as she stared up at him. "Hey," he grinned, releasing Clarise's hand and disentangling his arm just long enough to capture Columbine under the arms. With an exaggerated groan of effort that implied she was getting too big to be carried, he lifted her to perch on his hip, opposite Clarise.

"You are both so happy," she sighed, resting her head on his shoulder, her left arm hooking around his neck. He knew her right arm was wrapped around his back, but it wasn't until he saw her fingers protruding from her mother's grasp on Clarise's right-hand side that he realised she'd stretched her arm out two full adult body-widths to go around them both. Somehow the physical contact between them all felt right.

"We are," Clarise answered for him.

"Add another one!" Cora shouted, bringing his attention back to the missing member of their small family.

YHWH chuckled and shook his head. "Nine's a good number for your first try, Cora, and now that your parents are back, we'll probably be on the move again very soon."

"But I can do it!"

"I'm sure you can," Avis cut in, and, despite all the happiness he felt at that moment, he knew he'd rather eat his right arm then admit what he was about to say next. Nevertheless … "YHWH's right." —*blargh*— "We've lost enough time. Tonight, after the meal, you can practise some more before you go to bed."

Cora made an argumentative growl that didn't quite leave her throat, though one by one, each of her fireballs disappeared in a puff of lingering smoke as they reached the top of her arc. "Fine," she bellyached, dusting her hands against her legs once the last fireball vanished. "Go ruin my fun now that you've finished yours … see if I care."

Had her tone been serious, Avis would've reacted accordingly. As it was, he chuckled. "The privilege of being the real adult in the situation, tiger. I get to call all the shots."

YHWH cast his gaze across them all and beamed happily as well. In the next moment, the cherubim Columbine had been lying on rose onto its gold pins and rolled to its left to put the eagle side back on top in anticipation of flight; as if YHWH had whistled or spoken to it in some way. YHWH crossed the cloud to it and, grasping a single, outstretched talon for leverage, hoisted himself up onto its feathered mass. The talons then closed around his waist once more to prevent him from falling.

It was the first time Avis had actually registered his absolute lack of wings. "So are there a lot of angels that don't have wings?" It wasn't that he hadn't seen the missing wings. He'd just been too worked up about everything else to question some of the most basic principles of Heaven. Every angel he'd ever encountered before YHWH had the feathery wings which practically branded them as denizens of Heaven.

"Most do," YHWH answered, as the cherubim stood up, taking the young man with him. "In fact, the Third Choir are the only exception to that rule."

"Then how do *you* move through Heaven, sweetheart?" Clarise asked, as she took the reins of her own demon steed and eased onto its back. "I have seen how there is no land on the other side of the pearlescent wall for you to walk on."

Avis and the girls quickly mounted their own demon steeds, though he never took his eyes off YHWH as he settled in behind Hotspot's wings. Clarise raised a really good point. In a realm of endless sky, how did YHWH and the other Third Choir angels move around? He wasn't as bothered by Clarise's term of endearment as he had been. By her own admission the two of them had made a connection; just not the kind he'd been thinking. Friendship. Appreciation. The way a mature woman looked upon a young child whose behaviour pleased her. That was a relationship Avis could deal with.

YHWH smiled. "The thrones always ride with other angels," he said, patting the feathery hide of the cherubim beneath him. "They're what keep us all connected."

"And I assume the thrones is the designation of the Third Choir?" Clarise asked.

YHWH grinned and nodded. "Yes, ma'am."

"One more question before we head out," Avis said, since YHWH was in the mood to be informative.

YHWH lifted his chin and looked at Avis with such happiness in his eyes that tears began to fall. "Anything you want, Avis," he promised. "Ask me anything at all."

Avis barely refrained from rolling his own eyes at the over-dramatic reaction. Or maybe he didn't. Either way, if YHWH was inside his own realm and the Almighty was okay with his angels turning on the waterworks for stupid reasons, why should he care? "Why are the familial links so out of whack here in Heaven?"

YHWH blinked in surprise. "I don't understand," he admitted. "They're not— to my knowledge."

"Like hell they're not," Avis countered, stabbing his pointer finger into Hot Spot's fiery mane to reiterate his claim. "This whole realm's glowing like a noon-day sun every time we go to use them, and we can't get a fix on anyone. That's never happened to me before, and I've been around a *really* long time."

Understanding swept over YHWH and his ready smile returned to him. "Ahhh, I see." He then tilted his head to the side in apology. "That's my fault, I'm afraid. Part of my powerbase is set up so that I can be everywhere at once." He paused and gave a guilty shrug. "The downside to that is, my family can't see past *my* familial link to find anyone else's."

"You aren't our family," Avis argued, tired of having to point this out.

YHWH lifted his chin in challenge. "What if I was to tell you I am?"

Avis matched his chin-lift. "I'd call you a liar." It was a no-brainer. Angels, with the exception of a few expatriates from other realms, were constructs. Creations built by those with divine essence to bring into being something that didn't exist naturally. Although they were still a force to be reckoned with (especially since there appeared to be an endless supply of the little bastards), one on one with a true celest would have the construct obliterated in short order. Divinity was very one-sided like that. It looked after its own.

It was yet another reason why Mystal was so powerful. Not only was the pantheon filled with celestials with ranged abilities, but all of their people consisted of naturally birthed bending commoners. Born. Not constructed. At the time, Avis and his siblings hadn't realised just how many commoners had escaped the fringes of the Nexus over the eons, but with nowhere to go and no desire to be noticed, most of them had kept their heads down. That was, until Avis and his siblings set up Mystal. Then, those commoners turned up in droves, each swearing fealty on behalf of them and their descendants in exchange for a life of safety within the realm. Many of the originals from the Nexus had passed away by the time their descendants made it to Mystal, and as such, they had no idea why they were instinctually drawn to what they perceived was the comfort of having ranged benders in control.

"Beloved, it is also in their thrall to see everyone as one big family," Clarise said as a gentle reminder. "The angels all call each other brother and sister, despite having no blood between them. As an angel within Heaven, YHWH is no different."

"At least you're not yelling at me anymore," YHWH added, a cheeky half-grin crossing his features. "I'll take that as an improvement on our relationship."

"Give me ten minutes, brat." Avis may have meant the snarky comment, but the moment it left his lips, he couldn't help but smirk himself. Especially when YHWH threw his head back and laughed. Damn, the little shit was growing on him too ... now that he knew for sure that there was nothing going on between the little prick and his wife.

With a light chuckle still on his lips, Avis lifted his hand to his shoulder and dropped it forward at the wrist, sending them all into the sky. Perhaps his generosity towards YHWH stemmed from the kid's lack of wings, making him appear very Mystallian. He certainly wouldn't be able to tolerate any of YHWH's winged brethren in his vicinity. There was just too much bad blood between him and them to ever be on peaceful terms.

In fact, thinking about it, it was one of the very few things he ever really agreed with his father on. Theodrick hated Heaven's angels too. But unlike the rest of the pantheons who slaughtered the feathered fuckers on sight, his father kept them alive, as frozen statues beneath his throne room. To be used ... and abused at his leisure. For years Avis and his siblings had known they were there. They were probably still there being used even more, now that he and his brethren had fled from the realm. Avis had no desire to fuck an angel. None whatsoever. He just wanted them all dead. Was that really too much to ask? He shot a quick glance at the top of the wall, knowing the impenetrable line of Sixth Choir military followed their every movement.

Apparently, yes it was.

For several more hours, YHWH and Columbine led the way until the golden dot on Avis' glove edge indicated it was time to call it a night. But instead of raising his arm and indicating that the family needed to land (which neither YHWH or Columbine would see), Avis lifted his fingers to his lips and let out a sharp whistle to gain everyone's attention, before following through with the landing gesture.

Clarise's eyes had already taken on that insectoid feature that allowed her to see everything at once, and in the distance, grass sprouted through the clouds and unrolled across the grey surface like a rug towards them. Avis hadn't been able to keep his eyes off her for long all afternoon, and now was no exception. He loved Clarise so much, he wasn't sure what he'd do if she ever really left him. The very real possibility of that had eaten him alive during the last few months of internalisation (and the last few days in the physical realm). But thinking about it now that the threat had passed, it suddenly occurred to him that he'd never actually shown her that. Oh sure, they'd had sex just a few hours ago and lust was always at the forefront of his dance card, but how much had he been willing to yield that he didn't want to, to show her she meant everything to him? Not a lot, and definitely not often.

Maybe it's time I changed that.

"YHWH," he called, causing the boy to twist within the cherubim's talons towards him. "That invitation to dinner is still open, if you'd like to come."

Happiness inundated his body so thoroughly his mouth flew open and he had to fist his doublet and drag his knuckles across his chest to alleviate it. His other hand braced against Hotspot's neck, burying into its flames for support. "Enough!" he rasped when he could finally draw breath and hold it, not knowing how YHWH was doing it, but knowing he was. "For the love of Mystal, knock it off!" Almost as quickly as it came, the exhilaration abandoned him, confirming YHWH as the cause. He managed to retain enough of his own pleasure to know he'd done the right thing though; especially the way his family was beaming so happily at him. "Just one meal," he reiterated, holding up a single finger to physically represent the number involved.

YHWH smiled from ear to ear and shivered with excitement. He genuinely shivered. He looked at each of them in rapid succession, seemingly unable to believe the offer had been extended, then slid from his cherubim and danced on the lawn. "Yes! Yes, yes, yes, YES!"

"Oh, for Mystal's sake, knock it off, you lunatic! It's just a meal!"

YHWH spun on his heel to face him, his face red with delight and tears banked in his eyes. "But you invited me, brother! You! The leader of the others! And no one made you! That's huge!"

"I'm not your damned brother!" Avis was fed up to the back teeth with reminding him of that. He had exactly five brothers, and this nitwit in a child's body wasn't one of them.

Still dancing in circles by himself, YHWH's hands went up over his head with his fingers spread wide in what Avis first assumed was an apology. At least, it should have been, but with the rest of YHWH's erratic dance, it was hard to tell.

In a matter of minutes, Clarise had their home finished. However Avis, after spending months in this abode, saw straight away that the dimensions were off. Specifically, the left-hand side of the building was a good three metres wider from the central doors than the right.

He was about to ask why when she lifted her leg over her demon steed's back and dropped to the ground between them, holding her reins out for Tilu to take.

Avis immediately joined her on the ground, also passing his reins forward to Tilu. The second his hands were free, Clarise wrapped her arms around his neck and hugged him tightly. "Thank you," she whispered against his chest, as he locked his arms around her shoulders and held her close.

He pressed a kiss to her hair and replied, "Anything for you, sweetheart."

She purred against his chest, then twisted to stand at his side, sliding her arm across the small of his back under his cloak to sit on his opposite hip. He automatically draped his arm across her shoulders, holding her just as close.

"YHWH," she said. "I'm not sure what your powerbase allows you to do, so I have added an apartment at the end of the house for your benefit, should you wish to freshen up before the meal. Unfortunately, we have no extra servants to assist you, but there is a sitting room with a fireplace, a bedroom, and an ensuite, all of which are all at your disposal."

Well, that explained the added width to the house, though Avis hoped YHWH didn't take that as an extended invitation to stay the night. He wasn't quite ready for that ... just yet.

YHWH stopped dancing long enough to wrap his arms around his waist, though he still jiggled impatiently on the spot. "Mmm-hmmm," he said through lips that were bitten shut. His head bobbed in acknowledgement and his eyes sparkled in both anticipation and delight. Avis had seen his youngest brother Chance do that exact move a million times, when the runt wanted something he couldn't quite have, but knew he was going to get in the very near future.

The girls both slid to the ground and handed their reins to Tilu, who bowed to the family as a whole once she had all four sets and walked the demon steeds into their stable.

"C'mon! If we do this fast, we'll have time to juggle more before dinner!" Cora rushed to YHWH and had him by the hand before she finished her decree; all but hauling him towards the house.

"I said after dinner!" Avis bellowed after them.

"Let them play, beloved," Clarise chuckled, sliding her arm around his waist and resting her head against his pec. "With only Tilu to do all the work, it will give her more time to prepare everything."

Avis hadn't noticed any delay in their evening schedule thus far, but if Clarise said Tilu needed more time, she could have all the time in existence without a word of complaint. Well, until he got hungry. Then he might say something. "Time to go inside, princess," he said, holding his free hand out and wiggling his fingers for Columbine to take. "Say goodnight to the cherubim."

Just like they had every other night since the cherubim met them, every face of every beast arched skyward and howled at the thought of being separated from her. The blend of a bull's bellow, a lion's roar, a Mystallian's howl and an eagle's high-pitched screech times twenty-six was something Avis doubted he would ever get used to. For the ultimate, super vicious war monsters of celestial legend; they were absolutely pathetic.

"I will be back tomorrow," Columbine promised with all her heart, waving at them with her other hand. "Be good until then. I love you."

As if she'd issued a decree instead of a standard set of parental partings, all belligerent noise behind them ceased. The sudden silence made the ringing in his ears more profound, and when he looked over his shoulder at them, they had reassembled themselves in that same double line formation that they'd taken when YHWH first met him. Their faces were bright and alert and their chests were puffed in their determination to make her proud.

It was ... a bizarre sight.

Shaking his head at them, Avis led his family into the house, where another set of double doors was located behind his chair at the far-left hand side of the room. Both doors were wide open, beyond which were YHWH and Cora, just inside the doorway. Both had something in their hands, but it wasn't the fist-sized fireball that they'd been using earlier. This was ... smaller, about a third of the fireball's size. And it had rounded edges with a split down the middle, but was flat and gleaming like cut crystal both front and back. The only reason Avis knew this, was because Cora held hers still long enough for him to see it. YHWH, on the other hand, was rolling and spinning his 'whatever-it-was' across both of his forearms and bouncing it between his wrists and hands. A trail of glowing cord followed its movements until it looked as if YHWH was about to tangle himself hopelessly, but then a quick twist of his fingers and all the looped cords fell forward over his hands and landed in a complex spider's web pattern before him with just enough continuity to be deliberate. He looked at Cora's excited face and grinned. "Want me to show you again?" he asked, releasing the right-hand side of the web and dropping the circular thing until it spun in an endless loop near his feet. At that point, Avis realised the cord was tied to YHWH's middle finger ... which made the trick, not so impressive. A quick flick of the brat's wrist, and the thing flew up the cord and smacked into his palm, rolling the cord up with it as it went.

Cora looked at the similar, though smaller object in her own right hand. "No, I can do this ..." she said, though her face puckered into a tight frown of concentration that belied her confidence.

YHWH placed his hand over hers. "Okay, before you try that one, why don't we go over the basics, tiger?" He released her hand and gestured to the ground at her feet. "I want you to drop it down towards the ground. Just drop it, and let it spin."

Avis felt Columbine's fingers spasm with excitement against his palm and chuckled to himself. "Off you go princess," he said, releasing her hand with a small shove towards her sister. "Do you want to watch?" he asked, cocking his head to one side to look at Clarise.

"Oh, hey, sweet pea!" YHWH called, snatching Avis' attention away from his wife just in time to see YHWH go down on one knee with his arms outstretched in expectation of a hug. Like he hadn't been riding at her side ... all day.

Columbine wrapped her arms around his neck and gave him a tight squeeze, then turned inside his arms to look at the object in his right hand. "What is it?"

YHWH opened his hand further. "It's called a disc, sweet pea. Children from the next realm over have played with them for like ... ever. The harder tricks can be a bit difficult to master, but would you like to give it a try?"

He put both hands together around her, covering his disc, and when he pulled them apart, a second, smaller disc accompanied the first. Yet another powerplay, this one involving shifting. Avis would've loved to know the exact parameters of YHWH's powerbase. From what he'd seen so far, there didn't seem to be any limit.

"I was just showing your sister how to work out the balance between keeping it spinning and accepting defeat when it's gone flat." He looked over at Cora's still disk at the bottom of her string and smirked. "I'm afraid that's very flat. You'll have to roll it up now .... or not," he laughed, when Cora looked at her disc and it started to spin again. "Now, before it stops again, bounce your hand to try and bring it back up." He passed the second disk to Columbine, sliding the loop of cord over her middle finger to the first knuckle and curling her fingers around it. "Watch me, you two." He rose to his feet and opened his hand, allowing his disc to fall. But before it reached his feet, he gave it a quick jerk and it bottomed out and flew back up into his hand, just like it had the first time. He then gestured at them with both hands. "Okay. Now, you two try."

The trick was stupid and demeaning, and it was no shock that both girls picked it up straight away. Nevertheless, YHWH made their achievement seem incredible. "Awesome!" he said, with a profound clap of approval. "Next one. Roll your hand over like this …"

"YHWH is the perfect babysitter for young children," Clarise chuckled, resting her head against Avis' pec and smiling at how well the three of them played together. "When he is like this, he reminds me an awful lot of Chance."

Avis didn't want to admit he'd thought that too just a few minutes ago. Not that it changed anything. YHWH wasn't family, regardless of who said what or how he acted. Behaving like a blood relative didn't automatically make them one.

As the girls absorbed each of YHWH's disc lessons, Avis quickly grew bored with the way the toy dropped from the string, spun uselessly at the bottom and went back up the string. True, there were little tricks that complicated the falling process, but it was still ridiculously belittling.

Avis and Clarise turned and left them to it.

CHAPTER FORTY-THREE

The evening meal came and went with a familiarity that made Avis relax in his seat. Just like he had with the lunches, he put Cora on the same side of the table as Columbine and gave YHWH the side that faced the apartment doors, but no one seemed to mind. As always, YHWH made a lot of small talk that entertained the family, but through it all, Avis couldn't shake the feeling that he was trying too hard. It wasn't as blatant as it had been in the beginning, but every now and then, he caught the boy scanning each of their faces for their reaction before supplying his own. Even more rarely, a pucker of concern would cause his brow to twitch, only to be washed away moments later by a flash of bleak despair and replaced by his usual joviality. For the billionth time, Avis wished his bending would work on the angel. Then he wouldn't have to be guessing what was going on inside his head like this.

But by the end of the meal, after carefully scrutinising each of his guest's micro-expressions (and internalising with the rest of his Elder Court for a few minutes at each instance to ensure his siblings and their significant others concurred) Avis knew what he was looking at and was almost impatient for YHWH to be finished.

YHWH smiled in contentment and wiped his lips with a napkin. "That was wonderful," he said, lifting his chair away from the table. "Thank you for inviting me."

"A word before you go," Avis said, putting every ounce of command he could into that one statement.

The look of shock YHWH sent him would have been hilarious, if he didn't follow it so quickly with a despondent sigh that had him relaxing into his seat.

That's right, kid, Avis thought to himself. *I know, and you know I know. Time to 'fess up.*

YHWH watched Avis cautiously and leaned to his right; away from the Mystallian patriarch. He rubbed his fingers across his lips and hooked his right thumbnail between his teeth.

Avis caught Clarise staring at him, and when she had his full attention, she deliberately moved her gaze to where YHWH sat and back again. Twice more she did it.

I know, sweetheart. I know, Avis thought, nodding in agreement. He'd already worked out that the boy was hiding something, without her needing to point it out. *Leave it with me.*

Clarise gestured for Tilu, signalling that she was ready to stand. Tilu stood behind her chair and pulled it away as she rose to her feet. "Girls, come with me into Cora's room," she said.

Cora looked up from the pile of sweets she had yet to consume as if that was the worst idea she'd ever heard. By contrast, Columbine stared at YHWH, and even from where he sat, Avis could feel the combination of concern and sympathy pouring off her in waves.

"It's alright, princess. I'd just like a private word with YHWH. He's not in any trouble." He then shifted his attention to Cora. "Take your plate of desserts with you, tiger," he said in concession for it wasn't her fault she ate almost as much as

Tal and Griffith combined and as such hadn't quite finished. Diviten helped Columbine to her feet as Gingen stood with her hands on the back of Cora's seat.

Seeing her imminent eviction, Cora hastily reached forward and scooped a dozen more bite-sized treats to her already overflowing plate before she allowed herself to be helped out of her seat. She sent him a sideways look of disgust that she didn't act on, to which Avis grinned and winked at her in silent dismissal.

Less than a minute later, the room was vacant except for him and YHWH. Avis watched the boy grow more skittish with every passing second; his ready good humour seeming to fail him completely. "Out with it," Avis said, deciding he'd waited long enough. YHWH had the audacity to look at him as if he had no idea what he meant. "Don't play dumb with me, kid. To paraphrase my mother, you look like someone who can't decide if they want to shit or sing."

Instead of answering, YHWH froze for a few seconds with his wide-eyed gaze locked onto Columbine's double doors directly across from him. Just as Avis was about to repeat the demand, YHWH's breath escaped him in a huff and lowered his eyes to the table's edge. "She did say that, didn't she," he murmured, leaning forward to brace his elbows on the table. He steepled his fingers on either side of his nose and hooked his thumbs under his chin, then closed his eyes and breathed out slowly, his breath echoing against his palms. After three long breaths that allowed him to regain his composure, he lowered his hands to the table and turned to Avis with an eternity of regret in his eyes. "Do you ever miss her?"

With his entire discussion upended by what appeared to be a nonsense act, Avis leaned on the left arm of his chair, away from YHWH. "Who?"

"Belladonna, of course. Do you ever think of her much?"

Avis blinked in bewilderment and looked away, only to realise that was the act of someone bearing guilt. There was no way he was feeling guilty for escaping the Nexus, even if they had left their mother behind. If anything, it should've happened sooner. Snapping his gaze back to YHWH, he said icily, "Not a lot, no."

"Yeah, me either. Isn't that disgusting?" He looked back at Columbine's doors.

Avis wasn't interested in what YHWH or anyone else thought of his mother and scowled. "No, and quit avoiding the subject," he said, pulling himself off the chair arm to sit forward again. "What the fuck are you hiding?"

YHWH snorted and straightened in his seat. "That's a very non-specific question, Avis. As you can guess, someone like me houses a lot of people's secrets. Perhaps you could narrow it down a little?" He raised a hand and drew his thumb and forefinger together. "You know, so that we're not still sitting here at the end of eternity."

"Fine," Avis growled, knowing YHWH was deliberately being an ass. "I've been around a fucking long time, and I know when someone's sitting on something they know they're supposed to be sharing. You've been doing it the whole meal, so like I said; out with it. No more dodging the subject."

YHWH slowly licked his lips as if thinking about his next words. "The problem is, you have no idea how much I'm enjoying my time with you and Clarise and the girls. For so long, I've been on the outside looking in, watching everyone else interact with the people that mean everything to them. And now, after all this time, I'm finally experiencing it for myself. You will never know how much I'm treasuring it." He bit his bottom lip and shook his head. "I've always dreamed of one day meeting at least one of you, but I never thought it would be *you*, and I never thought it would be like this."

For the most part, Avis could relate to that. He'd been adrift as well, before he'd reconnected with Clarise and the girls. "So, what's the problem?"

"The problem is, you want to leave as soon as possible."

That had never been a big secret. "And?"

"And … I … know of a way to get you and the family to the Olympian border almost as fast as a single realm-step."

"WHAT?"

YHWH swung in his seat to face Avis, his face creased to the brink of tears and his hands reaching out pleadingly. "But then you'll leave! You have no idea how long I've been waiting to meet you, Avis. You can't. You've always had the others to lean on and support you, even when they weren't there. You've always had them in here!" He thumped the side of his head with his forefinger as he spoke, then slapped both hands against the table. "I've never had that!" YHWH pushed away from the table and stood up, instinctively turning away from Avis. "And until that happens to you, brother, you'll never understand the loneliness that comes with it."

Avis shot up after him, clamping his hand on YHWH's shoulder to prevent him from realm-stepping away from the house.

The panic that filled YHWH's eyes as they fell on Avis' restraining hand was unmistakable. It was gone as soon as it came, but for a moment, it was there. Avis had seen it. Yet again, for the umpteenth time, he wished his bending would work so he could see what was going on inside YHWH's head. It would make everything a whole lot easier.

Avis removed his hand and opened the fingers wide, showing without saying that he wasn't about to try anything. "You're okay, YHWH," he said, stepping away from the boy to rest his backside against the edge of the table. "Take a breath."

"I know. That—shouldn't have happened. I guess too many old memories have been stirred up this evening; both good and bad. I'm sorry."

Avis folded his arms and tilted his head to one side to scrutinise the boy. "If you were so determined to meet us, why didn't you come over and visit us yourself? It's not like you look like an angel or anything. You could walk in the front doors, and no one would ever know you were an angel."

YHWH shook his head, slowly at first but with more emphasis the longer the idea lingered between them. "I can't," he said, his bottom lip trembling even as he shook his head. "Besides, my thrall won't let me leave anymore, even if I wanted to." He turned towards the front doors. "But my resistance to your departure isn't just for me. Columbine has brought the cherubim back to life. I don't know how she's done it, but she has. Their thrall was very specific, because there was wasn't enough time to be creative. In the short space it took to set up the most basic powerbase and thrall, nineteen of the forty-five had already committed suicide, with more attempting it every second. Ever since then, they've done nothing but guard the entrances and exits of our innermost sanctums in much the same capacity as a stone golem would. They had no joy before this week. No life to speak of. All these years, I've wondered if the right thing had been done in keeping them alive, when everything that made them what they were had already been destroyed."

YHWH walked to the front door and opened it, stepping aside for Avis to see. "Those military lines have been the be-all and end-all of their existence ever since they were established, and their powerbase has kept them from needing sustenance or sleep. They guard. Yet one visit from young Columbine, and they broke free of their thrall and came to her. Think about that, brother, for it is my belief that they were waiting for her, as much as I was waiting for you."

"I won't allow you to keep us here by force."

YHWH looked shocked and quickly shook his head. "Of course not, brother. That's not what I meant at all. I would never keep you or your precious family prisoner, but can you blame me for not wanting to hasten your departure?"

"You really do need to stop calling us family, kid," Avis grumbled. He would've been more vocal, but YHWH's distress over losing them seemed genuine enough.

Avis folded his left arm across his waist, using the wrist as a ledge to balance his right elbow so he could stroke his jaw thoughtfully. As much as he wished otherwise, Clarise loved spending time in Heaven. So too, did the girls. He couldn't blame them. It was the first realm they'd come to since leaving Hell where they were genuinely welcomed with open arms. He was the only one that didn't want to be here. In the past, that would've been enough for Avis to move the Mystallians on. But he was trying to do better. "Alright," he said as the hint of an idea began to flicker to life in his mind. "How about we meet in the middle?"

YHWH moved to stand in front of him, his eyes sparkling with delight. "Yes!" he agreed, without bothering to hear any of the specifics.

Avis frowned at him. "Your negotiating skills suck, YHWH. What if I only agreed to one more day here?" He hadn't, but there was no way this angel could have possibly known that. Nor, it seemed, did he care.

"Then it's an extra day I get without guilt or coercion," he stated excitedly. "Do I get another day?"

Avis honestly wanted to slap some sense into him. "You really need to get out more, YHWH, if the thought of just one extra day of company has you bouncing off the walls like this."

Just when Avis hadn't thought it was possible, YHWH managed to dig deeper and find another level of stupid excitement. He danced on the spot like a kid half his apparent age and knotted his hands together, sucking on his bottom lip impatiently.

Avis watched his antics, and finally shook his head when the boy didn't seem to be winding down. "How does anyone believe you're capable of getting anything done?"

YHWH stopped dancing, but kept his hands clasped. "Too much?" he asked, hitching one eyebrow.

"Just a bit."

YHWH shrugged, but didn't remove his excited expression. "So what are you proposing, Avis?"

"Up until now, we've travelled all day, every day, and only stopped at night. The only social time you get to interact properly with Clarise and the girls is when we stop for meals, and that's either over a table or a picnic rug. So what if …" —Avis couldn't believe he was actually going to suggest this, but— "… what if we stay here. Right here. Spend the next … however long we choose to stay as if we were on vacation instead of spending every day riding. You would then have all day to be with Clarise and the girls, showing them whatever you want to about this place. And once *my* family (two could play the inclusion/exclusion game, after all) have had their fill, you agree to move us all straight to the boundary."

"What about you, Avis?"

The question surprised him. "What do you mean?"

"Is there no way I could get you to relax and maybe even enjoy your stay?"

Avis thought about that. "I don't suppose I could have a few angels to slow roast over an open firepit?" The mental image of at least two of those feathered fuckers tied back to back on a roasting spit that turned over an open fire had him smiling wistfully.

YHWH wasn't impressed. "Anything other than murdering the denizens of Heaven in cold blood," he clarified.

It had been on the tip of Avis' tongue to say, 'Cold's the last thing they'd be', but as things were going amicably at the moment, he bit his tongue. "Nothing comes to mind," he said with a casual shrug. "But I'll let you know."

"I appreciate that. So, are you okay with me spending some time this evening with the girls before they go to sleep?" he asked, rolling the pointer finger of both hands towards Cora's doors. "You did say Cora and I could work on our juggling after dinner, remember?"

"Don't do anything to make me regret this," Avis warned, though even as he spoke, he waved YHWH towards Cora's apartment.

"Never!" YHWH rushed past the Mystallian and around the table behind him, ducking into Cora's sitting room before Avis could change his mind.

A few moments later, Clarise emerged with a broad smile on her face and crossed the room to stand in front of him. "Everything will be fine, beloved," she promised, rising onto her tippy-toes to give him a light kiss on the cheek. "Not everything out of your control is destined to harm you."

Avis draped his arm across her shoulder and pulled her into his side. "Shall we recap?" he jeered, holding up the pointer of his left hand. "Your father is out of my control." He paused for dramatic effect, then added a second finger. "Uriel, while in either Heaven or Hell, is out of my control." He waved his hand, allowing the silence to remind her of the violent history all three shared. "And that's the grand total of exactly who sits outside my control from your side of things."

"So, you control me, do you?"

Avis smirked and kissed her forehead. "My blood is in your veins, sweetheart, so you don't count as one of them anymore."

Clarise chuckled and pulled him around the table to his recently abandoned chair, where she corralled him until he sat down. He wasn't sure what this new game was about, but since everyone was in such a good mood, he decided to play along. Especially when she slid across his lap and slipped her arms around his neck.

"And what about your side of things, Avis?"

The question was so unexpected that Avis stiffened in his seat, his fingers biting into the hand rests. He would have stood up, but her weight in his lap trapped him and he knew it wasn't an accident. Especially when she merged her lower anatomy with the chair to prevent his escape. Eyes wide with realisation, the heels of his boots scraped against the floor, searching for traction she wouldn't give him.

"Shhhh. No, Avis. The time for secrets between us is past and you will not run from me anymore. We are safe here, and the children are being entertained by YHWH as we speak." She gave him feather-light kisses all over his face to try and calm him down, ending with her forehead pressed to his. "I want you to tell me about the Nexus."

His heart hammered within his chest, but with her face filling his vision just as thoroughly as her fragrance filled his lungs, he didn't know what to do. Subconsciously, he clung to both, even if all he wanted to do was to distance himself from her until he could fortify his emotional defences. "Baby, don't go there," he finally pleaded. "Nothing good is in the Nexus, and I mean *nothing* good." He lifted his arms and rubbed her back in a half hug, willing her to believe him. "I won't permit his poison to ever touch you."

"Then tell me about your mother," she persisted.

Avis stared at her, willing her to drop the subject and let him go. And when that didn't happen, he breathed out slowly. "She was … everything Theodrick wasn't. She was kind. Caring. She did what she could to keep him away from us."

"Did he attack all of you, or just you?"

Avis tried to find something else to look at other than her eyes. In the farthest corner of his right eye, he caught a glimpse of the front doors and held it.

She must've realised he'd found the equivalent of a window to stare out of, for she shifted her weight just enough to block it. "Avis," she crooned, stroking his cheeks and throat. "Was it just you?"

Avis knew the answer was no, but he didn't want her to know that about the others. Theodrick hadn't just done the deed himself. He had forced them to pair off while he watched. The only small mercy they ever received while in the Nexus was their father had never allowed the women to change their biological status by falling pregnant.

She gently pulled his head forward to rest on her shoulder, at which point he closed his eyes and focused on breathing in as much of her calming scent as he could manage. "Beloved, you are strong in so many ways," she crooned, stroking his hair and massaging the back of his neck. "But this is not one of them. We are in this together for all eternity. I may be a Highborn Lady, but I am also the second born mistress of all Chaos. Hear my words when I say I will not permit you to deal with this alone anymore."

"I-I have the others …" he tried to argue.

"Avis, you cannot even bring yourself to look at me while I am restraining you to discuss this. You and I both know there has never been a time where you and your siblings have willingly sat down and discussed this in the hopes of getting past it."

"Why dwell on bad memories?" he asked, shaking his head against her shoulder. "We endured it and we survived. Reliving it isn't going to solve anything."

"No one is asking you to internalise and relive it, beloved. But pretending it didn't happen is almost as bad. It gives the memory the power to cripple you when it does choose to make an appearance."

Avis lifted his head and stubbornly shook it, making sure she saw his eyes as he made his stand. "I don't want to do this."

The gold in her eyes liquefied indulgently and she lightly pressed her lips against his. "I know, beloved. Just like I did not want to tell you about Charon, and you did not want to discipline Columbine earlier this week. Sometimes, for your own good and the good of others, you just need to do them anyway." She ran her fingers through his hair, softly scratching her nails against his scalp. "Trust me."

Avis did, with all his heart. But he had one last condition before they proceeded. "Promise me, if it goes too far, you'll tell me. I won't even start if I don't have your word on that."

Clarise kissed him passionately. "Absolutely," she said in a breathless whisper against his lips.

And so, for the next few hours, Avis poured it all out for her. All of it. Both what had been done to him, and what he'd been forced to do to the others. Every word he spoke, he watched her face, searching for any hint that he needed to stop. Her expression never changed, except to grow more sympathetic.

By the end, he'd expected to feel guilt-ridden. After all, the horrors of what he'd been through should never have been shared with another, especially someone who meant everything to him. But she'd stayed strong, and when he'd talked himself out, he felt ... lighter. He'd never considered those childhood memories to be a burden before. They were just something in the background to ignore. But now that he'd shared his past, he could see the effort it took to ignore them had been enormous.

"And that's why your thrall is so determined to keep you in charge at all costs," she said, nodding with new understanding. Avis hitched one shoulder a fraction, unable to deny it. She leaned back in his lap, placing her hands on his shoulders. "Well, now that I know all of that, I will know which triggers of yours to avoid in the future."

"I have triggers?" he asked, not realising he'd been so transparent in the past.

She kissed him again. "Oh, yes," she assured him with a secretive smile. "And tells that lead into them. But as of now you will not be dealing with them alone. I will redirect conversations as required to keep anyone else from seeing them."

Avis then thought about the look she'd sent him at the dinner table. Did YHWH have triggers too? Going back through his memories, he watched YHWH chew on his thumbnail and realised that yes, the boy most certainly did have tells, and his clever and beautiful wife had spotted them. Which meant she could've spotted something about himself that he didn't know about too. He stared up at her, waiting for her to explain herself, and when she didn't, he pouted. "You're really not going to tell me what they are, are you?"

"Not in the foreseeable future," she cooed, releasing him and stepping away from the chair towards their apartment. Her hips swayed suggestively as she moved, but she didn't look back at him until she reached the doors and opened them. "YHWH informed us of your concession to permit the family to stay here," she said, meeting his eyes with a sultry look. "Knowing how much you despise the angels, you should know I appreciate your benevolence almost as much as your honesty with me tonight." Her fingers danced across the edge of the door. "Are you coming?"

Avis was too miffed by her refusal to tell him what his tics were. He didn't think he had any, but if he had, even contrived ones, she should've told him what they were. It wasn't the first time she'd mentioned them. "In a minute," he replied, not wanting to be known as the god who was led by his dick.

Her left eyebrow arched into her hairline at his refusal and her beautiful lips pinched to one side in amusement. "Keeping me waiting will cost you, handsome," she purred in an unspoken promise, then sashayed through the doors and closed them behind her.

Avis was out of his seat and half way down the table before he caught himself. The voice in his head called him every sort of idiot for choosing now to make a point when sex would be the cost, but she hadn't said it wouldn't happen, only that it would cost him. He could think of plenty of fun ways in which that could be interpreted, and with a playful smile of his own, he made a point of going out the front doors instead.

* * *

Contrary to the way she had acted, as soon as there was a closed door between her and her husband, Clarise fell to her hands and knees and emptied her stomach onto the plush carpet. Avis had told her everything, and with each new horror, she had wanted to run into their bedroom and cover her head with as many pillows as she could find. But he'd needed her to be strong. It was clearly the first time he'd ever spoken of it outside the Nexus, and she knew if she broke now, he'd never mention it again. So, after sealing Cora's apartment doors to prevent any unwanted visitors, she drew on every nuance of her celestial birthright and kept herself physically cool, calm and non-judgemental; all the while her mind screamed and clawed for it to end inside her own physically numbed body.

She knew what would've happened if she told Avis she needed ten minutes alone to process it all. He'd have panicked, blaming himself for listening to her when in his mind he should've known better. So she deliberately provoked him with knowledge of his tells, then followed it up with a sexual dare, knowing her husband would resist coming straight in after her, without ever realising that delay was what she wanted in the first place.

"Milady!" Tilu cried, rushing across the room to kneel at her side.

Clarise ignored her, her mind swimming with all that Avis had told her. How could a father do that? To innocent children? His *own* children? Abused, in every way imaginable. Her father was by no means a gentle being, but punishment had to be earned, not dispensed for enjoyment and the thrill of control. No wonder Avis had lost his mind at the thought of seeing Columbine naked. Just the thought of it, after what he and his siblings had been through ...

She made a mental note to uphold what she'd originally thought was a foolish Mystallian tradition of bathing without family unless it was with a spouse. It had never occurred to her that the reason for this strange view was because of how they'd been raised. They were only safe in their bathrooms if they bathed quickly and alone. If one or more family members were brought in, it was for nefarious purposes, which made bathing alone a highly sought-after rarity.

When her stomach was empty, she dry heaved; her vision blurred by tears which streamed down her cheeks. Her husband's family was so strong. Everyone except her father feared the Mystallians. But that strength hadn't been brokered the way it was in Hell. Her family paraded their presence wherever they went, almost daring anyone to challenge them. By contrast, the Mystallians had clawed their way out of the filth of their existence to make something of themselves on their own. Pride may be at their core now but it hadn't been in the beginning. They worked as a team, leaning on each other during their moments of weakness. No other pantheon in existence had that unshakable foundation. A unity so powerful it drew lesser benders to them like a moth to a flame.

Clarise felt herself being lifted under the arms and guided through the rooms into the ensuite. "A bath will help, milady," Tilu assured her, already extending multiple limbs to pour the water, add the perfumed soaps and light the small row of tealight candles. Other hands went to relieve Clarise of her uniform, and in that instant, Clarise *became* a Mystallian. Snapping back to the present by the mere touch, she caught two of Tilu's hands by the wrists.

"A bath will," she agreed with ice in her tone despite the blubbering, vomiting mess she'd been moments earlier. "But if you ever attempt to remove my Mystallian uniform without permission again, you will never have the capacity to *possess* hands again either. Am I quite clear?" Clarise had never been more serious in her life. Avis' explanation went a long way to helping her understand the Mystallian need for owning the space instead of allowing another to own it for them, and as of this moment she would uphold that view until her dying day.

Extending her arms, Tilu dropped to her knees and pressed her forehead to the ground between Clarise's booted feet, relinquishing all control of her hands to her lady's whim. "Forgive me, mistress," she begged.

Clarise released her hands and began removing her cloak. "I will speak no more of it; however the forfeiture will remain in place indefinitely. Do not forget."

Tilu rose to her knees, her head and shoulders rolled forward in ongoing supplication. "As you wish, milady."

"Go. Clean up the mess in the sitting room. Leave me to my bath."

"Your will, milady," the servant shifted her body to have hundreds of legs, not unlike Diviten and Gingen, which allowed her to scurry backwards without standing up.

After the door had closed, Clarise looked around the bathroom, picturing what it must have been like for her husband as a child. According to him, something as simple as having a bath was an act of unmitigated terror, for they were more inclined to be attacked if they were naked. It showed just how determined Avis and his siblings were to take control of their own lives, that they could now bathe without panicking or even rushing the process. At some point, bathing had become pleasurable again for them.

She had never had to worry about that before. Shifters didn't believe in keeping the bloodlines pure. Like everything, it seemed, their views were the complete opposite. Outside blood was mandatory for any type of union to take place, and since only family had ranged shifting, no outsider was a threat to them.

Licking her teeth, Clarise grimaced on the horrible taste the vomit had left in her mouth and immediately shifted it clean. Avis wouldn't be far away. Despite his determination to do things his way, she'd seen his interest before he tried to quell it and knew sooner rather than later, he'd be joining her.

He may not have realised it yet, but what he'd achieved tonight was incredible. She hadn't expected him to be quite so forthcoming, but because he had been she felt more connected to him than anyone else alive. Perhaps even his own twin. He deserved a reward for all that honesty. A very special reward. One only she, as his wife would be permitted to give him. With a growing predatory smile, she knew just what to do.

CHAPTER FORTY-FOUR

Walking around the perimeter with a hard-on hadn't been as easy as it sounded, but Avis refused to go back inside until he had some semblance of control over himself.

As such, he was a little surprised to hear the front doors open a few minutes later. That was, until he saw YHWH making his way across the lawn towards him. The kid didn't look at him, but rather focused on the cherubim that stood before them in two straight lines. "I'm sorry, Avis," he said when he finally stood alongside him.

Avis was about to ask, 'for what?' but then remembered YHWH's powerbase allowed him to hear and see everything across the realm at once. Well, that certainly took care of his erection. He hadn't anticipated an audience when he emptied his spleen to Clarise. "You weren't meant to be a part of that," he said.

YHWH nodded softly in agreement. "I know. It's not going to mean much in consolation, but angels were sent in to try and save you."

Avis jerked his head to YHWH. "What?"

"All of those angels that were trapped under Theodrick's throne room weren't there to spread the views of Heaven. They were on a mission to get you and your siblings out of the Nexus, any way they could. A mission that was doomed to failure, but they were willing to try anyway."

"And just how the fuck did they even know we were there?"

YHWH looked a little guilty. "One or two of them may have stumbled into the crystal realm and reported back that Theodrick and Belladonna had birthed multiple children before they were silenced. Given Theodrick's propensity for keeping his bloodline pure and how much he hated watching his children grow up, I had a better idea than most about what he was doing to you all in the meantime, and I shared that knowledge with the choirs." He gave a tiny nod towards the mansion. "Hearing in your own words somehow makes it even worse, and it breaks my heart to know you all suffered like that."

Avis internalised for a few minutes, skimming back over the conversation he'd had with Clarise. He was pretty damned sure he hadn't mentioned the location of the imprisoned angels, and once that was confirmed, he returned to the physical realm and scowled. "I never said the angels were kept under Theodrick's throne room."

YHWH lifted his chin and sighed. "I'm not your enemy, Avis. I never was. If you and the others had made it to Heaven back then, I would've taken you all in. I'd hoped you'd come. Inasmuch as one of our kind can pray, I wanted to show you just how different things could be away from the Nexus. But subconsciously, you already knew that. It's why you took Chance before he was molested and escaped with everyone. You knew there was a better life waiting for you out here."

"If you knew all that, why didn't your precious Almighty bring us here as soon as we got out?"

For a moment, YHWH pressed his lips together. "I wasn't about to force you to do anything, brother. You'd all had enough of that already. You were finally free, and you were making your own way. I could respect that. But it didn't stop me from sending angels to keep an eye on you until you were established."

"So, you've been spying on us all this time?"

YHWH shook his head. "No. Once you became established, you made it impossible for the angels to visit, let alone live long enough to report back their findings. But before then, yes, I—watched from afar. It's …. kind of what I do."

"In other words, the Third Choir are supervisors, orchestrating what the rest of the realm does like a maestro."

"Somebody needs to be in charge," YHWH said, with a mocking smirk.

"I'm beginning to think your Almighty is one of the laziest pricks in existence."

That wiped the smile off YHWH's face and he slowly tilted his head towards the Mystallian. "How so?" he asked, with more than a little bite to his words.

Avis grinned, not surprised in the least by the angel's sudden defensiveness. Every warrior in Mystal would've had a much more violent reaction to an outsider speaking badly of him too. Nevertheless, he raised his left hand and waved at the realm around them. "He's got everyone doing everything for him. And I mean *everything*. He even leaves the day to day running of the place to you angels. At this rate, I'm surprised he even knows how to roll out of bed without a dozen of you pushing against his back."

As quickly as it came, the iciness in YHWH's features vanished and he chuckled lightly to himself. "Some days, it can certainly feel that way," he admitted ruefully. He then looked out over the realm once more. "Both Cora and Columbine are asleep in Cora's room and I fixed the hole they put between their rooms, but knowing them, they'll put it back just as soon as they notice. They're really tired, so I doubt they'll be up until after lunch."

"Why are you telling me this?"

YHWH's grin grew vivacious. "You'll figure it out soon enough," he answered with a quick waggle of his eyebrows. Then he flicked his left hand in a shoulder-high farewell and started off towards the double line of cherubim. "I'm the last person to fall for the seven deadly sins, but if I ever did, I'd be envious of you right about now …"

"Wait," Avis called after him. YHWH stopped and turned back. "Do you actually sleep?"

YHWH shrugged, self-consciously. "I haven't tried in a really long time. Why?"

Avis considered what he was about to say. The concession he was mulling over wasn't one he ever thought he'd offer an angel. "If you keep behaving yourself, that spare apartment at the end of the house is yours for the duration of our stay. Just because your thrall keeps you on top of everything that's happening within the realm, doesn't mean you can't sleep. Culkin knows everything that's going on in Mystal too, but he still gets his eight hours a night on average, same as the rest of us. I think you're just too scared to try."

As Avis thought, YHWH looked between him and the building and back again as if torn between wanting to attempt it, and concern that he might actually succeed. Since he didn't seem to be able to make up his mind, Avis, in his usual, diplomatic fashion, decided for him. "Get your ass back in the house, YHWH. I'll see you after lunch."

Avis watched as the boy's eyes rounded in shock, but then happiness exuded from him and he tore across the lawn with a high-pitched howl of delight. The way he caught the architrave of the door and swung tightly to his left, had Avis chuckling to himself. This felt right, and if the narcissistic Almighty loser with a stick up his ass had a problem with him kidnapping one of his angels for a couple of weeks, the vindictive prick could spin on it. Or roll his ass on out here to take it up with him. Avis didn't care which.

Enjoying the peace that settled over him, Avis followed in YHWH's wake, pausing just long enough in the doorway to be sure the doors to YHWH's apartment were firmly closed. Then he moved onto his own apartment at the other end of the house.

As he walked in, Tilu was kneeling in the sitting room. When she saw him, she pressed her forehead to the ground. Avis noted the unusual level of subservience and wondered what the female had done to aggravate his wife. Clearly something substantial, but until Clarise brought it up with him, he decided to leave it alone and carried on into the bedroom. Still no sign of Clarise. He paused beside the foot of the bed with his hand on the bedpost, his eyes searching again and again for her. *Nope, definitely not in here.*

And with the bedroom ruled out, that left only one space. His gaze settled on the closed ensuite doors. "Come out, come out," he whispered slyly to himself, eating up the distance in four large strides. His hand found the door handle but then he paused to consider his options. Should he try the sneaky approach and take her by surprise, or simply burst in on her?

Not wanting to scare her and ruin the moment, Avis carefully opened the door. It pleased him to find waves of steam coming off a freshly drawn bath (which in turn caused condensation to form along the walls) and a full decanter of ambrosia waiting on the bath's edge. Everything was just as he wanted to see it, minus what mattered most to him. Still, she was definitely in here somewhere. Hiding. The glorious aroma of her lavender, blending seamlessly with his own preferred scent of fresh pine betrayed her presence. To the best of his ability, he tried not to make his search of the room obvious as he began stripping off his clothes. The real challenge came with the removal of his pants and boots. The heightened anticipation along with the thrill of the hunt had him fully aroused once more, making any contact with that region almost too painful to bear. The boots he gave up on as a lost cause and used his toes on the heels to hook them off instead.

But he still couldn't find her. *What are you up to, sweetheart ...?* He couldn't help but wonder as he stepped into the bath and sat down on the bench seat, still pretending not to know she was there. He was a man who learned from his mistakes, and the last time she'd been this playful in the bathroom, he'd ruined her game. Not this time.

Allowing the heat to permeate his skin and soak into his muscles, Avis eventually closed his eyes and tilted his head back with a heartfelt sigh. It had been a *really* long day.

That was when he felt movement around his feet as first the water, and then a solid mass slid across his body. Avis' eyes flew open and he surged forward, only to find himself lip-locked with the most beautiful woman in creation. His fingers sifted through her hair of their own accord, while her arms wrapped around his chest and shoulders. "Trust me," he heard her words whisper seductively in the air, though her lips were still most definitely busy.

As focused as he was on kissing her, he couldn't help but notice he was being dragged to the edge of the seat. Doubting that she planned on standing up, Avis' first instinct was to grab the tub's edge to avoid the imminent dunking, and he'd be a liar if he said his fingers didn't flex with that need. But she had asked him to trust her, and after the number of times he'd said he'd willingly walk into hellfire for her, a bath filled with water wasn't that much to ask. Placing total trust in her, he wrapped his legs around hers and maintained his hold on her head, relinquishing any ability to resist.

In a single, effortless heave she dragged him off the seat and laid him across the bottom of the bath.

Air was then puffed into his mouth, which Avis inhaled with a gasp and breathed out his nose in a flurry of bubbles. Then another. He watched in fascination as her hair drifted softly in the water around them. High on adrenaline, he was not asking stupid questions like how she was breathing underwater for them. He'd had sex in a lot of strange places in his long life, especially in a bathroom, but weightlessly at the bottom of his own bath while his wife breathed for them both was something he'd never envisioned doing.

And he planned to make the most of it.

CHAPTER FORTY-FIVE

As was his habit, Avis woke early the following morning and after getting dressed, he made his rounds of the house, starting with Columbine. He let himself through her sitting room and into her bedroom, only to find the bed, and the whole room in general, untouched. Dread flooded his body as he rushed into the ensuite. There was no logical reason for why Columbine would be asleep in the bathroom, but it was the only room in the apartment he hadn't checked.

Nothing. Not even the brute squad guard. In a way, that latter took the edge off his panic, for wherever she was, she must've had her bodyguard with her. His eyes swept across the room faster than his mind could process—but when his brain caught up with what he'd seen, his vision returned to the filled-in spot where the girls had previously built their tunnel.

Which reminded him of the conversation he'd had with YHWH about blocking the hole, which in turn led to the earlier part where YHWH had said they were both asleep in Cora's room. Releasing the breath he was holding, Avis doubled over and braced his hands against his thighs. By the Twin Notes, he hated Heaven! Anywhere else, and a single look into his familial link would've told him exactly where they were!

Backtracking out of the empty apartment, he went through Cora's apartment and let himself into her bedroom. There he found both his daughters asleep, just as YHWH had said. Furniture had been moved to accommodate a second large bed adjacent to Cora's, which was something Avis hadn't even thought of at the time. Cora was a violent little shit when she slept in her Mystallian form, and no one who wanted to remain unharmed would share her bed for longer than a few minutes. It went to show just how tired Columbine was, that neither the heavy drone of Cora's snores, nor the destruction of her head and foot boards was sufficient to wake her.

Avis ducked into Cora's mind; not for any specific reason, just to run his eye over what they'd been up to while he and Clarise had been busy. It seemed Cora preferred to juggle fireballs over learning the intricacies of the spinning disc, whereas Columbine spent hours with the stringed toy. YHWH had challenged them both. When Cora had ten fireballs in the air, he began showing her alternating patterns that broke the steady rhythm she maintained. Simple things first, like snatching balls at random and throwing them sideways through the regular rotation, but ending with a sequence that looked horribly uncoordinated yet still kept everything off the ground. The mental discipline it took to keep everything under control in the face of such chaos was impressive.

Likewise, Columbine was being shown more and more complex tricks for her spinning disc. YHWH was patient. Even watching through the eyes of his other daughter, Avis could see simple mistakes she was making that would've had him losing his temper at her, but YHWH took it all in his stride. Not surprising, he supposed, when the Almighty leaned so heavily on him and his brethren to run the whole fucking realm in his stead. Realm-damned, lazy prick. Compared to that responsibility, babysitting two visiting kids would've been a finger snap.

After the girls were worn out, each of their governesses took them one at a time into Cora's ensuite for a bath. Then they were readied for bed. YHWH sat between them on Cora's bed with his back against the headboard. The girls sat on either side of him, leaning into his upper arms. His hands were open on his lap as if he were reading from a book, only instead of pages, a scene silently climbed off his hands to become a living story where he supplied all the vocals—both male and female voices, narration and subsequent sound effects. Somehow, (the realms only knew how) his story engaged the girls, reaching Cora on an adult level while appealing to Columbine's youthful naivety. They found different things to laugh at and were thoroughly enjoying themselves. As time went on, Cora's eyes began to sag and the words rolled together, leading into the clouded vision of her dreams where she played the primary role in YHWH's fanciful story.

Since the girls were asleep in two separate beds, Avis assumed that YHWH had arranged for them to stay within Cora's apartment, which led to the second bed being readied for Columbine.

As Cora was still in the midst of her dream, Avis backed out of her mind to allow it to continue. He saw the stooped poses of the two governesses in opposite corners of the room and withdrew from the room without a word to them. Columbine would know if he went poking around inside her mind, and while he would if he needed to, he had all the answers he was after from Cora. Getting another rendition of the same memories from Columbine's point of view was a pointless exercise to him.

Much happier now that he'd seen for himself what the girls had been up to, Avis made his way over to YHWH's apartment. Outwardly, the boy was a pubescant who appeared to need sleep almost as much as the girls, but after everything they'd been through, Avis knew that apparent age was an outright lie. He was a lot older. Older than Avis it seemed, and he was fucking ancient.

Which meant there was a very real chance that the kid was awake and he wouldn't be disturbing him at all.

Convinced of that probability, Avis rapped a single knuckle once against the double doors, and quietly let himself in a few seconds later when no one answered. Had he found YHWH asleep in the sitting room, he'd have backed out and let him be. But with no assigned servant to answer the door on his behalf, the Mystallian was confident that he'd be either in the bedroom or the bathroom beyond and thus unable to hear him.

His thoughts of YHWH's whereabouts were confirmed when he repeated his succinct knock on the bedroom doors and was told to come in.

YHWH sat cross-legged on the bed that didn't look as if it had been slept in.

"I thought I told you to get some sleep," Avis grizzled, unable to help himself.

YHWH looked up at him and smiled. It wasn't the childish one from yesterday or even last night. There was a stronger hint of maturity creeping into his expression. "I know, and while I truly appreciate the offer, there's absolutely zero chance of me falling asleep while you, Clarise and the girls are in the realm. Even while you're all sleeping, I'm savouring every moment of your presence to carry me through the times when you're not here."

Avis crossed the room until he stood by the foot of the bed, where he folded his arms and rested his hip and shoulder against the bedpost. "Why does this mean so much to you?"

Some of the levity left YHWH's eyes. "As you can imagine, my childhood wasn't a good one either, Avis. It's not something I particularly want to rehash any more than you did, but it's there, nonetheless. I was an only child, so there was no one else to share the brunt of Father's wrath. As such, it never stopped. Not once, and I was in danger of losing my mind for good. I only got out because of the courtiers who could see I wasn't going to make it much longer and intervened on my behalf. Choirmaster Raphael was one of those original courtiers, and I will be forever grateful for their timely assistance."

Avis tried to imagine what it would've been like if he'd been Theodrick and Belladonna's only child and shuddered uncontrollably. "Be grateful you didn't have my father," he said in commiseration as he slid down the bedpost to sit on the corner of the mattress. "Though it sounds like yours was just as big a piece of shit."

"Amen to that, brother."

Avis stiffened and leaned forward to snarl, but YHWH held up a hand in an unspoken apology, so he relaxed against the bedpost once more. "That bullshit aside, I still don't get why you're so fixated on us. What makes us so special?"

"Because you mean almost everything to me."

"But why, dammit?"

YHWH twisted his lips to one side and shook his head. "I have answered this many, many times over the last week, Avis. I'm not joking, and I'm not lying when I say we are brothers. But you won't have it. Even if I were to use superior bending on you right now to force you to believe me, it still wouldn't convince you, because I can see you've already accredited my mental superiority to my powerbase. And without using force to change your mind, there's nothing I can do to prove myself to you."

"You'd prove it fast enough if you stepped outside the realm." The answer was obvious. If YHWH left the realm, he'd be without his powerbase and he'd have to accept they weren't kin. Avis knew even before YHWH shook his head in denial that he'd never agree to that. Having convinced himself of the lie, YHWH didn't want to be proven wrong.

"I can't," the angel said, his eyes taking on a nervous gleam. "I-I … no. I won't go out there." YHWH shook his head more adamantly. "No."

Avis wasn't impressed. "So, you had a crappy childhood without any siblings, and when you heard I had a similarly crappy upbringing, you've somehow given your existence some kind of validation by deluding yourself into thinking you and I are all one big happy family."

YHWH closed his eyes and covered them with his hand. "How in Heaven's name can you be so right, yet so wrong at the same time?" he asked rhetorically, pinching the bridge of his nose. Then he dropped his hand and stared at Avis. "Yes, I've waited a long time to meet any of you. I've made no secret of that. But I never thought …" He paused and shook his head, ending it with his face pointed to the left where the rest of the family slept peacefully. "What you have is truly special, Avis. Do whatever it takes to hang onto it with both hands because it's real. Clarise loves you so much it almost hurts to look at her sometimes, and Columbine's only a hair's breadth behind her; in her own childlike way. Even Cora has come around, for the most part."

Despite his complimentary words, when YHWH turned back, there was such disapproval in his eyes that Avis almost pulled away. Almost. "Have you even acknowledged the stand she took against the Asgardians to be with you?"

Given his parental overtone, YHWH had to already know the answer, so Avis didn't dignify it with a response. But that didn't stop him from jumping ahead and seeing where this was going. Cora had made a monumental decision, and he'd been so desperate to get them all out of Asgard before Odin could retaliate, that he hadn't so much as acknowledged it. Then, once they arrived in Heaven, he'd been just as distracted with what he thought was the end of his marriage. It was no excuse, and once again he felt like a failure as a parent.

"The thing about children, it's never too late to make it up to them, Avis," YHWH said as if reading his thoughts. "You just have to keep trying."

"I have no intention of quitting," Avis growled, most assuredly.

YHWH's smile was sympathetic. "You and I both know that, but she doesn't and she's the priority here. Despite her adult perceptions, she's still just a little girl who wants to matter to her parents. It sounds so simple when I say it aloud, but you are fumbling the ball something fierce when it comes to her. And I'm not even talking about the way you constantly favour Columbine over her. She thinks she understands that, because everyone loves Columbine more than her, so why would you be any different?"

Avis bristled. "Now, hold on …"

YHWH held up a finger. "No, Avis. *You* hold on. I'm not saying you have to pander to Cora the way you do Columbine. If anything, she'd probably head-butt you for trying. But she still needs you to throw her a bone from time to time to show her you care. Now that you've agreed to stay here for a few weeks, why don't you take the time to get to know her, just like you would any other Mystallian? It's not like it was back on the Akheron River, where you had nothing at your disposal. Here, you can and will be supplied with anything you could ever want or need. Anything at all. You've already learned she can kick your ass in chess, so see what else you two can bond over. Find something, Avis. She's been reaching out for you for too long, and if you don't start reaching back soon, she's going to pull her hand back and be done with you again."

Avis lifted his eyes to the bed's canopy behind and above YHWH's head, his mind going back to just before the Asgardians turned up. Things between Cora and him had almost been at a breaking point, and if the Asgardians hadn't turned up and forced her hand, would she even be wearing the Mystallian uniform? Probably not. And since then, what had he done to welcome her into the family? Not a damned thing. He'd treated the most important decision of her young life like it was a non-event. Like *she* was a non-event. *Fucking hell!* He took a deep breath and raked the fingers of one hand through his hair, ending with them wrapped around the back of his neck. How in the realms was he going to make up for that?

"It's never too late to try," YHWH repeated, his eyes shining with conviction. "And now, you have plenty of time."

Avis' gaze narrowed as something occurred to him and he dropped his hand to the mattress. "So was it for you that you wanted us to stay the extra time socialising, or me?"

YHWH smirked. "What makes you think I'm limited to one reason?" His smirk then dimmed. "The truth is, ever since you arrived in Heaven, I have sensed the fractures within your family. Columbine has too. You were all on a dark path that would've ended in your family shattering irrevocably. If Clarise didn't tell you about her son, sooner or later, you'd have blamed someone else for supposedly catching her eye. Same goes for the way you refused to share your past with Clarise. That made her feel unworthy of being your wife because you didn't trust her with that knowledge. Cora's seen the tension between you two and assumed the worst, reinforcing her position with Columbine as someone her little sister can rely on, no matter what happens between you and Clarise. In effect, she's making herself Columbine's foundation and has prepared herself to bear the brunt of her sister's fall should your marriage to their mother collapse. She's six years old, Avis, and she's setting herself up as the primary caregiver for her younger sister. Do you have any idea how asinine that is?" YHWH waved haphazardly at the bedroom alongside his. "I've just spent half the night reminding her what it means to be a little girl, because she hasn't behaved like one in so long it's heartbreaking." He rolled his hand and stabbed the mattress with each of his next words. "And you. Haven't. Noticed."

"Alright, alright," Avis lifted a hand and waved the reprimand aside. "Enough, already. I don't know how to raise kids. I never said I did."

"No one's asking you to be an expert, Avis. But when someone who knows a little bit more about things offers you advice, you should get your head out of your ass and listen."

Avis's shoulders squared, though he leaned back into the bedpost, trying to work out how he wanted to react to that. Ripping YHWH's head off his shoulders and punting it to Asgard took positions one to twenty on his list of responses. Positions twenty-one to twenty-seven accepted the fact that the little bastard had a point. Twenty-eight and twenty-nine argued that he didn't need to do anything on principle, and only number thirty tried to convince him that he could use YHWH's help.

"A speechless Avis," YHWH drawled in amusement. "Did the other eight levels of Hell freeze over when I wasn't looking?"

"Oh, shut up, pipsqueak." Avis went to stand up again when something YHWH had said a while back flashed through his mind. "No, actually," he said with a frown, sliding back into his seat again. "Keep talking. You said ever since we arrived in Heaven you've been watching us. Since you see and hear everything all the time, how the fuck did we end up here?" It was something that still bothered him. 'The will of the gods' was what mortals said about them when it came to explaining the unexplainable. Everything in the celestial realm made sense, even if the answer was 'powerbase and thrall'. The thing about those two, they didn't work outside any given realm. For their transportation to be power based, the two realms would've had to have their respective gods meet at the border and pass Avis, his family *and their home* from one to the other and return to the pearlescent wall. Surely, the third choir overseer who missed nothing would've noticed that!

YHWH braced his elbows against his knees and pressed his fingertips into a steeple which he rested against his lips. "Now, that is a really interesting question," he admitted, after a lengthy pause, which meant at least Avis and the wingless wonder agreed on something.

"Interesting enough to tell me the answer?"

"Your house just appeared at the base of the pearlescent wall in all its glory, including the lawn and the security dome, in barely a fraction of an instant. It took the Sixth Choir longer to realise it was even there, and then, just as they flared their wings in response, you and your family appeared inside it." He pursed his lips and shook his head, parting his hands to scratch one eyebrow. "I completely freaked, Avis. I won't pretend I didn't. Something that big just … magically appearing that far inside Heaven's boundaries? Like you said. I'm supposed to hear and see everything, but someone put a freaking house inside my realm and to this day, I still have no idea who or how."

Avis thought about what he heard. "So we *were* moved …"

YHWH frowned. "Of course you were. This isn't Asgard. The moment you and your family arrived, I recognised you all and at that point, I didn't care who brought you to me. Nothing was going to stop me from meeting you after that." He cocked his other eyebrow. "Not even you, you stubborn pain in the butt." He dropped his hands into his lap. "Honestly, would it have killed you to just come inside and say hello?"

"And what does your Almighty have to say about all of this? I'd be losing my shit if someone dropped a domed house inside Mystallian territory with no clue as to how it got there or who brought it in."

YHWH opened his mouth to answer, but then a look of disappointment flashed across his face and he closed it again. "You'll figure it out soon enough," he said, then he rose to his knees and began shuffling to the edge of the bed. "The girls are up and on the move. I'll keep Columbine company while you see to Cora. That little girl's unique take on things is rather … refreshing."

"Agreed," Avis replied, rising to his feet. "Don't screw this up, YHWH."

"I never do."

Arrogant little shit, Avis thought to himself as they strode through YHWH's apartment and over to Cora's. Unlike his visit to YHWH's rooms, he let himself in without knocking and started across the sitting room. About halfway, the bedroom doors flew open and Columbine barrelled through, racing towards them. Avis automatically dropped to one knee with his arms outstretched and caught her around the waist. "Morning, Father!" she squealed, snapping her arms around his neck and squeezing.

"Morning to you too, princess," he returned her hug and lifted her off her feet, settling her to his right hip, where he supported her back with one hand and brushed her unbraided fringe out of her face with the other. She might've been dressed in her uniform, but the glossy locks that travelled past her backside showed her hair hadn't been styled yet.

That fact was confirmed when Diviten appeared moments later with a dozen brushes in many of her hands. The servant took one look at her ward in the safety of her father's arms and retreated with a bowed head to the bedroom.

Avis refocused on his daughter. "Did you sleep well?"

"Mmm-hmmm," she giggled, resting her head against his neck. "Would you like to see the disc tricks Uncle YHWH showed me last night? I learned lots and lots of new tricks!"

As much as Avis wanted to be excited for her, most of his happiness evaporated at the family designation she'd bestowed on YHWH and he turned to glare scathingly at the young angel who stood a short distance behind him.

Contrary to showing any remorse, YHWH smirked and shrugged. "That was her choice, Avis. She's not as pig-headed as you."

Avis gaze narrowed further, but determined to sort this mess out once and for all, he carried Columbine to one of the two high back lounge chairs that faced the fire and sat down. "Princess, you need to understand YHWH is working under a thrall. He's not really your uncle."

Columbine pushed herself out to arm's length; her tiny brows scrunching in confusion as she looked between them. "But ... he is ..." she insisted.

"No, baby. He isn't. His thrall is making him and everyone else think he is." Columbine's frown deepened and her bottom lip began to tremble. "It's not a bad thing," he quickly went on, before she turned on the waterworks that always destroyed him. "His thrall is making everyone think he's one of our family. But it's not real."

"But ... it is ..."

YHWH's brief snicker in the background did NOT help matters though of the two battlefronts, his priority was Columbine. "No, princess. It isn't."

"But ..."

Avis placed his finger over her lips. "No, Columbine. It isn't. It's his thrall. You've never seen a thrall in action, so you don't know how convincing it can be."

Columbine looked past him to where YHWH stood, and Avis could practically feel her silently begging him to intercede. Avis placed his hand on her jaw and brought her face back to him. "Look at me, princess. I'm the one talking to you. YHWH has a powerbase, just like your Uncle Uriel and some of the other angels in this realm. Do you understand that?"

Her head bobbed. "Yes, Father."

"And like all powerbases, there is a thrall that goes along with it. In this case, those angels see everyone as their brother or sister, just like the angelic constructs of this realm."

"But he is *Uncle* YHWH." She blinked in confusion, causing a tear to escape her right eye. Right on cue, his heart clenched in his chest.

Wiping her tear away, he pulled her into his chest and kissed her brow. "Okay, how about we do it this way, then. What if, for the duration of our stay, I'll let you call him 'uncle' YHWH," —he didn't appreciate how readily she nodded to that— "But that title isn't because he's blood, but because he's an older friend of the family."

Columbine frowned again. "So 'uncles' are not always uncles?"

Avis nodded. "Exactly."

"And 'aunts' are not always aunts?"

Avis made himself follow her logic. "I suppose," he said slowly, wondering where she was going with this.

"Then how many fathers do I have?"

"ONE!" Avis couldn't emphasise that quickly enough, even if in hindsight, that wasn't exactly accurate. As Belial had anointed her at birth, she technically had two, but he would never let her think that. Never. It was him, and only him. Belial was her grandfather.

Columbine gasped, but he quickly rubbed her shoulders and forced himself to think (thereby leading into feeling) pleasant things until she settled again. "Why would you think you have more than one father?" he asked.

"One real one, and lots of older friends of the family who are men."

"No, that's what false 'uncles' are called."

"Do I have any false mothers?"

Avis couldn't believe how horribly this supposedly straight forward discussion was going. It seemed he wasn't the only one.

"Now I know what it looks like to watch a mortal world fighting the gravitational pull of a black hole," YHWH mused, patting Avis' arm just below the shoulder. "Quit while you're behind, brother. You won't win this."

Fuck you! Avis decided to try a different angle. Quitting wasn't in his vocabulary. "You know how we have our family. Our *real* family." He repeated that last part for emphasis.

"Yes, Father."

"Well, sometimes, we have friends who mean so much to us that we wished they were family, even though they're not. Does that make sense?"

"Like Diviten and Gingen and Tilu?"

Avis rubbed his left temple. "No ... not like them. They're servants. Underlings. They take their orders from us, princess."

"So, I can't be friends with them?"

"You may be friendly with them if you wish, but no, they can never *be* your friends. There's a big difference. They have no rights or expectations where you're concerned. Your every whim is their life."

The muscle under Columbine's right eye spasmed, and he realised he'd slipped back into the habit of using adult words and connotations. He sighed and looked into the crackling fire for both inspiration and patience, knowing he had neither. "Okay. When you were in the Well of Hell and a servant was naughty, what happened to that servant?"

Columbine brightened, finally having an answer. "They went away and did not come back."

Well, that still didn't help Avis' cause in the slightest. Closing his eyes, he took a deep breath and mentally counted to ten. As a Highborn Hellion girl-child, he should've known they'd have raised her to see a subordinate's execution like that. "That's ... true," he agreed, searching fruitlessly for another way to make her understand. "But we're getting way off track here. What I'm trying to say is that a powerbase thrall will make things that are wrong, appear right."

Columbine frowned again. "So ... powerbases are wrong?"

"No!...no," he repeated, lowering his voice so as not to frighten her again. "Powerbases are very right. It's the thrall of a powerbase that can sometimes be wrong. It makes you think things are right when they're not."

By this stage, Columbine's bottom lip began to tremble and unshed tears gleamed in her eyes.

Avis was the one who now frowned in confusion. "What are the tears for, princess?"

"Can you not stop a thrall?"

"Not once it's in place, Columbine. It's almost impossible. Why?"

"Because I do not want you to think you are right when you are wrong, Father." *Wait … "What?"*

"Your thrall is making you think Uncle YHWH is not family when he is."

Avis' eyes shot open faster than his mouth, but thankfully, his tongue didn't react as quickly … or at all. For the first time in his long life, he was stunned speechless. *She-she … thinks …!* The first coherent string of words to return to him were not for Columbine's delicate ears, so he did another ten count, going as far as to grit his teeth and suppress a frustrated shudder as he pulled back all the profanity he longed to hurl. Only once he had a firm stranglehold on his temper, did he risk speaking. "No, this isn't my realm, so it's not my thrall, princess. YHWH is the one under the influence of a thrall here. Not me."

Columbine tilted her head. "In—flu—ence?" she asked, repeating the terminology though she broke it into three parts.

Avis nodded. "Thrall only affects a celestial if they are inside the realm of their powerbase. My powerbase and thrall are in Mystal. This one is YHWH's. He's the one who's mistaken."

"… But …"

Again, Avis placed a silencing finger on her lips, feeling for the first time he had the upper hand in the conversation. "No buts, princess. If YHWH was willing to leave this realm, we could show him and you that he's not really part of our family. But because he doesn't want to do that, and you won't understand until you're older just how much a powerbase and thrall change things, you need to take my word on that, okay?"

"But I am still allowed to call him Uncle YHWH while I am here?"

It was on the tip of his tongue to deny her since she didn't understand the difference between a false uncle and a real one, when it occurred to him that once this leg of the journey was over, she'd probably never set eyes on YHWH or Heaven again. If calling him 'Uncle' kept her happy for now, he had the rest of eternity to educate her on the finer points of a thrall. And the best part of his new plan? He wouldn't have to deal with those accursed tears of hers either.

Pleased with his solution, he smiled and tapped his pointer finger against the tip of her nose and nodded. "Just this once," he agreed. Happiness exploded through him, so overwhelmingly powerful that it bordered on painful, and she squeezed his neck in a bear hug once more. He tightened his own hold and enjoyed the moment until he felt her begin to pull away, at which point he opened his eyes and stared at her. "But just this one time, and only while we're here, okay?" He looked over his shoulder to where YHWH lingered and gave him an icy look of warning.

YHWH's smile was soft; his expression beatific. "Columbine, why don't you come with me and let your father spend some one-on-one time with Cora, okay? We can go outside and sit with the cherubim if you like."

Excitement swept through Avis with all the subtlety of a tornado as Columbine swung her head towards her father for confirmation. "All of them? At the same time? May I, Father?"

Avis scowled at YHWH, but then he looked at Columbine's pleading face and relented. "So long as YHWH's with you. The cherubim seem to behave themselves so long as he's about."

Columbine threw herself forward and gave him another tight hug, then she tore away from him and rushed over to YHWH. "Love you, Father!" she shouted over her shoulder, tugging YHWH out the door before he could change his mind.

CHAPTER FORTY-SIX

Rubbing out the dull ache that settled in his chest, Avis watched them go and shook his head with a widening smile. *Now*, she was behaving like a Mystallian. *About fucking time.* Of all the recent decisions he'd made, granting Columbine this concession was definitely one of his better ones, for it allowed her to prove she could be just as Mystallian as any of the family when the desire took her. More pleased with himself than he'd ever thought possible, Avis rose to his feet and made his way to Cora's open bedroom doors, knocking on the architrave.

The door was fully opened by Gingen, who bowed low as soon as she saw him. "Milord," she chimed.

As usual, Avis ignored her, stepping across the threshold of the doorway and scanning the otherwise empty space. "Where is she?" he demanded.

Before Gingen could answer, the hackles of his innate ability rose, not hard enough to indicate a clear and present danger, but not completely ruling it out either. His head jerked towards the ceiling, just in time to catch a glimpse of something falling on him from above.

Instinct caused him to internalise, freezing the scene. But instead of heading for his memories, he paused just inside the windows of his eyes and absorbed every detail of the slightly blurred mass frozen in time out there.

Cora, you little shit, he mused, folding his arms. She was poised in mid-air as if she were about to land on her hands and knees, or in this case, on his head and shoulders. He couldn't quite make out her expression, so he wasn't sure if this attack was meant in earnest, or in play.

His response would depend on which of those two it was.

Stepping away from the image, he journeyed back through the last few seconds of his memory, cataloguing each of Cora's changes despite the blurriness of her form. Then, he went over into his imagination and cleared away the visual distortion until he had a clearer picture of what he'd seen.

In the ceiling behind her, there were four sets of deep gouges, indicative of how she'd held herself up there. The impending ambush of a being with demonic claws was probably what triggered his innate ability to safeguard his own life in the first place. But as she fell towards him, everything about her returned to that of a little Mystallian girl.

So, she was just horsing around. But what did she hope to achieve by catching him unawares? Play had never been his forte. Fortunately, he knew who to ask.

An image of his youngest sibling appeared beside him. "Hey, bro, what ..." Chance's regular spiel ended abruptly as he took in the scene Avis had created. Specifically, the young girl in mid-fall over their heads. "Who's this?" he asked, walking around in a tight circle under Cora's prone form.

Not wanting to get bogged down on all the details and the subsequent fallout, Avis gave the Chance the knowledge that this was Cora—that she was fine—that she was on her way home—and most importantly, that he wasn't to flip out as her anointed father who hadn't seen her since she was a newborn. Once all of those modifications were in place, he gestured at the frozen image of his little girl. "She is playing, isn't she?" he asked, to clarify what he already suspected.

Chance dropped his chin to his chest and rolled his head and eyes towards him. "Naaah," he drawled derisively. "She's decided that murdering you in cold blood will give her the throne of Mystal and falling on you in her most non-lethal form from the top of a doorway is the best possible way to do that." As Avis wondered if that was even a remote possibility, Chance looked skyward with a huff of annoyance. "Yes, you moron. For the love of the realm, she's playing with you." An impish glint entered Chance's eyes, and his grin quickly followed suit. "So, how're you going to handle this, Mister I-Don't-Do-Fun?"

Avis sighed and rubbed two fingers in small circles against his right cheek. "That's what you're here for, runt. I've never had time for this shit. There's always been too much to do …"

"Spoken like a true first-time parent who thought they had an eternal career," Chance chuckled, glancing between his brother and the girl's image overhead. "Look, if she wants to play, would it really kill your pride to fall down with her on top of you?"

"What?" Avis was sure he'd misheard.

Chance shifted the point of view of the scene from first person to third, pushing the airborne Cora away from over their heads and out in front of them. A second version of Avis appeared beneath her, just as he was in the physical realm. "Something like this," he said, releasing the scene. Cora collided with Avis in a yowl of delight and drove him into the ground, ending with her sitting victoriously on his chest.

"Gotcha, Father!" she shouted, her eyes blazing with both excitement and triumph.

Avis froze the scene and glared in disgust at Chance. *You're out of your fucking mind if you think I'm going to do that!* While the idea of her exuding so much confidence might have sounded nice, he was never going to make the win so easy for her. It offered a hollow conquest that in time she would come to despise. Wins that weren't really wins were insulting.

"I know … I know …" Chance chided, patting his brother on the shoulder. "Losing to anyone kills the control freak in you. But sometimes for their sakes, you just have to suck it up and let it happen anyway, *Dad*. And don't be getting all defensive at me …" he added with a smirk, dropping his eyes to where Avis' hands had curled into tight fists. "This is a learning curve for both of you. So pull your head out of your ass and learn."

Avis gnashed his teeth as the red fog tinged the edges of his vision. Twice in five minutes? No one had dared to say that to him in eons, and twice in five minutes he'd been told to pull his head out of his ass? In a blur of movement, Avis held Chance off the ground by his doublet. "Who the fuck do you think you're talking to, you little shit!"

Chance's eyes widened, and his hands went up in supplication. "Easy, Brother," he crooned, waiting for Avis to put him down. "You brought me here, remember?"

Yes. Yes, he had. Closing his eyes, Avis started to count, and by the time he reached ten, he slowly opened his eyes and lowered the runt to the ground. The red was gone, and the shocked look on Chance's face as he lowered him was almost comical.

"That's new," he said, tilting his head to one side and running his eyes over Avis' face.

"A trick Clarise taught me. It works, for the most part."

"Wait … your 'ex' Clarise?"

Avis sighed at the oversight and added that information to the knowledge pool of this Chance, along with the restriction of 'you're not going to react to that either'. He wasn't in the mood for one of the runt's stupid outbursts. "Getting back to this," he said, gesturing at the image of Cora sitting on his chest. "Is that really my only option here?"

"You could always be a dick, and guarantee she'll never do it or anything else like it ever again."

Avis knew where he was going with this alternative option. It was where his own instincts led him. Smack her down, hard; physically or mentally or both. Only in his rhetoric, it had been for her good to make her try harder until her win was genuine. The dick part was an addition he didn't like.

"Something else to consider, bro," Chance said, coming to stand alongside him with one arm folded over his chest and the other hand stroking his chin. "Physically, she owns your ass. Mentally, you own hers." He looked across and up at his brother. "Do you really want this byplay to devolve into a dick waving contest?"

Avis didn't understand. "She doesn't own my ass physically. Her mother's blood in my veins prevents her from changing me that way."

"But she's a ranged shifter, and as much as it pains me to admit it, our forms aren't invulnerable, if you get my drift." Avis shot him a slitted look. "Seriously. She doesn't have to change your shape to nail you. She only has to change the air around you into something toxic to us, and you'll go down like a dying sun."

Avis hadn't considered that possibility and his chest puffed in challenge. "Not if I see her coming first, and she can't kill me …"

Chance didn't relent. "But she can keep you out of the game until she gets established, and then she'll have the same safety net you do. This all goes back to what I said earlier, bro. While things remain 'fun', neither one of you is serious about beating the other. But if you turn it into a contest where blood and pain are weapons of choice and the only way to win is by forcing the other to yield, someone's going to get seriously hurt. Probably both of you."

Avis had to concede that fact. If the clash was turned into a rite of passage, no one would win. The best way forward was to avoid trying to make one side of the celestial power-play more important than the other. Keep it light. Keep it … *fun*.

Avis looked at the image of himself under Cora and swallowed. "And what do I do after that?" he asked.

Chance shrugged. "That's up to you, Avis. Letting kids have little wins in the beginning isn't such a bad thing. Trust me. When they get older, they'll realise you were letting them win as children because you loved them and if anything, it'll go a long way toward cementing your adult relationship with them."

Avis couldn't see how that was possible, but he wasn't the child-maturing-into-adulthood expert here. "So, basically I have to let her land on me."

"I'd add a dash of 'pretending to be shocked' as well, just to give her ego that bit more of a kick," he suggested.

Avis rolled his eyes and shook his head in disgust. "Fuck me."

Chance barked out a laugh and punched him firmly in the arm. "No one said being a good parent was easy, bro. Most of us would tell you in a heartbeat that it's a hell of a lot easier to run a realm."

"Like any of you idiots would know," Avis snarled.

"Well, you make it look easy," Chance quipped, dodging away before Avis could react. He quickly sobered though and returned to his side. "All jokes aside, Avis, this is important. Really important. She needs to win more than she loses right now, whether the game is rigged or not. When the time comes for her play to evolve into reality, that's when you can make your stand as an unbeatable force. Until then, you need to fudge that hard-line you usually live by."

Clarise had more or less said the same thing back when they were on the Akheron River and he'd been teaching Cora how to play chess, but his way had triumphed because she had upped her game until she'd beaten him fair and square. But the reason that had ended so well was probably because the time it took for his little tiger to go from an amateur to a chess master was less than three weeks. If the process had taken years or decades, would Cora still have her easy-going opinion on her earlier losses, or would she start getting creative in order to win by any means?

He glanced at his youngest brother. "I don't know how to do this," he admitted.

Chance shrugged. "The hardest part in your case will be fighting your natural desire to be indomitable. Ever since ... well ... before, you've always been the pillar of strength that everyone else leaned on—even Amaro. If something got on top of you, you wouldn't let any of us see it. But perhaps this would be easier for you if you didn't see it as a weakening of your core values, and more along the lines of adding an extra layer of padding around the sharp edges of those views to protect your babies."

"They're not babies," Avis grizzled, to which Chance snorted irreverently.

"Brother, they're always going to be your babies. That's the first thing you're going to have to get your head around. Do you honestly think your protective instincts are going to go away just because they're a few billion years old and declaring themselves adults?"

Probably not.

Not knowing that Avis had already come to the same conclusion, Chance shook his head. "Of course not. You have no idea the grief I was going to unleash on Dionysus for getting my Emmalyn pregnant way back in the day, and that was a consensual union between two adults that led to us getting our own God of the Drink. If you think your protective instincts are on high alert now, wait till one of those beautiful little girls of yours comes home and tells you they're pregnant."

Chance lifted his right hand and made a motion of jumping over something with his extended finger. "Or, when *that* boy then grows up and comes to you with the, 'Grandad, I might have made an itty-bitty miscalculation last night ...' speech." Using the same hand to sweep away the story, he added, "That right there's a whole realm of not-fun. Especially when Emi's laughing her ass off in the background behind him."

"When the fuck did this become about you?" Avis snapped.

"Just proving it happens to everyone in the end. Even me." With a wicked gleam in his eyes, he added, "And especially you."

"No way," Avis declared, with absolute finality. Or if it did, the father who dared to get either of his girls pregnant would never be heard from again. Nor would the bastard's entire pantheon. Avis would finally consent to Armina taking the realm to war if anyone even thought about trying to cross that line.

Again, Chance's hand found Avis' bicep in a condescending pat. "Keep telling yourself that, old man. Once they hit their teen years and their libido kicks in …"

"Shut up before I have to fucking kill you."

Chance chuckled, his eyes dancing with amusement. "You're right," he said as if he were soothing Avis' ruffled feathers, but then he had to go and spoil his capitulation by adding, "That's future Avis' problem, and you're having a hard enough time dealing with present Avis' problems."

Avis already had too many historical points in his recent life that he wished he could go back and redo, without adding this one to it. "I can do this."

Chance sobered and nodded in full agreement. "I know you can. You can do anything, once you put your mind to it." His grin broadened. "That's why you're my big brother."

Avis wiped away the imaginary scene and returned to the physical realm, partially bracing himself for his daughter's impact around his head and shoulders; more to prevent himself from reacting as he normally would than anything else. He had to fall down and let Cora sit on his chest in triumph.

Everything went exactly as Chance had predicted. Cora wrapped her arms around his head and her legs landed on his shoulders, driving him backwards to the ground. But he couldn't quite let her win. He just couldn't do it. Instead, he gave her a moment that she could look back on as a framed memory where she appeared to have the upper hand. He even made his eyes widen and his body stiffen in what would've been interpreted as shock, but as they fell he twisted to face downwards with one hand outstretched to take the impact and the other cupping the back of Cora's neck with his forearm along her spine to support her fall. He allowed her butt to bump lightly against the ground while he suspended his full body weight between his booted toes and one hand, with Cora continuing to cling to him.

"I got you!" she crowed, releasing her arms and legs and rolling away from him, launching herself to her feet with her fisted hands thrust over her head in victory.

Avis lowered his body into the bottom end of a standard push up, only instead of extending his arm again, he shoved off his hand with enough strength to push himself all the way to his feet in one fluid motion. "Enjoy the win, brat," he grinned, dusting himself off even though no part of him had actually touched the ground.

All at once she stilled, and her hands fell to her sides. "You let me do that, didn't you?" she asked accusingly, though she already knew the answer. No one could ever accuse his little tiger of being an idiot.

Avis thought about lying to her and refused to do it. He never wanted there to be a time where she doubted the veracity of anything he said. "Does it really matter? I'm a lot older and a lot bigger than you." He lifted his eyes to the four sets of claw marks in the ceiling beside the door mouldings. "You did actually catch me by surprise when you first dropped on me, but then my innate ability to survive kicked in and I looked up. If anything, me figuring out it was you falling on me was in your best interest, tiger, because if you'd been anyone else, I'd have destroyed you."

Cora huffed in disappointment and looked away.

"Now, don't be like that," Avis chided. "If you were to see out the rest of eternity, do you honestly think there'll be any given point in your life where you could catch your grandfather Belial by surprise?"

"Of course not."

"Exactly. You beat me for a second. Most people don't even get that." He went over to her bed and sat on the edge, more to put them both on the same eye level than because he needed the seat. "Listen, we both know I suck at being a parent. Even if I wanted to, I can't do the cutesy-pretend-play stuff. It's not in my makeup." He paused to give her time to nod, though he wasn't surprised when she merely blinked at him; probably in an effort to figure out where he was going with this. "So, what if, you and I .." —he flicked his finger between them— "… meet in the middle?"

Cora cocked her head to one side. "How exactly do you propose we do that, Father?"

"Because while I can't do the cutesy stuff, I can teach you something that you've been chomping at the bit to learn ever since I properly met you."

The *very* first time they met back in her nursery didn't count in his mind.

He leaned back and dropped his hand to brace himself on the mattress without taking his eyes off Cora, and practically jumped out of his skin when his palm collided with a hard cool surface and sturdy edge. He swung his attention to that hand and found it poised over a long timber box roughly the width of his forearm and the length of his arm. Polished black timber, with the Mystallian insignia embossed in gold on the front.

It hadn't been there when he first sat down.

Lifting the lid, he saw inside two Mystallian longswords; one child-sized.

Okay, now you're just showing off, you wingless motherfucker, Avis fumed, without vocalising his thoughts.

"Is something wrong, Father?"

Avis shook his head and removed the child-sized sword first. "No. Actually, something is finally about to be made right." He rose to his feet and made a downwards stroke with the sword covering the shoulder to the hip of an imaginary attacker. Then he rolled his hand to the left in a disembowelling motion and ended the three-way manoeuvre with a reverse angular, upward sweep shoulder-width away from where he started. The sequence was done to test the blade for balance, and it annoyed him to admit YHWH had done a nice job of it. He rolled the sword towards himself with the tip of the blade resting close to his stomach and the hilt now facing Cora. "This one's yours," he said, beckoning her forward with the fingertips of his other hand. "Come and get it, tiger."

Cora looked from the weapon to his face and back to the weapon, her mouth hanging open in shock.

Avis grinned and waggled his eyebrows tauntingly. "Come on, tiger. You need to get back in touch with your birthright. The one your mother's people tried so damned hard and failed to drum out of you."

Cora hedged her way forward, her eyes still shifting from him to the sword in his hand and back again. Her hands were fisted, but she didn't hold them behind her back in outright denial of his claim. He could see, even without being privy to her mind that she wanted this so badly she ached for it. She just couldn't decide if he was being honest or if this was an elaborate hoax.

"As I said, this is yours," he said, holding the hilt out for her to take. "Don't waste any more time. If we were back home, your Aunt Armina would already have turned you into a minor prodigy with the blade, so you have a lot of catching up to do."

It took longer than Avis would've liked, but eventually, Cora took the blade from him and held it up for closer inspection. "This is like the one I had in the Well," she said, holding the blade at eye level to assess the honed edge. Again, Avis admired her warrior's instincts.

"Mystallian steel," he agreed, claiming the adult sword for himself. He turned a little away from Cora so as not to strike her and gave the blade the same weight and balance test he had the smaller one. Both blades were perfect. *Dammit.*

Cora watched his move, then imitated it with her own smaller blade. "Do you do that every time you pick up a sword?" she asked.

"Not that often," he replied. "If the blade was mine, I'd only be testing it every so often to make sure no one had messed with it. Likewise, if it were someone else's, I wouldn't test it at all unless I planned to use it."

He moved to Cora's side, twisting ever so slightly so she could see what he was doing with his sword arm and his feet but not impede her own attempts to mimic him. "Now, the first time you held the sword back in Hell, your grip was all wrong. You had your thumb above the crossguard here," he said, pointing to where, even now, her tiny thumb sat against the steel plate that locked the shoulder and tang of the blade into the hilt. "Which I have seen some people do, don't get me wrong. But the problem with that hold is ..." Avis brought his own blade to bear, placing the sharp edge against her thumb knuckle as if to sever it. "You've made it really easy for me to target the one digit that controls most of the blade's movement."

Cora covered the pommel of her sword with her other hand and pushed it until her primary hand was in the middle of the grip. "What's stopping me from shape shifting in another thumb if you did that?" she asked, not to be a smart-ass, but because she genuinely wanted to know. Curious fascination was plastered all over her young face.

Avis looked at her modified grip. "Primarily, in the heat of battle, you're usually too focused on staying alive to think about shifting in the digit you need to keep the fight going. In the time it takes you to regrow the thumb, your enemy has probably taken your head." With a wink, he added, "And that's the more important of the two, don't you think?"

"Right," Cora breathed, staring at her hand. She then glanced up at him. "Is this better?"

"Almost," he answered, tapping his own crossguard. "This metal plate here is called a crossguard. Roughly three finger-widths ahead of that is the balance point of your whole sword." To prove this, he held out a pointer finger, then placed the flat of his sword across it right where he'd indicated, with the hilt and three fingers on the left and the rest of the blade on the right. Then he released the blade.

Neither side moved, showing her as much as telling her the importance of a well-balanced blade. "This right here is the balancing point of your whole sword and you need your grip to be as close as comfortably possible to utilise that balance. The farther you are away from it, the harder it is to control the blade."

"If this is the best grip, why would I not meld my hand into the hilt to make sure it never changes?"

She was thinking. He had to give her that. "Because the hilt is constantly moving against your palm. While that grip you currently have does serve its purpose, it'll only do so for as long as you keep the balance point over the top of your hand." Pivoting towards her, he took the tip of her blade in his fingers and forcefully pulled it down until the blade sat horizontally in the air. "Now look at where the pommel is," he said, using his eyes to draw her attention to the hilt.

Instead of being curled between her little finger and the heel of her palm, the hilt had swivelled until the pommel rested against the bones of her wrist. It had moved a quarter of a turn. He watched her eyes widen in surprise and nodded. "This is the natural flow of your weapon. It's not a hammer, and it's not an axe. It's a bladed extension of your arm and you must treat it accordingly." To really make his point, Avis lifted his blade, twisting it in his hand so that the flat of the blade was facing him with his thumb resting against the blade. "What do you think I could achieve by holding my sword like this?"

"I'd say you'd either get yourself killed for not having the sharp edge facing your opponent or at the very least you're going to get your thumb cut off for sticking it over the crossguard," she replied.

Well, at least she'd been listening to what he said before. "True. Unless you have something special in mind." Stepping a safe distance away from her, he held out his free hand to prevent her from following him. Then, in a flurry of movement that had been perfected long before some universes came into being, he raised his sword into a horizontal position just above his head and made a series of circular sweeping moves that both protected his exposed head and gave way to a natural extension that would take out a supposed enemy's throat. "Forte cuts, and riposte back edge cuts," he said, bringing the blade to a halt in front of him. "But that's for the future when you get a better handle on things. For now, we'll start with the basics."

For the next two hours, Avis put her through her paces. Yes, he could have taken this training into her mind, but there was something to be said about physically holding a sword and swinging it, irrespective of the capability of the wielder. Once she was confident in her skills, then he'd take the training into her imagination and really lay on the heavy work.

CHAPTER FORTY-SEVEN

It didn't occur to Avis until much later that he and Cora had trained right through both breakfast and most of lunch. Clarise hadn't come looking for them either, so hopefully that meant she wasn't too annoyed with their absence. It was a weird situation. After so many months of having such a regimented schedule, monitoring the free time was going to take a little getting used to.

Lowering his sword so that it was angled backwards away from Cora, he held up his other hand for her to stop. Which, to her credit, she did. "What's wrong, Father? We were just getting to the fun part."

Avis grinned at her and returned to the bed where the box lay open, replacing the blade in its housing. "We can pick this up later," he said, waving her forward. "Neither one of us has eaten since last night, and you need nutrition."

"I'll shift it in," Cora said, not quite willing to give up her lessons just yet.

Mentally applauding her ingenuity (if not her shifting), Avis nevertheless shook his head and gestured to the empty spot in the box. "Not this time, tiger," he said. "We skipped breakfast, and I think your mother would sic' all the hordes of hell onto us if we missed lunch as well."

Cora snorted, unimpressed. "Mother's welcome to," she argued, placing her free hand on her hip rebelliously. "Two ranged benders and a ranged shifter up against a horde of touch shifters that can't do shit to either one of us?" She blew a raspberry and rolled her eyes. "Please."

Despite his disdain for that word, the derogatory way she said it let him know there wasn't any pleading in its meaning.

"That may be so, tiger, but I for one am not getting on your mother's bad side. Not over a meal. So put your blade away, give yourself a stimulation wave, and get your ass out to the dining table. I'll join you in a few minutes just as soon as I've freshened up in your ensuite."

"Spoilsport," she muttered, but crossed the room and placed her sword alongside his in the box. She cast the stimulation wave, cleansing herself of the sweat that clung to her skin and replacing it with a light floral scent. "Will we keep going after lunch?"

"I never promise anything I can't guarantee, tiger. It all depends on what your mother has planned for us." As she pouted and turned towards the doors, he gave her a half-hearted slap on the backside that made her yelp. "And the next time you sass your mother like that, it'll be *you* over my knee, along with a mental command to prevent you from healing yourself afterwards."

With her left hand rubbing where he'd smacked her, Cora spun back to him with wide eyes and Avis couldn't help but smile in a way that exposed all his teeth like an apex predator. "That's right, tiger. I know very well what you did to Columbine last week. But I also said that if your reasons are good enough; you'd have my support." He raised a finger at her in warning. "So long as your reasons *are* good enough."

Cora poked her tongue out at him and crossed her eyes. Since there was no malice in her surface thoughts, he stamped his foot in her direction, causing her to laugh and dart for the doors.

Gingen bowed from where she'd been standing near the ensuite. "Would you like me to draw you a bath, milord?"

Avis nodded his consent and waved her into the ensuite with one finger. Seconds later, the sound of running water had him closing his eyes, enjoying the tranquillity that was settling around him. He couldn't remember the last time everything felt so right in his life.

"Your bath is ready, milord," Gingen said shortly afterwards, breaking him from his musings. When he opened his eyes and looked, her upper half was bent at a right angle just inside the ensuite.

"Good," he said, striding past the servant, his hands already unfastening his cloak. "I won't need your assistance during my bath, but I'll utilise your speed in drying and dressing afterwards." Cleaning his uniform at the same time went without saying.

Gingen bowed deeper, almost folding herself in half. "Your will, milord."

Avis stripped and stepped into the bath that was about half the size of his own. *Fitting*, he thought, though there was plenty of room for him to bathe alone just the same. He reached for the cake of soap, then remembered this *was* his daughter's bathroom. That realisation gave him a definite sinking feeling and, cringing on what he feared he would find, he picked up the soap and gave it a tentative sniff. Pine. Not one of the more floral scents that the girls all wore. Gingen had swapped out the soap scents. Thank the Twin Notes. He had no desire to go to lunch smelling like a bouquet.

In less than five minutes he had washed and rinsed off by dunking below the waterline and was now standing outside the bath dripping wet. "Gingen," he called, holding his arms out to his sides.

The servant scuttled in with her head bowed lower than Avis' shoulder. "Milord," she asked, waiting for permission to approach him.

"You have your orders," he said, watching as she bowed again, then gathered up the various pieces of uniform and melded them into a single entity on her way over to him. Knowing not to initiate contact with him, she held out one of her many hands for him to take, and as soon as he did, all the moisture evaporated off his body. Then, the black mass that had been his uniform slithered along the hand she held and poured across his body, reforming into his pristine uniform starting with the toe of his left boot and ending with the glove of the hand she held. He released her hand and stretched his arms forward, finding the doublet had the same amount of give as it had originally. "Nice," he said in a complimentary fashion that had the servant ducking her head away to chitter happily to herself.

He was never going to get tired of watching a shifter dress him their way.

Without another word, he left the ensuite and went through the bedroom into the sitting room, raking his fingers through his hair as he went. That was one of the many joys of being a man. He didn't have the long tresses of the ladies that required hours of maintenance.

Dessert was being served just as Avis slid into his seat at the head of the table. "My apologies," he said, looking first at Clarise at the opposite end of the table, then Columbine to include her in that admission. If YHWH's feelings were hurt due to his omission, he wasn't exactly going to lose any sleep over it.

"Cora was just telling us how—interesting your day has been thus far," Clarise said, helping herself to a slice of blueberry mousse cake.

Avis smirked, reaching for a fresh apple instead of something sweet. "Most Mystallian women learn how to fight from an early age, sweetheart. If I didn't teach her, Armina would." In an attempt to further avoid the subject, Avis bit into the apple and turned his attention to Columbine. "And what have you been up to, apart from playing with the cherubim?" He had every intention of looking for himself at a later point in time, but for now, it was a good diversion. Columbine's answers were always safe.

"Uncle YHWH and I made up a game box and filled it up with lots of fun things to do," she answered excitedly.

"*Uncle* YHWH?" Both Clarise and Cora echoed in astonishment, as Avis choked and covered his eyes with one gloved hand. So much for safe answers.

"It was said in a moment of temporary insanity," he explained, deciding to go with the absolute truth.

"What kind of fun things are we talking about here?" Cora asked, not to intentionally interrupt her parents but because her curiosity had been piqued. More proof that she was becoming the Mystallian she should've always been.

"You should find out for yourself, once the meal has concluded," Clarise suggested pointedly, using a fork to break off the corner of her mousse cake before sliding it into her mouth. She savoured the fruity flavour with a sigh of contentment, then refocused on the older of their two daughters. "Assuming, of course, you have not made other arrangements?"

Cora's gaze immediately sliced to Avis, who chuckled and shrugged. "Like I said, tiger. No promises unless they can be guaranteed. The choice is still yours."

"But I'll only have today to squeeze it all in, because tomorrow we'll be heading out, won't we?"

"I would assume so," Clarise replied.

That was when Avis realised he hadn't told any of them of his change of plans.

Drumming the tips of three fingers across his lips, his eyes went to YHWH who, like the chicken-shit smartass he was, tried to hide his amusement behind a raised spoonful of whatever the hell he was eating. "I should have mentioned this earlier, *and* in private," he said, meeting Clarise's steady gaze with another apologetic one of his own. "I was talking things over with YHWH this morning, and he and I have come to an understanding. It seems he has the means to transport us instantly to the edge of Heaven. So rather than spend the next few weeks riding, I have accepted his invitation to stay for however long we wish to enjoy his hospitality, in exchange for immediate transport to the Olympian border when we are done."

"You make it sound like such a contractual hardship," YHWH mocked, his lips twisting to one side unimpressed. He then rolled his eyes to Clarise. "What he means is, I've invited you all to stay in one place and enjoy your first real family vacation together, instead of being constantly on the move." Avis watched as his gaze moved to each person at the table while his thumb flicked towards Avis. "Given that he's the single most stubborn being in all existence, I talked him into this first, believing everyone else here would welcome the reprieve with open arms." His eyes kept moving. "Am I mistaken?"

"Hell, no!" Cora laughed, jumping out of her seat and clapping her hands together excitedly. "I get to practice swordplay *and* find out what's in the game box!"

Cora's mouth flew open before Avis could reprimand her for her language and he knew the way she closed her eyes and grimaced in pain that her mother had beaten him to it. She maintained that tense pose for a few seconds then breathed out in a rush as the pain must have subsided, and opened her eyes.

Clarise was still looking at her very sharply.

"My apologies for my rudeness, Mother," she recanted, her breathing still hitched.

"Apology accepted," Clarise replied and returned to her dessert.

Cora turned her back to her mother and draped one arm over the back of her chair, pursing her lips into a silent O which she used to breathe through. After a few seconds, her eyes darted to Avis, and he couldn't help but raise an eyebrow in an unspoken 'well, what did you think would happen?'.

She in turn crossed her eyes at him, not quite willing to poke her tongue out in case her mother managed to see it.

Avis bit deeply into his apple to hide his amusement, almost tearing it in half.

"So, if you two young ladies are finished," YHWH said, sliding out of his seat to stand. "Why don't we go and see if we can find something for you both to do in that games box."

"Mother, may I be excused?" Columbine asked, her eyes alight with the same excitement Cora's had previously held.

Clarise smiled and nodded her consent. "Of course, sweetheart. Off you go." Her eyes moved to Cora. "Both of you."

Columbine slid off her chair and took her sister by the wrist, 'helping' her to her feet. "What shall we play first, Uncle YHWH?" she asked eagerly, as the pair did that combination walk/run thing that kids of all ages did when excitement got the better of them but running wasn't permitted. He took a small amount of perverse pleasure knowing they had chosen to go around him rather than their mother at the other end of the table to regroup with YHWH.

"Well, I think since Cora is the newcomer to our games, we should let her pick out the first one, don't you?" As YHWH herded them out the door, he looked over their heads in Avis' direction and shot him the same cautionary look that Clarise had sent Cora. And then they were gone, leaving him and Clarise alone with the servants.

Avis finished off the last of his apple and dropped the core onto his plate, trying without success to decipher the hidden meaning behind YHWH's warning.

Clarise gestured for Tilu to help her stand, then commanded, "Ladies, leave us," once she was upright. Tilu and the two governesses bowed and disappeared behind the closed doors of their respective ladies as Avis stilled.

"Is something the matter, sweetheart?" he asked, hoping to ferret out a hint as to the depth of trouble he was in.

Without saying another word, Clarise swept around the end of the table and made her way towards him. Avis decided to meet her in the middle, and when he did, he wrapped her in his arms and pressed his lips into her hair. "What's wrong?" he asked, determined to fix whatever was bothering her.

She looked up at him and hooked her hands around his neck, holding him close. "I have several things I wish to discuss with you over your recent conduct, but let us begin with the easiest one first." Raising her eyebrow she asked, *"Uncle* YHWH?"

Okay, he should've seen that one coming.

* * *

Clarise stroked the back of his neck and watched his eyes, waiting for his response. For nearly a week, he had refused to even consider the possibility that he and YHWH shared blood, though she had seen their similarities. He had valid reasons for his views, especially when almost all of her observations before last night had been physical ones. She of all people knew how easily an appearance could be manipulated. But when YHWH nibbled at his thumbnail because he was nervous, Clarise had seen Avis do that exact same thing for exactly the same reason.

It wasn't a physical affliction. It was psychological. And since Avis had no knowledge of having the tell, there was no way YHWH could have known how to replicate it so perfectly ... unless of course, YHWH had learned it from searching *her* memories. She couldn't in good conscience dismiss that possibility either. Avis had made a very compelling argument when he insisted YHWH was nothing more than the common child of awful parents, who'd made his way into the Almighty's realm and been given this ridiculous establishment field and subsequent thrall to make up for his bad start in life. So long as YHWH remained in Heaven, the realm and everything in it would believe in his thrall. Even the Almighty himself would believe it.

She'd spent her whole life studying the realms and everything that went into them. Still, what if YHWH *was* somehow related to Avis? In Chaos, one quickly learned anything was possible.

"He caught me at a moment of weakness."

"He did, or Columbine did?" Clarise asked.

Avis tensed, his expression clouding into a dark storm. "Why would you ask that?" he asked, probably to give her the opportunity to change her question before he exploded.

There was a time she would've heeded his warning and told him what he wanted to hear, but she hadn't been that person in a while. Ignoring his prickliness, she relaxed into his hold with a warm smile and stroked his cheek. "We both know Columbine is the one who has her father's heart wrapped around her little finger, not YHWH."

Avis closed his eyes and, as she was pressed tightly against him, she felt his tension grow into an all-over shudder that shook them both. But through it all, the one thing she noticed was he hadn't denied the charge.

"So how did Columbine manage to manipulate you into agreeing to this?"

"It wasn't so much of a manipulation," Avis argued, ever protective of his pride.

Clarise used the fingers of her right hand to comb his dark fringe. "My love, you have emphatically denied YHWH's connection to us for over a week now. In fact, you have made it your personal mission to throw it back in his face at every conceivable turn. I am extremely curious to hear what was said that convinced you to change your mind now."

Avis breathed out a sigh, and then gave her a veritable blow by blow accounting of the strange conversation he'd had with their daughter. He accomplished this with such precision that he must've ducked back into his memories half a dozen times to get the wording so exact, because she could actually hear their younger daughter pose such ludicrous questions. Had she been anyone else, Clarise would've accused her of being deliberately ambiguous. Fortunately for Columbine, Clarise knew that level of duplicity simply wasn't in her.

The designation of 'Uncle YHWH' seemed to please the childlike angel, but so much of his true history remained undetermined, and it all branched from his unwillingness to leave the realm. He wouldn't have to come out very far. Just far enough to separate himself from his thrall for a few minutes, and then everything would be made clear, one way or the other. Avis firmly believed the angel was a coward who'd prefer to live in denial than be dragged into the light of truth and YHWH was certainly not doing anything to disabuse him of that notion.

But YHWH did answer to the Almighty. Perhaps, since they were staying in one place, she could reach out to the ruler of the realm and see if he would be accommodating enough to force YHWH into stepping outside for just a few seconds. After all, it wasn't as if the Almighty hadn't already invited them inside the pearlescent walls and offered them an audience. Then, this could finally be put to rest.

Avis was studying her face, clearly attempting to interpret her every expression. "What are you thinking, sweetheart?" he asked.

"I was thinking I might go behind the pearlescent wall and speak to the Almighty directly." She had no reason to lie.

Avis' reaction was extreme to say the least. He locked his hands around her waist and arched away from her, staring at her as if she had gone temporarily insane. "Not just no, sweetheart, but *HELL*, no!" he roared, shaking his head in outright denial. "You are *not* going over that wall, and you are absolutely *not* going anywhere near that controlling bastard!"

"Avis …" Clarise chided, but he continued to shake his head.

"No way! That son of a bitch has been sending his angels to invade our realms since the Twin Notes first sang, and you would not believe some of the stories Odin and Zeus have told me about him over the eons! I am *not* letting him get his claws into you! No!" He pushed her out to his arm's length and shook her shoulders. "Promise me, sweetheart. Promise me you won't even think about it again, or I swear I'll never let you out of my sight."

"But he could order YHWH to leave the realm …"

"I don't care! I don't care enough about proving YHWH wrong to risk you! If he wants to live under his delusion, let him. We are staying on this side of the pearlescent wall, where it's safe."

Clarise was about to remind him that it wouldn't matter which side of the wall they were on since they were still within the boundary of Heaven, but decided against it. "Very well," she said, causing him to loosen his hold and draw her back into a cuddle. "If it means that much to you, beloved, I will continue to live in ignorance."

A huff of frustration left Avis. "Don't be like that, sweetheart. You don't know what he's like. His idea of fun is to force people into corners with expectations that he knows they can't meet, just so he can punish them for failing to meet those expectations. He's on par with Theodrick in terms of temper and cruelty and I don't want you anywhere near him."

"As you wish." She slipped her hands around his waist and squeezed, staring up at him to dedicate every line and contour of his face to memory. "There is something else we need to discuss at length, and although it is not going to be a particularly enjoyable discussion, it still needs to happen."

Looking at him as she had been, she saw the exact moment when the light in his eyes dimmed as he processed all that her words could entail. "After yesterday, what else could we possibly have left to discuss?" he asked, cautiously.

"That is something I would prefer to talk about in the comfort of our sitting room, since it will probably take up most of the afternoon."

Again, his eyes scrutinised her for some hint of subject matter, but Clarise held firm. She pulled away from him, sliding her left arm underneath his right hand until both hands clasped and she gave him an encouraging squeeze.

Avis said nothing, but just as it had the day before, she felt his pulse increase through two layers of gloves. Or, perhaps it was her own. Either way, she didn't try to tamp it down.

With ranged shifting, she opened the sitting room doors to their apartment and closed them again once they'd passed through. Then she walked one of the two single seated, high backed lounge chairs that faced the fireplace over to the other and merged them both into one stretch lounge large enough to seat them both together.

She led him to the lounge and, without a word, he slid into the seat closest to the fire. Clarise went to take the remaining seat, but he tightened his grip on her hand and tugged her into his lap. "Whatever this is about, sweetheart," he said, wrapping his arms around her waist to secure her to him, even as she lay her head against his shoulder and relaxed into him. "I want you right here as we work our way through it." With a nervous grin, he added, "Even if it's only to keep me here until we're done."

Clarise didn't laugh at his attempted humour, because chances were, he *would* rather leave than have the discussion she had in mind. "Avis, I need you to tell me exactly what you did and who you did it to after I left with Cora all those years ago."

Avis stiffened, but Clarise raised her hand and stroked the side of his neck and strong jawline. "It happened, beloved. You turned into a beast of a man. I am no longer afraid of it, but I do need to know what the Known Realms thinks of you and why. Perhaps in some cases, there may be room for reconciliation. Not by you specifically, but by the rest of the family. Either way, I am your wife, and I will know what trouble you have caused our family."

Avis' brows arched sharply upwards in distress, but she shushed his motion and kissed his furrowed brow, willing him to understand her reasons. "We will face each of them together, beloved; as husband and wife. You saw my shame and stood by me. Now let me help you bear yours."

After a little more convincing, her husband began a very, very long and painful recollection of events as he knew them.

* * *

CHAPTER FORTY-EIGHT

It took Clarise almost a week to come to terms with everything Avis had told her. It was one thing to generalise the title of 'monster', and another to be given a blow-by-blow accounting of how that title came about. In three years, it seemed he had managed to alienate almost every single realm in existence. It would take eons to work up enough good favour for even some of them to be on speaking terms with Mystal again. In cases such as Loki's, several unestablished kids of pantheons had died as a direct result of his actions and those pantheons would never forgive Mystal. Or, at the very least, forgive Avis, and given how unified Mystal was towards outsiders, most saw that as one and the same.

It took YHWH's insistence that everyone join him on the front lawn for 'an extra-special surprise' one morning for her to realise she was squandering this perfect opportunity to have a true vacation with her family. They had no responsibilities here except to each other. The sun didn't rely on them to wake up, and life and death within the realm were not their concern. Once they returned to Mystal, all that would change. Avis would have a realm to rule and as his queen, she would be at his side in all things. Until the children came of age and joined them in the pantheon, they would probably have more interaction with their governesses than the family. But that was the future. Right now, she was free to do anything she wanted with her family, and she was wasting it by dwelling on the past.

She and Avis followed the girls onto the lawn—and walked headlong into a glitter and streamer explosion. A large banner with the words 'Happy Birthday Cora' appeared over a pair of tables just above head height and the number six was represented in a range of mediums from floating balloons to looping tree trunks to the clouds overhead. Even the blades of grass were curled to represent the number six. Of the two tables, one was full of finger foods with a large cake in the middle bearing six lit candles, and the other had a single gift-wrapped square box about one and a half lengths of Avis' forearm. The box and its lid were wrapped separately in paper that changed patterns at least twice a second. The two were held together by a bright red bow that was bigger than the box.

"What is this?" Clarise asked, her eyebrows soaring into her fringe in surprise, as the girls ran through the glitter and streamers, laughing the whole time.

"It's Cora's birthday party, of course," YHWH answered, just as excited as the girls. "She turns six today."

"And … we're having a party for it, why?" Avis asked, frowning in confusion.

YHWH stopped and turned to look at them. "I told you," he said, shifting his focus from one to the other and back again. "Because she turned six. It's a big milestone for a little girl."

"But all children age a year every year," Clarise argued, beating Avis by half a second at best if the puffing of his cheeks was anything to go by. "Why would the natural progression of someone's age warrant an individual celebration?"

YHWH's eyes widened and his jaw went slack with disbelief. "Oh, you guys have got to be kidding me! You really haven't been celebrating any of their birthdays?"

Avis clearly didn't like the connotation that they as the parents had somehow deprived the girls of something meaningful. "One; we've been a little busy of late, brat. And two; no, we don't see the point. If we threw a party every single year on the date of our births, and those candles represent each the number of years we've been alive, the fire candle flames would challenge a star and there'd be more cake in the realm than anyone could possibly eat."

"I'm not talking about you as adults. Once you reach the point you can make your own decisions, you can throw your own parties for whatever reason you like. These birthday parties are for the kids. As children, they're often overlooked and not treated as the most special people in existence, so every year until they reach maturity, they're entitled to one day where everything revolves around them. It's...It's a mandate here."

"But there must be countless celebrations going on at any given time if Heaven abides by that stupid rule."

YHWH grinned as if Avis had offered him the greatest of compliments. "Exactly. No matter where you look in the mortal realm, you will find countless billions of children celebrating their special day with those that matter most to them, and as celestials we get to enjoy that ride with them."

He turned to the side and waved at Cora and Columbine, who were still tearing through the glitter and streamers. Well, Columbine was. Cora had paused to scoop up large fistfuls of glitter which she proceeded to pelt at her squealing sister. "And today's Cora's day. What's not to like about that?"

"And the gift?"

"That's for Cora; from me."

Although she made every effort to appear as if she wasn't eavesdropping, Cora whirled on her heel, the glitter clump in her hand all but forgotten. "*Wha—t?*" she shouted, wide-eyed, wanting to have that fact confirmed now that she'd inserted herself into the conversation.

YHWH chuckled at her astonishment and waved her towards the present. "Have at it, sweet pea, but don't be too rough. You don't want to hurt him."

Him?

Cora dropped the glitter ball and raced for the second table. Her hands slid around the wrapping paper until she clamped onto the back corners, then she dragged it from the table and eased it to the ground, kneeling as she went. Her movements were gentle, but it didn't stop whatever was inside from uttering a hollow growl that held no substance.

"YHWH, if she gets hurt I *will* find a way to murder you," Avis warned, stretching to his full height to try and see over the rim of the box to whatever was inside.

Clarise caught the sly gleam of condescension in YHWH's eyes, but it was gone before her husband saw it, to be quickly replaced by a broad smile as he raised both hands and patted the air. "Calm down, Avis. You'll see, it's okay," he promised. "It's my gift to her, and his personality suits her perfectly. You have my absolute word on that."

Cora tore the ribbon from the box and tossed it away, never once taking her eyes from the box. Her hands cupped the front corners of the box lid and she lifted it just enough to peek inside. "What the ...?" She slammed the lid down and swivelled on her toes to stare slack jawed at YHWH, then over to her and Avis; her eyes sparkling and tearing all at once.

"What is it?" Columbine asked, kneeling alongside her sister; somehow knowing the gift wasn't hers to touch.

"Well, don't leave him in there like that, baby," YHWH laughed, flicking his fingers to remove the box-lid. "You'll frighten him."

"No chance of that!" Cora flipped the lid off with such force it soared almost to the edge of the grass boundary, and before it landed she had both her hands inside the box. Columbine's hands covered her mouth and Clarise could see she was fighting back a squeal. Neither of their behaviours pleased her at that moment. Especially Columbine's.

Exposed to the light, the grumbling turned into an open-mouthed *rarr* of complaint that sounded like someone was attempting to strangle a scallye.

Avis stiffened, and YHWH raised a commanding finger at him. "I *said* it's okay," he repeated though this time with more bite, as if he wasn't in the habit of having his word questioned. "She's fine."

Cora lifted out a tiger cub that couldn't be more than a week or two old and snuggled it to her chest. "You are too adorable for words," she cooed, as the tiger cub growled and pushed its forepaws against Cora's neck and chest. She sat cross legged with its hindlegs resting in her lap and its chest flat against her own. Tears streamed down her face when she looked up at the adults. "And he's really mine?" she asked, her cheeks flushing with happiness.

"He is yours, Cora," Clarise decreed, knowing she needed to insert her parental authority before Avis took offence to the pet for it not being his idea. Besides, giving Cora something to care of may be what she needed to settle down. "Provided you see to his well-being."

* * *

Avis wasn't a man who liked surprises or challenges at the best of times, and he despised when they happened together. His first instinct was to tell YHWH where he could stuff the tiger cub, but then he saw the look on Cora's face and saw a vulnerability there that she'd spent the last year trying to pretend didn't exist. It gutted him harder than Columbine's tears, if only because he knew his little tiger would rather eviscerate herself than admit the weakness.

"He's yours, tiger," he said, adding his own weight to Clarise's proclamation. Ironically, Cora hadn't been the one he'd thought would become so emotional over a pet, but it just went to show how much he knew about kids.

Columbine's hands found the spots of fur around Cora's arms and between the two of them, the cub settled quickly; shifting from growling to purring. "It is a tiger cub," Columbine hissed, her voice caught between a high-pitched squeal and the need to be quiet. "Father showed me what they looked like when we were talking about baby animals. He is so soft and pretty."

Cora dropped her cheek to his head, rubbing her face against his fur. "He is," she agreed. "And he's mine!"

Ahh. Staking ownership. That, Avis could understand.

YHWH looked at Avis and grinned. "I felt it only fitting that Cora has a tiger for a companion, since she's taken them on as a namesake." He looked past Avis to where Clarise stood. "The decline in the latter half of his lifespan has been removed, so although he's still technically mortal, he won't die of old age. In fact, he won't age a day past his prime."

"But he'll still only live two decades at best, won't he?"

"Of course not," YHWH scoffed. "He can be killed at any time, but he no longer has a natural expiration date. His level of invulnerability and capability will be up to Cora." Looking at the girls, he smirked and added, "And if the way she's gushing over him is anything to go by, it'll take Amaro's touch while tapping into his powerbase to end him."

"And your Almighty is okay with that?" Avis asked, knowing how ... *upset* his twin would be if someone inside the family tried to circumvent his claim on even one mortal soul once it reached its expiration point.

"It was his idea," YHWH insisted with a wry grin, without taking his attention from the girls. Raising his voice, he asked, "Have you come up with a name for him, tiger? It'll get a bit weird if we call out 'tiger' and you both answer."

"Justin."

Avis stared slack-jawed at his older daughter. "Justin?" He said the name as if it was directly linked to something he scraped off the bottom of his boot, probably because that's precisely how he felt about it. "Of all the names in existence, why in the realms would you pick Justin?"

Cora's shoulder's straightened and she lifted her chin at him. "Why shouldn't I?" she shot back defensively.

"Because you couldn't pick a more common name in the entirety of existence— except maybe Jack."

Cora screwed up her nose. "I don't care. It suits him," she said, sliding her hand under the tiger cub's backside and rising to her feet. She snuggled her face against the cub's purring head and said quietly, "And when you grow up, you're going to eat anyone who makes fun of your name, aren't you, baby?"

"Justin's a good name," YHWH said with a nod of approval. "And it does suit both of you."

"I don't think Strahan's going to like this encroachment on his choice of companion," Avis muttered, just loud enough for Clarise and YHWH to hear him.

YHWH's gaze cut to him, and his grin lengthened into a lazy smile. "Strahan lives on the other side of Mystal from you. I'm sure you and Amaro can handle his hurt feelings in the matter." He paused when a young hand tugged on his slip and looked down at Columbine who was staring up at him.

"Will I get a party too?" she asked.

YHWH's smile softened indulgently as he went down on one knee in front of her. "I know it was your birthday only a few weeks ago, sweat pea," he said, cupping her chin with his palm and dusting her cheekbone with his thumb. "So, how about this? Since Cora had to wait until she was six before she had her first birthday party, how about next year when you turn six, I'll throw you a party that's all for you. That's fair, don't you think?"

"I guess," Columbine answered with a sigh, more out of resignation than because she wanted to agree with it.

"Wherever we happen to be, we will ensure you have a party of your own for your sixth birthday," Clarise declared. "Until then, sweetheart, you should go and enjoy your sister's party, for it will not last beyond the day."

"And I have plenty of games to play," YHWH added, as he slid his hand into Columbine's and squeezed it lightly. "We'll all have a great time, starting with the blowing out of the candles. Cora," he called, not because she'd gone far, but to gain her attention. As he led Columbine to the cake table, he used his free hand to wave Cora over. "You're up, tiger. Front and centre. But before you blow out the candles, you need to think of something to wish for."

"Like what?" Cora asked, returning to the first table.

"Well..." YHWH tilted his head a little in contemplation. "I bet when you were on the Akheron River, you spent every day wishing for an end to that raft ride."

"Try every minute of the never-ending day," she sneered in disgust.

"But the reason you wished for it, was because you didn't think it was likely to happen. That's what a wish is, tiger. Something that you want with all your heart that you're not sure you'll ever get."

Cora twisted her lips together in thought, then shook her head. "I don't think I have anything else I want to wish for," she admitted. "I can literally shapeshift into existence anything I want."

YHWH's smile grew indulgent. "That, and that alone is the only reason the second table over there isn't overflowing with more gifts than you could ever know what to do with. Technically, you're all still on the move, so I couldn't give you more than you could easily carry."

"I believe that is our cue," Clarise said, and from behind her back, she revealed a small, gift-wrapped parcel about the size of Avis' hands if he held them in a double fist. As he had no idea what his wife had created on the fly, he kept his mouth shut and watched on, giving the impression this had always had his stamp of approval.

Cora manoeuvred Justin so that he lay along her right forearm while she used her left forearm to secure him against her chest, freeing her hands at the wrists. "Thank you, Mother, Father," she said, looking to each of them before taking possession of the gift. Her fingers tore easily into the soft paper, revealing a small object made of supple black leather.

Once the paper was discarded, Avis saw it was a lady's pouch roughly the same size as his hand, with a long, braided, leather shoulder strap that became the intricate stitching which held the whole purse together. The pouch had a large flap over the top bearing the golden Mystallian sigil. It didn't quite sit flush with the pouch and had a pair of drawstrings hanging from under it. Sure enough, when Cora flipped open the cover, the opening of the pouch was crushed together by the drawstrings.

Justin chose that moment to squirm and Cora almost dropped him. "Damn it," she growled and grew a second set of extended arms to hold the purse while her original pair repositioned the tiger cub. "You are seriously gonna get yourself hurt if you keep wriggling like that, dum-dum," she grumbled, ruffling the fur over his forehead reproachfully.

"Welcome to parenthood," Avis mused, causing YHWH and Clarise to smirk with him.

With her second set of hands, Cora opened up the pouch to the size of a dinner plate and reached in ... all the way to her shoulder. She froze and looked back at her mother; who smiled and nodded. "It is able to carry anything you want," she said, her tone matter of fact. "The mouth of the purse will expand to admit any sized item you wish to store or retrieve, and once inside, it will be held indefinitely with no sense of time until it is retrieved."

Cora, it seemed, was keeping up with the capabilities of this thing better than Avis was.

"And how do I get out a specific item if I have a million things in there?" she asked.

"Picture in your mind what you are looking for and reach into the bag. That item will find your fingers."

Cora's gaze cut to her sister, and that sly grin of sibling mischief was one Avis recognised far too easily. "Don't even think about it, tiger," he warned, trying to keep the hint of amusement from his tone. He himself would love to stuff the runt in a bag like that for a few millennia. As he said: it was a sibling thing.

"You still have to make your wish," YHWH said, gesturing at the candled cake. Avis had seen a lot of cakes and even more lit candles in his time, but he'd never seen a cake being used as a candelabra before. That was just weird.

Changing her grip on Justin without fully letting him fully go, Cora ducked her head and one shoulder through the shoulder-strap and settled the purse on her opposite hip as if it had always been there. "We could've used that before we left the Well," she said, using one of her second set of hands to pat the purse possessively. "I would've loaded it up with everything imaginable, if I'd have known how long that stupid river ride was going to take."

Cora was focused on the cake as she spoke, and as such she probably hadn't seen the way he slid his gaze accusingly to her mother, who at least had the decency to blush in embarrassment. It took him all of two seconds to think of the only reason why Clarise hadn't done that herself, and the party mood within him vanished. "I *really* don't like your father," he growled with a shake of his head.

Clarise slid her hand into his and squeezed. "He has his reasons for what he does, Avis. Whether we understand them or not, we have to accept he always has a plan."

YHWH choked out a bark of laughter, which he attempted to cover up with a raised hand and a series of shallow coughs. "Sorry," he chuckled, his eyes dancing merrily when they both turned to look at him. "That's just usually my line." He was still snickering to himself as he shifted his focus to the table where the girls stood, leaving a very confused Avis in his wake. "So, have you thought of your wish yet, tiger?"

"Yeah, I..."

"Uh-uh!" YHWH cut in, immediately raising his finger and waggling it at her. "The only chance you've got of having it come true is if no one else finds out about it."

"What kind of a stupid rule is that?" Avis demanded. The ONLY chance a wish had of coming true was if someone else knew about it and made it happen. Especially if that someone was him.

"Mine," YHWH answered, moving that shaking finger around to tap Avis squarely in the chest. "And I don't want you poking around in her mind for what it is either, little brother. **This is Cora's secret sixth birthday wish, and you will let her keep it that way.**"

Avis wasn't sure what part he wanted to annihilate first. The physical contact that implied superiority or the bullshit claim that he—Avis—was somehow the little brother of this bastard. In fact, the only part of YHWH's spiel that he didn't have a problem with was Cora's desire to keep a childish secret from him. With everything else he had to worry about, her secret wish was so far down the list of his concerns that he wasn't even sure if it was on it.

Red seeped into Avis' vision and he wrapped his whole hand around YHWH's prodding finger. If it wasn't for the presence of the girls he'd have snapped that finger off and rammed it down the angel's throat. Instead, he leaned forward, still without releasing the finger. "If you ever, *ever* touch me again, angel-boy ..."

YHWH twisted so that his back was to the girls, and when he did, the youthfulness in his eyes hardened without any hint of remorse. "You're spoiling Cora's special day, Avis, and I'm going to have to insist that you **calm down,** at least **until the party's conclusion.**"

Avis blinked, the red in his vision vanishing, as if it had never been. He looked to his left where Clarise stood, apparently fascinated by their interaction. "Fine," he said, slipping his hand from Clarise's grip to lay his arm across her shoulders. He released YHWH's finger with a dismissive flick and turned his attention to Cora. "Make your wish, tiger."

YHWH beamed almost as if it was his birthday and slapped his hands together, swinging back to the table. "Just think it, tiger. Whatever it ... that! Whatever you're thinking right there, baby girl," YHWH declared, pointing at her with both hands decisively. "Whatever it is that's put that wistful look on your face. Hold onto it and blow out all six candles at once. That's another rule, if you want the wish to come true."

"Now I see why the adults don't have these types of birthday parties," Avis murmured into Clarise's hair, causing his beloved wife to look up at him curiously. "Could you imagine someone like us blowing out our annual age in candles on a single breath?" Chuckling at the imagery, he envisioned Armina's second youngest son who was Mystal's god of the Winds and added, "I don't think even young Rabbe's breath could pull that off, even if he tapped his powerbase."

"Indeed," Clarise mused, resting her head against his pec.

Cora drew in a deep breath and blew out all her candles in a single exhale, working her way across the cake three times to make sure they wouldn't reignite.

"Happy birthday to you ...!" The high-pitched operatic chorus that sprang from nowhere to fill the air scared the shit out of Avis and he instinctively drew Clarise closer to him and spun around, searching for the source in case it needed to be eliminated. The song itself was also new to him, but it wasn't until he looked up that he realised the soldiers along the pearlescent wall had been replaced by the regular parasitic kind that he *really* wanted to rip the wings off of. They held their hands out in front of them almost in worship as they continued to harmonise, but the biggest surprise was when YHWH joined in to repeat the first line, his deep baritone both complementing them and isolating him at the same time. Avis had not expected a voice that deep out of a child that apparently young.

Not knowing the words, Columbine hummed along with the tune, her knowledge of music giving her a rough idea of what to expect and when.

Poor Cora didn't know where to look or what to do, and it was with great heartache that Avis realised it was because she'd never been the sole centre of attention in a good way before. Her apprehension filled eyes slid from one adult to the next, holding 'Justin' (and by the Twin Notes, he was going to do *everything* in his power to get her to change that awful name!) like a shield, just waiting for the hammer to fall.

No wonder YHWH was so insistent that he tone down his temper. Cora was on tenterhooks already and needed all the positive reinforcement they could muster. He plastered a happy smile on his unwilling lips, if only to do just that.

At the end of the song, the lines of angels overhead cheered and applauded, as did YHWH. That part, Avis could get behind, and he and Clarise applauded as well.

"Don't ever tell anyone what you wished," YHWH repeated, moving around the table to slap his hands around Cora's shoulders, cuddling her close from behind. "Happy birthday, sweet pea."

Cora looked over her shoulder at him, torn between excitement and wariness. "So, what happens now?"

"Now, you get to decide who has what slice of cake that you cut up and in what order," he said.

"Wait … wait-wait … wait," she stammered. "It's *my* choice who gets what slice of cake I cut up?" Her eyes flickered to her parents and back to YHWH again.

YHWH nodded emphatically. "That's right, tiger, and no matter what you choose, we'll be happy with it." He looked over Cora's head to where Avis and Clarise stood. "Isn't that right, Avis?"

Avis wanted nothing more than to throttle YHWH at that moment. Ultimatums were one of his many pet peeves, but when he lowered his eyes to Cora, she had her gaze locked on him, awaiting his response. He had no doubt if he said 'no', she wouldn't question it and hand the job over to someone else. Clarise's light squeeze around the waist indicated she would support his decision, regardless of which way it went. "It's your day, tiger," he said, nodding his consent. "Like your mother said, make the most of it." *But do keep in mind, I'll be in charge of every other meal you have for the next year, so don't be getting any bright ideas about sandbagging me to make a point, tiger,* he added, if only to himself.

Cora's eyes twinkled and she turned and whispered something to YHWH.

"Of course," YHWH chuckled in response. The large cake-knife between them shimmered, and between one instant and the next snapped into a child's full-length sword; much like Cora had been using during their practice. Cora's grin was ear to ear as she used her other set of hands to pick up the blade that was quickly becoming second nature for her to carry. Avis' gut clenched at the obscene use of Mystallian steel, and for both Cora's and YHWH's sakes, he was glad Armina wasn't there to witness it.

Twisting Justin to the side so she could see what she was doing, she laid the sharp edge of the sword across the cake and pressed down, slicing it neatly in half. As it was a large, three layered circular cake, she took the baseplate it sat on and swivelled it ninety degrees, cutting it a second time. Two more cuts in rapid succession had the cake separated into eight equal parts.

Given that there were only four in the family and YHWH present, Avis wasn't sure who the other three slices were meant for. One might have been for Justin; except he was too young for anything other than milk. Perhaps they were for seconds. He glanced at YHWH. *If the cake was any good.*

Using the flat edge of the sword and her fingers, Cora placed each piece of cake on a small butter plate. The first two pieces, she carried to him and Clarise. Her bottom lip was nipped between her teeth as she waited for them to accept her offering.

"Thank you, sweetheart," Clarise said with a smile, unwinding her hand from his waist to receive her portion. Avis accepted his as well, adding another nod of approval to his smile. Equal portions for everyone. He should've expected nothing less from her.

Next to receive their slices were YHWH and Columbine, who munched happily on the cream and vanilla treat. Avis bit into his own slice, though he was more interested in Cora than the familiar flavour of the cake. She returned to the cake table with her back to him and after a few seconds of doing 'something', she twisted around to reveal a third right hand under the other two. Justin still took up her primary hands, but the other three each held a piece of her birthday cake on a plate. Avis eyes widened in surprise and he had to remind himself that the designation of the slices had been left up to her, and if she wanted to hoard three slices to herself, today was the only day she'd get away with it. That still left one on the table.

Cora gave her parents a wide berth as she walked past them towards the house, and Avis turned to watch her go, believing she was heading into her apartment where she could eat all three slices without ridicule. Instead, she drew to a halt in front of the three servants and held out the plates to them. "These are for you," she said, decisively.

Deep inside, Avis' fury and indignation reignited. No child of his would *ever* serve food to a servant, let alone do so before eating herself! It didn't matter that this was Cora's party and everything about this was supposed to be her choice! It just wasn't right! If only he could make himself care enough to voice it!

The cake churned in his gut as he watched the servants nervously accept the cake, their eyes constantly moving to him and Clarise to gauge their reaction to such a breach in protocol.

"Are you certain you approve of this, my love?" Clarise asked.

"No," Avis growled, with none of his usual aggression.

YHWH chose that moment to materialise alongside them. "It's her day, Avis. So long as she doesn't hurt or kill herself, or anything else, what she chooses to do today is up to her. If she wants to feed the servants, she will feed the servants. Don't make her second guess herself now that she's finally starting to make a few harmless decisions of her own."

"If we agree to this, it will only be for today, YHWH," Clarise said, stepping in on behalf of Avis. "This will not be happening tomorrow, or any other day of the year."

YHWH held up one finger. "It's just one day, guys. One day that's all about her, and every crazy, stupid thing she's ever wanted to do."

"One day," Avis ground out in agreement, nodding for Cora to continue.

After everyone had eaten their slice of cake and had their fill of the other finger foods, YHWH clapped his hands together for everyone's attention, and asked, "Now, who's up for some games?"

And with that, the rest of the day went by in a blur of childish entertainment that Avis had to admit was fun to observe. Many times YHWH tried to draw him and Clarise into the games, but both declined and chose to watch from the sidelines.

CHAPTER FORTY-NINE

The weeks that followed were some of the best memories Clarise had had to date. Somehow, despite his rank and power, YHWH was never required to leave them for a moment to see to other matters in the realm. Which, Clarise had to admit, was quite lovely of the Almighty. She couldn't picture any other celestial in the Known Realms being given nearly a two-month reprieve from their pantheon duties, especially one as important as YHWH seemed to be.

And YHWH had been the perfect houseguest, though how he could be seen as that when they were the ones visiting his realm, amused the Highborn Hellion in her. Columbine was still the only one to acknowledge his theoretical family connection by calling him Uncle YHWH, though he didn't seem to mind. Cora spent most of her time with her father, practicing swordplay of all things. Knowing that was the Mystallian way still didn't please Clarise, though she had to accept that Cora was following in her father's family's footsteps. Accept and adapt: the unofficial mantra of the Highborn Hellion Ladies.

Regardless of her lack of swordsmanship, Clarise grew to suspect that Cora's skill was improving at a rate faster than even her advanced maturity should have allowed for, though she refrained from asking the question of her husband. Not because he would lie, but because he would not. They seemed to have a considerable difference of opinion when it came to how long their children should remain locked inside their own minds.

Columbine, by contrast, spent the majority of her day out with the cherubim. Avis had relented early on in their vacation and permitted the huge creatures onto the lawn of their temporary home. He still drew the line at allowing them inside the house, but for now, every one of them took up roost in and around the brute squad guards. Something about the way they stood at their full heights and stared down at the Highborn Hellion Guard caught her eye, but she couldn't for the life of her give it a name. Something ominous. Maybe it was their lack of fear. Most beings tended to avoid her father's elite guards at all costs. These ones stood head and shoulders over them, and they stood with a combination of strength, purpose and something else …

* * *

It wasn't often that a vocal emotional response other than vulgar cursing permeated the air of the upper realm, and Belial wasn't particularly enjoying it this time. From his throne of the Damned, he watched as Theodrick lay over the left arm of his crystalline throne, one hand covering his eyes while the other pounded on the throne arm mercilessly. He was laughing so hard, tears streamed down his face and through his fingers. The occasional thump under the Table of Divinity meant even his feet were joining in his merriment. "Fucking serves you the fuck right!" he howled between breathless gusts of laughter. "Twenty-fucking-six of those dickless, cock-sucking motherfucking fuckers to four and those fuck-face fuckers have the fucking original butt-fucking intellect of their balless fucking

Pryde! I hope to fuck they fucking eat your realm-damned, fucked up precious fucking brute squad!"

All his profanity aside, Belial hadn't considered the possibility that the remaining true gryps with their knowledge of the past would hold a grudge against his brute squad for the virtual annihilation of their species. All those that were born after the near genocide were utterly terrified of both the brute squad and Theodrick's crystalline warriors on an essence level and ran as soon as their paths crossed. Belial knew this, because he'd tested the theory a few times over the eras by creating illusions around those surviving members. Even the mindless ones that Apollo kept as war-pets squealed and ran in panic from the sight of either Order or Chaos' pillar army. It had become genetically imbued in them to be beyond terrified, and that blind terror only increased with each new generation. By contrast, the cherubim of Heaven hadn't been born in fear. They were part of the original Pryde which lived as immortally as any descendant of an established celestial. Ironically, they could have lived any number of eons before enduring the loss of their Pryde, and like any blooded warrior who'd survived the near genocide of their species by a specific enemy, they were itching for payback. Especially when (as Theodrick so succinctly put it) the odds were twenty-six to four.

For a moment, Belial considered sending more of the Highborn Hellion Guard into the field as backup, but then decided against it. Even with their top speeds, it'd still take them too long to get into Heaven to save their colleagues. Beelzebub could cover the distance with time to spare, but that would betray just how powerful the pillar champion truly was to his daughter and her family. It would also lead them to deduce just who had been behind the construction of their home in Heaven and moved Columbine and her entire household to its safety in the space of a heartbeat. Better to potentially lose four basic warriors than risk that.

Besides, it seemed the cherubim were too interested in the presence of the Weaver to exact revenge for an ancient slaughter. And Columbine, with her adorably gentle heart, would be devastated if her brute squad guards were killed. The cherubim wouldn't risk upsetting her. They may not have understood what she was supposed to mean to them, but instinctually they knew their place was at her feet.

* * *

The weeks turned into nearly three months before Clarise noticed the slight changes in her husband to indicate he was growing restless. His smiles were not as genuine as they had been, and he'd started to sigh a lot under his breath. It was obvious to anyone with eyes that he knew how much his family was enjoying themselves, and was doing everything in his power to not spoil it for them; though clearly he'd had enough.

"Mother," Columbine said, one morning after lunch. "Father is not happy, and he will not tell me why. Am I doing something wrong?"

At that moment, Clarise knew their time in Heaven had drawn to a close. And if she knew it, YHWH would too. "No, sweetheart. You have not done anything improper. Your father misses his family in Mystal, and the longer we stay here, the longer it is before he sees them again. That is why he is sad. But because you, your sister and I are having such a lovely time here, he does not want to tell us that."

"Like the way I miss Charon?"

Clarise drew in a deep breath and released it slowly. "Yes, sweetheart. Exactly like the way you, Cora and I miss Charon."

Without waiting for permission, Columbine stepped forward and wrapped her arms around her mother's hips. "Maybe one day, Charon could come and live in Mystal with us?" she asked, resting her ear against her mother's waist.

Clarise's eyes glazed as she looked to the ceiling and softly petted her daughter's hair. "Then his father and the rest of the Highborn Hellions would miss him just as much as we do. That would not be very nice either, would it?" She avoided the subject of how the Mystallians would feel about a bastard son living amongst them because Columbine was too young to understand that complication.

"Father needs to go home," Columbine declared, with a slight lift of her chin.

A single blink had Clarise's eyes back to normal. "And are you alright with that?" she asked, genuinely interested in where her daughter's mind was at.

Columbine's shoulders sagged. "Uncle YHWH and the cherubim will be sad."

"YHWH already understands how your father is feeling, sweetheart, and the cherubim knew our time would draw to a close eventually. All good things must come to an end, in order for new good things to take their place." That was the way of Chaos.

"Like what?"

Clarise thought for a moment. "Well ... after everything you have heard about your father's family, are you not at least a little excited to meet them for yourself?" The wave of happiness that crashed through Clarise as her daughter's face lit up with excitement told her she'd chosen the right future subject. Relieved to have done so, she bent down and kissed Columbine's hair. "Go and take the rest of the day to say your farewells to the cherubim," she said, giving her younger daughter a soft push towards the doors. "In the morning, I will be asking YHWH to take us to the Olympian border."

Clarise knew the exact moment Columbine informed her gigantic friends of the family's decision to leave, for their caterwauling was so profound she heard it through the soundproofing of the house. Avis and Cora appeared a few minutes later, the former with his hands planted firmly over his ears. "What in the name of Mystal has gotten into them!" The question was a bellowed shout that shook the paintings in their sitting room, and Clarise realised that for the moment at least, he was without his hearing.

Choosing not to answer him with words he wouldn't hear, Clarise's eyes went to Cora to see if she was alright. Her answer was to grin and wink cheekily, then raise her left hand with her little and pointer fingers raised and the middle two fingers held against the palm by her thumb in Chaotian pride.

Clarise took Avis by the elbow and led him to the chair in front of the fire, where he dropped his weight without removing his hands from his ears. She sat on the arm of the chair beside him with her arm draped over his shoulders and waited for his hearing to come back. Cora stretched across the plush rug in front of the fire with her head propped up on one hand, also waiting. "We're going soon, aren't we?" she asked.

Clarise placed a finger against her own lips, knowing if she had this conversation outside of Avis' hearing, he would see it happening and go into Cora's mind and hear it for himself, then come back out with his own, shouted input, only to go back in again to hear their replies. That level of bending disjointedness didn't appeal to Clarise, who preferred all three of them to be in the physical realm discussing matters together.

It only took a few minutes, before Avis hesitantly cupped his hands around his ears and then slowly lifted them away. "What in the Twin Notes was that all about?" he demanded, after wiggling his jaw and swallowing hard to confirm the last of the buzzing had left his ears.

"I told Columbine to let the cherubim know we will be leaving in the morning."

Avis' head jerked towards her just moments before Cora's did. "We are?" they both asked, simultaneously.

Clarise draped her arms around his neck and pressed her forehead against his. "It is time," she said with a smile. "You have been more than gracious, my love, but if we stay any longer, I feel I might take root and never leave."

Avis smiled and kissed her lightly against the lips. "Can't have that, now can we?"

"Is this the point I need to leave?" Cora asked, deliberately drawing their attention to her presence before they went any further.

"Yes," Avis said, just as Clarise said, "No." At Avis' childish pout, Clarise slapped him in the chest. "Stop it."

"Yeah," Cora added, her lip curling in disgust. "Seriously. Stop it."

"Stop what?' Avis's look was purely predatorial as he snapped his arms around Clarise's waist and dragged her into his lap, his lips curling lasciviously.

"That's it! I'm out!" Cora declared, bouncing to her feet and heading for the door at a flat run. "And don't be doing anything until the door's shut. Like fused shut!"

Clarise's eyes flared at her total lack of respect for them as her parents, but Avis' bark of laughter prevented her from triggering every single pain receptor inside Cora's small body at once. "Avis …" she complained, after Cora had let herself out with an overly loud bang of the sitting room doors.

Avis shook his head. "She's just being a Mystallian, love. No one likes to picture their parents having sex." Holding her firmly against him, he slid off the chair to the plush rug Cora had abandoned. "And now that we have the room to ourselves," he purred, looming over the top of her.

Realising he was serious, Clarise squirmed. "You are incorrigible!"

Avis lowered his weight onto hers to pin her to the ground, then slid his hands along her arms until his fingers knotted into hers and kissed her passionately. "Absolutely," he whispered once he had thoroughly ravished her mouth; his voice thick with unspoken promises.

* * *

The meal that night was a sombre affair, which quite frankly surprised Avis. He was certainly keen to go; Cora had offered no opinion either way and Clarise seemed to have accepted the ending of their time in Heaven with all the grace of a

Highborn Hellion. Nevertheless, the mood that fell over the meal as Tilu and the governesses served YHWH and the family bordered on depression. Even Columbine stared at the food on her plate and pushed it around with her fork instead of eating.

Finally, of all people, it was YHWH who spoke up first. "This is unacceptable," he declared, putting his utensils down and pushing away from the table. Avis' gaze slid to his right where their house guest sat. In lieu of an explanation, the angel stood up and turned towards the doors, waving for them all to follow him. "C'mon. Our last night together shouldn't be like this." He never once looked back as he let himself out. "It feels more like a funeral."

All four of the Mystallians looked at each other, though Cora was the first to stand and charge out after the angel. Columbine waited just long enough for Avis to nod once in consent and she too was off, leaving Avis and Clarise at the table. "Shall we go and see what the lunatic's got in mind this time?" Avis asked, shaking his head in amusement. Over the last few weeks, the family had been introduced to a variety of new concepts; some not as enjoyable to him as others.

"I believe so," Clarise replied, making a hand gesture to bring Tilu forward to help her out of her seat. She then walked the length of the otherwise empty table and took Avis' hand in hers as he too stood up. "If only to keep an eye on what he gets the children up to."

When they walked outside, there was no sign of the lawn that reminded Avis so much of home. The bottom step of the stoop was half buried in the finest white sand he'd ever seen, sparkling under the flickering flames of the overhead bamboo torches that were set into the ground in short intervals to mark out a given path. The path was obvious, not just because it didn't sparkle like the sand, but because it was covered in tiny dots of coloured paper circles, roughly a quarter of his little finger's thickness. A wall of white curtains, halfway to the property perimeter, waved in the breeze. That same breeze when it reached Avis, reeked of the ocean. He could hear the girls laughing on the other side of the curtain, along with the heavy, quick beat of hand drums. The former was enough to lift his spirits, though the latter concerned him. Who else had joined them without his knowledge or permission?

Avis stepped out onto the paper covered path, only to rear back with a gasp of surprise as the paper flew upwards like reverse snowfall. "What in the Twin Notes ...?" he roared, as the paper spun for a few seconds, then settled back along the path. He had little love for the way Clarise tittered lightly at his side.

"I have heard of this," she said, her eyes gleaming mischievously as she raised one foot and held it out over the path. Looking at Avis, she tapped her toes against the path, sending the paper flying again. While it was still airborne, she tightened her grip on Avis and stepped out onto the path, forcing him to follow. "Relax, beloved," she laughed, releasing his hand to hold both at head height to try and catch as much of the crazy paper as possible.

Avis stood still. He was far more interested in the way the tiny pieces of paper were making his wife behave than the paper itself. He had never seen her show this playful side of her nature outside the bedroom, believing it 'too unruly' for public consumption. Yet here she was, dancing so happily that he couldn't help but smile at her, even if at times, he lost sight of her due to the quantity of paper.

When he hadn't thought it was possible, her eyes widened, and she whirled towards him. "Avis, it is edible!" she said, beaming. "It is sweet and bubbles on your tongue as soon as it lands."

If they'd have been anywhere else, her sudden playfulness would've triggered his protective instincts and he'd have hauled her out of the paper and back into the house until she had better control of herself. But YHWH considered them family and he belonged to a group of angels that only answered to the Almighty himself. Avis may not have believed in their supposed family connection, but he knew YHWH would never do anything to harm them. So, for once in his almost eternal life, Avis decided to lower his guard just enough to see where this would end. Already, his wife and girls were laughing more than they had been ten minutes ago, and that was a good thing—right? Right.

"Try it."

Avis opened his mouth to refuse, only to have the dancing paper fall against his moist lips, teeth and the tip of his tongue. The invasive nature of it had him scowling, but as Clarise had said, it bubbled and fizzed, releasing a battery of different flavours all heavily leaning towards sweet; and sweet made him smile. He eyed the hundreds of thousands of pieces of 'paper' dancing across his gloves and wondered if his guess on the flavours was accurate. Only one way to find out. He targeted a piece of green paper and tasted it. After the smallest fizzle on his tongue, he tasted the hint of sugared lime. Gold was caramel. Pink – strawberry; red – raspberry; yellow – pineapple; purple – grape ... and so forth.

"Stop analysing it and enjoy it for what it is," Clarise grinned, and before he could stop her, she shoved a small handful of the papered flakes into his mouth and burst out laughing as it all exploded into fizz on his tongue.

"Oh, you think that's funny do you?" he burbled in and around the mouthful of paper that was foaming so much he could feel it frothing through his lips; making him look like a rabid lunatic in the process.

She must've seen the way his hands scooped the air into a fist-sized ball of the stuff, for she squealed and ran off the path, streaking across the sparkling sand. Maintaining his hold on the paper ball, Avis tore after her, relishing the chase. As long as she remained in her Mystallian form, he had the size and strength advantage over her, but it wasn't until they did a full lap of the house that he cut across the fourth corner and caught her in a one-armed crash tackle around the waist.

The sand may have been soft, but as they fell, Avis still twisted so that he took the majority of the fall. As soon as they were down, he rolled partially on top of her, trapping her arm under his body. From there, Avis revealed he still had his makeshift weapon. Clarise giggled upon seeing it and squirmed in denial.

"Now, what do you suppose I should do with this?" he purred rhetorically, holding it just over Clarise's face.

"You would not dare ..."

He pulled the ball of flavoured fizz-paper away and loomed over her until their noses almost touched. "What're you gonna do to stop me, sweetheart?"

He felt a palm-wide pressure on the back of the hand holding the fizz-ball, and before he could connect the dots of her plan, she mashed the ball into the side of his face. The gold in her eyes sparkled almost as brightly as the sand around them as he blinked down at her through the pieces of coloured paper that clung to his cheek, ear and hair, unable to believe she'd actually done that. Clarise covered her mouth with her free hand to hide her laughter.

"Oh, now you're gonna get it," he promised.

However, the threat died when a very familiar young voice shouted, "Again?!" at them from across the beach.

Closing his eyes, Avis bowed his head against Clarise's forehead and muttered, "Why did we have kids again?"

Clarise's gaze sharpened and she slapped him hard in the chest as she shifted out from under him, causing him to end up on the sand face down. He rolled to his side and lifted himself into a seated position with one hand bracing his back against the sand. "Great timing, as always, tiger," he growled half-heartedly, bending one knee to balance his forearm on.

Clarise gave herself a stimulation wave, and as he continued to stare at her, he could feel and see the tiny pieces of paper and specks of sand vanishing from his face and uniform. By the time he sighed and pulled himself to his feet, there was nothing more to do than run his fingers through his hair and let it fall into its usual place. Which he did.

"So, what made you come looking for us?" he asked. Not that he really cared, but something needed to be said to break the silence. Clarise slipped under his arm with her hand around his back. His own arm dropped across her shoulders and held her close as if there'd been no other way between them.

"You're missing the show," Cora answered, spinning on her heel and charging back the way she'd come, all the while waving impatiently at them to follow her. "Come on!"

Avis still would've preferred to follow his own show to what promised to be a very satisfactory conclusion, but with Clarise urging him forward, they trailed Cora into the curtained area.

CHAPTER FIFTY

Stepping through the curtains, Avis found a longer, narrower dining table set into the sand facing long-ways away from him. After his eyes ran the length of the table, the next thing he noticed was YHWH sitting in his seat at the nearest end to him. "You cocky little mo-fo," he muttered under his breath, knowing his word choice skirted the profanity ban Clarise insisted on, but wanting something more aggressive than "Get the hell out of my seat, you little brat."

YHWH turned and looked up at him with a knowing smile and gestured with his raised goblet to the two empty seats located between the girls in the middle of the table length. "Front and centre of the show," he said, before Avis could jump down his throat. The goblet swung to his right, and following the gesture, Avis finally noticed the huge stage that dominated the scene. Four women knelt in the corners of the stage, each beating on a drum in a combination of their fingertips, fingers, palm and heel of their hands. The different strikes allowed for slight variations in sound which blended seamlessly into their counterparts'.

In the middle of the stage were two men, who danced and chanted while spinning short poles with flames on each end.

"Fire dancers?" he asked scornfully, as Clarise led him to the two empty seats. His wife had been born in the Well of Hell and his children were half Highborn Hellions, and YHWH wanted to impress them with fire?

As he spoke, he stood behind the seat closest to YHWH where Cora sat and tapped his fingers against the raised back. "Scoot over one, tiger," he said, flicking his finger towards the more central seats. The setting was nice enough, and YHWH had certainly proven over the last few months that he did indeed hold sway over much of Heaven, but when it came to mixed company Avis still felt the need to circle the wagons around his girls.

To his relief, he saw Clarise make a similar request of Columbine out of the left corner of his peripheral vision. Good. It hadn't escaped his notice that a sixth chair had been placed at the far end of the table where Clarise would normally be, and not knowing who that chair was meant for gnawed at his nerves. Five was the magic number of diners at their table when YHWH was present. Four without him. So, whoever the sixth chair was for, Avis did not want Columbine sitting next to them.

With the girls safely corralled between him and Clarise, Avis deliberately stared YHWH in the eye as he pulled the now vacant chair out far enough for him to use and sat down with a flare of his cloak and every bit of presence he could bring to bear as the ruler of a pantheon.

One side of YHWH's lips lifted in amusement and with half-closed eyes that were creased in the corners, he breathed out a light snort and slowly shook his head.

Avis arched an eyebrow sharply, all but daring him to speak his thoughts.

Taking a casual sip from his goblet, the angel chuckled again. "Don't ever change, Avis," he said, focusing more on his drink than his guest. "No one would ever recognise you."

Knowing there was an insult buried in there somewhere, Avis all but growled. What was that even supposed to mean? Of course, no one would recognise him if he changed. That was the crux of change and why he hated it so much.

Predictability meant everyone knew where they stood. Surprises were how people got killed. When he opened his mouth to voice this, a familiar set of feminine fingers caressed his forearm just below the elbow. The lavender fragrance that filled his senses identified his beloved wife as the source, but that didn't stop him from looking down and finding she'd stretched her left arm out behind both girls' chairs to reach him. The strangeness of her body modification didn't bother him as it once had, and without giving it another thought, he took his own left hand and placed it over hers, squeezing it lightly. As always, her presence calmed him, but he still couldn't let YHWH get away with his swipe completely. "Don't plan to, brat," he murmured, though he was willing to leave it at that, if YHWH was.

YHWH's lips kicked up again. "I was giving you and Clarise the best seats in the house, however this works just as well." The angel's eyes broke away from him and went to the wall of curtains separating them from the house. Although he didn't say anything else, a dozen or so wingless angels stepped out from behind the swaying fabric as if they'd been there all along, each bearing an oversized tray laden with mouth-watering food. Avis drew in the various scents, recognising each as either a personal favourite of his or a member of his family. Even ones he hadn't told his wife or their servants about yet. Seeing them all here, in one place, had him salivating.

He also noticed none of these angels bore wings and assumed YHWH had put in a call to his fellow Third Choir members, somehow coercing them into servitude for the evening. It was the only thing that made sense, though he felt it demeaning beyond words and knew he'd never make that expectation of one of his own in front of other pantheons. Maybe ('probably', if he were being honest with himself) certain pantheon members from the runt's side of things would jump at the chance to make sure the visitors had the best possible time from a party perspective, but this whole vassalage angle was one step too far. With the exception of Cora's birthday party, he'd never permit a member of his family behind a plate in servitude.

Avis helped himself to the meat platter first and wasn't disappointed as the savoury meats from a dozen different sources dissolved on his tongue, leaving him both groaning in delight and sighing for more. The breads, each with a knob of softened herb butter somewhere within them, were almost an afterthought. He was well on to his third plateful when he realised Cora had stopped eating and was tapping her fingers on the edge of the table in perfect rhythm with the music; her eyes shining as she followed every movement of the dancers.

Suddenly, she jumped out of her seat and squealed, "I can do that! That's easy!"

Knowing she meant the fire dancing; Avis wasn't so convinced of her capability. The fire itself wasn't his concern. She could make herself fireproof. No, it was the fragility of her Mystallian pride. She'd come a long way from that beaten-down little girl he'd met in Hell, but if something happened and she couldn't handle the spinning sticks without making a complete hash of it, her growing confidence would be set back months.

From the corner of his eye, he caught YHWH's broadening smile of encouragement as he majestically waved her towards the stage with his raised goblet.

And that was when he realised this had been YHWH's end goal all along; to give the family a chance to participate in the revelry instead of merely observing. As such, he was vouching for the strange angels' close proximity. There'd be hell to pay if this went sideways. Nevertheless … "Go for it, tiger," he said, adding his own consent to YHWH's. "Show us what you've got."

Cora charged around the table behind him and YHWH and leapt the short distance onto the stage. By the time she landed, she had a pair of lit firesticks in her hands, already spinning them to create the same illusion of a fire wheel as her dancing counterparts. Step by step, roll by roll, she matched them, adapting to their creative changes on the fly so that by the second rotation, she had each of their new moves down as well. He was enjoying the dance a lot more now that Cora had taken part and seemed to be having an absolute blast.

As that particular dance ended, the tempo of the drummers shifted drastically, taking the insane beat that would've left any untrained non-shifter gasping for breath, to an ominously slow one. The male dancer furthest to the right pulled back to that side of the stage and dipped his head respectfully. The one in the middle pulled back to stand between the rear drummers.

Wondering if Cora had any clue as to what was going on, Avis went into her mind and quickly deduced she didn't. Worse, she planned to go with the flow of things just to see where they led.

He hated that approach. It was such a … *shifter* way of dealing with an unknown. Wrangling control would always be the better option for him.

Speaking of wrangling control …

He drifted through her most recent memories and discovered she'd been internalising for over an hour to practice with the fire sticks with nothing more than an image of YHWH for guidance. Horror flooded him, for there was no way an imaginary YHWH would've had the necessary capability to keep everything real for her. Just to be sure, he sat through the entire hour's memory from beginning to end, ready to tweak anything that fell outside that would really happen. In the beginning, the fire-sticks had been awkward for her, but after accidentally burning herself (and burning down the stage twice), she had somehow managed to keep everything real.

All by herself.

Avis' chest swelled with pride. *That's my girl.* And without a backwards glance, he turned and withdrew from Cora's mind; missing the moment when the image of YHWH arched backwards to watch him go.

Cora continued to mirror the other dancers, and when they moved away from the centre of the stage to stand at the rear and left-hand side of the stage, she went to the right; though unlike them her head was up and her eyes alert. All three of their feet stepped in time with the darker rhythm.

Again, Avis looked to YHWH for confirmation that this was part of something he'd find acceptable and received a stern nod to indicate it was. So, okay then. But just to be on the safe side, the Mystallian still prepared himself for the worst.

High over the empty stage, a tower of four large fire rings whirled into existence. Each was easily the width of Avis' outstretched arms and together they created a pillar of fire that hovered in the air for several seconds.

From her seat between her parents, Columbine gasped and jerked her head towards Avis, though he quickly deduced it wasn't him she was seeking out. Following her gaze to his right, he just caught YHWH lowering a finger from his lips with a telling smile of hidden secrets. Avis abhorred secrets. Especially the kind he wasn't privy to. But he could fix this. He may not have been able to get into YHWH's head to find out, but Columbine was still a very viable option and one he had every intention of utilising.

Leave Columbine's mind alone for the next five minutes.

Where that thought came from, he wasn't really sure, but in its own way it did make a lot of sense. Especially when she'd know if he went in there. If he did this, it would look as if he didn't trust her, and that wasn't the case at all. If anything, he feared for her. She was so young and gullible that people could easily confuse her with big words she didn't understand.

But this was YHWH, and in all the time they'd been in Heaven, the kid hadn't once crossed the line with him. Nudged it a few times; sure. Pissed him off more times than he could count; absolutely. But he still hadn't crossed the line to make Avis consider him an enemy.

That in itself wouldn't have been enough to keep Avis from finding out what they'd shared. Only a fool turned his back on a non-family member without first guaranteeing a dagger wasn't going to be forthcoming, and Avis was no fool. Besides, Columbine seemed very excited by whatever she had deduced, and the blue happiness that filled her thoughts in moments like this was something he could swim in for hours. Provided, of course, she remained happy. His little princess was always so eager to please, that him turning up unexpectedly in her mind because he didn't trust what made her happy might be the very catalyst that brought it all crashing down. He couldn't do that to her. Especially not when it was a good surprise that would reveal itself in short order. He'd just have to wait. He could do that.

Breaking his gaze away from Columbine's dark hair, Avis glanced to his right and wasn't quite sure why YHWH had such a satisfied look on his face as he refocused on the stage. The cocky shit had nothing to be smug about. Nothing at all.

Avis felt his brow furrow.

So why are you?

Feeling frustrated by his own lack of answers and knowing exactly who was to blame for that, Avis took a moment to fantasize getting his hands on the Almighty for at least ten seconds. Just long enough to punch that fucker square in the nose (if he had one). Safeguarding a whole realm from someone like him was bullshit.

Having none of the answers he sought, Avis' heartrate picked up when the bottom of the fire tower concertinaed upwards and an adult male angel dropped out of the chamber to land on the stage in a crouch that didn't quite allow his knee to touch the platform. He was covered from head to toe, and wingtip to wingtip in a skin-tight black substance that made his head appear ambiguous, and when he rose to his feet, the Mystallian patriarch was grateful to see a loincloth covering what he didn't want his ladies to see.

In each of his outstretched hands, he had not one, but two spinning firesticks, bound in the middle somehow, whirling in a rhythm that Avis couldn't quite follow with his eyes. An arm length rope leashed each of his ankles to a fist sized fireball that spun like an orbit in time with his stamping feet. Avis had no idea how he didn't tangle himself up, but as he skipped and danced across the stage, the tethered ankle fireballs spun under the opposite raised foot, turning him into a blur of flames in motion.

The newcomer pranced across the stage until he was on the right-hand side opposite Cora where he stilled, though he managed to keep everything moving with the smallest of efforts. Only the cross bar of firesticks in his right hand stopped, and with a deliberate challenge, he held one of the points towards Cora, then rolled his wrist so his palm was under the stick and beckoned her with the very tips of his fingers.

Cora's sticks broke in half down the middle and pivoted, locking at ninety degrees into a pair of matching four-point firesticks. Her breathing increased with the difficulty, but nothing else gave away her apprehension. And then the two began to dance.

* * *

As time went on and more and more courses were added and taken away from the table, Avis' ultimate focus remained locked on the stage. Each time, the newcomer led with a dance that was even more intricate and difficult than the one before, and each time Cora matched his physical prowess move for move as if she'd known how to all along, much to Avis' delight. Complex acrobatics were added to the routines, along with fire hoops at the knees, waist, neck and elbows.

At the end of Cora's turns, Avis lifted his thumb and forefinger to his lips and whistled his approval, applauding loudly. Sticking it to an angel, in whatever form it took or whatever way a Mystallian could, would always receive his glowing endorsement.

After being soundly beaten (in Avis' mind), the angelic dancer crouched to the stage, then leapt vertically into the air. Fire continued to circle the angel, but as his wings worked to maintain his aerial position, the dancer touched his bare feet with his lit firestick.

Flames flew across his body, growing brighter as it burned, and not once did he cry out in pain. Brighter still. The blaze grew so intense that Avis had to half shut his eyes to continue looking at it.

And then it dawned on him. He knew that fire! He'd felt its insidious bite at least once an hour for almost two straight years! Fucking hellfire.

Whether it was a coincidence or the bastard had been waiting for Avis to make that deduction (the Mystallian wouldn't know which until their paths crossed outside of Heaven) the hellfire suddenly winked out, leaving the all-too familiar male with flame red hair and matching feathered wings which were flared to take his weight. Ice blue eyes, polished silver plate armour and a sheathed hellfire blade on his hip completed the unwelcome sight.

So much for good surprises.

"Uncle Uriel!" Columbine squealed, leaping to her feet to rush around the far end of the table.

Cora seemed no more thrilled to see the chaotic crown prince than he was, and he could well understand why. Not only had the bastard been a raving lunatic the last time they'd all crossed paths, but from a Highborn Hellion point of view, Cora had matched him move for move and he was a higher-ranking demon lord: a huge taboo amongst the Hellion Highborn.

Depending how his thrall took the slight, he could take extreme offence to her actions.

Not while Avis breathed.

Unwilling to waste time going around the table, Avis launched himself to his feet and vaulted over the cumbersome piece of furniture, determined to get to Cora and break Uriel's line of sight on her with his own body if he had to. If bending had still been an option, he'd have already put his brother-by-marriage in a realm of hurt to buy himself time.

Clarise also jumped to her feet and rushed as quickly as propriety allowed around the end of the table to reach her brother.

The only one who remained seated was YHWH.

Uriel ignored them all but Columbine. To face her, he turned in mid-air and dropped to the ground on one knee with his arms outstretched for her. This wasn't like the parting Avis had seen back in the Well of Hell, where everything had been nauseatingly proper. Or their most recent encounter either. Uriel's radiant smile was as out of place for Avis as the tears that poured down his cheeks, and Columbine rushed into his outstretched arms, wrapping her own around his neck and squeezing the life out of him. "I am so sorry I scared you, little one," he wept, burying his face into her hair.

Avis collected Cora under the arms and twisted himself to stand between his older daughter and the crown prince of Hell that was currently acting like anything but. He still wasn't happy that Uriel had his paws on either of his girls, but of the two, Columbine had always been Uriel's favourite and now was no exception. The archangel had been a psycho in front of both girls, but he was only crying into the hair of the one who mattered to him.

Despite her being a little too old for the move, Avis balanced Cora's backside on his hip and used both arms to cuddle her close, knowing without looking that his brave little tiger's silent tears dampened his doublet. *Bastard. Fuck him.* Cora was strong and didn't need the Highborn Hellions and their bullshit favouritism anyway. She had a real family elsewhere. She had him.

Using his cloak to hide her tears from everyone, Avis continued to carry her as he stepped away from the stage, wanting as much distance between him and his brother-by-marriage as he could possibly arrange. His eyes met Clarise's as they passed like ships in the night, and he made sure everything on his face told her how unhappy he was that Uriel was both here and he had Columbine in his arms. In return, he saw in her features that she was torn between the two sides and he couldn't blame her for that. She hadn't renounced her Highborn Hellion heritage, and he would never ask that of her, but the divide in the family at that moment was about as wide as it could possibly be.

It occurred to him as he returned to the table, that every step he took to separate himself from Uriel, was a step that separated him from Clarise and Columbine as well. His walk had been a physical representation of where the family stood emotionally; with him and Cora on one side and Uriel, Clarise and Columbine on the other. He didn't like that at all.

With his cloak still up and around Cora's head to keep her hidden, he turned just before the table and watched as Clarise took Columbine from Uriel's embrace and straightened with the girl in her arms. Uriel stood up alongside her, though it wasn't either his sister or his niece whose gaze he sought out. From across the fine white sand, ice-blue eyes locked with his, and although there was infinite strength in that look, with the gleam of tears still trailing his cheeks, there was also … vulnerability. The latter took Avis completely by surprise.

Uriel stepped off the stage and approached them. "Cora, your Uncle Uriel's heading this way," he murmured, warning her without saying that if she wanted to cast a stimulation wave before he saw her tears, now was the time to do it.

Cora used his cloak to wipe her eyes, then pushed it back out of the way and sat up straight on his hip, putting her head at the same height as his. He didn't know why she had chosen this path of strength, but as a Mystallian, he liked it better. It showed she wasn't ashamed of anything. Not even the aftermath of her tears. He turned to face Uriel squarely.

Uriel's eyes flicked once to Cora, then back to him. Clarise and Columbine walked a hairsbreadth behind. Not enough to give the demon prince any real lead, but enough for Clarise to show him some measure of Hellion dues. Avis eyed his brother-by-marriage suspiciously. "So, just how much influence does the Fifth Choir have you under right now?" he asked, for something had to be responsible for his emotional state. It sure as fuck wasn't natural, that's for sure.

"Actually," Uriel replied, in a similar lifeless monotone to his father as he lifted his chin to reveal a thick band of mud-flecked gold wrapped around his neck. "This is the real me."

Confused by the declaration, Avis turned his thoughts inwards to show his family what Uriel had just said, to see if they could make any kind of sense of it. Even they could only guess. "How so?" he finally had to ask the source.

"Consuming tefsla prevents a shifter from accessing any of their shifting abilities for however long it takes the poison to break down. Wearing it in a band like this, allows the process to be temporary. Much like a seclusion ring blocks a bender. For the first time in a very, very long time, I am outside the reach of my powerbases and subsequent thralls."

Avis had never seen the mud—no … *tefsla* flecked gold before. But now that he knew what it looked like, he planned on finding the source of the dull purple-grey substance for Mystal and stockpiling the shit out of it. Lifting his eyes to Uriel's ice blue gaze, Avis could see the exact moment he realised Avis' plan. The derisive snort that escaped the archangel was more like what Avis had come to expect from him, though in this case, he wasn't sure why.

"Avis, you and I will never be friends."

Understatement of the era, but since Uriel was making the effort to be amiable, Avis decided to play along. For now. "Probably not," he agreed, wondering where this was going.

"Yet, despite your past, I cannot in good conscience refute the care and love you have shown my sister and your daughters since your reunion. It is …" —he worked his jaw as if the next word had a chokehold on his tonsils— "… *commendable*."

Avis blinked at Uriel uncomprehendingly. *Is he …? Is this … a peace offering?*

The word coming from the demonic crown prince sounded so alien to Avis that he shook his head in outright denial. After everything they'd gone through, that could never be it. Never. But what if it was? He himself had literally just been thinking about how wide the divide in the family was, and Uriel chose now to approach him? Maybe his brother-by-marriage had been thinking about it too? And if so, why? Why now? Uriel had made his stand very clear back in Hell, and Avis had been willing to bet the entire realm of Mystal that his opinion would never change. If the crown prince of Hell suddenly hugged him, he'd have no choice but to throat punch the imposter.

Movement to Avis' left warned him moments before YHWH entered his peripheral vision bearing a neutral expression. "So long as you both cling to the anger and humiliation of the past, the future will forever remain in the shadow of what could be." He placed a hand under both Avis' elbow and Uriel's and squeezed lightly. "Neither of you has to like the other, to appreciate the love you both feel for the same people."

Avis caught the way Uriel's eyes slid across to Cora, just as his went to where Clarise and Columbine stood alongside the archangel. His free hand raised of its own accord for them, and without a word, Clarise stepped forward and turned to face her brother, at the same time sliding in under Avis' raised arm. She dropped the hand that had been supporting Columbine's back and snaked it across his lower back beneath his cloak, just as his draped across her shoulders with his fingers splayed across the back of Columbine's neck; massaging his thumb along the cord of her throat.

"Avis," Uriel said, drawing his attention back to the archangel. His hands were up as well, both reaching for Cora. His blue eyes burned with the question that neither of them expected him to voice.

"That's Cora's call," Avis answered, for she had been the one he'd snubbed and upset the most, and she'd be the one to decide how she'd react to that. As always, that space would be hers.

Uriel's eyebrows flexed ever so slightly, but then he shifted his focus to the girl in Avis' arms and rolled his hands to expose more of his palms. "Cora?" was all he asked.

On sheer principle, Avis would've made him say all the words. Every damn one of them. None of this silent dictation that the hellions loved. However, the combination of an acquiescent hand gesture and softer tone seemed to be enough for his little tiger, who released his neck and leaned out towards her uncle with outstretched arms. Uriel took her weight happily, though he baulked at the way she locked her legs around his hips and gripped his neck in a tight chokehold. Avis watched his brother-by-marriage recover quickly, closing one arm across her backside for support and the other across her back and shoulders, his head tilting to rub his cheek against her neck and shoulders. His eyes were closed and his breathing slow and deliberate, as if he fought to keep his emotions in check. Finally, after a minute or two of silence, he cleared his throat and managed to rasp, "It was never my intention to hurt you, little one. If you believe nothing else I have ever said in your young life, please believe that."

"I know." Cora pulled back to hold him at her tiny arm's length. Uriel still held her comfortably with his elbows bent. "I'm ... not Highborn Hellion anymore."

"Maybe not in title, little one, but that does not make you any less family to me," Uriel said and, despite the minor wobble in his voice at the beginning of his speech, by the end his words were filled with both promise and authority. He took the hand from around her back and placed it flat against her chest. "So long as my blood runs in your veins, I will only be a blood-link away from you." Cora had looked down to watch his fingers spread out across her chest, and as such showed no surprise when he lifted his hand away and used his pointer finger to lift her chin so that her eyes were on his mouth, where in his mind she'd be more inclined to heed him. "We are still family. Always."

The corners of YHWH's eyes creased as he smiled without saying a word.

CHAPTER FIFTY-ONE

Avis had no idea how long the family stood together in the empty space between the stage and the table, but eventually, YHWH said, "I think this calls for a more casual atmosphere."

That was all the warning Avis received before the temperature dropped and cool, moist air flowed across his face, carrying with it the forest scent he loved so much. The visual shift from sand to a deeper, richer greenery was also staggering.

Not liking the unexpected change at all, Avis turned his head to take in his surroundings as quickly as possible, then internalised to process what he'd seen. He didn't need his imagination for this—merely his memory. Millisecond by millisecond, he crawled the visual pan forward, pausing at every difference to figure out what that meant to him and his family.

The first change happened while he was still staring forward, and now that he'd frozen the scene, he could appreciate it for what it was. Uriel no longer stood between him and the stage. Both vanished, to be replaced by a wall of thin trees with exposed roots and thick overhead foliage framed a cresting waterfall in the distance. As water cascaded into the lake below, Avis estimated a good kilometre of cliff face separated the top of the waterfall from the bottom, and the line of churning white against the lush green was quite breath-taking.

Moving the memory to where he looked to his left, he saw the same bank of trees following the edge of the meadow like a privacy wall, not that they'd ever had to worry about that before. Clarise was still to his left, though she had now been seated with Columbine perched on her lap. Given that his point of view was only half a head over hers, Avis had to assume that he too had been involuntarily seated. *That's. Not. Cool.*

But there wasn't a damned thing he could do about it. Changes of this magnitude weren't the work of an overseeing angel. Not even a little bit. Which meant YHWH had reached out to his boss to pull off a minor 'miracle'. And because the biggest of Heaven's power players had intervened on his angel's behalf, Avis was in no way able to retaliate. Not unless he wanted the pleasant scene he found himself in to become far more sinister.

Years ago, that wouldn't have been a problem for him. Nothing the Almighty could do to him would be permanent. Not even the Hellion Highborn had been able to make it stick. But the very reason he'd been able to escape the Damned was the same reason he wouldn't take any risks now.

Uriel was in a chair semi-beside his sister with Cora on his lap, though his chair was ahead of theirs and twisted back to face them. Moving back to the starting point of this memory, he saw the cherubim both in and out of the water in the distance, almost as if they were playing. Avis highly doubted that was the case, but until he returned to the physical realm and watched them beyond this snapshot, he wouldn't know either way. YHWH was in a similar location to Avis' right as Uriel had been to the left, making the four of them seated in a casual horseshoe formation that faced each other.

Okay then. He could deal with this, provided the Almighty didn't try to make him do anything else.

Avis replayed the memory twice more at half speed just in case he'd missed anything, and once he was satisfied he hadn't, he returned to the physical realm. Of course, the first thing he focused on was the cherubim in the lake and to his astonishment, they *were* playing. Their wings sliced through the water as easily as the air, and when they lifted them high, water sprayed everywhere, causing all four faces to make noises of delight. Some took to the air and deliberately crashed into the water with a tidal surge that covered others, who in turn chased the bomber through the water. It was so light and carefree and as far removed from their dangerous legends that Avis had to once again remind himself of the peril they presented.

He took a deep breath and pushed his boot heels into the soft moss around his feet. However, instead of a solid, padded chair back that he could arch his spine into, Avis felt his lower torso push against a fabric that had way too much give in it to support his weight and nothing at all between his shoulders.

Sucking in a sharp breath, he straightened and turned, eyeing the ridiculous strip of canvas stretched between two metallic pieces of box frame that only came half-way up his back. The armrests were made of similar strips of stretched fabric, as was the seat itself, and he was sure it should've collapsed under his weight. U-shaped metal legs were crossed and bolted into place, making the whole thing appear incredibly fragile and slipshod. A cylindrical cut-out in the right arm of the seat held a similarly shaped cup of ambrosia.

A quick glance at everyone else found each of them in similar chairs, though granting the flimsy things the title of *chair* was pushing it in his mind.

"Relax, Avis," Uriel grinned, stretching his feet out in front of him and crossing his armoured boots at the ankle to prove he had absolute faith in the robustness of these seats. The lowness of the back gave his wings plenty of room.

"A casual setting requires casual seating," YHWH said by way of explanation as he relaxed into his own chair. "And family have nothing to hide from each other."

"Don't kid yourself," Avis grumbled, shooting Uriel a dirty look.

Uriel snorted, reaching for his own cup. "Amen to that," he agreed, tilting it towards Avis before taking a deep swig of his drink. Even Clarise smirked.

The only one who didn't find the rebuttal amusing was YHWH. "Perhaps I should have said family aren't *supposed* to hide things from each other," he said, and although it was loud enough to be heard, Avis got the distinct impression the statement was more for himself than his guests.

"So, what do you do here, Uncle Uriel, when you're not acting like a crazy psychopath?" Cora leaned away from the archangel as she spoke, holding his left shoulder for balance.

Avis felt his chest tighten apprehensively; not because his little tiger had posed a question she had every right to ask but in anticipation of Uriel's crappy reaction to it. Highborn Hellions as a whole did not take kindly to being talked to like that and if he did anything to her in retaliation (ie: anything at all), this would be the shortest truce in history.

And he knew from the way Uriel's gaze narrowed reprimandingly that his brother-by-marriage was considering that anyway. Then, he took another, longer swig of his drink and returned the cup to the drink holder in the arm. "I see your Mystallian tact is coming along remarkably," he said, with a disapproving shake of his head. "But to answer your question, little one, my powerbase here is not all that different to the one I have in Hell. Here, I am the archangel of vengeance. My actions are defined by the inappropriate behaviours and actions of others." Uriel tilted his head and sent Avis a sideways derogatory look that also had Cora's eyes moving to her father. "And sometimes, those behaviours are so reprehensible that bouts of temporary insanity are perfectly justified."

Avis arched his back, stretching his right hand over his head and his left out behind Clarise's head as if the subject bored him. Then, once he was sure that neither his wife nor his little princess could see it, he sharply rolled his left wrist and flipped off his brother-by-marriage.

Cora burst out laughing and slapped Uriel in the chest, while the archangel's eyes widened in shocked disbelief. Was it juvenile? Absolutely—but still very satisfying.

Clarise's head slowly canted towards him, her eyes glittering with wry suspicion.

Having half-expected to receive that look, Avis leaned farther back in his chair and smirked at her, not in the least bit apologetic.

After a few seconds, he moved his gaze to Columbine (still on her mother's lap) and noticed her eyes were locked on where the cherubim were playing, and a soft wistfulness had taken up residence. Sometimes he wished she wasn't so transparent in her desires, but other times, such as now, it made his life a lot easier. Leaning into the fabric strip that made up the left arm of his chair, he tilted his head towards her and said, "Princess, why don't you go and play with the cherubim on the shore where your mother and I can watch you?" As was their custom, he wasn't about to make it an order.

It was all the permission she needed. In a blur of instantaneous speed, she went from sitting in her mother's lap to reforming in a running pose that had her rushing across the moss towards the lake. "Stay out of the water!" he shouted after her, knowing first-hand how heavy the uniform could be when it became waterlogged. Just because she was an instantaneous shifter, didn't mean in a moment of panic she'd know how to save herself.

Just to be sure, Avis looked over his shoulder to where her personal bodyguard had been standing behind Clarise's seat and found the spot already vacant. *Good.*

The cherubim rushed out of the water as soon as they realised she was inbound, and they met in a chorus of happy sounds on the moss-covered shore. *They're legendary creatures of war … They're legendary creatures of war …* he repeated to himself, despite the fact they behaved more like sycophantic pets around his daughter.

As time rolled on, Avis discovered the tiny cup of ambrosia that he'd been given never actually emptied, and with a happy buzz, he found himself relaxing into the chair that seemed by design to encourage slouching. The structure was still strange to him, but after testing its boundaries, he'd found it could indeed support his weight regardless of which way he leaned.

Conversations quickly moved from the present to the larger and more pleasant story pool of the past. And unlike being with his own family, those currently with him hadn't heard any of his stories. With billions of eons to draw on, Avis easily kept up his end of the dialogue. The presence of Cora and the Highborn Hellions meant his stories had to be kept clean, but they were nonetheless entertaining. Likewise, some of the crazy scenarios Uriel had found himself in over the eras had

Avis practically crying with laughter. Clarise's stories might have been more subdued in comparison, but to Avis, they were just as important, and he made sure she was given plenty of opportunity to speak. YHWH added his own stories to the mix, describing at one point how he and Uriel had first met when the crown prince of Hell had returned a badly beaten Lucifer to Heaven and tossed him over the Pearly Gates with an unrepeatable threat to keep him out of Hell's business.

Avis looked across at Uriel, who shrugged unabashedly. "Long time ago," he said into his drink. "Father and the Almighty later came to an agreement. Hell would forever feature in Heaven's mythos and Lucifer would act as the fallen angel of Heaven who now ruled all of Hell. As the Lord of Lies, Father would reap the huge power boost from a whole realm believing in the lie."

Clarise nodded, both in understanding and agreement.

"It also meant I didn't have to deal with any potential troublemakers, as those unpleasant souls were and still are transported to the shores of the Akheron River for processing through Hell instead of here," YHWH added, with a thoughtful sip of his own drink. "The influx of mortal souls that would otherwise be denied to him was the sweetener that Lord Belial found irresistible."

Avis could well believe that. Heaven wasn't one of the bigger realms by any stretch, but laying claim to what had to be at least a fifth of Heaven's sapient mortal populace had him envious of Belial's deal. Many of the pantheons had a fixed number of mortal souls within the realm which they churned through via reincarnation, and here was Heaven, agreeing to a constant and rapid depletion of their worshippers. No wonder their Almighty constantly dispatched his angels to try and convert the mortals of other realms. He still didn't approve of their poaching ways, but at least now he understood them.

Even young Cora had stories to add, drawing on the hijinks she'd gotten up to in the Well, and much to Avis' delight and Uriel and Clarise's chagrin, not all of them had been discovered and disciplined by the hellion hierarchy.

Although he hated to admit it, this was turning out to be one of the most enjoyable nights he'd spent outside the bedroom. Sitting in a circle on what had to be the flimsiest chairs in creation, with the most basic of cups holding a never-ending supply of his favourite drink and shooting the breeze with people he had no interest in impressing; all the while laughing in return at their stories. No pressure. No expectations. It was fantastic.

CHAPTER FIFTY-TWO

The following 'morning' wasn't nearly as enjoyable, though it had started out well enough. Once the family had retired for the evening, Avis and YHWH took their conversation to the dining room, where they drank and chatted the rest of the night away. Just as he had suspected all along, YHWH was no child, and since it was only the two of them, Avis was able to speak more freely than he had before his family had gone to bed. In sharing true, unedited opinions on various subject matters, Avis discovered they actually had a lot in common.

Then, out of nowhere, high pitched animal noises blasted through the walls from outside. After several hours of relative quiet between him and YHWH, the unwelcome commotion had Avis wanting to cover his ears, despite the walls supposedly being sound-proofed. "What in the Twin Notes?" he demanded, as YHWH swivelled on his seat towards the front doors.

"Columbine's up," the angel said, his gaze narrowing. "And the cherubim know she's leaving this morning."

As if to confirm YHWH's appraisal, the door to Columbine's apartment opened and his darling little princess poked her head through the gap to look at them. "I-I could go and talk to them," she suggested, as she left the safety of her doorway and came to stand between him and YHWH with her hand on her father's knee. She was already dressed in her Mystallian uniform, but Avis doubted that had anything to do with putting on one piece of clothing at a time. He didn't need to look to know she'd rolled out of bed, snagged something for mass, and gone from bedraggled to perfectly dressed and presentable in seconds. "Before they wake up Mother and Cora."

No way was she going outside when things were clearly that far out of control, but YHWH beat him to the denial by about half a second. It was the first time the Mystallian had ever seen genuine fury crackle behind the boy's eyes as he rose to his feet and placed his hands on Columbine's shoulders. "Stay here with your father, sweet pea." The command was almost a growl and he never once removed his gaze from the front doors that separated them from the cherubim outside. He pressed his lips lightly to her forehead and pushed her further into her father's grasp. "I'll take care of this." And with that, he vanished in a clap of thunder and lightning that left the smell and taste of ozone in the air.

Avis clamped a hand on Columbine's shoulder to keep her with him and released a slow, silent whistle of surprise. He knew that move. Zeus may have been known for casting bolts of lightning as his establishment field required, but when he truly lost it, he didn't just throw a lightning bolt; he *became* the lightning bolt.

Avis almost felt sorry for what he assumed was about to happen to the cherubim, though now that he thought about the dynamics of Heaven, he wondered how YHWH was supposed to achieve that. The angelic overseer was a self-professed member of the Third Choir and the cherubim were Second. Those designations meant the cherubim should've outranked YHWH ... unless YHWH wasn't 'just' a Third Choir member. What if he was a choirmaster, like that Raphael angel? If he was, that'd also explain why the rest of the Third Choir had chosen to serve them last night at YHWH's behest. *Sunova bitch!* YHWH was downplaying his actual position of Third Choir choirmaster. *Cheeky little shit.*

Avis knew from personal experience that the Master Guardians of Hell's Nine Levels were feared by every other hellion without exception. And it didn't matter what level the individual hellions were assigned to, if any of the nine Master Guardians came through, everyone but the Highborn Hellions made room for them. If the same held true here, it would also explain why YHWH seemed to share such a personal connection with the Almighty. Putting Heaven and Hell in the same thought process also made Avis realise something else he hadn't considered before. There were Nine Levels of Hell, and nine choirs of Heaven? Coincidence? Or maybe after the deal YHWH and Uriel spoke of between Belial and the Almighty was in place, Heaven remodelled itself to show a level of unity between itself and the ancient realm of Chaos. It certainly would've made things easier for Heaven's mortals to swallow.

The noise outside ended as abruptly as it began, leaving an echo ringing in Avis' ears. It killed the control freak in him to not go outside and find out how YHWH had managed to muzzle the great beasts. Carrots were all well and good when rewarding a well-behaved subordinate, but every now and then a very large stick was required to prove the man—or in this case, the boy—in charge wasn't to be trifled with. Avis had definitely seen the latter in YHWH's eyes.

Truth be told, he would've gone and looked, if he hadn't noticed Columbine's brow crease in concern as her bottom lip began to tremble. *Shit!* He knew that look as well, and if he didn't do something to distract her quickly, the waterworks would soon follow.

Without wasting another second, he used his other hand to drag her into his lap and buried his fingers into her sides; using his greater mass to cage her against the arm of the chair. At first, she squealed in shock, then she laughed, squealed and laughed again, arching against him as he continued to tickle her unmercifully. Her laughter had him laughing as well, which was exactly what he was hoping for.

Nearly a full minute later, YHWH reappeared in the same spot he'd disappeared from. "My apologies," he said, looking from Avis to Columbine and back again to convey the depth of his sincerity. "The cherubim knew this day would come and they should not have acted out now that it was upon them."

Avis helped Columbine right herself to sit squarely on his lap. "They will miss us," she explained as if that wasn't already obvious. "And I will miss them."

YHWH looked down at her and smiled, allowing his features to return to the boyish charm Avis had come to associate with him. He leaned back against the table and brushed her hair off her shoulder, sliding his hand against her neck to dust his thumb against her jawline. "Never doubt for an instant just how much we will *all* miss you, sweet pea," he said, looking across at her so earnestly that even Avis believed him. "But if the cherubim make it too hard for you to leave, then you won't want to come back, and I have now made them very aware of that. Like me, they want you to come and visit us as often as you're able." His fingers curled loosely under her jaw and his thumb brushed against her cheek. "They've all promised to behave from now on. Just … keep in mind you mean so much to them that it's going to be really hard for them to say goodbye today."

Columbine's bottom lip quivered. "They do not want us to leave."

YHWH sighed sadly and straightened. "It's *you* they don't want to see leaving, sweet pea. You are what's so very special to them. But you don't want to stay here if the rest of your family is going, do you?"

Despite the rhetorical nature of the question, Avis couldn't help but bristle. Mystallians instilled their moral code into their children by offering them a limited range of acceptable choices that gave them a sense of owning their space. Questions should never be posed to a Mystallian child unless all of the available answers were acceptable ... and the other eight levels of Hell would freeze over before he'd leave Columbine behind.

He only relaxed when Columbine shook her head, though he didn't like the way her brow furrowed and her bottom lip rolled into a pout of misery again. Tears sprang into YHWH's eyes as he gathered her into his arms and lifted her off Avis' lap. "I know, baby. I'm going to miss you too." His gaze lifted to Avis. "Every single one of you. More than you could *ever* imagine." He held her close for several long moments, then pulled away and brushed her fringe from her tear glazed eyes, blinking his own back in the process. "But we'll be together again soon, I promise. I still owe you a birthday party next year, remember?" He then turned his head to look over his shoulder at Avis' apartment. "Good morning, Clarise," he called, just as those doors opened and Clarise stepped into the dining room.

"Have you and Avis really been up all night?" Clarise admonished as she approached them, looking from one to the other and back again.

Avis wasn't sure if YHWH knew where her incredulity came from, but he certainly did. For months she'd been trying every possible means at her disposal to coax him into building a friendship with YHWH, only to have it happen right before they were due to leave. Had their roles been reversed, he'd have been annoyed too.

He and YHWH grinned and shrugged their right shoulder at the same time, causing them both to look at the other and chuckle.

YHWH twisted to half sit on the table's edge, supporting Columbine's weight on his raised leg. "As I was just saying to Columbine and Avis, you and your Mystallian family will always be welcome and safe here. Should you ever need me, I'm here and I'll protect you. I know my angels aren't very popular in the Known Realms, but ..."

"Getting your Almighty to keep them out of Mystal will be a great start towards changing what I think of them," Avis interrupted, not believing for a second that YHWH had that much pull over his boss.

"Done," YHWH said without hesitation. "From now on, they'll only enter Mystal after you or one of your people has extended an invitation for them to do so." He slapped his free hand against his standing leg as if to seal the deal. "In fact, I'll even sweeten the deal. Should you ever grant them entrance ..."

"I won't."

YHWH flicked his wrist to dismiss the interruption and carried on. "But should you ever do it, from this day forward they'll stay out of Mystal's mortal realm, so there won't be any chance of them accidentally influencing your mortals' beliefs." His eyes sparkled with excitement as he pulled himself off the table to stand alongside Avis's chair, perching Columbine on his hip. "Apart from Heshbon, of course."

Heshbon; Griffith's wife and mother to the Triplets of Construction. She was the former Seventh Choir angel who possessed the freedom to go wherever she wanted in Mystal, because in their eyes, she was as Mystallian as her husband and sons.

"Anything else?"

As much as Avis would've loved to see YHWH's declaration come to fruition, the boy's arrogance needed to be kneecapped; if only for his own good. It wasn't as if he was the guy in charge, after all. Avis stood himself, casting a derogatory look at YHWH as he reached out and took Columbine from him. "Don't you think you should run something like that past your Almighty before you start making promises on his behalf?" he asked, settling his little girl on his hip.

The right hand corner of YHWH's lips twitched as he fought to suppress a smile. "What makes you think he doesn't already know?" he asked with a wry cluck of his tongue against the roof of his mouth.

The sudden bout of humour at his expense didn't impress Avis. YHWH seemed to sense this, for he drew in a deep breath and, when he released it, all humour vanished from his expression. "All jokes aside, I had hoped to share one last breakfast with you all, but between the heartache that the cherubim are broadcasting and the way their misery is affecting Columbine, it's probably more prudent to forego the meal and head straight for the border." He met Avis' probing gaze and asked, "Would you object to me bringing Uriel in to expedite matters? Using the ..." —he glanced momentarily at Clarise— "... *fire rings*, we can only transport up to seven beings at a time."

Had YHWH asked that question yesterday, Avis' answer would've been a categorical 'Fuck yes, I have a realm-damned problem with that!', but things had changed a little between himself and his wife's oldest brother. As Uriel had said, they'd never be friends, but that didn't mean they couldn't be in the same space without trying to kill each other. At least, not while his brother-by-marriage wore his tefsla infused choker that kept him from going into a homicidal rage. "Go ahead," he said, not bothering to add the prerequisite of the choker, because YHWH knew of its importance as much as he did.

"I will see that Cora is made ready," Clarise said, and removed herself from both the conversation and the room.

Initially, Avis wondered how YHWH was going to get the message through to Uriel when the archangel was blocked from all outside influences. But the answer had been obvious once he thought about it. YHWH had the ability to hear and see all things at once, which meant he would know not only where Uriel was but who was with him, and get a message through to him that way. Being a choirmaster had its perks like that.

Whether he'd done it as Avis surmised or undertaken a different method, a few seconds later the tower of fire that he and his family had been introduced to the night before appeared in the space between YHWH's apartment doors and Avis' seat at the head of the dining table. Knowing what to expect, Avis waited for the fire to concertina upward to reveal the archangel.

It really was an interesting transport system to have within a realm; just not one he'd want in Mystal. He didn't like the way people could travel anywhere they wanted to on a whim, bypassing all manner of guardians and barriers.

Avis watched as the fiery rings shrank to the size of regular golden bracelets adorned with circular dots of colour just above Uriel's head-height and fell into the archangel's outstretched hand. Uriel then drew his hellfire blade and fed the sword through the rings until all four reached the hilt, at which point the hellfire overtook the rings and they vanished from sight. The roll of Uriel's wrist as he sheathed his blade made Avis think he'd done that move countless times over the eons. His eyes settled on YHWH. "You summoned me, milord?" he asked.

"The cherubim are not happy with Columbine's departure," the choirmaster answered, on behalf of everyone. "And since I have no inkling as to why they're behaving this way, I see no point in exacerbating it. Avis concurs, so whilst Clarise is seeing to Cora, I'd like you to collect the demon steeds from the stables outside and bring them here for immediate transport to the Olympian border. Preferably in one of their alternate forms that will make them easier for you to carry in your hands."

Uriel immediately bowed. "As you wish," he said, stepping away from them and heading out the front doors.

"I could watch that level of acquiescence from him all day," Avis grinned after the doors were firmly closed behind Uriel.

"If you hadn't made such an enemy of the archangel of vengeance and his family, you might have been privy to it more often," YHWH replied, with more than a hint of reprimand.

Avis shrugged. "Whatever."

Clarise came out with a fully dressed Cora just a few seconds before Uriel returned with the demon steeds (in the same tiny statuette form that they'd held in both Yaru and Rangi-Tuarea) in his left hand. In the other, he held the four gold rings with the coloured embellishments from before. "Do you wish me to take these four and a servant?" he, once again meeting YHWH's gaze.

YHWH shook his head. "No, I'd prefer you to take one of their guards instead of the servant, in anticipation of our arrival. I'll bring Avis and his family through afterwards, along with two other guards. That'll leave one guard behind to keep the servants at ease. You may then return to the house and bring across the remainder of their party."

Uriel again dipped his head in acknowledgement of the instruction and moved into the space near the front doors. As if it too had been summoned, one of the outside guards appeared at his side. With a flick of his wrist, Uriel tossed the four rings into the air so that they began to spin. They ignited on the first turn and grew larger with every passing second. Then, once they were wide enough to encompass Uriel and the guard, they dropped over the pair and thickened until they became a solid wall of fire. Then they vanished.

"That would be our cue," YHWH said, waving the family into the open space behind Avis' chair. Columbine's bodyguard and one other from outside joined them. YHWH passed his left hand behind his right, and as it came back into view, he held a set of his own rings. "Ready?" he asked, looking at the family.

Avis nodded. "Let's go."

Like Uriel, the boy threw his hand upwards and released them with a last-minute wrist-snap that sent them spinning over his head. Avis followed the movement with his eyes. The last-minute flick seemed to be what ignited them and when they hovered overhead, they grew in size and dropped over the gathered party, surrounding them in bands of fire. Avis said nothing, but in reflex he pressed Columbine's head into his shoulder and twisted her into the middle of the group; suspiciously eyeing the fire rings that whirled within a hand-width of his cloak. No heat poured off the rings as he'd expected, but the visual they presented was just as daunting. He kept his eyes on the dining room table through one of the gaps until the rings expanded to connect with each other, creating a wall of fire.

Avis had endured enough close proximity to fire to last a thousand lifetimes. He didn't even enjoy the aromatic crackling of timber as it burned in a fireplace anymore, unless there was a protective screen in front of it. But he wasn't going to let his family know how uncomfortable the prospect of being surrounded by flames made him, so he did what he'd always done when facing difficulty. He put his shoulders back, lifted his chin as if he owned the situation and held on to that superior pose as if his life depended on it.

Just as quickly as the fire wall had formed, it broke apart again into the four thick rings of flames, which thinned and lifted completely out of the way.

Already? Avis blinked in disbelief and quickly looked around to get his bearings.

They were no longer alongside the pearlescent wall, but the military that lined the outer border just a few metres away was one he definitely recognised. Large, circular shields of white with realistic flashes of three-tiered lightning bolts silently animating the surface. Pressed-gold helmets peeked over the top with an occasional red crest indicating an officer. A single, solid gold plate protected their torsos and strips of thick, studded leather fell to their knees. Gold shin guards and toeless sandals completed the outfit, reminding Avis of their shifter bloodlines.

Unlike the pantheon itself, these common Olympians were from the standard demonic stock, and as such, they were able to alter their own shape into any form they liked. Had their bipedal form been their only form, no army worth their salt would've left the top of the foot so exposed, especially where the officers were concerned. In the middle of hand to hand combat, a well-placed solid boot heel would shatter the bones of the foot and completely incapacitate them. Boots, say … like his Mystallian soldiers wore.

Uriel was standing to one side with the demon steeds still cupped in his left hand like a jumbled mass of toys. The guard with Uriel stood in front of the archangel and to his left, while the guard that had travelled with Avis took up a matching position to his right. Not enough to interfere with the Mystallian's line of sight, but enough to make their presence as protective escorts known. Columbine's guard remained at Avis' side.

Uriel passed the four statuettes to his sister. "I will return momentarily," he said, stepping away from them and back to the spot where his fire rings still spun furiously over the archangel's head.

Avis ignored his brother-by-marriage and turned his attention to the border. Technically, there were two realms that identified themselves as 'Olympus', but Avis knew this was the one ruled by his best friend. He knew because apart from the lightning on their shields versus the double face of Janus (which was the pantheon sigil of the other Olympus—no one could ever accuse that two-faced bastard of being modest) the lines of warriors that faced him consisted solely of men.

Considering Mystal's stance on women in the military, their exclusion here had been a highly contentious point between him and Zeus over the eons. It didn't help that Avis had always seen Ares as an annoying little upstart who (apart from a single, elite battalion of Amazons) didn't trust women in his army because he feared their loyalty would ultimately revert to his older sister Athena. In that regard, he was probably right, because Athena was Olympus' original Goddess of War and, unlike her idiot younger brother, she didn't make mistakes. Victory was literally built into her establishment. It was one of the many reasons why Armina got along so well with her, provided they didn't challenge each other over anything.

Frustration itched through Avis' veins every time he was confronted with the absolute lunacy of Zeus' current army. *Idiots,* he fumed. Ares, for having effectively halved the Olympians' combative capability, and Zeus for not supporting the original war goddess the way he himself supported Armina. As the red plumes of the officers moved through the ranks to reach the front of their lines, Avis thought he might have recognised one or two individuals amongst them. It was quite probable, given how much time he'd spent in his friend's realm. Unfortunately, their faces were the extent of his recognition. *Hey, you,* was all he'd ever needed for names.

Five cylindrical towers of fire appeared high above Avis and his family, but before they could crush together to reveal their passengers, all twenty-six cherubim poured from the bases, banking sharply in every direction to avoid colliding with those below. They roared and creeled to make their presence known, not that anyone would miss the gigantic guardians as they circled the area.

Then, on what appeared to be an unspoken command, the whole choir landed behind them in a synchronised WHOOMP that shook the ground, forming the same militant half circle on either side of YHWH that they had when the Third Choirmaster first introduced himself all those months ago. YHWH's reaction to their landing was perfect. Apart from the tousling of his dark hair and the flap of his slip, nothing else about him moved; not even to blink. Whether he had done it to prove his control to the Olympians, or it was merely a by-product of his natural comfort around the Second Choir, Avis couldn't be sure. Either way; it was a damned fine piece of intimidation.

Avis cast his gaze over the dual row of beasts and noticed each of them had their heads positioned so that at least two sets of eyes were on Columbine, while a third retained a constant vigil on the Olympians. It seemed they weren't taking any chances either.

Uriel returned with the final guard and the three remaining servants, which meant it was time to go. "Say your goodbyes to the cherubim, princess," Avis said, lowering her to the ground and nudging her towards the line of great beasts. He knew she'd want to make physical contact with each of them, and he trusted YHWH to keep them from doing anything stupid.

Sure enough, one by one she cuddled them, weeping as they each folded their wings around her and held her close for a few seconds before pushing her to the next in line. Avis turned away and rubbed at the deep ache that grew in his chest, focusing on his breathing to keep it level and steady. Seeing his daughter in tears always tore at his heart, but in this case, it was a necessary evil. They had to leave. This was inevitable.

YHWH tapped Cora on the shoulder, then went down on one knee with his arms outstretched for her as she turned to face him. Cora's stiff upper lip melted and she flew voluntarily into his arms. "I'm going to miss you all so much," he said as he arched his back and lifted her off her feet, his voice on the verge of breaking.

"I'm gonna miss you too, YHWH," Cora sobbed in return, crushing the life out of his neck. Once she loosened her hold, she leaned back to look down at him. "Do I get another party next year too?"

YHWH laughed, even as tears streamed down his cheeks. "Absolutely, tiger," he promised, mussing her hair until she ducked away and scowled at him through her own tears. He held up a finger. "One party every year until you reach maturity. That's our way."

Avis ground his teeth and tried to not roll his eyes. In just three sentences that were barely statements, YHWH had managed to finagle not just a return visit during the following year, but two a year for the next decade and a half. Worse, if Avis said or did anything to prevent it from happening, he would be the one stuck with dealing with the fallout. *Nicely played, you little dick,* he admitted begrudgingly, if only to himself.

YHWH hugged her briefly once more, then released her with a pinched smile and rose to his feet, fixing his tear glazed eyes on Clarise.

As he did so, she glanced at the demon steeds that still encumbered her hands then across to where Tilu stood. Fortunately for the servant, Tilu caught her implied message and immediately came and relieved her of the steeds.

Once Clarise's hands were free, she opened them invitingly to YHWH. "Until our paths cross again, YHWH."

Tears dripped from YHWH's chin as he stepped into the embrace and wrapped his arms around her middle, squeezing tightly. Avis hadn't noticed just how close in height they were before. "Take good care of this stubborn fool," YHWH whispered at the conclusion of the hug, his head tipping ever so slightly towards Avis.

At that, Avis *did* roll his eyes.

Clarise merely smiled in her usual serene way. "I will," she promised.

After clinging to her for a few more seconds, YHWH broke away from her and moved to stand in front of Avis. "We're better than we were, aren't we?" he asked, lifting his chin to look Avis in the eye.

Avis released a long breath as he considered the words, then finally nodded. "Yeah, brat. We are."

YHWH's immediate smile was dazzling and fresh tears of joy poured down his cheeks as he launched himself at Avis, wrapping his arms around the Mystallian's neck and standing on his tiptoes to bury his face into Avis' clavicle.

Stunned, Avis froze with his hands locked at forty-five degree angles from his sides. When he searched Clarise's face for what to do, she was rubbing her hands together in front of her lips and smiling happily at them. In fact, everyone seemed to be happy with their hug, except him. He knew he needed to do something, but since he was unwilling to return YHWH's embrace, Avis gave the boy's shoulders an uncomfortable pat. "C'mon, kid. You're embarrassing both of us here," he whispered thickly, knowing the Olympians were bearing witness to this.

It was enough to have YHWH step back and wipe away his tears with the back of his hand. "Come back with the girls, if you're able, Avis," he said, beseechingly. "I'd really, really love it, if you did."

Avis could see that. YHWH had made no secret of his adoration for him and his family. Nevertheless … "I won't promise what I can't guarantee," he replied with a negative shake of his head.

"Then give me your word you'll at least try."

Yes, the brat really was that desperate. "I'll *try*," Avis replied, purposefully leaving out the oath. YHWH beamed as if he'd received it anyway and stepped forward with his arms spread wide again, to which Avis threw out a hand to stop him. "Don't you dare hug me again," he growled, curling three of his four fingers against his palm to point at him in warning. "I mean it."

YHWH stopped and dropped his hands to his sides, but the broad grin remained. "One day," he said, as he turned side on to watch Columbine continue making her way down the double line of cherubim.

Not likely. "Maybe."

Uriel took the end of their discussion as his chance to speak, and after he made a hand movement that was meant to catch Avis' eye, he slid up beside YHWH and said, "We both know you will have more to worry about than me if you ever set foot in Hell again, but have Clarise blood-link me should you ever find the need to return to Heaven. If I'm within these hallowed halls and the safeguards are not put in place before your arrival, I will try to destroy you."

'Try' being the operative word, Avis thought to himself, but rather than voice his poisonous thoughts and part on bad terms, he nodded briefly in acknowledgement and turned his attention back to the Olympians.

Every set of eyes over there was glued in fear to the four Highborn Hellion Guards that accompanied them, and most fidgeted nervously. Because the brute squad had been silently accompanying Avis and his family for almost a year now, he'd almost forgotten how intimidating they could be to other celestials. It was a colossal reminder of just how much power their small group wielded.

Word spread along the Olympian lines like wildfire, with more and more troops arriving every second to bolster their numbers. Double, then triple their original quota. Not that it would have made a lick of difference to the Highborn Hellion Guard. If the brute squad were there to start something, they were the only force Avis knew of that could take on a pantheon and not give a damn about the powerbase that supported it. They destroyed powerbases. They destroyed pantheons. They could almost do it single-handedly. He often wondered if his father's crystalline soldiers were a match for that, but as they never left the Nexus (thankfully), it wasn't something he'd ever know for sure.

CHAPTER FIFTY-THREE

Once Columbine had completed her goodbyes, Clarise placed a protective arm across Cora's shoulders and drew her closer to her side, while Avis hooked Columbine under the arms and lifted her into the air, resettling her on his hip. The two sides then said their final farewells and Avis led his family to the Olympus/Heaven border.

As he did so, he pretended not to notice the way Columbine's hand lifted off his shoulder to continue to wave at those they were leaving behind.

Although it was a short walk across the lawn, by the time Avis and his party arrived at the very edge of Heaven's border, Athena stood in front of her troops with her faceplate up; as close as the former war goddess ever went to lowering her guard. Between her long, free-flowing hair that was as yellow as the sun and the white plume of her helmet amidst the sea of officer red, no one would ever mistake the pantheon goddess for anyone else. Her lips twitched when her eyes met Avis' but sobered as she deliberately took in each of the brute squad guards around him.

"Lady Athena," Avis said in greeting.

Storm grey eyes collided once more with his. "*Lord* Avis," she replied with a hint of mockery in her voice. Her gaze then dropped to Clarise at his side and she smiled politely. "Aunt Clarise."

Aunt…wha…? And then it hit him. *Gaia.*

Gaia was the primordial goddess of Zeus' pantheon, and Avis wanted to slap himself for forgetting this realm's original goddess of creation was also his wife's only older sister. He'd just been thinking about how the Olympians used shifting during battle, and he'd overlooked the fundamental fact of how that came to be for their pantheon.

Clarise smiled in return, and after guiding Cora across her body to stand with him, she stepped up to the border's edge with both hands raised in greeting.

Judging by Athena's reaction, the former war goddess had clearly been expecting a more subdued Highborn Hellion greeting from her prestigious aunt. Her eyes flared in surprise, but it was gone so quickly Avis had to review his memory to be sure he'd seen it. Nevertheless, Athena's welcoming smile grew and she leaned forward to accept her aunt's embrace.

Dropping his gaze to their feet, Avis couldn't help but notice the boundary line still ran between them. Proof that a formal invitation to cross into Olympus hadn't been issued yet.

"It is a pleasure to finally meet you, sweetheart."

"You too, Aunt Clarise."

When they pulled apart, Clarise said, "Of course, I speak as a Mystallian, not as a Highborn Hellion. As I am sure you are aware, if I were still under my father's sigil …"

Athena dismissed the matter with a carefree wave of her hand. "Yes, I know. I don't want you to take this the wrong way, Aunt Clarise, but the Hellion Highborn have been giving us the cold shoulder for so long, I'm surprised we aren't frozen right along with Antenora. I had assumed the presence of your Mystallian family meant your allegiance had shifted, though I must admit, I wasn't quite as prepared for the personality shift that went with it." She returned her focus to the brute squad guards. "Am I also correct in assuming they're here to protect you and the little ones?"

Just as Athena had gauged Clarise's loyalty by her clothing, Avis could tell the jury was still out with the Olympian as far as the brute squad was concerned.

"Avis has made quite a few enemies in recent times, and my father wished to ensure we made it to our destination unharmed," Clarise answered.

"And where exactly would that destination be?" Ever the war strategist, Athena had heard a possible threat and reacted accordingly.

Clarise held her ground. "We have yet to decide on a final destination, sweetheart, which is why we require sanctuary to consider our options."

Athena once again eyed the imposing guards. "Do I have your word, both as a Mystallian and as a Hellion Highborn, that you have complete control of them? I speak for everyone on this side of the border when I say we are not comfortable with their presence inside Olympus."

"Their orders are to safeguard the four of us," Avis intervened, moving forward to stand alongside his wife rather than be kept in the shadows of the conversation. Cora came with him of her own volition, though his outstretched hand across her chest prevented her from crossing the border line. "If you doubt their ability to adhere to those orders, you'll need to take it up with Lord Belial directly."

Athena's gaze cut to him, and what he read there wasn't flattering. "At least now I know how you made it this far in one piece, Uncle Avis."

Uncle Avis. From Zeus' pantheon. His best friend was now also his distant nephew. That was going to take some time to get his head around. The rest, he couldn't really fault.

"I had assumed Ares would have been the one to meet us at the border, sweetheart," Clarise said, bringing the conversation back to her. "Is he unwell?"

Athena snorted and twisted her lips to one side. "He's fine, Aunt Clarise. When word of the brute squad's presence reached the capital, it wasn't hard for me to convince Father that I should be the one to meet you all at the border. Given Hell's utter disdain for us, it was my belief that the sudden arrival of four brute squad guards would be the result of a visiting Highborn Hellion or ten instead of a legitimate threat to Olympus. My younger brother attempted to counter my claim by insisting that an assault on the Highborn Hellion Guards while their guard was down would be the kind of victory Olympus needed to finally be on equal footing with Chaos."

"Well, he's got a serious death wish," Cora snorted, fighting the wave of laughter that swept over her and failing miserably.

"He does have a rather inflated belief in his own capabilities," Athena agreed, her eyes glittering in amusement. "Fortunately, cooler heads prevailed and I was sent to greet you instead." Still smirking, she moved her attention to Avis. "Father will be most happy to see you again, Uncle Avis."

"So, are we welcome to cross, dear?" Clarise asked, seeking that confirmation.

Athena dipped her head and twisted to the side, making a long, majestic wave of welcome with her right hand. The wordless way the troops parted for them only reiterated in Avis' mind why Athena should never have been stripped of her establishment field. There was no way the men would've broken apart so smoothly, if Ares had been the one trying to move them.

"Of course," she answered, watching as the two advancing brute squad guards crossed the line first to ensure the family had enough room to pass between them unhindered. "Though if you don't mind me asking, what were those creatures that flanked Lord YHWH?"

It was no surprise to Avis that Athena knew the choirmaster by name. "They're the Second Choir, called cherubim. From what I'm told, they're a really vicious piece of work, though they didn't show that side of their nature to us while we were there."

Athena's face screwed up as if she'd tasted something incredibly vile. "Cherubim? *Really?*" She took a deep breath and bellowed her next question at those still gathered around YHWH. "That's your rendition of a true gryps?" Her expression of disgust increased with every passing second until she finally shook her head and turned back to the Mystallians. "*Trelos!* You can't half tell that idiot's never set foot outside of Heaven, if that's what he thinks the true gryps look like. They're not even close!"

Remembering what YHWH had said about hiding the true gryps in plain sight, Avis pinched his lips together in a tight smirk and refrained from commenting.

What came next wasn't nearly as amusing.

"And I must say, *Iliachtida* – you're the last person I thought I'd ever see Lord YHWH hugging without taking the opportunity to rip him to pieces. Did he ensorcel you or something, because you've certainly never made a secret about how much you hate him and his angels."

Iliachtida. Or, in Mystallian, *Sunray.* The Olympian version of Sunshine. Avis was so intent on following her speech that it took him a little while to realise what else she'd said. When he did, his expression soured. "My stance on *winged* angels has never changed," he argued, disliking the need to explain himself. "I don't hold the wingless ones stuck in Heaven responsible for the actions of their winged brethren."

Athena's eyes widened once more, and she searched each member of the family for any hint that this was some kind of cosmic joke being played on her. "You really don't know," she finally said, returning to Avis. Then, she threw her head back and laughed, and laughed, and laughed some more, until she was forced to fold forward at the waist and brace both hands against her thighs to support herself, and continued to laugh.

Finally, when the last of the spasms left her body, she straightened and wiped the tears from her eyes and sighed. "Oh, thank you for that, Uncle Avis. I haven't laughed that hard in centuries. But you've got it backwards. Lord YHWH's not an angel! He's …"

"I know who he is!" Avis snapped, hating the thought of being laughed at even more than the need to justify himself. "He's the Third Choir's choirmaster …!"

With her face still flushed with humour, Athena lifted her left hand and stabbed a finger back at where YHWH and the others stood. "Those realm-damned rings of fire that the cherubim came through with are the Third Choir of Heaven, you fool! They're the ophanim! Not Lord YHWH! Lord YHWH *IS* the Almighty of Heaven!"

"*WHAT?*" Avis swung on his heel, the entirety of his vision turning a near-blinding red. For three long months he'd had the creator of those angelic constructs in his grasp, and not only had he never once tried to murder the bastard, he'd invited him to stay with them! *NO!!*

YHWH wore a serene smile as he held his hands in a relaxed pose on either side of his body with his palms facing forward. As he bent his elbow and raised them to waist-height, a blinding glow surrounded him and lifted him into the air. He still bore the appearance of the boy Avis knew, but the power that cascaded from him in all directions was anything but angelic. Hovering in the air, his glow stretched out and plucked each of the cherubim and Uriel off the ground, lifting them all to levitate just below his hands.

Until our paths cross again, little brother. Grace be with you.

The words flashed through Avis' surface thoughts. Then YHWH, and everyone travelling with him, was gone.

MOTHERFUCKER!

* * *

Clarise was also in shock, though she cast her memory as best she could over the numerous conversations she'd had with YHWH, wondering if his powerbase of being all-powerful had somehow interfered with her ability to recognise the truth. But as she recalled each one, it occurred to her that he had never actually lied. What he'd said at the time was "The Third Choir had no wings", and from that, she and Avis had incorrectly *assumed* he was a member of that wingless choir. At no point did he ever actually say he was.

Seeing the truth as it stood now explained many of the cryptic things he'd alluded to about his relationship with the Almighty. "I see what he meant by hiding in plain sight," she said, with a displeased purse of her lips.

"Pardon?" Athena asked.

Clarise drew in a deep breath and released it forcing her exterior to return to its usual serenity. It was done now. There was nothing she or anyone else could do about it. "Never mind, dear," she said with a soft smile.

Heavy, choppy breaths were as much an indicator of her husband's irate state as the bone deep shudders that swept through him. He was trying to manage it though, which in her eyes showed just how far he'd come from the god he'd been.

She placed her hand on his elbow and squeezed. "Beloved, you need to calm down before you upset Columbine," she warned, knowing the mention of their younger daughter's well-being would be enough to offset any rage he felt, especially if he happened to be carrying her.

* * *

Avis felt so much indignant fury that he couldn't see straight. He wanted to rant, and rave! He wanted to kill everything in Heaven! For months, the Almighty had made a fool out of him by pretending to be a dumb, friendly kid, just to get him to lower his guard! And how fucking stupid was he to fall for it? He, a ranged bender who'd spent two fucking years in the original home realm of all shifters! He was married to a shifter, had two daughters capable of shifting, and had three fucking hellion servants for Mystal's sake! He was literally surrounded by celestials that could become anything they wanted! He should have known better!

His fury almost broke its mental banks when he felt Clarise's hand on his elbow. Between that, her lavender scent and the reminder of Columbine on his hip, his inner tirade stopped dead in its tracks. Columbine's tiny face was twitching in anger and she had a dangerous gleam in her eyes. Her entire body was rigid except the muscles along her neck and shoulders that shivered with unbridled hatred. Her eyes glowed and her face was contorted in fury.

Realisation drained all the blood from his face and limbs until his fingers grew numb. *By the Twin Notes of all creation … no … no!*

They'd gone to incredible lengths to shield Columbine from the touch-wrath of the Asgardians, only to have her blindsided by his rage now?

At that moment, the Olympians didn't matter to Avis. YHWH didn't matter. Nothing mattered but getting himself back under control, for Columbine's sake. Clarise's steely gaze bored into him, but she must have approved of what she saw for she didn't do or say anything to interfere.

"I'm so sorry, princess," he whispered, pressing his lips to her hair and rubbing her back and shoulders, willing them to soften.

Ever so slowly, Columbine's body began to relax and move of its own accord. Her hands unwound from his neck and slid over his shoulders to his chest, fisting his doublet somewhere around his pecs. The tension in her face also fell away, until she twisted her head and buried her face in the soft line of his throat. "That's it, princess. Let it go. It was never yours to have in the first place. I've got you." He didn't want to think about how he had been the one to cause this. Him and his stupid temper.

"*We've* got you, short-horns," Cora corrected.

Glancing down, he saw Cora had gripped her sister's knee in unconditional support, and nodded in appreciation. "We've got you," he agreed.

"If I hadn't seen it, I wouldn't have believed it," Athena remarked, drawing Avis' focus away from his daughters. The former war goddess was staring at him with the same level of shock she'd had when she realised they hadn't recognised YHWH. For the life of him, he couldn't think why. To add insult to injury, she then shook her head. "In fact, I *am* seeing it and I still don't believe it. When in the realms did you become such a family man, old timer?"

Avis sensed his wife's disgruntlement at such an impertinent question, though he understood Athena's stand. At no time throughout his long history had he ever claimed to be a family man. In fact, he'd gone out of his way to prove the opposite. Countless hours had gone into ridiculing Zeus for marrying Hera when he clearly didn't love her, and that was before the subject of their numerous rug-rats came up.

But this was different. He was different. He didn't see Clarise and his girls as a weight around his neck, dragging him through the eons. They lifted him up and made him a better man, and there wasn't a damn thing he wouldn't do for them. "When I finally met a woman who made me realise an eternity without someone meaningful to share it with was just another form of torture." He didn't care what it sounded like. For him it was the truth.

Athena closed her eyes and rubbed her forehead with two fingers. "I don't know whether to congratulate you, or vomit all over you," she said, poking her tongue into her cheek, even as she cracked one eye open to observe his reaction. When he didn't offer her any, she straightened. "Going back to our original topic, how long were you planning on staying in Olympus?"

"A while," Avis answered, keeping his response vague until he caught up with Zeus to assess the status of their friendship for himself. He stepped forward, leading his family across the threshold of the two realms, then turned to face the former war goddess. "The exact length of time will depend on a variety of things, the first being how long your father is willing to let us stay."

"Ask him yourself, Uncle Avis."

Keen to do just that, Avis' hand left Columbine's shoulders in a bid to blood-link with his new 'nephew'. But just as he was about to roll his wrist and speak Zeus' name, he remembered that his best friend had no problem answering anyone's blood-links, no matter where he was or what (or even *who*) he was doing. And with Columbine in his arms and Cora holding onto Columbine, the last thing he wanted was for either of them to get an eyeful of that. Unfortunately, due to his own heinous actions, Cora already knew too much about the subject and he had no interest in adding to her education if his friend happened to be in the midst of a drunken orgy.

"Athena, if you wouldn't mind, I'd prefer it if you reached out to your father first on our behalf," he said, lowering the raised hand to Cora's shoulder possessively. He looked down at Cora, then across to Columbine still on his hip, then pointedly at Athena in the hopes that she would catch onto his unspoken reasons.

Her snort and disbelieving headshake said as much. "This side of you is going to take a whole lot of getting used to, old man," she mused, still shaking her head as she raised her hand and called, "Zeus." Her eyes shifted to see something that wasn't there, and Avis knew the connection had been made. "Yes, he's here, Father. And it's as I said; the brute squad are with them for protective purposes only. Aunt Clarise and their two children are with them, along with three serv…yes, two."

She held up two fingers to emphasise the number as she spoke, and it wasn't lost on Avis that she held them up with the back of her hand facing her father, instead of rotating it at the wrist to imply peace. One of the many ways Athena had shown her father subtle disrespect for demoting her in favour of her little brother. "They have two children. And you're going to love this. Avis wanted me to reach out to you, because he didn't want to scar the girls for life with visions of what you might have been up to." She angled her body so that she could see Avis and his family by looking to her right, but not far enough that they were visible to her father. The smirk she carried as she shot Avis a wry look had the Mystallian patriarch straightening where he stood. "Because he won't put his children down long enough to talk to you himself, I assume." The whole family was included in her next visual sweep. "Yes, their familial links are working, so you can reach him directly, if you want."

Avis hadn't tried using their familial links since they had been proven so useless in Heaven. But now that he was out, he opened himself to the glow of family and found it just as Athena had described. Clarise and the girls, Athena, and two other individuals buried amongst the troops registered as kin. There could be any number of reasons for why that unnamed pair kept their heads down, up to and including military training, the designation for a bastard offspring, or because having ranged shifters interspersed with regular self-shifters would take an enemy by surprise. Neither of them interested Avis.

"I'll let him know." Athena's eyes refocused on the family. Avis in particular. "He's decent, and he says if he has to contact you, he's keeping all the ambrosia for himself, and the only way you'll get any the whole time you're here is if he needs to …" —she suddenly glanced at Clarise and quickly amended it to— "… well, he said you'll get it second hand."

Avis couldn't help but snort; both at the empty threat that had circulated between the three realm rulers almost as long as their friendship had existed, and the way Athena danced around the vulgar punchline for Clarise's sake. Thankfully, the cross in-joke went over the girls' heads … and from the look on Clarise's face, hers as well. But Clarise's cool gaze also had a 'you-will-explain-this-later' aspect to it that Avis read loud and clear. If that was what she wanted, he would of course tell her, but he would also give her the chance to remain ignorant before doing so. "A long-standing joke between three drunks," he said, to smooth things over for now. He lifted his hand from Cora's shoulder and called out to his friend, using the ending arc of that hand to shield Columbine's face, just in case anything at all was inappropriate on the other side of that link. Even if his friend wasn't doing anything, his decorative tastes bordered on pornographic.

Zeus appeared stretched out on a silk covered kline, fully dressed in a chiton with his sandalled feet crossed at the ankle. His upper body was draped over the raised head of the kline and he drank from a gem-encrusted goblet. Behind his shoulders within easy reach was a side table with a bowl overflowing with fruits and honeyed sweets. Curtains swayed in the background, exposing from time to time a set of open balcony doors. Avis knew that room. Zeus' private sanctum in the rear of his palace.

"Hey," Avis said, still a little wary after the complete blindside he'd undergone in Asgard.

Zeus took a heavy swallow of ambrosia and wiped his mouth with the back of his wrist. "Hey, yourself," he replied with a lazy grin, dropping his feet to the floor and sitting up. One elbow pressed itself against his knee and the other hand rested loosely on his hip. The move had been perfected so long ago that not a single drop of ambrosia fell. "What in the realms are you up to now, Avis?"

"My family and I need sanctuary while we plan our next move. The brute squad are with us purely to ensure our safety. I never have, and to my current knowledge will never make a move against you or Olympus." Avis knew better than to promise the future. They all did.

Zeus looked down at Columbine who was still snuggled against her father, and further down to where Cora stood at Avis' side. Cora met his appraising gaze with a measured one of her own. When Zeus raised an eyebrow, Cora followed suit. "Ooh, I like this one," he purred, gesturing a finger at Cora while lifting his eyes to Avis once more. "She's got pluck."

"She's Mystallian," Avis answered with pride, placing a hand on Cora's shoulder possessively. He never for one second thought Zeus meant anything lewd. Like himself, his friend's taste in lovers only started once they reached puberty.

Cora looked up at her father first, then across to Zeus, sending him a a silent chin-lift to acknowledge the Olympian ruler.

"I see what you mean," Zeus chuckled. He finished the last of his ambrosia and tossed the goblet aside, sliding effortlessly to his feet. "You have a lot of explaining to do, my friend, but you can't do it from over there."

A wave of relief washed over Avis as he watched his friend's hand come up in invitation and he released the breath he hadn't realised he'd been holding. "Agreed." He couldn't say the word quickly enough. "However, one of the brute squad must come across first." The words were more for his friend than anyone on his side of the conversation. He saw Zeus' face contort into a scowl and hastily added, "I trust you, my friend. I do. But if I didn't send one of the brute squad through first to act as a sentry for Clarise and the girls, they'd find a way to get there first anyway, and then you'd really get your chiton in a twist."

Zeus snorted and rolled his eyes. "Right. Like they could beat a single step into my personal abode," he guffawed. He drew in a deep breath to laugh outright, then noticed Avis hadn't joined him in the joke. "Seriously?" he asked, closing his hand into a fist of denial and staring at the monstrosities behind Avis. The other two guards were still in front of Avis, and as such out of Zeus' line of sight.

Avis raised one shoulder in a shrug. "Remind me again, how long it took six of them to destroy all of Teon?"

Everyone had heard of Teon's fate. The three friends had often spoke of the destruction over drinks and whores, all agreeing that the number of brute squad required had to be higher. Thousands, possibly millions. Avis was no longer of that opinion, but even if they took the highest figure of their estimate, millions had still been able to destroy hundreds of billions of galaxies in very short order.

Zeus' gaze turned glacial. "And yet you have four acting as bodyguards?"

Avis knew what he had to be thinking, and was grateful that their friendship meant he hadn't acted on those thoughts, *yet*. He decided to lighten the mood at his own expense. "It's a known fact how protective Lord Belial is of his females, and it's also safe to say he doesn't think too highly of my ability to achieve that." He kept the tenuous relationship between himself and Belial non-specific for Columbine's sake. Everyone else knew the score.

That broke the ice for Zeus, and without warning he roared with laughter. Avis grinned as well. *Asshole.*

The fingers of Zeus' hand uncurled once more. "Send one over," he said. "And once the ladies are settled, you're going to tell me exactly what you did to upset our old friend Odin. I haven't been able to get a civil word out of him in over a year where you're concerned."

That wasn't a conversation Avis was looking forward to, but Zeus had earned the right to know why his two best friends were no longer on speaking terms. He waved the first of the guards forward with his free hand, then reached through and accepted Zeus' outstretched hand. The guard placed a hand on Avis' bicep and reached through to Zeus. A step later, he was on that side of the conversation. The rest of his family and their servants followed, (though Tilu had passed each of the demon steeds through one at a time to either Diviten or Gingen) until he was the last one to go through. Then, with a smile and an appreciative nod at Athena, he stepped through to rejoin his family.

CHAPTER FIFTY-FOUR

Two hours later, Avis had Clarise and the girls settled into a two-storey villa on the outskirts of the palace grounds. The entire mountain was considered one of the three capital cities of Olympus, but because of the disruptive presence of the brute squad, Zeus had given them the use of the guest villa at the base of the mountain, as far from his city proper as he possibly could. There was a time when such a blatant segregation would've offended Avis' sensibilities, but this time round he actually preferred the privacy. None of the Olympians wanted to be in the same space as the brute squad, and Avis certainly didn't want them getting too curious about Columbine. Besides, it wasn't as if he or his family had to hike up the mountain every time they wanted something from the palace. Now that they were kin, the entire Olympian pantheon was a simple blood-link away.

Also, as Clarise had pointed out, the villa did have a lovely view; combining her beachfront preferences on one side with his love of greenery on the other. Each bedroom had a balcony that overlooked either a fine white sandy beach that bled out into a rich, crystal blue ocean or an exquisite private garden with sandstone steps leading into a flower covered, timber pergola.

Gaia had appeared almost the second the family walked in the front door, and while she'd glowered at him over her sister's head, it still amused him to see his tiny wife being engulfed in the bosom of her hugely endowed older sister. Clearly, the pair were thrilled to be reunited, and as much as he wanted to catch up with Zeus, it bore nothing on the two sisters. Gaia had been on the outs with the Hellion Highborn ever since she married her son and slept with him to produce most of the other gods of the Olympian pantheon, and Zeus was two generations after that. With the obedience expected of all Highborn Hellion ladies, Clarise hadn't so much as mentioned her sister's name in all that time.

The pair went straight through the villa and settled on the three-seater rattan lounge that led down to the beach out the back. It barely took a handful of words between them before Avis realised his manliness could only stomach so much talk of who was married to whom and how many children they'd all had. Wanting nothing to do with the hurricane of mindless feminine drivel, Avis retreated upstairs to check on the girls.

From Columbine's balcony on the second level, he found Cora down on the beach, attempting to kick back each of the waves as they crashed over her and howling with delight as the salt-water covered her before withdrawing back into the ocean. She dropped her head and shoulders forward and shook herself all over, then squared up in anticipation of the next wave.

Chuckling at her antics, Avis scanned the area around him in search of a guard. Apprehension stirred when he couldn't find one, but the one direction he hadn't looked, was up. Stepping out to the balcony's edge, he turned and looked at the roofline overhead. Sure enough, perched at the apex of the fascia was one of the four guards, looking for all the realm like an oversized, golden gargoyle. He then dropped his gaze into the bedroom where another stood between the queen-sized bed and the doors that led to the ensuite. Like its peer on the roof, its head rotated constantly, letting Avis know without words that it was alive and on duty in the otherwise unmoving shell.

As he ran his eyes over the sleeping form in the middle of the bed, he saw the muscles of Columbine's face had relaxed, indicating she was no longer under the influence of his vile mood. That was good. Sleep was the best thing for getting over a rage-fest. He knew that better than most.

Ignoring the centipede-like governess hunched in the corner, he went to the bed and used one gloved finger to brush her fringe out of her face. At the same time, he rolled his hand and stroked the back of his knuckles across her cheek, smiling at the way she subconsciously sought out his touch. His darling little girl.

Wanting to leave the villa in search of his own adult conversation, Avis lifted his head and glanced back at the open balcony doors. His smile grew as he considered jumping over the rail and landing alongside his wife and sister-by-marriage below, but quickly decided against that. Scaring the crap out of two shifters when one could turn him into a sardine and the other could withhold bedroom privileges did not make a whole lot of logical sense to him; funny or not. So, he backed out of Columbine's room and made his way down the marble stairs that led to the sitting area out the back. Both women stopped speaking as he approached. "Columbine's asleep and Cora's on the beach playing in the waves. There's a guard on the roof overseeing Cora, and Columbine has her usual guard. Are you alright to keep an eye on them if I go up and see Zeus for a while?"

Clarise smiled and nodded her accord, but the stunned look on Gaia's face would be one Avis would treasure for a long time. What the snarky cow said next; not so much. "Who are you, what have you done with the real Avis, and how many boons do we have to offer you to keep that snake imprisoned indefinitely?"

As he had with Uriel, Avis used his body's position to keep his left hand hidden from Clarise as he flipped off his sister-by-marriage with a heartfelt sneer.

Clarise on the other hand, was far more forceful. She slapped her sister's leg sharply in reprimand and went to stand as if her sister's presence offended her, but Avis held out his other hand to keep her seated. "Let it go, sweetheart. We both know I deserve that and a whole lot worse, and so long as the girls aren't here to hear it, I don't care who says what. Enjoy your afternoon with your sister. I'll probably lose track of time with Zeus, so if it gets too late, let me know."

Clarise's shoulders softened as she rose and took his outstretched hand anyway. Her free hand hooked him around the neck and he allowed her to pull his head down so she could kiss him lightly on the lips. "I will let you know when the evening meal is ready, beloved," she said. Considering lunch was still hours away, giving him until the evening meal was plenty of time to catch up with Zeus. With her lips still lingering over his, she whispered, "Do not drink too much, my love."

Avis wasn't in the habit of going from sober to rotten drunk in just a few hours. But then, it had been years since he'd gone on a bender, and there was no doubt that was what Zeus had planned for them that day. Perhaps that had been another reason why his old friend had put the visiting family so far from the palace—to distance Clarise and the girls from their revelry. Not that it mattered. He was never getting that shit-faced again. *Ever.* "Promise," he whispered in return, kissing her more passionately: present company be damned.

With more effort than he thought he could manage; he broke away from Clarise and both uttered a soft sigh of contentment. His eyes were still fixed on her as he raised his hand into the air, but just as he was about to call on his old friend, he heard Gaia say, "I like this new version of you, Avis."

Avis slid his gaze to his sister-by-marriage, maintaining his grin as he winked at her and finished the hand gesture. "Zeus."

Moments later, the ladies were blocked out by a vision of Zeus who already had dozens of undressed women draped over every piece of furniture behind him in anticipation of his arrival. Zeus was entertaining himself with a busty redhead he had bent over the head of the kline, and paused, it seemed, just long enough to accept Avis' blood-link. "Ready to party long and hard, old friend?" the Olympian asked, his hand lifting off the redhead's bare back for him to take.

This … this right here, was why he'd covered Columbine's face earlier. If he could've grown a third arm, he'd have covered Cora's eyes too. You could never trust Zeus not to be … *busy* when he accepted a blood-link. He was definitely glad neither Clarise nor Gaia could see what he was looking at. Clarise would've have kittens … or turned her distant nephew into one.

Before they could, he took his friend's hand and stepped through the link.

Soft, unfamiliar hands immediately fell upon him, caressing while attempting to undress him at the same time. Not knowing who to knock away first, he backed himself into a corner of the room and shot out a series of mental barbs to keep the women at bay. He wanted to spend the afternoon talking to his friend and probably share a few drinks along the way—not partake in this drunken orgy. It didn't take Zeus long to notice his friend's growing agitation (or the way the women fell away from the Mystallian, holding their heads and screaming) and he cleared the room. Still naked, the Olympian walked over to a credenza where a carafe of ambrosia and several untouched goblets sat. Zeus' personal liquor supply. The women wouldn't have touched it without invitation, and they were never going to receive it. He poured two full goblets and walked back to Avis, holding one out to the Mystallian. "Tell me you've given up the liquor as well, and I'll revoke your visitation," he promised, only half-jokingly.

Avis pulled himself out of the corner and took the goblet, taking a deep swallow just to show his friend he hadn't changed that much. "Your Aunt Clarise is the only woman I want touching me like that, Zeus."

Zeus hmphed and took another mouthful of his own drink. "Never thought I'd live to see the day where a lone woman managed to leash your balls."

"My balls, and every other part of me," Avis agreed with pride, taking another long drink. "Get used to it."

Zeus looked at him in disgust, then turned and retraced his steps to the kline, where he made himself comfortable. "So, what did you do to piss Odin off so much?"

Avis took a seat on a second kline that faced Zeus, allowing them to still see each other. He even went as far as to lift his booted feet and stretch himself across the base of it, much like his best friend had. "The bastard's accusing me of killing Balder, but the whole fucking thing is thrall bullshit. I didn't lay a finger on that boy. I liked him."

Zeus looked across at him with a frown. "Given that this is the end of an exceedingly long friendship between all of us, you're going to have to do better than that."

Avis frowned. "What's my fight with Odin got to do with your friendship to him?"

Zeus shrugged and rolled onto his back. "Odin's trying to force me into picking a side. If I'm your friend, I can't be his." He rolled his head back to look at Avis and shrugged. "His words."

"Oh, that fucking ..." It suddenly occurred to him just how dangerous things could be if his Olympian friend *had* sided with Odin and was only *pretending* to be his friend all this time. Avis froze, his mind already working out how quickly he could regroup with his family and escape Olympus before the boom dropped.

The problem with long, celestial friendships was moves like that were anticipated way before they were acted on, and a soft, cylindrical cushion struck Avis in the nose with enough force to smack his head against the raised kline arm. "Don't even think about it," Zeus growled, his right hand and his eyes already glowing in readiness of a more dangerous lightning strike. The cushion had been but a warning. "The day I let anyone tell me who I will and won't be friends with, is the day I hand Mt. Olympus over to my brothers and retire to the mortal realm."

Avis relaxed against his seat and smiled at his friend. Olympus wasn't like Mystal, in the way their families operated. Zeus' rulership wasn't because he had the support of his two brothers. It was more a case of three brothers divvying up the realm after they jointly murdered their father. For Zeus to say he would hand over Mt Olympus to his brothers meant he had no intention of doing whatever preceded that statement; which in turn meant their friendship was still solid. Avis would never take that for granted again.

"Thank me, and I'll ram a lightning bolt so far up your ass your teeth will glow for a month," Zeus warned, still reading Avis like a book.

Avis chuckled and took another mouthful of ambrosia. "Wouldn't dream of it," he lied. For the next hour, Avis explained the situation between himself and Odin. Ironically, it was one of the few instances where Avis felt he was being unfairly treated. He didn't regret killing Loki's braggart of a son, and Odin certainly hadn't blamed him at the time. "Loki's fucking thrall is making the bastard untouchable. Everyone keeps seeing everything he does as an act of mischief, so no one's holding him accountable for anything!"

He saw Zeus' lips twitch and knew (just as his friend had known previously what he'd been thinking) that the prick was in possession of knowledge to the contrary. "Spill, you shapeshifting shithead," he commanded, rolling forward to bring himself that much closer to the Olympian. "What don't I know?"

Instead of being insulted, Zeus' grin expanded. "If I've got my timing right, just after you left Asgard, Odin must've told Frigg what you said about going to get Balder instead of just bitching about his loss, because she sent one of their other sons down to Hel to make a deal for his release. I didn't realise you were tied up in his original death, but the way I heard it ..." He paused deliberately, but Avis refused to pick up the bait. Zeus would always reward impatience with a drawn-out version that made the listener want to murder him. "If everyone in Asgard, both celestial and mortal, agreed to weep for Balder, the Asgardians could have their beloved son back."

Avis had a feeling he knew where this was going, but he still didn't interrupt.

"And Loki refused to weep. Of course, the gutless bastard didn't do it in his own form. That would've been too easy. Instead, he took on the form of a frost giantess in the hopes of stirring shit between them and the Aesir and didn't think anyone would be smart enough to see through his disguise." He took a swallow of ambrosia to moisten his tongue and continued. "To say Odin noticed was an understatement, and the whole realm felt his and Frigg's rage. Realising he'd finally pushed his establishment field too far, Loki tried shifting into a salmon to escape them."

"And I assume Odin had deep fried fish for dinner?" Avis couldn't stay out of it forever.

"No, but once they caught him, they used his dead son's intestines to bind him to a dark cave floor and had a venomous snake drip poison non-stop into his mouth. Word has it his wife is doing her best to keep most of the poison off him, but trust me, my friend, he's suffering now."

"About fucking time."

"So, what about you?" Zeus rolled back onto his side to face his friend. "You may love your wife and daughters now, but one whiff of your thrall and you'll be back to stepping on their necks just to get to the next pretty piece of ass."

Avis stared at his reflection in the half-finished ambrosia in his goblet, hearing the truth of his friend's words. The thought of going back to that made him sick beyond words, and with an agonising sigh, he rolled forward and placed the goblet on the floor. "If my thrall can't be changed, I'm not going back to Mystal."

Zeus pulled himself up onto one elbow, shock blanching his face. "Come again?"

Avis's gaze narrowed and he slowly licked his lips. "You heard me. If my thrall can't or won't be amended to accept the way I feel about my wife and girls right now, I'm not going back."

"But-but what in the realms will you do? You can't hide here forever."

"No," Avis agreed, picturing the inevitable outcome of overstaying his welcome. "But if I have to, I—we can start again in the Unknown Realms. I've already discussed the matter with Clarise, and she agrees."

Zeus' eyes went even wider. "Seriously?"

"I won't go back to the way I was." He closed his eyes against the possibility and shook his head. "I won't."

"So, what's your plan, old friend, and how can I help?"

And that was why Avis was never going to take this friendship for granted ever again. He relaxed on his back and stared up at the ceiling with his fingers interlocked on his chest. "Once I have Clarise and the girls fully settled, I plan to reach out to Amaro. Out of everyone over there, he's the only one who won't try and guilt-trip me into coming home before things are changed."

"That's assuming they even want you back," Zeus supplied unhelpfully. When Avis scowled and cast a gimlet eye at him, he explained, "You burned a lot of bridges in recent years, my friend, and I don't think you realise just how accountable most of the Known Realms is holding Mystal for what you did. Right now, outside of blood, Mystal's reputation has all but been destroyed, and if they take you back after everything you've done, that's likely to become a permanent state of affairs."

"Shit." Avis parted his hands and dragged his fingers through his hair to cup them behind his head. He hadn't thought of that. It was one thing to bear the blame when he'd been the one responsible for it, but another entirely to drag all of Mystal down with him. He didn't share Zeus' concerns about them turning their backs on him. His concerns were the reverse. He knew his siblings only too well and there was never any doubt that they'd all stand by him just like they always had and weather the hatred of the Known Realms that wasn't theirs to weather. The only chance Mystal had of smoothing things over and eventually standing proud once more was if he kept his distance from them.

By the Twin Notes, he couldn't even risk contacting Amaro anymore. In his heart he'd always planned to go back, so Chance's luck wouldn't push the runt to choose that moment to visit Death with Peace at his side. Luck was a silver-tongued bastard when he wanted to be, and with Paz backing him up, they could talk anyone into anything; up to and including making him willingly step through the blood-link and accept his thrall just as it was.

The thought of never seeing any of them again outside his imagination was beyond heart-breaking, and the lump that grew in his throat threatened to choke him. He ground his teeth and swallowed several times, until the muscles in his jaw ached and the burn in the back of his eyes no longer threatened to turn into waterworks. Then, once he felt he had himself under control, he cleared his throat and said, "Change of plans then. Once the girls have rested, we'll head straight out into the Unknown Realms. I'm not going to make things even worse for Mystal than they already are, and I'm not going to make them worse for you either." With that decided, there was no point delaying the inevitable.

A strange look entered Zeus' eyes. "So, this is the real you outside your thrall," he said, running his eyes ever so slowly over the Mystallian sitting opposite him. "I think I prefer the Avis that thought Mystal existed for him, not the other way around."

Avis didn't argue the point. He was too busy picking up the pieces of his shattered heart. Never was a long time for someone who'd see out eternity because so long as Mystal survived, so would he. Perhaps Zeus was right. Perhaps, with all of his power and thrall stripped away, this was the real Avis. At the very least it was the closest he'd been to his older self, back when they'd first escaped the Nexus. In retrospect, he knew he and Amaro could've made that run at the border wall all by themselves, but it hadn't occurred to either of them to abandon their siblings that way. It hadn't even been within the realms of possibility. Either they all got out, or none of them would. He himself had been the last to jump down from the wall, once he'd pushed Tal off into Griffith's outstretched arms. His family's safety had always been important to him, and they had responded in kind. When was the last time he could honestly say he'd have done that before his time in Hell?

"You're not going anywhere for at least a year or two," Zeus proclaimed, breaking him out of his morbid thoughts long enough to stir his ire.

No one ... *no one*, but him and Clarise dictated his actions, present company included.

"And I'm not saying that for your benefit, before you get yourself all worked up. Grandmother Gaia is the only one of us who originated in Hell, and you're not taking her sister away from her before they've finished catching up. The last thing I need or want is that woman tearing strips off me because I kneecapped her long-awaited family reunion."

Avis could appreciate that.

"And I think you should still reach out to your twin before you decide your next move."

Avis' gaze narrowed irritably, to which Zeus laughed and waved him off.

"Seriously. Don't be making decisions without having all the facts. Your wider family's as much a part of this as Clarise and the girls. Mystal's a unified pantheon, or so you've always told me. If they figure out you've fallen on your sword for them without their input, they're going to be pissed."

Yes … yes they would be. In fact, pissed would be an understatement. On the other hand, too bad. Like him, they'd just have to get over it. Scratching at his bottom lip, he decided as soon as Clarise signalled she was ready to go, they'd leave and start again in the Unknown Realms.

And, if he was lucky, time would one day ease his wounded heart.

A flash of light followed by a loud boom both blinded and deafened him. In the seconds it took for his vision to clear and his hearing to return, he was sitting on the edge of the kline with his upper body covered in ambrosia and the goblet he'd placed on the floor a molten puddle of gems and golden slag. "Really?" he growled savagely as he shook out his hands, using the clean portion of his doublet sleeve to dry his face.

"Really," Zeus snapped with a matching scowl, his hand still smouldering from where the lightning had been released. "I wasn't making a suggestion, you dumb *malakis*, and I sure as hell don't appreciate being discounted like a mortal. You need to blood-link Lord Amaro before you decide to write off Mystal, and if you don't, I will."

Avis' blood went cold. He detested threats. Like, a lot. "You don't share blood with Amaro." Hanging onto that truth was what kept him from completely losing his shit at his friend.

"I don't have to. Yitzak is my grandson, and I'll get that boy to link me to your twin if I have to. You're not getting out of this, you bastard, so get that stupid idea out of your idiotic head." Zeus seemed just as determined to win, and in Olympus, the arrogant fucker held the upper hand.

Fury coursed through Avis' veins as he rose to his feet. Or rather, as he began to rise to his feet. Partway between the two, the bowl of fruit and honeyed sweets that he'd noticed hours ago collided heavily with his stomach, pushing him back into the kline. "Sit your ass back down, you stubborn fool, and have something to eat. Just because you're not getting your own way doesn't mean it's not being done for your benefit."

The old Avis would've thrown the fruit bowl in Zeus' face and told him where he could shove it for trying to tell him what to do. But then, the old Avis would've blood-linked with someone in Mystal and gotten the fuck out of Olympus before Zeus could retaliate with a flurry of painful lightning bolts.

Still fuming, Avis took an apricot from the bowl and tore into its flesh with his teeth, making a point of staring daggers at his friend as he chewed. The anger evaporated from Zeus the moment Avis complied, and with a smirk that said he understood Avis' frustration, he stood up with his own goblet still in his hand and went back to the credenza. Refilling his goblet, he then filled another and brought the latter over to Avis. "Neither of us likes to be told what to do," he admitted, as Avis took the goblet and drank a little to wash down the apricot pulp.

"No, we don't," Avis agreed.

"Perhaps this will make it easier for you to tolerate. In exchange for offering you and your young family temporary sanctuary, I want you to contact your twin and see how things are in Mystal before you decide to turn your back on all the Known Realms." With a tip of his goblet towards Avis to let him know the condition was non-negotiable, Zeus returned to his kline and sat down. "At the very least, I will miss your annoying company if you were to disappear for good." He took a sip, using the motion to relax into the arm of the kline. "Not too many people are willing to go toe to toe with me anymore."

Avis took another bite of his apricot, this time appreciating the tart sweetness of the fruit. "I used to think that too. Turns out, if you rub certain people the wrong way, there's a whole realm of Highborn Hellions that are willing to do more than just go toe to toe with the likes of us."

Zeus chuckled and lifted his drink in agreement, not that Avis found the statement very funny at all.

And speaking of things that weren't funny … "YHWH is the Almighty."

Zeus paused and slid his eyes towards him. "Your point?"

"Both you and Odin told me what an overbearing prick he was."

The Olympian relaxed and nodded. "He was."

"So what changed?"

Zeus shrugged. "No idea," he admitted, honestly. "A few months ago, it was like he had a complete personality shift and went from a ruthless overlord to a benevolent custodian in the blink of an eye. It took everyone by surprise." He finished his ambrosia in several long mouthfuls and placed the goblet on the floor. "From what Athena said, you have probably got more to do with it than anyone else."

"*Me?*" Avis couldn't hide the shock.

"Well, he's older than all of us, yet you're the one he was clinging to and bawling all over like a baby right before you left Heaven. What was that all about?"

Little brother. Avis shook his head, clearing the echo of YHWH's parting words. "Don't remind me," he said, refusing to answer his friend's question. "I didn't know an established god could change their personality like that."

"First I've ever heard of it," Zeus agreed.

"Have you ever heard the Almighty call anyone else 'brother'?"

Zeus looked at him as if he'd just grown a second head. "What?"

Well, that answers that, Avis thought, though he still refused to believe it.

For the next few hours, the two discussed anything and everything that came to mind, carefully avoiding the subject of Odin. Zeus wanted to know in exacting detail what Avis had done to whom during his time on the run, and more disturbingly, what the Hellions had done to punish him once they'd caught him.

Avis was happy to fill him in on all the regular punishments, but he avoided the ones that destroyed his pride as a man. Those he tried not to even think about.

Several times during the afternoon, scantily dressed men and women came in to top up Zeus' carafe and replace the fruits and sweets bowl with more substantial foods, but on the whole, the two were left alone.

It didn't surprise Avis when the pulse of a blood-link eventually rippled through him, and he rolled sideways to place his goblet on the floor before answering it. "That time already, sweetheart?" he asked, dropping his booted feet to the floor and sitting up. The question was rhetorical. He knew from the glowing bead on his glove how long he'd been gone and Clarise's blood-link signified an end to his social respite with his friend.

Clarise smiled with her hands clasped before her. Thankfully, he and Zeus were still on their respective klines, and as such, Zeus was behind her image and outside her line of sight. The Olympian still hadn't felt the need to get dressed, and Clarise might not be so pleased if she saw that. Had he still been lying down looking at the ceiling when he accepted the link, Clarise would've seen Zeus on Avis' left. Hence the initial sideways roll.

"Did you have a nice time with Zeus?"

Avis closed his eyes and chuckled, rubbing his gloved forefinger across one eyebrow. No way was he answering that in front of Zeus. Not when doing so would make him sound no older than the girls. Instead, he pushed off the kline and rose to his feet, twisting himself just enough to see Zeus and give him a quick chin-lift in farewell. "Later, Zeus," he said, reaching out to his wife. He didn't wait for Zeus' response, mainly because he didn't want Clarise to hear it. The look of absolute disgust on his friend's face that he was answering his wife's summons said plenty.

CHAPTER FIFTY-FIVE

The end of that step found him in the space between the head of the table where he always sat and the front doors behind his chair. The girls were already seated, waiting for him to join them. He interlaced his fingers with Clarise's and walked her down the length of the table to the seat closest to the beach where she would smell the salty ocean breeze. Tilu drew out the chair for her and Avis helped her sit, then returned to his own seat. A dismissive gesture kept Tilu with her mistress, where she belonged as far as he was concerned. The girls' governesses lingered on either side of the room, and Columbine's personal guard stood between the two columns behind Clarise that led out into the external sitting area. Its choice of location gave it the best vantage point of everything on the lower level of the house; the stairs and most of the indoor balcony that covered three sides of the upper floor as well as sitting area outside. As a regular guard, it would've been too far away to be of any use to Columbine, but speed wasn't exactly a problem for them

"Did you enjoy Gaia's visit?" Avis asked, returning to their previous discussion but flipping the question on her.

Clarise's face lit up at the mention of her long-lost sister, and any ill-will he felt towards Zeus for being such a dick right before he left vanished in a wave of happiness that settled across him. "I did, thank you. She has done incredibly well for herself, even without the support of the family."

As they spoke, the three servants disappeared and returned carrying dishes of various hot meats and vegetables along with the accompanying condiments and bread rolls. Avis gestured to the baked fish as his first choice, unable to keep the mischievous grin from working its way across his face as he did so.

"Something amuses you, beloved?" Clarise asked, as Tilu served him the fish, along with his preferred choices of vegetables and white sauce.

Avis dragged his fork through the tender flesh and lifted it to his lips, savouring the smell a moment before sliding it into his mouth. It dissolved almost on contact with his tongue, leaving a buttery aftertaste behind. "Just something Zeus told me this afternoon, sweetheart," he assured her, still preferring his final outcome over what the Asgardians chose for that trouble-making asswipe. "Nothing to concern yourself with." He lifted his goblet and took a sip, then looked to his right where Cora sat. "So, who won the fight between you and the ocean, tiger?" he asked, if only to change the subject.

"Me, of course," Cora replied with an emphatic nod, as if that end result was never in doubt.

"Gaia and I found it necessary to intercede on her behalf when Poseidon rode in on one of the waves and Cora kicked him in the shins by accident," Clarise added.

Recognising the danger, all humour disappeared and Avis narrowed his gaze reproachfully at his older daughter; who seemed just as determined to maintain her facade of innocence. "You mistook a two-and-a-half-metre god carrying a three-metre trident for a one-metre wave?" He wanted to see if she'd be hubristic enough to try that line of crap on him. The very notion was preposterous, though somehow she'd managed to convince her mother of her sincerity.

Cora shrugged and met his eyes without flinching. "It wasn't intentional. I was caught up in the fun of the moment and didn't notice him in the surf. It's not as if I was looking above the wave crest I was kicking."

That … actually rang true. During their vacation in Heaven, he'd seen her loosen up more than he ever had before, and during those times she'd become so entrenched in the enjoyment that she'd lose track of everything else. It was perhaps the only aspect of her inner workings that vaguely resembled her physical age, and he was in no rush to strip it from her.

Avis slipped into her mind, not because he doubted her anymore, but because he wanted to see the look on Poseidon's face when he realised a tiny little six-year-old Mystallian girl had kicked him in the shins.

It was as priceless as he'd expected, and after freezing the memory of the Oceanic God staring down at her in utter disbelief, Avis laughed until tears blurred his vision and his side hurt, forcing him to sit down. His little tiger was proving every day just how Mystallian her essence really was, and he could not be any prouder. Especially when he unfroze the memory and watched her square her shoulders and yell up at him, "Hey, what's your problem, bozo?"

Her derogatory tone was enough to snap Poseidon out of his daze. His hands clenched around his trident and a dangerous look entered his eyes; behind him, the ocean began to churn in response to his anger. The next moment was a snatched blur that ended with Cora back in her bedroom upstairs. Through her linear memories, he watched her blink in confusion, then replay her memories just as he was doing now, slowing down that blurred moment to an absolute crawl until she saw the tell-tale hint of gold.

Cora huffed and returned to the physical realm, where she faced the open doors of her balcony. She could hear adult voices down on the beach and went to join them, only to run headlong into a golden monstrosity that looked even more intimidating from her height. "Aw, come on!" she shouted up at it, after ducking sharply to either side in an attempt to slip between its three legs and resorting to a gelatinous mass didn't help. "I wasn't doing anything wrong! Let me out!"

Avis skipped over the next half hour of boredom that she was forced to endure before Clarise and Gaia entered the room and dismissed Gingen. "I didn't do anything wrong," Cora insisted, though not as emphatically as she had with the guard.

"Striking one of Olympus' three kings and insulting him is acceptable behaviour to you?" Clarise asked, the ice in her words alone cutting through Cora's posturing.

The way Cora's point of view widened then shifted to the empty wall beside her mother's head; Avis deduced she hadn't recognised the Oceanic ruler. "He-he didn't say who he was …" she argued feebly, confirming his suspicion.

"You need to go and apologise to him."

Cora's point of view snapped back to her mother, and Avis could feel the horror clouding her thoughts. "B-But I didn't do anything wrong," she insisted.

Avis completely agreed with her and his lips curled in a blend of repulsion and vexation. *This is the past,* he reminded himself. It couldn't be changed … but by the Twin Notes, he'd have handled it very differently if he'd been there. Bullying a Mystallian into apologising to someone outside the pantheon grated on every nerve he had.

"You will apologise for your deplorable actions," Clarise insisted, pointing at the balcony windows. "In fact, you will do it right this moment, young lady. Your cousin Poseidon is waiting for you on the beach."

Cora's vision shuttered as her eyes closed, and he could almost feel the frustration and fury that bubbled up inside her. This was why no one should ever try to browbeat a Mystallian into anything. It rarely ever worked, especially when their personal space was so blatantly commandeered.

A few seconds later, the blackness of her vision parted in the middle to indicate she'd opened her eyes and was looking from her mother to her aunt and back again. "Fine," she growled, turning on her heel to stalk past the guard. On her way to the balcony, she snagged the corner of a blanket and absorbed its mass.

"Make it sincere!" Clarise called after her.

"I will!" Cora shouted back as she stepped up onto the rails and launched herself into the air. Gravity drew her downwards, until she used her excess mass to unfurl her demonic wings. She levelled out over the rattan furniture and flew to where Poseidon awaited her. His arms were folded as he watched her approach, but instead of landing at his feet where she would have to look up at him, Cora hovered at head height just outside of arms' reach.

"You have something you wish to say to me, child?" he asked, his expression so smug even Avis wanted to knock him on his ass for it.

"Yeah," Cora said, straightening up with her hands on her hips. "I'm sorry you weren't looking where you were going."

That wiped the smirk right off Poseidon's face. "*What?*" he snarled.

Cora held her position, causing Avis to freeze the scene and laugh even harder than he had previously. This was fantastic! Like all Mystallians before her, Cora wasn't backing down one bit and had found an end-run around her mother's directive.

Only once the last chuckle left his chest did he restart the memory.

"I was told I had to apologise sincerely to you, and since I didn't do anything wrong, the only thing left to apologise for is the fact that you weren't looking where you were going." She cocked her head to one side. "You didn't even tell me you were the king, and it's not like you have it tattooed across your forehead, so how was I supposed to know?" **So, calm the fuck down.**

Avis' eyes widened in surprise at the mental command that was so perfectly delivered, though it was quickly followed by a wave of genuine pride. *That's my girl,* he cheered, as anger abandoned the king of the high seas and his stiff posture relaxed.

"You know now though, child, correct?"

"Yeah, but for the record, the 'child' has a name. I'm Cora."

"And I am Lord Poseidon."

Cora shook her head. "Uh-uh. You and I are blood, and Father said we're allowed to drop the titles if we're kin."

Poseidon raked his gaze over the girl hovering in front of his face, specifically the black uniform with gold embellishments. "So, you're Avis' spawn," he said, almost accusingly.

The term was meant to be derogatory, but given where she'd been raised, Cora rolled her arms to the sides and bowed with all the grandeur of a Highborn Hellion lady (though she kept her eyes fixed on Poseidon because she wasn't an idiot). "All day long, big guy." She straightened up and asked, "So, what brings you to our little neck of the woods?"

Poseidon looked at her incredulously, then snorted and shook his head. "Do you honestly think I'm going to answer that, child?"

"I told you, my name is Cora."

"And perhaps in a few millennia, I might get around to calling you that, peanut."

Cora stiffened and lifted her chin, but her mother's voice intervened before she could say what Avis guessed was so clearly written on her face. "Cora, go and play up the other end of the beach. Your aunt and I wish to have words with your cousin Poseidon."

Cora's point-of-view swivelled to the two women making their way down the beach towards them, then back to Poseidon. "Sure," she said with a shrug, as if she were done with the King of the High Seas anyway. Then, with a flick of her leathery wings, she shot to the far end of their little beachfront paradise where she resumed her booted assault on the surf.

After three average waves, a huge tidal surge came at her in a wall of water almost five times her height. Squeaking in surprise, she scrambled backwards a few steps then turned and launched herself into the air. She made it about halfway to the mansion house when the crest of the wave snatched her out of the air and dragged her back into the ocean proper.

Panic overtook her for a few seconds as she realised her Mystallian form couldn't breathe through the briny water that surrounded her. Then she got mad. *Water ... meet HELLFIRE!* She shifted her Mystallian flesh into a Mystallian profile of living hellfire, evaporated several body-lengths of water around her to provide her with a clear escape window to the sky above. A guard hovered overhead, no doubt waiting to see if she needed its help before intervening.

Leaving a dissipating trail of hellfire behind her, Cora blasted through the air and pulled up alongside the golden brute squad guard. She then shifted into her demonic form with her wings flared to maintain her airborne position and swung to face the three congregating adults. The women's backs were to her, so neither of them saw what happened.

A quick scan of the dry beach told her that she had been targeted specifically by the wave, following her flight pattern without touching the beach below until it overtook her like a giant hand grabbing her out of the air.

That deduction brought her venomous glare to Poseidon, whose lips twitched with amusement even though he was supposedly focusing his attention on the two women in front of him. His broad arms were folded over his chest; one hand still holding the trident that was the icon of his oceanic establishment field. *ASSHOLE!* She flicked both middle fingers at her aquatic cousin, noting the way he slid his eyes slyly in her direction and how his wry grin intensified accordingly.

A combination of irritation and grudging respect bloomed inside Cora's mind for Poseidon, and after poking her forked tongue through her fangs at him in a disrespectful raspberry, she turned and flew back to the mansion to see if Columbine was awake yet.

Avis pulled out of Cora's mind, smirking at the harmless byplay. From what he'd seen, Poseidon saw her audacity as amusing, though that could possibly change once his thrall threw out the conditioning that was keeping his infamous temper in check. Just to make sure things didn't get out of hand there, Avis knew he'd be keeping a close eye on Poseidon whenever those two crossed paths, not that the Olympian would ever know it. So far, it looked as if Cora might have found a kindred spirit in the water king.

The thought pleased him.

Leaning forward in his seat, Avis cleared his throat, knowing it would garner the whole family's attention. "The journey to get us home has certainly had its share of challenges, but I believe those challenges have made us stronger. I've also come to realise during this time, that 'home' is not a location. Family is what makes a home, and so long as we have each other, we are whole."

Clarise nodded in agreement and quickly raised her goblet. "To family," she toasted, her eyes meeting his as she spoke, before moving to include the girls. "Wherever this journey takes us."

Although Avis hadn't finished what he was going to say, he couldn't argue with the toast when it epitomised everything he felt inside. The girls lifted their fruit-juice filled goblets in agreement, and as Avis already had his goblet off the table, he lifted it that much higher to add it to the toast. "To family," he and the girls concurred, each taking a mouthful of their drink.

Avis kept drinking, long after Clarise and the girls had placed their goblets back on the table and resumed their meal, emptying its contents entirely. With each swallow, he thought about the journey his life had taken in recent years and imagined what would happen if the Avis of last decade met the man sitting in his seat right now. Everything about him, including the future he was planning for, would've mortified his old self. But that was the crux of life outside the Nexus. Change was the only constant, and despite what Zeus had said, he needed to accept that Mystal was no longer in his future. The home he'd helped establish so long ago with his siblings was now as much a part of his past as his friendship with Odin.

It seemed even the gods couldn't change certain outcomes.

At least he still had his girls, and the future was theirs for the taking.

In the end, that was all that really mattered.

EPILOGUE

Hours after the meal had concluded and everyone had retired for the night, Clarise lay with her ear on the chest of her sleeping husband, listening to his steady heartbeat and feeling each breath he took. She wasn't fooled by his bravado at the evening meal. Something drastic had happened during his visit with Zeus. Something he had yet to discuss with her. Up until this morning, he'd made no secret of his desire to eventually return to Mystal, yet his impromptu speech at dinner this evening implied a major change of heart. She had deliberately thrown out the toast to family to interrupt whatever else he'd been going to say, because it was a discussion the two of them needed to have in private first. Especially if it affected the whole family.

The problem with that plan was in the hours that followed the girls going to bed, she and Avis had been ... otherwise engaged. Clarise had always known of Zeus' propensity for aimless sex and could well imagine how hard he'd tried to push Avis into joining him. The hunger in her husband's eyes the moment they were alone spoke volumes, and he'd given Clarise just enough time to soundproof their apartment before he set about claiming her on practically every piece of furniture in all three rooms of their apartment.

As always, their concluding union was in their bed, where Avis finally fell into a deep, blissful sleep with his arms wrapped firmly around her waist; leaving Clarise awake enough to start mulling things over. It wasn't just his change of heart that bothered her. From out of nowhere, a potential solution to the YHWH enigma had occurred to her, and now that it had taken up residence, it battered the inside of her mind like a wasp that refused to land.

Eventually, carefully, she extracted herself from Avis' hold and slipped to the edge of the bed. Avis sighed at her movement and rolled into the space she'd vacated. His fingers slid across the sheets in a subconscious search for her, and when he didn't make contact, his breathing hitched.

Before he became too alert, Clarise crafted a generic body pillow out of the pooled blankets; one that shared her heat, general shape and lavender fragrance. It was enough to fool his lethargic senses and after cuddling the pillow close, he let out a more relaxed sigh and slipped back into a deeper sleep.

He seemed so childlike when he slept—like it was the only time in his life he ever truly let down his guard. Clarise smiled and resisted the urge to run her fingers through his fringe. She could watch him sleep like this for hours, but there was something else she needed to do first.

Rising to her feet, she created a silk negligee and matching wrap, then cast a stimulation wave to make herself presentable. Her long, bedraggled hair that Avis had fisted throughout their lovemaking swept up and rolled itself into a neat bun complete with a decorative rose woven into the twist, and her skin took on a fresh look of vibrancy. Satisfied that the stimulation wave had done its job, Clarise crossed the room towards the balcony, pausing every few steps to ensure her husband remained asleep.

She paused once more at the glass doors, then pushed them open and let herself out.

Avis had chosen for them the second apartment that faced the beach opposite Columbine's, knowing how much happier she'd be with the chaotic nature of the ocean over the more serene greenery that would've been his first choice. As such, the salt air with a hint of sea-spawn woven into it filled her senses and she allowed herself a small smile of delight as she turned and closed the glass doors behind her.

Giving her appearance one final inspection in the glass door's reflection for any imperfections, Clarise twisted once more towards the beach and raised her hand. "YHWH," she whispered, as she rolled her hand.

Immediately, her view of the balcony rail and the oceanfront behind it disappeared, and in its place an endless domain of sky and clouds appeared. In the distance, angels flew from one point to another or hovered in small groups, but it was the entity who appeared at the forefront of the scene that had her eyes widening in surprise.

For this was not the pubescent child who had stayed with them over the last few months. It was an older man with the same towering height, build and supreme presence as her husband. Dressed in a white robe, he bore shoulder-length grey-white hair with a light wave to it and a matching grey-white beard. His lips parted in a joyous smile that continued to grow until the top row of his teeth was fully exposed. Clarise lifted her chin to see the sparkle of happiness in his ancient obsidian eyes; the same eyes she saw every time she looked up at her husband. "So, it is true," she said, finding his joy contagious. If the family connection didn't truly exist, an attempted blood-link from outside his realm would never have worked.

"It is indeed, little sister."

There weren't many people in existence who could rightfully call her that, but YHWH had proven himself to be one. This also explained why the familial links had gone so insane. YHWH *was* real family and his powerbase as the Almighty of Heaven put him everywhere in Heaven at once, which in turn put his familial link *everywhere at once*. How ironic that the realm-wide glow which prevented the family from finding each other would only affect the Mystallians.

"I must say, this is quite different from the image you portrayed all those months you lived with us."

Although she hadn't thought it possible, YHWH's smile grew until creases formed at the sides of his eyes. "And as my siblings would say, *'pot, meet kettle'*. Like you and all of your kind, I am able to choose ..."

Clarise raised and held a single finger between them. "Do not make comparisons when there is a realm of difference between your shifting and mine, YHWH. Older or not, that level of condescension is intolerable."

YHWH lifted both of his open palms to placate her. "My apologies, little sister. It's difficult to not treat everyone with a certain level of supercilious sovereignty when you've lived and ruled as long as I have."

Which answered two questions at once. "So, you are the Almighty as well as the older sibling of Avis?" Given how Heaven had existed long before Mystal had been established, Clarise knew the answers already, but she wanted to hear the actual words from YHWH to confirm it.

YHWH lowered his hands to his sides and nodded. "Yes, on both counts. As the true firstborn of Theodrick and Belladonna of the Nexus, I am much, much older than your husband."

Clarise was far from convinced. "And how exactly could you know that for sure? I mean, all this time, Avis thought he was the eldest ..."

The soft, almost indulgent smile returned to YHWH's lips. "I know I was our mother's first experiment into motherhood, because she told me so and she never lied about anything. After watching what happened to me, she must have realised there was something to be said about the safety of numbers if she ever wanted any of her children to survive to adulthood. Especially after our father culled many of his courtiers who he suspected may have even thought that my escape had been somehow justified."

"How did you escape?"

"I spoke of this briefly with Avis. As I said to him, a few of our father's courtiers smuggled me out of the Nexus when it became apparent I wasn't going to survive much longer with my sanity intact. I was ... not in any condition to assist them, but thankfully, I didn't need to be. The only downside to my escape was that I took all of the sympathetic touch benders with me, leaving no network of support for Avis and the others when they came along. They were completely on their own, and I've never forgiven myself for that."

"Why not simply blood-link to them, and pull them out that way?" The solution seemed simple enough to Clarise.

Apparently, just the suggestion was enough to drain the colour from YHWH's face. He swallowed heavily and shook his head, the tip of his tongue rubbing across his upper lip. "Contact them whilst they were still *inside* the Nexus?" he barely whispered. His eyes skirted the immediate area around her, as if she had drawn herself to that beast of a man's attention by merely suggesting it.

Lord Theodrick's domination over his offspring was still absolute. Even as all-powerful as they had become, they were still completely terrified of him.

"How long did you suffer at Theodrick's hand before you escaped?"

YHWH's expression deadpanned until his eyes closed and he slowly shook his head. "It's not something I dwell on anymore. The past is where those memories belong."

Supremacy via evasion. Yet another family trait he shared with Avis.

"As you wish," she said, determined to garner as many answers as possible from this meeting. "Something more recent then. Avis once compared you directly to your father in matters of cruelty and temper. I find it hard to believe he could get your temperament so incredibly wrong ..."

YHWH gently rubbed the length of his bottom lip with his thumb and forefinger; his eyes filling with something akin to shame. "He didn't." Whatever he was thinking, it must've been too much for him to bear, for he broke eye contact and looked at the stucco wall beside her head to gather his thoughts.

Then, after a moment where he'd probably spent who knew how long inside his own mind in reflection, he returned his attention to her. "It's quite ... *enlightening* to see what your own sibling thinks of you when they don't know you're snooping." He winced and swallowed, but carried on. "In all my years, it never occurred to me to make that comparison. Nor did it please me to see another, one I hold so dear, do so now. Avis' views caused me to do an immediate re-evaluation of myself and I found I didn't like what I saw. I wanted my siblings and their families to feel welcome in my realm; not run in fear of it."

Clarise smirked. "You had best not repeat that within your siblings' hearing."

YHWH also broke into a light, wry chuckle. "Yes, I know. Fear is a reminder of our childhood, and to be avoided at all costs."

Had that been the underlying reason behind why Avis and his siblings became so aggressive around the mere insult of being frightened? If so, it made an awful kind of sense.

She had one last question to ask. One that may help reunite her beloved husband with his siblings quicker. "Avis also spoke of needing months, maybe even a year or two away from Mystal while the family changed his establishment and thrall. I realise there is a substantial size difference between Mystal and Heaven, but that does not refute you had yours modified in the short time we slept. How were you able to make such a radical change to your establishment and thrall so quickly?"

YHWH's smile was gratifying. "Because I am the embodiment of everything," he answered, opening his hands once more to show her his palms. "And thus, with a few very minor exceptions that have carried over from my time in the Nexus, I have no thrall to speak of." He drew his hands together and clasped them before him, much as she had done. "I love my family with all my heart, little sister, and you must believe me when I say I will do whatever it takes to make peace with them."

"By pretending to be an excitable child for all those months?" she asked, raising an eyebrow as if she'd caught him out, though her dry chuckle took all the sting out of her reprimand.

She was shocked to see his cheeks flush in embarrassment. "That—wasn't entirely acting," he admitted, hiding his mouth behind his fingertips sheepishly. "From the day I found out about my siblings' existence, I have always wanted to meet them, and by extension, the rest of you. I sent angels to sing my praises, thinking that would entice them to come. Instead, they were slaughtered, and I never did understand why until recently.

Eons came and went with no contact. Then, from out of nowhere, Avis was suddenly here. My own brother. My blood." The look in his eyes sharpened and pierced straight through her. "You will never know how hard it was for me to let you all go yesterday morning, when I had the power to keep you with me indefinitely. But I wanted what so many of my mortals here take for granted. A family who *wanted* to spend time with me, because they chose it for themselves. Not because I forced it upon them."

Clarise had forgotten that little detail. YHWH's seniority would've given him the bending advantage over all of them, including her husband. The fact that he hadn't (to her knowledge) was a huge plus for him in her eyes.

"Have you really been alone all this time?"

Although she hadn't intended to be so blunt, YHWH's lower lip quivered until he broke eye contact and drew in a deep breath to calm himself. Then he nodded somewhat awkwardly. "When it comes to blood family, yes. I have since created my own family here, but it's never quite felt the same."

"Constructs will rarely ever fill that void," Clarise agreed. She reached out for his hand in solidarity and although apprehension flashed across his face once he noticed it, she was pleased when he smiled and slid his fingers through hers. "We are family now, YHWH," she declared, squeezing his hand and willing him to believe it.

"And my heart truly sings for it," he replied, a single tear sliding down his cheek. "You and the girls will always be welcome here, little sister. Always. No matter what happens or where you are. Never forget I am only a blood-link away."

Overwhelmed by the sincerity in his voice, Clarise went up on her tiptoes and hooked her free hand around his neck. Then she withdrew her other hand from his and hugged him with all the love he had shown Avis that morning. "It may take time, but I will convince your brother to make contact with you again," she promised, closing her eyes and gripping him tightly.

YHWH relaxed and returned her embrace whole-heartedly. "I would truly appreciate that, Clarise."

Clarise had no idea how long they held each other like that, but eventually she gave his shoulders a parting squeeze and pulled back when his hold lessened. "Until our paths cross again, brother," she said, lightly kissing him on the cheek in farewell.

"Until our paths cross again, little sister," he whispered in kind, pressing his lips into her hair. "Grace be with you."

When they broke apart, the image of YHWH winked out and her view of the oceanfront returned.

Still reeling from everything that had been revealed to her, she went to the edge of the balcony and curled her fingers around the rail. No matter what the future held, she had an ally in her husband's only older brother. A true ally, whose first instinct when dealing with Avis wouldn't be one of torture. Someone she could just talk to, should the need arise.

Suddenly, all the tension that she hadn't known she was carrying fled her body, leaving her light-headed. She bowed her head between her arms to stare at her bare feet …

… and almost leapt over the rail when someone stepped up behind her and slid their broad hands over her back and shoulders. "Is everything alright, sweetheart?" Avis asked, pressing his lips between her shoulder blades and nibbling his way across the thin silk to the nape of her neck.

She pulled herself off the rail and turned inside his arms, sliding her own around his neck to stare into his dark eyes. "Honestly, my love, it could not be better."

And she meant every word of it.

ACKNOWLEDGEMENTS

As before, thanks must go out to the friends and family who have continued to support me through this crazy journey. To my husband Wayne, and my three girls. We're still on that bumpy ride called life, but so long as we have each other's backs, we'll make it. To Alan (Ack), who remains steadfast in his faith in me, even when at times I haven't believed in myself.

To my mother, Jan, who continues to be a daily inspiration for me.

And lastly, to Drew Hassell. An American editor I encountered shortly after the first book of this series was published, whose praises I cannot sing highly enough of. His dedication to his job is matched only by his passion and belief in unsung authors.

Each of you has made this journey a complete joy, and my love goes out to you all.

RECOMMENDATIONS

Arkos Sloth Editing at arkossloth1@gmail.com

ABOUT THE AUTHOR

Karen Buckeridge is an author who has always been interested in things just outside the veil of normality. She lives a quiet life in North Queensland with her husband and the youngest of her three children. Her older two have grown up and moved on to create families of their own, though they still stay in touch.

Karen loves creating realistic characters with recognisable flaws and personality types despite their power levels, and fun, interesting story arcs that leave the reader wondering "Maybe?"

She's an avid reader of all things supernatural, paranormal and romance … not necessarily in that order or exclusively.